SUE GRAFTON

Three Complete Novels

SUE GRAFTON

Three Complete Novels

"**D**" is for Deadbeat

"**E**" is for Evidence

"**F**" is for Fugitive

WINGS BOOKS
New York

This 2001 edition is published by Wings Books®, an imprint of Random House Value Publishing, Inc., 280 Park Avenue, New York, NY 10017, by arrangement with Henry Holt and Company, Inc.

Wings Books® and colophon are registered trademarks of Random House Value Publishing, Inc.

Random House
New York • Toronto • London • Sydney • Auckland
http://www.randomhouse.com/

Printed in the United States of America

A catalog record for this title is available from the Library of Congress

ISBN: 0-517-16271-7

8 7 6 5 4 3 2 1

CONTENTS

"D" is for Deadbeat

For my sister, Ann,
and the memories of Maple Hill.

The author wishes to acknowledge the invaluable asistance of the following people: Steven Humphrey, Florence Clark, Joyce Mackewich, Steve Stafford, Bob Ericson, Ann Hunnicutt, Charles and Mary Pope of the Rescue Mission, Michael Thompson of the Santa Barbara Probation Department, Michelle Bores and Bob Brandenburg of the Santa Barbara Harbor Master's Office, Mary Louise Days of the Santa Barbara Building Department, and Gerald Dow, Crime Analyst, Santa Barbara Police Department.

1

Later, I found out his name was John Daggett, but that's not how he introduced himself the day he walked into my office. Even at the time, I sensed that something was off, but I couldn't figure out what it was. The job he hired me to do seemed simple enough, but then the bum tried to stiff me for my fee. When you're self-employed, you can't afford to let these things slide. Word gets out and first thing you know, everybody thinks you can be had. I went after him for the money and the next thing I knew, I was caught up in events I still haven't quite recovered from.

My name is Kinsey Millhone. I'm a private investigator, licensed by the state of California, operating a small office in Santa Teresa, which is where I've lived all my thirty-two years. I'm female, self-supporting, single now, having been married and divorced twice. I confess I'm sometimes testy, but for the most part I credit myself with an easygoing disposition, tempered (perhaps) by an exaggerated desire for independence. I'm also plagued with the sort of doggedness that makes private investigation a viable proposition for someone with a high school education, certification from the police academy, and a constitutional inability to work for anyone else. I pay my bills on time, obey most laws, and I feel that other people should do likewise . . . out of courtesy, if nothing else. I'm a purist when it comes to justice, but I'll lie at the drop of a hat. Inconsistency has never troubled me.

It was late October, the day before Halloween, and the weather was mimicking autumn in the Midwest—clear and sunny and cool. Driving into town, I could have sworn I smelled woodsmoke in the air and I half expected the leaves to be turning yellow and rust. All I actually saw were the same old palm trees, the same relentless green everywhere. The fires of summer had been contained and the rains hadn't started yet. It was a typical California *un*season, but it *felt* like fall and I was responding with inordinate good cheer, thinking maybe I'd drive up the pass in the afternoon to the pistol range, which is what I do for laughs.

I'd come into the office that Saturday morning to take care of some bookkeeping chores—paying personal bills, getting out my statements for the month. I had my calculator out, a Redi-Receipt form in the typewriter, and four completed statements lined up, addressed and stamped, on the desk to my left. I was so intent on the task at hand that I didn't realize anyone was standing in the doorway until the man cleared his throat. I reacted with one of those little jumps you do when you open the evening paper and a spider runs out. He apparently found this amusing, but I was having to pat myself on the chest to get my heart rate down again.

"I'm Alvin Limardo," he said. "Sorry if I startled you."

"That's all right," I said, "I just had no idea you were standing there. Are you looking for me?"

"If you're Kinsey Millhone, I am."

I got up and shook hands with him across the desk and then suggested that he take a seat. My first fleeting impression had been that he was a derelict, but on second glance, I couldn't find anything in particular to support the idea.

He was in his fifties, too gaunt for good health. His face was long and narrow, his chin pronounced. His hair was an ash gray, clipped short, and he smelled of citrus cologne. His eyes were hazel, his gaze remote. The suit he wore was an odd shade of green. His hands seemed huge, fingers long and bony, the knuckles enlarged. The two inches of narrow wrist extending, cuffless, from his coat sleeves suggested shabbiness though his clothing didn't really look worn. He held a slip of paper which he'd folded twice, and he fiddled with that self-consciously.

"What can I do for you?" I asked.

"I'd like for you to deliver this." He smoothed out the piece of paper then and placed it on my desk. It was a cashier's check drawn on a Los Angeles bank, dated October 29, and made out to someone named Tony Gahan for twenty-five thousand dollars.

I tried not to appear as surprised as I felt. He didn't look like a man with money to spare. Maybe he'd borrowed the sum from Gahan and was paying it back. "You want to tell me what this is about?"

"He did me a favor. I want to say thanks. That's all it is."

"It must have been quite a favor," I said. "Do you mind if I ask what he did?"

"He showed me a kindness when I was down on my luck."

"What do you need me for?"

He smiled briefly. "An attorney would charge me a hundred and twenty dollars an hour to handle it. I'm assuming you'd charge considerably less."

"So would a messenger service," I said. "It's cheaper still if you do it yourself." I wasn't being a smart-mouth about it. I really didn't understand why he needed a private detective.

He cleared his throat. "I tried that, but I'm not entirely certain of Mr. Gahan's current address. At one time, he lived on Stanley Place, but he's not there now. I went by this morning and the house is empty. It looks like it hasn't been lived in for a while. I want someone to track him down and make sure he gets the money. If you can estimate what that might run me, I'll pay you in advance."

"That depends on how elusive Mr. Gahan turns out to be. The credit bureau might have a current address, or the DMV. A lot of inquiries can be done by phone, but they still take time. At thirty bucks an hour, the fee does mount up."

He took out a checkbook and began to write out a check. "Two hundred dollars?"

"Let's make it four. I can always refund the balance if the charges turn out to be less," I said. "In the meantime, I've got a license to protect so this better be on the up and up. I'd be happier if you'd tell me what's going on."

This was where he hooked me, because what he said was just offbeat enough to be convincing. Liar that I am, it still didn't occur to me that there could be so much falsehood mixed in with the truth.

"I got into trouble with the law awhile back and served some time. Tony Gahan was helpful to me just before I was arrested. He had no idea of my circumstances so he wasn't an accessory to anything, nor would you be. I feel indebted."

"Why not take care of it yourself?"

He hesitated, almost shyly I thought. "It's sort of like that Charles Dickens book, *Great Expectations*. He might not like having a convicted felon for a benefactor. People have strange ideas about ex-cons."

"What if he won't accept an anonymous donation?"

"You can return the check in that case and keep the fee."

I shifted restlessly in my chair. What's wrong with this picture, I asked myself. "Where'd you get the money if you've been in jail?"

"Santa Anita. I'm still on parole and I shouldn't be playing the ponies at all, but I find it hard to resist. That's why I'd like to pass the money on to you. I'm a gambling man. I can't have that kind of cash around or I'll piss it away, if you'll pardon my French." He closed his mouth then and looked at me, waiting to see what else I might ask. Clearly, he didn't want to volunteer more than was necessary to satisfy my qualms, but he seemed amazingly patient. I realized later, of course, that his tolerance was probably the function of his feeding me so much bullshit. He must have been entertained by the game he was playing. Lying is fun. I can do it all day myself.

"What was the felony?" I asked.

He dropped his gaze, addressing his reply to his oversized hands, which were folded in his lap. "I don't think that pertains. This money is clean and I came by it honestly. There's nothing illegal about the transaction if that's what's worrying you."

Of *course* it worried me, but I wondered if I was being too fastidious. There was nothing wrong with his request on the face of it. I chased the proposition around in my head with caution, wondering what Tony Gahan had done for Limardo that would net him this kind of payoff. None of my business, I supposed, as long as no laws had been broken in the process. Intuition was telling me to turn this guy down, but it happens that the rent on my apartment was due the next day. I had the money in my checking account, but it seemed providential to have a retainer drop in my lap unexpectedly. In any event, I didn't see a reason to refuse. "All right," I said.

He nodded once, pleased. "Good."

I sat and watched while he finished signing his name to the check. He tore it out and pushed it toward me, tucking the checkbook into the inner pocket of his suit coat. "My address and telephone number are on that in case you need to get in touch."

I pulled a standard contract form out of my desk drawer and took a few minutes to fill it in. I got his signature and then I made a note of Tony Gahan's last known address, a house in Colgate, the township just north of Santa Teresa. I was already feeling some low-level dread, wishing I hadn't agreed to do anything. Still, I'd committed myself, the contract was signed, and I figured I'd make the best of it. How much trouble could it be, thought I.

He stood up and I did too, moving with him as he walked toward the door. With both of us on our feet, I could see how much taller he was than I . . . maybe six-four to my five-foot-six. He paused with his hand on the knob, gazing down at me with the same remote stare.

"One other thing you might need to know about Tony Gahan," he said.

"What's that?"

"He's fifteen years old."

I stood there and watched Alvin Limardo move off down the hall. I should have called him back, folks. I should have known right then that it wasn't going to turn out well. Instead I closed the office door and returned to my desk. On impulse, I opened the French doors and went out on the balcony. I scanned the street below, but there was no sign of him. I shook my head, dissatisfied.

I locked the cashier's check in my file cabinet. When the bank opened on Monday, I'd put it in my safe deposit box until I located Tony Gahan and then turn it over to him. Fifteen?

At noon, I closed up the office and went down the back stairs to the parking lot, where I retrieved my VW, a decaying sedan with more rust than paint. This is not the sort of vehicle you'd choose for a car chase, but then most of what a P.I. does for a living isn't that exciting anyway. I'm sometimes reduced to serving process papers, which gets hairy now and then, but much of the time I do preemployment background checks, skip-tracing, or case-and-trial preparation for a couple of attorneys here in town. My office is provided by California Fidelity Insurance, a former employer of mine. The company headquarters is right next door and I still do sporadic investigations for them in exchange for a modest two rooms (one inner, one outer) with a separate entrance and a balcony overlooking State Street.

I went by the post office and dropped the mail in the box and then I stopped by the bank and deposited Alvin Limardo's four hundred dollars in my checking account.

Four business days later, on a Thursday, I got a letter from the bank, informing me that the check had bounced. According to their records, Alvin Limardo had closed out his account. In proof of this, I was presented with the check itself stamped across the face with the sort of officious looking purple ink that makes it clear the bank is displeased.

So was I.

My account had been debited the four hundred dollars and I was charged an additional three bucks, apparently to remind me, in the future, not to deal with deadbeats. I picked up the phone and called Alvin Limardo's number in Los Angeles. A disconnect. I'd been canny enough to ignore the search for Tony Gahan until the check cleared, so it wasn't as if I'd done any work to date. But how was I going to get the check replaced? And what was I going to do with the twenty-five grand in the meantime? By then, the cashier's check was tucked away in my safe deposit box, but it was useless to me and I didn't want to proceed with delivery until I knew I'd be paid. In theory, I could have dropped Alvin Limardo a note, but it might have come bouncing back at me with all the jauntiness of his rubber check, and then where would I be? Crap. I was going to have to drive down to L.A. One thing I've learned about collections—the faster you move, the better your chances are.

I looked up his street address in my *Thomas Guide to Los Angeles Streets*. Even on the map, it didn't look like a nice neighborhood. I checked my watch. It was then 10:15. It was going to take me ninety minutes to reach L.A., probably another hour to locate Limardo, chew him out, get the check replaced, and grab a bite of lunch. Then I'd have to drive ninety minutes back, which would put me in the office again at 3:30 or 4:00. Well, that wasn't too bad. It was tedious, but necessary, so I decided I might as well quit bellyaching and get on with it.

By 10:30, I'd gassed up my car and I was on the road.

2

I left the Ventura Freeway at Sherman Oaks, taking the San Diego Freeway south as far as Venice Boulevard. I exited, turning right at the bottom of the off-ramp. According to my calculations, the address I wanted was somewhere close. I doubled back toward Sawtelle, the street that hugs the freeway on a parallel route.

Once I saw the building, I realized that I'd spotted the rear of it from the freeway as I passed. It was painted the color of Pepto-Bismol and sported a sagging banner of Day-Glo orange that said NOW RENTING. The building was separated from the roadway by a concrete rain wash and protected from speeding vehicles by a ten-foot cinderblock wall sprayed with messages for passing motorists. Spiky weeds had sprung up along the base of the wall and trash had accumulated like hanging ornaments in the few hearty bushes that managed to survive the gas fumes. I had noted the building because it seemed so typical of L.A.: bald, cheaply constructed, badly defaced. There was something meanspirited about its backside, and the entrance turned out to be worse.

The street was largely made up of California "bungalows," small two-bedroom houses of wood and stucco with ragged yards and no trees. Most of them had been painted in pastel hues, odd shades of turquoise and mauve, suggestive of discount paints that hadn't quite covered the color underneath. I found a parking space across the street and locked my car, then crossed to the apartment complex.

The building was beginning to disintegrate. The stucco looked mealy and dry, the aluminum window frames pitted and buckling. The wrought-iron gate near the front had been pulled straight out of the supporting wall, leaving holes large enough to stick a fist into. Two apartments at street level were boarded up. The management had thoughtfully provided a number of garbage bins near the stairs, without (apparently) paying for adequate trash removal services. A big yellow dog was scratching through this pile of refuse with enthusiasm, though all he seemed to net for his efforts was a quarter moon of pizza. He trotted off, the rim of crust clenched in his jaws like a bone.

I moved into the shelter of the stairs. Most of the mailboxes had been ripped out and mail was scattered in the foyer like so much trash. According to the address on the face of the check, Limardo lived in apartment 26, which I surmised was somewhere above. There were apparently forty units, only a few marked with the occupants' names. That seemed curious to me. In Santa Teresa, the post office won't even deliver junk mail unless a box is provided, clearly marked, and in good repair. I pictured the postman, emptying out his mail pouch like a wastepaper basket, escaping on foot then before the inhabitants of the building swarmed over him like bugs.

The apartments were arranged in tiers around a courtyard "garden" of loose gravel, pink paving stones, and nut grass. I picked my way up the cracked concrete steps.

At the second-floor landing, a black man was seated in a rickety metal folding chair, whittling with a knife on a bar of Ivory soap. There was a magazine open on his lap to catch the shavings. He was heavyset and shapeless, maybe fifty years old, his short-cropped frizzy hair showing gray around his ears. His eyes were a muddy brown, the lid of one pulled askew by a vibrant track of stitches that cut down along his cheek.

He took me in at a glance, turning his attention then to the sculpture taking form in his hands. "You must be looking for Alvin Limardo," he said.

"That's right," I said, startled. "How'd you guess?"

He flashed a smile at me, showing perfect teeth, as snowy as the soap he carved. He tilted his face up at me, the injured eye creating the illusion of a wink. "Baby, you ain't live here. I know ever'body live here. And from the look on your face, you ain't thinkin' to rent. If you knew where you were going, you'd be headed straight there. Instead, you be lookin' all around like somethin' might jump out on you, including me," he said and then paused to survey me. "I'd say you do social work, parole, something like that. Maybe welfare."

"Not bad," I said. "But why Limardo? What made you think I was looking for him?"

He smiled then, his gums showing pink. "We *all* Alvin Limardo 'round here. It's a joke we play. Just a name we take when we jivin' folk. I been Alvin Limardo myself lass week at the food stamp line. He get welfare checks, disability, AFDC. Somebody show up lass week wid a warrant on him. I tole 'em, 'Alvin Limardo's done leff. He gone. Ain't nobody here by that name about now.' The Alvin Limardo you want . . . he be white or black?"

"White," I said and then described the man who'd come into my office on Saturday. The black man started nodding about halfway through, his knife blade still smoothing the surface of the soap. It looked like he'd carved a sow lying on her side with a litter of piglets scrambling over her to nurse. The whole of it couldn't have been more than four inches long.

"That's John Daggett. Whooee. He bad. He the one you want, but he gone for sure."

"Do you have any idea where he went?"

"Santa Teresa, I heard."

"Well, I know he was up there last Saturday. That's where I ran into him," I said. "Has he been back since then?"

The man's mouth drooped with skepticism. "I seen him on Monday and then he gone off again. Only other peoples must want him too. He ack like a man who's runnin' and don't want to be caught. What you want wid him?"

"He wrote me a bum check."

He shot me a look of astonishment. "You take a check from a man like that? Lord God, girl! What's the matter wid you?"

I had to laugh. "I know. It's my own damn fault. I thought maybe I could catch him before he skipped out permanently."

He shook his head, unable to sympathize. "Don't take nothin' from the likes of him. That's your first mistake. Comin' 'round this place may be the next."

"Is there anybody here who might know how to get in touch with him?"

He pointed the blade of his knife toward an apartment two doors down. "Axe Lovella. She might know. Then again, she might not."

"She's a friend of his?"

"Not hardly. She's his wife."

I felt somewhat more hopeful as I knocked at apartment 26. I was afraid he'd moved out altogether. The door was a hollowcore with a hole kicked into the bottom about shin high. The sliding glass window was open six inches, a fold of drapery sticking out. A crack ran diagonally across the pane, held together by a wide band of electrician's tape. I could smell something cooking inside, kale or collard greens, with a whisper of vinegar and bacon grease.

The door opened and a woman peered out at me. Her upper lip was puffy, like the kind of scrape children get falling off bicycles when they first learn to ride. Her left eye had been blackened not long ago and it was streaked now with midnight blue, the surrounding tissue a rainbow of green and yellow and gray. Her hair was the color of hay, parted in the middle and snagged up over each ear with a bobby pin. I couldn't even guess how old she might be. Younger than I expected, given John Daggett's age, which had to be fifty plus.

"Lovella Daggett?"

"That's right." She seemed reluctant to admit that much.

"I'm Kinsey Millhone. I'm looking for John."

She licked uneasily at her upper lip as if she was still unfamiliar with its new shape and size. Some of the scraped area had formed a scab, which resembled nothing so much as half a moustache. "He's not here. I don't know where he's at. What'd you want him for?"

"He hired me to do some work, but he paid me with a bum check. I was hoping we could get it straightened out."

She studied me while she processed the information. "Hired you to do what?"

"Deliver something."

She didn't believe a bit of that. "You a cop?"

"No."

"What are you, then?"

I showed her the photostat of my license by way of reply. She turned and walked away from the door, leaving it open behind her. I gathered this was her method of inviting me in.

I stepped into the living room and closed the door behind me. The carpeting was that green cotton shag so admired by apartment owners everywhere. The only furniture in the room was a card table and two plain wooden chairs. A six-foot rectangle of lighter carpeting along one wall suggested that there'd once been a couch on the spot, and a pattern of indentations in the rug indicated the former presence of two heavy chairs and a coffee table, arranged in what decorators refer to as "a conversational grouping." Instead of conversation these days, Daggett apparently got right down to busting her chops, breaking anything else that came to hand. The one lamp I saw had been snapped off at the socket and the wires were hanging out like torn ligaments.

"Where'd the furniture go?"

"He hocked it all last week. Turns out he used the payments for his bar bill. The car went before that. It was a piece of junk, anyway, but I'd paid for it. You ought to see what I've got for a bed these days. Some peed-on old mattress he found out on the street."

There were two bar stools at the counter and I perched on one, watching as Lovella ambled into the small space that served as a kitchen. An aluminum saucepan sat on a gas flame on the stove, the water in it boiling furiously. On one of the back burners, there was a battered aluminum kettle filled with simmering greens.

Lovella wore blue jeans and a plain white tee shirt wrong-side out, the Fruit of the Loom label visible at the back of her neck. The bottom of the shirt had been pulled tight and knotted to form a halter, leaving her midriff bare. "You want coffee? I was just fixing some."

"Yes, please," I said.

She rinsed a cup under the hot water faucet and gave it a quick swipe with a paper towel. She set it on the counter and spooned instant coffee into it and then used the same paper towel as a potholder when she reached for the saucepan. The water sputtered against the edge of the pan as she poured. She added water to a second cup, gave a quick stir to the contents, and pushed it toward me with the spoon still resting up against the rim.

"Daggert's a jerk. They should lock him up for life," she remarked, almost idly, I thought.

"Did he do that to you?" I asked, my gaze flicking across her bruised face.

She fixed a pair of dead gray eyes on me without bothering to reply. Up close, I could see that she wasn't much more than twenty-five. She leaned forward, resting her elbows on the counter, her coffee cup cradled in her hands. She wasn't wearing a bra and her breasts were big, as soft and droopy as balloons filled with water, her nipples pressing against the tee-shirt fabric like puckered knots. I wondered if she was a hooker. I'd known a few with the same careless sexuality—all surface, no feeling underneath.

"How long have you been married?"

"You care if I have a cigarette?"

"It's your place. You can do anything you want," I said.

That netted me a wan smile, the first I'd seen. She reached for a pack of Pall Mall 100s, flipped on the gas burner, and lit her cigarette from it, tilting her head so her hair wouldn't catch fire. She took a deep drag and exhaled it, blowing a cloud of smoke at me. "Six weeks," she said, answering my question belatedly. "We were pen pals after he got sent to San Luis. Wrote for a year and then I married him the minute he got out. Dumb? Jesus. Can you believe I did that?"

I shrugged noncommittally. She didn't really care if I believed it or not. "How'd you connect in the first place?"

"A buddy of his. Guy named Billy Polo I used to date. They'd sit and talk about women and my name came up. I guess Billy made me sound like real hot stuff, so Daggett got in touch."

I took a sip of my coffee. It had that flat, nearly sour taste of instant, with tiny clumps of coffee powder floating at the edge. "Do you have any milk for this?"

"Oh, sure. Sorry," she said. She moved over to the refrigerator where she took out a small can of Carnation.

It wasn't quite what I had in mind, but I added some to my coffee, intrigued as evaporated milk rose to the surface in a series of white dots. I wondered if a fortune teller could read the pattern, like tea leaves. I thought I spied some indigestion in my future, but I wasn't sure.

"Daggett's a charmer when he wants," she said. "Give him a couple drinks, though, and he's mean as a snake."

That was a story I'd heard before. "Why don't you leave?" said I, as I always do.

"Because he'd come after me is why," she said snappishly. "You don't know him. He'd kill me without giving it a second thought. Same thing if I called the cops. Talk back to that man and he'll punch your teeth down your throat. He hates women is what's the matter with him. Of course, when he sobers up, he can charm your socks off. Anyway, I'm hoping he's gone for good. He got a phone call Monday morning and he was out of here like a shot. I haven't heard from him since. Of course, the phone was disconnected yesterday so I don't know how he'd reach me even if he wanted to."

"Why don't you talk to his parole officer?"

"I guess I could," she said reluctantly. "He reports to the guy every time he turns around. For two days he had a job, but he quit that. Of course, he's not supposed to drink. I guess he tried to play by the rules at first, but it was too much."

"Why not get out while you have the chance?"

"And go where? I don't have a nickel to my name."

"There are shelters for battered women. Call the rape crisis center. They'll know."

She gestured dismissively. "Jesus, I love people like you. You ever had a guy punch you out?"

"Not one I was married to," I said. "I wouldn't put up with that shit."

"That's what I used to say, sister, but I'll tell you what. You don't get away as easy as all that. Not with a bastard like Daggett. He swears he'd follow me to the ends of the earth and he would."

"What was he in prison for?"

"He never said and I never asked. Which was also dumb. It didn't make any difference to me at first. He was fine for a couple weeks. Just like a kid, you know? And sweet? Lord, he trotted around after me like a puppy dog. We couldn't get enough of each other and it all seemed just like the letters we wrote. Then he got into the Jack Daniel's one night and the shit hit the fan."

"Did he ever mention the name Tony Gahan?"

"Nuh-uh. Who's he?"

"I'm not sure. Some kid he asked me to find."

"What'd he pay you with? Can I see the check?"

I took it out of my handbag and laid it on the counter. I thought it best not to mention the cashier's check. I didn't think she'd take kindly to his giving money away. "I understand Limardo is a fabricated name."

She studied the check. "Yeah, but Daggett did keep some money in this account. I think he cleaned it out just before he left." She took a drag of her cigarette as she handed back the check. I managed to turn my head before she blew smoke in my face again.

"That phone call he got Monday, what was it about? Do you know?"

"Beats me. I was off at the Laundromat. I got home and he was still on the phone, his face as gray as that dish rag. He hung up quick and then started shovin' stuff in a duffel. He turned the place upside down lookin' for his bank book. I was afraid he'd come after me, thinkin' I took it, but I guess he was too freaked out to worry about me."

"He told you that?"

"No, but he was cold sober and his hands were shaking *bad*."

"You have any idea where he might have gone?"

A look flashed through her eyes, some emotion she concealed by dropping her gaze. "He only had one friend and that was Billy Polo up in Santa Teresa. If he needed help, that's where he'd go. I think he used to have family up there too, but I don't know what happened to them. He never talked much about that."

"So Polo's out of prison?"

"I heard he got out just recently."

"Well, maybe I'll track him down since that's the only lead I have. In the meantime, would you find a phone and call me if you hear from either one?" I took out a business card and jotted my home address and phone on the back. "Call collect."

She looked at both sides of the card. "What do you think is goin' on?"

"I don't know and I don't much care. As soon as I run him down, I'll clean up this business and *bail out*."

3

As long as I was in the area, I went by the bank. The woman in charge of customer service couldn't have been less helpful. She was dark haired, in her early twenties, and new at the job I gathered because she greeted my every request with the haunted look of someone who isn't quite sure of the rules and therefore says no to everything. She would not verify "Alvin Limardo's" account number or the fact that the account had been closed. She would not tell me if there was, perhaps, another account in John Daggett's name. I knew there had to be a registered copy of the cashier's check itself, but she refused to verify the information he'd given at the time. I kept thinking there was some other tack I might take, especially with that much money at stake. Surely, the bank must care what happened to twenty-five thousand dollars. I stood at the counter and stared at the woman, and she stared back. Maybe she hadn't understood.

I took out the photostat of my license and pointed. "Look," I said, "You see this? I'm a private investigator. I've got a real problem here. I was hired to deliver a cashier's check, but now I can't find the man who gave it to me and I don't know the whereabouts of the person who's supposed to receive it and I'm just trying to get a lead so I can do what I was hired to do."

"I understand that," she said.

"But you won't give me any information, right?"

"It's against bank regulations."

"Isn't it against bank regulations for Alvin Limardo to write me a bad check?"

"Yes."

"Then what am I supposed to do with it?" I said. I really knew the answer . . . eat it, dum-dum . . . but I was feeling stubborn and perverse.

"Take him to small claims court," she said.

"But I can't find him. He can't be hauled into court if nobody knows where he is."

She stared at me blankly, offering no comment.

"What about the twenty-five thousand?" I said. "What am I supposed to do with that?"

"I have no idea."

I stared down at the desk. When I was in kindergarten, I was a biter and I still struggle with the urge. It just feels good, you know? "I want to speak to your supervisor."

"Mr. Stallings? He's gone for the day."

"Well, is there anybody else here who might give me some help on this?"

She shook her head. "I'm in charge of customer service."

"But you're not doing a thing. How can you call it customer service when you don't do shit?"

Her mouth turned prim. "Please don't use language like that around me. It's very offensive."

"What do I have to do to get help around here?"

"Do you have an account with us?"

"If I did, would you help?"

"Not with this. We're not supposed to divulge information about bank customers."

This was silly. I walked away from her desk. I wanted to make a withering remark, but I couldn't think of one. I knew I was just mad at myself for taking the job to begin with, but I was hoping to lay a little ire off on her . . . a pointless enterprise. I got back in my car and headed toward the freeway.

When I reached Santa Teresa, it was 4:35. I bypassed the office altogether and went home. My disposition improved the minute I walked in. My apartment was once a single-car garage and consists now of one room, fifteen feet on a side, with a narrow extension on the right that serves as a kitchenette, separated from the living area by a counter. The space is arranged with cunning: a stackable washer-dryer tucked in beside the kitchenette, bookshelves, drawers and storage compartments built into the wall. It's tidy and self-contained and all of it suits me absolutely. I have a six-foot convertible sofa that I usually sleep on as is, a desk, a chair, an endtable, and plump pillows that serve as additional seating if anyone comes over to sit. My bathroom is one of those preformed fiberglass units with everything molded into it, including a towel bar, a soap holder, and a cutout for a window that looks out at the street. Sometimes I stand in the bathtub, elbows resting on the sill, and stare at passing cars, just thinking how lucky I am. I love being single. It's almost like being rich.

I dropped my handbag on the desk and hung my jacket on a peg. I sat on the couch and pulled off my boots, then padded over to the refrigerator and took out a bottle of white zinfandel and a corkscrew. At intervals, I try to behave like a person with class, which is to say I drink wine from a bottle instead of a cardboard box. I pulled the cork and poured myself a glass. I crossed to the desk, taking the telephone book from the top drawer, trailing telephone cord, directory, and wine glass over to the sofa. I set the wine glass on the endtable and thumbed through the book to see if Billy Polo was listed. Of course, he wasn't. I looked up the name Gahan. No dice. I drank some wine and tried to think what to do next.

On an impulse, I checked for the name Daggett. Lovella had mentioned that he once lived up here. Maybe he still had relatives in town.

There were four Daggetts listed. I started dialing them in

order, saying the same thing each time. "Oh, hi. I'm trying
to reach a John Daggett, who used to live in this area. Can
you tell me if this is the correct number?"

On the first two calls, I drew a blank, but with the third,
the man who answered responded to my query with one of
those odd silences that indicate that information is being processed.

"What did you want with him?" he asked. He sounded like
he was in his sixties, his phrasing tentative, alert to my response, but undecided how much he was willing to reveal.

He was certainly skipping right down to the tricky part.
From everything I'd heard about Daggett, he was a bum, so
I didn't dare claim to be a friend of his. If I admitted he owed
me money, I was going to have the phone slammed down in
my ear. Ordinarily, in a situation like this, I'd insinuate that
I had money for *him*, but somehow I didn't think that would
fly. People are getting wise to that shit.

I laid out the first lie that occurred to me. "Well, to tell you
the truth," I said, "I've only met John once, but I'm trying to
get in touch with a mutual acquaintance and I think John has
his address and telephone number."

"Who were you looking to get in touch with?"

That caught me off-guard, as I hadn't made that part up
yet. "Who? Um . . . Alvin Limardo. Has John ever mentioned
Alvin?"

"No, I don't believe so. But, now, you may have the wrong
party. The John Daggett that used to live here is currently in
prison and he's been there, oh I'd say nearly two years." His
manner suggested a man whose retirement has invested even
a wrong number with some interesting possibilities. Still, it
was clear I'd hit pay dirt.

"That's the one I'm talking about," I said. "He was up in
San Luis Obispo."

"He still is."

"Oh, no. He's out. He was released six weeks ago."

"John? *No,* ma'am. He's still in prison and I hope he stays there. I don't mean to speak ill of the man, but you'll find he's what I call a problematic person."

"Problematic?"

"Well, yes. That's how I'd have to put it. John is the type of person that creates problems and usually of a quite serious nature."

"Oh, really," I said. "I didn't realize that." I loved it that this man was willing to chat. As long as I could keep him going, I might figure out how to get a bead on Daggett. I took a flyer. "Are you his brother?"

"I'm his brother-in-law, Eugene Nickerson."

"You must be married to his sister then," I said.

He laughed. "No, he's married to *my* sister. She was a Nickerson before she became a Daggett."

"You're Lovella's brother?" I was trying to picture siblings with a forty-year age span.

"No, Essie's."

I held the receiver away from my ear and stared at it. What was he talking about? "Wait a minute. I'm confused. Maybe we're *not* talking about the same man." I gave a quick verbal sketch of the John Daggett I'd met. I didn't see how there could be two, but there was something going on here.

"That's him all right. How did you say you knew him?"

"I met him last Saturday, right here in Santa Teresa."

The silence on the other end of the line was profound.

I finally broke into it. "Is there some way I might stop by so we can talk about this?"

"I think you'd best," he said. "What would your name be?"

"Kinsey Millhone."

He told me how to get to the place.

The house was white frame with a small wooden porch, tucked into the shadow of Capillo Hill on the west side of town. The street was abbreviated, only three houses on each side before the blacktop petered out into the gravel patch that formed a parking pad beside the Daggett residence. Beyond the house, the hill angled upward into sparse trees and underbrush. No sunlight whatever penetrated the yard. A sagging chicken wire fence cut along the lot lines. Bushes had been planted at intervals, but had failed to thrive, so that now there were only globes of dried twigs. The house had a hangdog look, like a stray being penned up until the dogcatcher comes.

I climbed the steep wooden steps and knocked. Eugene Nickerson opened the door. He was much as I had pictured him: in his sixties, of medium height, with wiry gray hair and eyebrows drawn together in a knot. His eyes were small and pale, his lashes nearly white. Narrow shoulders, thick waist, suspenders, flannel shirt. He carried a Bible in his left hand, his index finger closed between the covers, keeping his place.

Uh-oh, I thought.

"I'll have to ask your name again," he said as he admitted me. "My memory's not what it was."

I shook his hand. "Kinsey Millhone," I said. "Nice to meet you, Mr. Nickerson. I hope I didn't interrupt anything."

"Not at all. We're preparing for our Bible class. We usually get together on Wednesday nights, but our pastor has been down with the flu this week, so the meeting was postponed. This is my sister, Essie Daggett. John's wife," he said, indicating the woman seated on the couch. "You can call me Eugene if you like," he added. I smiled briefly in assent and then concentrated on her.

"Hello. How are you? I appreciate your letting me stop by like this." I moved over and offered my hand. She allowed a few fingers to rest in mine briefly. It was like shaking hands with a Playtex rubber glove.

She was broad-faced and colorless, with graying hair in an unbecoming cut and glasses with thick lenses and heavy plastic frames. She had a wen on the right side of her nose about the size of a kernel of popcorn. Her lower jaw jutted forward aggressively, with protrusive cuspids on either side. She smelled virulently of lilies of the valley.

Eugene indicated that I should have a seat, my choice being the couch where Essie sat, or a Windsor chair with one of the wooden spokes popped out. I opted for the chair, sitting forward slightly so as not to pop anything else. Eugene seated himself in a wicker rocker that creaked under his weight. He took up the narrow purple ribbon hanging out of the Bible and marked his place, then set the book on the table in front of him. Essie had said nothing, her gaze fixed on her lap.

"May I get you a glass of water?" he asked. "We don't hold with caffeinated beverages, but I'd be happy to pour you some 7-Up, if you like."

"I'm fine, thanks," I said. I was seriously alarmed. Being with devout Christians is like being with the very rich. One senses that there are rules at work, some strange etiquette that one might inadvertently breech. I tried to hold bland and harmless thoughts, hoping I wouldn't blurt out any four-letter words. How *could* John Daggett be related to these two?

Eugene cleared his throat. "I was explaining to Essie this confusion we're having over John Daggett's whereabouts. Our understanding is that John is still incarcerated, but now you seem to have a different point of view."

"I'm as baffled as you are," I said. I was thinking fast, wondering how much information I might elicit without giving anything away. As bugged as I was with Daggett, I still didn't feel I should be indiscreet. Not only was there the issue of his being out on parole—there was Lovella. I didn't want to be the one to spill the beans about this new bride of his to a woman he was apparently still married to. "Do you happen to have a picture of him?" I asked. "I suppose it's possible the man I talked to was simply claiming to be your brother-in-law."

"I don't know," Eugene said, dubiously. "It surely sounded like him from what you described."

Essie reached over and picked up a color studio photograph in an ornate silver frame. "This was taken on our thirty-fifth wedding anniversary," she said. Her voice had a nasal cast and a grudging undertone. She passed the photograph to her brother as though he'd never seen it before and might like to have a peek.

"Shortly before John left for San Luis," Eugene amended, passing the photo to me. His tone suggested John was off on a business trip.

I studied the picture. It was Daggett all right, looking as self-conscious as someone in one of those booths where you dress up as a Confederate soldier or a Victorian gent. His collar looked too tight, his hair too slicked down with pomade. His face looked tight too, as if any minute he might cut and run. Essie was seated beside him, as placid as a blancmange. She was wearing what looked like a crepe de chine dress in lilac, with shoulder pads and glass buttons, a big orchid corsage pinned to her left shoulder.

"Lovely," I murmured, feeling guilty and false. It was a terrible picture. She looked like a bulldog and John looked like he was suppressing a fart.

I handed the picture to Essie again. "What sort of crime did he commit?"

Essie inhaled audibly.

"We prefer not to speak of that," Eugene interjected smoothly. "Perhaps you should tell us of your own acquaintance with him."

"Well, of course, I don't know him well. I think I mentioned that on the phone. We have a mutual friend and he's the one I was hoping to get in touch with. John mentioned that he had family in this area and I just took a chance. I'm assuming you haven't spoken to him recently."

Essie shifted on the couch. "We stuck by him as long as we could. The pastor said in his opinion we'd done enough. We don't know what John might be wrestling with in the dark of his soul, but there's a limit to what others can *take*." The edge was there in her voice and I wondered what it was made of: rage, humiliation perhaps, the martyrdom of the meek at the hands of the wretched.

I said, "I gather John's been a bit of a trial."

Essie pressed her lips together, clutching her hands in her lap. "Well, it's just like the Bible says. '*Love* your enemies, *bless* them that curse you, do *good* to them that hate you, and pray for them which despitefully use you and persecute you'!" Her tone was accusatory. She began to rock with agitation.

Whoa, I thought, this lady's heat gauge has shot right up into the red.

Eugene creaked in his chair, snagging my attention with a gentle clearing of his throat. "You said you saw him on Saturday. May I ask what the occasion was?"

I realized then that I should have devoted a lot more time to the fib I'd told because I couldn't think how to respond, I was so unnerved by Essie Daggett's outburst that my mind went blank.

She leaned forward then. "Have you been saved?"

"Excuse me, what?" I said, squinting.

"Have you taken Jesus into your heart? Have you set aside *sin*? Have you *repented*? Have you been washed in the Blood of the *Lamb*?"

A spark of spit landed on my face, but I didn't dare react. "Not lately," I said. What is it about me that attracts women like this?

"Now Essie, I'm sure she didn't come by to ponder the state of her soul," Eugene said. He glanced at his watch. "My goodness, I believe it's time for your medication."

I took the opportunity to rise. "I don't want to take up any more of your time," I said, conversationally. "I really appreciate your help on this and if I need any more information, I'll give you a call." I fumbled in my handbag for a business card and left it on the table.

Essie had kicked into high gear by now. " 'And they shall stone thee with stones, and *thrust* thee through with their swords. And they shall burn thine houses with fire, and execute judgments upon thee in the sight of many women; and I will cause thee to *cease* from playing harlot, and thou also shalt give no hire anymore . . .' "

"Well, okay now, thanks a lot," I called, easing toward the door. Eugene was patting Essie's hands, too distracted to worry about my departure.

I closed the door and trotted back to my car at a quick clip. It was getting dark and I didn't like the neighborhood.

4

Friday morning I got up at 6:00 and headed over to the beach for my run. For much of the summer, I'd been unable to jog because of an injury, but I'd been back at it for two months and I was feeling good. I've never rhapsodized about exercise and I'd avoid it if I could, but I notice the older I get, the more my body seems to soften, like butter left out at room temp. I don't like to watch my ass drop and my thighs spread outward like jodhpurs made of flesh. In the interest of tight-fitting jeans, my standard garb, I jog three miles a day on the bicycle path that winds along the beach front.

The dawn was laid out on the eastern skyline like water-colors on a matte board: cobalt blue, violet, and rose bleeding together in horizontal stripes. Clouds were visible out on the ocean, plump and dark, pushing the scent of distant seas toward the tumbling surf. It was cold and I ran as much to keep warm as I did to keep in shape.

I got back to my apartment at 6:25, showered, pulled on a pair of jeans, a sweater, and my boots, and then ate a bowl of cereal. I read the paper from front to back, noting with interest the weather map, which showed the radiating spiral of a storm sweeping toward us from Alaska. An 80 percent chance of showers was forecast for the afternoon, with scattered showers through the weekend, clearing by Monday night. In Santa Teresa, rain is not a common event, and it takes on a festive air when it comes. My impulse, always, is to shut myself inside and curl up with a good book. I'd just picked up a new Len Deighton novel and I was looking forward to reading it.

At 9:00, reluctantly, I dug out a windbreaker and picked up my handbag, locked the apartment, and headed over to the office. The sun was shining with a brief show of warmth while the bank of charcoal clouds crept in from the islands twenty-six miles out. I parked in the lot and went up the back stairs, passing the glass double doors of California Fidelity, where business was already under way.

I unlocked my office and dropped my bag on the chair. I really didn't have much to do. Maybe I'd put in a little bit of work and then head home again.

My answering machine showed no messages. I sorted through the mail from the day before and then typed up the notes from my visit with Lovella Daggett, Eugene Nickerson, and his sister, Essie. Since no one seemed to know where John Daggett was, I decided I'd try to get a line on Billy Polo instead. I was going to need data for an effective paper search. I put a call through to the Santa Teresa Police Department and asked to be connected to Sergeant Robb.

I'd met Jonah back in June when I was working on a missing persons case. His erratic marital status made a relationship between us inadvisable from my point of view, but I still eyed him with interest. He was what they call Black Irish: dark-haired, blue-eyed, with (perhaps) a streak of masochism. I didn't know him well enough to determine how much of his suffering was of his own devising and I wasn't sure I wanted to find out. Sometimes I think an unconsummated affair is the wisest course, in any event. No hassles, no demands, no disappointments, and both partners keep all their neuroses under wraps. Whatever the surface appearances, most human beings come equipped with convoluted emotional machinery. With intimacy, the wreckage starts to show, damage rendered in the course of passions colliding like freight trains on the same track. I'd had enough of that over the years. I wasn't in any better shape than he was, so why complicate life?

Two rings and the call was picked up.

"Missing Persons, Sergeant Robb."

"Hello, Jonah. It's Kinsey."

"Hey, babe," he said, "What can I do for you that's legal in this state?"

I smiled. "How about a field check on a couple of ex-cons?"

"Sure, no sweat," he said.

I gave him both names and what little information I had. He took it down and said he'd get back to me. He'd fill out a form and have the inquiry run through the National Crime Information Computer, a federal offense since I'm really not entitled to access. Generally, a private investigator has no more rights than the average citizen and relies on ingenuity, patience, and resourcefulness for facts that law enforcement agencies have available as a matter of course. It's a frustrating, but not impossible, state of affairs. I simply cultivate relationships with people plugged into the system at various points. I have contacts at the telephone company, the credit bureau, Southern California Gas, Southern Cal Edison, and the DMV. Occasionally I can make a raid on certain government offices, but only if I have something worthwhile to trade. As for information of a more personal sort, I can usually depend on people's tendencies to rat on one another at the drop of a hat.

I made up a check sheet for Billy Polo and went to work.

Knowing Jonah, he'd call Probation and pick up Polo's current address. In the meantime, I wanted to tag some bases of my own. A personal search always pays unexpected dividends. I didn't want to bypass the possibility of surprise, as that's half the fun. I knew Polo wasn't listed in the current phone book, but I tried information, thinking he might have had a phone put in. There was no new listing for him.

I put a call through to my pal at the utility company, inquiring about a possible service connection. Their records showed nothing. Apparently he hadn't applied for water, gas, or electricity in the area in his own name, but he could be renting a room somewhere, paying a flat rate, with utilities thrown in.

I put calls through to five or six fleabag hotels on lower State Street. Polo wasn't registered and nobody seemed to spark to the name. While I was at it, I tried John Daggett's name and got nowhere.

I knew I wouldn't get so much as a by-your-leave from the local Social Security office and I doubted I'd find Billy Polo's name among the voter registration files.

Which left what?

I checked my watch. Only thirty minutes had passed since I talked to Jonah. I wasn't sure how long it would take him to call back and I didn't want to waste time sitting around until I heard from him. I grabbed my windbreaker, locked the office, and went down the front stairs to State Street, walking two blocks over and two blocks up to the public library.

I found an empty table in the reference department and hauled out Santa Teresa telephone directories for the past five years, checking back year by year. Four books back, I found Polo. Great. I made a note of the Merced Street address, wondering if his prison sentence accounted for the absence of a listing since then.

I went over to the section on Santa Teresa history and pulled out the city directory for that year. In addition to an alphabetical listing by name, the city directory lists *addresses* alphabetically so that if you have an address and want to know the resident, you can thumb to the street and number and pick up the name of the occupant and a telephone number. In the back half, telephone numbers are listed sequentially. If all you have is a telephone number, the city directory will provide you with a name and address. By cross referencing

the address, you can come up with the name again, an occupation, and the names of neighbors all up and down the
same street. In ten minutes, I had a list of seven people who
had lived in range of Billy Polo on Merced. By checking for
those seven in the current directory, I determined that two
were still living there. I jotted down both current telephone
numbers, returned the books to their proper places, and headed
back toward my office.

The sunlight, intermittent for the last hour, was now largely
blocked by incoming clouds which had crowded out blue sky,
leaving only an occasional patch, like a hole in a blanket. The
air was beginning to cool rapidly, a damp breeze worrying at
women's hems. I looked toward the ocean and spotted that
silent veil of gray that betokens rain already falling some miles
out. I quickened my pace.

Once in my office again, I entered the new information in
the file I'd opened. I was just on the verge of closing up for
the day when I heard a tap at the door. I hesitated, then
crossed to the door and peered out.

There was a woman standing in the corridor, late thirties,
expressionless and pale.

"Can I help you?" I said.

"I'm Barbara Daggett."

Quickly, I prayed this wasn't wife number three. I tried the
optimistic approach. "John Daggett's daughter?"

"Yes."

She was one of those icy blondes, with skin as finely textured
as a percale bedsheet, tall, substantially built, with short coarse
hair fanning straight back from her face. She had high cheekbones, a delicate brow, and her father's piercing gaze. Her
right eye was green, her left eye blue. I'd seen a white cat like
that once and it had had the same disconcerting effect. She
was wearing a gray wool business suit and a prim, high-necked
white blouse with a froth of lace at the throat. Her heels were
a burgundy leather and matched her shoulder bag. She looked

like an attorney or a stockbroker, someone accustomed to power.

"Come on in," I said, "I was just trying to figure out how to get in touch with him. I take it your mother told you I stopped by."

I was making small talk. She wasn't having any of it. She sat down, turning those riveting eyes on me as I moved around to my side of the desk and took a seat. I thought of offering her coffee, but I really didn't want her to stay that long. Even the air around her seemed chilly and I didn't like the way she looked at me. I rocked back in my swivel chair. "What can I do for you?"

"I want to know why you're looking for my father."

I shrugged, underplaying it, sticking to the story I'd started with. "I'm not really. I'm looking for a friend of his."

"Why weren't we told Daddy was out of prison? My mother's in a state of collapse. We had to call the doctor and have her sedated."

"I'm sorry to hear that," I said.

Barbara Daggett crossed her legs and smoothed her skirt, her movements agitated. "Sorry? You don't know what this has done to her. She was just beginning to feel safe. Now we find out he's in town somewhere and she's very upset. I don't understand what's going on."

"Miss Daggett, I'm not a parole officer," I said. "I don't know when he got out or why nobody notified you. Your mother's problems didn't start yesterday."

A bit of color came to her cheeks. "That's true. Her problems started the day she married him. He's ruined her life. He's ruined life for all of us."

"Are you referring to his drinking?"

She brushed right over that. "I want to know where he's staying. I have to talk to him."

"At the moment, I have no idea where he is. If I find him, I'll tell him you're interested. That's the best I can do."

"My uncle tells me you saw him on Saturday."

"Only briefly."

"What was he doing in town?"

"We didn't discuss that," I said.

"But what did you talk about? What possible business could he have had with a private detective?"

I had no intention of giving her information, so I tried her technique and ignored the question.

I pulled a legal pad over and picked up a pen. "Is there a number where you can be reached?"

She opened her handbag and took out a business card which she passed across the desk to me. Her office address was three blocks away on State and her title indicated that she was chairman and chief executive officer of a company called FMS.

As if in response to a question, she said, "I develop financial management software systems for manufacturing firms. That's my office number. I'm not listed in the book. If you need to reach me at home, this is the number."

"Sounds interesting," I remarked. "What's your background?"

"I have a math and chemistry degree from Stanford and a double masters in computer sciences and engineering from USC."

I felt my brows lift appreciatively. I couldn't see any evidence that Daggett had ruined *her* life, but I kept the observation to myself. There was clearly more to Barbara Daggett than her professional status indicated. Maybe she was one of those women who succeeds in business and fails in relationships with men. As I'd been accused of that myself, I decided not to make a judgment. Where is it written that being part of a couple is a measure of anything?

She glanced at her watch and stood up. "I have an appointment. Please let me know if you hear from him."

"May I ask what you want with him?"

"I've been urging Mother to file for divorce, but so far she's refused. Maybe I can persuade him instead."

"I'm surprised she didn't divorce him years ago."

Her smile was cold. "She says she married him 'for better or for worse.' To date, there hasn't been any 'better.' Maybe she's hoping for a taste of that before she gives up."

"What about his imprisonment? What was that for?"

Something flickered in her face and I thought at first she wouldn't answer me. "Vehicular manslaughter," she said, finally. "He was drunk and there was an accident. Five people were killed, two of them kids."

I couldn't think of a response and she didn't seem to expect one. She stood up, closed the conversation with a perfunctory handshake, and then she was gone. I could hear her high heels tapping away down the corridor.

5

By the time I closed up the office and got down to my car, the clouds overhead looked like dark gray vacuum cleaner fluff and the rain had begun to splatter the sidewalk with polka dots. I stuck Daggett's file on the passenger seat and backed out of my space, turning right from the parking lot onto Cannon, and right again onto Chapel. Three blocks up, I made a stop, ducking into the supermarket to pick up milk, Diet Pepsi, bread, eggs, and toilet paper. I was into my siege mentality, looking forward to pulling up the drawbridge and waiting out the rain. With luck, I wouldn't have to go out for days.

The phone was ringing as I let myself in. I put the grocery bag on the counter and snatched up the receiver.

"God, I was just about to give up," Jonah said. "I tried the office, but all I got was your answering machine."

"I closed up for the day. I can work at home if I'm in the mood, which I'm not. Have you seen the rain?"

"Rain? Oh yeah, so there is. I haven't even looked out the window since I got in. God, that's great," he said. "Listen, I have some of the information you're looking for and the rest will have to wait. Woody's got a priority request and I had to back off. I'm working tomorrow so I can pick it up then."

"You're working Saturday?"

"I'm filling in for Sobel. My good deed for the week," he said. "Got a pencil? Polo's the one I got a line on."

He rattled out Billy Polo's age, date of birth, height, weight, hair and eye color, his a.k.a, and a hasty rundown of his record, all of which I noted automatically. He'd picked up the name of Billy's parole officer, but the guy was out of the office and wouldn't be available until Monday afternoon.

"Thanks. In the meantime, I'm nosing around on my own," I said. "I bet I'll get a line on him before you do." He laughed and hung up.

I put groceries away and then sat down at my desk, hauling out the little portable Smith-Corona I keep in the knee hole. I consigned the data Jonah'd given me to index cards and then sat and stared at it. Billy Polo, born William Polokowski, was thirty years old, five-foot-eight, a hundred and sixty pounds, brown hair, brown eyes, no scars, tattoos, or "observable physical oddities." His rap sheet sounded like a pop quiz on the California Penal Code, with arrests that ranged from misdemeanors to felonies. Assault, forgery, receiving stolen property, grand theft, narcotics violations. Once he was even convicted of "injuring a public jail," a misdemeanor in this state. Had this occurred in the course of an escape attempt, the charge would have been bumped up to a felony. As it was, he'd probably been caught scratching naughty words on the jail house walls. A real champ, this one.

Apparently, Billy Polo was pretty shiftless when it came to breaking the law and had never even settled on an area of expertise. He'd been arrested sixteen times, with nine convictions, two acquittals, five dismissals. Twice, he'd been put on probation, but nothing seemed to have affected the nature of his behavior, which appeared nearly pathological in its thrust. The man was determined to screw up. Since the age of eighteen, he'd spent an accumulated nine years in jail. No telling what his juvenile record looked like. I assumed his acquaintance with John Daggett dated from his latest offense, an armed robbery conviction, for which he'd served two years and ten months at the California Men's Colony at San Luis Obispo, a medium security facility about ninety miles north of Santa Teresa.

I pulled out the telephone book again and checked for a listing under the name Polokowski. Nothing. God, why can't anything be simple in this business? Oh well. I wasn't going to worry about it for the moment.

By now, I could hear the rain tapping on the glass-enclosed breezeway that connects my place to Henry Pitt's house. He's my landlord and has been for nearly two years. In dry weather, he places an old Shaker cradle out there, filled with rising bread. When the sun is out, the space is like a solar oven, warm and sheltered, dough puffing up above the rim of the cradle like a feather pillow. He can proof twenty loaves at a time, then bake them in the big industrial-sized oven he had installed when he retired from commercial baking. Now he trades fresh bread and pastries for services in the neighborhood and stretches his Social Security payments by clipping coupons avidly. He picks up additional income constructing crossword puzzles which he sells to a couple of those pint-sized "magazines" you can purchase in a supermarket check-out line. Henry Pitts is eighty-one years old and everyone knows I'm half in love with him.

I considered popping over to see him, but even the fifty-foot walk seemed like too much to deal with in the wet. I put some tea water on and picked up my book, stretching out on the sofa with a quilt pulled over me. And that's how I spent the rest of the day.

During the night, the rain escalated and I woke up twice to hear it lashing at the windows. It sounded like somebody spraying the side of the place with a hose. At intervals, thunder rumbled in the distance and my windows flickered with blue light, tree branches illuminated briefly before the room went black again. It was clear I'd have to cancel my 6:00 A.M. run, an obligatory day off, so I burrowed into the depths of my quilt like a little animal, delighted at the idea of sleeping late.

I woke at 8:00, showered, dressed, and fixed myself a soft-boiled egg on toast with lots of Lawry's Seasoned Salt. I'm not going to give up salt. I don't care what they say.

Jonah called as I was washing my plate. He said, "Hey, guess what? Your friend Daggett showed."

I tucked the receiver into the crook of my neck, turning off the water and drying my hands. "What happened? Did he get picked up?"

"More or less. A scruffy drifter spotted him face down in the surf this morning, tangled up in a fishing net. A skiff washed ashore about two hundred yards away. We're pretty sure it connects."

"He died last night?"

"Looks like it. The coroner estimates he went into the water sometime between midnight and five A.M. We don't have a determination yet on the cause and manner of death. We'll know more after the autopsy's done, of course."

"How'd you find out it was him?"

"Fingerprints. He was over at the morgue listed as a John Doe until we ran the computer check. You want to take a look?"

"I'll be right there. What about next of kin? Have they been notified?"

"Yeah, the beat officer went over as soon as we made the I.D. You know the family?"

"Not well, but we've met. I wouldn't want to be quoted on this, but I think you'll find out he's a bigamist. There's a woman down in L.A. who also claims she's married to him."

"Cute. You better come talk to us when you leave St. Terry's," he said and hung up.

The Santa Teresa Police Department doesn't really have a morgue of its own. There's a coroner-sheriff, an elected office in this county, but the actual forensic work is contracted out among various pathologists in the tri-county area. The morgue space itself is divided between Santa Teresa Hospital (commonly referred to as St. Terry's) and the former County General Hospital facility on the frontage road off 101. Daggett was apparently at St. Terry's, which was where I headed as soon as I'd rounded up my slicker, an umbrella, and my handbag.

The visitors' lot at the hospital was half empty. It was Saturday and doctors would probably be making rounds later in the day. The sky was thick with clouds and, high up, I could see the wind whipping through like a fan, blowing white mist across the gray. The pavement was littered with small branches, leaves plastered flat against the ground. Puddles had formed everywhere, pockmarked by the steady rainfall. I parked as close to the rear entrance as I could and then locked my car and made a dash for it.

"Kinsey!"

I turned as I reached the shelter of the building. Barbara Daggett hurried toward me from the far side of the lot, her umbrella tilted against the slant of the rain. She was wearing a raincoat and spike-heeled boots, her white-blonde hair forming a halo around her face. I held the door open for her and we ducked into the foyer.

"You heard about my father?"

"That's why I'm here. Do you know how it happened?"

"Not really. Uncle Eugene called me at eight-fifteen. I guess they tried to notify Mother and he interceded. The doctor has her so doped up it doesn't make any sense to tell her yet. He's worried about how she'll take it, as unstable as she is."

"Is your uncle coming down?"

She shook her head. "I said I'd do it. There's no doubt it's Daddy, but somebody has to sign for the body so the mortuary can come pick it up. Of course, they'll autopsy first. How did you find out?"

"Through a cop I know. I'd told him I was trying to get a line on your father, so he called me when they got a match on the fingerprints. Did you manage to locate him yesterday?"

"No, but it's clear someone did." She closed her umbrella and gave it a shake, then glanced at me. "Frankly, I'm assuming somebody killed him."

"Let's not be too quick off the mark," I said, though privately, I agreed.

The two of us moved through the inner door and into the corridor. The air was warmer here and smelled of latex paint.

"I want you to look into it for me, in any event," she said.

"Hey, listen. That's what the police are for. I don't have the scope for that. Why don't you wait and see what they have to say first?"

She studied me briefly and then moved on. "They don't give a damn what happened to him. Why would they care? He was a drunken bum."

"Oh come on. Cops don't have to *care*," I said. "If it's homicide, they have a job to do and they'll do it well."

When we reached the autopsy room, I knocked and a young black morgue attendant came out, dressed in surgical greens. His name tag indicated that his name was Hall Ingraham. He was lean, his skin the color of pecan wood with a high-gloss finish. His hair was cropped close and gave him the look of a piece of sculpture, his elongated face nearly stylized in its perfection.

"This is Barbara Daggett," I said.

He looked in her direction without meeting her eyes. "You can wait right down here," he said. He moved two doors down and we followed, pausing politely while he unlocked a viewing room and ushered us in.

"It'll be just a minute," he said.

He disappeared and we took a seat. The room was small, maybe nine by nine, with four blue molded-plastic chairs hooked together at the base, a low wooden table covered with old magazines, and a television screen affixed, at an angle, up in one corner of the room. I saw her gaze flick to it.

"Closed circuit," I said. "They'll show him up there."

She picked up a magazine and began to flip through it distractedly. "You never really told me why he hired you," she said. An ad for pantyhose had apparently caught her eye and she studied it as if my reply were of no particular concern.

I couldn't think of a reason not to tell her at this point, but I noticed that I censored myself to some extent, a habit of long standing. I like to hold something back. Once information is out, it can't be recalled so it's better to exercise caution before you flap your mouth. "He wanted me to find a kid named Tony Gahan," I said.

That remarkable two-toned gaze came up to meet mine and I found myself trying to decide which eye color I preferred. The green was more unusual, but the blue was clear and stark. The two together presented a contradiction, like the signal at a street corner, flashing Walk and Don't Walk simultaneously.

"You know him?" I asked.

"His parents and a younger sister were the ones killed in the accident, along with two other people in the car with them. What did Daddy want with him?"

"He said Tony Gahan helped him once when he was on the run from the cops. He wanted to thank him."

Her look was incredulous. "But that's bullshit!"

"So I gather," I said.

She might have pressed for more information, but the television screen flashed with snow at that moment and then flipped over to a closeup of John Daggett. He was lying on a gurney, a sheet neatly pulled up to his neck. He had the blank, plastic look that death sometimes brings, as if the human face were no more than an empty page on which the lines of emotion and experience are transcribed and then erased. He looked closer to twenty years old than fifty-five, with a stubble of beard and hair carelessly arranged. His face was unmarked.

Barbara stared at him, her lips parting, her face diffused with pink. Tears rose in her eyes and hung there, captured in the well of her lower lids. I looked away from her, unwilling to intrude any more than I had to. The morgue attendant's voice reached us through the intercom.

"Let me know when you're done."

Barbara turned away abruptly.

"Thank you. That's fine," I called. The television screen went dark.

Moments later, there was a tap at the door and he reappeared with a sealed manila envelope and a clipboard in hand.

"We'll need to know what arrangements you want made," he said. He was using that tone of studied neutrality I've heard before from those who deal with the bereaved. Its effect is impersonal and soothing, liberating one to transact business without intrusive emotionalism. He needn't have bothered. Barbara Daggett was a businesswoman, bred to that awesome poise that so unsettles men accustomed to female subservience. Her manner now was smooth and detached, her tone as impassive as his.

"I've talked to Wynington-Blake," she said, indicating one of the funeral homes in town. "If you'll notify them once the autopsy's done, they'll take care of everything. Is that form for me?"

He nodded and held the clipboard out to her with a pen attached. "A release for his personal effects," he said.

She dashed off a signature as if she were signing an autograph for a pesky fan. "When will you have the autopsy results?"

He handed her the envelope, which apparently contained Daggett's odds and ends. "Probably by late afternoon."

"Who's doing the post?" I asked.

"Dr. Yee. He's scheduled it for two-thirty."

Barbara Daggett glanced at me. "She's a private investigator. I want all information released to her. Will I need to sign a separate authorization for that?"

"I don't know. There's probably some procedure, but it's a new one on me. I can check into it and contact you later, if you like."

She slipped her business card under the clamp as she handed the clipboard back to him. "Do that."

His eyes met hers for the first time and I could see him register the oddity of the mismatched irises. She brushed past him, moving out of the room. He stared after her. The door closed.

I held my hand out. "I'm Kinsey Millhone, Mr. Ingraham."

He smiled for the first time. "Oh yeah. I heard about you from Kelly Borden. Nice to meet you."

Kelly Borden was a morgue attendant I'd met during a homicide investigation I'd worked on in August.

"Nice to meet you too," I said. "What's the story on this one?"

"I can't tell you much. They brought him in about seven, just as I was coming to work."

"Do you have any idea how long he'd been dead?"

"I don't know for sure, but it couldn't have been long. The body wasn't bloated and there wasn't any putrefaction. From what I've seen of drowning victims, I'd guess he went in the water late last night. Don't quote me on that. The watch he had on was stopped at two thirty-seven, but it could have been broken. It's a crummy watch and looks all beat up. It's in with his effects. Hell, what do I know? I'm just a flunkie, lowest of the low. Dr. Yee hates it if we talk to people like this."

"Believe me, I'm not going to say anything. I'm just asking for my own purposes. What about his clothing? How was he dressed?"

"Jacket, pants, shirt."

"Shoes and socks?"

"Well, shoes. He didn't have socks on and he didn't have a wallet or anything like that."

"Any signs of injury?"

"None that I've seen."

I couldn't think of anything else I wanted to ask for the moment so I thanked him and said I'd be in touch.

Then I went out to look for Barbara Daggett. If I was going to work for her, we needed to get business squared away.

6

I found her standing in the foyer, looking out at the parking lot. The rain was falling monotonously, occasional gusts of wind tossing the treetops. Cozy-looking lights were on in all the buildings that rimmed the parking lot, which only emphasized the dampness and the chill outside. A nurse, her white uniform flashing from the flaps of a dark blue raincoat, approached the doorway, leaping over puddles like a kid playing hopscotch. Her white hose were speckled with flesh-colored blotches where the rain had soaked through and the tops of her white shoes were spattered with mud. She reached the entrance and I held the door for her.

She flashed me a smile. "Whoo! Thanks. It's like an obstacle course out there." She shook the water from her raincoat and padded down the hallway, crepe soles leaving a pattern of damp footprints in her wake.

Barbara Daggett seemed rooted to the spot. "I have to go to Mother's," she said. "Somebody has to tell her." She turned and looked at me. "How much do you charge for your services?"

"Thirty an hour, plus expenses, which is standard for the area. If you're serious, I can drop a contract off at your office this afternoon."

"What about a retainer?"

I made a quick assessment. I usually ask for an advance, especially in a situation like this, when I know I'll be talking to the cops. There's no concept of privilege between a P.I.

and a client, but at least the front money makes it clear where my loyalties lie.

"Four hundred should cover it," I said. I wondered if the figure came to mind because of Daggett's bounced check. Oddly enough, I felt protective of him. He'd conned me—there was no doubt of that—but I *had* agreed to work for him, and in my mind, I still had a duty to discharge. Of course, I might not have felt as charitable if he were still alive, but the dead are defenseless, and somebody in this world has to look out for them.

"I'll have my secretary cut you a check first thing Monday morning," she said. She turned back, looking out the double doors into the gloom. She leaned her head against the glass.

"Are you okay?"

"You don't know how many times I've wished him dead," she said. "Have you ever dealt with an alcoholic?"

I shook my head.

"They're so maddening. I used to look at him and I was convinced he could quit drinking if he wanted to. I don't know how many times I talked to him, begging him to stop. I thought he didn't understand. I thought he just wasn't aware of what we were going through, my mother and me. I can remember the look he'd get in his eyes when he was drunk. Little pink piggy eyes. His whole body radiated this odor. Bourbon. God, I hate that stuff. He smelled like somebody'd dropped a bottle of Early Times down a heater vent . . . waves of smell. He reeked of it."

She looked over at me, her eyes dry and pitiless. "I'm thirty-four and I've hated him with every cell in my body for as long as I can remember. And now I'm stuck with it. He won, didn't he? He never changed, never straightened up, never gave us an inch. He was such a shitheel. It makes me want to smash this glass door out. I don't even know why I care how he died.

I should be relieved, but I'm pissed. The irony is that he's probably still going to dominate my life."

"How so?"

"Look what he's done to me already. I think of him every time I have a drink. I think of him if I decide *not* to have a drink. If I even *meet* a man who drinks or if I see a bum on the street or smell bourbon, his face is the first thing that comes to mind. Oh God, and if I'm around someone who's had too much, I can't stand it. I disconnect. My life is filled with reminders of him. His apologies and his phony, whee-dling charm, his boo-hooing when the booze got to him. The times he fell, the times he got put in jail, the times he spent every dime we had. When I was twelve, Mother got religion and I don't know which was worse. At least Daddy woke up most days in okay shape. She had Jesus for breakfast, lunch, and dinner. It was grotesque. And then there were the joys of being an only child."

She broke off abruptly and seemed to shake herself. "Oh hell. What difference does it make? I know I sound sorry for myself, but it's been such a bitch and there's no end in sight."

"Actually, you look like you've done pretty well," I said.

She turned her gaze back to the parking lot and I could see her faint, bitter smile reflected in the glass. "You know what they say about living well as the best revenge. I did well because it was the one defense I had. Escape has been the motivating force in my life. Getting away from him, getting away from her, putting that household behind me. The funny thing is, I haven't moved an inch, and the harder I run, the faster I keep slipping back to them. There are spiders that work like that. They bury themselves and create a little pocket of loose dirt. Then when their prey comes along, the soil gives way and the victim slides right down into the trap. There are laws for everything except the harm families do."

She turned, shoving her hands down in her raincoat pock-ets. She pushed the door open with her backside and a draft of cold air rushed in. "What about you? Are you leaving or will you stick around?"

"I guess I'll hit the office as long as I'm out," I said.

She pressed a button on the handle of her umbrella and it lifted into the open position with a muffled *thunk*. She held it for me and we walked toward my car together. The raindrops tapping on the umbrella fabric made a muted sound, like popcorn in a covered saucepan.

I unlocked my car and got in, while she moved off toward hers, calling back over her shoulder. "Try me at the office as soon as you hear anything. I should be there by two."

My office building was deserted. California Fidelity is closed on weekends so their offices were dark. I let myself in, picking up the batch of morning mail that had been shoved through the slot. There were no messages on my answering machine. I pulled a contract out of my top drawer and spent a few minutes filling in the blanks. I checked Barbara Daggett's business card to verify the address, then I locked up again and went down the front stairs.

I walked the three blocks and dropped the contract off at her office, then headed over to the police station on Floresta. The combination of the weekend and the bad weather lent the station much the same deserted air as my office building. Crime doesn't adhere to a forty-hour week, but there are days when even the criminals don't seem to feel like doing much. The linoleum showed a gridwork of wet footprints, like a pattern of dance steps too complex to learn. The air smelled of cigarette smoke and damp uniforms. I could see where someone had fashioned a folded newspaper into a rain hat and then abandoned it on the wooden bench just inside the door.

One of the clerks in the identification and records section buzzed Jonah and he came out to the locked foyer door and admitted me.

He wasn't looking good. During the summer, he'd shed an excess twenty pounds and he'd told me he was still working out at the gym, so it wasn't that. His dark hair seemed poorly trimmed and the lines around his eyes were pronounced. He also had that weary aura that unhappiness seems to breed.

"What happened to you?" I asked as we walked back to his office. He'd been reconciled with his wife since June, after a year's separation, and from what I'd gathered, it was not going well.

"She wants an open relationship," he remarked.

"Oh come *on*," I said, with disbelief.

That netted me a tired smile. "That's what the lady says." He held the door open for me and we passed into an L-shaped room, furnished with big wooden desks.

Missing Persons is included in Crimes Against Persons, which in turn is considered part of the Investigations Division, along with Crimes Against Property, Narcotics, and Special Investigations. The room was deserted at the moment, but people came and went at intervals. From the interview room off the inside corridor, I could hear the rise and fall of a shrill female voice and I guessed that an interrogation was under way. Jonah closed the hall door, automatically protective of department business.

He filled two Styrofoam cups with coffee and brought them over, handing me packets of Cremora and Equal. Just what I needed, a cup of hot chemicals. We went through the motions of doctoring the coffee, which smelled like it'd been on the burner too long.

I took a few minutes to lay out the Daggett situation. At this point, we didn't have the results of the autopsy, so the idea of murder was purely theoretical. Still, I told Jonah what had gone on to date, detailing the principal characters. I was talking to him as a friend instead of a cop and he listened as an interested, but unofficial, party.

"So how long was he up here before he died?" Jonah asked.

"Since Monday presumably," I said. "It's possible he went

somewhere else first, but Lovella seemed to think he'd head straight for Billy Polo if he needed help."

"Did that information on Polo do you any good?"

"Not yet, but it will. I'm just waiting to see what we've got on our hands before I proceed. Even if the death was accidental, I suspect Barbara Daggett will want me to look into it. I mean, for starters, what was he doing on a boat in a rainstorm? And where has he been all this time?"

"Where have *you* been?" Jonah asked.

I focused on him and realized he'd shifted the subject. "Who, me? I've been around."

He picked up a pencil and began to tap out a beat, like a man auditioning for a tiny blues band. He was giving me a look I'd seen before, full of heat and speculation. "Are you dating anyone?"

I shook my head, smiling slightly. "The only good men I know are married." I was being flirtatious and he seemed to like that.

His blue eyes locked into mine and the color rose in his face. "What do you do for sex?"

"Jog on the beach. How about you?"

He smiled, breaking off eye contact. "In other words, it's none of my business."

I laughed. "I'm not avoiding the question. I'm telling the truth."

"Really? That's funny. I always pictured you out raising hell."

"I did some of that years ago, but I can't stand it these days. Sex is a bonding process. I'm careful who I connect up with. Besides, you don't know what the marketplace is like. A one-night stand is more like a wrestling match with a couple of quick take-downs. Talk about demoralizing. I'd rather be alone."

"I know what you mean. I was out there hustling some the year she was gone, but I never got the hang of it. I'd go in a bar and some babe would sidle up to me, but I never made the right moves. Couple of times, women told me I was rude when I just thought I was making small talk."

"It's worse if you're successful at it," I said. "Be grateful you never learned the gamesmanship. I know a couple of guys on the circuit and they're hard as nails, you know? Unhappy. Hostile toward women. They get laid, but that's about all they get."

Behind him, Lieutenant Becker came in and took a seat at a desk across the room. Jonah's pencil tapping started again and then stopped. He tossed it aside and rocked back in his chair.

"I wish life were simple," he said.

I kept my tone of voice mild. "Life *is* simple. You're the one making things complex. You were doing great without Camilla, as far as I could see. She crooks her finger, though, and you go running back. And now you can't figure out what went wrong. Quit acting like a victim when you did it to yourself."

This time he laughed. "God, Kinsey. Why don't you just say what's on your mind."

"Well, I don't understand voluntary suffering. If you're unhappy, change something. If you can't make it work, then bail out. What's the big deal?"

"Is that what you did?"

"Not quite. I dumped the first and the second one dumped me. With both, I did my share of suffering, but when I look back on it, I can't understand why I endured so long. It was dumb. It was a big waste of time and cost me a lot."

"I've never even heard you mention those guys."

"Yeah, well I'll tell you about them sometime."

"You want to have a drink when I get off work?"

I looked at him briefly and then shook my head. "We'd end up in bed, Jonah."

"That's the point, isn't it?" He smiled and did a Groucho Marx wiggle with his eyebrows.

I laughed and turned the subject back to Daggett as I got up. "Call me when Dr. Yee has results on the post."

"I'll call for more than that."

"Get your life squared away first."

When I left, he was still staring after me, and it was all I could do to get out of there. I had this troubling urge to gallop over and leap onto his lap, laughing while I covered his face with licks, but I didn't think the department would ever be the same. As I glanced back, I could see Becker giving us a speculative look while he pretended to check his "in" box.

7

Daggett's death was ruled accidental. Jonah called me at home at 4:00 to give me the news. I'd spent the afternoon again wrapped up in a quilt, hoping to finish the book. I'd just put on a fresh pot of coffee and I was scurrying back under the covers as the phone rang. When he told me, I was puzzled, but I wasn't convinced. I kept waiting for the punchline, but there wasn't one.

"I don't get it," I said. "Does Yee know the background on this?"

"Babe, Daggett's blood alcohol was point three-five. You're talking acute ethanol intoxication, almost coma stage."

"And that was the cause of death?"

"Well no, he drowned, but Yee says there's no evidence of foul play. None. Daggett went out in a boat, got tangled up in a fishing net, and fell overboard, too drunk to save himself."

"Bullshit!"

"Kinsey, some people die accidentally. It's a fact."

"I don't believe it. Not this one."

"The crime scene investigation unit didn't find a thing. Not even a *hint*. What can I say? You know these guys. They're as good as they come. If you think it's murder, come up with some evidence. In the meantime, we're calling it an accident. As far as we're concerned, the case is closed."

"What was he doing dead drunk in a boat?" I asked. "The man was broke and it was raining cats and dogs. Who'd he rent the boat from?"

I could hear Jonah sigh. "He didn't. Apparently, he took

a little ten-foot skiff from its mooring off the dock at Marina One. The harbor master identified the boat and you can see where the line was cut."

"Where'd they find it?"

"On the beach near the pier. There weren't any usable prints."

"I don't like it."

"Look, I know what you're saying and you've got a point. I tend to agree, if that makes you feel any better, but who's asking us? Look at it as a gift. If the death is ruled a homicide, you can't get near it. This way, you've got carte blanche . . . within limits, of course."

"Does Dolan know I'm interested?" Lieutenant Dolan was an assistant division commander and an old antagonist of mine. He hated private investigators getting involved in police business.

"The case is Feldman's. He won't give a shit. You want me to talk to him?"

"Yeah, do that," I said. "And clear it with Dolan, while you're at it. I'm tired of getting my hand smacked."

"Okay. I'll get back to you first thing Monday then," Jonah said. "In the meantime, let me know if anything turns up."

"Right. Thanks."

I put a call through to Barbara Daggett, repeating the information I'd just received. When I finished, she was silent.

"What do you think?" she asked, finally.

"Let's put it this way. *I'm* not satisfied, but it's your money. If you like, I can nose around for a couple of days and if nothing turns up, we'll dump the whole business and you'll just have to live with it."

"What are the odds?"

"I have no idea. All I know to do is pick up a thread and see where it leads. We may come up with six dead ends, but at least you'll know we gave it a shot."

"Let's do it."

"Great. I'll be in touch."

I pushed the quilt aside and got up. I hoped Billy Polo was still around. I didn't know where else to start.

I unplugged the coffeepot, poured the balance of the coffee into a thermos, and then made myself a peanut butter and dill pickle sandwich, which I put in a brown paper bag like a school kid. I had just about that same feeling in my gut too . . . the dull dread I'd experienced when I was eight, trudging off to Woodrow Wilson Elementary. I didn't want to go out in the rain. I didn't want to connect up with Billy Polo, who was probably a creep. He sounded like one of the sixth-grade boys I'd been so fearful of . . . lawless, out of control, and mean.

I searched through my closet until I found my slicker and an umbrella. I left my warm apartment behind and drove over to Billy Polo's old address on Merced. It was 4:15 and getting prematurely dark. The neighborhood had probably been charming once, but it was gradually being overtaken by apartment buildings and was now no more than a hapless mix of the down-at-the-heel and the bland. The little gingerbread structures were wedged between three-story stucco boxes with tenant parking underneath and everywhere there was evidence of the same tasteless disregard for history.

I parked under a pepper tree, using the overhanging branches as brief shelter while I put up my umbrella. I checked the names and house numbers of the two former neighbors, hoping one of them could give me a lead on Polo's current whereabouts.

The first door I knocked on was answered by an elderly woman in a wheelchair, her legs wrapped in Ace bandages and stuffed into lace-up shoes with slices cut out of the sides to accommodate her bunions. I stood on her leaky front porch, talking to her through the screen door, which she kept latched. She had a vague recollection of Billy, but had no idea what had happened to him or where he'd gone. She did direct me to a little rental unit at the rear of the property next door. This was not one of the addresses I'd picked up from the city directory. She said Billy's family had lived in the front house, while the rear was still occupied by an old gent named Talbot, who had been there for the last thirty years. I thanked her and picked my way down the rain-slicked stairs and back along the driveway.

The front unit must have been one of the early houses in the area—a story and a half of white frame, with a peaked roof, two dormers, and a front porch that was screened in now and furnished with junk. I could see the coils on the backside of an old refrigerator and beside it, what looked like a pillar of milk cartons, filled with paperback books. Hydrangeas and bougainvillea grew together in a tangle along the side of the house and the runoff from the rain gutter threw a gush of water out on the drive, forcing me to cut wide to the right.

The rear unit looked like it was originally a tool shed, with a lean-to attached to the left side and a tiny carport on the right. There was no car visible and most of the sheltered space was taken up by a cord of firewood, stacked against the wall. There was room left for a bicycle maybe, but not much else.

The structure was white frame, propped up on cinderblocks, with a window on either side of a central door, and a tiny chimney poking up through the roof. It looked like the drawing we all did in grade school, even to the smoke curling up from the chimney pipe.

I knocked and the door was opened by a wizened old man with no teeth. His mouth was a wide line barely separating the tip of his nose from the upward thrust of his chin. When he caught sight of me and realized that I was no one he knew, he left the doorway briefly and returned with his dentures, smiling slightly as he shifted them into place. His false teeth made a crunching sound like a horse chewing on a bit. He looked to be in his seventies, frail, his pale skin speckled with red and blue. His white hair was brushed into a pompadour in front, shaggy over his ears and touching his collar in the back. He wore a shirt that looked soft from years of washing and a cardigan sweater that probably belonged to a woman at some point. The buttons were rhinestone and the button-holes were on the wrong side. He smoothed his hair back with a trembling hand and waited to see what I could possibly want.

"Are you Mr. Talbot?"

"Depends on who's asking," he said.

"I'm Kinsey Millhone. The woman next door suggested that I talk to you. I'm looking for Billy Polo. His family lived in that front house about five years ago."

"I know Billy quite well. Why are you looking for him?"

"I need some information about a friend of his," I said and then gave him a brief explanation. I couldn't see any reason to prevaricate so I simply stated my purpose and left it at that.

He blinked at me. "Billy Polo's a very bad fella. I wonder if you're aware of that." His voice was powdery and I noticed that he had a tremor, his head oscillating as he spoke. I guessed that he suffered from some form of parkinsonism.

"Yeah, I am. I heard he was up at the California Men's Colony until recently. I think that's where he met the man I'm referring to. Do you have any idea how I might reach him?"

"Well, you know, his mother is the one who owned that place," he said, nodding toward the front house. "She sold it about two years ago when she remarried."

"Is she still here in town?"

"Yes, and I believe she's living on Tranvia. Her married name is Christopher. Just a minute and I'll give you the ad-dress." He shuffled away and a few moments later was back with a small address book in hand. "She's a lovely woman. Sends me a card every year at Christmastime. Yes, here it is.

Bertha Christopher. Goes by the nickname of Betty. If you chance to see her, I wish you'd give her my best."

"I'll do that, Mr. Talbot. Thanks so much."

Tranvia turned out to be a wide, treeless street off Milagro on the east side of town, a neighborhood of one-story frame houses on small lots, with chicken wire fences, unruly head-high poinsettia bushes pelted by the rain, and soggy children's toys abandoned in driveways paved with parallel strips of concrete. The level of maintenance here seemed erratic, but the address I now had for Bertha Christopher showed one of the better-kept houses on the block, mustard-colored with dark brown trim. I parked my VW on the opposite side of the street, about fifty yards away, so I could sit and watch the place inconspicuously. Most of the parked cars were crummy so mine fit right in.

It was now after 5:00 and the light was fading fast, the chill in the air more pronounced. The rain had eased somewhat so I left my umbrella where it was. I grabbed my yellow slicker and slipped into it, pulling up the hood. I locked the car and crossed the street, splashing through puddles that darkened the leather of my boots. The rain drummed against the fabric of the slicker with a pocking sound that made me feel like I was in a pup tent.

The Christopher property was surrounded by a low rock wall, constructed with sandstone boulders the size of canta-loupes, held together with concrete. A row of hanging plant-ers screened the front windows from the street and a set of glass windchimes, suspended in one corner of the porch, tin-kled with the wind. There were two lightweight aluminum lawn chairs arranged on either side of a metal table. Every-thing was soggy and smelled of wet grass.

There was no doorbell, but I tapped on the pane of glass in the front door, cupping a hand so I could peer in. The interior was in shadow, no lights showing from the rear of the house. I moved to the porch rail and checked the adjacent houses, both of which were dark. My guess was that many of these people were off at work. After a few minutes, I went back to my car.

I started the engine and ran the heater for a while, fogging up the windows until I could barely see. I rubbed a clear spot in the middle of the windshield and then sat and stared. Street-lights came on. At 5:45, I ate my sandwich just for something to do. At 6:15, I drank some coffee and flipped on my car radio, listening to a talk-show host interview a psychic. Fifteen minutes later, right after the 6:30 news, a car approached and slowed, turning into the Christophers' driveway.

A woman got out, dimly illuminated by the street light. She paused as if to raise her umbrella and then apparently decided to make a dash for it. I watched her scuttle up the driveway and around toward the back of the house. Moments later, the lights went on in sequence . . . first the rear left room, prob-ably a kitchen, then the living room, and finally the front porch light. I gave her a few minutes to get her coat hung up and then I returned to her front door.

I knocked again. I could see her peer into the hallway from the rear of the house and then approach the front door. She stared at me blankly, then leaned her head close to the glass for a better look.

She appeared to be in her fifties, with a sallow complexion and a deeply creased face. Her hair was too uniform a shade to be a natural brown. She wore it parted on the side with big puffy bangs across her lined forehead. Her eyes were the size and color of old pennies and her makeup looked like it needed renewing at this hour of the day. She wore a uniform I'd seen before, brown pants and a brown-and-yellow-checked tunic. I couldn't place the outfit offhand.

"Yes?" she called through the glass.

I raised my voice against the sound of the rain. "I'm looking for Billy. Is he back yet?"

"He don't live here, hon, but he said he'd be by at eight o'clock. Who are you?"

I picked a name at random. "Charlene. Are you his mother?"

"Charlene who?"

"A friend of his said I should look him up if I was ever in Santa Teresa. Is he at work?"

She gave me an odd look, as if the notion of Billy working had never crossed her mind. "He's out checking the used car lots for an automobile."

She had one of those faces that seemed tantalizingly familiar and it dawned on me, belatedly, that she was a checker at the supermarket where I shop now and then. We'd even chatted idly about the fact that I was a P.I. I eased back out of the porch light, hoping she hadn't recognized me at the same time I recognized her. I held the corner of the slicker up as though to shield my face from the wind.

She seemed to pick up on the fact that something odd was going on. "What'd you want him for?"

I ignored that, pretending I couldn't hear. "Why don't I come back when he gets home?" I hollered. "Just tell him Charlene stopped by and I'll catch up with him when I can."

"Well, all right," she said reluctantly. I gave her a casual wave as I turned. I went down the porch steps and into the dark, aware that she was peering after me suspiciously. I must have disappeared from her field of vision then because she turned the porch light off.

I got back in my car with one of those quick, involuntary shudders that racks you from head to toe. When I caught up with Billy, I might well admit who I was and what I wanted with him, but for the moment, I didn't want to tip my hand. I checked my watch and settled in, prepared to wait. Already, it was feeling like a long night.

8

Four hours passed. The rain stopped. It became apparent that Billy was not only late, but possibly not coming at all. Maybe he'd bought a car and hightailed it out of town, or maybe at some point he'd phoned his mother and decided to skip the visit when he heard about "Charlene." I finished all the coffee in the thermos, my brain fairly crackling from caffeine. If I smoked cigarettes, I could have gone through a pack. Instead, I listened to eight more installments of the news, the farm report, and an hour of Hispanic music. I pondered the possibility of learning the Spanish language by simply listening to these gut-wrenching tunes. I thought about Jonah and the husbands I'd known. Surely, if my heart broke again, it would sound just like this, though for all I knew, the lyrics were about cut worms and inguinal hernias, matters only made soulful through soaring harmonies. Altogether, I came perilously close to boring myself insensible with my own mental processes, so it was with real relief that I saw the car approach and pull into the curb in front of the house across the street. It looked like a 1967 Chevrolet, white, with a temporary registration sticker on the windshield. I couldn't tell much about the guy who got out, but I watched with interest as he took the porch steps in two bounds and rang the bell.

Betty Christopher came to the door to let him in. The two of them disappeared. A moment later, shadows wavered against the kitchen light. I figured they'd sit down for a couple of beers and a heart-to-heart talk. The next thing I knew, however, the front door opened again and he came out. I slipped down on the car seat until my eyes were level with the bottom of the window. The cloud cover was still heavy, obscuring the moon, and the cars along the curb created deeper shadows still. He stared out at the street, taking in the line of parked cars one by one. I felt my heart start to thump as I watched him come down the steps and head in my direction.

He paused in the middle of the street. He moved over to a van parked two cars away from mine. He flicked on a flashlight and opened the door on the driver's side, apparently to check the registration. I lost sight of him. Moments went by. I watched the shadows, wondering if he'd crept around the other side and was coming up on my right. I heard a muffled sound as he closed the door to the van. The beam from his flashlight swept over the car in front of me and flashed across my windshield, the light too diffused by the time it reached me to illuminate much. He flicked it off. He waited, scanning the street on both sides. Apparently, he decided there was nothing to worry about. He crossed back to the house. As he reached the porch, she came out, clutching a robe around her. They talked for a few minutes and then he got in his car and took off. The minute she went inside, I started the VW and did a big U-turn, following. I hoped this wasn't all some elaborate ruse to flush me into the open.

He had already made a left turn and then a right by the time I caught sight of him two blocks ahead of me. We were driving along the back streets with no traffic lights at all and only an occasional stop sign to slow our progress. I had to close the gap or risk losing him. A "one-man" tail is nearly pointless unless you know who you're following and where he's going to begin with. At this hour, there were very few cars on the road, and if he drove far, he'd realize the presence of my VW was no accident.

I thought he was headed toward the freeway, but before he reached the northbound on-ramp, he slowed and made a right-hand turn. By then, I was only half a block back so I whipped over to the curb and parked, killing the engine. I locked the car and took off on foot, heading diagonally across the corner lot at a dead run. I caught sight of his taillights half a block ahead. The car was making a left-hand turn into a shabby trailer park.

Puente is a narrow street that parallels Highway 101 on the east side of town, with the trailer park itself squeezed into the space between the two roadways, screened off from the highway by a ten-foot board fence and masses of oleander. I was covering ground at a quick clip. The houses I passed were dark, driveways crowded with old cars, most of them sporting dents. The street lighting here was poor, but ahead of me I caught traces of light from the trailer park, which was strung with small multicolored bulbs.

By the time I got to the entrance, there was no sign of the Chevrolet, but the place was small and I didn't think the car would be hard to spot. The road twisting through the trailer park was two lanes wide. The blacktop still glistened from the rain and water was dripping from the eucalyptus trees that towered at intervals. There were signs posted everywhere: SLOW. SPEED BUMPS. TENANT PARKING ONLY. DO NOT BLOCK DRIVEWAY.

Most of the trailers were "single-wides," fifteen to twenty feet long, the kind that once upon a time you could actually hitch to your car and travel in. Nomad, Airstream, and Concord seemed to predominate. Each had a numbered cardboard sign in the window, indicating the number of the lot on which it sat. Some were moored in narrow patches of grass, temporary camper spaces for RVs passing through, but many were permanent and, by the look of them, had been there for years. The lots were stingy squares of poured concrete, surrounded by sections of white picket fence two feet high, or separated from one another by sagging lengths of bamboo matting. The yards, when they existed, harbored an assortment of plastic deer and flamingos.

It was almost eleven and many of the trailers were dark. Occasionally, I could see the blue-gray flicker of a TV set. I found the Chevrolet, hood warm, the engine still ticking, parked beside a dark green battered trailer with a torn awning and half the aluminum skirting ripped away. From inside, I could hear the dull thump of rock and roll music being played too loudly in too small a space.

The trailer windows were ovals of hot yellow light, positioned about a foot higher than eye level. I edged around to the right-hand side, easing in as close as I could, checking the area to see if any of the neighbors had spotted me. The trailer next door had a FOR RENT sign taped to the siding, and the one across the lane had the curtains pulled. I turned back to the window and got up on tiptoe, peering in. The window was opened slightly and the air seeping out was hot and smelled of fried onions. The curtains consisted of old cotton dish towels, with a brass rod threaded through one end, hanging crookedly enough to provide a clear view of Billy Polo and the woman he was talking to. They were both seated at a flop-down table in the galley, drinking beer, mouths working, words inaudible in the thumping din of music. The interior of the trailer was a depressing collage of cheap paneled walls, dirty dishes, junk, torn upholstery, newspapers, and canned goods stacked on counter tops. A bumper sticker pasted above the front door said, I'VE BEEN TO ALL 48 STATES!

There was a small black-and-white television set perched on a cardboard box, tuned to what looked like the tag end of a prime-time private-eye show. The action was speeding up. A car careened out of control, flipping end over end before it went off a cliff, exploding in midair. The picture cut to two men in an office, one talking on the phone. Neither Billy nor his companion seemed to be watching and the music must have made it impossible for them to hear the dialogue anyway.

I could feel a cramp forming in my right calf. I cast about for something to stand on to ease the strain. The yard next door was a jungle of overgrown shrubs, the parking space choked with discards. There was a set of detached wooden steps tucked up under the trailer door. I blundered through the bushes, my jeans and boots getting drenched in the process. I was counting on the thunder of music to cover the sound of my labors as I hefted the box steps, tramped back through the shrubs, and set the steps under the window.

Cautiously, I mounted, peering in again. Billy Polo had a surprisingly boyish face for a man who'd lived his thirty years as a thug. His hair was dark, a curly mass standing out around his face. His nose was small, his mouth generous, and he had a dimple in his chin that looked like a puncture wound. He wasn't a big man, but he had a wiry musculature that suggested strength. There was something manic about him, a hint of tension in his gestures. His eyes were restless and he tended to stare off to one side when he spoke, as if direct eye contact made him anxious.

The woman was in her early twenties, with a wide mouth, strong chin, and a pug nose that looked as if it was made of putty. She wore no makeup and her fair hair was dense, a series of tight ripples that she wore shoulder length, brittle and illcut. Her skin was very pale, mottled with freckles. She was wearing a man's oversized silk bathrobe and apparently nursing a cold. She kept a wad of Kleenex in her pocket which she honked into from time to time. She was so close to me I could see the chapping where the frequent blowing had reddened her nose and upper lip. I wondered if she was an old girlfriend of Billy's. There was no overt sexuality in the way they related to one another, but there was a curious intimacy. An old love affair gone flat perhaps.

The continuous rock and roll music was driving me nuts. I was never going to hear what they were saying with that stuff booming out all over the place. I got down off the steps and went around the other side of the trailer to the front door. The window to the right was wide open, though the curtains were pinned shut.

I waited until there was a brief pause between cuts. I took a deep breath and pounded on the door. "Hey! Could you cut the goddamn noise," I yelled. "We're tryin' to get some sleep over here!"

From inside the trailer, the woman hollered, "Sorry!" The music ceased abruptly and I went back around to the other side to see how much of their conversation I could pick up.

The quiet was divine. The volume on the television set must have been turned all the way down, because the string of commercials that now appeared was antic with silence and I could actually catch snatches of what they were saying, though they mumbled unmercifully.

". . . course, she's going to say that. What did you expect?" she said.

"I don't like the pressure. I don't like havin' her on my back . . ." He said something else I couldn't make out.

"What difference does it make? Nobody forced her. Shit, she's free, white, and twenty-one . . . the point is . . . getting into . . . just so she doesn't think . . . the whole thing, right?"

Her voice had dropped and when Billy answered, he had one hand across his mouth so I couldn't understand him at all. He was only half attentive anyway, talking to her with his gaze straying to the television picture. It must have been 11:00 because the local news came on. There was the usual lead-in, a long shot of the news desk with two male newscasters, one black, one white, like a matched set, sitting there in suits. Both looked properly solemn. The camera cut to a head shot of the black man. A photograph of John Daggett appeared briefly behind him. There was a quick shot of the beach. It took me a moment to realize that it must have been the spot where Daggett's body had been found. In the background, I could see the mouth of the harbor and the dredge.

Billy jerked upright, grabbing the woman's arm. She swiveled around to see what he was pointing to. The announcer talked on, smoothly moving the top sheet of paper aside. The camera cut to the co-anchor and the picture shifted to a still shot of a local waste disposal site.

Billy and the woman traded a long, anxious look. Billy started cracking his knuckles. "Christ!"

The woman snatched up the paper and tossed it at him. "I told you it was him the minute I read some bum washed up on the beach. Goddamn it, Billy! Everything with you comes down to the same old bullshit. You think you're so smart. You got all the angles covered. Oh sure. Turns out you don't even know what you're talking about!"

"They don't even know we knew him. How would they know that?"

She gave him a scornful look, exasperated that he'd try to defend himself. "Give the cops some credit! They probably identified him by his fingerprints, right? So they know he was up in San Luis. It's not going to take a genius to figure out you were up there with him. Next thing we know somebody's coming around knocking at the door. 'When'd you last see this guy?' Shit like that."

He got up abruptly. He crossed to a kitchen cabinet and opened it. "You got any Black Jack?"

"No, I don't have any Black Jack. You drank it all last night."

"Get some clothes on. Let's go over to the Hub."

"Billy, I've got a cold! I'm not going out at this hour. You go. Why do you need a drink anyway?"

He reached for his jacket, hunching into it. "You have any cash? All I got on me is a buck."

"Get a job. Pay your own way. I'm tired of givin' you money."

"I said you'd get it back. What are you worried about? Come on, come on," he said, snapping his fingers impatiently.

She took her time about it, but she did root through her

purse, coming up with a crumpled five-dollar bill, which he took without comment.

"Are you crashing here?" she asked.

"I don't know yet. Probably. Don't lock up."

"Well, just keep it down, okay? I feel like hell and I don't want to be woke up."

He put his hands on her arms. "Hey," he said. "Cool it. You worry too much."

"You know what your problem is? You think all you have to do is say shit like that and it's all okay. The world doesn't work that way. It never did."

"Yeah, well there's always a first time. Your problem is you're a pessimist. . . ."

At that point, I figured I'd better cut out and head back to my car. I eased down off my perch, debating briefly about whether I should move the steps or leave them there. Better to move them. I hefted them, swiftly pushing through the undergrowth to a cleared space where the junk was stacked up. I set the box down and then took off through the darkened trailer park and out to the street.

I jogged to my car, started it, and did another U-turn, anticipating that Billy would head back the same way he came. Sure enough, in my rearview mirror I saw the Chevrolet make a left turn onto the main thoroughfare, coming up behind me. He followed me for a block and a half, tailgating, a real A-type. With an impatient toot of the horn, he passed me, squealed into another left-hand turn, and zoomed off toward Milagro. I knew where he was headed so I took my time. There's a bar called the Hub about three blocks up. I walked into the place maybe ten minutes after he did. He'd already bought his Jack Daniel's, which he was nursing while he played pool.

9

The Hub is a bar with all the ambience of a converted ware-house. The space is too vast for camaraderie, the air too chill for relaxation. The ceiling is high, painted black, and covered with a gridwork of pipes and electrical conduits. The tables in the main room are sparse, the walls lined with old black-and-white photographs of the bar and its various clientele over the years. Through a wide archway is a smaller room with four pool tables. The juke box is massive, outlined in bands of yellow, green, and cherry red, with bubbles blipping through the seams. The place was curiously empty for a Sat-urday night. A Willie Nelson single was playing, but it wasn't one I knew.

I was the only woman in the bar and I could sense the male attention shift to me with a bristling caution. I paused, feeling sniffed at, as if I were a dog in an alien neighborhood. Cig-arette smoke hung in the air, and the men with their pool cues were caught in the hazy light, bent above the tables in silhouette. I identified Billy Polo by the great puff of hair around his head. Upright, he was taller than I'd pictured him, with wide, hard shoulders and slim hips. He was playing pool with a Mexican kid, maybe twenty-two, with a gaunt face, tattooed arms, and a strip of pinched-looking chest which was visible in the gap of the Hawaiian shirt he wore unbuttoned to the waist. He sported maybe six chest hairs in a shallow depression in the middle of his sternum.

I crossed to the table and stood there, waiting for Billy to finish his game. He glanced at me with disinterest and lined up the cue ball with the six ball, which he smacked smartly into a side pocket. He moved around the table without pause, lining up the two ball which he fired like a shot into the corner pocket. He chalked his cue, eyeing the three ball. He tested an angle and rejected it, leaning into the table then with a shot that sent the three ball rocketing into the side pocket, while the five ball glanced off the side, rolled into range of the corner pocket, hung there, and finally dropped in. A trace of a smile crossed Billy's face, but he didn't look up.

Meanwhile, the Mexican kid stood there and grinned at me, leaning on his cue stick. He mouthed, "I love you." One of his front teeth was rimmed in gold, like a picture frame, and there was a smudge of blue chalk near his chin. Behind him, Billy cleaned up the table and put his cue stick back in the rack on the wall. As he passed, he plucked a twenty from the kid's shirt pocket and tucked it into his own. Then, with his face averted, he said, "You the chick came looking for me at my mom's house earlier?"

"That's right. I'm a friend of John Daggett's."

He cocked his head, squinting, his right hand cupped behind his ear. "Who?"

I smiled lazily. We were apparently playing charades. I raised my voice, enunciating. "Daggett. John."

"Oh, yeah, him. How's he doing these days?" He started snapping his fingers lightly to the music, which had switched from Willie Nelson to a George Benson tune.

"He's dead."

I have to credit him. He did a nice imitation of casual surprise, not overdoing it. "You're shittin' me. Daggett's dead? Too bad. What happened to the dude, heart attack?"

"Drowned. It just happened last night, down at the marina." I wagged a thumb over my shoulder in the direction of the beach so he'd know which marina I meant.

"Here in town? Hey, that's tough. I didn't know that. He was in L.A. last I heard."

"I'm surprised you didn't see it on the news."

"Yeah, well I never pay attention to that shit, you know? Bums me out. I got better things to do with my time."

His eyes were all over the place and his body was half turned away. I had to guess that he was busy trying to figure out who I was and what I was up to. He flicked a look at me. "I'm sorry. I didn't catch your name."

"Kinsey Millhone."

He studied me fleetingly. "I thought my mom said the name was Charlene."

I shook my head. "I don't know where she got that."

"And you do what?"

"Basic research. I free-lance. What's that got to do with it?"

"You don't look like a friend of Daggett's. He was kind of a lowlife. You got too much class for a scumbag like him."

"I didn't say we were close. I met him recently through a friend of a friend."

"Why tell me about it? I don't give a damn."

"I'm sorry to hear that. Daggett said if anything happened to him, I should talk to you."

"Me? Naww," he said with disbelief. "That's fuckin' weird. You must have got me mixed up with somebody else. I mean, I knew Daggett, but I didn't *know* him, you dig?"

"That's funny. He told me you were the best of friends."

He smiled and shook his head. "Old Daggett gave you a bum steer, baby doll. I don't know nothin' about it. I don't even remember when I saw him last. Long time."

"What was the occasion?"

He glanced at the Mexican kid who was eavesdropping shamelessly. "Catch you later, man," he said to him. Then under his breath, with contempt, he said, "Paco." Apparently, this was a generic insult that applied to all Hispanics.

He touched my elbow, steering me into the other room. "These beaners are all the same," he confided. "Think they know how to play pool, but they can't do shit. I don't like talking personal in front of spics. Can I buy you a beer?"

"Sure."

He indicated an empty table and held a chair out for me. I hung my slicker over the back and sat down. He caught the bartender's eye and held up two fingers. The bartender pulled out two bottles of beer which he opened and set on the bar.

Billy said, "You want anything else? Potato chips? They make real nice french fries. Kinda greasy, but good."

I shook my head, watching him with interest. At close range, he had a curious charisma . . . a crude sexuality that he probably wasn't even aware of. I meet men like that occasionally and I'm always startled by the phenomenon.

He ambled over and picked up the beers, dropping a couple of crumpled bills on the bar. He said something to the bartender and then waited while the guy placed a glass upside down on each bottle, shooting a smirk in my direction.

He came back to the table and sat down. "Jesus, ask for a glass in this place and they act like you're puttin' on airs. Bunch of bohunks. I only hang out here because I got a sister works here three nights a week."

Ah, I thought, the woman in the trailer.

He poured one of the beers and pushed it over to me, taking his time then as he poured his own. His eyes were deepset, and he had dimples that formed a crease on either side of his mouth. "Look," he said, "I can see you got your mind made up I know something I don't. The truth is, I didn't like Daggett much and I don't think he liked me. Where you got this yarn about me bein' some pal of his, I don't know, but it wasn't from him."

"You called him Monday morning, didn't you?"

"Nuh-uh. Not me. Why would I call him?"

I went on as though he hadn't said anything. "I don't know what you told him, but he was scared."

"Sorry I can't help you out. Must have been somebody else. What was he doin' up here anyway?"

"I don't know. His body washed up in the surf this morning. I thought maybe you could fill me in on the rest. Do you have any idea where he was last night?"

"Nope. Not a clue." He'd gotten interested in a speck of dust in the foam on his beer and he had to pick that out.

"When did you see him last? I don't think you said."

His tone became facetious. "Geez, I don't have my Day-Timer with me. Otherwise, I could pin it down. We might've had lunch at some little out of the way place, just him and me."

"San Luis perhaps?"

There was a slight pause and his smile dimmed a couple of watts. "I was at San Luis with him," he said, cautiously. "Me and thirty-seven hundred other guys. So what?"

"I thought maybe you'd kept in touch."

"I can tell you didn't know Daggett too good. Being with him is like walking around with dog-do on your shoe, you know? It's not something you'd seek out."

"Who else did he know here in town?"

"Can't help you there. It's not my week to keep track."

"What about your sister? Did he know her?"

"Coral? No way. She don't hang out with bums like that. I'd break her neck. I don't get why you're goin' on and on about this. I told you I don't know nothin'. I didn't see him, didn't hear from him. Why can't you just take my word for it?"

"Because I don't think you're telling the truth."

"Says who? I mean, you came lookin' for me, remember? I don't have to talk to you. I'm doin' you a favor. I don't know who you are. I don't even know what the fuck you're up to."

I shook my head, smiling slightly. "God, Billy. Such foul talk. I didn't think you dealt with women that way. I'm shocked."

"Now you're makin' fun of me, right?" He scrutinized my face. "You some kind of cop?"

I ran my thumbnail down the bottle, snagging an accordion strip of label, which I picked off. "Actually I am."

He snorted. Now he'd heard everything. "Come on. Like what," he said.

"I'm a private investigator."

"Bullshit."

"It's a fact."

He tipped back in his chair, amused that I'd try to lay such a line on him. "Jesus, you're too much. Who do you think you're talkin' to? I might have been born at night, but it wasn't *last* night. I know the private eyes around town and you ain't one, so try somethin' else."

I laughed. "All right, I'm not. Maybe I'm just a nosy chick looking into the death of a man I once met."

"Now, that I'd buy, but it still don't explain why you're crankin' on my case."

"You introduced him to Lovella, didn't you?"

That stopped him momentarily. "You know Lovella?"

"Sure. I met her down in L.A. She has an apartment on Sawtelle."

"When was this?"

"Day before yesterday."

"No foolin'. And she told you to look me up?"

"How else would I know where you were?"

He stared at me, going through some sort of mental debate.

I thought a little coaxing might loosen his tongue. "Are you aware that Daggett's been beating the shit out of her?"

That made him restless and his eyes dropped away from mine. "Yeah, well Lovella's a big girl. She has to learn how to take care of herself."

"Why don't you help her out?"

He smiled bitterly. "I know people who'd laugh at the notion of me helping anyone," he said. "Besides, she's tough. You don't want to underestimate that one, I'm tellin' you."

"You've known her a long time, haven't you?"

His knee had started to jump. "Seven years, eight. I met
her when she was seventeen. We lived together for a while,
but it didn't work out. We used to knock heads too much.
She's a bullheaded bitch, but I loved her a lot. Then I got
busted on a burglary rap and me and her, hell, I don't know
what it was. We wrote to each other for a while, but you can't
go back to something once it's dead, you know? Anyway, now
we're friends, I guess. At least I dig her. I don't know how
she feels about me."

"Have you seen her recently?"

The knee stopped. "No, I haven't seen her recently," he
said. "What about you? Why'd you go down there?"

"I was looking for Daggett. The phone was disconnected."

"What exactly did she say?"

I shrugged. "Nothing much. I wasn't there long and she
wasn't feeling that good. She was nursing a big black eye."

"Jesus," he said. He rocked back in his chair. "Tell me
something. How come women do that? Let guys punch 'em
out?"

"I have no idea."

He drained his beer glass and set it down. "I bet you don't
take crap from anyone, am I right?"

"We all take crap from someone," I said.

Billy got up. "Sorry to cut this off, but I gotta split." He
turned, tucking his shirt down into his pants more securely.
His body language said he'd already taken off and hoped his
clothing would catch up with him by the time he hit the street.

I got up, reaching for my slicker. "You're not leaving town,
are you?"

"What business is it of yours?"

"It doesn't seem like a good idea with Daggett's death hanging fire. Suppose the cops want to talk to you."

"About what?"

"Where you were last night, for starters."

His tone rose. "Where *I* was? What are you talkin' about?"

"They might want to know about the connection between Daggett and you."

"What connection? That's a crock. I don't know where you come up with that."

"It's not me you have to worry about. It's the cops who count."

"What cops?"

I shook my head. "You know who your friendly local cops are," I said. "If somebody puts a bug in the wrong ear, you'll be sitting in the hot seat."

He was all outrage. "Why would you do that to me?"

"Because you're not leveling with me, William."

"I *am* leveling with you! I've told you everything I know."

"I don't think so. I think you knew about Daggett's death. I think you saw him this week."

He put his hands on his hips and looked off across the room, shaking his head. "Man, this is all I need. This is no lie. I've been straight. I'm minding my own business, doing like I been told. I didn't even know the dude was up here."

"You can stick to your story if you like," I said, "but I'll give you a word of advice. I've got the license number of that car you bought. You bolt and I'm calling Lieutenant Dolan down at Homicide."

He seemed as much puzzled as dismayed. "What is this? A shakedown? Is that what this is about?"

"What's to shake? You don't have a cent. I want information, that's all."

"I don't *have* any information. How many times I gotta tell you that?"

"Look," I said patiently. "Why don't I let you think about the situation and then we can talk again."

"Why don't you go fuck yourself!"

I put my slicker on, tucking the strap of my handbag over my shoulder. "Thanks for the beer. I'll buy yours next time."

He made an exaggerated gesture of dismissal, too pissed

off to reply. He headed toward the door and I watched him go. I glanced at my watch. It was well after midnight and I was exhausted. My head was starting to ache and I knew everything about me smelled like stale cigarette smoke. I wanted to go home, strip down, shower, and then crawl into the folds of my quilt. Instead, I took a deep breath and went after him.

10

I gave him a good head start, then followed him back to the trailer. The temperature felt like it had dropped into the fifties. The eucalyptus trees were still tossing occasional showers at me when the wind cut through, but for the most part, the night was clear. Above me, I could see pale puffs of rain cloud receding, wide patches of starry sky breaking through. I parked half a block away and padded into the park on foot as I had before. Billy's car was parked beside the trailer. I was getting bored, but I had to be certain he wasn't heading off to consult with some confederate I didn't know about.

The same lights were on in the galley, but a dim light now glowed at the rear of the trailer, where I imagined the bedroom to be. I picked my way through the bushes to that end. Curtains were pulled across the windows, but the venting system was piping a murmured conversation right out through a mesh-covered opening. I hunkered down by the torn skirting, leaning my head against the aluminum. I could smell cigarette smoke, which I guessed was Coral's.

". . . want to know why she showed up now," she was saying. "That's what we have to worry about. For all we know, they're in it together."

"Yeah, but doin' what? That's what I can't figure out."

"When'd she say she'd get in touch?"

"She didn't. Said I should think about the situation. Jesus. How'd she get a bead on the Chevy so fast? That's what bugs me. I had that car two hours."

"Maybe she followed you, dimwit."

The silence was profound. "Goddamn it," he said.

I heard footsteps thump toward the front of the trailer. By the time the door banged open I was easing my way around the end. I peered out into the carport. The nose of the Chevy was about six feet away, the space on either side of it crowded with junk.

The door to the trailer had been flung open. Light poured out, washing as far as the point where the asphalt began. With a quick look over my shoulder, I waded into the refuse, picking my way around to the far side of the car, where I crouched, listening intently. Sometimes I feel like I spend half my life this way. I heard Billy fumble his way around the bedroom end of the trailer just as I had.

"Jesus!" he hissed.

Coral peered out the side window, whispering hoarsely. "What's wrong?"

"Shut up! Nothing. I banged my goddamn shin on the trailer hitch. Why don't you clean up this crap?"

My sentiments exactly.

Coral laughed and the curtain dropped back into place.

Billy appeared again at the far end of the carport, rubbing his left shin. He did a quick visual survey, apparently convinced by then there wasn't anybody lurking about the premises. He shook his head and thumped up the steps, banging the door shut behind him. The carport went dark. I let out my breath.

I could hear them murmuring together, but by then I didn't really care what else they discussed. As soon as I was convinced it was safe, I crept out of the driveway and headed for my car.

Sunday morning was overcast. The very air looked gray, and dampness seemed to rise up out of the earth like a mist. I went through my usual morning routine, getting a three-mile run in before the skies opened up again. At 9:00, I put a call through to Barbara Daggett at home. I brought her up to date, filling her in on my night's activities.

"What now?" she asked.

"I'm going to let Billy Polo stew for a day or two and then get back to him."

"What makes you think he won't skip?"

"Well, he *is* on parole and I'm hoping he won't want to mess that up. Besides, it feels like a waste of money to pay me to sit there all day."

"I thought you said he was the only lead you had."

"Maybe not," I said cautiously. "I've been thinking about Tony Gahan and the other people killed in the accident."

"Tony Gahan?" she said with surprise. "How could he be involved in this?"

"I don't know. Your father hired me originally to track him down. Maybe he found the kid himself and that's where he was early in the week."

"But Kinsey, why would Daddy want to track him down? That boy must hate his guts. His whole family was wiped out."

"That's my point."

"Oh."

"Do you have any idea how to locate him? Your father had an address on Stanley Place, but the house was apparently empty. I can't find a Gahan listed in the telephone book."

"He lives with his aunt now, I think, somewhere in Colgate. Let me see if I've got an address."

Colgate is the bedroom community, attached to Santa Teresa like a double star. The two are just about the same size, but Santa Teresa has all the character and Colgate has the affordable housing, along with hardware stores, paint companies, bowling alleys, and drive-in theaters. Colgate is the Frostee-Freeze capital of the world.

There was a pause and I could hear pages rattle. She came back on the line. "My mistake. They live near the Museum. Her last name is Westfall. Ramona."

"I wonder why your father didn't know about her."

"I don't know. She was there for the trial. I do remember that, because someone pointed her out to me. I wrote her a note afterwards, saying that of course we'd do anything we could to help, but I never heard back."

"You know anything else about her? Is she married, for instance?"

"I think so, yes. Her husband manufactures industrial supplies or something like that. Actually, now that I think about it, she *was* working at that kitchenware place on Capilla because I spotted her when I was in there shopping a couple of months ago. Maybe you could catch her this afternoon if she still works there."

"On Sunday?"

"Sure, they're open from twelve to five."

"I'll try her first and see how far I get," I said. "What about your mother? How's she holding up?"

"Surprisingly well. Turns out she handles death like a champ. If it's covered in the Bible, she trots out all the appropriate attitudes and goes through the sequence automatically. I thought she'd flip out, but it seems to have put her back on her feet. She's got church women sitting with her, and the pastor's there. The kitchen table's stacked with tuna casseroles and chocolate cakes. I don't know how long it will last, but for now, she's in her element."

"When's the funeral?"

"Tuesday afternoon. The body's been transported to the mortuary. I think they said he'd be ready for viewing early this afternoon. Are you coming by?"

"Yes, I think I will. I can tell you then if I've talked to this Westfall woman or the kid."

Jorden's is a gourmet cook's fantasy, with every imaginable food preparation device. Rack after rack of cookware, utensils, cookbooks, linens, spices, coffees, and condiments; chafing dishes, wicker baskets, exotic vinegars and oils, knives, baking pans, glassware. I stood in the entrance for a moment, amazed by the number and variety of food-related implements. Pasta machines, cappuccino makers, food warmers, coffee grinders, ice cream freezers, food processors. The air smelled of chocolate and made me wish I had a mother. I spotted three saleswomen, all wearing wraparound aprons made of mattress ticking, with the store's name embroidered in maroon across the bib.

I asked for Ramona Westfall and was directed toward the rear aisle. She was apparently doing a shelf count. I found her perched on a small wooden stool, clipboard in hand, checking off items on a list that included most of the non-electrical gadgets. She was sorting through a bin of what looked like small stainless steel sliding boards with a blade across the center that would slice your tiny ass off.

"What are those?" I asked.

She glanced up at me with a pleasant smile. She appeared to be in her late forties, with short, pale sandy hair streaked with gray, hazel eyes peering at me over a pair of half-glasses which she wore low on her nose. She used little if any makeup, and even seated, I could tell she was small and slim. Under the apron, she wore a white, long-sleeved blouse with a Peter Pan collar, a gray tweed skirt, hose, and penny loafers.

"That's a mandoline. It's made in West Germany."

"I thought a mandolin was a musical instrument."

"The spelling's different. This is for slicing raw vegetables. You can waffle-cut or julienne."

"Really?" I said. I had sudden visions of homemade French fries and cole slaw, neither of which I've ever prepared. "How much is that?"

"A hundred and ten dollars. With the slicing guard, it's one thirty-eight. Would you like a demonstration?"

I shook my head, unwilling to spend that much money on behalf of a potato. She got to her feet, smoothing the front of her apron. She was half a head shorter than I and smelled like a perfume sample I'd gotten in the mail the week before. Lavender and crushed jasmine. I was impressed with the price of the stuff, if not the scent. I stuck it in a drawer and I'm assailed with the fragrance now every time I pull out fresh underwear.

"You're Ramona Westfall, aren't you?"

Her smile was modified to a look of expectancy. "That's right. Have we met?"

I shook my head. "I'm Kinsey Millhone. I'm a private investigator here in town."

"Is there something I can help you with?"

"I'm looking for Tony Gahan. I understand you're his aunt."

"Tony? Good heavens, what for?"

"I was asked to locate him on a personal matter. I didn't know how else to get in touch with him."

"What personal matter? I don't understand."

"I was asked to deliver something to him. A check from a man who's recently deceased."

She looked at me blankly for a moment and then I saw recognition leap in her eyes. "You're referring to John Daggett, aren't you? Someone told me it was on the news last night. I assumed he was still in prison."

"He's been out for six weeks."

Her face flooded with color. "Well, isn't that typical," she snapped. "Five people dead and he's back on the streets."

"Not quite," I said. "Could we go someplace and talk?"

"About what? About my sister? She was thirty-eight, a beautiful person. She was decapitated when he ran a stoplight and plowed into them. Her husband was killed. Tony's sister was crushed. She was six, just a baby. . . ." She bit off her sentence abruptly, suddenly aware that her voice had risen. Nearby, several people paused, looking over at us.

"Who were the others? Did you know them?" I asked.

"You're the detective. You figure it out."

In the next aisle, a dark-haired woman in a striped apron

caught her eye. She didn't open her mouth, but her expression said, "Is everything all right?"

"I'm taking a break," Ramona said to her. "I'll be in the back room if Tricia's looking for me."

The dark-haired woman glanced at me briefly and then dropped her gaze. Ramona was moving toward a doorway on the far side of the room. I followed. The other customers had lost interest, but I had a feeling that I'd be facing an unpleasant scene.

By the time I entered the back room, Ramona was fumbling in her handbag with shaking hands. She opened a zippered compartment and took out a vial of pills. She extracted a tablet and broke it in half, downing it with a slug of cold coffee from a white mug with her name on the side. On second thought, she took the second half of the tablet as well.

I said, "Look, I'm sorry to have to bring this up . . ."

"Don't apologize," she spat. "It doesn't do any good." She searched through the bag and came up with a hard pack of Winston's. She pulled out a cigarette and tamped it repeatedly on her thumbnail, then lit it with a Bic disposable lighter she'd tucked in her apron pocket. She hugged her waist with her left arm, propping the right elbow on it so she could hold the cigarette near her face. Her eyes seemed to have darkened and she fixed me with a blank, rude stare. "What is it you want?"

I could feel my face warm. Somehow the money was suddenly beside the point and seemed like too paltry a sum in any event. "I have a cashier's check for Tony. John Daggett asked me to deliver it."

Her smile was supercilious. "Oh, a *check*. Well, how much is it for? Is it per *head* or some sort of lump sum payment by the carload?"

"Mrs. Westfall," I said patiently.

"You can call me Ramona, dear, since the subject matter's so intimate. We're talking about the people I loved best in this world." She took a deep drag of her cigarette and blew smoke toward the ceiling.

I clamped down on my temper, controlling my response. "I understand that the subject is painful," I said. "I know there's no way to compensate for what happened, but John Daggett was making a gesture, and regardless of your opinion of him, it's possible that Tony might have a use for the money."

"We provide for him very nicely, thanks. We don't need anything from John Daggett *or* his daughter or from *you*."

I plowed on, heading into the face of her wrath like a swimmer through churning surf. "Let me just say something first. Daggett came to me last week with a cashier's check made out to Tony."

She started to speak, but I held up one hand. "Please," I said.

She subsided, allowing me to continue.

"I put the check in a safe deposit box until I could figure out how to deliver it, as agreed. You can toss it in the trash for all I care, but I'd like to do what I said I'd do, which is to see that Tony Gahan gets it. In theory, it's Tony's to do with as he sees fit, so I'd appreciate it if you'd talk to him before you do anything else."

She thought about that one, her eyes locked on mine. "How much?"

"Twenty-five thousand. That's a good chunk of education for Tony, or a trip abroad. . . ."

"I get the point," she cut in. "Now maybe you'll allow me to have my say. That boy has been with us for almost three years now. He's fifteen years old and I don't think he's slept a full eight hours since the accident. He has migraines, he bites his nails. His grades are poor, school attendance is *shit*. We're talking about a kid with an I.Q. right off the charts. He's a wreck and John Daggett did that to him. There's no way . . . no *way* anyone can ever make up to Tony for what that man did."

"I understand that."

"No, you don't." Her eyes filled suddenly with tears. She was silent, hands shaking again so badly now that she could scarcely get the Winston to her lips. She managed to take another drag, fighting for control. The silence lengthened. She seemed to shudder and I could almost see the tranquilizer kick in. She turned away abruptly, dropped the cigarette, and stepped on it. "Give me a number where I can reach you. I'll talk to my husband and see what he says."

I handed her my card, taking a moment to jot down my home address and telephone number on the back, in case she needed to reach me there.

11

After I left Ramona Westfall, I stopped by my apartment and changed into pantyhose, low heels, and my all-purpose dress. This garment, which I've owned for five years, is made of some magic fabric that doesn't wilt, wrinkle, or show dirt. It can be squashed down to the size of a rain hat and shoved in the bottom of my handbag without harm. It can also be rinsed out in any bathroom sink and hung to dry overnight. It's black, lightweight, has long sleeves, zips up the back, and should probably be "accessorized," a women's clothing concept I've never understood. I wear the dress "as is" and it always looks okay to me. Once in a while I see this look of recognition in someone's eye, but maybe it's just a moment of surprise at seeing me in something other than jeans and boots.

The Wynington-Blake Mortuary—Burials, Cremation, and Shipping, Serving All Faiths—is located on the east side of town on a shady side street with ample parking. It was originally built as a residence and retains the feeling of a substantial single-family dwelling. Now, of course, the entire first floor has been converted into the equivalent of six spacious living rooms, each furnished with metal folding chairs and labeled with some serene-sounding word.

The gentleman who greeted me, a Mr. Sharonson, wore a subdued navy blue suit, a neutral expression, and used a public library voice. John Daggett was laid out in "Meditation," which was just down the corridor and to my left. The family, he murmured, was in the Sunrise Chapel if I cared to wait.

I signed in. Mr. Sharonson removed himself discreetly and I was left to do as I pleased. The room was rimmed with chairs, the casket at the apex. There were two sprays of white gladioli that looked somehow like pristine fakes provided by the mortuary, instead of wreaths sent by those who mourned Daggett's passing. Organ music was being piped in, a nearly subliminal auditory cue meant to trigger thoughts about the brevity of life.

I tiptoed across the room to have a peek at him. The color and texture of Daggett's skin looked about like a Betsy-Wetsy doll I'd had as a kid. His features had a flattened appearance, which I suspected was a side effect of the autopsy process. Peel somebody's face back and it's hard to line it all up again. Daggett's nose looked crooked, like a pillowcase put on with the seam slightly skewed.

I was aware of a rustling behind me and Barbara Daggett appeared on my right. We stood together for a moment without a word. I don't know why people stand and study the dead that way. It makes about as much sense as paying homage to the cardboard box your favorite shoes once came in. Finally, she murmured something and turned away, moving toward the entrance where Eugene Nickerson and Essie Daggett were just coming in through the archway.

Essie was wearing a dark navy dress of rayon jersey, her massive arms dimpled with pale flesh. Her hair looked freshly "done," puffed and thick, sprayed into a turban of undulating gray. Eugene, in a dark suit, steered her by the elbow, working her arm as if it were the rudder on a ship. She took one look at the casket and her wide knees buckled. Barbara and Eugene caught her before she actually hit the floor. They guided her to an upholstered chair and lowered her into the seat. She fumbled for a handkerchief, which she pressed to her mouth as if she meant to chloroform herself.

"Sweet Jesus Lord," she mewed, her eyes turned up piteously. "Lamb of God . . ." Eugene began to pat at her hand and Barbara sat down beside her, putting one arm around her protectively.

"You want me to bring her some water?" I asked.

Barbara nodded and I moved toward the doorway. Mr. Sharonson had sensed the disturbance and had appeared, his face forming a question. I passed the request along and he nodded. He left the room and I returned to Mrs. Daggett's side. She was having a pretty good time by now, rolling her head back and forth, reciting scriptures in a high-pitched voice. Barbara and Eugene were working to restrain her and I gathered that Essie had expressed a strong desire to fling herself into the coffin with her beloved. I might have given her a boost myself.

Mr. Sharonson returned with a paper envelope full of water, which Barbara took, holding it to Essie's lips. She jerked her head back, unwilling to accept even this small measure of solace. "By night on my bed, I sought him whom my soul loveth," she warbled. "I sought him, but I found him not. I will rise now, and go about the city in the streets, and in the broad ways I will seek him whom my soul loveth. The watchmen that go about the city found me . . . Lord in Heaven . . . O God. . . ."

With surprise, I realized she was quoting fragments from the Song of Solomon, which I recognized from my old Methodist Sunday School days. Little kids were never allowed to read that part of the Bible as it was considered too smutty, but I was real interested in the idea of a man with legs like pillars of marble set upon sockets of fine gold. There was some talk of swords and thighs that caught my attention too. I believe I lasted three Sundays before my aunt was asked to take me down the street to the Presbyterians.

Essie was rapidly losing control, whipping herself into such an agitated state that Eugene and Mr. Sharonson had to assist her to her feet and help her out of the room. I could hear her cries becoming feebler as she was moved down the hall. Barbara rubbed her face wearily. "Oh God. Count on Mother," she said. "How has your day been?"

I sat down beside her. "This doesn't seem like the best time to talk," I said.

"Oh, don't worry about it. She'll calm down. This is the first she's seen of him. There's some kind of lounge upstairs. She can rest for a while and she'll be fine. What about Ramona Westfall? Did you talk to her?"

I filled her in on my brief interview, bringing the subject around to my real question at this point, which had to do with the two other victims in the accident. Barbara closed her eyes, the matter clearly causing her pain.

"One was a little friend of Hilary Gahan's. Her name was Megan Smith. I'm sure her parents are still in the area. I'll check the address and telephone number when I get home. Her father's name is Wayne. I forget the name of the street, but it's probably listed."

I took my notebook out and jotted the name down. "And the fifth?"

"Some kid who'd bummed a ride with them. They picked him up at the on-ramp to the freeway to give him a lift into town."

"What was his name?"

"Doug Polokowski."

I stared at her. "You're kidding."

"Why? Do you know him?"

"Polokowski is Billy Polo's real last name. It's on his rap sheet."

"You think they're related?"

"They'd almost have to be. There's only one Polokowski family in town. It's got to be a cousin or a brother, *something*."

"But I thought Billy Polo was supposed to be Daddy's best friend. That doesn't make sense."

Mr. Sharonson returned to the room and caught her eye. "Your mother is asking for you, Miss Daggett."

"You go ahead," I said. "I've got plenty to work on at this point. I'll call you later at home."

Barbara followed Mr. Sharonson while I headed out to the foyer and hustled up a telephone book. Wayne and Marilyn Smith were listed on Tupelo Drive out in Colgate, right around the corner from Stanley Place, if my memory served me correctly. I considered calling first, but I was curious what the reaction would be to the fact of Daggett's death, if the news hadn't already reached them. I stopped to get gas in the VW and then headed out to the freeway.

The Smiths' house was the single odd one in a twelve-block radius of identical tract homes and I guessed that theirs was the original farmhouse at the heart of what had once been a citrus grove. I could still spot orange trees in irregular rows, broken up now by winding roads, fenced lots, and an elementary school. The Smiths' mailbox was a small replica of the house and the street number was gouged out of a thick plank of pine, stained dark and hung above the porch steps. The house itself was a two-story white frame with tall, narrow windows and a slate roof. A sprawling vegetable garden stretched out behind the house, with the garage beyond that. A tire swing hung by a rope from a sycamore that grew in the yard. Orange trees extended on all sides, looking twisted and barren, their producing years long past. It was probably cheaper to leave them there than to tear them out. An assortment of boys' bicycles in a rack on the porch suggested the presence of male offspring or an in-progress meeting of a cycling club.

The bell consisted of a metal twist in the middle of the door. I cranked it once and it trilled harshly. As with the Christopher house, the upper portion of the door was glass, allowing me a glimpse of the interior—high ceilings, waxed pine floors, a scattering of rag rugs, and Early American antiques that looked authentic to my untrained eye. The walls were covered with patchwork quilts, the colors washed out to pale shades of mauve and blue. Numerous children's jackets hung from a row of pegs to the left, rainboots lined up underneath.

A woman in jeans and an oversized white shirt trotted down the stairs, trailing one hand along the banister. She gave me a quick smile and opened the front door.

"Oh hi. Are you Larry's mom?" She read instantly from my expression that I hadn't the faintest idea what she was talking about. She gave a quick laugh. "I guess not. The boys got back from the movie half an hour ago and we've been waiting for Larry's mother to pick him up. Sorry."

"That's all right. I'm Kinsey Millhone," I said. "I'm a private investigator here in town." I handed her my card.

"Can I help you with something?" She was in her midthirties, her blonde hair pulled straight back from her face in a clumsy knot. She was dark-eyed, with the tanned good looks of someone who works outdoors. I imagined her to be the kind of mother who forbade her children to eat refined sugar and supervised the television shows they watched. Whether such vigilance pays off or not, I'm never sure. I tend to place kids in a class with dogs, preferring the quiet, the smart, and the well trained.

"John Daggett was killed here in town Friday night," I said.

Something flickered across her face, but maybe it was just the realization that a painful subject was coming up again. "I hadn't heard about that. What happened?"

"He fell out of a boat and drowned."

She thought about that briefly. "Well, that's not too bad. Drowning's supposed to be fairly easy, isn't it?" Her tone of voice was light, her expression pleasant. It took me a minute to realize the savagery of the sentiment. I wondered what kind of torture she'd wished on him.

"Most of us don't get to choose our death," I said.

"My daughter certainly didn't," she said tartly. "Was it an accident or did someone give him a nice push?"

"That's what I'm trying to find out," I said. "I heard he came up from L.A. on Monday, but nobody seems to know where he spent the week."

"Not here, I can assure you. If Wayne so much as set eyes on him, he'd have. . . ." The words tapered off to a faint smile and her tone became almost bantering. "I was going to say, he'd have killed him, but I didn't mean that literally. Or maybe I did. I guess I shouldn't speak for Wayne."

"What about you? When did you see him last?"

"I have no idea. Two years ago at least."

"At the trial?"

She shook her head. "I wasn't there. Wayne sat in for a day, but he couldn't take it after that. He talked to Barbara Daggett once, I think, but I'm sure there's been nothing since. I'm assuming somehow that the man was murdered. Is that what you're getting at?"

"It's possible. The police don't seem to think so, but I'm hoping they'll revise their opinion if I can come up with some evidence. I get the impression a lot of people wanted Daggett dead."

"Well, I sure did. I'm thrilled to hear the news. Somebody should have killed him at birth," she said. "Would you like to come in? I don't know what I can tell you, but we might as well be comfortable." She glanced at my business card again, double-checking the name and then tucking it in her shirt pocket.

She held the door and I passed over the threshold, pausing to see where she meant for us to go. She led me into the living room.

"You and your husband were home Friday night?"

"Why? Are we suspects?"

"There isn't even a formal investigation yet," I said.

"I was here. Wayne was working late. He's a C.P.A."

She indicated a chair and I sat down. She took a seat on the couch, her manner relaxed. She was wearing a thin gold bracelet on her right wrist and she began to turn that, straightening a kink in the chain. "Did you ever meet John Daggett yourself?" she asked.

"Once. He came to my office a week ago Saturday."

"Ah. Out on parole, no doubt. He must have served his ten minutes."

I made no comment, so she went on.

"What was he doing in Santa Teresa? Returning to the scene of the slaughter?"

"He was trying to locate Tony Gahan."

This seemed to amuse her. "To what end? It's probably none of my business, but I'm curious."

I was discomfited by her attitude, which seemed an odd mix of the wrathful and the jocular. "I'm not really sure what his intentions were," I said carefully. "The story he told me wasn't true anyway, so it's probably not worth repeating. I gathered he wanted to make restitution."

Her smile faded, dark eyes boring into mine with a look that chilled me. "There's no such thing as 'restitution' for what that man did. Megan died horribly. Five-and-a-half years old. Has anyone given you the details?"

"I have the newspaper clippings in the car. I talked to Ramona Westfall too, and she filled me in," I said, lying through my teeth. I didn't want to hear about Megan's death. I didn't think I could bear it, whatever it was. "Have you kept in touch with the other families?"

For a moment, I didn't think I could distract her. She was going to sit there and tell me some blood-curdling tale that I was never going to forget. Cruel images seemed to play across her face. She faltered and her expression underwent that transformation that precedes tears—her nose reddening, mouth changing shape, lines drawing down on either side. Then her self-control descended and she looked at me with clouded eyes. "I'm sorry. What?"

"I was wondering if you'd talked to the others recently. Mrs. Westfall or the Polokowskis."

"I've hardly even talked to Wayne. Megan's death has just about done us in."

"What about your other children? How are they handling it?"

"Better than we are, certainly. People always say, 'Well, you still have the boys.' But it doesn't work that way. It's not like you can substitute one child for another." Belatedly, she took out a Kleenex and blew her nose.

"I'm sorry I had to bring it all up again," I said. "I've never had children, but I can't imagine anything more painful than losing one."

Her smile returned, fleeting and bitter. "I'll tell you what's worse. Knowing there's a man out there doing a few months in jail for 'vehicular manslaughter' when he murdered five people. Do you know how many times he got picked up for drunk driving before that accident? Fifteen. He paid a few fines. He got his hand smacked. Once he did thirty days, but most of the time. . . ." She broke off, then changed her tone. "Oh hell. What difference does it make? Nothing changes anyway and it never ends. I'll tell Wayne you stopped by. Maybe he knows where Daggett was."

12

I sat in the car and shuddered. I couldn't think when an interview had made me feel so tense. Daggett *had* to have been murdered. I just didn't see how it could come down any other way. What I couldn't figure out was how to get my thinking straight. Usually the morality of homicide seems clear to me. Whatever the shortcomings of the victim, murder is wrong and the penalties levied against the perpetrator had better be substantial to balance out the gravity of the crime. In this case, that seemed like a simplistic point of view. It was *Daggett* who had caused the world to tilt on its axis. Because of him, five people had died, so that his death, whatever the instrument, was swinging the planet upright again, restoring a moral order of sorts. At the moment, I still didn't know whether his desire to make restitution was sincere or part of some elaborate con. All I knew was that I'd been caught up in the loop and I had a part to play, though I had no idea yet what it was.

I started the car and headed back to my place. The sky was clouding over again. It was after 5:00 and a premature twilight already seemed to be spilling down the mountainside. I pulled up in front of my apartment and switched off the ignition. I glanced over at my windows, which were dark. I was feeling edgy and I wasn't ready to go home yet. On impulse, I started the car again and headed for the beach, drawn by the scent of salt in the air. Maybe a walk would ease my restlessness.

I pulled into one of the municipal lots and parked, slipping out of my shoes and pantyhose, which I tossed in the back seat along with my handbag. I zipped up my windbreaker and locked the car, tucking my keys in my jacket pocket as I crossed the bike path to the beach. The ocean was silver, but the breaking waves were a muddy brown and the sand along the surf line was peppered with rocks. This was the winter beach, dark boulders having surfaced with the shifting coastal sands. Gulls hovered overhead, eyeing the thundering waves for signs of edible sea life.

I walked along the wet sand with a buffeting wind at my back. A windsurfer clung to the crossbar on a bright green sail, arching himself against the force of the wind, his board streaking toward the beach. Two big fishing boats were chugging into the marina. Everywhere there was the sense of urgency and threat—the torn white of storm surf, the darkening gray of the sky. Across the harbor, the ocean drove at the shore without pity, pounding at the breakwater with a grudging monotony. A rocketing spray shot straight up on impact, fanning along the seawall. I could almost hear the splats as successive waves hit the concrete walkway on the landward side.

I passed the entrance to the wharf. Ahead the beach widened, curving left toward the marina where the bare masts of sailboats tilted in the wind like metronomes. The sand was softer here, deeper too, so that walking became a labor. I turned and walked backwards for a few steps, trying to get my bearings. Somewhere along this part of the beach was the spot where Daggett's body had been found. A brief glimpse of the site had appeared on the newscast and I was hoping now to get a fix on the place. I thought it was probably this side of the boat launch. Ahead and to my right was the kiddie park with its playground equipment and a fenced-in area with a wading pool.

The newscast had shown a portion of the dredge in the background, intersected by the breakwater and a line of rocks. I trudged on until I had the three lined up in the same configuration. The dry sand was trampled and there were signs that vehicles had crossed the beach. Where waves slapped against the shore, all traces of activity had been erased. The crime scene investigators had, no doubt, done at least a cursory search. I scanned the area without any expectation of finding "evidence." If you murder a man by tossing him, dead drunk, out of a rowboat, there aren't any telltale clues to dispose of afterward. The boat itself had been left to drift and, from what Jonah said, must have washed ashore closer to the pier.

I drank in the heady perfume of the sea, watching the restless surge of the waves, turning myself slowly until the ocean was at my back and I was staring at the line of motels across the boulevard. Daggett had apparently died sometime between midnight and 5:00 A.M. I wondered if it would be productive to canvas the neighborhood for witnesses. It was possible, of course, that Daggett had actually cut the line on the skiff himself, rowing out of the harbor alone. With a 0.35 blood alcohol level, it seemed unlikely. By the time blood alcohol concentrations reach 0.40 percent, a drunk is essentially in a state of deep anesthesia, incapable of anything so athletic as working an oar. He might have maneuvered his way out of the harbor first and *then* sat in the bobbing boat, drinking himself insensible, but I couldn't picture that. I kept visualizing somebody with him . . . waiting, watching . . . finally hefting his feet and toppling him backwards. "A lesson in the back flip, Daggett. Oh shit, you blew it. Too bad, sucker. You die."

Getting him in the boat in the first place might have been a trick, as drunk as he was, but the rest of it must have been a snap.

I glanced to my right. An old bum with a shopping cart was picking through a trash container. I crossed the sand, heading toward him. As I approached, I could see that his skin was nearly gray with accumulated filth, tanned by the wind, with an overlay of rosiness from recent sunburn or

Mogen David wine . . . Mad Dog 20–20, as it's better known among the scruffy drifters. He looked in his seventies and was bulked up by layers of clothing. He wore a watch cap, his gray hair hanging out of it like mop strings. He smelled as musky as an old buffalo. The odor radiated from his body in nearly visible wavy lines, like a cartoon rendition of a skunk.

"Hello," I said.

He went about his business, ignoring me. He pulled out a pair of spike heels, inspecting them briefly before he tucked them into one of his plastic trash bags. A two-day-old newspaper didn't interest him. Beer cans? Yes, he seemed to like those. A Kentucky Fried Chicken barrel was a reject. A skirt? He held it up with a critical eye and then shoved it into the trash bag with the shoes. Someone had discarded a plastic beach ball with a hole punched in it. The old man set that aside.

"Did you hear about the guy they found in the surf yesterday?" I asked. No response. I felt like an apparition, calling to him from the netherworld. I raised my voice. "I heard somebody down here spotted him and called the cops. Do you happen to know who?"

I guess he didn't care to discuss it. He resolutely avoided eye contact. I didn't have my handbag with me so I didn't have a business card or even a dollar bill as a letter of reference. I had no choice but to let it drop. I moved away. By then, he had worked his way down in the bin, his head almost out of sight. So much for my interviewing techniques.

By the time I got back to the parking lot, the light had faded, so I registered the fact that something was wrong long before I realized what it was. The door on the passenger side of my car was ajar. I stopped in my tracks.

"Oh no," I said.

I approached with caution, as if the vehicle might be booby-trapped. It looked like someone had run a coathanger in through the wind-wing in an attempt to jimmy the lock. Failing that, the shitheel had simply smashed the window out on the passenger side and had opened the door. The glove compartment hung open, the contents spilling out across the front seat. My handbag was missing. *That* generated a flash of irritation, swiftly followed by dread. I jerked the seat forward and hauled out my briefcase. The strap that secured the opening had been cut and my gun was gone.

"Oh nooo," I wailed. I gave vent to a string of expletives. In high school, I had hung out with some bad-ass boys who taught me to cuss to perfection. I tried some combinations I hadn't thought of in years. I was mad at myself for leaving the stuff in plain sight on the seat and mad at the jerk who ripped me off. Mine was one of the last cars left in the lot and had probably stood out like a beacon. I slammed the car door shut and headed off across the street, still barefoot, gesturing and muttering to myself like a mental case. I didn't even have the spare change to call the cops.

There was a hamburger stand close by and I conned the fry cook into making the call for me. Then I went back and waited until the black-and-white arrived. The beat officers, Pettigrew and Gutierrez (Gerald and Maria, respectively), I'd encountered some months before when they made an arrest in my neighborhood.

She took the report now, while he made sympathetic noises. Somehow the two of them managed to console me insofar as that was possible, calling for a crime scene investigator who obligingly came out and dusted for prints. We all knew it was pointless, but it made me feel better. Pettigrew said he'd check the computer for the serial number on my gun, which was registered, thank God. Maybe it would turn up later in a pawn shop and I'd get it back.

I love my little semiautomatic, which I've had for years . . . a gift from the aunt who raised me after my parents' death. That gun was my legacy, representing the odd bond between us. She'd taught me to shoot when I was eight. She had never married, never had children of her own. With me, she'd exercised her many odd notions about the formation of female character. Firing a handgun, she felt, would teach me to appreciate both safety and accuracy. It would also help me develop good hand-eye coordination, which she thought was useful. She'd taught me to knit and crochet so that I'd learn patience and an eye for detail. She'd refused to teach me to cook as she felt it was boring and would only make me fat. Cussing was okay around the house, though we were expected to monitor our language in the company of those who might take offense. Exercise was important. Fashion was not. Reading was essential. Two out of three illnesses would cure themselves, said she, so doctors could generally be ignored except in case of accident. On the other hand, there was no excuse for having bad teeth, though she viewed dentists as the persons who came up with ludicrous schemes for the human mouth. Drilling out all of your old fillings and replacing them with gold, was one. She had dozens of these precepts and most are still with me.

Rule Number One, first and foremost, above and beyond all else, was financial independence. A woman should never, never, never be financially dependent on anyone, especially a man, because the minute you were dependent, you could be abused. Financially dependent persons (the young, the old, the indigent) were inevitably treated badly and had no recourse. A woman should *always* have recourse. My aunt believed that every woman should develop marketable skills, and the more money she was paid for them the better. Any feminine pursuit that did not have as its ultimate goal increased self-sufficiency could be disregarded. "How to Get Your Man" didn't even appear on the list.

When I was in high school, she'd called Home Ec "Home Ick" and applauded when I got a D. She thought it would make a lot more sense if the boys took Home Ec and the girls took Auto Mechanics and Wood Shop. Make no mistake about it, she liked (some) men a lot, but she wasn't interested in tending to one like a charwoman or a nurse. She was nobody's mother, said she, not even mine, and she didn't intend to behave like one. All of which constitutes a long-winded account of why I wanted my gun back, but there it is. I didn't have to explain any of this to G. Pettigrew or M. Gutierrez. They both knew I'd been a cop for two years and they both understood the value of a gun.

By the time everyone left the parking lot, it was fully dark and starting to rain again. Oh perfect.

I drove home and started making out a list of items I'd have to replace, including my driver's license, gasoline charge card, checkbook, and God knows what else. While I was at it, I looked up three "800" numbers, phoning in the loss of my credit cards from the Xerox copy I keep in my file drawer at home. I'd only been carrying about twenty bucks in cash, but I resented the loss. It was all too irritating to contemplate for long. I showered, pulled on jeans, boots, and a sweater, and headed up to Rosie's for a bite to eat.

Rosie's is the tavern in my neighborhood, run by herself, a Hungarian woman in her sixties, short and top-heavy, with dyed red hair that recently had looked like a cross between terra cotta floor tile and canned pumpkin pie filling. Rosie is an autocrat—outspoken, overbearing, suspicious of strangers. She cooks like a dream when it suits her, but she usually wants to dictate what you should eat at any given meal. She's protective, sometimes generous, often irritating. Like your best friend's cranky grandmother, she's someone you endure for the sake of peace. I hang out at her establishment because it's unpretentious and it's only half a block away from my place. Rosie apparently feels that my patronage entitles her to boss me around . . . which is generally true.

That night when I walked in, she took one look at my face and poured me a glass of white wine from her personal supply. I moved to my favorite booth at the rear. The backs are high, cut from construction grade plywood and stained dark, with side pieces shaped like the curve of a wingback chair. Within moments, Rosie materialized at the table and set the glass of wine in front of me.

"Somebody just busted out the window of my car and stole everything I hold dear, including my gun," I said.

"I've got some *sóska leves* for you," she announced. "And after that, you gonna have a salad made with celery root, some chicken paprikas, some of Henry's good rolls, cabbage strudel, and deep-fried cherries if you're good and clean up your plate. It's on the house, on account of your troubles, only think about this one thing while you eat. If you had a good man in your life, this would never happen to you and that's all I'm gonna say."

I laughed for the first time in days.

13

The next morning, Monday, I began the laborious process of replacing the contents of my handbag. I hit the DMV first, since the offices opened at 8:00 A.M. I set in motion the paperwork for a new driver's license, paying three dollars for a duplicate. The minute the bank opened, I closed out my checking account and opened a new one. I stopped by the apartment then and put a call through to Sacramento to the Bureau of Collection and Investigative Services, Department of Consumer Affairs, requesting application for a certified replacement for my private investigator's registration card. I armed myself with a batch of business cards from my ready supply and hunted up an old handbag to use until I could buy a new one. I drove over to the drugstore and made purchases to replace at least a few of the odds and ends I carry with me as a matter of course, birth control pills being one. At some point, I'd have to have my car window replaced, too. Irksome, all of it.

I didn't reach the office until almost noon and the message light on my answering machine was blinking insistently. I tossed the morning mail aside and punched the playback button as I passed the desk, listening to the caller as I opened the French doors to let in some fresh air.

"Miss Millhone, this is Ferrin Westfall at 555-6790. My wife and I have discussed your request to speak with our nephew, Tony, and if you'll get in touch, we'll see what we can work out. Please understand, we don't want the boy upset. We trust you'll conduct whatever business you have with him dis-

creetly." There was a click, breaking the connection. His tone
had been cold, perfectly suited to his formal, well-organized
speaking voice. No "uh"s, no hesitations, no hiccups in the
presentation. I lifted my brows appreciatively. Tony Gahan
was in capable hands. Poor kid.

I made myself a pot of coffee and waited until I'd downed
half a cup before I returned the call. The phone rang twice.

"Good morning. PFC," the woman said.

PFC turned out to be Perforated Formanek Corporation,
a supplier of industrial abrasives, grinders, clamps, epoxy,
cutters, end mills, and precision tools. I know this because I
asked and she recited the entire inventory in a sing-song tone,
thinking perhaps that I was in the market for one of the above.
I asked to speak to Ferrin Westfall and was thanked for my
request.

There was a click. "Westfall," said he.

I identified myself. There was a silence, meant (perhaps)
to intimidate. I resisted the urge to rush in with a lot of
unnecessary chatter, allowing the pause to go on for as long
as it suited him.

Finally, he said, "We'll see that Tony's available this evening
between seven and eight if that's acceptable." He gave me the
address.

"Fine," I said. "Thank you." Ass, I added mentally. Then
I hung up.

I tipped back in my swivel chair and propped my feet up.
So far, it was a crummy day. I wanted my handbag back. I
wanted my gun. I wanted to get on with life and quit wasting
time with all this clerical nonsense. I glanced out at the balcony. At least it wasn't raining at the moment. I pulled the
mail over and started going through it. Most of it was junk.

I was feeling restless again, thinking about John Daggett
and his boat trip across the harbor. Yesterday, at the beach,
the notion of canvassing the neighborhood for witnesses had
seemed pointless. Now I wasn't so sure. Somebody might have

seen him. Public drunkenness is usually conspicuous, especially at an hour when not many people are about. Weekend guests at the beach motels had probably checked out by now, but it might still be worth a shot. I grabbed my jacket and my car keys, locked the office, and headed down the back stairs.

My VW was looking worse every time I turned around. It's fourteen years old, an oxidized beige model with dents. Now the window was smashed out on the passenger side. Not a class act by any stretch of the imagination, but it was paid for. Every time I think about a new car, it makes my stomach do a flip-flop. I don't want to be saddled with car payments, a jump in insurance premiums, and hefty registration fees. My current registration costs me twenty-five dollars a year, which suits me just fine. I turned the ignition key and the engine fired right up. I patted the dashboard and backed out of the space, taking State Street south toward the beach.

I parked on Cabana, just across from the entrance to the wharf. There are eight motels strung out along the boulevard, none with rooms for under sixty dollars a night. This was the "off" season and there were still no vacancies. I started with the first, the Sea Voyager, where I identified myself to the manager, found out who'd been working the night desk the previous Friday, jotted down the name, and left my card with a handwritten note on the back. As with many other aspects of the job I do, this door-to-door inquiry requires dogged patience and a fondness for repetition that doesn't really come naturally. The effort has to be made, however, on the off chance that someone, somewhere can fill in a detail that might help. Having worked my way to the last motel, I returned to my car and headed on down the boulevard toward the marina, half a mile away.

I parked this time near the Naval Reserve Building, in the lot adjacent to the harbor. There didn't seem to be much foot traffic in the area. The sky was overcast, the air heavy with the staunch smells of fresh fish and diesel fuel. I ambled along

the walk that skirts the waterfront, with its eighty-four acres
of slips for eleven hundred boats. A wooden pier, two lanes
wide, juts out into the water topped with a crane and pulleys
for hoisting boats. I could see the fuel dock and the city guest
dock, where two men were securing the lines on a big power
boat that they'd apparently just brought in.

On my right, there was a row of waterfront businesses—a
fish market with a seafood restaurant above, a shop selling
marine and fishing supplies, a commercial diving center, two
yacht brokers. The building fronts are all weathered gray
wood, with bright royal blue awnings that echo the blue canvas
sail covers on boats all through the harbor. For a moment, I
paused before a plate glass window, scanning the snapshots
of boats for sale—catamarans, luxury cabin cruisers, sailboats
designed to sleep six. There's a small population of "live-
aboards" in the harbor—people who actually use their boats
as a primary residence. The idea is mildly appealing to me,
though I wonder about the reality of chemical toilets in the
dead of night and showering in marina restrooms. I crossed
the walk and leaned on the iron railing, looking out across
the airy forest of bare boat masts.

The water itself was a dark hunter green. Big rocks were
submerged in the gloomy depths, looking like sunken ruins.
Few fish were visible. I spotted two little crabs scuttling along
the boulders at the water's edge, but for the most part, the
shallows seemed cold and sterile, empty of sea life. A beer
bottle rested on a shelf of sand and mud. Two harbor patrol
boats were moored not far away.

I spotted a line of skiffs tied up at one of the docks below
and my interest perked up. Four of the marinas are kept
locked and can only be entered with a card key issued by the
Harbor Master's Office, but this one was accessible to the
public. I moved down the ramp for a closer look. There were
maybe twenty-five small skiffs, wood and fiberglass, most of
them eight to ten feet long. I had no way of knowing if one

of these was the boat Daggett had taken, but this much seemed clear: if you cut the line on one of these boats, you'd have to row it out around the end of the dock and through the harbor. There was no current here and a boat left to drift would simply bump aimlessly against the pilings without going anyplace.

I went up the ramp again and turned left along the walkway until I reached Marina One. At the bottom of the ramp, I could see the chain-link fence and locked gate. I loitered on the walk, keeping an eye on passersby. Finally, a middle-aged man approached, his card key in one hand, a bag of groceries in the other. He was trim and muscular, tanned to the color of rawhide. He wore Bermuda shorts, Topsiders, and a loose cotton sweater, a mat of graying chest hairs visible in the V.

"Excuse me," I said. "Do you live down there?"

He paused, looking at me with curiosity. "Yes." His face was as lined as a crumpled brown grocery bag pressed into service again.

"Do you mind if I follow you out onto Marina One? I'm trying to get a line on the man who washed up on the beach Saturday."

"Sure, come on. I heard about that. The skiff he stole belongs to a friend of mine. By the way, I'm Aaron. You are?"

"Kinsey Millhone," I said, trotting down the ramp after him. "How long have you lived down here?"

"Six months. My wife and I split up and she kept the house. Nice change, boat life. Lot of nice people. You a cop?"

"Private investigator," I said. "What sort of work do you do?"

"Real estate," he said. "How'd you get into it?" He inserted his card and pushed the gate open. He held it while I passed through. I paused on the other side so he could lead the way.

"I was hired by the dead man's daughter," I said.

"I meant how'd you get into investigative work."

"Oh. I used to be a cop, but I didn't like it much. The law enforcement part of it was fine, but not the bureaucracy. Now I'm self-employed. I'm happier that way."

We passed a cloud of sea gulls converging rapidly on an object bobbing in the water. The screeches from the birds were attracting gulls from a quarter of a mile away, streaking through the air like missiles.

"Avocado," Aaron said idly. "The gulls love them. This is me." He had paused near a thirty-seven-foot twin-diesel trawler, a Chris Craft, with a flying bridge.

"God, it's a beautiful boat."

"You like it? I can sleep eight," he said, pleased. He hopped down into the cockpit and turned, holding a hand out to me. "Pop your boots off and you can come on board and take a look around. Want a drink?"

"I better not, thanks. I've got a lot of ground to cover yet. Is there any way you can introduce me to the guy whose skiff was stolen?"

Aaron shrugged. "Can't help you there. He's out on a fishing boat all day, but I can give him your name and telephone number if you like. I think the police impounded the skiff, so if you want to see that, you better talk to them."

I didn't expect anything to come of it, but I thought I'd leave the door open just in case. I took out a business card, jotting down my home number on the back before I passed it on to him. "Have him give me a call if he knows anything," I said.

"I'll tell you who you might want to talk to. Go down here six slips and see if that guy's in. *The Seascape* is the name of the boat. His is Phillip Rosen. He knows all the gossip down here. Maybe he can help."

"Thanks."

The Seascape was a twenty-four-foot Flicka, a gaff-rigged sloop with a twenty-foot mast, teak deck, and a fiberglass hull that mimicked wood.

I tapped on the cabin roof, calling a hello toward the open doorway. Phillip Rosen appeared, ducking his head as he came up from down below. His emerging was like a visual

joke: he was one of the tallest men I'd seen except on a basketball court. He was probably six-foot-ten and built on a
grand scale—big hands and feet, big head with a full head of
red hair, a big face with red beard and moustache, bare-chested
and barefoot. Except for the ragged blue jean cut-offs, he
looked like a Viking reincarnated cruelly into a vessel un-
worthy of him. I introduced myself, mentioning that Aaron
had suggested that I talk to him. I told him briefly what I
wanted.

"Well, I didn't see them, but a friend of mine did. She was
coming down here to meet me and passed 'em in the parking
lot. Man and a woman. She said the old guy was drunk as a
skunk, staggering all over the place. The little gal with him
had a hell of a time trying to keep him upright."

"Do you have any idea what she looked like?"

"Nope. Dinah never said. I can give you her number though,
if you want to ask her about it yourself."

"I'd like that," I said. "What time was this?"

"I'd say two-fifteen. Dinah's a waitress over at the Wharf
and she gets off at two. I know she didn't close up that night
and it only takes five minutes to get here. Shoot, if she walked
on water, she could skip across the harbor in the time it takes
her to get to the parking lot."

"Is she at work now by any chance?"

"Monday afternoon? Could be. I never heard what her
schedule was this week, but you can always try. She'd be up
in the cocktail lounge. A redhead. You can't miss her if she's
there."

Which turned out to be true. I drove the half mile from
the marina to the wharf, leaving my car with the valet who
handles restaurant parking. Then I went up the outside staircase to the wooden deck above. Dinah was crossing from the
bar to a table in the corner, balancing a tray of margaritas.
Her hair was more orange than red, too carroty a shade to
be anything but natural. She was probably six feet tall in heels,

wearing dark mesh hose, and a navy blue "sailor" suit with a
skirt that skimmed her crotch. She had a little sailor cap pinned
to her head and an air about her that suggested she'd known
starboard from port since the day she reached puberty.

I waited until she'd served the drinks and was on her way
back to the bar. "Dinah?"

She looked at me quizzically. Up close, I could see the
overlay of pale red freckles on her face and a long, narrow
nose. She wore false eyelashes, like a series of commas encir-
cling her pale hazel eyes, lending her a look of startlement.
I gave her a brief rundown, patiently repeating myself. "I
know who the old guy is," I said. "What I'm trying to get a
fix on is the woman he was with."

Dinah shrugged. "Well, I can't tell you much. I just saw
them as I went past. I mean, the marina's got *some* lights, but
not that great. Plus, it was raining like a son of a bitch."

"How old would you say she was?"

"On the young side. Twenties, maybe. Blonde. Not real big,
at least compared to him."

"Long hair? Short? Buxom? Flat-chested?"

"The build, I don't know. She was wearing a raincoat. Some
kind of coat, anyway. Hair was maybe shoulder length, not a
lot of curl. Kind of bushy."

"Pretty?"

She thought briefly. "God, all I remember thinking was
there was something off, you know? For starters, he was such
a mess. I could smell him ten feet away. Bourbon fumes. Phew!
Actually, I kind of thought she might be a hooker on the
verge of rolling him. I nearly said something to her, but then
I decided it was none of my business. He was having a great
old time, but you know how it is. Drunk as he was, she really
could have ripped him off."

"Yeah, well, she did. *Dead* is about as ripped off as you can
get."

14

By the time I pulled out of the restaurant parking lot, it was 2:00 and the air felt dank. Or maybe it was only the shadowy image of Daggett's companion that chilled me. I'd been half convinced there was someone with him that night and now I had confirmation—not proof of murder, surely, but some sense of the events leading up to his death, a tantalizing glimpse of his consort, that "other" whose ghostly passage I tracked.

From Dinah's description, Lovella Daggett was the first name that popped into my head. Her trashy blonde looks had made me think she was hooking when I met her in L.A. On the other hand, most of the women I'd run across to date were on the young side and fair-haired—Barbara Daggett, Billy Polo's sister Coral, Ramona Westfall, even Marilyn Smith, the mother of the other dead child. I'd have to start pinning people down as to their whereabouts the night of the murder, a tricky matter as I had no way to coerce a reply. Cops have some leverage. A P.I. has none.

In the meantime, I went by the bank and removed the cashier's check from my safe deposit box. I ducked into a coffee shop and grabbed a quick lunch, then spent the afternoon in the office catching up on paperwork. At 5:00, I locked up and went home, puttering around until 6:30 when I left for Ferrin and Ramona Westfall's house to meet Tony Gahan.

The Westfalls lived in an area called the Close, a deadend street lined with live oaks over near the Natural History Museum. I drove through stone gates into the dim hush of privacy. There are only eight homes on the cul-de-sac, all Victorian, completely restored, immaculately kept. The neighborhood looks, even now, like a small, rural community inexplicably lifted out of the past. The properties are surrounded by low walls of fieldstone, the lots overgrown with bamboo, pampas grass, and fern. It was fully dark by then and the Close was wreathed in mist. The vegetation was dense, intensely scented, and lush from the recent rain. There was only one street light, its pale globe obscured by the branches of a tree.

I found the number I was looking for and parked on the street, picking my way up the path to the front. The house was a putty-colored, one-story wood frame with a wide porch, white shutters and trim. The porch furniture was white wicker with cushions covered in a white-and-putty print. Two Victorian wicker plant stands held massive Boston ferns. All too perfect for my taste.

I rang the bell, refusing to peer in through the etched glass oval in the door. I suspected the interior was going to look like something out of *House and Garden* magazine, an elegant blend of the old, the new, and the offbeat. Of course, my perception was probably colored by Ferrin Westfall's curt treatment of me and Ramona's outright hostility. I'm not above holding grudges.

Ramona Westfall came to the door and admitted me. I kept my tone pleasant, but I didn't fall all over myself admiring the place, which, at a glance, did appear to be flawlessly done. She showed me into the front parlor and removed herself, closing the oak-paneled sliding doors behind her. I waited, staring resolutely at the floor. I could hear murmuring in the hall. After a moment, the doors slid open and a man entered, introducing himself as Ferrin Westfall . . . as if I hadn't guessed. We shook hands.

He was tall and slim, with a cold, handsome face and silver hair. His eyes were a dark green, as empty of warmth as the harbor. There were hints of something submerged in the depths, but no signs of life. He wore charcoal gray pants and a soft gray cashmere sweater that fairly begged to be stroked. He indicated that I should have a seat, which I did.

He surveyed me for a moment, taking in the boots, the faded jeans, the wool sweater beginning to pill at the elbows. I was determined not to let his disapproval get through to me, but it required an effort on my part. I stared at him impassively and warded off his withering assessment by picturing him on the toilet with his knickers down around his ankles.

Finally, he said, "Tony will be out in a moment. Ramona's told me about the check. I wonder if I might examine it."

I removed the check from my jeans pocket and smoothed it out, passing it to him for his inspection. I wondered if he thought it was forged, stolen, or in some way counterfeit. He scrutinized it, fore and aft, and returned it, apparently satisfied that it was legitimate.

"Why did Mr. Daggett come to you with this?" he asked.

"I'm not really sure," I said. "He told me he'd tried to find Tony at an old address. When he had no luck, he asked me to track him down and deliver it."

"Do you know how he acquired the money?"

Again, I found myself feeling protective. It was really none of this man's business. He probably wanted to assure himself that Daggett hadn't come by the money through some tacky enterprise—drugs, prostitutes, selling dogs and kitty cats to labs for medical experiments.

"He won it at the track," I said. Personally, I hadn't quite believed this part of Daggett's tale, but I didn't mind if Ferrin Westfall got sucked in. He didn't seem any more convinced than I. He shifted the subject.

"Would you prefer to be alone with Tony?"

I was surprised at the offer. "Yes, I would. I'd really like to go off somewhere with him and have a Coke."

"I suppose that would be all right, as long as you don't keep him too long. This is a school night."

"Sure. That's very nice of you."

There was a tap at the door. Mr. Westfall rose and crossed the room. "This will be Tony," he said.

The doors slid back and Tony Gahan came in. He looked like an immature fifteen. He was maybe five-foot-six, a hundred and twenty-five pounds. His uncle introduced me. I proferred my hand and we fumbled through a handshake. Tony's eyes were dark, his hair a medium brown, attractively cut, which struck me as odd. Most of the high school kids I've seen lately look like they're being treated for the same scalp disease. I suspected Tony's hairstyle was a concession to Ferrin Westfall's notions of good taste and I wondered how that sat with him.

His manner was anxious. He seemed like a kid trying desperately to please. He shot a cautious look at his uncle, searching for visual cues as to what was expected of him and how he was meant to behave. It was painful to watch.

"Miss Millhone would like to take you out for a Coke, so she can talk to you," Mr. Westfall said.

"How come?" he croaked. Tony looked like he was going to drop dead on the spot and I remembered in a flash how much I'd hated eating and drinking in the presence of strange adults when I was his age. Meals represent a series of traps when you haven't yet mastered the appropriate social skills. I hated adding to his distress, but I was convinced I'd never have a decent conversation with him in this house.

"She'll explain all that," Mr. Westfall said. "Obviously, you're not required to go. If you'd prefer to stay here, simply say so."

Tony seemed unable to get a reading from his uncle's statement, which was neutral on the surface, but contained some tricky side notes. It was the word "simply" that tripped him, I thought, and the "obviously" didn't help.

Tony glanced at me with a half shrug. "It's okay, I guess. Like, right now?"

Mr. Westfall nodded. "It won't be for long. You'll need a jacket, of course."

Tony moved out into the hall and I followed, waiting until he found his jacket in the hall closet.

At fifteen, I thought he could probably figure out if he needed a jacket or not, but neither of them consulted me on the subject. I opened the front door and held it while he went out. Mr. Westfall watched us for a moment and then closed the door behind us. God, it was just like a date. I nearly swore I'd have him home by 10:00. Absurd.

We made our way down the path in the dark. "You go to Santa Teresa High School?"

"Right."

"What year?"

"Sophomore."

We got in the car. Tony tried to roll down the smashed window on his side without much success. A shard of glass tinkled down into the door frame. He finally gave up.

"What happened to this?"

"I was careless," I said, and let it go at that.

I did a U-turn in the lane and I headed for the Clockworks on State Street, a teen hangout generally regarded as seedy, unclean, and corrupt, which it is . . . a training ground for junior thugs. Kids come here (stoned, no doubt) to drink Cokes, smoke clove cigarettes, and behave like bad-asses. I'd been introduced to the place by a seventeen-year-old pink-haired dope dealer named Mike, who made more money than I did. I hadn't seen him since June, but I tend to look for him around town.

We parked in a small lot out back and went in through the rear entrance. The place is long and narrow, painted charcoal gray, the high ceiling rimmed with pink and purple neon. A series of mobiles, looking like big black clock gears, revolve in the smoky air. The noise level, on weekends, is deafening, the music so loud it makes the floor vibrate. On week nights, it's quiet and oddly intimate. We found a table and I went over to the counter to pick up a couple of Cokes. There was a tap on my shoulder and I turned to find Mike standing there. I felt a rush of warmth. "I was just thinking about you!" I said. "How are you?"

A pink tint crept across his cheeks and he gave me a slow seductive smile. "I'm okay. What are you doin' these days?"

"Nothing much," I said. "Great hair." Formerly, he'd sported a Mohawk, a great cockscomb of pink down the center of his head, with the sides shaved close. Now it was arranged in a series of purple spurts, each clump held together with a rubber band, the feathery tips bleached white. Aside from the hair, he was a good-looking kid, clear skin, green eyes, good teeth.

I said, "Actually, I'm about to have a talk with that guy over there . . . a schoolmate of yours."

"Yeah?" He turned and gave Tony a cursory inspection.

"You know him?"

"I've seen him. He doesn't hang out with the kind of people I do." His gaze returned to Tony and I thought he was going to say more, but he let it pass.

"What are you up to?" I asked. "Still dealing?"

"Who me? Hey, no. I told you I'd quit," he said, sounding faintly righteous. The look in his eyes, of course, suggested just the opposite. If he was doing something illegal, I didn't want to know about it anyway, so I bypassed the subject.

"What about school? You graduate this year?"

"June. I got college applications out and everything."

"Really?" I couldn't tell if he was putting me on or not.

He caught the look. "I get good grades," he protested. "I'm not just your average high school dunce, you know. The bucks I got, I could go anyplace I want. That's what private enterprise is about."

I had to laugh. "For sure," I said. The "bar maid" set two Cokes on the counter and I paid her. "I have to get back to my date."

"Nice seeing you," he said. "You ought to come in sometime and talk to me."

"Maybe I'll do that," I said. I smiled at him, mentally shaking my head. Flirtatious little shit. I moved over to the table where Tony was sitting. I handed him a Coke and sat down.

"You know that guy?" Tony asked cautiously.

"Who, Mike? Yes, I know him."

Tony's eyes strayed to Mike and back again, resting on my face with something close to respect. Maybe I wasn't such a geek after all.

"Did your uncle tell you what this is about?" I asked.

"Some. He said the accident and that old drunk."

"You feel okay discussing it?"

He shrugged by way of reply, avoiding eye contact.

"I take it you weren't in the car," I said.

He smoothed the front of his hair to the side. "Uh-uh. Me and my mom got into this argument. They were going to my granny's for this Easter egg hunt and I didn't want to go."

"Your grandmother's still in town someplace?"

He shifted in his chair. "In a rest home. She had a stroke."

"She's your mother's mother?" I didn't care particularly about any of this. I was just hoping the kid would relax and open up.

"Yeah."

"What's it like living with your aunt and uncle?"

"Fine. No big deal. He comes down on my case all the time, but she's nice."

"She said you were having some problems at school."

"So?"

"Just curious. She says you're very smart and your grades are in the toilet. I wondered what that was about."

"It's about school sucks," he said. "It's about I don't like people butting into my fuckin' business."

"Really," I said. I took a sip of Coke. His hostility was like a sewer backing up and I thought I'd give the efflux a chance to subside. I didn't care if he cussed. I could outcuss him any day of the week.

When I didn't react, he filled the silence. "I'm trying to get my grades pulled up," he said somewhat grudgingly. "I had to take all this bullshit math and chemistry. That's why I didn't do good."

"What's your preference? English? Art?"

He hesitated. "You some kind of shrink?"

"No. I'm a private investigator. I assumed you knew that."

He stared at me. "I don't get it. What's this got to do with the accident?"

I took out the check and laid it on the table. "The man responsible wanted me to look you up and give you this."

He picked the check up and glanced at it.

"It's a cashier's check for twenty-five thousand dollars," I said.

"What for?"

"I'm not really sure. I think John Daggett was hoping to make restitution for what he did."

Tony's confusion was clear and so was the anger that accompanied it. "I don't want this," he said. "Why give it to me? Megan Smith died too, you know, and so did that other guy, Doug. Are they gettin' money too, or just me?"

"Just you, as far as I know."

"Take it back then. I don't want it. I hate that old bastard." He tossed the check on the table and gave it a push.

"Look. Now just wait and let me say something first. It's your choice. Honestly. It's up to you. Your aunt was offended by the offer and I understand that. No one can force you to accept the money if you don't want it. But just hear me out, okay?"

Tony was staring off across the room, his face set.

I lowered my voice. "Tony, it's true John Daggett was a drunk, and maybe he was a totally worthless human being, but he did something he felt bad about and I think he was trying to make up for it. Give him credit for that much and don't say no without giving it consideration first."

"I don't *want* money for what he did."

"I'm not done yet. Just let me finish this."

His mouth trembled. He made a dash at his eyes with the sleeve of his jacket, but he didn't get up and walk away.

"People make mistakes," I said. "People do things they never meant to do. He didn't kill anyone deliberately . . ."

"He's a fuckin' drunk! He was out on the fuckin' street at fuckin' nine in the morning. Dad and Mom and Hilary . . ." His voice broke and he fought for control. "I don't want anything from him. I hate his guts and I don't want his crummy check."

"Why don't you cash it and give it all away?"

"No! You take it. Give it back to him. Tell him I said he could get fucked."

"I can't. He's dead. He was killed Friday night."

"Good. I'm glad. I hope somebody cut his heart out. He deserved it."

"Maybe so. But it's still possible that he felt something for you and wanted to give you back some of what he took away."

"Like what? It's done. They're all dead."

"But you're not, Tony. You have to find a way to get on with life . . ."

"Hey! I'm doing that, okay? But I don't have to listen to this bullshit! You said what you had to say and now I want to go home."

He got up, radiating rage, his whole body stiff. He moved swiftly toward the rear entrance, knocking chairs aside. I snatched up the check and followed.

When I reached the parking lot, he was kick-boxing the remaining glass out of the smashed window of my car. I started to protest and then I stopped myself.

Oh why not, I thought. I had to replace the damn thing anyway. I stood and watched him without a word. When he was done, he leaned against the car and wept.

15

By the time I got Tony home again, he was calm, shut down, as if nothing out of the ordinary had occurred. I pulled up in front of the house. He got out, slammed the door, and headed up the path without a word. I was reasonably certain he wouldn't mention his outburst to his aunt and uncle, which was fortunate as I'd sworn I could talk to him without his getting upset. I was, of course, still in possession of Daggett's check, wondering if I'd be toting it around for life, trying in vain to get someone to take it off my hands.

When I got back to my place, I spent twenty minutes unloading my VW. While I tend to maintain an admirable level of tidiness in the apartment, my organizational skills have never extended to my car. The back seat is usually crowded with files, law books, my briefcase, piles of miscellaneous clothing—shoes, pantyhose, jackets, hats, some of which I use as "disguises" in the various aspects of my trade.

I packed everything in a cardboard box and then proceeded around to the backyard where the entrance to my apartment is located. I opened the padlock on the storage bin attached to the service porch and stowed the box, snapping the padlock into place again.

As I reached my door, a dark shape loomed out of the shadows. "Kinsey?"

I jumped, realizing belatedly that it was Billy Polo. I couldn't distinguish his features in the dark, but his voice was distinctly his own.

"Oh Jesus, what are you doing here?" I said.

"Hey, I'm sorry. I didn't mean to scare you. I wanted to talk to you."

I was still trying to recover from the jolt he'd given me, my temper rising belatedly. "How'd you know where to find me?"

"I looked you up in the telephone book."

"My home address isn't in the book."

"Yeah, I know. I tried your office first. You weren't in, so I asked next door at that insurance place."

"California Fidelity gave you my home address?" I said. "Who'd you talk to?" I didn't believe for a minute that CF would release that kind of information to him.

"I didn't get her name. I told her I was a client and it was urgent."

"Bullshit."

"No, it's the truth. She only gave it to me because I leaned on her."

I could tell he wasn't going to budge on the point, so I let it pass. "All right, what is it?" I said. I knew I sounded cranky, but I didn't like his coming to my place and I didn't believe his tale about how he found out where it was.

"We're just gonna stand around out here?"

"That's right, Billy. Now get on with it."

"Well, you don't have to get so huffy."

"Huffy! What the hell are you talking about? You loom up out of the dark and scare me half to death! I don't know you from Jack the Ripper so why should I invite you in?"

"Okay, okay."

"Just say what you have to say. I'm beat."

He did some fidgeting around . . . for effect, I thought. Finally, he said, "I talked to my sister, Coral, and she told me I should be straight with you."

"Oh goody, what a treat. Straight about what?"

"Daggett," he mumbled. "He did get in touch."

"When was this?"

"Last Monday when he got to town."

"He called you?"

"Yeah, that's right."

"How'd he know where you were?"

"He tried my mom's house and talked to her. I wasn't home at the time, so she got his number and I called him back."

"Where'd he call from?"

"I don't know for sure. Some dive. There was all this noise in the background. He was drunk and I figured he must have parked himself in the first bar he found."

"What time of day was this?"

"Maybe eight at night. Around in there."

"Go on."

"He said he was scared and needed help. Somebody called him down in Los Angeles and told him he was dead meat on account of a scam he pulled up in prison just before he got out."

"What scam?"

"I don't know all the details. What I heard was his cellmate got snuffed and Daggett helped himself to a big wad of cash the guy had hidden in his bunk."

"How much?"

"Nearly thirty grand. It was some kind of drug deal went sour, which is why the guy got killed in the first place. Daggett walked off with the whole stash and somebody wanted it back. They were comin' after him. At least that's what they told him."

"Who?"

"I don't want to mention names. I got a fair idea and I could find out for sure if I wanted to, but I don't like puttin' my neck in a noose unless I have to. The point is I shined him on. I wasn't going to help that old coot. No way. He got himself in a hole, let him get himself out. I didn't want to be involved. Not with those guys after him. I'm too fond of my health."

"So what happened? You talked on the phone and that was it?"

"Well, no. I met him for a drink. Coral said I should level with you about that."

"Really," I said. "What for?"

"In case something came up later. She didn't want it to look like I was holding out."

"So you think they caught up with him?"

"He's dead, ain't he?"

"Proving what?"

"Don't ask me. I mean, all I know is what Daggett said. He was on the run and he thought I'd help."

"How?"

"A place to hide."

"When did you meet with him?"

"Not till Thursday. I was tied up."

"Pressing social engagements, no doubt."

"Hey, I was looking for work. I'm on parole and I got requirements to meet."

"You didn't see him Friday?"

"Uh-uh. I just saw him once and that was Thursday night."

"What'd he do in the meantime?"

"I don't know. He never said."

"Where'd you meet him?"

"At the bar where Coral works."

"Ah, now I see. She got worried I'd ask around and some-body'd say they saw you with him."

"Well, yeah. Coral don't like me to mess with the law, es-pecially with me on parole anyway."

"How come it took the bad guys so long to catch up with him? He's been out of prison for six weeks."

"Maybe they didn't figure it was him at first. Daggett wasn't the brightest guy, you know. He never did nothin' right in his life. They prob'ly figured he was too dumb to stick his hand in a mattress and walk off with the cash."

"Did Daggett have the money with him when you talked to him?"

"Are you kidding? He tried to borrow ten bucks from me," Billy said, aggrieved.

"What was the deal?" I asked. "If he gave the money back, they'd let him off the hook?"

"Probably not. I doubt that."

"So do I," I said. "How do you think Lovella figures into this?"

"She doesn't. It's got nothing to do with her."

"I wouldn't be too sure about that. Somebody saw Daggett down at the marina last Friday night, dead drunk, in the company of a trashy-looking blonde."

Even in the dark, I could tell Billy Polo was staring at me.

"A blonde?"

"That's right. She was on the young side from what I was told. He was staggering, and she had to work to keep him on his feet."

"I don't know nothin' about that."

"Neither do I, but it sure sounded like Lovella to me."

"Ask her about it then."

"I intend to," I said. "So what happens next?"

"About what?"

"The thirty thousand, for starters. With Daggett dead, does the money go back to the guys who were after him?"

"If they found it, I guess it does," he said, uncomfortably.

"What if they didn't find it?"

Billy hesitated. "Well, I guess if it's stashed somewhere, it'd belong to his widow, wouldn't it? Part of his estate?"

I was beginning to get the drift here, but I wondered if he did. "You mean Essie?"

"Who?"

"Daggett's widow, Essie."

"He's divorced from her," Billy said.

"I don't think so. At least not as far as the law is concerned."

"He's married to Lovella," he said.

"Not legally."

"You're shittin' me."

"Come to the funeral tomorrow and see for yourself."

"This Essie has the money?"

"No, but I know where it is. Twenty-five thousand of it, at any rate."

"Where?" he said, with disbelief.

"In my pocket, sweetheart, in the form of a cashier's check made out to Tony Gahan. You remember Tony, don't you?"

Dead silence.

I lowered my voice. "You want to tell me who Doug Polokowski is?"

Billy Polo turned and walked away.

I stood there for a moment and then followed reluctantly, still pondering the fact that he had my home address. Last time I'd talked to him, he didn't even buy the fact that I was a private investigator. Now suddenly he was seeking me out, having confidential chats about Daggett on my front step. It didn't add up.

I heard his car door slam as I reached the street. I hung back in the shadows, watching as he swung the Chevrolet out of a parking place four doors down. He gunned it, speeding off toward the beach. I debated about whether to pursue him, but I couldn't bear the thought of lurking about outside Coral's trailer again. Enough of that stuff. I turned back and let myself into my apartment. I kept thinking about the fact that my car was broken into, my handbag stolen, along with all of my personal identification. Had Billy Polo done that? Is that how he came up with my home address? I couldn't figure out how he'd tracked me to the beach in the first place, but it would explain how he knew where to find me now.

I was sure he was maneuvering, but I couldn't figure out what he'd hoped to get. Why the yarn about Daggett and the bad guys in jail? It did fit with some of the facts, but it didn't have that nice, untidy ring of truth.

I hauled out a stack of index cards and wrote it all down anyway. Maybe it would make sense later, when other information came to light. It was 10:00 by the time I finished. I pulled the white wine out of the refrigerator, wiggled the cork loose, and poured myself a glass. I stripped my clothes off, turned the lights out, and toted the wine into the bathroom where I set it on the window sill in the bathtub and stared out at the darkened street. There's a streetlight out there, buried in the branches of a jacaranda tree, largely denuded now by the rain. The window was half opened and a damp slat of night wind wafted in, chilly and secretive. I could hear rain begin to rattle on my composition roof. I was restless. When I was a young girl, maybe twelve or so, I wandered the streets on nights like this, barefoot, in a raincoat, feeling anxious and strange. I don't think my aunt knew about my nocturnal excursions, but maybe she did. She had a restless streak of her own and she may have honored mine. I was thinking a lot about her, of late, perhaps because of Tony. His family had been wiped out in a car accident, just as mine had, and he was being raised now by an aunt. Sometimes, I had to admit to myself . . . especially on nights like this . . . that the death of my parents may not have been as tragic as it seemed. My aunt, for all her failings, was a perfect guardian for me . . . brazen, remote, eccentric, independent. Had my parents lived, my life would have taken an altogether different route. There was no doubt of that in my mind. I like my history just as it is, but there was something else going on as well.

Looking back on the evening, I realized how much I'd identified with Tony's kicking my car window out. The rage and defiance were hypnotic and touched off deep feelings of my own. Daggett's funeral was coming up the next afternoon and that touched off something else . . . old sorrows, good friends gone down into the earth. Sometimes I picture death as a wide stone staircase, filled with a silent procession of those being led away. I see death too often to worry about it much, but I miss the departed and I wonder if I'll be docile when my turn comes.

I finished my wine and went to bed, sliding naked into the warm folds of my quilt.

16

The dawn was accompanied by drizzle, dark gray sky gradually shading to a cold white light. Ordinarily, I don't run in the rain, but I hadn't slept well and I needed to clear away the dregs of nagging anxiety. I wasn't even sure what I was worried about. Sometimes I awaken uncomfortably aware of a low-level dread humming in my gut. Running is the only relief I can find short of drink and drugs, which at 6:00 A.M. don't appeal.

I pulled on a sweat suit and hit the bike path, jogging a mile and a half to the recreation center. The palm trees along the boulevard had shed dried fronds in the wind and they lay on the grass like soggy feathers. The ocean was silver, the surf rustling mildly like a taffeta skirt with a ruffle of white. The beach was a drab brown, populated by sea gulls snatching at sand fleas. Pigeons lifted in a cloud, looking on. I have to admit I'm not an outdoor person at heart. I'm always aware that under the spritely twitter of birds, bones are being crunched and ribbons of flesh are being stripped away, all of it the work of bright-eyed creatures without feeling or conscience. I don't look to Nature for comfort or serenity.

Traffic was light. There were no other joggers. I passed the public restrooms, housed in a cinderblock building painted flesh pink, where two bums huddled with a shopping cart. One I recognized from two nights before and he watched me now, indifferently. His friend was curled up under a cardboard comforter, looking like a pile of old rags. I reached the turnaround and ran the mile and a half back. By the time I

got home, my Etonics were soaked, my sweat pants were darkened by the drizzle, and the mist had beaded in my hair like
a net of seed pearls. I took a long hot shower, optimism returning now that I was safely home again.

After breakfast, I tidied up and then checked my automobile insurance policy and determined that the replacement
of my car window was covered, after a fifty-dollar deductible.
At 8:30, I started soliciting estimates from auto glass shops,
trying to persuade someone to work me in before noon that
day. I zipped myself into my all-purpose dress again, resur-
rected a decent-looking black leather shoulder bag that I use
for "formal" wear and filled it with essentials, including the
accursed cashier's check.

I dropped the car off at an auto glass shop not far from
my office and hoofed it the rest of the way to work. Even with
low-heeled pumps, my feet hurt and my pantyhose made me
feel like I was walking around with a hot, moist hand in my
crotch.

I let myself into the office and initiated my usual morning
routines. The phone rang as I was plugging in the coffeepot.

"Miss Millhone, this is Ramona Westfall."

"Oh hello," I said. "How are you?" Secretly, my stomach
did a little twist and I wondered if Tony Gahan had told her
about his freak-out at the Clockworks the night before.

"I'm fine," she said. "I'm calling because there's something
I'd like to discuss with you and I hoped you might have some
time free this morning."

"Well, my schedule's clear, but I don't have a car. Can you
come down here?"

"Yes, of course. I'd prefer that anyway. Is ten convenient?
It's short notice, I know."

I glanced at my watch. Twenty minutes. "That's fine," I
said. She made some good-bye noises and clicked off. I depressed the line and then put a call through to Barbara Dag-

gett at her mother's house to verify the time of the funeral. She was unavailable to come to the phone, but Eugene Nickerson told me the services were at 2:00 and I said I'd be there.

I took a few minutes to open my mail from the day before, posting a couple of checks to accounts receivable, then made a quick call to my insurance agent, giving her the sketchy details about my car window. I'd no more than put the phone down when it rang again.

"Kinsey, this is Barbara Daggett. Something's come up. When I arrived here this morning, there was some woman sitting on the porch steps who says she's Daddy's wife."

"Oh God. Lovella."

"You know about her?"

"I met her last week when I was down in L.A., trying to get a line on your father's whereabouts."

"And you knew about this claim of hers?"

"I never heard the details, but I gathered they were living in some kind of common-law relationship."

"Kinsey, she has a marriage certificate. I saw it myself. Why didn't you tell me what was going on? I was speechless. She stood out on the front porch, screaming bloody murder until I finally had to call the police. I can't believe you didn't at least *mention* it."

"When was I supposed to do that? At the morgue? Over at the funeral home with your mother in a state of collapse?"

"You could have called me, Kinsey. Any time. You could have come to my office to discuss it."

"Barbara, I could have done half a dozen things, but I didn't. Frankly, I was feeling protective of your father and I was hoping you wouldn't have to find out about this 'alleged' marriage. That certificate could be a fake. The whole thing could be trumped up, and if not, you've still got problems enough without adding bigamy to his list of personal failings."

"That isn't yours to decide. Now Mother wants to know

what the ruckus was about and I have no idea what to say."

"Well, I can see why you're upset, but I'm not sure I'd do it any differently."

"I can't believe you'd take that attitude! I don't appreciate being kept in the dark," she said. "I hired you to investigate and I expect you to pass on whatever comes to light."

"Your father hired me long before you did," I said.

That silenced her for a moment and then she took off again. "To do what? You never did specify."

"Of course I didn't. He talked to me confidentially. It was all bullshit, but it's still not mine to flap around. I couldn't stay in business if I blabbed all the information that came my way."

"I'm his daughter. I have a right to know. Especially if my father's a *bigamist*. What else am I paying you for?"

"You might be paying me to exercise a little judgment of my own," I said. "Come on, Barbara. Be reasonable. Suppose I'd told you. What purpose would that have served? If your parents are still legally married, Lovella has no claim whatever and, for all I know, she's perfectly aware of that. Why add to your grief when she might well have slunk away without a word?"

"How did she know he died in the first place?"

"Not from me, I can tell you that. I'm not an idiot. The last thing in the world I wanted was her up here camping out on your doorstep. Maybe she read it in the paper. Maybe she heard it on the news."

She murmured something, temporarily mollified.

"What happened when the cops got there?" I asked.

There was another pause while she debated whether to move on or continue berating me. I sensed that she enjoyed chewing people out and it was hard for her to give up the opportunity. From my point of view, she wasn't paying me enough to take much guff. A little bit, perhaps. I probably should have told her.

"The two officers took her aside and had a talk with her. She left a few minutes ago."

"Well, if she shows up again, I'll take care of it," I said.

"Again? Why would she do that?"

I remembered then that aside from the matter of her father's apparent bigamy, I hadn't told her about the infamous twenty-five thousand dollars, which Billy Polo assumed was part of Daggett's "estate." Maybe Lovella had come up here to collect. "I think we better have a chat soon," I said.

"Why? Is there something *else*?"

I looked up. Ramona Westfall was standing in my doorway. "There's always something else," I said. "That's what makes life so much fun. I've got someone here. I'll talk to you this afternoon."

I hung up and rose to my feet, shaking hands with Mrs. Westfall across the desk. I invited her to take a seat and then poured coffee for us both, using social ritual as a way of setting her at ease, or so I hoped.

She was looking drawn, the fine skin under her mild eyes smudged with fatigue. She wore a tan poplin shirtwaist with shoulder epaulets and carried a mesh-and-canvas handbag that looked like it could be packed for a quick safari somewhere. Her pale hair had the sheen of a Breck shampoo ad in a magazine. I tried to picture her in a raincoat, lurching around the marina with Daggett's arm draped over her shoulder. Could she have flipped him, ass over teakettle, right out of that skiff? Hey, sure. Why not?

She stared at me uneasily, reaching out automatically to straighten some items on my desk. She lined up three pencils with the points facing me, like little ground-to-air missiles, and then she cleared her throat.

"Well. We were wondering. Tony never said anything so we thought perhaps we should ask you about it. Did you tell Tony about the money when you talked to him last night?"

"Sure," I said. "Not that it did any good. I got nowhere. He was adamant. He wouldn't even discuss it."

She colored slightly. "We're thinking to take it," she said. "Ferrin and I talked about it last night while Tony was out with you and we're beginning to believe we should put the money in a trustee account for him . . . at least until he's eighteen and really has a sense of what he might do with it."

"What brought about the change?"

"Oh everything, I guess. We've been in family counseling and the therapist keeps hoping we can work through some of the anger and the grief. He feels Tony's migraines are stress-related in part, a sort of index of his unwillingness . . . or maybe inability is a better word . . . to process his loss. I've been wondering how much I've contributed to that. I haven't dealt with Abby's death that well and it can't have helped him." She paused and then shook her head slightly as though embarrassed. "I know it's a reversal. I suppose we've been unnecessarily rude to you and I'm sorry."

"You don't have to apologize," I said. "Personally, I'd be delighted to have you take the check. At least then I could feel I'd discharged my responsibilities. If you change your mind later, you can always donate the money to a worthy cause. There are lots of those around."

"What about his family? Daggett's. They may feel they're entitled to the money, don't you think? I mean, I wouldn't want to take it if there are going to be any legal ramifications."

"You'd have to talk to an attorney about that," I said. "The check is made out to Tony, and Daggett hired me to deliver it to him. I don't think there's any question about his intention. There may be other legal issues I don't know about, but you're certainly welcome to talk to someone first." Secretly, I wanted her to take the damn thing and be done with it.

She stared at the floor for a moment. "Tony said . . . last night he mentioned that he might want to go to the funeral.

Do you think he should? I mean, does that seem like a good idea to you?"

"I don't know, Mrs. Westfall. That's way out of my line. Why don't you ask his therapist?"

"I tried, but he's out of town until tomorrow. I don't want Tony any more upset than he is."

"He's going to feel what he feels. You can't control that. Maybe it's something he has to go through."

"That's what Ferrin says, but I'm not sure."

"What's the story on the migraines? How long has that been going on?"

"Since the accident. He had one last night as a matter of fact. It's not your fault," she added hastily. "His head started bothering him about an hour after he got home. He threw up every twenty minutes or so from midnight until almost four A.M. We finally had to take him over to the emergency room at St. Terry's. They gave him a shot and that put him out, but he woke up a little while ago and he's talking now about going to the funeral. Did he mention it to you?"

"Not at all. I told him Daggett was dead, but he didn't react much at the time, except to say he was glad. Is he well enough to go?"

"He will be, I think. The migraines are odd. One minute you think he's never going to pull out of it and the next minute he's on his feet and starving to death. It happened last Friday night."

"Friday?" I said. The night of Daggett's death.

"That episode wasn't quite as bad. When he came home from school, he knew he was on the verge of a headache. We tried to get some medication down him to head it off, but no luck. Anyway, he pulled out of it after a while and I ended up fixing him two meatloaf sandwiches in the kitchen at two A.M. He was fine. Of course, he had another headache on Tuesday, and then the one last night. Two the week before that. Ferrin thinks maybe his going to the funeral will have some symbolic significance. You know, finish it off for him and set him free."

"That's always possible."

"Would Barbara Daggett object?"

"I don't see why she would," I said. "I suspect she feels as guilty as her father did, and she's offered to help."

"I guess I'll see how he's doing when I get home, then," she said. She glanced at her watch. "I better go."

"Let me give you the check." I pulled my handbag out of the bottom drawer and took out the check, which I passed across the desk to her. As her husband had done the night before, she smoothed out the folds, looking at it closely as if it might be some preposterous fake. She folded it up again and slipped it in her bag as she got to her feet. She hadn't touched her mug of coffee. I hadn't drunk mine either.

I told her the time and place of the services and walked her to the door. After she left, I sat down at my desk again, reviewing everything she'd said. At some point, I wanted to take Tony Gahan aside and see if he could verify her presence at the house the night Daggett died. It was hard to picture her as a killer, but I'd been fooled before.

17

John Daggett's funeral service took place in the sanctuary of some obscure outpost of the Christian church. The building itself was a one-story yellow stucco, devoid of ornament, located just off the freeway—the sort of chapel you glimpse through the bushes when you're going someplace else. I arrived late. I'd retrieved my VW from the auto glass shop at 1:45 after countless delays, and I confess I'd spent a few contented moments cranking my new car window up and down. The drizzle was beginning to turn serious and I was heartened by the notion that it wouldn't blow straight in on me.

When I reached the gravel parking lot beside the church, there were already fifty cars jammed into space for thirty-five. Some vehicles had nosed out into the vacant lot next door and some hugged the fence along the frontage road. I was forced to pass the place, snag a spot at the end of a long line of cars, and walk back. I could already hear electronic organ music thumping out in a style better suited to a skating rink than a house of God. I noticed from the sign out front that the minister was called a pastor instead of "Reverend" and I wondered if that was significant. Pastor Howard Bowen. The church name was composed of a long string of words and reminded me uneasily of the outfit that distributes pamphlets door-to-door. I hoped they weren't keen on converts.

Mr. Sharonson, from Wynington-Blake, was standing by himself on the low front steps and he gave me a pained look as he passed me a mimeographed copy of the program with a hand-drawn lily on the front. His manner suggested that

the services were spiritually second-rate, this being the K mart
of churches.

I went in. An usher peeled a metal folding chair from a
stack near the door and flipped it open for me. The congregation had risen to its feet to sing so I stood in the back row,
wedged in among other late arrivals. The woman on my left
offered to share her hymnal and I took my half, my gaze
sliding over the page in haste. They were on verse four of a
ditty that went on and on about blood and sin. I made some
mouth noises which I hoped were being lost in the general
din. Aside from the fact I don't believe in this stuff, I don't
sing too good and I was worried I might be denounced on
both counts.

Way up at the front, I thought I spotted Barbara Daggett's
blonde head, but I didn't see anyone else I knew. We sat down
with a rustle of clothing and the scrape of metal chair legs.
While Pastor Bowen, in a matte black suit, talked about what
wretches we were, I stared at the brown vinyl tile floor and
studied the staunch row of stained glass windows which de-
picted forms of spiritual torment that made me squirm. Already, I could feel a burgeoning urge to repent.

I could see Daggett's casket up by the altar, looking somehow like one of those boxes magicians use when they cut folk
in half. I checked my program. We'd whipped through the
opening prayer and the invocation, and now that we'd dis-
pensed with the first hymn, we were apparently settling in for
an energetic discourse on the temptations of the flesh, which
put me in mind of the numerous and varied occasions on
which I'd succumbed. That was entertaining.

Pastor Bowen was in his sixties, balding, a small man with
a tight round face, who looked like he would suffer from
denture breath. He'd chosen as his subject matter a passage
from Deuteronomy: "The Lord shall smite thee in the knees,
and in the legs, with a sore botch that cannot be healed, from
the sole of thy foot unto the top of thy head," and I heard

more on that subject than I thought possible without falling asleep. I was curious what he could find to say about John Daggett, whose transgressions were many and whose repentances were few, but he managed to tie Daggett's passing into "He shall lend to thee, and thou shalt not lend to him; he shall be the head, and thou shalt be the tail," and sailed right into an all-encompassing prayer.

When we stood for the final hymn, I felt someone's eyes on me and I looked over to spot Marilyn Smith two rows down, in the company of a man I assumed to be her husband, Wayne. She was wearing red. I wondered if she would leap up and do a tap dance on the coffin lid. The congregation by now was really getting into the spirit of things and hosannas were being called out on all sides, accompanied by amens, huzzahs, and much rending and tearing of clothes. I wanted to excuse myself, but I didn't dare. This was beginning to feel like soul-aerobics.

The woman next to me began to sway, her eyes closed, while she hooted out an occasional "Yes, Lord." I'm not given to this sort of orthodox public outburst and I commenced to edge my way to the door. I could see now that the minister, doing what looked like deltoid releases, was leading his merry band of church elders in the equivalent of a canonical conga line with Essie Daggett bringing up the rear.

At the exit, I came face to face with Billy Polo and his sister, Coral. He took me by the arm and pulled me aside as the service drew to a close behind me and people began to crowd through the door. Essie Daggett was wailing, nearly borne aloft like a football coach after a big win. Barbara Daggett and Eugene Nickerson had arranged themselves on either side, giving her what protection they could. For some reason, the other mourners were reaching out to touch and pat and grasp at Essie, as if her grief lent her healing powers.

The pallbearers came last, pulling the coffin along on a rolling cart instead of toting it. None of the six of them ap-

peared to be under sixty-five and Wynington-Blake may have
worried that they'd collapse, or topple their cargo right out
into the aisle. As it was, the cart seemed to have one errant
wheel which caused it to meander, squeaking energetically.
The coffin, as though with a will of its own, headed for the
chairs first on one side and then the other. I could see the pallbearers struggle to maintain mournful expressions while correcting its course, dragging it up the aisle like a stubborn dog.

I caught sight of Tony Gahan briefly, but he was gone again
before I could speak to him. The hearse pulled up in front
and the coffin was angled down the low steps and into the
rear. Behind it, the limousine pulled up and Essie was helped
into the back seat. She was wearing a black suit, with a broad-
brimmed black straw hat, swathed in veiling. She looked more
like a beekeeper than anything else. Stung by the Holy Spirit,
I thought. Barbara Daggett wore a charcoal gray suit and black
pumps, her two-toned eyes looking almost electric in the pale
oval of her face. The rain was falling steadily and Mr. Sharonson was distributing big black umbrellas as people ducked
off the porch and hurried to the parking lot.

Cars were being started simultaneously in a rumble of ex-
haust fumes, gravel popping as we pulled out onto the frontage road and began the slow procession to the cemetery, maybe
two miles away. Again, we parked in a long line, car doors
slamming as we crossed the soggy grass. This was apparently
a fairly new cemetery, with few trees—a wide flat field planted
to an odd crop. The headstones were square cut and low,
without any of the worn beauty of stone angels or granite
lambs. The grounds were well kept, but consisted primarily
of asphalt roadways winding among sections of burial plots
that had apparently been sold "pre-need." I wondered if
cemeteries, like golf courses, had to be designed by experts
for maximum aesthetic effect. This one felt like a cut-rate
country club, low membership fees for the upstart dead. The
rich and respectable were buried someplace else and John

Daggett couldn't possibly qualify for inclusion among them.

Wynington-Blake had set up a canopy over the grave itself and, nearby, a second larger one with folding chairs arranged under it. No one seemed to know who was supposed to go where and there was a bit of milling around. Essie and Barbara Daggett were led into the big tent and placed in the front row, with Eugene Nickerson on one side and a fat woman on the other in a set of four folding chairs connected at the base. The back legs were already beginning to sink into the rain-softened soil, tilting the four of them backward at a slight angle. I had a brief image of them trapped like that, staring at the tent top, legs dangling, unable to right themselves again. Why is it that grief always seems edged with absurdity?

I eased over to one side, under shelter, but remained standing. Most of the mourners appeared to be elderly and (perhaps) needed folding chairs more than I. It looked like the entire church membership had turned out in Essie Daggett's behalf.

Pastor Bowen had declined a raincoat and he stood now in the open air, rain collecting on his balding head, waiting patiently for everyone to get settled. At this range, I saw evidence of a hearing aid tucked into the tiny ear cave on his right. Idly, he fiddled with the device, keeping his expression benign so as not to call attention to himself. I wondered if the battery was shorting out from the damp. I could see him tap on the aid with his index finger, flinching then as though it had suddenly barked to life again.

On the far side of the tent, I saw Marilyn and Wayne Smith, and behind them Tony Gahan, accompanied by his aunt Ramona. He looked like the perfect prep school gentleman in gray wool slacks, white shirt, navy blazer, rep tie. As though sensing that he was being watched, his eyes strayed to mine, his expression as empty as a robot's. If he was expunging raw hate or an old sorrow, there was no sign of it. Billy Polo and his sister stood outside the tent in the rain, sharing an um-

brella. Coral looked miserable. She was apparently still caught
up in the throes of a cold, clutching a fistful of Kleenex. She
belonged in bed with a flannel rag on her chest reeking of
Vick's Vaporub. Billy seemed restless, scanning the crowd with
care. I followed his gaze, wondering if he was looking for
someone in particular.

"Dear friends," the minister said in a powdery voice. "We
are gathered here on the sad occasion of John Daggett's death,
to witness his return to the earth from which he was formed,
to acknowledge his passing, to celebrate his entry into the
presence of our Lord Jesus. John Daggett has left us. He is
free now of the cares and worries of this life, free of sin, free
of his burdens, free of blame. . . ."

From somewhere near the back, a woman hollered out
"Yes, Lord!" and a second woman yelled out "Buulllshiit!" in
just about the same tone. The minister, not hearing that well,
apparently took both as spiritual punctuation marks, Biblical
whoopees to incite him to greater eloquence. He raised his
voice, closing his eyes as he began quoting admonitions against
sin, filth, defiled flesh, lasciviousness, and corruption.

"John Daggett was the biggest asshole who ever lived so get
it straight!" came the jeering voice again. Heads whipped
around. Lovella had gotten to her feet near the back. The
people turned to stare, their faces blank with amazement.

She was drunk. She had the little bitty pink eyes that suggest
some high-grade marijuana toked up in addition to the booze.
Her left eye was still slightly puffy, but the bruising had light-
ened up to a mild yellow on that side and she looked more
like she was suffering from an allergy than a rap up the side
of the head from the dead man. Her hair was the same blonde
bush I remembered, her mouth a slash of dark red. She'd
been weeping copiously and her mascara was speckled under
her lower lids like soot. Her skin was splotchy, her nose hot
pink and running. For the occasion she'd chosen a black sequined cocktail dress, low cut. Her breasts looked almost

transparent and bulged out like condoms inflated as a joke. I couldn't tell if she was weeping out of rage or grief and I didn't think this crowd was prepared to deal with either one.

I was already headed toward the rear. Out of the corner of my eye, I saw Billy Polo make a beeline toward her on the far side of the tent. The minister had figured out by now that she was not on his team and he shot a baffled look at Mr. Sharonson, who motioned the ushers to take charge. We all reached her just about at the same time. Billy grabbed her from behind, pinning her arms back. Lovella flung him off, kicking like a mule, yelling "Fuck-heads! You scum-sucking hypocrites!" One usher snagged her by the hair and the other took her feet. She shrieked and struggled as they carried her toward the road. I followed, glancing back briefly. Barbara Daggett was obscured by the mourners who'd stood up for a better look, but I saw that Marilyn Smith was loving every trashy minute of Lovella's performance.

By the time I reached Lovella, she was lying in the front seat of Billy Polo's Chevrolet, hands covering her face as she wept. The doors were open on both sides of the car and Billy knelt by her head, shushing and soothing her, smoothing her rain-tangled hair. The two ushers exchanged a look, apparently satisfied that she was under control at that point. Billy bristled at their intrusion.

"I got her, man. Just bug off. She's cool."

Coral came around the car and stood behind him, holding the umbrella. She seemed embarrassed by Billy's behavior, uncomfortable in the presence of Lovella's excess. The three of them formed an odd unit and I got the distinct impression that the connection between them was more recent than Billy'd led me to believe.

The graveside service, I gathered, was drawing to a close. From the tent came the thin, discordant voices of the mourners as they joined in an a cappella hymn. Lovella's sobs had taken on the intensity of a child's—artless, unself-conscious.

Was she truly grieving for Daggett or was something else going on?

"What's the story, Billy?" I said.

"No story," he said gruffly.

"Something's going on. How'd she find out about his death? From you?"

Billy laid his face against her hair, ignoring me.

Coral shifted her gaze to mine. "He doesn't know anything."

"How about you, Coral? You want to talk about it?"

Billy shot her a warning look and she shook her head.

Murmurs and activity from the tent. The crowd was breaking up and people were beginning to move toward us.

"Watch your head. I'm closing the car doors," Billy said to Lovella. He shut the door on the driver's side and moved around the front to catch the door on the passenger side. He paused with his hand on the handle, waiting for her to pull her knees up to make clearance. Idly, he surveyed the mourners still huddled under the cover of the tent. As the crowd shifted, I saw his gaze flicker. "Who's that?"

He was looking at a small group formed by Ramona Westfall, Tony, and the Smiths. The three adults were talking while Tony, his hands in his pockets, passed his shoe over the rung of a folding chair, scraping the mud from the sole. Barbara Daggett was just behind him, in conversation with someone else. I identified everyone by name. I thought Wayne was the one who seemed to hold his attention, but I wasn't positive. It might have been Marilyn.

"How come the Westfalls showed up for this?"

"Maybe the same reason you did."

"You don't know why I came," he said. He was agitated, jingling the car keys, his gaze drifting back to the mourners.

"Maybe you'll tell me one of these days."

His smirk said don't count on it. He signaled to Coral and she got in the back seat. He got in the car and started it, pulling out then without a backwards glance.

18

Barbara Daggett invited me back to her mother's house after the funeral, but I declined. I couldn't handle another emotional circus act. After I've spent a certain amount of time in the company of others, I need an intermission anyway. I retreated to my office and sat there with the lights out. It was only 4:00, but dark clouds were massing again as though for attack. I slipped my shoes off and put my feet up, clutching my jacket around me for warmth. John Daggett was in the ground now and the world was moving on. I wondered what would happen if we left it at that. I didn't think Barbara Daggett gave a damn about seeing justice done, whatever that consisted of. I hadn't come up with much. I thought I was on the right track, but I wasn't sure I really wanted an answer to the question Daggett's death had posed. Maybe it was better to forget this one, turn it under again like top soil, worms and all. The cops didn't consider it a homicide anyway and I knew I could talk Barbara Daggett out of pursuing the point. What was there to be gained? I wasn't in the business of avenging Daggett's death. Then what was I uneasy about? It was the only time in recent memory that I'd wanted to drop a case. Usually I'm dogged, but this time I wanted out. I think I could have talked myself into it if nothing else had occurred. As it happened, my phone rang about ten minutes later, nudging me into action again. I took my feet off the desk for form's sake and picked up on the first ring. "Millhone."

A young-sounding man said hesitantly: "Is this the office or an answering service?"

"The office."

"Is this Kinsey Millhone?"

"Yes. Can I help you?"

"Yeah, well my boss gave me this number. Mr. Donagle at the Spindrift Motel? He said you had some questions about Friday night. I think maybe I saw that guy you were asking about."

I reached for a lined yellow pad and a pen. "Great. I appreciate your getting in touch. Could you tell me your name first?"

"Paul Fisk," he said. "I read in the paper some guy drowned and it just sure seemed like an odd coincidence, but I didn't know if I should say anything or not."

"You saw him Friday night?"

"Well, I think it was him. This was about quarter of two, something like that. I'm on night desk and sometimes I step outside for some air, just to keep myself awake." He paused and I could hear him shift gears. "This is confidential, isn't it?"

"Of course. Strictly between us. Why? Did your girlfriend stop by or something like that?"

His laugh was nervous. "Naw, sometimes I smoke a little weed is all. Place gets boring at two A.M., so that's how I get through. Get loaded and watch old black-and-white movies on this little TV I got. I hope you don't have a problem with that."

"Hey, it's your business, not mine. How long have you worked at the Spindrift?"

"Just since March. It's not a great job, but I don't want to get fired. I'm trying to get myself out of debt and I need the bucks."

"I hear you," I said. "Tell me about Friday night."

"Well, I was on the porch and this drunk went by. It was raining pretty hard so I didn't get a real good look at him at the time, but when I saw the news, the age and stuff seemed pretty close."

"Did you see the picture of him by any chance?"

"Just a glimpse on TV, but I wasn't paying much attention so I couldn't say for sure it was him. I guess I should have called the cops, but I didn't have anything much to report and I was afraid it'd come out about the . . . about that other stuff."

"What was he doing, the drunk?"

"Nothing much. It was him and this girl. She had him by the arm. You know, kind of propped up. They were laughing like crazy, wandering all over the place on account of his being so screwed up. Alcohol'll do that, you know. Bad stuff. Not like weed," he said.

I bypassed the sales pitch. "What about the woman? Did you get a good look at her?"

"Not really. Not to describe."

"What about hair, clothing, things like that?"

"I noticed some. She had these real spiky heels and a raincoat, a skirt, and let's see . . . a shirt with this sweater over it. Like, what do you call 'em, preppies wear."

"A crewneck?"

"Yeah. Same color green as the skirt."

"You saw all that in the dark?"

"It's not that dark there," he said. "There's a streetlight right out in front. The two of them fell down in a heap they were laughing so hard. She got up first and kind of looked down to see if her stockings were torn. He just lay there in a puddle on his back till she helped him up."

"Did they see you?"

"I don't think so. I was standing in the shadow of this overhang, keeping out of the wet. I never saw 'em look my way."

"What happened after the fall?"

"They just went on toward the marina."

"Did you hear them say anything?"

"Not really. It sounded like she was teasing him about falling down, but other than that nothing in particular."

"Could they have had a car?"

"I don't think so. Anyway, not that I saw."

"What if they'd parked it in that municipal lot across the street?"

"I guess they could have, but I don't know why they'd walk to the marina in weather like that. Seems like if they had a car it'd be easier to drive and then park it down there."

"Unless he was too drunk. He'd had his driver's license yanked too."

"She could have driven. She was half sober at least."

"You've got a point there," I said. "What about public transportation? Could they have come by bus or cab?"

"I guess, except the buses don't run that late. A cab maybe. That'd make sense."

I was jotting down information as he gave it to me. "This is great. What's your home phone in case I need to get in touch?"

He gave me the number and then said, "I usually work eleven to seven on weekdays."

I made a quick note. "Do you think you'd recognize the girl if you saw her again?"

"I don't know. Probably. Do you know who she is?"

"Not yet. I'm working on that."

"Well, I wish you luck. You think this'll help?"

"I hope so. Thanks for calling. I really appreciate it."

"Sure thing, and if you catch up with her, let me know. Maybe you can do like a police lineup or something like that."

"Great and thanks."

He clicked off and I finished making notes, adding this information to what I had. Dinah had spotted Daggett and the girl at 2:15 and Paul Fisk's sighting placed them right on

Cabana thirty minutes before. I wondered where they'd been before that. If they'd arrived by cab, had she taken one home from the marina afterward? I didn't get it. Most killers don't take taxis to and from. It isn't good criminal etiquette.

I hauled out the telephone book and turned to the Yellow Pages to look up cab companies. Fortunately, Santa Teresa is a small town and there aren't that many. Aside from a couple of airport and touring services, there were six listed. I dialed each in turn, patiently explaining who I was and inquiring about a 2:00 A.M. Saturday fare with a Cabana Boulevard drop off. I was also asking about a pickup anywhere in that vicinity sometime between 3:00 and 6:00 A.M. According to the morgue attendant, the watch Daggett had been wearing was frozen at 2:37, but anybody could have jimmied that, breaking the watch to pinpoint the time, then attaching it to his wrist before he was dumped. If she'd left the boat and swum ashore or rowed to the wharf and abandoned it there, it was still going to take her a little time to organize herself for the cab ride home.

All the previous week's trip sheets, of course, had been filed and there were some heavy sighs and grumblings all around at the notion of having to look them up. Ron Coachella, the dispatcher for Tip Top, was the only cheerful soul in the lot, primarily because he'd done a records search for me once before with good results. I couldn't talk anyone into doing the file check right then, so I left my name and number and a promise that I'd call again. "Whoopee-do," said one.

While I was talking, I'd been doodling on the legal pad, running my pencil around idly so that the line formed a maze. I circled the note about the green skirt. Hadn't that old bum pulled a pair of spike heels and a green skirt out of a trash bin at the beach? I remembered his shoving discarded clothing into one of the plastic bags he kept in his shopping cart. Hers? Surely she hadn't made her way home in the buff. She did have the raincoat, but I wondered if she might have had a change of clothes stashed somewhere too. She'd sure gone to a lot of trouble if she were setting Daggett up. This didn't look like an impulsive act, done in the heat of the moment. Had she had help? Someone who picked her up afterward? If the cab companies didn't come up with a record of a fare, I'd have to consider the possibility of an accomplice.

In the meantime, I thought I'd better head down to the beach and look for my scruffy drifter friend. I'd seen him that morning near the public restrooms when I did my run. I tore the sheet off the legal pad and folded it, shoving it in my pocket as I grabbed up my handbag, locked the office, and headed down the back stairs to my car.

It was now nearly quarter to five, getting chillier by the minute, but at least it was dry temporarily. I cruised along Cabana, peering from my car window. There weren't many people at the beach. A couple of power walkers. A guy with a dog. The boulevard seemed deserted. I doubled back, heading toward my place, passing the wharf on the left and the string of motels across the street. Just beyond the boat launch and kiddie pool, I pulled up at a stoplight, scanning the park on the opposite corner. I could see the band shell where bums sometimes took refuge, but I didn't see any squatters. Where were all the transients?

I circled back, passing the train station. It occurred to me that this was probably the bums' dinner hour. I cut over another block and a half and sure enough, there they were—fifty or so on a quick count, lined up outside the Redemption Mission. The fellow I was looking for was near the end of the line, along with his pal. There was no sign of their shopping carts, which I thought of as a matched set of movable metal luggage, the derelict's Louis Vuitton. I slowed, looking for a place to park.

The neighborhood is characterized by light industry, factory outlets, welding shops, and quonset huts where auto body repair work is done. I found a parking spot in front of a place that made custom surfboards. I pulled in, watching in my

rearview mirror until the group outside the mission had shuffled in. I locked the car then and crossed the street.

The Redemption Mission looks like it's made out of papier-
mâché, a two-story oblong of fakey-looking fieldstone, with
ivy clinging to one end. The roofline is as crenellated as a
castle's, the "moat" a wide band of asphalt paving. City fire
codes apparently necessitated the addition of fire escapes that
angle down the building now on all sides, looking somehow
more perilous than the possibility of fire. The property is
considered prime real estate and I wondered who would house
the poor if the bed space were bought out from under them.
For most of the year, the climate in this part of California is
mild enough to allow the drifters to sleep outdoors, which
they seem to prefer. Seasonally, however, there are weeks of
rain . . . even occasionally someone with a butcher knife intent
on slitting their throats. The mission offers safe sleeping for
the night, three hot meals a day, and a place to roll cigarettes
out of the wind.

I picked up cooking odors as I approached—bulk hamburger with chili seasoning. As usual, I couldn't remember
eating lunch and here it was nearly dinnertime again. The
sign outside indicated prayer services at 7:00 every night and
Hot Showers & Shaves on Mondays, Wednesdays, and Sat-
urdays. I stepped inside. The walls were painted glossy beige
on top and shoe brown down below. Hand-lettered signs pointed
me to the dining room and chapel on the left. I followed the
low murmur of conversation and the clatter of silverware.

On the right, through a doorway, I spotted the dining room—
long metal folding tables covered with paper, metal folding
chairs filled with men. Nobody paid any attention to me. I
could see serving plates stacked high with soft white bread,
bowls of applesauce sprinkled with cinnamon, salads of ice-
berg lettuce that glistened with bottled dressing. The table
seated twenty, already bent to their evening meal of chili served
over elbow macaroni. Another fifteen or twenty men sat obe-

diently in the "chapel" to my left, which consisted of a lectern, an old upright piano, orange molded plastic chairs, and an imposing cross on the wall.

The scruffy drifter I was looking for sat in the back row with his friend. Slogans everywhere assured me that Jesus cared, and that certainly seemed true here. What impressed me most was the fact that Redemption Mission (according to the wall signs) was supported by private donations, with little or no connection to the government.

"May I help you?"

The man who'd approached me was in his sixties, heavyset, clean-shaven, wearing a red short-sleeved cotton shirt and baggy pants. He had one normal arm and one that ended at the elbow in a twist of flesh like the curled top of a Mr. Softee ice cream cone. I wanted to introduce myself, shaking hands, but the stump was on the right and I didn't have the nerve. I took out a business card instead, handing it to him.

"I wonder if I might have a word with one of your clients?"

His beefy brow furrowed. "What's this about?"

"Well, I think he retrieved some articles I'm looking for from a trash can at the beach. I want to find out if he still has them in his cart. It will only take a minute."

"You see him in here?"

I indicated the one who interested me.

"You'll have to talk to the both of them," the man said. "Delphi's the fellow you want, but he don't talk. His buddy does all the talking. His name is Clare. I'll bring them out if you'll wait out there in the corridor. They got their shopping carts on the back patio. I'd go easy about them carts. They get a might possessive of their treasures sometimes."

I thanked him and retraced my steps, lingering in the entranceway until Delphi and Clare appeared. Delphi had shed some of his overcoats, but he wore the same dark watch cap and his skin had the same dusky red tone. His friend Clare was tall and gaunt with a very pink tongue that crept out of his mouth through the gap left by his missing front teeth. His hair was a silky white, rather sparse, his arms long and stringy, hands huge. Delphi made no eye contact at all, but Clare turned out to have some residual charm, left over perhaps from the days before he started to drink.

I explained who I was and what I was looking for. I saw Delphi look at Clare with the haunted subservience of a dog accustomed to being hit. Clare may have been the only human being in the world who didn't frighten or abuse him and he evidently depended on Clare to handle interactions of this kind.

"Yep. I know the ones. High heels in black suede. Green wool skirt. Delphi here was pleased. Usually it's slim pickin's around that bin. Aluminum cans is about the best you can hope for, but he got lucky, I guess."

"Does he still have the items?"

The tongue crept out with a crafty life of its own, so pink it looked like Clare had been sucking red hots. "I can ask," he said.

"Would you do that?"

Clare turned to Delphi. "What do you think, Delph? Shall we give this little gal what she wants? Up to you."

Delphi gave no evidence whatever of hearing, absorbing, or assenting. Clare waited a decent interval.

"Now that's tough," Clare said to me. "That was his best day and he likes that green skirt."

"I could reimburse him," I said tentatively. I didn't want to insult these guys.

Out came the tongue, like some shy creature peering from its lair. Delphi's hearing seemed to improve. He shifted slightly. I left Clare to translate this movement into dollars and cents.

"A twenty might cover it," Clare said at length.

I only had a twenty on me, but I took it out of the zippered compartment in my black handbag. I offered it to Delphi. Clare interceded. "Hold that until we've done our business. Let's step outside."

I filed after them along a short corridor to a back exit that opened on a small concrete patio surrounded on three sides by an openwork fence made of lathing. Someone had "landscaped" the entire area in annuals planted in coffee cans and big industrial-sized containers that had held green beans and applesauce. Delphi stood by, looking on anxiously, while Clare pawed through one of the shopping carts. He seemed to know exactly where the shoes and skirt were located, whisking them out in no time flat. He passed them over to me and I handed him the twenty. It felt somehow like an illicit drug sale and I had visions of them buying a jug of Mad Dog 20–20 after I'd left. Clare held the bill up for Delphi to inspect, then he glanced at me.

"Don't you worry. We'll put this in the collection plate," Clare said. "Delphi and me have give up drink." I thought Clare seemed happier about it than Delphi did.

19

My dinner that night was cheese and crackers, with a side of chili peppers just to keep my mouth awake. I'd changed out of my all-purpose dress into a tee shirt, jeans, and fuzzy slippers. I ate sitting at my desk, with a Diet Pepsi on the rocks. I studied the skirt and shoes. I tried the right shoe on. Too wide for me. The back of the heel was scuffed, the toe narrowing to a bunion-producing point. The manufacturer's name on the inner sole had been blurred by sweat. A pair of Odor-eaters wouldn't have been out of line here. The skirt was a bit more informative, size 8, a brand I'd seen at the Village Store and the Post & Rail. Even the lining was in good shape, though wrinkled in a manner that suggested a recent soaking. I touched my tongue to the fabric. Salt. I checked the inseam pockets, which were empty. No cleaner's marks. I thought about the women connected, even peripherally, with Daggett's death. The skirt might fit any one of them, except for Barbara Daggett maybe, who was big-boned and didn't seem like the type for the preppy look, especially in green. Ramona Westfall was a good candidate. Marilyn Smith, perhaps. Lovella Daggett or Billy's sister, Coral, could probably both wear an 8, but the style seemed wrong . . . unless the outfit had been lifted from a Salvation Army donation box. Maybe in the morning I'd stop by a couple of clothing stores and see if any of the salesclerks recognized the skirt. Fat chance, I thought. A better plan would be to show it, along with the shoes, to all five women and see if anyone would admit ownership. Unlikely under the circumstances. Too bad I couldn't do a little breaking and entering. The matching green sweater might come to light in someone's dresser drawer.

I padded into the kitchen and rinsed my plate. Eating alone is one of the few drawbacks to single life. I've read those articles that claim you should prepare food just as carefully for yourself as you would for company. Which is why I do cheese and crackers. I don't cook. My notion of setting an elegant table is you don't leave the knife sticking out of the mayonnaise jar. Since I usually work while I eat, there isn't any point in candlelight. If I'm not working, I have *Time* magazine propped up against a stack of files and I read it back to front as I munch, starting with the sections on books and cinema, losing interest by the time I reach Economy & Business.

At 9:02, my phone rang. It was the night dispatcher for Tip Top Cab Company, a fellow who identified himself as Chuck. I could hear the two-way radio squawking in the background.

"I got this note from Ron says to call you," said he. "He pulled the trip sheets for last Friday night and said to give you the information you were asking about, but I'm not really sure what you want."

I filled him in and waited briefly while he ran his eye down the sheet. "Oh yeah. I guess this is it. He's got it circled right here. It was my fare. That's probably why he asked me to call. Friday night, one twenty-three . . . well, you'd call that early Saturday. I dropped a couple off at State and Cabana. Man and a woman. I figured they were booked into a motel down there."

"I've heard the man was drunk."

"Oh yeah, very. Looked like she'd been drinking too, but not like him. He was a mess. I mean, this guy smelled to high heaven. Stunk up the whole back seat and I got a pretty fair tolerance for that kind of thing."

"What about her? Can you tell me anything?"

"Can't help you on that. It was late and dark and raining to beat the band. I just took 'em where they said."

"Did you talk to them?"

"Nope. I'm not the kind of cabbie engages in small talk with a fare. Most people aren't interested and I get sick of repeating myself. Politics, weather, baseball scores. It's all bull. They don't want to talk to me and I don't want to talk to them. I mean, if they ask me something I'm polite, don't get me wrong, but I can't manufacture chitchat to save my neck."

"What about the two of them? They talk to each other?"

"Who knows? I tuned 'em out."

God, this was no help at all. "You remember anything else?"

"Not offhand. I'll give it some thought, but it wasn't any big deal. Sorry I can't be a help."

"Well, at least you've verified a hunch of mine and I appreciate that. Thanks for your time."

"No problem."

"Oh, one more thing. Where'd the fare originate?"

"Now *that* I got. You know that sleazeball bar on Milagro? That place. I picked 'em up at the Hub."

I sat and stared at the phone for a moment after he hung up. I felt like I was running a reel of film backwards, frame by frame. Daggett left the Hub Friday night in the company of a blonde. They apparently had a lot of drinks, a lot of laughs, staggered around in the rain together, fell down, and picked themselves up again. And little by little, block by block, she was steering him toward the marina, herding him toward the boat, guiding him out into the harbor on the last short ride of his life. She must have had a heart of stone and steadier nerves than mine.

I made some quick notes and tossed the index cards in the top drawer of my desk. I kicked off my slippers and laced up my tennies, then pulled on a sweatshirt. I snatched up the skirt and shoes, my handbag, and car keys and locked up, heading out to the VW. I'd start with Coral first. Maybe she'd

know if Lovella was still in town. I was remembering now the
fragment of conversation I'd overheard the night I eaves-
dropped on Billy and Coral. She'd been talking to Billy then
about some woman. I couldn't remember exactly what she'd
said, but I did remember that. Maybe Coral had seen the
woman I was looking for.

When I reached the trailer park, I found the trailer dimly
lighted, as if someone had gone out and left a lamp burning
to keep the burglars at bay. Billy's Chevrolet was in the carport, the hood cold to the touch. I knocked on the door. After
a moment, I heard footsteps bumping toward the front.

"Yeah?" Billy's muffled voice came through the door.

"It's Kinsey," I said. "Is Coral here?"

"Uh-uh. She's at work."

"Can I talk to you?"

He hesitated. "About what?"

"Friday night. It won't take long."

There was a pause. "Wait a sec. Let me throw some clothes
on."

Moments later, he opened the door and let me in. He had
pulled on a pair of jeans. Aside from that, he was barefoot
and naked to the waist. His dark hair was tousled. He looked
like he hadn't worked out recently, but his arms and chest
were still well developed, overlaid by a fine mat of dark hair.

The trailer was disordered—newspapers, magazines, dinner dishes for two still out on the table, the counters covered
with canned goods, cracker boxes, bags of flour, sugar, and
corn meal. There wasn't a clear surface anywhere and no place
to sit. The air was dense, smelling faintly of fresh cigarette
smoke.

"Sorry to disturb you," I said. He looked like he'd been
screwing his brains out and I wondered who was in the bedroom. "You have company?"

He glanced toward the rear, his dimples surfacing. "No, I
don't. Why, are you interested?"

I smiled and shook my head, at the same time caught up in a flash fantasy of me and Billy Polo tangled up in sheets that smelled like him, musky and warm. His skin exuded a masculine perfume that conjured up images of all the trashy things we might do if the barriers went down. I kept my expression neutral, but I could feel my face tint with pink. "I have some questions I was hoping Coral might help me with."

"So you said. Try the Hub. She'll be there till closing time."

I laid the skirt and shoes across the television set, which was the only bare surface I could find. "Do you know if these are hers?"

He glanced at the items, too canny to bite. "Where'd you get 'em?"

"A friend of a friend. I thought you might know whose they were."

"I thought this was supposed to be about Friday night."

"It is. I talked to a cabbie who picked Daggett up at the Hub Friday night and dropped him off down near the wharf."

"I'll bite. So what?"

"A blonde was with him. The cabbie took them both. I figure she met him at the Hub, so I thought Coral might have had a look at her."

Billy knew something. I could see it in his face. He was processing the information, trying to decide what it meant.

I was getting impatient. "Goddamn it, Billy, level with me!"

"I am!"

"No, you're not. You've been lying to me since the first time you ever opened your mouth."

"I have not," he said hotly. "Name one thing."

"Let's start with Doug Polokowski. What's your relation to him? Brother?"

He was silent. I stared at him, waiting him out.

"Half-brother," he said grudgingly.

"Go on."

His tone of voice dropped, apparently with embarrassment.

"My mom and dad split up, but they were still legally married when she got pregnant by somebody else. I was ten and I hated the whole idea. I started gettin' in trouble right about then so I spent half my time in Juvenile Hall anyway, which suited me just fine. She finally had me declared a whaddyou call 'em. . . ."

"An out-of-control minor?"

"Yeah, one of them. Big deal. I didn't give a fat rat's ass. Let her dump us. Let her have a bunch more kids. She didn't have any more sense than that, then to hell with her."

"So you and Doug were never close?"

"Hardly. I used to see him now and then when I'd come home but we didn't have much of a relationship."

"What about you and your mother?"

"We're okay. I got over it some. After Doug got killed, we did better. Sometimes it happens that way."

"But you must have known Daggett was responsible."

"Sure I knew. Of course I did. Mom wrote and told me he was bein' sent up to San Luis. At first, I thought I'd get even with him. For her sake, if nothin' else. But it didn't work out like that. He was too pathetic. Know what I mean? Hell, I ended up almost feeling sorry for him. I despised him for the whiny little fucker that he was, but I couldn't leave him alone. It's like I had to torment him. I liked to watch him squirm, which maybe makes me weird but it don't make me a killer. I never murdered anybody in my life."

"What about Coral? Where was she in all this?"

"Hey, you ask her."

"Could she have been the one with Daggett that night? It sounds like Lovella to me, but I can't be sure."

"Why ask me? I wasn't there."

"Did Coral mention it?"

"I don't want to talk about this," he said, irritably.

"Come on. You talked to Daggett Thursday night. Did he mention this woman?"

"We didn't talk about women," Billy said. He began to snap the fingers of his right hand against his left palm, making a soft, hollow pop. I could feel myself going into a terrier pup mode, worrying the issue like a rawhide bone, knotted on both ends.

"He must have known who she was," I said. "She didn't just materialize out of the blue. She set him up. She knew what she was doing. It must have been a very carefully thought-out plan."

The popping sound stopped and Billy's tone took on a crafty note. "Maybe she was connected to the guys who wanted their money back," he said.

I looked at him with interest. That really hadn't occurred to me, but it didn't sound bad. "Did you tip them off?"

"Listen, babe, I'm not a killer and I'm not a snitch. If Daggett had a beef with somebody, that was his lookout, you know?"

"Then what's the debate? I don't understand what you're holding back."

He sighed and ran a hand through his hair. "Lay off, okay? I don't know nothin' else so just leave it alone."

"Come on, Billy. What's the rest of it?" I snapped.

"Oh, shit. It wasn't Thursday," he blurted out. "I met Daggett Tuesday night and that's when he asked me to help him out."

"So he could hide from the guys at San Luis," I said, making sure I was following.

"Well, yeah. I mean, they'd called him Monday morning and that's why he'd hightailed it up here. We talked on the phone late Monday. He was drunk. I didn't feel like putting myself out. I'd just got home and I was bushed so I said I'd meet him the next night."

"At the Hub?"

"Right."

"Which is what you did," I said, easing him along.

"Sure, we met and talked some. He was already in a panic so I kind of fanned the flames, just twitting him. There's no harm in that."

"Why lie about it? Why didn't you tell me this to begin with?" I was crowding him, but I thought it was time to persist.

"It didn't look right somehow. I didn't want my name tied to his. Thursday night sounded better. Like I wasn't all that hot to talk to him. You know, like I didn't rush right out. I can't explain it any better than that."

It was just lame enough to make sense to me. I said, "All right. I'll buy it for now. Then what?"

"That's all it was. That's the last I saw of him. He came in again Friday night and Coral spotted him, so she called me, but by the time I got there, he'd left."

"With the woman?"

"Yeah, right."

"So Coral did see her."

"Sure, but she didn't know who she was. She thought it was some babe hittin' on him, like a whore, something like that. The chick was buyin' him all these drinks and Daggett was lappin' 'em up. Coral got kind of worried. Not that either of us really gave a shit, but you know how it is. You don't want to see a guy get taken, even if you don't like him much."

"Especially if you've heard he's got thirty thousand dollars on him, right?" I said.

"It wasn't thirty. You said so yourself. It was twenty-five." Billy was apparently feeling churlish now that he'd opened up. "Anyway, what are you goin' on and on about? I told you everything I know."

"What about Coral? If you lied, maybe she's been lying too."

"She wouldn't do that."

"What'd she say when you got there?"

The look on Billy's face altered slightly and I thought I'd hit on something. I just didn't know what. My mind leapt ahead. "Did Coral *follow* them?" I asked.

"Of course not."

"What'd she say then?"

"Coral wasn't feeling so hot," he replied, uneasily.

"So she'd what, gone home?"

"Not really. She was coming down with this cold and she'd taken a cold cap. She was feeling zonked so she went back in the office and lay down on the couch. The bartender thought she'd left. I get there and I'm pissed because I can't find her, I can't find Daggett. I don't know what's goin' on. I hang around for a while and then I come back here, thinking she's home. Only she's not. It was a fuck-up, that's all. She was at the Hub the whole time."

"What time did she get home?"

"I don't know. Late. Three o'clock. She had to wait till the owner closed out the register and then he only gave her a lift partway so she had to walk six blocks in the rain. She's been sick as a dog ever since."

I stared at him, blinking, while the wheels went round and round. I was picturing her at the wharf with Daggett and the fit was nice.

"Why look at me like that?" he said.

"Let me say this. I'm just thinking out loud," I said. "It could have been Coral, couldn't it? The blonde who left the Hub with him? That's what's been worrying you all this time."

"No, uh-uh. No way," he said. His eyes had settled on me with fascination. He didn't like the line I was taking, but he'd probably thought about it himself.

"You only have her word for the fact that this other woman even exists," I said.

"The cabbie saw her."

"But it could have been Coral. She might have been the one buying Daggett all those drinks. He knew who she was and he trusted her too, because of you. She could have called the cab and then left with him. Maybe the reason the bartender thought she was gone was because he saw her leave."

"Get the hell out of here," Billy whispered.

His face had darkened and I saw his muscles tense. I'd been so caught up in my own speculation I hadn't been paying attention to the effect on him. I picked up the skirt and shoes, keeping an eye on him while I edged toward the door. He leaned over and opened it for me abruptly.

I had barely cleared the steps when the door slammed behind me hard. He shoved the curtain aside, staring at me belligerently as I backed out of the carport. The minute the curtain dropped, I cut around to the trailer window where I'd spied on him before. The louvers were closed, but the curtain on that side gaped open enough to allow me a truncated view.

Billy had sunk down on the couch with his head in his hands. He looked up. The woman who'd been in the back bedroom had now emerged and she leaned against the wall while she lit another cigarette. I could see a portion of her heavy thighs and the hem of a shortie nightgown in pale yellow nylon. Like a drowning man, Billy reached for her and pulled her close, burying his face between her breasts. Lovella. He began to nuzzle at her nipples through the nylon top, making wet spots. She stared down at him with that look new mothers have when they suckle an infant in public. Lazily, she leaned over and stubbed out her cigarette on a dinner plate, then wound her fingers into his hair. He grabbed her at the knees and lowered her to the floor, pushing her gown up around her waist. Down, down, down, he went.

I headed over to the Hub.

20

It looked like another slow night at the Hub. The rain had picked up again and business was off. The roof was leaking in two places and someone had put out galvanized pails to catch the drips . . . one on the bar, one by the ladies' room. The place, at its best, was populated by neighborhood drinkers—old women with fat ankles in heavy sweaters who started at 2:00 in the afternoon and consumed beer steadily until closing time, men with nasal voices and grating laughs whose noses were bulbous and sunburned from alcohol. The pool players were usually young Mexicans who smoked until their teeth turned yellow and squabbled among themselves like pups. That night the pool room was deserted and the green felt table tops seemed to glow as though lighted from within. I counted four customers in all and one was asleep with his head on his arms. The jukebox was suffering from some mechanical quirk that gave the music a warbling, underwater quality.

I approached the bar, where Coral was perched on a high-backed stool with a Naugahyde top. She was wearing a Western-cut shirt with a silver thread running through the brown plaid, tight jeans rolled up at the ankles, and heels with short white socks. She must have recognized me from the funeral because when I asked if I could talk to her, she hopped down without a word and went around to the other side of the bar.

"You want something to drink?"

"A wine spritzer. Thanks," I said.

She poured a spritzer for me and pulled a draft beer for

herself. We took a booth at the back so she could keep her eye on the clientele in case someone needed service. Up close, her hair looked so bushy and dry I worried about spontaneous combustion. Her makeup was too harsh for her fair coloring and her front teeth were decayed around the edges, as if she'd been eating Oreo cookies. Her cold must have been at its worst. Her forehead was lined and her eyes half squinted, like a magazine ad for sinus medication. Her nose was so stopped up she was forced to breathe through her mouth. In spite of all that, she managed to smoke, lighting up a Virginia Slim the minute we sat down.

"You should be home in bed," I said, and then wondered why I'd suggested such a thing. Billy and Lovella were currently back there groveling around on the floor, probably causing the trailer to thump on its foundations. Who could sleep with that stuff going on?

Coral put her cigarette down and took out a Kleenex to blow her nose. I've always wondered where people learn their nose-blowing techniques. She favored the double-digit method, placing a tissue over her hands, sticking the knuckles on both index fingers up her nostrils, rotating them vigorously after each honk. I kept my eyes averted until she was done, wondering idly if she was aware of Lovella's current whereabouts.

"What's the story on Lovella? She seemed distraught at the funeral."

Coral paused in her endeavors and looked at me. Belatedly, I realized she probably didn't know what the word distraught meant. I could see her put the definition together.

"She's fine. She had no idea they weren't legally married to each other. That's why she fell apart. Freaked her out." She gave her nose a final Roto-rooting and took up her cigarette again with a sniff.

"You'd think she'd be relieved," I said. "From what I hear, he beat the shit out of her."

"Not at first. She was crazy about him when he first got out. Still is, actually."

"That's probably why she called him the world's biggest asshole at the funeral," I remarked.

Coral looked at me for a moment and then shrugged noncommittally. She was smarter than Billy, but not by much. I had the same feeling here that I'd had with him. I was tapping into a matter they'd hoped to bury, but I didn't know enough to pursue the point.

I tried fishing. "I thought Lovella and Billy had a thing at one time."

"Years ago. When she was seventeen. Doesn't count for shit."

"She told me Billy set her up with Daggett."

"Yeah, more or less. He talked to Daggett about her and Daggett wrote and asked if they could be pen pals."

"Too bad he never mentioned his wife," I said. "I do want to talk to Lovella, so when you see her please tell her to get in touch." I gave her a business card with my office number on it, which she acknowledged with a shrug.

"I won't see Lovella," she said.

"That's what you think," said I.

Coral's attention strayed to the bartender who was holding a finger aloft. "Hang on."

She crossed to the bar where she picked up a couple of mixed drinks and delivered them to the one other table that was occupied. I tried to picture her flipping Daggett backwards out of a rowboat, but I couldn't quite make it stick. She fit the description, but there was something missing.

When she got back to the booth, I held up the high heels. "These yours?"

"I don't wear suede," she said flatly.

I loved it. Like suede was against her personal dress code. "What about the skirt?"

She took a final drag of the cigarette and crushed it in the metal ashtray, blowing out a mouthful of smoke. "Nope. Whose is it?"

"I think the blonde who killed Daggett wore it Friday night. Billy says she picked him up in here."

Belatedly, she focused on the skirt. "Yeah, that's right. I saw her," she said, as if cued.

"Does this look like the skirt she wore?"

"It could be."

"You know who she is?"

"Uh-uh."

"I don't mean to be rude about this, Coral, but I could use a little help. We're talking murder."

"I've been all tore up about it too," she said, bored.

"Don't you give a shit about any of this?"

"Are you kidding? Why should I care about Daggett? He was scum."

"What about the blonde? Do you remember anything about her?"

Coral shook another cigarette out of the pack. "Why don't you give it a rest, kid. You don't have the right to ask us any of this shit. You're not a cop."

"I can ask anything I want," I said, mildly. "I can't force you to answer, but I can always ask."

She stirred with agitation, shifting in her seat. "Know what? I don't like you," she said. "People like you make me sick."

"Oh really. People like what?"

She took her time extracting a paper match from a packet, scratching the tip across the striking area until it flared. She lit her cigarette. The match made a tiny tinking sound when she dropped it in the ashtray. She rested her chin on her palm and smiled at me unpleasantly. I wanted her to get her teeth fixed so she'd be prettier. "I bet you've had it real easy, haven't you?" she said, her voice heavy with sarcasm.

"Extremely."

"Nice white-collar middle-class home. The whole mommy-hubby trip. Bet you had little brothers and sisters. Nice little fluffy white dog . . ."

"This is amazing," I said.

"Two cars. Maybe a cleaning woman once a week. I never went to college. I never had a daddy giving me all the advantages."

"Well, that explains it then," I said. "I did meet your mom, you know. She looks like someone who's worked hard all her life. Too bad you don't appreciate the effort she made in your behalf."

"What effort? She works in a supermarket checkout line," Coral said.

"Oh, I see. You think she should do something classy like you."

"I'm sure not going to do *this* for life, if that's what you think."

"What happened to your father? Where was he in all this?"

"Who knows? He bugged out a long time ago."

"Leaving her with kids to raise by herself?"

"Skip it. I don't even know why I brought it up. Maybe you should get to the point and let me get back to work."

"Tell me about Doug."

"None of your business." She slid out of the booth. "Time's up," she said, and walked away. God, and here I was being friendly.

I picked up the shoes and skirt and dropped a couple of bucks on the table. I moved to the entranceway, pausing in the shelter of the doorway before I stepped out into the rain. It was 10:17 and there was no traffic on Milagro. The street was shiny black and the rain, as it struck the pavement, made a noise like bacon sizzling in a pan. A mist drifted up from the manhole covers that dotted the block, and the gutters gushed in a widening stream where water boiled back out of the storm drains.

I was restless, not ready to pack it in for the night. I thought about stopping by Rosie's, but it would probably look just like the Hub—smoky, drab, depressing. At least the air outside, though chilly, had the sweet, flowery scent of wet concrete. I started the car and did a U-turn, heading toward the beach, my windshield stippled with rain.

At Cabana, I turned right, driving along the boulevard. On my left, even without a moon visible, the surf churned with a dull gray glow, folding back on itself with a thundering monotony. Out in the ocean, I could see the lights on the oil derricks winking through the mist. I'd pulled up at a stoplight when I heard a car horn toot behind me. I checked my rear-view mirror. A little red Honda was pulling over into the lane to my right. It was Jonah, apparently heading home just as I was. He made a cranking motion. I leaned over and rolled the window down on the passenger side.

"Can I buy you a drink?"

"Sure. Where?"

He pointed at the Crow's Nest to his right, a restaurant with exterior lights still burning. The light changed and he took off. I followed, pulling into the lot behind him. We parked side by side. He got out first, hunching against the rain while he opened an umbrella and came around to my door. We huddled together and puddle hopped our way to the front entrance. He held the door and I ducked inside, holding it for him then while he lowered the umbrella and gave it a quick shake.

The interior of the Crow's Nest was done in a halfhearted nautical theme which consisted primarily of fishing nets and rigging draped along the rafters and mariner's charts sealed into the table tops under a half-inch of polyurethane. The restaurant section was closed, but the bar seemed to be doing all right. I could see maybe ten tables occupied. The level of conversation was low and the lighting was discreet, augmented by fat round jars where candles glowed through orange glass.

Jonah steered us past a small dance floor toward a table in the corner. The place had an aura of edgy excitement. We were protected by the weather, drawn together like the random souls stranded in an airport between flights.

The waitress appeared and Jonah glanced at me.

"You decide," I said.

"Two margaritas. Cuervo Gold, Grand Marnier, shaken, no salt," he said. She nodded and moved off.

"Very impressive," I said.

"I thought you'd like that. What brings you out?"

"Daggett, of course." I filled him in, realizing as I summed it up that I'd had just about as much of Billy Polo and his ilk as I could take for one night.

"Let's don't talk about him," I said when I was done. "Tell me what you're working on."

"Hey, no way. I'm here to relax."

The waitress brought our drinks and we paused briefly while she dipped neatly, knees together, and placed a cocktail napkin in front of each of us, along with our drinks. She was dressed like a boatswain except that her high-cut white pants were spandex and her buns hung out the back. I wondered how long uniforms like that would last if the night manager was required to squeeze his hairy fanny into one.

When the waitress left, Jonah touched his glass to mine. "To rainy nights," he said. We drank. The tequila had a little "wow" effect as it went down and I had to pat myself on the chest. Jonah smiled, enjoying my discomfiture.

"What brings you out so late?" I asked.

"Catching up on paperwork. Also, avoiding the house. Camilla's sister came down from Idaho for a week. The two of them are probably drinking wine and carving me up like a roast."

"Her sister doesn't like you, I take it."

"She thinks I'm a dud. Camilla came from money. Deirdre doesn't think either one of them should take up with guys on salary, for God's sake. And a cop? It's all too bourgeois. God, I gotta watch myself here. All I do is complain about life on the home front. I'm beginning to sound like Dempsey."

I smiled. Lieutenant Dempsey had worked Narcotics for years, a miserably married man whose days were spent complaining about his lot. His wife had finally died and he'd turned around and married a woman just like her. He'd taken early retirement and the two of them had gone off in an RV. His postcards to the department were amusing, but left people uncomfortable, like a stand-up comic making mean-spirited jokes at a spouse's expense.

Conversation dwindled. The background music was a tape of old Johnny Mathis tunes and the lyrics suggested an era when falling in love wasn't complicated by herpes, fear of AIDS, multiple marriages, spousal support, feminism, the sexual revolution, the Bomb, the Pill, approval of one's therapist, or the specter of children on alternate weekends.

Jonah was looking good. The combination of shadow and candlelight washed the lines out of his face, and heightened the blue of his eyes. His hair looked very dark and the rain had made it look silkier. He wore a white shirt, opened at the neck, sleeves rolled up, his forearms crosshatched with dark hair. There's usually a current running between us, generated I suppose by whatever primal urges keep the human race reproducing itself. Most of the time, the chemistry is kept in check by a bone-deep caution on my part, ambivalence about his marital status, by circumstance, by his own uneasiness, by the knowledge on both our parts that once certain lines are crossed, there's no going back and no way to predict the consequences.

We ordered a second round of drinks, and then a third. We slow danced, not saying a word. Jonah smelled of soap and his jaw line was smooth and sometimes he hummed with a rumbling I hadn't heard since I sat on my father's lap as a very young child, listening to him read to me before I knew

what words meant. I thought about Billy Polo lowering Lovella
to the trailer floor. The image was haunting because it spoke
so eloquently of his need. I was always such a stoic, so careful
not to make mistakes. Sometimes I wonder what the difference is between being cautious and being dead. I thought
about rain and how nice it is to sink down on clean sheets. I
pulled my head back and Jonah looked down at me quizzically.

"This is all Billy Polo's fault," I said.

He smiled. "What is?"

I studied him for a moment. "What would Camilla do if
you didn't come home tonight?"

His smile faded and his eyes got that look. "She's the one
who's talking about an open relationship," he said.

I laughed. "I'll bet that applies to her, not you."

"Not anymore," he said.

His kiss seemed familiar.

We left soon afterward.

21

I drove to the office at 9:00. The rain clouds were hunched above the mountains moving north, while above, the sky was the blue white of bleached denim. The city seemed to be in sharp focus, as if seen through new prescription lenses. I opened the French doors and stood on the balcony, raising my arms and doing one of those little butt wiggles so favored by the football set. *That* for you, Camilla Robb, I thought, and then I laughed and went and had a look at myself in the mirror, mugging shamelessly. Amazing Grace. I looked just like myself. Where tears erase the self, good sex transforms and I was feeling energized.

I put the coffee on and got to work, typing up my case notes, detailing the conversations I'd had with Billy and Coral. Cops and private eyes are always caught up in paperwork. Written records have to be kept of everything, with events set out so that anyone who comes along afterward will have a clear and comprehensive résumé of the investigation to that point. Since a private eye also bills for services, I have to keep track of my hours and expenses, submitting statements periodically so I can make sure I get paid. I prefer fieldwork I suspect we all do. If I'd wanted to spend my days in an office, I'd have studied to be an underwriter for the insurance company next door. Their work seems boring 80 percent of the time while mine only bores me about one hour out of every ten.

At 9:30, I touched base with Barbara Daggett by phone, giving her a verbal update to match the written account I was putting in the mail to her. The duplication of effort wasn't really necessary, but I did it anyway. What the hell, it was her money. She was entitled to the best service she could get. After that, I did some filing, then locked up again, taking the green skirt and heels with me down the back stairs to my car, heading out to Marilyn Smith's. I was beginning to feel like the prince in search of Cinderella, shoe in hand.

I took the highway north, drinking in the newly washed air. Colgate is only a fifteen-minute drive, but it gave me a chance to think about events of the night before. Jonah had turned out to be a clown in bed . . . funny and inventive. We'd behaved like bad kids, eating snacks, telling ghost stories, returning now and then to a lovemaking which was, at the same time, intense and comfortable. I wondered if I'd known him in another life. I wondered if I'd know him again. He was so generous and affectionate, so amazed at being with someone who didn't criticize or withhold, who didn't withdraw from his touch as though from a slug's. I couldn't imagine where we'd go from here and I didn't want to start worrying. I'm capable of screwing things up by trying to solve all the problems in advance instead of simply taking care of issues as they surface.

I missed my off-ramp, of course. I caught sight of it as I sped by, cursing good-naturedly as I took the next exit and circled back.

By the time I reached Wayne and Marilyn Smith's house, it was nearly 10:00. The bicycles that had been parked on the porch were gone. The orange trees, though nearly leafless with age, still carried the aura of ripe fruit, a faint perfume spilling out of the surrounding groves. I parked my car in the gravel drive behind a compact station wagon I assumed belonged to her. A peek into the rear, as I passed, revealed a gummy detritus of fast-food containers, softball equipment, school papers, and dog hair.

I cranked the bell. The entrance hall was deserted, but a

golden retriever bounded toward the front door, toenails ticking against the bare floors as it skittered to a stop, barking
joyfully. The dog's entire body waggled like a fish on a hook.

"Can I help you?"

Startled, I glanced to my right. Marilyn Smith was standing
at the bottom of the porch steps in a tee shirt, drenched jeans,
and a straw hat. She wore goatskin gardening gloves and
bright yellow plastic clogs that were spattered with mud. When
she realized it was me, her expression changed from pleasant
inquiry to a barely disguised distaste.

"I'm working in the garden," she said, as if I hadn't guessed.
"If you want to talk you'll have to come out there."

I followed her across the rain-saturated lawn. She tapped
a muddy trowel against her thigh, distractedly.

"I saw you at the funeral," I remarked.

"Wayne insisted," she said tersely, then looked over her
shoulder at me. "Who was the drunk woman? I liked her."

"Lovella Daggett. She thought she was married to him, but
it turned out the warranty hadn't run out on his first wife."

When we reached the vegetable patch, she waded between
two dripping rows of vines. The garden was in its winter
phase—broccoli, cauliflower, dark squashes tucked into a spray
of wide leaves. She'd been weeding. I could see the trampled-
looking spikes scattered here and there. Farther down the
row, there was evidence that the earth had been turned, heavy
clods piled up near a shallow excavation site.

"Too wet for weeding, isn't it?"

"The soil here has a high clay content. Once it dries out,
it's impossible," she said.

She shucked the gardening gloves and began to tear widths
from an old pillow case, tying back the masses of sweet pea
plants that had drooped in the rain. The strips of white rag
contrasted brightly with the lime green of the plants. I held
up the skirt and shoes I'd brought.

"Recognize these?"

She scarcely looked at the articles, but the chilly smile appeared. "Is that what the killer wore?"

"Could be."

"You've made progress since I saw you last. Three days ago, you weren't even certain it was murder."

"That's how I earn my pay," I said.

"Maybe Lovella killed him when she found out he was a bigamist."

"Always possible," I said, "though you still haven't said for sure where you were that night."

"Oh, but I did. I was here. Wayne was at the office and neither of us has corroborating witnesses." She was using that bantering tone again, mild and mocking.

"I'd like to talk to him."

"Make an appointment. He's in the book. Go down to the office. The Granger Building on State."

"Marilyn, I'm not your enemy."

"You are if I killed him," she replied.

"Ah, yes. In that case, I would be."

She tore off another strip of pillow case, the width of cotton dangling from her hand like something limp with death. "Sounds like you have suspects. Too bad you're short on proof."

"But I do have someone who saw her and that should help, don't you think? This is just preliminary work, narrowing the field," I said. It was bullshit, of course. I wasn't sure the motel clerk could identify anybody in the dark.

Her smile dimmed by a watt. "I don't want to talk to you anymore," she whispered.

I raised my hands, as if she'd pulled a gun. "I'm gone," I said, "but I have to warn you, I'm persistent. You'll find it unsettling, I suspect."

I kept my eyes on her as I moved away. I'd seen the muddy hoe she was using and I thought it best not to turn my back.

I cruised by the Westfalls on my way into town. I was going to have to show the skirt to Barbara Daggett at some point,

but the Close was on my way. The low fieldstone wall surrounding the place was still a dark gray from the passing rain.
I drove through the gates and parked along the road as I had
before, pulling over into dense ivy. By day, the eight Victorian
houses were enveloped in shade, sunlight scarcely penetrating
the branches of the trees. I locked the car and picked my way
up the path to the front steps. In the yard, the trunks of the
live oak were frosted with a fungus as green as the oxidized
copper on a roof. Tall palms punctuated the corners of the
house. The air felt cool and moist in the wake of the storm.

The front door was ajar. The view from the hallway was a
straight shot through to the kitchen and I could see that the
back door was open too, the screen door unlatched. A portable
radio sat on the counter and music blasted out, the *1812
Overture*. I rang the bell, but the sound was lost against the
booming of cannons as the last movement rose to a thunder
pitch.

I left the front porch and walked around to the back, peering in. Like the rest of the house, the kitchen had been redone,
the owners opting here to modernize, though the Victorian
character had been retained. There was a small floral print
paper on the walls, lots of wicker, oak, and fern. The cabinet
doors had been replaced with leaded glass, but the appliances
were all strictly up-to-date.

There was no one in the room. A door on the left was open,
the oblong of shadow suggesting that the basement stairs must
be located just beyond. Two brown grocery bags sat on the
kitchen table and it looked like someone had been interrupted
in the course of unloading them. There was an electric per-
colator plugged into the outlet on the stove. While I was watching, the ready-light went on. Belatedly, I picked up the smell
of hot coffee.

The music ended and the FM announcer made his con-
cluding remarks about the piece, then introduced a Brahms
concerto in E minor. I knocked on the frame of the screen

door, hoping someone would hear me before the music started up again. Ramona appeared from the depths of the basement. She was wearing a six-gore wool skirt in a muted gray plaid, with a line of dark maroon running through it. Her pullover sweater was dark maroon, with a white blouse under it, the collar pinned sedately at the throat by an antique brooch. For effect, I decided not to mention the heels and wool skirt I'd brought.

"Tony?" she said. "Oh, it's you."

She had an armload of ragged blue bath towels which she dumped on a chair. "I thought I heard someone knock. I couldn't see who it was through the screen." She turned the radio off as she passed and then she opened the screen door to admit me.

"Tony's bringing groceries in from the garage. We just got back from the market. Have a seat. Would you like a cup of coffee? The pot's fresh."

"Yes, please. That's nice." I moved the pile of rags out of the chair and sat down, putting the skirt and shoes on the table in front of me. I saw her eyes stray to them, but she made no comment.

"Isn't this a school day for him?" I asked.

"They're giving the sophomores some sort of academic placement tests. He finished early so they let him go. He's got an appointment with his therapist shortly anyway."

I watched her move about the kitchen, fetching cups and saucers. She had one of those hairstyles that settle into perfect shape with a flick of the head. I butcher my own at six-week intervals with a pair of nail scissors and a two-way mirror, causing salon stylists to pale when they see me. "Who *did* that to you?" they always ask. I wanted perfect waves like hers, but I didn't think I could achieve the effect.

Ramona poured two cups of coffee. "There's something I probably should have mentioned before," she said. She took a ceramic pitcher from the cupboard and filled it with milk, realizing then that I was waiting for her to continue. Her smile was thin. "John Daggett called here Monday night, asking to talk to Tony. I took his number, but Ferrin and I decided it wasn't a good idea. It might not matter much at this point, but I thought you should be aware."

"What made you think of it?"

She hesitated. "I came across the number on the pad by the phone. I'd forgotten all about it."

I could feel a tingle at the back of my neck—that clammy feeling you get when your body overloads on sugar. Something was off here, but I wasn't sure what it was.

"Why bring it up now?" I asked.

"I thought you were tracking his activities early in the week."

"I wasn't aware that I'd told you that."

Her cheeks tinted. "Marilyn Smith called me. She mentioned it."

"How'd Daggett know where to reach you? When I talked to him on Saturday, he had no idea where Tony was and he certainly didn't have your name or number."

"I don't know how he got it," she said. "What difference does it make?"

"How do I know you didn't make a date to meet him Friday night?"

"Why would I do that?" she said.

I stared at her. A millisecond later she realized what I was getting at.

"But I was here Friday night."

"I haven't heard that verified so far."

"That's ridiculous! Ask Tony. He knows I was here. You can check it out yourself."

"I intend to," I said.

Tony thumped up the wooden porch steps, armed with two more grocery bags, his attention diverted as he groped for the screen door handle, missing twice. "Aunt Ramona, can you give me a hand with this?"

She crossed to the door and held it open. Tony spotted me and the green skirt at just about the same time and I saw his gaze jump to his aunt's face quizzically. Her expression was neutral, but she busied herself right away, pushing canned goods aside so he could set one bag on the table top. The second bag she took herself and placed on the counter. She sorted through and lifted out a carton of ice cream. "I better get this put away," she murmured. She crossed to the freezer.

"What are you doing here?" Tony said to me.

"I was curious how you were feeling. Your aunt mentioned that you had a migraine Monday night."

"I feel okay."

"What'd you think about the funeral?"

"Bunch of freaks," he said.

"Let's get these unloaded, dear," his aunt said. The two of them began to put groceries away while I sipped my coffee. I couldn't tell if she was deliberately distracting him or not, but that was the effect.

"You need some help?" I asked.

"We can manage," she murmured.

"Who was that lady who went nuts?" Tony asked. Lovella had made a big impression on everyone.

Ramona held up a soft drink in a big plastic bottle. "Stick this in the refrigerator while you're there," she said.

She released the bottle an instant before he'd gotten a good grip on it and he had to scramble to catch it before it toppled to the floor. Had she done that deliberately? He was waiting for my reply so I gave him a brief rendition of the tale. It was gossip, in some ways, but he was as animated as I'd seen him and I hoped to keep his attention.

"I don't mean to interrupt, but Tony does have homework to take care of. Finish your coffee, of course," she said. Her tone suggested that I suck it right down and scram.

"I'm due back at the office anyway," I said, getting up. I looked at Tony. "Could you walk me to my car?"

He glanced at Ramona, whose gaze dropped away from his. She didn't protest. He ducked his head in assent.

He held the door for me while I gathered the skirt and shoes and turned back to her. "I nearly forgot. Are these yours, by any chance?"

"I'm sure not," she said to me, and then to him, "Don't be long."

He looked like he was on the verge of saying something, but he shrugged instead. He followed me out on the porch and down the steps. I led the way as we circled the house. The path to the street was paved with stepping-stones spaced oddly, so that I had to watch my feet to gauge the distances.

"I have a question," I said as we reached the car.

He was watching me warily by then, interested but on guard.

"I was curious about the migraine you had Friday night. Do you remember how long that one lasted?"

"Friday night?" His voice had a croak in it from surprise.

"That's right. Didn't you have a migraine that night?"

"I guess."

"Think back," I said. "Take your time."

He seemed uncomfortable, casting about for some visual clue. I'd seen him do this before, reading body language so he could adjust his response to whatever was expected of him. I waited in silence, letting his anxiety accumulate.

"I think that's the day I got one. When I came home from school," he said, "but then it cleared."

"What time was that?"

"Real late. After midnight. Maybe two . . . two-thirty, something like that."

"How'd you happen to notice the time?"

"Aunt Ramona made me a couple of sandwiches in the kitchen. It was a real bad headache and I'd been throwing up for hours so I never had dinner. I was starving. I must have looked at the kitchen clock."

"What kind of sandwiches?"

"What?"

"I was wondering what kind she made."

His gaze hung on mine. The seconds ticked away. "Meat-loaf," he said.

"Thanks," I said. "That helps."

I opened the VW on the driver's side, tossing skirt and shoes on the passenger seat as I got in. His version was roughly the same as his aunt's, but I could have sworn the "meatloaf" was a wild guess.

I started the car and did a U-turn, heading toward the gates. I caught a glimpse of him in the rearview mirror, already moving toward the house.

22

It's a fact of life that when a case won't break, you have to go through the motions anyway, stirring up the waters, rattling all the cages at the zoo. To that end, on my way into town I did a long detour that included a stop at the trailer park, in hopes that Lovella would still be there. It was obvious to me, as I'm not a fool, that toting a green wool skirt and a pair of black suede heels all over town was a pointless enterprise. No one was going to claim them and if someone did, so what? The articles proved nothing. No one was going to break down sobbing and confess at the mere sight of them. The pop quiz was simply my way of putting them all on notice, making the rounds one more time to announce that I was still on the job and making progress, however insignificant it might appear.

I knocked at the trailer door, but got no response. I jotted a note on the back of a business card, indicating that Lovella should call. I tucked it in the doorjamb, went back to my car, and headed for town.

Wayne Smith's office was located on the seventh floor of the Granger Building in downtown Santa Teresa. Aside from the clock tower on the courthouse, the Granger is just about the only structure on State Street that's more than two stories high. Part of the charm of the downtown area is its low-slung look. The flavor, for the most part, is Spanish. Even the trash containers are faced with stucco and rimmed with decorative tile. The telephone booths look like small adobe huts and if you can ignore the fact that the bums use them for urinals, the effect is quaint. There are flowering shrubs along the walk, jacaranda trees, and palms. Low ornamental stucco walls widen in places to form benches for weary shoppers. Everything is clean, well kept, pleasing to the eye.

The Granger Building looks just like hundreds of office buildings constructed in the twenties—yellow brick, symmetrical narrow windows banded with granite friezes, topped by a steeply pitched roof with matching gables. Along the roofline, just below the cornice, there are decorative marble torches affixed to the wall with inexplicable half shells mounted underneath. The style is an anomaly in this town, falling as it does between the Spanish, the Victorian, and the pointless. Still, the building is a landmark, housing a movie theater, a jeweler's, and seven stories of office space.

I checked the wall directory in the marble foyer for Wayne Smith's suite number, which turned out to be 702. Two elevators serviced the building and one was out of order, the doors standing open, the housing mechanism in plain view. It's not a good idea to scrutinize such things. When you see how elevators actually work, you realize how improbable the whole scheme is . . . raising and lowering a roomful of people on a few long wires. Ridiculous.

A fellow in coveralls stood there, mopping his face with a red bandanna.

"How's it going?" I asked, while I waited for the other elevator doors to open.

He shook his head. "Always something, isn't it? Last week it was that one wouldn't work."

The doors slid open and I stepped in, pressing seven. The doors closed and nothing happened for a while. Finally, with a jolt, the elevator began its ascent, stopping at the seventh floor. There was another interminable delay. I pressed the "DOOR OPEN" button. No dice. I tried to guess how long I could survive on just that one ratty piece of chewing gum at the bottom of my handbag. I banged the button with the flat of my hand and the doors slid open.

The corridor was narrow and dimly illuminated, as there was only one exterior window, located at the far end of the hall. Four dark, wood-paneled doors opened off each side, with the names of the professional tenants in gold-leaf lettering that looked as if it had been there since the building went up. There was no activity that I could perceive, no sounds, no muffled telephones ringing. Wayne Smith, C.P.A., was the first door on the right. I pictured a receptionist in a small waiting area, so I simply turned the knob and walked in without knocking. There was only one large room, tawny daylight filtering in through drawn window shades. Wayne Smith was lying on the floor with his legs propped up on the seat of his swivel chair. He turned and looked at me.

"Oh sorry! I thought there'd be a waiting room," I said. "Are you okay?"

"Sure. Come on in," he said. "I was resting my back." He removed his legs from the chair, apparently in some pain. He rolled over on his side and eased himself into an upright position, wincing as he did. "You're Kinsey Millhone. Marilyn pointed you out at the funeral yesterday."

I watched him, wondering if I should lend him a hand. "What'd you do to yourself?"

"My back went out on me. Hurts like a son of a bitch," he said. Once he was on his feet, he dug a fist into the small of his back, twisting one shoulder slightly as if to ease a cramp. He had a runner's body—lean, stringy muscles, narrow through the chest. He looked older than his wife, maybe late forties while I pegged her in her early thirties. His hair was light, worn in a crewcut, like something out of a 1950s high school annual. I wondered if he'd been in the military at some point. The hairstyle suggested that he was hung up in the past, his persona fixed perhaps by some significant event. His eyes were pale and his face was very lined. He moved to the windows and raised all three shades. The room became unbearably bright.

"Have a seat," he said.

I had a choice between a daybed and a molded plastic chair with a bucket seat. I took the chair, doing a surreptitious visual survey while he lowered himself into his swivel chair as though into a steaming sitz bath. He had six metal bookcases that looked like they were made of Erector sets, loosely bolted and sagging slightly from the weight of all the manuals. Brown accordion file cases were stacked up everywhere, his desk top virtually invisible. Correspondence was piled on the floor near his chair, government pamphlets and tax law updates stacked on the window sill. This was not a man you'd want to depend on if you were facing an I.R.S. audit. He looked like the sort who might put you there.

"I just talked to Marilyn. She said you came by the house. We're puzzled by your interest in us."

"Barbara Daggett hired me to investigate her father's death. I'm interested in everyone."

"But why talk to us? We haven't seen the man in years."

"He didn't get in touch last week?"

"Why would he do that?"

"He was looking for Tony Gahan. I thought he might have tried to get a line on him through you."

The phone rang and he reached for it, conducting a business-related conversation while I studied him. He wore chinos, just a wee bit too short, and his socks were the clinging nylon sort that probably went up to his knees. He switched to his good-bye tone, trying to close out his conversation. "Uh-huh, uh-huh. Okay, great. That's fine. We'll do that. I got the forms right here. Deadline is the end of the month. Swell."

He hung up with an exasperated shake of his head.

"Anyway," he said, as a way of getting back to the subject at hand.

"Yeah, right. Anyway," I said, "I don't suppose you remember where you were Friday night."

"I was here, doing quarterly reports."

"And Marilyn was home with the kids?"

He sat and stared at me, a smile flickering off and on. "Are you implying that we might have had a hand in John Daggett's death?"

"Someone did," I said.

He laughed, running a hand across his crewcut as if checking to see if he needed a trim. "Miss Millhone, you've got a hell of a nerve," he said. "The newscast said it was an accident."

I smiled. "The cops still think so. I disagree. I think a lot of people wanted Daggett dead. You and Marilyn are among them."

"But we wouldn't do a thing like that. You can't be serious. I despised the man, no doubt about that, but we're not going to go out and track a man down and kill him. Good God."

I kept my tone light. "But you did have the motive and you had the opportunity."

"You can't hang anything on that. We're decent people. We don't even get parking tickets. John Daggett must have had a lot of enemies."

I shrugged by way of agreement. "The Westfalls," I said. "Billy Polo and his sister, Coral. Apparently, some prison thugs."

"What about that woman who set up such a howl at the funeral?" he said. "She looked like a pretty good candidate to me."

"I've talked to her."

"Well, you better go back and talk to her again. You're wasting time with us. Nobody's going to be arrested on the basis of 'motive' and 'opportunity.' "

"Then you don't have anything to worry about."

He shook his head, his skepticism evident. "Well. I can see you have your work cut out for you. I'd appreciate it if you'd lay off Marilyn in this. She's had trouble enough."

"I gathered as much." I got up. "Thanks for your time. I hope I won't have to bother you again." I moved toward the door.

"I hope so too."

"You know, if you did kill him, or if you know who killed him, I'll find out. Another few days and I'm going to the cops anyway. They'll scrutinize that alibi of yours like you wouldn't believe."

He held his hands out, palms up. "We're innocent until proven otherwise," he said, smiling boyishly.

23

Waiting for the elevator, I replayed the conversation, trying to figure out what I'd missed. On the surface, there was nothing wrong with his response, but I felt irritated and uneasy, maybe just because I wasn't getting anyplace. I banged on the DOWN button. "Come on," I said. The elevator door opened partway. Impatiently, I shoved it back and got on. The doors closed and the elevator descended one floor before it stopped again. The doors opened. Tony Gahan was standing in the corridor, a shopping bag in hand. He seemed as surprised to see me as I was to see him.

"What are you doing here?" he said. He got on the elevator and we descended.

"I had to see someone upstairs," I said. "What about you?"

"A shrink appointment. He's been out of town and now his return flight was delayed. His secretary's supposed to pick him up in an hour so she said to come back at five."

We reached the lobby.

"How are you getting home? Need a ride?" I asked.

He shook his head. "I'm going to hang around down here." He gestured vaguely at the video arcade across the street where some high school kids were horsing around.

"See you later then," I said.

We parted company and I returned to the parking lot behind the building. I got in my car and circled the four blocks to the lot behind my office where I parked. For the time being, I left the skirt and shoes in the backseat.

There were no messages on my answering machine, but

the mail was in and I sorted through that, wondering what else to do with myself. Actually, I realized I was exhausted, the emotional charge from Jonah having drained away. I'm not used to drinking that much, for starters, and I tend, being single, to get a lot more sleep. He'd left at 5:00, before it was light, and I'd managed maybe an hour's worth of shut-eye before I'd finally gotten up, jogged, showered, and fixed myself a bite to eat.

I tilted back in my swivel chair and propped my feet up on the desk, hoping no one would begrudge me a snooze. The next time I was aware of anything, the clock hands had dissolved magically from 12:10 to 2:50 and my head was pounding. I staggered to my feet and trotted down the hall to the ladies' room. I peed, washed my hands and face, rinsed my mouth out, and stared at myself in the mirror. My hair was mashed flat in the back and standing straight up everywhere else. The fluorescent light in the room made my skin look sickly. Was this the consequence of illicit sex with a married man? "Well, I soitonly hope so," I said. I ducked my head under the faucet and then dried my hair with eight rounds of hot air from a wall-mounted machine that had been installed (the sign said) to help protect me from the dangers of diseases that might be transmitted through paper towel litter. Idly, I wondered what diseases they were worried about. Typhus? Diphtheria?

I could hear my office phone from halfway down the hall and I started to run. I snagged it on the sixth ring, snatching up the receiver with a winded hello.

"This is Lovella," the glum voice said. "I got this note to call you."

I took a deep breath, inventing as I went along. "Right," I said. "I thought we should touch base. We really haven't talked since I saw you in L.A." I sidled around my desk and sat down, still trying to catch my breath.

"I'm mad at you, Kinsey," she said. "Why didn't you tell me you had Daggett's money?"

"To what end? I had a cashier's check, but it wasn't made out to you. So why mention it?"

"Because I'm standing around telling you I'm married to a guy who'd just as soon kill me as look at me and you're telling me to call the rape crisis center, some bullshit like that. And all the time, Daggett had thousands of dollars."

"But he stole the money. Didn't Billy tell you that?"

"I don't care where it came from. I'd just like to have a little something for myself. Now he's dead and she gets everything."

"Who, Essie?"

"Her and that daughter."

"Oh come on, Lovella. He couldn't have left them enough to worry about."

"More than he left me," she said. "If I'd known about the money, I might have talked him out of some."

"Yeah, right. As generous as he was," I said drily. "If you'd gotten your hands on it, you might be dead now instead of him. Unless Billy's been lying to me about the punks from San Luis who were after him." I'd never really taken that story seriously, but maybe it was time I did.

She was silent. I could practically hear her shifting gears. "All I know is I think you're a shit and he was too."

"I'm sorry you feel that way, Lovella. John hired me, and my first loyalty was to him . . . misguided, as it turned out, but that's where I was coming from. You want to vent a little more on the subject before we turn to something else?"

"Yeah. I should have got the money, not someone else. I was the one who got banged around. I still got two cracked ribs and an eye looks like it's all sunk in on one side from the bruise."

"Is that why you freaked out at the funeral?"

Her tone of voice became tempered with sheepishness. "I'm sorry I did that, but I couldn't help myself. I'd been sittin' in some bar drinkin' Bloody Marys since ten o'clock and I guess

I got outta hand. But it bugged me, all that Bible talk. Daggett never went to church a day in his life and it didn't seem right. And that old fat-ass claimed she was married to him? I couldn't believe my eyes. She looked like a bulldog."

I had to laugh. "Maybe he didn't marry her for her looks," I said.

"Well, I hope not."

"When did you see him last?"

"At the funeral home, where else?"

"Before that, I mean."

"Day he left L.A.," she said. "Week ago Monday. I never saw him after he took off."

"I thought maybe you hopped a bus on Thursday after I left."

"Well, I didn't."

"But you could have, couldn't you?"

"What for? I didn't even know where he went."

"But Billy did. You could have come up to Coral's last week. You might have met him at the Hub Friday night and bought him a couple of drinks."

Her laugh was sour. "You can't pin that on me. If that was me, how come Coral didn't recognize me, huh?"

"For all I know, she did. You're friends. Maybe she just kept her mouth shut."

"Why would she do that?"

"Maybe she wanted to help you out."

"Coral doesn't even like me. She thinks I'm a slut so why would she help me?"

"She might've had reasons of her own."

"I didn't kill him, Kinsey, if that's what you're getting at."

"That's what everyone says. You're all wide-eyed and innocent. Daggett was murdered and nobody's guilty. Amazing."

"You don't have to take my word for it. Ask Billy. Once he gets back, he can tell you who it was for sure, anyway."

"Oh hey, sounds great. How's he going to manage that?"

There was a pause, as if she'd said something she really wasn't authorized to say. "He thought he recognized somebody at the funeral and then he figured out where he'd seen 'em before," she said reluctantly.

I blinked at the telephone receiver. In a quick flash, I remembered Billy's staring at the little group formed by the Westfalls, Barbara Daggett, and the Smiths. "I don't understand. What's he up to?"

"He set up a meeting," she said. "He wants to find out if his theory's right and then he said he'd call you."

"He's going to *meet* with her?"

"That's what I said, isn't it?"

"He shouldn't be doing that by himself. Why didn't he notify the police?"

"Because he doesn't want to make a fool of himself in front of them. Suppose he's wrong? He doesn't have any proof, anyway. Just a hunch is all and even that's not a hundred percent."

"Do you have any idea who he was talking about?"

"Uh-uh. He wouldn't tell, but he was pretty happy with himself. He said we might get some money after all."

Oh God, I thought, not blackmail. I could feel my heart sink. Billy Polo wasn't smart enough to pull that off. He'd blow it like he did every other crime he tried. "Where's the meeting taking place?"

"What makes you ask?" she said, turning cagey.

"Because I want to go!"

"I don't think I should tell."

"Lovella, don't do this to me."

"Well, he didn't say I could."

"You've told me this much. Why not the rest? He could be in trouble."

She hesitated, mulling it over. "Down at the beach somewhere. He's not dumb, you know. He made sure it was public.

He figured in broad daylight, there wouldn't be any problem, especially with other people around."

"Which beach?"

"What if he gets mad at me?"

"I'll square it with him myself," I said. "I will *swear* I forced the information out of you."

"He's not going to like it if you show up and spoil everything."

"I won't spoil it. I'll lurk in the background and make sure he's okay. That's all I'm talking about."

Silence. She was so slow I thought I'd scream. "Look at it this way," I said. "He might be happy for the help. What if he needs backup?"

"Billy wouldn't need backup from a *woman*."

I closed my eyes, trying to keep my temper in check. "Just give me a hint, Lovella, or I'll come over to the trailer and rip your heart out by the roots." That, she heard.

"You better never tell him I told," she warned.

"Cross my heart and hope to die. Now come on."

"I think it's that parking lot near the boat launch. . . ."

I banged the phone down and snagged my handbag. I locked the office in haste and ran down the hall, going down the back stairs two and three at a time. I'd had to park my car at the far end of the lot and once I got to the pay booth, there were three other cars in front of mine. "Come on, come on," I murmured, banging on the steering wheel.

Finally, it was my turn. I showed the attendant my parking permit and shot through the gate as soon as the bar went up.

Chapel is one way, heading up from the beach, so I had to turn right, take a left, and hit the one-way street going down again. I caught the light wrong at 101 so that delayed me. I didn't want to miss this one. I didn't want to show up two minutes late and miss the only chance I might have. I pictured a citizen's arrest . . . me and Billy Polo saving the day.

The light turned green and I crossed the highway. Two

blocks more and I reached Cabana where I took a right turn. The entrance to the lot I wanted was all the way around the bend near Santa Teresa City College. I got a ticket from the machine and threaded my way along the perimeter of the lot. I scanned the parked cars, hoping for a glimpse of Billy's white Chevy. The marina was on my right, the sun reflecting starkly from the white sails of a stately boat as it glided out of the harbor. The boat launch itself was at the very end of the parking lot, through a second parking gate. I pulled a second ticket and the arm went up. I found a slot and left my car, proceeding on foot.

Four joggers passed me. There were people on the boat dock, people on the walk, people by the snack shop and the public restrooms. I broke into a trot, searching the landscape ahead of me for some sign of Billy or the blonde. I heard three hollow pops in quick succession dead ahead. I ran. No one else was reacting, but I could have sworn it was the sound of shots.

I reached the boat launch, where the parking lot slants down into the water. There was no one in sight. No one running, no one leaving the scene in haste. The air was still, the water lapping softly at the asphalt. Two pontoon piers extend into the water about thirty feet, but both were empty, no boats or pedestrians in sight. I did a three-sixty turn, surveying every foot of the area. And then I spotted him. He was lying on his side by a boat trailer, one arm caught under him awkwardly. He struggled, gasping, and turned himself over on his back. I crossed the macadam rapidly.

A man in cutoffs had come out of a snack shop and he peered at me as I went past. "Is that guy okay?"

"Call the cops. Get an ambulance," I snapped.

I knelt beside Billy, angling so he could see me. "It's me," I said. "Don't panic. You'll be fine. We'll have help here in a second."

Billy's eyes strayed to mine. His face was gray and there

was a widening puddle of quite red blood spreading out under him. I took his hand and held it. A crowd was beginning to collect, people running from all directions. I could hear them buzzing at my back.

Somebody handed me a beach towel. "You want to cover him with this?"

I grabbed the towel. I let go of him long enough to unbutton his shirt, opening it so I could see what I was dealing with. There was a hole in his belly. He must have been shot from behind, because what I was looking at was an exit wound, ragged, welling with blood. The slug must have severed the abdominal aorta. A coil of his lower intestine was visible, gray and glistening, bulging through the hole. I could feel my hands start to shake, but I kept my expression neutral. He was watching me, trying to read my face. I made a pad of the towel, pressing it against the wound to staunch the flow of blood.

He groaned, breathing rapidly. He had one hand resting on his chest and his fingers fluttered. I took his hand again, squeezing hard.

He tilted his head. "Where's . . . my leg? I can't feel nothin' down there."

I glanced down at his right knee. The pantleg looked like it had caught on a nail. Blood and bone seemed to blossom through the tear.

"Don't sweat it. They can fix that. You'll be fine," I said. I didn't mention the blood soaking through the towel. I thought he probably knew about that.

"I'm gut-shot."

"I know. Relax. It's not bad. The ambulance is on its way."

The hand I held was icy, his fingers pale. There were questions I should have asked, but I didn't. I couldn't. You don't intrude on someone's dying with a bullshit interrogation like you're some kind of pro. This was just me and him and nothing else entered into it.

I studied his face, sending love through my eyes, willing him to live. His hair looked curlier than I remembered it. With my free hand, I moved it away from his forehead. Sweat beaded on his upper lip.

"I'm goin' . . . I can feel myself goin' out . . ." He clutched my hand convulsively, bucking against a surge of pain.

"Take it easy. You'll be fine."

He began to hyperventilate and then his struggle subsided. I could see the life drain away, see it all fade—color, energy, awareness, pain. Death comes in a gathering cloud that settles like a veil. Billy Polo sighed, his gaze still pinned on my face. His hand relaxed in mine, but I held on.

24

I sat on the curb near the snack shop and stared at the asphalt. The proprietor had brought me a can of Coke and I held the cold metal against my temple. I felt sick, but there wasn't anything wrong with me. Lieutenant Feldman had appeared and he was hunkered over Billy's body, talking to the lab guys, who were bagging his hands. The ambulance had backed around and waited with its doors open, as if to shield the body from the public view. Two black-and-whites were parked nearby, radios providing a squawking counterpoint to the murmurs of the gathering crowd. Violent death is a spectator sport and I could hear them trading comments about the way the final quarter had been played. They weren't being cruel, just curious. Maybe it was good for them to see how grotesque homicide really is.

The beat officers, Gutierrez and Pettigrew, had arrived within minutes of Billy's demise and they'd radioed for the CSI unit. The two of them would probably drive over to the trailer park to break the news to Coral and Lovella. I felt I should ride along, but I couldn't bring myself to volunteer yet. I'd go, but for the moment, I was having trouble coping with the fact of Billy's death. It had happened so fast. It was so irrevocable. I found it hard to accept that we couldn't rewind the tape and play the last fifteen minutes differently. I would arrive earlier. I would warn him off and he could walk away unharmed. He'd tell me his theory and then I'd buy him the beer I'd promised him that first night at the Hub.

Feldman appeared. I found myself staring at his pantlegs, unable to look up. He lit a cigarette and came down to my level, perching on the curb. I hugged my knees, feeling numb. I barely know the man, but what I've seen of him I've always liked. He looks like a cross between a Jew and an Indian—a large flat face, high cheekbones, a big hooked nose. He's a big man, probably forty-five, with a cop haircut, cop clothes, a deep rumbling voice. "You want to bring me up to speed on this?" he said.

It was the act of opening my mouth to speak that brought the tears. I held myself in check, willing them back. I shook my head, struggling with the nearly overwhelming rush of regret. He handed me a handkerchief and I pressed it to my eyes, then folded it, addressing my remarks to the oblong of white cotton. There was an "F" embroidered in one corner with a thread coming loose.

"Sorry," I murmured.

"That's okay. Take your time."

"He was such a screw-up," I said. "I guess that's what gets me. He thought he was so smart and so tough."

I paused. "I guess you never know which people will affect your life," I said.

"He never said who shot him?"

I shook my head. "I didn't ask. I didn't want the last minutes of his life taken up with that stuff. I'm sorry."

"Well, he might not have said anyway. What was the setup?"

I started talking, saying anything that came to mind. He let me ramble till I finally took control of myself and began to lay it out systematically. After hundreds of reports, I know the drill. I cited chapter and verse while he nodded, making notes in a battered black notebook.

When I finished, he tucked his ballpoint pen away and shoved the notebook back into the inside pocket of his suitcoat. He got up and I rose with him, automatically.

"What next?" I asked.

"Actually, I got Daggett's file sitting on my desk," he said. "Robb told me you tagged it a homicide and I thought I'd take a look. We had a double killing, one of those execution-style shootings, up on the Bluffs late yesterday and we've had to put a lot of manpower on that one, so I haven't had a chance as yet. It'd help if you came down to the station and talked to Lieutenant Dolan yourself."

"Let me see Billy's sister first," I said. "This is the second brother she's lost in the whole Daggett mess."

"You don't think there's any chance she's the one who plugged him?"

I shook my head. "I thought she might connect to Daggett's death, but I can't picture her involved in this. Unless I'm missing something big. For one thing, he wouldn't have to meet her out in public like this. It was someone at the funeral, I'm almost sure."

"Make a list and we'll take it from there," he said.

I nodded. "I can also stop by the office and make some copies of my file reports. And Lovella may know more than she's told us so far." It felt good, turning everything over to him. He could have it all. Essie and Lovella and the Smiths.

Pettigrew approached, holding a small plastic Ziploc bag by one corner. In it were three empty brass casings. "We found these over by that pickup truck. We're sealing off the whole parking lot until the guys have a chance to go over it."

I said, "You might check the trash bins. That's where I found the skirt and shoes after Daggett was killed."

Feldman nodded, then gave the shells a cursory look. "Thirty-twos," he remarked.

I felt a cold arrow shoot up my spine. My mouth went dry. "My thirty-two was stolen from my car a few days ago," I said. "Gutierrez took the report."

"A lot of thirty-twos around, but we'll keep that in mind," Feldman said to me, and then to Pettigrew, "Let's hustle these folk out of here. And be polite."

Pettigrew moved away and Feldman turned to study me. "Are you all right?"

I nodded, wishing I could sit down again, afraid once I did I'd be stuck.

"Anything you want to add before I let you go?"

I closed my eyes for a moment, thinking back. I know the snapping sound a .32 makes when fired and the shots I'd heard weren't like that. "The shots," I said. "They sounded odd to me. Hollow. More like a pop than a bang."

"A silencer?"

"I've never heard one except on TV," I said, sheepishly.

"I'll have the lab take a look at the slugs, though I don't know where anybody'd get a silencer in this town." He made another quick note in his book.

"You can probably order one from the back of a magazine," I said.

"Ain't that the truth."

The photographer was snapping pictures and I could see Feldman's gaze flick in that direction. "Let me tend to this guy. He's new. I want to make sure he covers everything I need."

He excused himself and crossed to Billy's body where he engaged in a conversation with the forensic photographer, using gestures to describe the various angles he wanted.

Maria Gutierrez came up to me. "We're going out to the trailer park. Gerry said you might want to come."

"I'll follow in my car," I said. "You know where it is?"

"We know the park. We can meet you there if you want."

"I'm going to see if Billy's car is here in the lot. I'll be along shortly, but don't wait on my account."

"Right," she said.

I watched them pull out and then I worked my way through the lot, checking the vehicles in the area adjacent to the boat launch. I spotted the Chevy three rows from the entrance, tucked between two RVs. The temporary sticker was still on the windshield. The windows were down. I stuck my head in without touching anything. The car looked clean to me. Nothing in the front seat. Nothing in the back. I went around to the passenger window and peered in, checking the floorboards from that side. I don't even know what I was hoping for. A hint, some suggestion of where we might go from here. It looked as if Feldman might initiate a formal investigation after all, and glad as I was to turn it over to him, I still couldn't quite let go.

I stopped by my car and picked up the skirt and shoes, which I handed over to Lieutenant Feldman. I told him where to find Billy's car and then I finally got back in mine and took off. In my heart, I knew I'd been stalling to allow Pettigrew and Gutierrez a chance to deliver the news of Billy's death. That has to be the worst moment in anybody's life, finding two uniformed cops at your door, their expressions somber, voices grave.

By the time I got to the trailer park, the word had apparently spread. By some telepathic process, people were collecting in twos and threes, all staring at the trailer uncomfortably, chatting in low tones. The trailer door was closed and I heard nothing as I approached, but my appearance had generated conversation at my back.

A fellow stepped forward. "You a family friend? Because she's had bad news. I wasn't sure if you were aware," he said.

"I was there," I said. "She knows me. How long ago did the officers leave?"

"Two minutes. They were real good about it . . . talked to her a long time, making sure she was all right. I'm Fritzy Roderick. I manage the park," he said, offering me his hand.

"Kinsey Millhone," I said. "Is anybody with her now?"

"I don't believe so, and we haven't heard a peep. We were just talking among ourselves here . . . the neighbors and all . . . wondering if someone ought to sit with her."

"Is Lovella in there?"

"I don't know the name. Is she a relative?"

"Billy's ex-girlfriend," I said. "Let me see if I can find out what's going on. If she needs anything, I'll let you know."

"I'd appreciate that. We'd like to help any way we can."

I knocked at the trailer door, uncertain what to expect. Coral opened it a crack and when she saw it was me, she let me in. Her eyes were reddened, but she seemed in control. She sat down on a kitchen chair and picked up her cigarette, giving the ash a flick. I sat down on the banquette.

"I'm sorry about Billy," I said.

She glanced at me briefly. "Did he know?"

"I think so. When I found him, he was already in shock and fading fast. I don't think he suffered much if that's what you're asking."

"I'll have to tell Mom. The two cops who came said they'd do it, but I said no." Her voice trailed off, hoarse from grief or the head cold. "He always knew he'd die young, you know? Like when we'd see old people on the street, crippled or feeble. He said he'd never end up like them. I used to beg him to straighten up his act, but he had to do everything his way." She lapsed into silence.

"Where's Lovella?"

"I don't know," Coral said. "The trailer was empty when I got here."

"Coral, I wish you'd fill me in. I need to know what was going on. Billy told me three different versions of the same tale."

"Why look at me? I don't know anything."

"But you know more than I do."

"That wouldn't take much."

"Level with me. Please. Billy's dead now. There's nothing left to protect. Is there?"

She stared at the floor for a moment and then she sighed and stubbed out her cigarette. She got up and started clearing the table, running water in the tiny stainless steel kitchen sink.

She squirted in Ivory Liquid, dropping silverware and plates into the mounting suds, talking in a low monotone as she worked. "Billy was already up at San Luis when Daggett got there. Daggett had no idea Doug was related to us, so Billy struck up an acquaintance. We were both of us bitter as hell."

"Billy told me he and Doug were never close."

"Bullshit. He just told you that so you wouldn't suspect him. The three of us were always thick as thieves."

"So you did intend to kill him," I said.

"I don't know. We just wanted to make him pay. We wanted to punish him. We figured we'd find a way once we got close. Then Daggett's cellmate died and he got all that money."

"And you thought that would compensate?"

"Not me. I knew I'd never be happy till the day Daggett died, but I couldn't do it myself. I mean, kill someone in cold blood. Billy was the one who said the money would help. We couldn't bring Doug back, but at least we'd have something. He always knew Daggett lifted the cash, but he didn't think he'd get away with it. Daggett gets out of prison and sure enough, he's home free. He starts throwin' money around. Lovella calls Billy and we decide to go for it."

"So the guys up at San Luis never did figure it out," I said.

"Nope. Once Billy saw Daggett was in the clear, we decided to rip him off."

"And Lovella was part of it?"

Coral nodded, rinsing a plate, which she placed in the dish rack. "They got married the same week he got out, which suited us just fine. We figured if she didn't talk him out of it, she could steal it. . . ."

"And failing that, what?"

"We never meant to kill anyone," she said. "We just wanted the money. We didn't have much time anyway because he'd already spent part of it. He went through five grand before

we could bat an eye and we knew if we didn't move fast, he'd
blow the whole wad."

"You didn't realize he intended to give the rest of it to Tony
Gahan?"

"Of course not," she said with energy. "Billy couldn't believe
it when you told him about that. We thought most of it was
still around somewhere. We thought we could still get our
hands on it."

I watched her face, trying to compute the information she
was giving me. "You mean you set Daggett up with Lovella
so you could con him out of twenty-five thousand bucks?"

"That's right," she said.

"You were splitting it three ways! That's a little over eight
grand apiece."

"So?"

"Coral, eight grand is nothing."

"Bullshit, it's nothing! Do you know what I could do with
eight grand? How much do you have? Do you have eight
grand?"

"No."

"So, all right. Don't tell me it's nothing."

"All right. It's a fortune," I said. "What went wrong?"

"Nothing at first. Billy called him up and said the guys at
San Luis heard about the money and they wanted it back. He
told Daggett they were coming after him, so that's when Daggett split."

"How'd you know he'd hightail it up here?"

"Billy told Daggett he'd help him out," she said with a shrug.
"And then when Daggett got into town, Billy started working
on him, trying to get him to fork it over to us. He said he'd
act as a go-between, smooth it all over and get him off the
hook."

"He'd already given it to me at that point, right?"

"Sure, but we didn't know that. He acted like he still had

it handy. He acted like he might turn it over to Billy, but that was all crap. Of course, he was drunk all the time by then."

"So he was conning you while you conned him."

"He was just stringing us along!" she said indignantly. "Billy met him Tuesday night and Daggett was real cagey. Said he needed time to get his hands on it. He said he'd bring it in Thursday night, so Billy met him at the Hub again, only Daggett said he needed one more day. Billy really laid into him. He said these guys were getting very pissed and might kill Daggett anyway, whether he gave 'em the money or not. Daggett got real nervous and swore he'd have it the next night, which was Friday."

"The night he died."

"Right. I was working that night, and I was supposed to keep an eye on him, which I did. Billy decided to come late, just to make him sweat, and before I knew what was happening this woman showed up and started buying him drinks. You know the rest."

"Billy told me you took some kind of cold cap and crashed in the back room. Was that true?"

"I was just laying low," she said. "When I saw Daggett leave, I knew Billy'd have a fit. I already felt bad enough without putting up with his bullshit."

"And Billy finally figured out who she was?"

"I don't know. I guess. I wasn't here this morning, so I don't know what he was up to."

"Look. I have to go down to the police station and tell Lieutenant Dolan what's been going on. If Lovella comes back, please tell her it's urgent that she get in touch. Will you do that?"

Coral wedged the last clean dish against the pile in the rack. She filled a glass with water and poured it over the lot of them, rinsing off the few remaining suds. She turned to look at me with a gaze that chilled. "Do you think she killed Billy?"

"I don't know."

"Will you tell me if you find out it's her?"

"Coral, if she did it, she's dangerous. I don't want you in the middle of this."

"But will you tell me?"

I hesitated. "Yes."

"Thank you."

25

I had a brief chat with the manager of the trailer park. I gave him my card and asked him to call me if Lovella came back. I didn't really trust Coral to do it. The last I saw of him, he was tapping at her door. I got in my car and headed over to the police station. I asked for Lieutenant Dolan at the desk, but he and Feldman were in a section meeting. The clerk buzzed Jonah for me and he came as far as the locked door, admitting me into the corridor beyond. Both of us were circumspect—pleasant, noncommittal. No one observing us could have guessed that mere hours ago, we'd been cavorting stark naked on my Wonder Woman sheets.

"What happened when you got home?" I asked.

"Nothing. Everybody was asleep," he said. "We have something in the lab you might want to see." He moved down the hall to the right and I followed. He looked back at me. "Feldman had the guys check the trash bins at your suggestion. We think we found the silencer."

"You did?" I said, startled.

He opened the half-door into the crime lab, holding it for me as I passed in front of him. The lab tech was out, but I could see Billy's bloody shirt, tagged, on the counter, along with an object I couldn't at first identify.

"What's that," I said. "Is *that* it?" What I was looking at was a large plastic soft drink bottle, painted black, lying on its side with a hole visible in the bottom.

"A disposable silencer. Handmade. A sound suppressor, in effect. It's been wiped clean of prints," Jonah said.

"I don't understand how it works."

"I had to have Krueger explain it to me. The bottle's filled with rags. Take a look. The barrel of the gun is usually wrapped with tape and the bottle affixed to it with a one-inch hose clamp. The soda bottle has a reinforced bottom, but it's only effective for a few shots because the noise level increases each time as the exit hole gets larger. Obviously, the device works best at close range."

"God, Jonah. How do people know about these things? I never heard of it."

He picked up a paperbound booklet from the counter behind me, flipping through it carelessly so I could see. Every page was filled with diagrams and photographs, illustrating how disposable silencers could be made out of common household objects. "This is from a gun shop down in Los Angeles," he said. "You ought to see what you can do with a length of window screen or a pile of old bottle caps."

"Jesus."

Lieutenant Becker stuck his head in the door. "Line one for you," he said to Jonah and then disappeared. Jonah glanced at the lab phone, but the call hadn't been transferred.

"Let me take this and I'll be right back," Jonah said. "Hang on."

"Right," I murmured. I leaned toward the silencer, trying to remember where I'd seen something similar. Through the hole in the bottom, I caught a glimpse of the blue terrycloth filling the interior. When I realized what it was, my mental processes clicked in, and the interior machinery fired up. I knew.

I straightened up and crossed to the door, checking the corridor, which was empty. I headed for my car. I could still see Ramona Westfall coming up the basement stairs with an armload of ragged blue bath towels, which she'd dumped on the chair. The plastic bottle had been filled with a soft drink which she nearly dropped as she passed it to Tony to refrigerate.

I stopped by the office long enough to try the Westfalls' number. The phone rang four times and then the machine clicked in.

"Hello. This is Ramona Westfall. Neither Ferrin nor I can come to the phone right now, but if you'll leave your name, telephone number, and a brief message, we'll get back to you as soon as possible. Thank you." I hung up at the sound of the tone.

I checked my watch. It was 4:45. I had no idea where Ramona was, but Tony had a 5:00 appointment just a few blocks away. If I could intercept him, I could lean on him some about her alibi since he represented the only confirmation she had. How had she pulled it off? He had to be on heavy medication for the migraine, so she might have slipped out while he was sleeping, adjusting the kitchen clock when she got back so she'd be covered for the time of Daggett's death. Once she was home again, Tony had wakened— she'd probably made sure of that so she'd have someone to corroborate the time. She'd fixed the sandwiches, chatting pleasantly while he ate, and as soon as he went back to bed, she changed the clock again. Or maybe it wasn't even as complicated as that. Maybe the watch Daggett wore had been set for 2:37 and then submerged. She could have killed him earlier and been home by 2:00. Tony may have realized what she'd done and tried to shield her when he understood how close my investigation was bringing me. It was also possible that he was in cahoots with her, but I hoped that wasn't the case.

I locked my office and went down the front stairs, trotting up State Street on foot. The Granger Building was only three blocks up and it made more sense than hopping in my car and driving all the way around to the parking lot behind the building. Tony might still be hanging out at the arcade across the street. I had to get to him before she had a chance to intercept. I didn't want him going home. She had to realize things were getting hot, especially since I'd shown up at the house with the shoes and skirt. All I needed from him was an indication I was on the right track and then I'd call Feldman. I thought about the Close, which I knew would be gloomy with the gathering twilight. I didn't want to go back there unless I had to.

I checked the arcade. Tony was at the rear, on the right-hand side, playing a video game. He was concentrating fully and I didn't think he was aware of me. I waited, watching small creatures being blasted off the screen. His scores weren't that good and I was tempted to have a try at it myself. The creatures suddenly froze into place, random weapons firing off here and there without regard to his manipulations. He looked up. "Oh hi."

"I need to talk to you," I said.

His eyes moved to the clock. "I got an appointment in five minutes. Can it wait?"

"I'll walk you over. We can talk on the way."

He picked up his package and we moved out to the street. The fading afternoon sun seemed bright after the darkness of the arcade. Even so, the fog was rolling in, November twilight beginning to descend. I punched the button at the crosswalk and we waited for the light to change. "Last Friday . . . the night Daggett died, do you remember where your uncle was?"

"Sure. Milwaukee, on a business trip."

"Are you on medication for the migraines?"

"Well, yeah. Tylenol with codeine. Compazine if I'm throwing up. How come?"

"Is it possible your aunt went out while you slept?"

"No. I don't know. I don't understand what you're getting at," he said.

I thought he was stalling, but I kept my mouth shut. We'd reached the Granger Building and Tony moved into the lobby ahead of me.

The elevator that had been out of order was now in operation, but the other one was immobilized, doors open, the housing visible, two sawhorses in front of the opening with a warning sign.

Tony was watching me warily. "Did she say she went out?"

"She claims she was home with you."

"So?"

"Come on, Tony. You're the only alibi she has. If you were zonked on medication, how do you know where she was?"

He pressed the elevator button.

The doors opened and we got on. The doors closed without incident and we went up to six. I checked his face as we stepped into the hallway. He was clearly conflicted, but I didn't want to press just yet. We headed down the corridor toward the suite his psychiatrist apparently occupied.

"Is there anything you want to talk about?" I asked.

"No," he said, his voice breaking with indignation. "You're crazy if you think she had anything to do with it."

"Maybe you can explain that to Feldman. He's in charge of the case."

"I'm not talking to the cops about her," Tony said. He tried the office door and found it locked. "Shit, he's not here."

There was a note taped to the door. He reached up to snatch the piece of paper, turning the movement into an abrupt shove. Next thing I knew, I was on my hands and knees and he'd taken off. He banged on the elevator button and then veered right. I was up and running when I heard the door leading to the stairway slam back against the wall. I ran, banging into the stairwell only seconds after he did. He was already heading up.

"Tony! Come on. Don't do this."

He was moving fast, his footsteps scratching on the concrete stairs. His labored breathing echoed against the walls as he went up. I don't keep fit for nothin', folks. He had youth on me, but I was in good shape. I flung my bag aside and grabbed the rail, starting up after him, mounting the steps two at a time. I peered upward as I ran, trying to catch sight of him. He reached the seventh floor and kept on going. How many floors did this building have?

"Tony. Goddamn it! Wait up! What are you doing?"

I heard another door bang up there. I stepped up my pace.

I reached the landing at the top. The elevator repairman had apparently left the door to the attic unlocked and Tony had shot through the gap, slamming the door behind him. I snatched the handle, half expecting to find it locked. The door flew open and I pushed through, pausing on the threshold. The space was dim and hot and dry, largely empty except for a small door opening off to my right where the elevator brake, sheave, and drive motors were located. I ducked my head into the cramped space briefly, but it appeared to be empty. I pulled out and peered around. The roof was another twenty feet up, the rafters steeply pitched, timbers forming a ninety-degree angle where they met.

Silence. I could see a square of light on the floor and I looked up. A wooden ladder was affixed to the wall to my right. At the top, a trap door was open and waning daylight filtered down. I scanned the attic. There was an electrical panel sitting on some boxes. It looked like some kind of old light board from the theater on the ground floor. For some reason, there was a massive papier-mâché bird standing to one side . . . a blue jay, wearing a painted business suit. Wooden chairs were stacked, seat to seat, to my left.

"Tony?"

I put a hand on one of the ladder rungs. He might well be hiding somewhere, waiting for me to head up to the roof so he could ease out and down the steps again. I started up, climbing maybe ten feet so I could survey the attic from a better vantage point. There was no movement, no sound of breathing. I looked up again and started climbing cautiously. I'm not afraid of heights, but I'm not fond of them either. Still, the ladder seemed secure and I couldn't figure out where else he might be.

When I got to the top, I pulled myself into a sitting position and peered around. The trap came out in a small alcove, hidden behind an ornamental pediment, with a matching pediment halfway down the length of the roof. From the ground, the two of them had always looked strictly decorative, but I could see now that one disguised a brace of air vents. There was only a very narrow walkway around the perimeter of the roof, protected by a short parapet. The steep pitch of the roof would make navigating hazardous.

I peered down into the attic, hoping to see Tony dart out of hiding and into the stairwell. There was no sign of him up here, unless he'd eased around to the far side. Gingerly, I got to my feet, positioning myself between the nearly vertical roofline on my left and the ankle-high parapet on my right. I was actually walking in a metal rain gutter that popped and creaked under my weight. I didn't like the sound. It suggested that any minute now the metal would buckle, toppling me off the side.

I glanced down eight floors to the street, which didn't seem that far away. The buildings across from me were two stories high and lent a comforting illusion of proximity, but pedestrians still seemed dwarfed by the height. The streetlights had come on, and the traffic below was thinning. To my right, half a block away, the bell tower at the Axminster Theater was lighted from within, the arches bathed in tawny gold and warm blue. The drop had to be eighty feet. I tried to remember the velocity of a falling object. Something-something per foot per second was as close as I could come, but I knew the end result would be an incredible splat. I paused where I was and raised my voice. "Tony!"

I caught a flash of movement out of the corner of my eye and my heart flew into my throat. The plastic bag he'd been carrying was eddying downward, floating lazily. Coming from where? I peered over the parapet. I could see one of the niches that cut into the wall just below the cornice molding. The frieze that banded the building had always looked like marble from the street, but I could see now that it was molded plaster, the niche itself down about four feet and to the left. A half shell extended out maybe fifteen inches at the bottom edge and it held what was probably meant to be some sort of lamp with a torch flame, all molded plaster like the frieze. Tony was sitting there, his face turned up to mine. He'd climbed over the edge and he was now perched in the shallow ornamental niche, his arm locked around the torch, legs dangling. He'd taken a wig out of the bag he carried, donning it, looking up at me with a curious light in his eyes.

I was looking at the blonde who'd killed Daggett.

For a moment, we stared at each other, saying nothing. He had the cocky look of a ten-year-old defying his mom, but under the bravado I sensed a kid who was hoping someone would step in and save him from himself.

I put a hand on the pediment to steady myself. "You coming up or shall I come down?" I kept my tone matter-of-fact, but my mouth was dry.

"I'll be going down in a minute."

"Maybe we could talk about that," I said.

"It's too late," he said, smiling impishly. "I'm poised for flight."

"Will you wait there until I reach you?"

"No grabbing," he warned.

"I won't grab."

My palms were damp and I wiped them on my jeans.

I squatted, turning to face the roof, extending a foot tentatively down along the frieze. I glanced down, trying to find some purchase. Garlands of pineapple, grapes, and fig leaves formed a bas relief design that wound across the face of the building. "How'd you do this?" I asked.

"I didn't think about it. I just did it. You don't have to come down. It won't help."

"I just don't want to talk to you hanging over the edge," I said, lying through my teeth. I was hoping to get close enough to nab him, ignoring visions of grappling with him at that height. I steadied myself, tucking a toe into the shallow crevice formed by a curling vine. The niche was only four feet away. At ground level, I wouldn't have given it a thought.

I sensed that he was watching me, but I didn't dare look. I held onto the parapet, lowering my left foot.

He said, "You're not going to talk me out of this."

"I just want to hear your side of it," I said.

"Okay."

"You won't try to kill me, will you?" I asked.

"Why would I? You never did anything to me."

"I'm glad you recognize that. Now I feel really confident." I heard him laugh lightly at my tone.

I've seen magazine pictures of a man who can climb a vertical cliff face in a pair of tennis shoes, holding himself with the tips of his fingers tucked into small cracks that he discovers as he ascends. This has always seemed like a ludicrous pursuit and I usually flip to an article that makes more sense. The sight of the photographs makes me hyperventilate, especially the ones taken from his vantage point, staring down into some yawning crevasse. Maybe, if the truth be known, I'm more anxious about heights than I let on.

I allowed my right foot to inch down again as far as the lip of the niche. I found a handhold, down and to the right. Felt like a pineapple, but I wasn't sure. Pinning my safety to a phony piece of fruit. I had to be nuts.

The hardest part was actually letting go of the coping once my foot was resting safely in the recess. I had to bend my knees, turning slightly to the right, sinking little by little until I could take a seat. Tony, ever gallant, actually gave me a hand, steadying me until I eased down next to him. I'm not a brave soul. I'm really not. I just didn't want him flying off the side of that building while I looked on. I locked my left arm around the torch, just below his, holding onto my wrist with my right hand. I could feel sweat trickle down my sides.

"I hate this," I said. I was winded, not from effort but from apprehension.

"It's not bad. Just don't look down."

Of course I did. The minute he said that I had an irresistible desire to peek. I was hoping somebody would spot us, like they always do on TV. Then the cops would come with nets and the fire engines would arrive and somebody would talk him out of this. I'm an organism of the earth, a Taurus. I was never born of air, of water, or of fire. I'm a creature of gravity and I could feel the ground whisper. The same thing happens to me in old hotels when I'm staying on the twenty-second floor. I open a window and want to fling myself out.

"Oh, Jesus. This is such a bad idea," I said.

"For you maybe. Not for me."

I tried to think back to my short life as a cop and the standard procedure for dealing with potential suicides. Stall for time was the first rule. I didn't recall anything about hanging your ass off the side of a building, but here I was. I said, "What's the story, babe. You want to tell me what's been going on? "

"There's not much to it. Daggett called the house on Monday. Aunt Ramona made a note of the number so I called him back. I dreamed about killing him. I couldn't wait. I had fantasies for months, every night before I went to sleep. I wanted to catch him with a wire around his neck and twist till it bit into his windpipe and his tongue bugged out. It doesn't take that long. I forget what that's called now . . ."

"Garroting," I supplied.

"Yeah, I would have liked that, but then I figured it was better if it looked like an accident because that way I could get away with it."

"Why'd he call?"

"I don't know," Tony said uncomfortably. "He was drunk and blubbering, said he was sorry and wanted to make it up to me for what he did. I go, 'Fine. Why don't we meet and talk?' And he goes, 'It would mean so much to me, son.' " Tony was acting out the parts, using a quavering falsetto for Daggett. "So then I tell him I'll meet him the next night at this bar he's calling from, the Hub, which didn't give me much time to put together this getup."

"Was that Ramona's skirt?"

"Nah, I got it at the Salvation Army thrift store for a buck. The sweater was another fifty cents and the shoes were two bucks."

"Where'd the sweater go?"

"I tossed it in another trash can a block away from the first. I thought it would all end up at the dump."

"What about the wig?"

"That was Aunt Ramona's from years ago. She didn't even know it was gone."

"Why'd you keep it?"

"I don't know. I was going to put it back in her closet where I got it, in case I needed it again. I had it on at the beach, but then I remembered Billy already knew who I was." He broke off, obviously confused. "I might have told my shrink about the whole thing if he'd been here. Anyway, the wig's expensive. This is real hair."

"The color's nice too," I said. I mean, where else could I go with this? Even Tony recognized the absurdity and he flashed me a look.

"You're humoring me, right?"

"Of course I'm humoring you!" I snapped. "I didn't come down here so we could have an argument."

He did a half shrug, smiling sheepishly.

I said, "Did you actually meet him there Tuesday night?"

"Not really. I went. I had it all worked out by then, only when I walk in, he's sittin' at this table talking to some guy. Turned out to be Billy Polo, but I didn't know it at the time. Billy was sitting in this booth with his back to the door. I saw Daggett, but I didn't realize he had company till I was right there in front of him. I veer off the minute I spot Billy, but by then he's had a good look at me. I'm not worried. I figure I'll never see him again anyway. I hang around for a while but they're really into it. I can tell Billy's leaning all over him and isn't likely to let up so I take a hike and go home."

"Was this one of the nights you had a migraine?"

"Yeah," he said. "I mean, some are real and some are fake, but I have to have a pattern, know what I mean? So I can come and go as I please."

"How'd you get down to the Hub, by cab?"

"My bike. The night I killed him, I rode down and left it at the marina and then I called a cab from a pay phone and took it over to the Hub."

"How'd you know he'd show up?"

"Because he called again and I said I'd be there."

"He never twigged to the fact that you'd showed up the first time in drag?"

"How was he going to know? He hadn't seen me since way before the trial. I was twelve, thirteen, something like that, a fat boy back then. I figured even if he guessed, I'd do it anyway, kill his ass . . . and once he was dead, who would know?"

"What went wrong?"

His brow furrowed. "I don't know. Well, I do. The plan went fine. It was something else." His eyes met mine and he looked every bit of fifteen, the blonde wig adding softness and dimension to a face that was nearly formless with youth. I could see how he'd pass as a woman, slim, with a clear complexion, sweet smile on his wide mouth. He looked down at the street and for a moment I thought he meant to swing out into space.

"When I was eight, I had these pet mice," he said. "Really sweet. I kept 'em in this cage with a wheel and a water bottle hanging upside down. Mom didn't think I'd take care of 'em but I did. I'd cut up strips of paper in the bottom of the cage so they could nest. Anyway, the girl mouse had these babies. They couldn't have been as long as this." He was indicating the end of his little finger. "Bald," he went on. "Just little bitty old things. We had to go out of town one weekend and when we got back the cat had tried to get in the cage. Knocked it off the desk and everything. The mice were gone. Probably the cat got 'em except for this one that had been laying in all these paper shreds. Well, the water had spilled so the paper was damp and the little thing must have had pneumonia or something because it was panting, like it couldn't breathe good. I tried to keep it warm. I watched it for hours and it just kept getting worse and worse so I decided I better . . . you know, do away with it. So it wouldn't suffer anymore."

He leaned forward, swinging his feet back and forth.

"Don't do that," I murmured anxiously. "Finish the story. I want to know what happened next."

He looked over at me then, his tone of voice mild. "I tossed it in the toilet. That's the only way I could think of to kill it. I couldn't crush it, so I just figured I'd flush it away. The little thing was half dead anyway and I thought I'd be doing it a favor, putting it out of its misery. But before I could do it, that little tiny hairless baby started struggling. You could tell

it was in a total panic, trying to get out of there, like it knew
what was happening . . ." He paused, dashing at his eyes.
"Daggett did that and now I can't get away from the look on
his face, you know? I see it all day long. He knew. Which was
fine with me. I wanted that. I wanted him to know it was me
and his life wasn't worth two cents. I just didn't think he'd
care. He was a drunk and a bum and he killed all those people.
He should have died. He shoulda been glad to go. I was
putting him out of his misery, you know? So why'd he have
to make it so hard?"

He fell silent and then he let out a deep breath. "Anyway,
that's how that went. I can't sleep anymore. I dream about
that stuff. Makes me sick."

"What about Billy? I assume he figured it out when he saw
you at the funeral."

"Yeah. That was weird. He didn't give a shit about Daggett,
but he felt like he should get part of the money if he kept his
mouth shut. I would have given him all of it, but I didn't
believe him. You should have seen him. Swaggering around,
making all these threats. I figured he'd start bragging one
night about what he knew and there I'd be."

The edge of the niche was beginning to cut into my rear
end. I was hanging on so tightly that my arm was getting
numb, but I didn't dare ease up. I couldn't figure out how to
get us out of this, but I knew I'd better start talking fast.

"I killed a man once," I said. I meant to say more, but that'
all I could get out. I clamped my teeth together, trying to
force the feelings back down where I'd been keeping them.
It surprised me that after all this time, it was still so painful
to think about.

"On purpose?"

I shook my head. "Self-defense, but dead is dead."

His smile was sweet. "You can always come with me."

"Don't say that. I'm not going to jump and I don't want

you to either. You're fifteen years old. There are lots of other ways out."

"I don't think so."

"Your parents have money. They could hire Melvin Belli if they wanted to."

"My parents are dead."

"Well, the Westfalls, then. You know what I mean."

"But Kinsey, I murdered two people and it's first degree because I looked it up. How'm I gonna get away with that?"

"The way half the killers in this country do," I said with energy. "Hell, if Ted Bundy's still alive, why shouldn't you be?"

"Who's he?"

"Never mind. Someone who did a lot worse than you."

He thought for a moment. "I don't think it would work. I hurt too bad and I don't see the point."

"There isn't a point. That's the part you invent."

"Could you do me a favor."

"All right. What's that?"

"Could you tell my aunt I said good-bye? I meant to write her a note, but I didn't have a chance."

"Goddamn it, Tony! Don't do this. She's had enough pain."

"I know," he said, "but she's got my Uncle Ferrin and they'll be okay. They never really knew what to do with me anyway."

"Oh, I see. You've got this all worked out."

"Well, yeah, I do. I've been reading up on this stuff and it's no big deal. Kids kill themselves all the time."

I hung my head, almost incapable of framing a response. "Tony, listen," I said finally. "What you're talking about is dumb and it doesn't make any sense. Do you have any idea how crummy life seemed when I was your age? I cried all the time and I felt like shit. I was ugly. I was skinny. I was lonely. I was mad. I never thought I'd pull out of it, but I did. Life is hard. Life hurts. So what? You tough it out. You get through and then you'll feel good again, I swear to God."

He tilted his head, watching me intently. "I don't think so. Not for me. I'm in too deep. I can't bear any more. It's too much."

"Tony, there are days when none of us can bear it, but the good comes around again. Happiness is seasonal, like anything else. Wait it out. There are people who love you. People who can help."

He shook his head. "I can't do that. It's kind of like I made a deal with myself to go through with this. She'll understand."

I could feel my temper snapping. "You want me to tell her that? You took a flying leap because you made a fucking *deal* with yourself?" His face clouded with uncertainty. I pressed on in a softer tone. "You want me to tell her we sat up here like this and I couldn't talk you out of it? I can't let you do it. You'll break her heart."

He looked down at his lap, his eyes remote, face coloring up the way boys do in lieu of tears. "It doesn't have anything to do with her. Tell her it was me and she did just great. I love her a lot, but it's my life, you know?"

I was silent for a moment, trying to figure out where to go next.

His face brightened and he held up an index finger. "I nearly forgot. I have a present for you." He shifted, letting go of the torch with a move that made me snatch at him instinctively. He laughed at that. "Take it easy. I'm just reaching in the waistband of my jeans."

I looked to see what he'd produced. My .32 lay across his palm. He held his hand out so I could take it, realizing belatedly that I couldn't free up a hand to reach for it.

"That's okay. I'll put it right here," he said kindly. He set it in the niche, behind the ornamental torch I was clinging to.

"How'd you get it?" Stalling, stalling.

"Same way I did everything else. I used my head. You put your home address on that business card you gave Aunt Ramona, so I rode over on my bike and waited till you got home. I was going to introduce myself, you know, and act like this real polite kid with good manners and a nifty haircut and stuff like that. Real innocent. I wasn't sure how much you knew and I thought maybe I could steer you off. I saw the car and you almost stopped, but then you took off again. I had to pedal my ass off to keep up with you and then you parked at the beach and I saw a chance to go through your stuff."

"You killed Billy with that?"

"Yeah. It was handy and I needed something quick."

"How'd you know about disposable silencers?"

"Some kid at school. I can make a pipe bomb too," he said. Then he sighed. "I gotta go soon. Time's nearly up."

I glanced down at the street. It was really getting dark up here, but the sidewalk was bright, the arcade across the way lit up like a movie house. Two people on the far side of the street had spotted us, but I could tell they hadn't figured out what was going on. A stunt? A movie being shot? I looked at Tony, but he didn't seem to be aware. My heart began to bang again and it made my chest feel tight and hot.

"I'm getting tired," I said casually. "I may go back up, but I need some help. Can you give me a hand?"

"Sure," he said. And then he paused, his whole body alert. "This isn't a trick, is it?"

"No," I said, but I could hear my voice shake and the lie cut my tongue like a razor blade. I've always lied with ease and grace, with ingenuity and conviction and I couldn't get this one out. I saw him make a move. I grabbed him, hanging on for dear life, but all he had to do was give his arm a quick twist and my hand came loose. I reached again, but it was too late. I saw him push out, lifting off. For a moment, he seemed to hover there, like a leaf, and then he disappeared from my line of sight. I didn't look down again after that.

I thought I heard a siren wailing, but the sound was mine.

I billed Barbara Daggett for $1,040.00, which she paid by return mail. It's nearly Christmas now and I haven't slept well for six weeks. I've thought a lot about Daggett and I've changed my mind about one thing. I suspect he knew what was going on. From a distance, Tony might have passed for a woman, but up close, he looked like exactly what he was . . . a young kid playing dress-up, smart beyond his years, but not wise enough by half. I don't think Daggett was fooled. Why he went along with the game, I'm not sure. If he believed what Billy'd told him, he must have figured he was dead either way. Maybe he felt he owed Tony that last sacrifice. I'll never know, but it makes more sense to me that way. Some debts of the human soul are so enormous only life itself is sufficient forfeit. Perhaps in this case, all of the accounts are now paid in full . . . except mine.

—Respectfully submitted,
Kinsey Millhone

"E" is for Evidence

For my two mothers,
past and present:
Viv and Lillian

The author wishes to acknowledge the invaluable assistance of the following people: Steven Humphrey; Jim Hetherington, President, and Dorcas Lube, Office Manager, Hetherington, Inc.; Bruce Boller, First Vice-President, Institutional Services, Robert W. Baird, Inc.; Joyce Mackewich and Kim Nelson of Montgomery, Fansler & Carlson Insurance; Dennis W. Leski; William Pasich; Robert Snowball; Caroline Ware, Santa Barbara Travel; Elisa Moran, Santa Barbara County Registrar of Voters; Kathleen Hotchkiss, Culinary Alliance and Bartenders Local 498; Anne Reid; Frank and Florence Clark; Lynn Herold, Ph.D., Senior Criminalist, Department of Chief Medical Examiner-Coroner, Los Angeles County; George Donner, A-1 Tri-Counties Investigations; Detective Robert J. Lowry, Investigative Division, Santa Barbara Police Department; and Deputy Juan Tejeda, Santa Barbara County Sheriff's Department.

1

It was Monday, December 27, and I was sitting in my office, trying to get a fix on the mood I was in, which was bad, bad, bad, comprised of equal parts irritation and uneasiness. The irritation was generated by a bank notice I'd just received, one of those windowed numbers with a yellow carbon showing through. At first, I assumed I was overdrawn, but what I pulled out was a slip, dated Friday, December 24, showing a five-thousand-dollar deposit to my checking account.

"What the hell is this?" I said.

The account number was correct, but the deposit wasn't mine. In my experience, banks are the least helpful institutions on earth, and the notion of having to stop what I was doing to straighten out an error was nearly more than I could bear. I tossed the notice aside, trying to reclaim my concentration. I was getting ready to write up the preliminary report on an insurance case I'd been asked to look into, and Darcy, the secretary at California Fidelity, had just buzzed to say that Mac wanted the file on his desk right away. Mentally, I'd come up with a tart suggestion about what she could do with herself, but I'd kept my mouth shut, showing (I thought) admirable restraint.

I turned back to my portable Smith-Corona, inserting the proper form for a property-insurance-loss register. My nimble fingers were poised to type while I reviewed my notes. That's where I was stuck. Something was off and I couldn't figure out what it was. I glanced at the bank notice again.

Almost with an eye toward the comic relief, I called the
bank, hoping the diversion would help me focus on what was
bothering me about the situation at Wood/Warren, a local
company manufacturing hydrogen furnaces for industrial use.
They'd had a fire out there on December 19 that had destroyed a warehouse.

"Mrs. Brunswick, Customer Service. May I help you?"

"Well, I hope so," I said. "I just received a notice saying I
put five thousand dollars in my checking account last Friday
and I didn't do that. Is there any way you can straighten it out?"

"May I have your name and account number, please?"

"Kinsey Millhone," I said, supplying my account number
in slow, measured tones.

She put me on hold briefly while she called up the records
on her computer terminal. Meanwhile, I listened to the bank's
rendition of "Good King Wenceslas," which I've personally
never understood. What's the Feast of Stephen?

Mrs. Brunswick clicked back in. "Miss Millhone, I'm not
certain what the problem is, but we do show a cash deposit
to this account number. Apparently, it was left in the night-
deposit slot and posted over the weekend."

"You still have one of those night-deposit slots?" I asked
with amazement.

"At our downtown branch, yes," she said.

"Well, there's some kind of mistake here. I've never even
seen the night-deposit slot. I use my twenty-four-hour instant-
teller card if I need to transact bank business after hours.
What do we do now?"

"I can track down a copy of the deposit slip," she said
skeptically.

"Would you do that, please? Because I didn't make a deposit
of any kind last Friday and certainly not five thousand dollars'
worth. Maybe somebody transposed some numbers on the

deposit slip or something, but the money sure doesn't belong to me."

She took my telephone number and said she'd get back to me. I could tell I was in for countless phone calls before the correction could be made. Suppose somebody was merrily writing checks against that five grand?

I went back to the task at hand, wishing I felt more enlightened than I did. My mind kept jumping around. The file on the fire claim at Wood/Warren had actually come into my hands four days before, late Thursday, the 23rd. I'd been scheduled to have a farewell drink with my landlord, Henry Pitts, at four, and then take him out to the airport and put him on a plane. He was flying back to Michigan to spend the holidays with his family, some of whom are edging into their nineties with their vigor and good spirits still in evidence. Henry's pushing eighty-one, a mere kid, and he was about as excited as one at the prospect of the trip.

I was still at the office that afternoon with my paperwork caught up and some time to kill. I went out onto my second-floor balcony, peering off to my right at the V of Pacific Ocean visible at the foot of State Street, ten blocks down. This is Santa Teresa, California, ninety-five miles north of Los Angeles. Winter here is a grand affair, full of sunshine and mild temperatures, vibrant magenta bougainvillea, gentle winds, and palm trees waving fronds at the sea gulls as they wheel overhead.

The only signs of Christmas, two days away, were the garlands of tinsel strung along the main streets. The stores, of course, were packed with shoppers, and there was a trio of Salvation Army horn players tooting away at "Deck the Halls." In the interests of feeling jolly, I thought I'd better work out my strategy for the next two days.

Anyone who knows me will tell you that I cherish my un-

married state. I'm female, twice divorced, no kids, and no
close family ties. I'm a private detective by trade. Usually I'm
perfectly content to do what I do. There are times when I
work long hours on a case and times when I'm on the road
and times when I hole up in my tiny apartment and read
books for days. When the holidays come around, however, I
find that I have to exercise a certain cunning lest the absence
of loved ones generate unruly depression. Thanksgiving had
been a breeze. I spent the day with Henry and some pals of
his, who'd cooked and sipped champagne and laughed and
told tales about days long past, making me wish I were their
age instead of my own, which is thirty-two.

Now Henry was leaving town, and even Rosie, who runs
the dingy neighborhood tavern where I often eat, was closing
down until January 2, refusing to tell a soul what she meant
to do with herself. Rosie is sixty-six, Hungarian, short, top-
heavy, bossy, and often rude, so it wasn't as though I was
worried I'd miss any touching heart-to-heart chats. The fact
that she was closing her eatery was simply one more uncomfortable reminder that I was out there in the world all by
myself and had best find a way to look after me.

At any rate, I'd glanced at my watch and decided I might
as well head on home. I switched on the answering machine,
grabbed my jacket and handbag, and was just locking up when
Darcy Pascoe, the receptionist from the insurance company
next door, popped her head in. I had worked for California
Fidelity full time at one point, doing investigations on fire and
wrongful death claims. Now the arrangement is informal. I'm
more or less on call, doing a certain number of investigations
for them, as needed, in exchange for downtown office space
I couldn't otherwise afford.

"Oh, wow. I'm glad I caught you," Darcy said. "Mac told
me to give you this."

She handed me a file, which I glanced at automatically. The

blank form inside indicated that I was being asked to do a fire-scene inspection, the first in months.

"Mac did?" Mac is the CF vice-president. I couldn't imagine him handling routine paperwork.

"Well, actually, Mac gave it to Andy and Andy said I should give it to you."

There was a memo attached to the file cover, dated three days before and marked RUSH. Darcy caught my look and her cheeks tinted faintly.

"It was stuck under a big pile of stuff on my desk or I'd have gotten it to you sooner," she said. Darcy's in her late twenties and something of a flake. I crossed to my desk, tossing the file on top of some others I was working on. I'd catch it first thing in the morning. Darcy lingered in the doorway, guessing my intent.

"Is there any way you can get to that today? I know he's anxious to get somebody out there. Jewel was supposed to handle it, but she's taking two weeks off, so Mac said maybe you could do it instead."

"What's the claim?"

"A big warehouse fire out in Colgate. You probably heard it on the news."

I shook my head. "I've been down in L.A."

"Well, the newspaper clippings are in there, too. I guess they want someone out there superquick."

I was annoyed at the pressure, but I opened the manila folder again and checked at the property-loss notice, which was posted on top. "Wood/Warren?" I said.

"You know the company?"

"I know the Woods. I went to high school with the youngest girl. We were in the same homeroom."

She looked relieved, as if I'd just solved a problem for her. "That's great. I'll tell Mac maybe you can get out there this afternoon."

"Darcy, would you knock that off? I've got to take somebody to the airport," I said. "Trust me. I'll make an appointment for the earliest possible moment."

"Oh. Well, I'll make a note then so they'll know you're taking care of it," she said. "I have to get back to the phones. Let me know when you have the report and I'll come pick it up."

"Terrific," I said. She must have decided she had pushed me far enough because she excused herself and disappeared in haste.

As soon as she left, just to get it over with, I put a call through to Wood/Warren and arranged to meet with the company president, Lance Wood, at 9:00 the next morning, Christmas Eve day.

Meanwhile, as it was 3:45, I tucked the file in my handbag, locked up, and headed down the back stairs to the lot where my VW was parked. I was home ten minutes later.

During our little pre-Christmas celebration, Henry gave me a new Len Deighton novel and I gave him a periwinkle-blue mohair muffler, which I had crocheted myself—a little-known talent of mine. We sat in his kitchen and ate half a pan of his homemade cinnamon rolls, drinking champagne out of the matching crystal flutes I'd given him the year before.

He took out his plane ticket and checked the departure time again, his cheeks flushed with anticipation. "I wish you'd come with me," he said. He had the muffler wrapped around his neck, the color setting off his eyes. His white hair was soft and brushed to one side, his lean face tanned from California sun.

"I wish I could, but I just picked up some work that'll get my rent paid," I said. "You can take lots of pictures and show 'em to me when you get back."

"What about Christmas Day? You're not going to be by yourself, I hope."

"Henry, would you quit worrying? I've got lots of friends." I'd probably spend the day alone, but I didn't want him to fret.

He raised a finger. "Hold on. I almost forgot. I have another little present for you." He crossed to the counter by the kitchen sink and picked up a clump of greenery in a little pot. He set it down in front of me, laughing when he saw the expression on my face. It looked like a fern and smelled like feet.

"It's an air fern," he said. "It just lives on air. You don't even have to water it."

I stared at the lacy fronds, which were a nearly luminous green and looked like something that might thrive in outer space. "No plant food?"

He shook his head. "Just let it sit."

"I don't have to worry about diffuse sunlight or pinching back?" I asked, tossing around some plant terms as if I knew what they meant. I'm notoriously bad with plants, and for years I've resisted any urge whatever to own one.

"Nothing. It's to keep you company. Put it on your desk. It'll jazz the place up a bit."

I held the little pot up and inspected the fern from all sides, experiencing this worrisome spark of possessiveness. I must be in worse shape than I thought, I thought.

Henry fished a set of keys out of his pocket and passed them over to me. "In case you need to get into my place," he said.

"Great. I'll bring in your mail and the papers. Is there anything else you need done while you're gone? I can mow the grass."

"You don't need to do that. I've left you the number where I can be reached if the Big One hits. I can't think of anything else." The Big One he referred to was the major earthquake we'd all been expecting any day now since the last one in 1925.

He checked his watch. "We better get a move on. The airport is mobbed this time of year." His plane wasn't leaving until 7:00, which left us only an hour and a half to make the twenty-minute trip to the airport, but there wasn't any point in arguing. Sweet man. If he had to wait, he might as well do it out there, happily chatting with his fellow travelers.

I put on my jacket while Henry made a circuit of the house, taking a few seconds to turn the heat down, making sure the windows and doors were secured. He picked up his coat and his suitcase and we were on our way.

I was home again by 6:15, still feeling a bit of a lump in my throat. I hate to say goodbye to folks and I hate being left behind. It was getting dark by then and the air had a bite to it. I let myself into my place. My studio apartment was formerly Henry's single-car garage. It's approximately fifteen feet on a side, with a narrow extension on the right that serves as my kitchenette. I have laundry facilities and a compact bathroom. The space has been cleverly designed and apportioned to suggest the illusion of living room, dining room, and bedroom once I open my sofa bed. I have more than adequate storage space for the few things I possess.

Surveying my tiny kingdom usually fills me with satisfaction, but I was still battling a whisper of Yuletide depression, and the place seemed claustrophobic and bleak. I turned on some lights. I put the air fern on my desk. Ever hopeful, I checked my answering machine for messages, but there were none. The quiet was making me feel restless. I turned on the radio—Bing Crosby singing about a white Christmas just like the ones he used to know. I've never actually seen a white Christmas, but I got the gist. I turned the radio off.

I sat on a kitchen stool and monitored my vital signs. I was hungry. One thing about living alone . . . you can eat any time you want. For dinner that night I made myself a sandwich of olive-pimento cheese on whole-wheat bread. It's a source of comfort to me that the brand of olive-pimento cheese I buy has tasted exactly the same since the first time I remember eating it at the age of three and a half. Resolutely I veered off *that* subject, since it connected to my parents, who were killed when I was five. I cut the sandwich into four fingers, as I always did, poured myself a glass of white wine, and took my plate over to the couch, where I opened the book Henry had given me for Christmas. I checked the clock.

It was 7:00 P.M. This was going to be a very long two weeks.

2

The next morning, December 24, I jogged three miles, showered, ate a bowl of cereal, packed a canvas tote with supplies,
and was heading toward Colgate by 8:45, a quick ten-mile
drive. I'd reviewed the file over breakfast, and I was already
puzzled about what the big rush was. The newspaper account
indicated that the warehouse was gutted, but there was no
telltale closing line about arson, investigations pending, or any
speculation that the nature of the blaze was suspect. The fire-
department report was included, and I'd read that twice. It
all looked routine. Apparently the origin of the fire was a
malfunction in the electrical system, which had simultaneously
shorted out the sprinklers. Since the materials stored in the
two-story structure were largely paper goods, the 2:00 A.M.
fire had spread rapidly. According to the fire inspector at the
scene, there was no sign of firetraps, no gasoline or other
flammables, and no sign of obstacles placed so as to impede
the work of the firemen. There was no indication that doors
or windows had been left open to create favorable drafts and
no other physical evidence of incendiary origin. I'd read dozens of reports just like this one. So what was the big deal here?
I wondered. Maybe I was missing a crucial piece of information, but as far as I could see, this was a standard claim. I
had to guess that somebody at Wood/Warren was putting the
squeeze on California Fidelity for a speedy settlement, which
might explain Andy's panic. He's a nail-biter by inclination,

anxious for approval, worried about censure, in the middle of marital problems, from what I'd heard. He was probably the source of the little note of hysteria that had crept into the case. Maybe Mac was leaning on him, too.

Colgate is the bedroom community that adjoins Santa Teresa, providing affordable housing for average working folk. While new construction in Santa Teresa is closely regulated by the Architectural Board of Review, building in Colgate has proceeded according to no known plan, though it leans toward the nondescript. There is one major street lined with donut shops, hardware stores, fast-food establishments, beauty salons, and furniture stores that feature veneer and laminate, velour and Naugahyde. From the main thoroughfare, tract homes stretch out in all directions, housing styles appearing like concentric rings on a tree stump, spiraling out decade by decade until the new neighborhoods peter out into raw countryside, or what's left of it. In isolated patches there are still signs of the old citrus groves that once flourished there.

Wood/Warren was located on a side street that angled back toward an abandoned drive-in theater that functions as a permanent location for weekend swap sales. The lawns of the neighboring manufacturing plants were a close-clipped green, and the shrubs were trimmed into perfect rectangles. I found a parking place out front and locked up. The building was a compact story and a half of stucco and fieldstone. The address of the warehouse itself was two blocks away. I'd inspect the fire scene after I talked to Lance Wood.

The reception area was small and plain, furnished with a desk, a bookcase, and an enlarged photograph of the FIFA 5000 Hydrogen/Vacuum Furnace, the mainstay of the company fortunes. It looked like an oversized unit for an efficiency kitchen, complete with stainless-steel counter and built-in microwave. According to the data neatly framed nearby, the front-loading FIFA 5000 provided five thousand cubic inches of uniform hot zone for hydrogen or vacuum brazing, for metallizing ceramics, or for manufacturing ceramic-to-metal seals. I should have guessed.

Behind me, the receptionist was returning to her desk with a fresh cup of coffee and a Styrofoam container that smelled of sausage and eggs. The laminated plastic sign on her desk indicated that her name was Heather. She was in her twenties and apparently hadn't yet heard about the hazards of cholesterol and fat. She would find the latter on her fanny one day soon.

"May I help you?" Her smile was quick, exposing braces on her teeth. Her complexion was still ruddy from last night's application of an acne cure that so far hadn't had much effect.

"I have an appointment with Lance Wood at nine," I said. "I'm with California Fidelity Insurance."

Her smile faded slightly. "You're the arson investigator?"

"Well, I'm here on the fire claim," I said, wondering if she mistakenly assumed that "arson" and "fire" were interchangeable terms.

"Oh. Mr. Wood isn't in yet, but he should be here momentarily," she said. The braces infused her speech with a sibilance that amused her when she heard herself. "Can I get you some coffee while you wait?"

I shook my head. There was one chair available and I took a seat, amusing myself by leafing through a brochure on the molybdenum work rack designed specifically for metallizing alumina at 1450°C. in a bell-style hydrogen furnace. These people had about as many laughs as I do at home, where a prime source of entertainment is a textbook on practical aspects of ballistics, firearms, and forensic techniques.

Through a doorway to my left, I could see some of the office staff, casually dressed and busy, but glum. I didn't pick up any sense of camaraderie among them, but maybe hydrogen furnace-making doesn't generate the kind of good-natured bantering I'm accustomed to with California Fidelity. Two desks were unoccupied, bare of equipment or accouterments.

Some attempt had been made to decorate for Christmas. There was an artificial tree across the room from me, tall and skeletal, hung with multicolored ornaments. There didn't seem to be any lights strung on the tree, which gave it a lifeless air and only pointed up the uniformity of the detachable limbs stuck into pre-bored holes in the aluminum shaft. The effect was dispiriting. From the information I'd been given, Wood/Warren grossed close to fifteen million bucks a year, and I wondered why they wouldn't pop for a live pine.

Heather gave me a self-conscious smile and began to eat. Behind her was a bulletin board decorated with garlands of tinsel and covered with snapshots of the family and staff. H–A–P–P–Y H–O–L–I–D–A–Y–S was spelled out in jaunty store-bought silver letters.

"Mind if I look at that?" I asked, indicating the collage.

By then, she had a mouth full of breakfast croissant, but she managed assent, holding a hand in front of her mouth to spare me the sight of her masticated food. "Help yourself."

Most of the photographs were of company employees, some of whom I'd seen on the premises. Heather was featured in one, her fair hair much shorter, her face still framed in baby fat. The braces on her teeth probably represented the last vestige of her teens. Wood/Warren must have hired her right out of high school. In one photograph, four guys in company coveralls stood in a relaxed group on the front doorstep. Some of the shots were stiffly posed, but for the most part they

seemed to capture an aura of goodwill I wasn't picking up on
currently. The founder of the company, Linden "Woody"
Wood, had died two years before, and I wondered if some of
the joy had gone out of the place with his demise.

The Woods themselves formed the centerpiece in a studio
portrait that looked like it was taken at the family home. Mrs.
Wood was seated in a French Provincial chair. Linden stood
with his hand resting on his wife's shoulder. The five grown
children were ranged around their parents. Lance I'd never
met before, but I knew Ash because I'd gone to high school
with her. Olive, older by a year, had attended Santa Teresa
High briefly, but had been sent off to a boarding school in
her senior year. There was probably a minor scandal attached to that, but I wasn't sure what it was. The oldest of
the five was Ebony, who by now must be nearly forty. I remembered hearing that she'd married some rich playboy
and was living in France. The youngest was a son named
Bass, not quite thirty, reckless, irresponsible, a failed actor
and no-talent musician, living in New York City, the last I'd
heard. I had met him briefly eight years before through
my ex-husband Daniel, a jazz pianist. Bass was the black
sheep of the family. I wasn't sure what the story was on
Lance.

Seated across his desk from him sixty-six minutes later, I
began to pick up a few hints. Lance had breezed in at 9:30.
The receptionist indicated who I was. He introduced himself
and we shook hands. He said he had a quick phone call to
make and then he'd be right with me. I said "Fine" and that
was the last I saw of him until 10:06. By then, he'd shed his
suit coat and loosened his tie along with the top button of
his dress shirt. He was sitting with his feet up on the desk, his
face oily-looking under the fluorescent lights. He must have
been in his late thirties, but he wasn't aging well. Some com-

bination of temper and discontent had etched lines near his
mouth and spoiled the clear brown of his eyes, leaving an
impression of a man beleaguered by the Fates. His hair was
light brown, thinning on top, and combed straight back from
his face. I thought the business about the phone call was
bullshit. He struck me as the sort of man who pumped up his
own sense of importance by making people wait. His smile
was self-satisfied, and the energy he radiated was charged with
tension.

"Sorry for the delay," he said. "What can I do for you?"
He was tipped back in his swivel chair, his thighs splayed.

"I understand you filed a claim for a recent fire loss."

"That's right, and I hope you're not going to give me any
static over that. Believe me, I'm not asking for anything I'm
not entitled to."

I made a noncommittal murmur of some sort, hoping to
conceal the fact that I'd gone on "fraud alert." Every insurance
piker I'd ever met said just that, right down to the pious little
toss of the head. I took out my tape recorder, flicked it on,
and set it on the desk. "The company requires that I tape the
interview," I said.

"That's fine."

I directed my next few remarks to the recorder, establishing
my name, the fact that I worked for California Fidelity, the
date and time of the interview, and the fact that I was speaking
to Lance Wood in his capacity as president and CEO of Wood/
Warren, the address of the company, and the nature of the
loss.

"Mr. Wood, you do understand that this is being taped," I
said for the benefit of the record.

"Yes."

"And do I have your permission to make this recording of
the conversation we're about to have?"

"Yes, yes," he said, making that little rolling hand gesture that means "Let's get on with it."

I glanced down at the file. "Can you tell me the circumstances of the fire that occurred at the Wood/Warren warehouse at 606 Fairweather on December nineteenth of this year?"

He shifted impatiently. "Actually, I was out of town, but from what I'm told . . ." The telephone intercom buzzed and he snatched up the receiver, barking at it like a dog. "Yes?"

There was a pause. "Well, goddamn it, put her through." He gave me a quick look. "No, wait a minute, I'll take it out there." He put the phone down, excused himself brusquely, and left the room. I clicked off the recorder, mentally assessing the brief impression I'd had of him as he passed. He was getting heavy in the waist and his gabardine pants rode up unbecomingly, his shirt sticking to the center of his back. He smelled harshly of sweat—not that clean animal scent that comes from a hard workout, but the pungent, faintly repellent odor of stress. His complexion was sallow and he looked vaguely unhealthy.

I waited for fifteen minutes and then tiptoed to the door. The reception area was deserted. No sign of Lance Wood. No sign of Heather. I moved over to the door leading into the inner office. I caught a glimpse of someone passing into the rear of the building who looked very much like Ebony, but I couldn't be sure. A woman looked up at me. The name plate on her desk indicated that she was Ava Daugherty, the office manager. She was in her late forties, with a small, dusky face and a nose that looked as if it had been surgically tampered with. Her hair was short and black, with the glossy patina of hair spray. She was unhappy about something, possibly the fact that she'd just cracked one of her bright-red acrylic fingernails.

"I'm supposed to be meeting with Lance Wood, but he's disappeared. Do you know where he went?"

"He left the plant." She was licking the cracked nail experimentally, as if the chemistry of her saliva might serve as adhesive.

"He left?"

"That's what I said."

"Did he say how soon he'd be back?"

"Mr. Wood doesn't consult with me," she said snappishly. "If you'd like to leave your name, I'm sure he'll get back to you."

A voice cut in. "Something wrong?"

We both looked up to find a dark-haired man standing in the doorway behind me. Ava Daugherty's manner became somewhat less antagonistic. "This is the company vice-president," she said to me. And to him, "She's supposed to be in a meeting with Lance, but he left the plant."

"Terry Kohler," he said to me, holding out his hand. "I'm Lance Wood's brother-in-law."

"Kinsey Millhone, from California Fidelity," I said, shaking hands with him. "Nice to meet you." His grip was hard and hot. He was wiry, with a dark moustache and large, dark eyes that were full of intelligence. He must have been in his early forties. I wondered which sister he was married to.

"What's the problem? Something I can help you with?"

I told him briefly what I was doing there and the fact that Lance Wood had abandoned me without a word of explanation.

"Why don't I show you the warehouse?" he said. "At least you can go ahead and inspect the fire scene, which I'm assuming is one of your responsibilities."

"I'd appreciate that. Is anybody else out here authorized to give me the information I need?"

Terry Kohler and Ava Daugherty exchanged a look I couldn't decipher.

"You better wait for Lance," he said. "Hold on and I'll see if I can find out where he went." He moved toward the outer office.

Ava and I avoided small talk. She opened her top right-hand drawer and took out a tube of Krazy Glue, ignoring me pointedly as she snipped off the tip and squeezed one clear drop on the cracked fingernail. She frowned. A long dark hair was caught in the glue and I watched her struggle to extract it.

Idly I tuned into the conversation behind me, three engineers in a languid discussion about the problem before them.

"Now maybe the calculation is off, but I don't think so," one was saying.

"We'll find out," someone interjected. All three men laughed.

"The question came up . . . oh, this has occurred to me many times . . . What would it take to convert this to a pulse power supply for the main hot cell?"

"Depends on what your pulsing frequency is."

"About ten hertz."

"Whoa."

"Anything that would allow you to modulate a signal away that was being influenced by the juice going through the susceptors. You know, power on for nine-tenths of a second, off for a tenth. Take measurements . . ."

"Um-hum. On for a half a second, off for a tenth of a second. You can't really do it easily, can you?"

"The PID controller could send the output that fast. I'm not sure what that would do to the NCRs. To the VRT setup itself, whether that would follow it . . ."

I tuned them out again. They could have been plotting the end of the world for all I knew.

It was another ten minutes before Terry Kohler reappeared. He was shaking his head in apparent exasperation.

"I don't know what's going on around here," he said. "Lance had to go out on some emergency and Heather's still away from her desk." He held up a key ring. "I'll take you over to the warehouse. Tell Heather I've got these if she shows up."

"I should get my camera," I said. "It's with my handbag."

He tagged along patiently while I moved back to Lance Wood's office, where I retrieved the camera, tucked my wallet in my tote, and left my handbag where it was.

Together we retraced a path through the reception room and the offices beyond. Nobody actually looked up as we passed, but curious gazes followed us in silence, like those portraits where the eyes seem to move.

The assembly work was done in a large, well-ventilated area in the back half of the building with walls of corrugated metal and a floor of concrete.

We paused only once while Terry introduced me to a man named John Salkowitz. "John's a chemical engineer and consulting associate," Terry said. "He's been with us since 'sixty-six. You have any questions about high-temperature processing, he's the man you want to ask."

Offhand, I couldn't think of one—except maybe about that pulse power supply for the main hot cell. That was a poser.

Terry was moving toward the rear door, and I trotted after him.

To the right, there was a double-wide rolling steel door that could be raised to accommodate incoming shipments or to load finished units ready for delivery. We went out into the alleyway, cutting through to the street beyond.

"Which of the Wood sisters are you married to?" I asked. "I went to high school with Ash."

"Olive," he said with a smile. "What's your name again?"

I told him and we chatted idly for the remainder of the short walk, dropping into silence only when the charred skeleton of the warehouse loomed into view.

3

It took me three hours to examine the fire scene. Terry went through the motions of unlocking the front door, though the gesture seemed ludicrous given the wreckage the fire had left. Most of the outer shell of the building remained upright, but the second story had collapsed into the first, leaving a nearly impenetrable mass of blackened rubble. The glass in the first-floor windows had been blown out by the heat. Metal pipes were exposed, many twisted by the weight of the walls tumbling inward. Whatever recognizable objects remained were reduced to their abstract shapes, robbed of color and detail.

When it became apparent that I was going to be there for a while, Terry excused himself and went back to the plant. Wood/Warren was closing early that day as it was Christmas Eve. He said if I was finished soon enough, I was welcome to stop by and have some punch and Christmas cookies. I had already taken out my measuring tape, notebook, sketch pad, and pencils, mentally laying out the order in which I intended to proceed. I thanked him, scarcely aware of his departure.

I circled the perimeter of the building, noting the areas of severest burning, checking the window frames on the first floor for signs of forced entry. I wasn't sure how quickly the salvage crew would be coming in, and since there was no apparent evidence of arson, I didn't feel California Fidelity could insist on a delay. Monday morning, I would do a background check on Lance Wood's financial situation just to make

sure there wasn't any hidden profit motive for the fire itself . . . a mere formality in this case, since the fire chief had
already ruled out arson in his report. Since this was probably
the only chance we'd have to survey the premises, I photographed everything, taking two rolls of film, twenty-four ex-
posures each.

As nearly as I could tell, the probable point of origin of
the fire was somewhere in the north wall, which seemed con-
sistent with the theory of an electrical malfunction. I'd have
to check the wiring diagram from the original blueprints, but
I suspected the fire chief had done just that in coming up
with his analysis. The surface of charred wood bore the typical
pattern of crevices known as "alligatoring," the deepest char-
ring and the smallest check in the pattern localized in this
rear portion of the building. Since hot gases rise and fire
normally sweeps upward, it's usually possible to track the course
of the flames, which will tend to rise until an obstacle is encountered, then project horizontally, seeking other vertical
outlets.

Much of the interior had been reduced to ashes. The load-
bearing walls remained, as black and brittle as cinder. Gingerly, I picked my way through the char-broiled junk, making
a detailed map of the ruins, noting the degree of burning,
general appearance, and carbonization of burned objects. Every
surface I encountered had been painted with the black and
ashen pallor of extreme heat. The stench was familiar: scorched
wood, soot, the sodden odor of drenched insulation, the lingering chemical aroma of ordinary materials reduced to their
elements. There was some other odor as well, which I noted
but couldn't identify. It was probably connected to materials
stored there. When I'd called Lance Wood the day before, I'd
requested a copy of the inventory sheets. I'd review those to
see if I could pinpoint the source of the smell. I wasn't crazy

about having to inspect the fire scene before I'd had a chance to interview him, but I didn't seem to have much choice, now that he'd disappeared. Maybe he'd be back for the office Christmas party and I could pin him down then about an appointment first thing Monday morning.

At 2:00 P.M., I packed my sketch pad away and brushed off my jeans. My tennis shoes were nearly white with ash, and I suspected that my face was smudged. Still, I was reasonably content with the job I'd done. Wood/Warren was going to have to get several contractors' estimates, and those would be submitted to CF along with my recommendation regarding payment of the claim. Using the standard rule, I was guessing five hundred thousand dollars' replacement cost, with additional payment for the inventory loss.

The Christmas party was indeed in progress. The festivities were centered in the inner offices, where a punch bowl had been set up on a drafting table. Desks had been cleared and were covered with platters of cold cuts, cheeses, and crackers, along with slices of fruitcake and homemade cookies. The company employees numbered about sixty, so the noise level was substantial, the general atmosphere getting looser and livelier as the champagne punch went down. Some sort of Reggae version of Christmas carols was being blasted through the intercom system.

There was still no sign of Lance Wood, but I spotted Heather on the far side of the room, her cheeks rosy with wassail. Terry Kohler caught my eye and shouldered his way in my direction. When he reached me, he leaned down close to my ear.

"We better get your handbag before this gets out of control," he said. I nodded vigorously and inched my way behind him through the reception area to Lance's office. The door was standing open and his desk was being used as a bar. Liquor bottles, ice, and plastic glasses were arranged across the surface, with several people helping themselves to both the booze and the comfort of the boss's furniture. My handbag had been tucked into a narrow slot between a file cabinet and a bookcase jammed with technical manuals. I put away my camera and sketch pad, hefting the bag onto my right shoulder. Terry offered to fetch me some punch, and after a moment of hesitation, I agreed. Hey, why not?

My first impulse was to leave as soon as I could gracefully extricate myself. I don't generally do well in group situations, and in this instance I didn't know a soul. What kept me was the sure knowledge that I had nowhere else to go. This might be the extent of my holiday celebration, and I thought I might as well enjoy it. I accepted some punch, helped myself to cheese and crackers, ate some cookies with pink and green sugar on top, smiled pleasantly, and generally made myself amenable to anyone within range. By 3:00, when the party was really getting under way, I excused myself and headed out the door. I had just reached the curb when I heard someone call my name. I turned. Heather was moving down the walk behind me, holding out an envelope embossed with the Wood/Warren logo.

"I'm glad I caught you," she said. "I think Mr. Wood wanted you to have this before you left. He was called away unexpectedly. This was in my out box."

"Thanks." I opened the flap and peered at the contents: inventory sheets. "Oh great," I said, amazed that he'd remembered in the midst of his vanishing act. "I'll call on Monday and set up a time to talk to him."

"Sorry about today," she said. "Merry Christmas!" She waved and then moved back to the party. The door was now propped open, cigarette smoke and noise spilling out in equal parts. Ava Daugherty was watching us, her gaze fixed with curiosity on the envelope Heather'd given me, which I was just tucking into my handbag. I returned to my car and drove back into town.

When I stopped by the office, I passed the darkened glass doors of California Fidelity. Like many other businesses, CF had shut down early for Christmas Eve. I unlocked my door, tossed the file on my desk, and checked for messages. I put a call through to the fire chief for a quick verification of the information I had, but he, too, was gone. I left my number and was told he probably wouldn't return the call until Monday.

By 4:00, I was back in my apartment with the drawbridge pulled up. And that's where I stayed for the entire weekend.

Christmas Day I spent alone, but not unhappily.

The day after that was Sunday. I tidied my apartment, shopped for groceries, made pots of hot tea, and read.

Monday, December 27, I was back in harness again, sitting at my desk in a poinky mood, trying to wrestle the fire-scene inspection into a coherent narrative.

The phone rang. I was hoping it was Mrs. Brunswick at the bank, calling back to tell me the five-thousand-dollar snafu had been cleared up. "Millhone Investigations," I said.

"Oh hi, Kinsey. This is Darcy, next door. I just wondered when I could pop over and pick up that file."

"Darcy, it's only ten-fifteen! I'm working on it, okay?" Please note: I did not use the "F" word, as I know she takes offense.

"Well, you don't have to take that tone," she said. "I told Mac the report wouldn't be ready yet, but he says he wants to review the file first anyway."

"Review the file before what?"

"I don't know, Kinsey. How am I supposed to know? I called because there's a note in the action file on my desk."

"Oh, your 'action' file. You should have said so before. Come pick the damn thing up."

Ill temper and intuition are not a good mix. Whatever inconsistency was nagging at me, I could hardly get a fix on it with Darcy breathing down my neck. My first act that morning had been to fill out a form for the Insurance Crime Prevention Unit, asking for a computer check on Lance Wood. Maybe at some point in the past I'd come across a previous fire claim and that's what was bugging me. The computer check wouldn't come back for ten days, but at least I'd have covered my bases. I adjusted the tabs on my machine, typed in the name of the insured, the location, date, and time of loss.

When Darcy arrived to pick up the file, I spoke without looking up. "I dropped the film off at Speedee-Foto on my way in. They'll have prints for me by noon. I haven't had a chance to talk to Lance Wood or the fire chief yet."

"I'll tell Mac," she said, her tone cool.

Oh well, I thought. She's never been a pal of mine anyway.

As there was no slot or box where unspecified hunches could be typed in, I kept my report completely neutral. When I finished, I rolled it out of the machine, signed it, dated it, and set it aside. I had an hour before I could pick up the photographs, so I cleaned up the sketch of the warehouse layout and attached that to the report with a paper clip.

The phone rang. This time it was Andy. "Could you step into Mac's office for a few minutes?"

I quelled my irritation, thinking it best not to sass the CF claims manager. "Sure, but I won't have the pictures for another hour yet."

"We understand that. Just bring what you've got."

I hung up, gathered up the report and the sketch, locked

the office behind me, and went next door. What's this "we" shit? I thought.

The minute I stepped into Mac's office, I knew something was wrong. I've know Maclin Voorhies since I started working for California Fidelity nearly ten years ago. He's in his sixties now, with a lean, dour face. He has sparse gray hair that stands out around his head like dandelion fuzz, big ears with drooping lobes, a bulbous nose, and small black eyes under unruly white brows. His body seems misshapen: long legs, short waist, narrow shoulders, arms too long for the average sleeve length. He's smart, capable, stingy with praise, humorless, and devoutly Catholic, which translates out to a thirty-five-year marriage and eight kids, all grown. I've never seen him smoke a cigar, but he's usually chewing on a stub, the resultant tobacco stains tarnishing his teeth to the color of old toilet bowls.

I took my cue not so much from his expression, which was no darker than usual, but from Andy's, standing just to his left. Andy and I don't get along that well under the best of circumstances. At forty-two, he's an ass-kisser, always trying to maneuver situations so that he can look good. He has a moon-shaped face and his collar looks too tight and everything else about him annoys me, too. Some people just affect me that way. At that moment he seemed both restless and smug, studiously avoiding eye contact.

Mac was leafing through the file. He glanced over at Andy with impatience. "Don't you have some work to do?"

"What? Oh sure. I thought you wanted me in this meeting."

"I'll take care of it. I'm sure you're overloaded as it is."

Andy murmured something that made it sound like leaving was his big idea. Mac shook his head and sighed slightly as the door closed. I watched him roll the cigar stub from one corner of his mouth to the other. He looked up with surprise, as if he'd just realized I was standing there. "You want to fill me in on this?"

I told him what had transpired to date, sidestepping the fact that the file had sat on Darcy's desk for three days before it came to me. I wasn't necessarily protecting her. In business, it's smarter not to bad-mouth the help. I told him I had two rolls of film coming in, that there weren't any estimates yet, but the claim looked routine as far as I could see. I debated mention of my uneasiness, but discarded the idea even as I was speaking. I hadn't identified what was bothering me and I felt it was wiser to stick to the facts.

The frown on Mac's face formed about thirty seconds into my recital, but what alarmed me was the silence that fell when I was done. Mac is a man who fires questions. Mac gives pop quizzes. He seldom sits and stares as he was doing in this case.

"You want to tell me what this is about?" I asked.

"Did you see the note attached to the front of this file?"

"What note? There wasn't any note," I said.

He held out a California Fidelity memo form, maybe three inches by five, covered with Jewel's curlicue script. "Kinsey . . . this one looks like a stinker. Sorry I don't have time to fill you in, but the fire chief's report spells it out. He said to call if he can give you any help. J."

"This wasn't attached to the file when it came to me."

"What about the fire-department report? Wasn't that in there?"

"Of course it was. That's the first thing I read."

Mac's expression was aggrieved. He handed me the file, open to the fire-department report. I looked down at the familiar STFD form. The incidental information was just as I remembered. The narrative account I'd never seen before.

The fire chief, John Dudley, had summed up his investigation with a no-nonsense statement of suspected arson. The newspaper clipping now attached to the file ended with a line to the same effect.

I could feel my face heat, the icy itch of fear beginning to assert itself. I said, "This isn't the report I saw." My voice had dropped into a range I scarcely recognized. He held his hand out and I returned the file.

"I got a phone call this morning," he said. "Somebody says you're on the take."

I stared. "What?"

"You got anything to say?"

"That's absurd. Who called?"

"Let's not worry about that for the moment."

"Mac, come on. Somebody's accusing me of a criminal act and I want to know who it is."

He said nothing, but his face shut down in that stubborn way of his.

"All right, skip that," I said, yielding the point. I thought it was better to get the story out before I worried about the characters. "What did this unidentified caller say?"

He leaned back in his chair, studying the cold coin of ash on the end of his cigar. "Somebody saw you accept an envelope from Lance Wood's secretary," he said.

"Bullshit. When?"

"Last Friday."

I had a quick flash of Heather calling to me as I left the plant. "Those were inventory sheets. I asked Lance Wood to have them ready for me and he left 'em in his out box."

"What inventory sheets?"

"Right there in the file."

He shook his head, leafing through. From where I stood, I could see there were only two or three loose papers clipped in on one side. There was nothing resembling the inventory sheets I'd punched and inserted. He looked up at me. "What about the interview with Wood?"

"I haven't done that yet. An emergency came up and he disappeared. I'm supposed to set up an appointment with him for today."

"What time?"

"Well, I don't know. I haven't called him yet. I was trying to get the report typed up first." I couldn't seem to avoid the defensiveness in my tone.

"This the envelope?" Mac was holding the familiar envelope with the Wood/Warren logo, only now there was a message jotted on the front. "Hope this will suffice for now. Balance to follow as agreed."

"Goddamn it, Mac. You can't be serious! If I were taking a payoff, why would I leave that in the file?"

No answer. I tried again. "You really think Lance Wood paid me off?"

"I don't think anything except we better look into it. For your sake as well as ours . . ."

"If I took money, where'd it go?"

"I don't know, Kinsey. You tell me. If it was cash, it wouldn't be that hard to conceal."

"I'd have to be a fool! I'd have to be an idiot and so would he. If he's going to bribe me, do you think he'd be stupid enough to put the cash in an envelope and write a note to that effect? Mac, this whole thing has frame-up written all over it!"

"Why would anyone do that?" At this point, his manner wasn't accusatory. He seemed genuinely puzzled at the very idea. "Who would go to such lengths?"

"How do I know? Maybe I just got caught in the loop. Maybe Lance Wood is the target. You know I'd never do such a thing. I'll bring you my bank statements. You can scrutinize my accounts. Check under my mattress, for God's sake. . . ." I broke off in confusion.

I saw his mouth move, but I didn't hear the rest of what he said. I could feel the trap close and something suddenly made sense. In the morning mail, I'd gotten notice about five thousand dollars credited to my account. I think I knew now what that was about.

4

I packed up my personal belongings and my current files. California Fidelity had suspended our relationship until the Wood/Warren matter could be "straightened out," whatever that meant. I had until noon to clear the premises. I called the telephone company and asked to have calls forwarded to my home until further notice. I unplugged the answering machine and placed it on top of the last cardboard box, which I toted down the back steps to my car. I had been asked to turn in my office keys before I left, but I ignored the request. I had no intention of giving up access to five years' worth of business files. I didn't think Mac would press the point and I didn't think anyone would bother to have the locks changed. Screw 'em. I know how to pick most locks, anyway.

In the meantime, I was already analyzing the sequence of events. The Wood/Warren folder had been sitting on my desk the entire weekend, so the fire-department reports could have been switched at any point. I'd worked from notes that morning without reference to the file itself, so I had no way of knowing if the inventory sheets were in the file or not. I might not have registered the loss had I looked. My office door and the French doors opening out onto the balcony showed no signs of forced entry, but my handbag, along with my keys, had sat in Lance Wood's office for three hours on Friday. Anybody could have gotten into that bag and had duplicate keys made. My checkbook was there, too, and it didn't take a wizard to figure out how somebody could have lifted a deposit slip, filled it out, stuck it in an envelope with five grand, and put the whole of it in the night-deposit slot at my bank. Obviously my instant-teller card couldn't be used because my code number wasn't written down anyplace.

I drove out to Wood/Warren, my brain clicking away, fired by adrenaline. The moment I'd understood what was going on, the anger had passed and a chill of curiosity had settled in. I'd felt my emotions disconnect and my mind had cleared like a radio suddenly tuned to the right frequency. Someone had gone to a lot of trouble to discredit me. Insurance fraud is serious damn shit, punishable by two, three, or four years in the state prison. That wasn't going to happen to me, folks.

Heather stared at me, startled, as I moved through the Wood/Warren reception area, scarcely slowing my pace. "Is he in?"

She looked down at the appointment book with confusion. "Do you have an appointment this morning?"

"Now I do," I said. I knocked on the door once and went in. Lance was meeting with John Salkowitz, the chemical engineer I had been introduced to on my earlier visit. The two men were bending over a set of specs for an item that looked like a giant diaper pin.

"We need to talk," I said.

Lance took one look at my face and then flicked a signal to Salkowitz, indicating that they'd continue some other time.

I waited until the door closed and then leaned on Lance's desk. "Somebody's trying to shove one up our collective rear end," I said. I detailed the situation to him, citing chapter and verse in a way that left no room for argument. He got the point. Some of the color left his face.

He sank into his swivel chair. "Jesus," he said. "I don't believe it." I could see him computing possibilities the same way I had.

I drew up a chair and sat down. "What was the emergency that pulled you out of here so fast Friday afternoon?" I asked. "It has to be connected, doesn't it?"

"How so?"

"Because if I'd questioned you as I intended to, you probably would have mentioned arson, and then I'd have known the fire-department report was counterfeit."

"My housekeeper called. I'm in the middle of a nasty divorce and Gretchen showed up at the house with two burly guys and a moving van. By the time I got home, she'd cleared out the living room and was working on the den."

"Does she have the wherewithal to set up a deal like this?"

"Why would she do that? It's in her best interest to keep me alive and well and earning money hand over fist. Right now, she's collecting over six grand a month in temporary support. Insurance fraud is the last thing she'd want to stick me with. Besides, she's been in Tulsa since March of this year."

"Or so she claims," I said.

"The woman is a twit. If you knew her, you wouldn't suspect her of anything except licking a pencil point every time she has to write her name."

"Well, somebody sure wanted to blacken your name," I said.

"What makes you think it's me they're after? Why couldn't it be you?"

"Because no one could be sure I'd be called in on this. These fire claims are assigned almost randomly, according to who's free. If it's me they wanted, they'd have to go about it differently. They're not going to burn down your warehouse on the off-chance that I'll be called to investigate."

"I suppose not," he said.

"What about you? What's going on in your life, aside from the divorce?"

He picked up a pencil and began to loop it through his fingers, end over end, like a tiny baton. He watched its progress and then shot me an enigmatic look. "I have a sister who moved back here from Paris three months ago. Rumor has it she wants control of the plant."

"Is this Ebony?"

He seemed surprised. "You know her?"

"Not well, but I know who she is."

"She disapproves of the way I run things."

"Enough to do this?"

He stared at me for a moment and then reached for the phone. "I better call my attorney."

"You and me both," I said.

I left and headed back into town.

As far as I knew, the D.A.'s office hadn't been notified, and no charges had been filed. A valid arrest warrant has to be based on a complaint supported by facts showing, first of all, that a crime has been committed, and second, that the informer or his information is reliable. At this point, all Mac had was an anonymous telephone call and some circumstantial evidence. He'd have to take action. If the accusation was correct, then CF had to be protected. My guess was that he'd go back through my workload, case by case, to see if there was any whisper of misconduct on my part. He might also hire a private detective to look into the affairs of Wood/Warren, Lance Wood, and possibly me—a novel idea. I wondered how my life would hold up if it were subjected to professional scrutiny. The five grand would certainly come to light. I wasn't sure what to do about that. The deposit was damning in itself, but if I tried to move the money, it would look even worse.

I remember the rest of the day in fragments. I talked to Lonnie Kingman, a criminal attorney I'd done some work for in the past. He's in his early forties, with a face like a boxer; beetle-browed, broken nose. His hair is shaggy and his suits usually look too tight across the shoulder blades. He's about five foot four and probably weighs two hundred and five. He lifts weights at the same gym I do and I see him in there doing squats with three hundred pounds of plates wobbling on either end of the bar like water buckets. He graduated summa cum laude from Stanford Law School and he wears silk shirts with his monogram on the cuff.

Attorneys are the people who can say things in the mildest of tones that make you want to shriek and rend your clothes. Like doctors, they seem to feel obliged to acquaint you with the full extent of the horror you could face, given the current path your life is on. When I told him what was happening, he tossed out two possible additions to the allegation of insurance fraud: that I'd be named with Lance Wood as co-conspirator, and charged as an aider and abettor to arson after the fact. And *that* was just what he came up with off the top of his head.

I could feel myself pale. "I don't want to hear this shit," I said.

He shrugged. "Well, it's what I'd go for if I were D.A.," he said offhandedly. "I could probably add a few counts once I had all the facts."

"Facts, my ass. I never saw Lance Wood before in my life."

"Sure, but can you prove it?"

"Of course not! How would I do that?"

Lonnie sighed like he was going to hate to see me in a shapeless prison dress.

"Goddamn it, Lonnie, how come the law always helps the other guy? I swear to God, every time I turn around, the bad guys win and the little guys bite the Big Wienie. What am I supposed to do?"

He smiled. "It's not as bad as all that," he said. "My advice is to keep away from Lance Wood."

"How? I can't just sit back and see what happens next. I want to know who set me up."

"I never said you couldn't look into it. You're an investigator. Go investigate. But I'd be careful if I were you. Insurance fraud is bad enough. You don't want to take the rap for something worse."

I was afraid to ask him what he meant.

I went home and unloaded the boxes full of office files. I took a few minutes to reword the message on my answering machine at home. I put a call through to Jonah Robb in Missing Persons at the Santa Teresa Police Department. As a lady in distress, I don't ordinarily call on men. I've been schooled in the notion that a woman, these days, saves herself, which I was willing to do if I could just figure out where to start.

I'd met Jonah six months before while I was working on a case. Our paths had crossed more than once, most recently in my bed. He's thirty-nine, blunt, nurturing, funny, confused, a tormented man with blue eyes, black hair, and a wife named Camilla who stalks out intermittently with his two little girls, whose names I repress. I had ignored the chemistry between us for as long as I could, too wise (said I) to get pulled into a dalliance with a married gent. And then one rainy night I'd run into him on my way home from a depressing interview with a hostile subject. Jonah and I started drinking margaritas in a bar near the beach. We danced to old Johnny Mathis tunes, talked, danced again, and ordered more drinks. Somewhere around "The Twelfth of Never," I lost track of my resolve and took him home with me. I never could resist the lyrics on that one.

We were currently at that stage in a new relationship where both parties are tentative, reluctant to presume, quick to feel injured, eager to know and be known as long as the true frailties of character are concealed. The risking felt good, and as a consequence the chemistry felt good, too. I smiled a lot when I thought of him and sometimes I laughed aloud, but the warmth was undercut by a curious pain. I've been married twice, done in more times than I care to admit. I'm not as trusting as I used to be and with good reason. Meanwhile, Jonah was in a constant state of upheaval according to the fluctuations in Camilla's moods. Her most recent claim was that she wanted an "open" marriage, his guess being that the sexual liberties were intended more for her than for him.

"Missing Persons. Sergeant Schiffman."

For an instant my mind went absolutely blank. "Rudy? This is Kinsey. Where's Jonah?"

"Oh, hi, Kinsey. He's out of town. Took his family skiing for the holidays. It came up kind of sudden, but I thought he said he'd let you know. He never called?"

"I guess not," I said. "Do you know when he's expected back?"

"Just a minute. Let me check." He put me on hold and I listened to the Norman Luboff Choir singing "Hark, the Herald Angels Sing." Christmas was over. Hadn't anybody heard? Rudy clicked back in. "Looks like January third. You want to leave a message?"

"Tell him I hung myself," I said and rang off.

I have to confess that in the privacy of my own home, I burst into tears and wept with frustration for six minutes flat. Then I went to work.

The only line of attack I could think of was through Ash Wood. I hadn't spoken to her since high school, nearly fourteen years. I tried the directory. Her mother, Helen Wood, was listed and so was Lance, but there was no sign of Ash, which probably meant that she'd moved away or married. I tried the main house. A woman answered. I identified myself and told her I was trying to locate Ash. Often I tell lies in a situation like this, but the truth seemed expedient.

"Kinsey, is that really you? This is Ash. How are you?" she said. All the Wood girls have voices that sound the same; husky and low, underlaid with an accent nearly Southern in its tone. The inflection was distinct, not a drawl, but an indolence. Their mother was from Alabama, if my memory hadn't failed me.

"I can't believe my luck," I said. "How are you?"

"Well, darlin', we are in a world of hurt," she replied, "which is why I'm so glad to hear from you. Lance mentioned that he'd seen you at the plant last Friday. What's happening?"

"That's what I called to ask you."

"Oh Lord. I'd love to bring you up-to-date. Are you free for lunch by any chance?"

"For you . . . anything," I said.

She suggested the Edgewater Hotel at 12:30, which suited me. I'd have to change clothes first. My standard outfit consists of boots or tennis shoes, form-fitting jeans, and a tank top or a turtleneck, depending on the season. Sometimes I wear a windbreaker or a denim vest, and I've always got a large leather shoulder bag, which sometimes (but not often) contains my little .32. I was relatively certain Ashley wouldn't appear in public like this. I hauled out my all-purpose dress, panty hose, and low heels. One day soon, I gotta get myself something else to wear.

5

The Edgewater Hotel sits on twenty-three acres of ocean-front property, with lawns sweeping down to the sea. An access road cuts through, not ten feet from the surf, with a sea wall constructed of local sandstone. The architecture of the main building is Spanish, with massive white stucco walls, arched doorways, and deeply recessed windows. Horizontal lines of red tile define the roof. A glass-walled dining patio juts out in front, white umbrella tables sheltering the patrons from sunlight and buffeting sea winds. The grounds are landscaped with juniper and palm, hibiscus, bottle brush and fern, flower beds filled year round with gaudy annuals in hot pink, purple, and gold. The day was chill, the sky icy white and overcast. The drab olive-green surf was churned up by the outer fringes of a storm system that had passed us to the north.

The valet parking attendant was far too discreet to remark, even with a look, the battered state of my ancient car. I moved into the hotel lobby and down a wide corridor furnished with a series of overstuffed couches, interspersed with rubber plants. The ceiling overhead was wood-beamed, the walls tiled halfway up, sounds muffled by a runner of thick carpet patterned with flowers the size of dinner plates.

Ash had reserved a table in the main dining room. She was already seated, her face turned expectantly toward me as I approached. She looked much as she had in high school; pale-red hair, blue eyes set in a wide, friendly face mottled with freckles. Her teeth were very white and straight and her smile was engaging. I had forgotten how casually she dressed. She was wearing a blue wool jumpsuit with a military cut, and over it a bulky white sheepskin vest. I thought, with regret, of my jeans and turtleneck.

She was still maybe twenty pounds overweight, and she moved with all the enthusiasm of an ungainly pup, leaping up to hug me when I arrived at the table. There had always been a guileless quality about her. Despite the fact she came from money, she had never been snobbish or affected. Where Olive had seemed reserved, and Ebony intimidating, Ash seemed utterly unselfconscious, one of those girls everybody liked. In our sophomore year, we had ended up sitting in adjoining homeroom seats and we'd often chatted companionably before classes began. Neither of us was a cheerleader, an honor student, or a candidate for prom queen. The friendship that sprang up between us, though genuine, was short-lived. I met her family. She met my aunt. I went to her house and thereafter neatly bypassed her coming to mine. While the Woods were always gracious to me, it was obvious that Ash functioned at the top of the social heap and I at the bottom. Eventually the disparity made me so uncomfortable that I let the contact lapse. If Ash was injured by the rejection, she did a good job of covering it. I felt guilty about her anyway and was relieved the next year when she sat somewhere else.

"Kinsey, you look great. I'm so glad you called. I ordered us a bottle of Chardonnay. I hope that's okay."

"Fine," I said, smiling. "You look just the same."

"Big rump, you mean," she said with a laugh. "You're just as thin as you always were, only I half expected you to show up in jeans. I don't believe I ever saw you in a dress."

"I thought I'd act like I had some class," I said. "How are you? When I didn't find you listed in the phone book, I thought you'd probably gotten married or left town."

"Actually, I've been gone for ten years and just got back.

What about you? I can't believe you're a private detective. I always figured you'd end up in jail. You were such a rebel back then."

I laughed. I was a misfit in high school and hung out with guys known as "low-wallers" because they loitered along a low wall at the far end of the school grounds. "You remember Donan, the boy with the gold tooth who sat right in front of you in homeroom? He's an Ob-Gyn in town. Got his teeth fixed and went to med school."

Ash groaned, laughing. "God, that's one way to get your hand up a girl's skirt. What about the little swarthy one who sat next to you? He was funny. I liked him."

"He's still around. Bald now and overweight. He runs a liquor store up on the Bluffs. Who was that girlfriend of yours who used to shoplift? Francesca something."

"Palmer. She's living with a fellow in Santa Fe who designs furniture. I saw her about a year ago when I was passing through. God, she's still a klepto. Are you married?"

"Was." I held up two fingers to indicate the number of husbands who had come and gone.

"Children?" she asked.

"Oh God, no. Not me. You have any?"

"Sometimes I wish I did." Ash was watching me with shining eyes and somehow I knew anything I said would be fine with her.

"When did we see each other last? It's been years, hasn't it?" I asked.

She nodded. "Bass's twenty-first birthday party at the country club. You were with the most beautiful boy I ever saw in my life."

"Daniel," I said. "He was husband number two."

"What about number one? What was he like?"

"I better drink some first."

The waiter appeared with the wine, presenting the label

for her inspection before he opened it. She waved aside the ritual of the sniffing of the cork and let him go ahead and pour for both of us. I noticed that the waiter was smiling to himself, probably charmed as most people are by Ash's breezy manner and her impatience with formality. He was tall and slim, maybe twenty-six years old, and he told us about the specials as if we might want to take notes. "The sea bass is being served today with a green chili *beurre blanc*, gently poached first with fresh tomatoes, cilantro, lemon, and white wine, garnished with jalapeños and accompanied by a pine-nut rice pilau. We're also offering a fillet of coho salmon . . ." Ash made little mewing sounds, interrupting now and then for clarification of some culinary subtlety.

I let her order for us. She knew all the waiters by name and ended up in a long chat with ours about what we should eat. She settled on steamed clams in a broth with Pernod, a salad of field greens lightly dressed, and said we'd think about dessert if we were good girls and cleaned our plates.

While we ate, I told her about my connection to Wood/Warren and the irregularities that had come to light.

"Oh, Kinsey. I feel awful. I hope Lance isn't responsible for the trouble you're in."

"Believe me, I do, too. What's the story on him? Is he the type to burn down the family warehouse?"

Ash didn't leap to his defense as I'd expected her to. "If he did, I don't think he'd snitch on himself," she said.

"Good point. Who'd go after him like that?"

"I don't know. That whole situation got very screwed up once Daddy died. He was crazy about the boys, but Bass was a dilettante and Lance raised hell half the time."

"I seem to remember that. Your father must have had conniption fits."

"Oh, he did. You know how straight he was. Daddy had real strong ideas about parenting, but most of them were wrong. He had no idea how to implement them anyway. He wanted to control and mold and dominate but he couldn't even do that very well. Kids just don't behave like company employees. Daddy thought he'd have more control at home, but the truth was, he had less. Both Lance and Bass were determined to thwart him. Bass never has straightened out."

"He's still in New York?"

"Oh, he comes home now and then—he was here for a week at Thanksgiving—but for the most part, he's gone. New York, Boston, London. He spent a year in Italy and swears he's going back. Much as I love him, he's a waste of time. I don't think he's ever going to get his act together. Of course, Lance was that way for years. They're both smart enough, but they always partied hard and Lance had a few scrapes with the law. It drove Daddy up the wall."

The clams arrived. Each of us was presented with a plate piled high with small, perfect shells, swaddled in cloth to keep the broth piping hot. She speared a tender button of clam flesh and placed it on her tongue, her eyes closing in a near-swoon as she swallowed. I watched her butter a crescent of French bread and dip it in the bowl, sopping up clam liquor. As she bit into it, she made a little sound low in her throat like something out of an X-rated video.

"Your lunch okay?" I asked dryly.

"Fine," she said. "Good." She realized belatedly that I was teasing her and she smiled, her cheeks tinted becomingly with pink. "Someone asked me once which I'd rather have—sex or a warm chocolate-chip cookie. I still can't decide."

"Go for the cookies. You can bake 'em yourself."

She wiped her mouth and took a sip of wine. "Anyway, about the last six or seven years, Lance took hold, more or less, and started showing an interest in the business. Daddy was thrilled. Wood/Warren was Daddy's life. He loved us, but he couldn't manage us the way he did the business. By the time Bass came along, the last in line, Daddy'd pretty much given up any hopes for a successor."

"What about Ebony?"

"Oh, she's been passionate about the company since she was a kid, but she didn't believe Daddy'd ever let her have a hand in it. He was old-fashioned. A man leaves his business to his oldest son. Period. He knew Ebony was smart, but he didn't think she was tough enough, and he didn't think she'd stay with it. Women get married and have babies and spend money. That was his attitude. Women join the country club and play tennis and golf. They don't go head-to-head with chemical engineers and systems analysts. She even went off to Cal Poly and started working on an engineering degree, but Daddy made it clear it wouldn't help her cause, so she went to Europe and got married instead."

"Thus fulfilling his prophecy," I said.

"That's right. Of course, at that point, Daddy did a turnaround and swore he'd have left her the company if she'd stuck it out. She hated him for that, and I didn't blame her a bit. He was a real shit sometimes."

"She's back now, isn't she?"

"Right. She got home in August, minus Julian, which is no big loss. He was a dud if I ever saw one. A real bore. I don't know how she put up with him."

"Lance says she wants to take over."

"I've heard that, too, though it's not anything she talks to me about. I get along with Ebony, but we're not real close."

"What about Olive? Is she interested?"

"Peripherally, I guess. She married one of the chemical engineers who worked for Daddy. He's vice-president now, but they met when she was still in college and he'd just hired on."

"Is that Terry Kohler?"

She nodded. "You met him?"

"When I was out there. What's he like?"

"Oh, I don't know. Smart. Moody. Intense. Pleasant enough, but sort of humorless. Good at what he does. Crazy about her, I must say. He worships the ground she walks on. 'Slavish' is the word."

"Lucky girl. Is he ambitious?"

"He used to be. He wanted to go out on his own at one point and form his own company, but I guess it didn't work out. He kind of lost heart after that, and I don't know . . . being married to the boss's daughter probably takes the heat off."

"How does he get along with Lance?"

"They clash now and then. Terry's easily offended. You know the type. He gets his nose bent out of shape at the least little thing."

"What about John Salkowitz?"

"He's a sweetie. He's what Daddy wanted Lance to be."

"You said Lance had a couple of scrapes with the law. What was that about?"

"He stole some things from the plant."

"Really. When was this?"

"In high school. He came up with a scheme to make some money, but it didn't work out. It was part of an economics class and I guess his grade depended on how well he did. When he realized his little enterprise was failing, he stole some equipment—nothing big—but he tried to sell it to a fence. The guy got uneasy and called the cops."

"Not too smart."

"That's what pissed Daddy off, I suspect."

"Did he press charges?"

"Are you kidding? Of course. He said that was the only way Lance would ever learn."

"And did he?"

"Well, he got in trouble again, if that's what you mean. Lots of times. Daddy finally threw his hands up and sent him off to boarding school."

The subject veered off. We finished lunch, chatting about other things. At 2:00, Ash glanced at her watch. "Oh Lord. I've got to go. I promised Mother I'd take her shopping this afternoon. Come along if you like. I know she'd love to see you." She signaled for the check.

"I better take care of some other business first, but I do want to talk to her."

"Give us a call and come up to the house."

"Are you living there now?"

"Temporarily. I just bought a place of my own and I'm having some work done. I'll be staying with Mother for another six weeks."

When the check arrived, I reached for my handbag, but she waved me off. "I'll take care of it. I'll claim it as a business lunch and charge it off to the company. It's the least I can do with the bind you're in."

"Thanks," I said. I got Ebony's personal telephone number from her and we walked out together. I was relieved that the valet service brought her car first. I watched her pull away in a little red Alfa-Romeo. My car appeared. I tipped the fellow more than I should have and got in with care, humping myself onto the seat to avoid snagging my panty hose behind the knee. The valet slammed the door and I turned the key. Honest to God, it started right up and I felt a surge of pride. The damn thing is paid for and only costs me ten bucks a week in gas.

I drove home and let myself in the gate, steadfastly disregarding the yawning air of emptiness about the place. The winter grass seemed ragged and the dead heads on the zinnias and marigolds had multiplied. Henry's house stood silent, his back door looking blank. Usually the scent of yeast or cinnamon lies on the air like a heady perfume. Henry's a retired commercial baker who can't quite give up his passion for kneading dough and proofing bread. If he isn't in the kitchen, I can usually find him on the patio, weeding the flower beds or stretched out on a chaise inventing crossword puzzles filled with convoluted puns.

I let myself into my apartment and changed back into jeans, my whole body sighing with relief. I hauled the mower out of the toolshed and had a run at the yard, and then I got down on my hands and knees and clipped all the dead blossoms from the beds. This was very boring. I put the lawn mower away. I went inside and typed up my notes. As long as I was investigating in my own behalf, I decided to do it properly. This was boring, too.

Since Rosie's was closed, I ate dinner at home, preparing a cheese-and-pickle sandwich, which entertained me no end.

I'd finished the Len Deighton and I didn't have anything else in the house to read, so I switched on my little portable television set.

Sometimes I wonder if my personal resources aren't wearing a little thin.

6

Tuesday morning, I went into the gym at 6:00 A.M. As I no longer had an office to go to, I could well have waited until later in the morning, but I like the place at that hour. It's quiet and half empty, so there's no competition for equipment. The free weights are neatly reracked. The mirrors are clean and the air doesn't smell like yesterday's sweat socks. Weight-lifting apparatus are a curious phenomenon—machines invented to replicate the backbreaking manual labor the Industrial Revolution relieved us of. Lifting weights is like a meditation: intermittent periods of concentrated activity, with intervals of rest. It's a good time for thinking, as one can do little else. I did ab crunches first; thirty-five, then thirty, then twenty-five. I adjusted the bench on one of the Nautilus machines and started doing seated military presses, three sets, ten reps each, using two plates. The guys lift anywhere from ten to twenty plates, but I work just as hard, and I'm not really preparing for the regional body-building championship.

I was thinking back over the details of the frame-up . . . a clever piece of work, dependent on a number of events coming together just as they had. The phone call to Mac must have come from Ava Daugherty, but who put her up to it? Surely she didn't cook up that trouble by herself. Someone had access to the Wood/Warren file, and while it was possible that the office keys had been lifted from my bag, who at Wood/ Warren knew enough to make a mockup of a fire-department report? That must have been done by someone who knew the procedure at CF. Insurance investigations usually follow a format. An outsider simply couldn't guarantee that all the paper switching could be done in the necessary sequence. Darcy could have managed it. Andy might have, or even Mac. But why?

I worked through biceps and triceps. Since I jog six days a week, my prime interest in the gym is the three A's—arms, abs, and ass—a routine that takes forty-five minutes three times a week. I was finished by 7:15. I went home to shower and then I started out again, dressed in jeans, turtleneck, and boots. Darcy was due at work at 9:00, but I'd spotted her three days out of five having breakfast first, coffee and a Danish in the coffee shop across the street. She used the time to chitchat, read the newspaper, and do her nails.

There was no sign of her when I got there at 8:00. I bought a paper and settled into the back booth where she usually sits. Claudine came by and I ordered breakfast. At 8:12, Darcy came through the door in a lightweight wool coat. She stopped when she saw me, checked her stride, and slid into an empty booth halfway down. I picked up my coffee cup and joined her, loving the sour look that crossed her face when she realized what I was up to.

"Mind if I join you?" I asked.

"Well, actually, I'd prefer to have the time to myself," she said, avoiding my gaze.

Claudine arrived with a steaming plate of bacon and scrambled eggs, which she set down in front of me. Claudine is in her fifties, with a booming voice and calves knotted with varicose veins.

"Morning, Darcy. What'll you have today? We're out of cheese Danish, but I laid back a cherry in case you're interested."

"That's fine. And a small orange juice."

Claudine made a note and tucked her order pad in her

apron pocket. "Just a second and I'll bring you a coffee cup." She was gone again before Darcy could protest. I could see her do a quick visual survey, looking for an empty seat. The place was filling up rapidly and it looked like she was trapped.

While I ate, I studied her in a manner that I hoped was disconcerting. She eased out of her coat, making a big deal out of standing up so she could fold it just so. She's one of those women a glamour magazine should "make over" as a challenge to their in-house experts. She has baby-fine hair that defies styling, a high, bulging forehead, pale-blue eyes. Her skin is milky white and translucent, with a tracery of veins showing through like faded laundry marks. I'd heard Darcy's boyfriend was a mail carrier, dealing drugs on the side, and I wondered if he delivered junk mail and junk on the same run. I could tell I was ruining her day, which improved my appetite.

"I'm assuming you heard about the trouble I'm in."

"It'd be hard not to," she said.

I opened a plastic locket of grape jelly and spread half on a triangle of whole-wheat toast. "Got any ideas about who set me up?"

Claudine returned with a cup and saucer and the coffeepot. Darcy judiciously elected to refrain from comment until her cup was filled and mine had been topped off. When Claudine departed, Darcy's expression turned prim and her coloring altered like a mood ring, shifting down a grade from woeful to glum. Actually, the change was not unappealing. She's big on pastel shades, imagining, I suppose, that washed-out colors are somehow more flattering to her than bold ones. She wore a pale-yellow sweater about the hue of certain urine samples I've seen where the prognosis isn't keen. The pink in her cheeks gave her back an air of health.

She leaned forward. "I didn't do anything to you," she said.

"Great. Then maybe you can help."

"Mac told us specifically not to talk to you."

"How come?"

"Well, obviously, he doesn't want you to get information you're not supposed to have."

"Such as?"

"I'm not going to discuss it with you."

"Why don't I tell you my theory," I said sociably. I half expected her to stick her fingers in her ears and start singing aloud to drown me out, but I noticed that she was not completely uninterested and I took heart from that. "I suspect maybe Andy's at the bottom of this. I don't know what he's getting out of it, but it's probably some form of financial gain. Maybe somebody's throwing business his way, or giving him a kickback. Of course, it crossed my mind that it might be you, but I don't really think so at this point. I think if you'd done it you'd be friendly, to convince me of your goodwill, if nothing else."

Darcy opened a paper sugar packet and measured out half a teaspoon, which she stirred into her coffee. I went right on, talking aloud as if she were a pal of mine and meant to help.

"CF hires other outside investigators, so I'm imagining that any one of us could have been implicated. It was just my dumb luck that I was up at bat. Not that Andy wouldn't take a certain satisfaction from the fact. He's never been fond of me and he always hated it that Mac let me have office space. Andy wanted to knock the wall out and take that corner for himself. At any rate, I have to assume Lance Wood is the real focus of the frame, though I don't know why yet. What I'll probably do is try working both sides of the street here and just see where all the paths intersect. Should be fun. I've never worked for me before and I'm looking forward to it. Cuts down on the paperwork."

I checked her reaction. Those pale eyes were focused on mine and I could see that her mental gears were engaged.

"Come on, Darcy. Help me out," I coaxed. "What do you have to lose?"

"You don't even like me."

"You don't like me either. What's that got to do with it? We both hate Andy. *That's* the point. The guy's a shit-heel."

"Actually he is," she said.

"You don't think Mac had anything to do with it, do you?"

"Well, no."

"So who else could it be?"

She cleared her throat. "Andy has been hanging around my desk a lot."

Her voice was so low I had to lean forward. "Go on."

"It started the day Jewel left on vacation and Mac told him to farm out her work. Andy was the one who suggested you for the Wood/Warren fire claim."

"He probably thought it'd be easier to pressure me."

Claudine brought Darcy's OJ and the cherry Danish. Darcy broke the Danish into small pieces, buttering each with care before she popped it in her mouth. Jesus, maybe I'd have one.

She was just warming up on the subject of Andy Motycka, who was apparently no fonder of her than he was of me. "What irritates me," she said, "is that I got in trouble with Mac because Andy said the file sat on my desk for three days before it got to you. That's an outright lie. Andy took it home with him. I saw him put it in his briefcase Tuesday when the fire-department report came in."

"Did you tell Mac that?"

"Well, no. Why bother? It sounds like I'm trying to defend myself by pushing all the blame off on him."

"You're right. I found myself in the same position," I said. "Look, if Andy falsified the fire-department report, he probably did the dirty work at home, don't you think?"

"Probably."

"So maybe we can turn up some proof if we look. I'll nose around at his place if you'll try his office."

"He moved, you know. He's not at the house. He and Janice are in the process of splitting up."

"He's getting divorced?"

"Oh, sure. It's been going on for months. She's hosing him, too."

"Really. Well, that's interesting. Where's he living?"

"One of those condos out near Sand Castle."

I'd seen the complex: one hundred and sixty units across from a public golf course called Sand Castle, out beyond Colgate in the little community of Elton. "What about his office? Is there any way you could check that out?"

Darcy smiled for the first time. "Sure. I'll do that. It would serve him right."

I got her home number and said I'd call later. I paid both checks and took off, figuring it wouldn't be a good idea to get caught in Darcy's company. While I was downtown, I hoofed it over to the credit bureau and had a discreet chat with a friend of mine who works as a key-punch operator. I'd done some work for her years before, checking into the background of a certain seedy gent who had hoped to relieve her of a burdensome savings account. She'd had the bucks in hand to pay me, but I sensed that both of us would benefit from a little bartering—"professional courtesies," as they're known. Now I check out any new fellow in her life and, in return, she pirates occasional confirmation copies of computer runs. One drawback is that I have to wait until a periodic updating of the master file is scheduled, which usually happens once a week. I asked her to give me anything she had on Lance Wood and she promised me something in a day. On an impulse, I asked her to check out Andy Motycka while she was at it. Financial information on Wood/Warren I'd have to get from the local equivalent of Dun & Bradstreet. My best source of information was going to be California Fidelity itself, for whom Lance Wood had no doubt filled out countless forms in applying for coverage. I was hoping I could enlist Darcy's aid again on that one. It was amazing to me how much more appealing she seemed now that she was on my team. I trotted back to pick up my car.

As I pulled out of the parking lot behind the building, Andy was just pulling in, pausing while the machine stamped and spat a ticket through the slot. He pretended he didn't see me.

I drove back to my apartment. I'd never paid much attention to the looming importance of the office in my life. I conduct maybe 40 percent of all business in my swivel chair, telephone in the crook of my neck, files close at hand. Sixty percent of the time I'm probably on the road, but I don't like feeling cut off from my reference points. It puts me at a subtle disadvantage.

It was only 10:05 and the day loomed ahead. Out of habit, I hauled out my little portable Smith-Corona and started typing up my notes. That done, I caught up with some filing, prepared some bills for a couple of outstanding accounts, and then tidied up my desk. I hate sitting around. Especially when I could be out getting into trouble. I gave Darcy a call at CF and got Andy's new address and telephone number. She assured me he was sitting in his office even as we spoke.

I dialed his apartment and was reassured to hear the answering machine pick up. I changed into a pair of blue-gray slacks with a pale stripe along the seam and a matching pale-blue shirt with Southern California Services stitched around a patch on the sleeve. I added hard black shoes left over from my days on traffic detail with the Santa Teresa Police Department, tacked on a self-important key ring with a long chain, and grabbed up a clipboard, my key picks, and a set of master keys. I checked myself out in the mirror. I looked like a uniformed public servant just about to make a routine service check—of what, I wasn't sure. I looked like I could read meters and make important notes. I looked like I could verify downed lines and order up repair crews on the mobile phone in my county-owned maintenance vehicle. I hopped in my car and headed out to Andy's condominium for a little B & E.

7

The Copse at Hurstbourne is one of those fancy-sounding titles for a brand-new tract of condominiums on the outskirts of town. "Copse" as in "a thicket of small trees." "Hurst" as in "hillock, knoll, or mound." And "bourne" as in "brook or stream." All of these geological and botanical wonders did seem to conjoin within the twenty parcels of the development, but it was hard to understand why it couldn't have just been called Shady Acres, which is what it was. Apparently people aren't willing to pay a hundred and fifty thousand dollars for a home that doesn't sound like it's part of an Anglo-Saxon land grant. These often quite utilitarian dwellings are never named after Jews or Mexicans. Try marketing Rancho Feinstein if you want to lose money in a hurry. Or Paco Sanchez Park. Middle-class Americans aspire to tone, which is equated, absurdly, with the British gentry. I had already passed Essex Hill, Stratford Heights, and Hampton Ridge.

The Copse at Hurstbourne was surrounded by a high wall of fieldstone, with an electronic gate meant to keep the riffraff out. The residents were listed on a mounted panel beside a telephone handset with push-buttons, and an intercom. Each occupant was assigned a personal entry code that one had to have in order to gain admittance. I know because I tried several sequences at random and got nowhere. I pulled over and waited until another car approached. The driver punched in his code. When the gate rolled back, I tucked my car in behind his and sailed through. No alarms went off. I wasn't set upon by dogs. Security measures, like the property's pedigree, were largely in the minds of the marketing team.

There were maybe twenty buildings in all, eight units each, gray frame with white trim in a Cape Cod style, all angles, mullioned windows, and wooden balconies. Sycamore and eucalyptus trees still graced the terrain. Winding roads led in two directions, but it was clear that both came together in the same rear parking lot rimmed with carports. I found a visitor's space and pulled in, checking the building directory, which sported a plot map of units.

Andy Motycka's was number 364, located, happily, at the far reaches of the property. I took my clipboard and a flashlight and tried to look as officious as I could. I passed the recreational facility, the spa, the laundry rooms, the gym, and the sales office. There were no signs of children. Judging from the number of empty carports, my guess was that many of the residents were off at work somewhere else. Wonderful. A band of thugs could probably sweep through and clean the place out in half a day.

I moved around some Cape Cod-style garbage bins and went up a set of outside stairs to the second floor of building number 18. The landing of the apartment next door to Andy's was attractively furnished with shoulder-high ficus and assorted potted plants. Andy's porchlet was bare. Not even a doormat. The drapes were open, and there were no interior lights on. No sound of a television set, stereo, or toilets flushing. I rang the bell. I waited a decent interval, easing back slightly so I could check for tenants on either side. No signs of activity. It looked like I had the building to myself.

The front-door lock was a Weiss. I sorted through my key picks and tried one or two without luck. Picking a lock is time-consuming shit and I didn't feel I could stand out there indefinitely. Someone might pass and wonder why I was jiggling that length of thin metal in the keyhole and cursing mildly to myself. On an impulse I raised my hand and felt along the top of the doorjamb. Andy'd left me his key. I let myself in.

I dearly love being in places I'm not supposed to be. I can empathize with cat burglars, housebreakers, and second-story men, experiencing, as I've heard some do, adrenaline raised to a nearly sexual pitch. My heart was thudding and I felt extraordinarily alert.

I did a quick walking survey, eyeballing the two bedrooms, walk-in closets and both bathrooms, just to determine that no one was tossing the apartment but me. In the master bedroom, I opened the sliding glass door and the screen. I went out on the balcony that connected the two bedrooms and devised an escape route in case Andy came home unexpectedly. Against the side wall, around the corner to the right, was an ornamental trellis with a newly planted bougainvillea at its base. In a pinch, I could scamper down like an orangutan and disappear.

I eased back into the apartment and began my search. Andy's bedroom floor was densely matted with dirty clothes, through which a narrow path had been cleared. I picked my way past socks, dress shirts, and boxer shorts in a variety of vulgar prints. In lieu of a chest of drawers, he kept his clean clothes in four dark-blue plastic stacking crates. His newfound bachelorhood must be taking him back to his college days. None of the bins contained anything of interest. I spent fifteen minutes sliding my hand into all the coat pockets on his hanging rod, but all I came up with were some woofies, a handkerchief full of old boogers, and a ticket for a batch of cleaning he hadn't yet retrieved. The second bedroom was smaller. Andy's bicycle was propped against one wall, the back tire flat. He had a rowing machine, eight cardboard moving boxes, unlabeled and still taped shut. I wondered how long he'd been separated.

I'd met Andy's wife, Janice, at a couple of California Fidelity

office parties and hadn't thought much of her until I saw what
she'd left him with. The lady had really done a thorough
shakedown. Andy had always complained about her extrav-
agance, making sure we all knew she shopped at the best stores
in town. It was a measure of his success, of course, that she
could charge with impunity. What was clear now was that she
played for keeps. Andy'd been granted a card table, four
aluminum lawn chairs with webbed seats, a mattress, and some
flatwear with what must have been his mother's monogram.
It looked like Janice had been sticking it in the dishwasher
for years because the finish was dull and the silver plate was
worn off the handles.

The kitchen cabinets held paper plates and insulated cups,
along with a sorry assortment of canned goods. This guy ate
worse than I did. Since the condos were brand-new, the appliances were up-to-date and immaculate: self-cleaning oven,
big refrigerator (empty except for two six-packs of no-brand
beer) with an ice-maker clattering away, dishwasher, microwave, disposal, trash compactor. The freezer was stacked with
cartons of Lean Cuisine. He favored Spaghetti and Chicken
Cacciatore. A bottle of aquavit lay on its side and he had a
bag of frozen rock-hard Milky Way bars that were just an
invitation to break off a tooth.

The dining area was actually a simple extension of the small
living room, the kitchen separated by a pass-through with bi-
fold shutters painted white. There was very little in the way
of furnishings. The card table seemed to double as dining-
room table and home office. The telephone sat there, plugged
into the answering machine, which showed no messages. The
surface was littered with typing supplies, but there was no
typewriter in sight. His bottle of white-out was getting as sluggish as old nail polish. The wastebasket was empty.

I went back into the kitchen and slid open the compactor,
which was loosely packed, but full. Gingerly, I rooted through,

spotting crumpled sheets of paper about three layers down. I removed the liner and inserted a fresh one. I doubted Andy would remember whether he'd emptied his trash or not. He'd probably spent most of his married life being waited on hand and foot, and my guess was he took household chores for granted, as if the elves and fairies crept in at night and cleaned pee off the rim of the toilet bowl whenever he missed. I glanced at my watch. I'd been in the place thirty-five minutes and I didn't want to press my luck.

I closed and locked the sliding glass door again, made a final pass to see if I'd overlooked anything, and then let myself out the front, taking his trash bag with me.

By noon, I was home again, sitting on Henry's back patio with Andy's garbage spread around me like a beggar's picnic. Actually, the debris was fairly benign and didn't make me feel I needed a tetanus booster just to sort through. He was heavy into pickles, olives, anchovies, jalapeño peppers, and other foodstuffs in which no germs could live. There were no coffee grounds or orange peels. No evidence whatever that he ate anything fresh. Lots of beer cans. There were six plastic Lean Cuisine pouches, layers of junk mail, six dunning notices rimmed in red or pink, a notice of a Toastmaster's roast of a local businessman, a flyer from a carwash, and a letter from Janice that must have left him incensed, as he had crumpled it into a tiny ball and bitten down on it. I could see the perfect impression of his teeth in the wadded paper. She was bugging him about a temporary support check that was late *again*, said she, underlined twice and bracketed with exclamation points.

At the bottom of the bag was the back end of a pad of checks, deposit slips still attached, with the name of Andy's bank and his checking-account number neatly printed thereon. I saved that for future reference. I had set aside the crumpled papers that were shoved into the bag halfway down. I smoothed them out now—six versions of a letter to someone he referred to variously as "angel," "beloved," "light of my life," "my dar-ling," and "dearest one." He seemed to remember her anat-omy in loving detail without much attention to her intellect. Her sexual enthusiasms still had him all aflame and had thus, apparently, impaired his typing skills—lots of strikeovers in the lines where he reviewed their "time together," which I gathered was on or about Christmas Eve. In recalling the experience, he seemed to struggle with a paucity of adjectives, but the verbs were clear enough.

"Well, Andy, you old devil," I murmured to myself.

He said he longed to have her suckle the something-something from his xxxxxxx . . . all crossed out. My guess was that it was related to flower parts and that his botanical knowledge had failed him. Either that or the very idea had caused emotional dyslexia. Also, he couldn't quite decide what tone to take. He vacillated somewhere between groveling and reverential. He said several things about her breasts that made me wonder if she might benefit from surgical reduction. It was embarrassing reading, but I tried not to shrink from my responsibilities.

Having finished, I made a neat packet of all the papers. I'd make a separate holding file for them until I could decide if any might be of use. I shoved the trash back in the bag and tossed it in Henry's garbage can. I let myself into my apart-ment and checked my answering machine. There was one message.

"Hi, Kinsey. This is Ash. Listen, I talked to my mother yesterday about this business with Lance and she'd like to meet with you, if that's okay. Give me a call when you get in and we'll set something up. Maybe this afternoon sometime if that works for you. Thanks. Talk to you soon. Bye."

I tried the number at the house, but the line was busy. I changed into my jeans and made myself some lunch.

By the time I got through to Ash, her mother was resting

and couldn't be disturbed, but I was invited to tea at 4:00.

I decided to drive up the pass to the gun club and practice target shooting with the little .32 I keep locked in my top desk drawer in an old sock. I shoved the gun, clip, and a box of fifty cartridges into a small canvas duffel and tucked it in the trunk of my car. I stopped for gas and then headed north on 101 to the junction of 154, following the steep road that zig-zags up the mountainside. The day was chilly. We'd had several days of unexpected rain and the vegetation was a dark green, blending in the distance to an intense navy blue. The clouds overhead were a cottony white with ragged underpin-nings, like the torn lining on the underside of an old box spring. As the road ascended, fog began to mass and dissipate, traffic slowing to accommodate the fluctuating visibility. I downshifted twice and pulled the heater on.

At the summit, I turned left onto a secondary road barely two lanes wide, which angled upward, twisting half a mile into back country. Massive boulders, mantled in dark-green moss, lined the road, where the overhanging trees blocked out the sun. The trunks of the live oaks were frosted with fungus the color of a greened-out copper roof. I could smell heather and bay laurel and the frail scent of woodsmoke drifting from the cabins tucked in along the ridge. Where the roadside dropped away, the canyons were blank with fog. The wide gate to the gun club was open and I drove the last several hundred yards, pulling into the gravel parking lot, deserted except for a lone station wagon. Aside from the man in charge, I was the only person there.

I paid my four bucks and followed him down to the cinder-block shed that housed the restrooms. He opened the padlock to the storage room and extracted an oblong of cardboard mounted on a piece of lathing, with a target stapled to it.

"Visibil'ty might be tough now in this fog," he warned.

"I'll chance it," I said.

He eyed me with misgiving, but finally handed over the target, a staple gun, and two additional targets.

I hadn't been up to the practice range for months, and it was nice to have the whole place to myself. The wind had picked up and mist was being blown across concrete bunkers like something in a horror movie. I set up the target at a range of twenty-five yards. I inserted soft plastic earplugs and then put on hearing protectors over them. All outside noises were damped down to a mild hush, my breathing audible in my own head as though I were swimming. I loaded eight cartridges into the clip of my .32 and began to fire. Each round sounded like a balloon popping somewhere close by, followed by the characteristic whiff of gunpowder I so love.

I moved up to the target and checked to see where I was hitting. High and left. I circled the first eight holes with a Magic Marker, went back to the bench rest and loaded the gun again. A sign just behind me read: "Guns as we use them here are a source of pleasure and entertainment, but one moment of carelessness or foolishness can bring it all to an end forever." Amen, I thought.

The hard-packed dirt just in front of me was as littered with shells as a battlefield. I saved my brass, collecting the casings after each firing, tucking them neatly back into the Styrofoam brick that cradled the live rounds.

By 3:15 I was cold, and most of my ammunition was gone. I can't claim that my little semiautomatic is wildly accurate at twenty-five yards, but at least I was feeling connected to the process again.

8

At 3:55, I was turning into the circular drive to the Wood family home, located on seven acres of land that sat on the bluffs overlooking the Pacific. Their fortunes on the rise, they'd moved since I'd last visited. This house was enormous, done in a French Baroque style—a two-story central structure flanked by two prominent tower wings. The stucco exterior was as smooth and white as frosting on a wedding cake, roofline and windows edged with plaster garlands, rosettes, and shell motifs that might have been piped out of a pastry tube. A brick walk led from the driveway around to the seaward-facing front of the house and up two steps to a wide, uncovered brick porch. A series of arched French doors spanned the facade, which curved outward around a conservatory on one end and a gazebo on the other. A heavy black woman in a white uniform admitted me. I followed her, like a stray pup, across a foyer tiled in black and white marble squares.

"Mrs. Wood asked if you'd wait in the morning room," the maid said, without pausing for a reply. She departed on thick crepe soles that made no sound on the polished parquet floors.

Oh, sure, I thought, that's where I usually hang out at my place . . . the morning room, where else?

The walls were apricot, the ceiling a high dome of white. Large Boston ferns were arranged on stands between high curving windows through which light streamed. The furniture was French Provincial; round table, six chairs with cane backs. The circle of Persian carpeting was a pale blend of

peach and green. I stood at one of the windows, looking out
at the rolling sweep of the grounds (which is what rich people
call their yards). The C-shape of the room cupped a view of
the ocean in its lower curve and a view of the mountains in
its hook, so that the windows formed a cyclorama. Sky and
sea, pines, a pie wedge of city, clouds spilling down the distant
mountainside . . . all of it was perfectly framed, wheeling gulls
picked out in white against the dark hills to the north.

What I love about the rich is the silence they live in—the
sheer magnitude of space. Money buys light and high ceilings,
six windows where one might actually do. There was no dust,
no streaks on the glass, no scuff marks on the slender bowed
legs of the matching French Provincial chairs. I heard a whisper of sound, and the maid returned with a rolling serving
cart, loaded with a silver tea service, a plate of assorted tea
sandwiches, and pastries the cook had probably whipped up
that day.

"Mrs. Wood will be right with you," she said to me.

"Thanks," I said. "Uh, is there a lavatory close by?" "Bathroom" seemed like too crude a term.

"Yes, ma'am. Turn left into the foyer. Then it's the first
door on the left."

I tiptoed to the loo and locked myself in, staring at my
reflection in the mirror with despair. Of course, I was dressed
wrong. I never could guess right when it came to clothes. I'd
gone to the Edgewater Hotel in my all-purpose dress to eat
lunch with Ashley, who'd worn an outfit suitable for bagging
game. Now I had down-dressed to the point where I looked
like a bum. I didn't know what I'd been thinking of. I knew
the Woods had money. I'd just forgotten how much. The
trouble with me is I have no class. I was raised in a two-
bedroom stucco bungalow, maybe eight hundred and fifty
square feet of space, if you counted the little screened-in utility
porch. The yard was a tatty fringe of crabgrass surrounded

by the kind of white picket fence you bought in sections and stuck in the ground where you would. My aunt's notion of "day-core" was a pink plastic flamingo standing on one foot, which I'd thought was pretty classy shit until I was twelve.

I blocked the bathroom out of my visual field, but not before I got a glimpse of marble, pale-blue porcelain, and gold-plated hardware. A shallow dish held six robin's-egg-sized ovals of soap that had never been touched before by human hands. I peed and then just ran my hands under the water and shook them off, not wanting to soil anything. The terry hand towels looked as though they'd just had the price tags removed from the rims. There were four guest towels laid out beside the basin like big decorative paper napkins, but I was way too smart to fall for that trick. Where would I put a used one afterward—in the trash? These people didn't make trash. I finished drying my hands on the backside of my jeans and returned to the morning room feeling damp around the rear. I didn't dare sit down.

Presently, Ash appeared with Mrs. Wood holding on to her arm. The woman walked slowly, with a halting gait, as if she'd been forced to ambulate with a pair of swim fins for shoes. I was startled to realize she must be in her early seventies, which meant that she'd had her children rather late. Seventy isn't that old out here. People in California seem to age at a different rate than the rest of the country. Maybe it's the passion for diet and exercise, maybe the popularity of cosmetic surgery. Or maybe we're afflicted with such a horror of aging that we've halted the process psychically. Mrs. Wood apparently hadn't developed the knack. The years had knocked her flat, leaving her knees weak and her hands atremble, a phenomenon that seemed to cause her bitter amusement. She appeared to watch her own progress as if she were having an out-of-body experience.

"Hello, Kinsey. It's been a long time," she said. She lifted her face to mine at that point, her gaze dark and snappish. Whatever energy had been drained from her limbs was being concentrated now in her eyes. She had high cheekbones and a strong chin. The skin hung from her face like tissue-thin kid leather, lined and seamed, yellowing with the years like a pair of cotillion gloves. Like Ashley, she was big: wide through the shoulders, thick through the waist. Like Ash, too, she might have been a redhead in her youth. Now her hair was a soft puff of white, gathered on top and secured by a series of tortoiseshell combs. Her clothes were beautifully made— a softly draped kimono of navy silk over a dark red silk wrap-around dress. Ashley helped her into a chair, pulling the tea cart within range so her mother could supervise the pouring of tea.

Ash glanced over at me. "Would you prefer sherry? The tea is Earl Grey."

"Tea's fine."

Ash poured three cups of tea while Helen selected a little plate of cookies and finger sandwiches for each of us. White bread spread with butter, sprigs of watercress peeping out. Wheat bread with curried chicken salad. Rye layered with herbed cream cheese and lox. There was something about the ritual attention to detail that made me realize neither of them cared what I was wearing or whether my social status was equivalent to theirs.

Ashley flashed me a smile when she handed me my tea. "Mother and I live for this," she said, dimples appearing.

"Oh, yes," Helen said, with a smile. "Food is my last great vice and I intend to sin incessantly as long as my palate holds out."

We munched and sipped tea and laughed and chatted about old times. Helen told me that both she and Woody had sprung from the commonplace. His father had owned a hardware store in town for years. Her father was a stonemason. Each had inherited a modest sum which they'd pooled to form Wood/Warren sometime in the forties. The money they'd amassed was all fun and games as far as they were concerned. Woody was dead serious about the running of the company, but the profits had seemed like a happy accident. Helen said he'd carried nearly two million dollars' worth of life insurance on himself, considering it a hot joke as it was the only investment he knew of with a guaranteed payoff.

At 5:00, Ash excused herself, leaving the two of us alone.

Helen's manner became brisk. "Now tell me about this business with Lance."

I brought her up-to-date. Ash had apparently filled her in, but Helen wanted to hear it all again from me.

"I want you to work for me," she said promptly when I finished.

"I can't do that, Helen. For starters, my attorney doesn't want me anywhere near Lance, and I certainly can't accept employment from the Wood family. It already looks like I'm being paid off."

"I want to know who's behind this," she said.

"So do I. But suppose it turns out to be one of you. I don't mean to offend, but we can't rule that out."

"Then we'd have to put a stop to it. I don't like underhanded dealings, especially when people outside the company are affected. Will you keep me informed?"

"If it's practical, of course. I'm willing to share anything I find. For once, I don't have a client to protect."

"Tell me how I can help."

"Fill me in on the details of Woody's will, if that's not too personal. How was his estate divided? Who controls the company?"

A flash of irritation crossed her face. "That was the only thing we argued about. He was determined to leave the business to Lance, which I didn't disagree with in principle. Of all the children, Lance seemed to be the best qualified to carry on once his father was gone. But I felt Woody should have given him the clout to go with it. Woody wouldn't do it. He absolutely refused to give him control."

"Meaning what?"

"Fifty-one percent of the stock, that's what. I said, 'Why give him the position if you won't give him the power to go along with it? Let the boy run it his way, for God's sake, you old goat!' But Woody wouldn't hear of it. Wouldn't even *consider* the possibility. I was livid, but that old fool wouldn't budge. Lord, he could be stubborn when he made his mind up."

"What was he so worried about?"

"He was afraid Lance would run the business into the ground. Lance's judgment *is* sometimes faulty. I'd be the first to admit it. He doesn't seem to have a feel for the market like Woody did. He doesn't have the relationships with suppliers or customers, not to mention employees. Lance is impetuous and he has very grandiose schemes that never quite pan out. He's better now, but those last few years before Woody died, Lance would go off on a tear, all obsessed with some muddleheaded idea he'd got hold of. While Woody was alive, he could rein him in, but he was petrified that Lance would make a disastrous mistake."

"Why leave him the company in the first place? Why not put someone he trusted at the helm?"

"I suggested that myself, but he wouldn't hear of it. It had to be one of the boys, and Lance was the logical choice. Bass was . . . well, you know Bass. He had no desire to follow in Woody's footsteps unless they led straight to the bank."

"What about Ebony? Ash mentioned she was interested."

"I suppose she was, but by the time Woody made out this last will of his, she was off in Europe and showed no signs of coming back."

"How was the stock divided?"

"Lance has forty-eight percent. I have nine, our attorney has three percent, and Ebony, Olive, Ash, and Bass each have ten."

"An odd division, isn't it?"

"It's set up so Lance can't act alone. To make up a majority, he has to persuade at least one of us that what he's proposing makes good business sense. For the most part he's free to do as he sees fit, but we can always rally and outvote him in a pinch."

"That must drive him crazy."

"Oh, he hates it, but I must say I begin to see Woody's point. Lance is young yet and he's not that experienced. Let him get a few years under his belt and then we'll see how things stand."

"Then the situation could change?"

"Well, yes, depending on what happens to my shares when I die. Woody left that entirely up to me. All I have to do is leave three shares to Lance. That would make him a majority stockholder. No one could touch him."

"Sounds like the stuff of which soap operas are made."

"I can wield power like a man if it comes to that. Next to eating, it's what I enjoy best." She glanced at the watch that was pinned to her dress, then reached over to the wall and pressed a button that apparently signaled the maid somewhere in the house. "Time for my swim. Would you care to join me? We have extra suits and I'd enjoy the company. I can still do a mile, but it bores me to death."

"Maybe another time. I tend to be a land animal, given my choice." I got up and shook her hand. "Tea was lovely. Thanks for the invitation."

"Come again, any time. Meanwhile, I'll see that Ebony and Olive give you any information you need."

"I'd appreciate that. I'll see myself out."

As I moved toward the foyer, the maid was returning with a portable wheelchair.

Behind her the front door opened, and Ebony came in. I hadn't seen her since I was seventeen. She must have been twenty-five then, which seemed very mature and sophisticated to me. She still had the power to intimidate. She was tall, rail-thin, high cheekbones, dark-red lipstick. Her hair was jet-black and pulled back dramatically, worn with a bow at her neck. She'd gone to Europe originally as a fashion model and she still walked like she was whipping down a runway. She'd been at Cal Poly for two years, had quit, had tried photography, dance, design school, and free-lance journalism before she turned to modeling. She'd been married maybe six years to a man whose name had recently been linked with Princess Caroline of Monaco. As far as I knew, Ebony had no children and, at forty, seemed an unlikely prospect for motherhood.

She paused when she caught sight of me, and for a moment I wasn't sure if she remembered who I was. She flicked me a chill smile and continued toward the stairs.

"Hello, Kinsey. Come upstairs. I think we should talk."

I followed her. She was wearing a wide-shouldered black suit, nipped in at the waist, a stark white shirt, knee-high glossy black boots with heels sharp enough to pierce a cheap floor covering. She smelled of a high-powered perfume, dark and intense, faintly unpleasant at close range. A trail of it wafted back at me like diesel fuel. This was going to give me a headache, I could tell. I was already annoyed by her attitude, which was peremptory at best.

The second floor was carpeted in pale beige, a wool pile so dense I felt as if we were slogging through dry sand. The hallway was wide enough to accommodate a settee and a massive antique armoire. It surprised me somehow that she was living at home. Maybe, like Ash, she was here temporarily until she found a permanent residence somewhere else.

She opened a bedroom door and stepped back, waiting for me to pass in front of her. She should have been a school principal, I thought. With a tiny whip, she could have done a thriving trade in dominance. As soon as I'd entered the room, she closed the door and leaned against it, still holding on to the knob at the small of her back. Her complexion was fine, loose powder lending a matte finish to her face, like the pale cast of hoarfrost.

9

There was an alcove to the left, done up as a little sitting room with a coffee table and two easy chairs. "Sit down," she said.

"Why don't you just tell me what you want and let's get on with it?"

She shrugged and crossed the room. She leaned down and plucked a cigarette from the crystal box on the coffee table. She sat down in one of the upholstered chairs. She lit her cigarette. She blew the smoke out. Every gesture was separate and deliberate, designed to call maximum attention to herself.

I moved to the door and opened it. "Thanks for the trip upstairs. It's been swell," I said, as I started out the door.

"Kinsey, wait. Please."

I paused, looking back at her.

"I'm sorry. I apologize. I know I'm rude."

"I don't care if you're rude, Ebony. Just pick up the pace a bit."

Her smile was wintry. "Please sit, if you would."

I sat down.

"Would you like a martini?" She set her burning cigarette in the ashtray and opened a small refrigerator unit built into the coffee table. She extracted chilled glasses, a jar of pitted green olives, and a bottle of gin. There was no vermouth in sight. Her nails were so long they had to be fake, but they allowed her to extract the olives without getting her fingers wet. She inserted an acrylic tip and pierced the olives one by one, lifting them out. I watched her pour gin with a glint in her eye that suggested a thirst springing straight from her core.

She handed me a drink. "What happened with you and Lance?"

"Why do you ask?"

"Because I'm curious. The company's affected by whatever affects him. I want to know what's going on." She picked up her cigarette again and took a deep drag. I could tell the nicotine and alcohol were soothing some inner anxiety.

"He knows as much as I do. Why don't you ask him?"

"I thought you might tell me, as long as you're here."

"I'm not sure that's such a good idea. He seems to think you're part of it."

Her smile returned, but it held no mirth. "In this family, I'm not part of anything. I wish I were."

I felt another surge of impatience. I said, "Jesus, let's quit fencing. I hate conversations like this. Here's the deal. Someone set me up and I don't like it. I have no idea why and I don't much give a shit, but I'm going to find out who it was. At the moment I'm self-employed, so the only client I have to answer to is me. If you want information, hire a private detective. My services are spoken for."

Her expression hardened like plaster of Paris, dead white. I suspected if I reached out to touch her, her skin would have had the same catalytic heat. "I hoped you'd be reasonable."

"What for? I don't know what's going on, and what I've seen so far, I don't like. For all I know, you're at the bottom of this or you know who is."

"You don't mince words, do you?"

"Why should I mince words? I don't work for you."

"I made a simple inquiry. I can see you've decided to take offense." She stubbed out her cigarette at the halfway mark.

She was right. I was hot and I wasn't sure why. I took a deep breath and calmed myself. Not for her sake, but for mine. I tried again. "You're right. I'm out of line. I didn't think I was pissed off, but clearly I am. Somehow I've gotten caught up in family politics and that doesn't sit well with me."

"What makes you so sure it's family politics? Suppose it's someone outside the company?"

"Like who?"

"We have competitors like anybody else." She took a sip of her martini and I could see her savor the icy liquid as it flooded through her mouth. Her face was narrow, her features fine. Her skin was flawless and unlined, giving her the bland expression of a Madame Alexander doll. Either she'd already had plastic surgery or she'd somehow learned not to have the kinds of feelings that leave telltale marks. It was hard to imagine that she and Ash were sisters. Ash was earthy and open with a sunny disposition, generous, good-natured, easygoing, relaxed. Ebony was as lean as a whip, all edges—brittle, aloof, controlled, arrogant. It was possible, I thought, that the differences between them were related, in part, to their relative positions in the family constellation. Ebony was the oldest daughter, Ash the youngest. Woody and Helen had probably expected perfection of their first child. By the time they got down to Ash, and beyond her to Bass, they must have given up expecting anything.

Ebony touched the olive in her drink, turning it. She eased the fingernail into the hole and plucked it out, laying the green globe on her tongue. Her lips closed around her finger and she made a faint sucking noise. The gesture had obscene overtones and I wondered suddenly if she was coming on to me.

She said, "I don't suppose you'll tell me what Mother wanted."

I could feel my temper climb again. "Don't you people talk to each other? She invited me for tea. We had a few laughs about old times. I'm not going to run straight up here and spill it all to you. If you want to know what we talked about, ask her. When I find out what's going on, I'll be delighted to dump the whole thing in your lap. In the meantime, I don't think it's smart to run around telling everything I know."

Ebony was amused. I could see the corners of her mouth turning up.

I stopped what I was saying. "Have you got some kind of problem with that?"

She laughed. "I'm sorry. I don't mean to condescend, but you were always like this. All that energy. So fiery and defensive."

I stared at her, stumped for a response.

"You're a professional," she went on pleasantly. "I understand that. I'm not asking you to divulge any confidences. This is my family and I'm concerned about what goes on. That's my only point. If I can be of any help, just tell me how. If something you discover has a bearing on me, I'd like to hear about it. Is that so unreasonable?"

"Of course not. Sorry," I said. I circled back through our conversation, returning to something she'd said earlier. "You mentioned that the trouble might originate from someone outside the company. Were you talking in general or specific terms?"

She shrugged languidly. "General, really, though I do know of someone who hates us bitterly." She paused, as though trying to decide how to frame her explanation. "There was an engineer who worked for us for many years. A fellow named Hugh Case. Two years ago, a couple of months before my father died, as a matter of fact, he—um, killed himself."

"Was there a connection?"

She seemed faintly startled. "With Daddy's death? Oh, no, I'm sure not, but from what I'm told, Hugh's wife was convinced Lance was responsible."

"How so?"

"You'd have to ask someone else for the details. I was in

Europe at the time, so I don't know much except that Hugh shut himself up in his garage and ran his car until he died of carbon monoxide poisoning." She paused to light another cigarette and then sat for a moment, using the spent match to rake the ash into a neat pile in the ashtray.

"His wife felt Lance drove him to it?"

"Not quite. She thought Lance murdered him."

"Oh, come on!"

"Well, he was the one who stood to benefit. There was a rumor floating around at the time that Hugh Case intended to leave Wood/Warren and start a company of his own in competition with us. He was in charge of research and development, and apparently he was on the track of a revolutionary new process. The desertion could have caused us serious harm. There are only fifteen or so companies nationwide in our line of work, so the defection would have set us back."

"But that's ridiculous. A man doesn't get murdered because he wants to change jobs!"

Ebony arched an eyebrow delicately. "Unless it represents a crippling financial loss to the company he leaves."

"Ebony, I don't believe this. You'd sit there and say such a thing about your own brother?"

"Kinsey, I'm reporting what I heard. I never said *I* believed it, just that she did."

"The police must have investigated. What did they find?"

"I have no idea. You'd have to ask them."

"Believe me, I will. It may not connect, but it's worth checking out. What about Mrs. Case? Where is she at this point?"

"I heard she left town, but that might not be true. She was a bartender, of all things, in that cocktail lounge at the airport. Maybe they know where she went. Her name is Lyda Case. If she's remarried or gone back to her maiden name, I don't know how you'd track her down."

"Anybody else you can think of who might want to get to Lance?"

"Not really."

"What about you? I heard you were interested in the company. Isn't that why you came back?"

"In part. Lance has done some very foolish things since he took over. I decided it was time to come home and do what I could to protect my interests."

"Meaning what?"

"Meaning just what it sounds like. He's a menace. I'd like to get him out of there."

"So if he's charged with fraud, it won't break your heart."

"Not if he's guilty. It would serve him right. I'm after his job. I make no bones about it, but I certainly wouldn't need to go about it in an underhanded way, if that's what you're getting at," she said, almost playfully.

"I appreciate your candor," I said, though her attitude irritated me. I'd expected her to be defensive. Instead, she was amused. Part of what offended me in Ebony was the hint of superiority that underscored everything she did. Ash had told me Ebony was always considered "fast." In high school, she'd been daring, a dazzler and wild, one of those girls who'd try anything once. At an age when everyone else was busy trying to conform, Ebony had done whatever suited her. "Smoked, sassed adults, and screwed around" was the way Ash put it. At seventeen she'd learned not to give a shit, and now she seemed indelibly imprinted with an air of disdain. Her power lay in the fact that she had no desire to please and she didn't care what your opinion of her was. Being with her was exhausting and I was suddenly too tired to press her about the little smile that played across her mouth.

It was 6:15. High tea wasn't doing much for someone with my low appetites. I was suddenly famished. Martinis give me

a headache anyway and I knew I smelled of secondhand cigarette smoke.

I excused myself and headed home, stopping by Mc-
Donald's to chow down a quarter-pounder with cheese, large
fries, and a Coke. This was no time to torment my cells with
good nutrition, I thought. I finished up with one of those
fried pies full of hot glue that burns the fuck out of your
mouth. Pure heaven.

When I got back to my place, I experienced the same disconcerting melancholy I'd felt off and on since Henry got on
the plane for Michigan. It's not my style to be lonely or to
lament, even for a moment, my independent state. I like being
single. I like being by myself. I find solitude healing and I
have a dozen ways to feel amused. The problem was I couldn't
think of one. I won't admit to depression, but I was in bed
by 8:00 P.M. . . . not cool for a hard-assed private eye waging
a one-woman war against the bad guys everywhere.

10

By 1:00 the next afternoon, I had tracked Lyda Case by telephone to a cocktail lounge at the Dallas/Fort Worth airport, where she was simultaneously tending bar and hanging up in my ear with a force that made me think I'd have to have my hearing rechecked. Last May I'd been compelled to shoot someone from the depths of a garbage bin and my ears have been hissing ever since. Lyda didn't help this . . . especially as she said a quite rude word to me before she smacked the phone down. I was deeply annoyed. It had taken me a bit of doing to locate her and she'd already hung up on me once that day.

I'd started at 10:00 A.M. with a call to the Culinary Alliance and Bartenders Local 498, which refused to tell me anything. I've noticed lately that organizations are getting surly about this sort of thing. It used to be you could ring them right up, tell a plausible tale, and get the information you wanted within a minute or two. Now you can't get names, addresses, or telephone numbers. You can't get service records, bank balances, or verification of employment. Half the time, you can't even get confirmation of the facts you already have. Don't even bother with the public schools, the Welfare Department, or the local jail. They won't tell you nothin'.

"That's privileged," they say. "Sorry, but that's an invasion of our client's privacy."

I hate that officious tone they take, all those clerks and receptionists. They *love* not telling you what you want to know.

And they're smart. They don't fall for the same old song and dance that worked a couple of years ago. It's too aggravating for words.

I reverted to routine. When all else fails, try the county clerk's office, the public library, or the DMV. They'll help. Sometimes there's a small fee involved, but who cares?

I whipped over to the library and checked back through old telephone directories year by year until I found Hugh and Lyda Case listed. I made a note of the address and then switched to the crisscross and found out who their neighbors had been two years back. I called one after another, generally bullshitting my way down the block. Finally, someone allowed as how Hugh had died and they thought his widow moved to Dallas.

It worried me briefly that Lyda Case might be unlisted, but I dialed Information in Dallas and picked up a home phone number right away. Hot damn, this was fun. I tried the number and someone answered on the third ring.

"Hello."

"May I speak to Lyda Case?"

"This is she."

"Really?" I asked, amazed at my own cleverness.

"Who is this?" Her voice was flat.

I hadn't expected to get through to her and I hadn't yet made up a suitable fib, so I was forced to tell the truth. Big mistake. "My name is Kinsey Millhone. I'm a private detective in Santa Teresa, California. . . ."

Bang. I lost some hearing in the mid-range. I called back, but she refused to answer the phone.

At this point, I needed to know where she was employed and I couldn't afford to call every bar in the Dallas/Fort Worth area, if indeed that's the sort of work she still did. I tried Information again and picked up the telephone number of the Hotel and Restaurant Employees Union Local 353 in Dal-

las. I had my index finger poised to dial when I realized I
would need a ruse.

I sat and thought for a moment. It would help to have Lyda
Case's Social Security number, which might lend a little air of
credibility to my bogus pursuit. Never try to get one of these
from the Social Security Office. They're right up there with
banks in their devotion to thwarting you at every turn. I was
going to have to get the information through access to public
records of some sort.

I grabbed my handbag, a jacket, and my car keys and headed
over to the courthouse. The Registrar of Voters is located in
the basement, down a flight of wide red-tile steps with a
handrail made out of antique rope as big around as a boa
constrictor.

I followed the signs down a short corridor to the right,
pushing into the office through a glass door. Two clerks were
working behind the counter, but no one paid any attention
to me. There was a computer terminal on the counter and
I typed in Lyda Case's name. I closed my eyes briefly, offering up a small prayer to whichever of the gods is in charge
of bureaucracies. If Lyda had registered to vote any time
in the last six years, the revised form wouldn't show her Social Security number. That question had been deleted in
1976.

The name flashed up, line after line of green print streaking out. Lyda Case had first registered to vote October 14,
1974. The number of the original affidavit was listed on
the bottom line. I made a note of the number and gave it
to the clerk who had approached when she saw I needed
help.

She disappeared into a back corridor where the old files
are kept. She returned a few minutes later with the affidavit
in hand. Lyda Case's Social Security number was neatly filled
in. As a bonus, I also picked up her date of birth. I started

laughing at the sight of it. The clerk smiled and I knew from
the look we exchanged that she felt as I did about some things.
I love information. Sometimes I feel like an archaeologist, digging for facts, uncovering data with my wits and a pen. I made
notes, humming to myself.

Now I could go to work.

I went home again and picked up the phone, redialing the
Bartenders Local in Santa Teresa.

"Local Four-Ninety-eight," the woman said.

"Oh, hi," said I. "Who am I speaking to, please?"

"I'm the administrative assistant," she said primly. "Perhaps
you'll identify yourself."

"Oh, sorry. Of course. This is Vicky with the Chamber of
Commerce. I'm addressing invitations for the annual Board
of Supervisors dinner and I need your name, if you'd be so
kind."

There was a dainty silence.. "Rowena Feldstaff," she said,
spelling it out for me carefully.

"Thank you."

I dialed Texas again. The phone on the other end rang
four times while two women in teeny, tiny voices laughed
about conditions in the Inky Void. Someone picked up.

"Hotel and Restaurant Employees Local Three-Five-Three.
This is Mary Jane. Can I he'p you?" She had a soft voice and
a mild Texas accent. She sounded like she was about twenty.

"You sure can, Mary Jane," I said. "This is Rowena Feldstaff
in Santa Teresa, California. I'm the administrative assistant
for Bartenders Local Four-Ninety-eight and I'm trying to do
a status check on Lyda Case. That's C–A–S–E . . ." Then I
rattled out her date of birth and her Social Security number,
as though from records of my own.

"Can I have a number so I can call you back?" said the
ever-cautious Mary Jane.

"Sure," I said and gave her my home phone.

Within minutes, my phone rang again. I answered as Bartenders Local 498, and Mary Jane very kindly gave me Lyda Case's current place of employment, along with the address and phone number. She was working at one of the cocktail lounges at the Dallas/Fort Worth airport.

I called the bar and one of the waitresses told me Lyda would be there at 3:00 Dallas time, which was 1:00 where I was.

At 1:00, I called back and lost another couple of decibels' worth of hearing. Whoo, that lady was quick. I'd have to walk around with a horn sticking out of my ear at this rate.

If I'd been working off an expense account, I'd have hired myself out to the Santa Teresa airport and jumped on a plane for Dallas. I can be pretty cavalier with someone else's money. My own, I think about first, as I'm very cheap.

I hopped in my car and drove over to the police station. Jonah Robb, my usual source of illicit information, was out of town. Sergeant Schiffman, sitting in for him, was not all that swift and didn't really like to bend the rules, so I bypassed him and went straight to Emerald, the black clerk in Records and Identification. Technically she's not supposed to give out the kind of information I needed, but she's usually willing to help if no one's around to catch her.

I leaned on the counter in the reception area, waiting while she finished typing a department memo. She took her time getting to me, probably sensing that I was up to no good. She's in her forties, with a medium complexion about the color of a cigar. Her hair is cut very short and it curls tensely around her head, a glistening, wet-looking black with gray frizz at the tips. She's probably fifty pounds overweight and it's all solidly packed into her waist, her belly, and her rump.

"Uh-uhn," she said to me as she approached. Her voice is

higher than one would imagine for a woman her size, and it has a nasal cast to it, with just the faintest suggestion of a lisp. "What do you want? I'm almost afraid to ask."

She was wearing a regulation uniform, a navy-blue skirt and a white short-sleeved blouse that looked very stark and clean against the tobacco brown of her arms. The patch on her sleeve said Santa Teresa Police Department, but she's actually a civilian clerk.

"Hello, Emerald. How are you?"

"Busy. You better cut right down to what you want," she said.

"I need you to look something up for me."

"Again? I'm gonna get myself fired one of these days because of you. What is it?" Her tone was offset by a sly smile that touched off dimples in her cheeks.

"A suicide, two years back," I said. "The guy's name was Hugh Case."

She stared at me.

Uh-oh, I thought. "You know who I'm talking about?"

"Sure, I know. I'm surprised you don't."

"What's the deal? I assume it wasn't routine."

She laughed at that. "Oh, honey, no way. No waay. Uh-un. Lieutenant Dolan still gets mad when he hears the name."

"How come?"

"How come? Because the evidence disappeared, that's how come. I know two people at St. Terry's got fired over that."

Santa Teresa Hospital, St. Terry's, is where the hospital morgue is located.

"What evidence came up missing?" I asked.

"Blood, urine, tissue samples, the works. His weren't the only specimens disappeared. The courier picked 'em up that day and took 'em out to County and that's the last anybody ever saw of the whole business."

"Jesus. What about the body? Why couldn't they just redo the work?"

Emerald shook her head. "Mr. Case'd been cremated by the time they found out the specimens were missing. Mrs. Case had the ashes what-do-you-call-'em . . . scattered at sea."

"Oh, shit, you're kidding."

"No ma'am. Autopsy'd been done and Dr. Yee'd already released the body to the mortuary. Mrs. Case didn't want any kind of funeral, so she gave the order to have him cremated. He was gone. People had a fit. Dr. Yee turned St. Terry's upside down. Nothing ever did show. Lieutenant Dolan was beside himself. Now I hear they got this whole new policy. Security's real tight."

"But what was the assumption? Was it an actual theft?"

"Don't ask me. Like I said, lot of other stuff disappeared at the same time so the hospital couldn't say what went on. It could have been a mistake. Somebody might have thrown all that stuff out by accident and then didn't want to admit it."

"Why was Dolan involved? I thought it was a suicide."

"You know nobody will make a determination on the manner and cause of death until the reports come back."

"Well, yeah," I said. "I just wondered if the lieutenant had any initial doubts."

"Lieutenant always has doubts. He'll have some more he catches you sniffin' around. Now I got work to do. And don't you tell nobody I told you this stuff."

I drove over to the Pathology Department at St. Terry's, where I had a quick chat with one of the lab techs I'd dealt with before. She confirmed what Emerald had told me, adding a few details about the mechanics of the episode. From what she said, a courier from the coroner's office did a daily run in a blood-transport vehicle, making a sweep of labs and law-enforcement agencies. Specimens to be picked up were sealed, labeled, and placed in insulated cold packs, like picnic supplies. The "hamper" itself was stored in the lab refrigerator until the driver showed up. The lab tech would fetch the hamper. The courier would sign for the evidence and away he'd go. The Hugh Case "material," as she so fastidiously referred to it, was never seen again once it left the hospital lab. Whether it disappeared en route or after it was delivered to the coroner's lab, no one ever knew. The clerk at St. Terry's swore she gave it to the driver and she had a signed receipt to show for it. She assumed the hamper reached its destination as it had every day for years. The courier remembered putting it in the vehicle and assumed it was among the items delivered at the end of his run. It was only after some days had passed and Dr. Yee began to press for lab results on the toxicological tests that the disappearance came to light. By then, of course, as Emerald had indicated, Hugh Case's remains had been reduced to ashes and flung to the far winds.

I used one of the pay phones in the hospital lobby to call my travel agent and inquire about the next flight to Dallas. There was one seat left on the 3:00 shuttle from Santa Teresa to Los Angeles, arriving at LAX at 3:35. With a two-hour layover, I could pick up a United flight that would get me into Dallas that night at 10:35, CST. If Lyda clocked into the bar at 3:00 and worked an eight-hour shift, she should be getting off at 11:00. A delay at any point in the journey would get me there too late to connect with her. I couldn't get a flight back to Santa Teresa until morning anyway, because the airport here shuts down at 11 P.M. I was going to end up spending a night in Dallas in any event. The air fare itself was nearly two hundred bucks, and the notion of paying for a hotel room on top of that made me nearly giddy with anxiety. Of course, I could always sleep listing sideways in one of those molded-plastic airport chairs, but I didn't relish the idea. Also, I wasn't quite sure how I could contrive to eat on the ten bucks in cash I had on me. I probably couldn't even afford to retrieve my VW from the long-term parking lot when I got home again.

My travel agent, Lupe, was breathing patiently into my ear while I did these lightning-quick calculations.

"I don't want to bug you, Millhone, but you got about six minutes to make up your mind about this."

I glanced at my watch. It was 2:17. I said, "Oh hell, let's go for it."

"Done," she said.

She booked the seats. I charged the tickets to my United credit card, which I had just gotten paid off. Curses, I thought, but it had to be done. Lupe said the tickets would be waiting for me at the ticket counter. I hung up, left the hospital, and headed out to the airport.

My handsome travel wardrobe that day consisted of my boots, my ratty jeans, and a cotton turtleneck, navy blue with the sleeves only slightly stretched out of shape. I had an old windbreaker in the back seat of my car. Happily, I hadn't used it recently to clean off my windshield. I also keep a small overnight case in the back seat, with a toothbrush and clean underwear.

I boarded the plane with twelve minutes to spare and tucked my overnight case under the seat in front of me. The aircraft was small and all fifteen seats were occupied. A hanging curtain separated the passengers from the cockpit. Since I was only two seats back, I could see the whole instrument panel, which didn't look any more complicated than the dashboard of a new Peugeot. When the flight attendant saw me rubbernecking, she pulled the curtain across the opening, as if the pilot and copilot were doing something up there we were better off not knowing about.

The engines sounded like lawn mowers and reminded me vaguely of the Saturday mornings of my youth when I would wake late to hear my aunt out cutting the grass. Over the din, the intercom system was worthless. I couldn't hear a word the pilot said, but I suspected he was reciting that alarming explanation of what to do in the "unlikely" event of a water landing. Most planes crash and burn on land. This was just something new to worry about. I didn't think my seat cushion was going to double as a flotation device of any kind. It was barely adequate to keep my rear end protected from the steel-reinforced framework of the seat itself. While the pilot droned on, I looked at the plastic card with its colorful cartoon depicting the aircraft. Someone had placed two X's on the diagram. One said, "You are here." A second X out on the wing tip said, "Toilet is here."

The flight only took thirty-five minutes, so the flight attendant, who wore what looked like a Girl Scout uniform, didn't have time to serve us complimentary drinks. Instead, she whipped down the aisle, passing a little basket of Chiclets chewing gum in tiny boxes. I spent the flight time trying to get my ears to unpop, looking, I'm sure, like I was suffering from some kind of mechanical jaw disease.

My United flight left right on time. I sat in the no-smoking section being serenaded by a duet of crying babies. Lunch consisted of a fist of chicken breast on a pile of rice, covered with what looked like rubber cement. Dessert was a square of cake with a frosting that smelled like Coppertone. I ate every bite and tucked the cellophane-wrapped crackers in my purse. Who knew when I'd get to eat again.

Once we landed in Dallas, I grabbed up my belongings and eased my way toward the front of the plane as we waited for the jetway to thump against the door. The stewardess released us like a pack of noisy school kids and I dogtrotted toward the gate. By the time I actually hit the terminal, it was 10:55.

The cocktail lounge I was looking for was in another satellite, typically about as far away as you could get. I started running, grateful, as usual, that I keep myself fit. I reached the bar at 11:02. Lyda Case had left. I'd missed her by five minutes and she wasn't scheduled to work again until the weekend. I won't repeat what I said.

11

I had Lyda paged. I had passed a Traveler's Aid station, an L-shaped desk, where the airline-terminal equivalent of a candy-striper was posted. This woman was in her fifties, with an amazingly homely face: gaunt and chinless, with one eye askew. She was wearing a Salvation Army uniform, complete with brass buttons and epaulets. I wasn't sure what the deal was. Maybe distraught mothers of lost toddlers and foreign-speaking persons in need of Kaopectate were meant to garner spiritual comfort along with the practical kind. She was just shutting down her station for the night, and at first she didn't seem to appreciate my request for help.

"Look," I said, "I just flew in from California to speak with a woman who's on her way out of the terminal. I've got to catch her before she hits the parking lot, and I have no idea which exit she's using. Is there any way to have her paged?"

The woman fixed me with the one eye while the other moved to the one-page directory she kept taped to her desk top. Without a word, she picked up the phone and dialed. "What's the name?" she asked.

"Lyda Case."

She repeated the name and within moments I heard Lyda Case being paged to the Traveler's Aid station, Terminal 2. I was profuse in my thanks, though she didn't seem to require much in the way of appreciation. She finished packing up and, with a brief word, departed.

I had no idea if Lyda Case would show. She might have been out of the building by the time her name was called. Or she might have been too tired and cranky to come back for any reason. On an impulse, I rounded the desk and sat down in the chair. A man passed with a rolling suitcase that trailed after him reluctantly, like a dog on its way to the vet. I glanced at my watch. Twelve minutes had passed. I checked the top desk drawer, which was unlocked. Pencils, pads of paper, tins of aspirin, cellophane-wrapped tissue, a Spanish-language dictionary. I read the list of useful phrases inside the back cover. *"Buenas tardes,"* I murmured to myself. *"Buenas noches."* Good nachos. I was starving to death.

"Somebody paging me? I heard my name on the public-address system and it said to come here." The accent was Texan. Lyda Case was standing with her weight on one hip. Petite. No makeup. All freckles and frizzy hair. She was dressed in dark slacks and a matching vest—one of those all-purpose bartender uniforms that you can probably order wholesale from the factory. Her name was machine-embroidered on her left breast. She had on a diamond-crusted watch, and in her right hand she held a lighted cigarette, which she dropped and crushed underfoot.

"What's the matter, baby? Did I come to the wrong place?" Mid-thirties. Lively face. Straight little nose and a sharp, defiant chin. Her smile revealed crooked eyeteeth and gaps where her first molars should have been. Her parents had never gone into debt for *her* orthodontia work.

I got up and held my hand out. "Hello, Mrs. Case. How are you?"

She allowed her hand to rest in mine briefly. Her eyes were the haunting, surreal blue of contact lenses. Distrust flickered across the surface. "I don't believe I know you."

"I called from California. You hung up on me twice."

The smile drained away. "I thought I made it clear I wasn't interested. I hope you didn't fly all this way on my account."

"Actually, I did. You'd just gone off duty when I got to the lounge. I'm hoping you'll spare me a few minutes. Is there some place we can go to talk?"

"This is called talkin' where I come from," she snapped.

"I meant, privately."

"What about?"

"I'm curious about your husband's death."

She stared at me. "You some kind of reporter?"

"Private detective."

"Oh, that's right. You mentioned that on the phone. Who all are you working for?"

"Myself at the moment. An insurance company before that. I was investigating a warehouse fire at Wood/Warren when Hugh's name came up. I thought you might fill me in on the circumstances of his death."

I could see her wrestling with herself, tempted by the subject. It was probably one of those repetitious nighttime tales we tell ourselves when sleep eludes us. Somehow I imagined there were grievances she recited endlessly as the hours dragged by from 2:00 to 3:00. Something in the brain comes alive at that hour and it's usually in a chatty mood.

"What's Hugh got to do with it?"

"Maybe nothing. I don't know. I thought it was odd his lab work disappeared."

"Why worry about it? No one else did."

"It's about time then, don't you think?"

She gave me a long look, sizing me up. Her expression changed from sullenness to simple impatience. "There's a bar down here. I got somebody waiting, so I'll have to call home first. Thirty minutes. That's all you get. I worked my butt off today and I want to rest my dogs." She moved off and I followed, trotting to keep up.

We sat in captain's chairs at a table near the window. The night sky was thick with low clouds. I was startled to realize it was raining outside. The plate glass was streaked with drops blown sideways by a buffeting wind. The tarmac was as glossy as black oilcloth, with runway lights reflected in the mirrored surface of the apron, pebbled with raindrops. Three DC-10s were lined up at consecutive gates. The area swarmed with tow tractors, catering vehicles, boom trucks, and men in yellow slickers. A baggage trailer sped by, pulling a string of carts piled high with suitcases. As I watched, a canvas duffel tumbled onto the wet pavement, but no one seemed to notice. Somebody was going to spend an irritating hour filling out "Missing Baggage" claim forms tonight.

While Lyda went off to make her phone call, I ordered a spritzer for me and a Bloody Mary for her, at her request. She was gone a long time. The waitress brought the drinks, along with some Eagle Snack pretzels in a can. "Lyda wanted somethin' to snack on, so I brought you these," she said.

"Can we run a tab?"

"Sure thing. I'm Elsie. Give a holler if you need anything else."

Ground traffic was clearing and I saw the jetway retract from the side of the plane nearest us. On the runway beyond, an L-1011 lumbered by with a stripe of lighted windows along its length. The bar was beginning to empty, but the smoke still sat on the air like a visible smudge on a photograph. I heard high heels clopping toward the table, and Lyda was back. She'd peeled off her vest, and her white blouse was now unbuttoned to a point just between her breasts. Her chest was as freckled as a bird's egg and it made her look almost tanned.

"Sorry it took me so long," she said. "I got this roommate in the middle of a nervous breakdown, or so she thinks." She used her celery stalk to stir the pale cloud of vodka into the

peppered tomato juice down below. Then she popped the top
off the can of pretzels.

"Here, turn your hand up and lemme give you some," she
said. I held my hand out and she filled my palm with tiny
pretzels. They were shaped like Chinese pagodas encrusted
with rock salt. Her hostility had vanished. I'd seen that before—people whose mistrust takes the form of aggressiveness
at first, their resistance like a wall in which a sudden gate
appears. She'd decided to talk to me and I suppose she saw
no point in being rude. Besides, I was buying. With ten bucks
in my pocket, I couldn't afford more than thirty minutes'
worth of drinks anyway.

She had taken out a compact and she checked her makeup,
frowning at herself. "God. I am such a mess." She plunked
her bag up on the table and rooted through until she found
a cosmetics pouch. She unzipped it and took out various items,
and then proceeded to transform herself before my very eyes.
She dotted her face with liquid foundation and smoothed it
on, erasing freckles, lines, discolorations. She took out an
eyeliner and inked in her upper and lower lids, then brushed
her lashes with mascara. Her eyes seemed to leap into prom-
inence. She dusted blusher high on each cheek, lined the
contour of her mouth with dark red and then filled her lips
in with a lighter shade. Less than two minutes passed, but by
the time she glanced at me again, the rough edges were gone
and she had all the glamour of a magazine ad. "What do you
think?"

"I'm impressed."

"Oh, honey, I could make you over in a minute. You ought
to do a little more with yourself. That hair of yours looks like
a dog's back end."

I laughed. "We better get down to business if thirty minutes
is all I get."

She waved dismissively. "Don't worry about that. I changed my mind. Betsy's workin' on an overdose and I don't feel like going home yet."

"Your roommate took an overdose?"

"She does that all the time, but she never can get it right. I think she got a little booklet from the Hemlock Society and takes half what she needs to do the job. Then I get home and have to deal with it. I truly hate paramedics trooping through my place after midnight. They're all twenty-six years old and so clean-cut it makes you sick. Lot of times she'll date one afterwards. She swears it's the only way to meet nurturing men."

I watched while she drained half her Bloody Mary. "Tell me about Hugh," I said.

She took out a pack of chewing gum and offered me a piece. When I shook my head, she unwrapped a stick and doubled it into her mouth, biting down. Then she lit a cigarette. I tried to imagine the combination . . . mint and smoke. It was an unpleasant notion even vicariously. She wadded up the gum wrapper and dropped it in the ash-tray.

"I was just a kid when we met. Nineteen. Tending bar. I went out to California on the Greyhound bus the day I turned eighteen, and went to bartending school in Los Angeles. Cost me six hundred bucks. Might have been a rip-off. I did learn to mix drinks but I probably could have done that out of one of them little books. Anyway, I got this job at LAX and I've been working airport bars ever since. Don't ask me why. I just got stuck somehow. Hugh came in one night and we got talkin' and next thing I knew, we fell in love and got married. He was thirty-nine years old to my nineteen, and I was with him sixteen years. I knew that man. He didn't kill himself. He wouldn't do that to me."

"What makes you so sure?"

"What makes you sure the sun's coming up in the east ever' day? It just does, that's all, and you learn to count on that the way I learned to count on him."

"You think somebody killed him?"

" 'Course I do. Lance Wood did it, as sure as I'm sittin' here, but he's not going to admit it in a million years and neither will his family. Have you talked to them?"

"Some," I said. "I heard about Hugh's death for the first time yesterday."

"I always figured they paid off the cops to keep it hush. They got tons of money and they know ever'one in town. It was a cover-up."

"Lyda, these are honorable people you're talking about. They'd never tolerate murder and they wouldn't protect Lance if they thought he had anything to do with it."

"Boy, you're dumber than I am, if you believe that. I'm tellin' you it was murder. Why'd you fly all this way if you didn't think so yourself?"

"I don't know what to think. That's why I'm asking you."

"Well, it wasn't suicide. He wasn't depressed. He wasn't the suicidal type. Why would he do such a thing? That's just dumb. They knew him. They knew what kind of man he was."

I watched her carefully. "I heard he was planning to leave the company and start a business of his own."

"He talked about that. He talked about a lot of things. He worked for Woody fifteen years. Hugh was loyal as they come, but everybody knew the old man meant to leave the company to Lance. Hugh couldn't stand the idea. He said Lance was a boob and he didn't want to be around to watch him mess up."

"Did the two of them have words?"

"I don't know for sure. I know he gave notice and Woody talked him out of it. He'd just bid on a big government contract and he needed Hugh. I guess Hugh said he'd stay until word came through whether Woody got the bid or not. Two days later, I got home from work, opened the garage door, and there he was. It looked like he fell asleep in the car, but his skin was cherry red. I never will forget that."

"There's no way it could have been an accident?"

She leaned forward earnestly. "I said it once and I'll say it again. Hugh wouldn't kill himself. He didn't have a reason and he wasn't depressed."

"How do you know he wasn't holding something back?"

"I guess I don't, if you put it like that."

"The notion of murder doesn't make any sense. Lance wasn't even in charge at that point, and he wouldn't kill an employee just because the guy wants to move on. That's ludicrous."

Lyda shrugged, undismayed by my skepticism. "Maybe Lance worried Hugh would take the business with him when he went."

"Well, aside from the fact he wasn't gone yet, it still seems extreme."

She bristled slightly. "You asked for my opinion. I'm tellin' you what I think."

"I can see you believe it, but it's going to take more than that to talk me into it. If Hugh was murdered, it could have been someone else, couldn't it?"

"Of course it could. I believe it was Lance, but I can't *swear* to it. I don't have any proof, anyhow. Sometimes I think it's not worth foolin' with. It's over and done, so what difference does it make?"

I shifted the subject. "Why'd you have him cremated so fast?"

She stared at me. "Are you thinking *I* had a hand in it?"

"I'm just asking the questions. What do I know?"

"He *asked* to be cremated. It wasn't even my idea. He'd been dead for two days. The coroner released the body and the funeral director suggested we go ahead with it, so I took his advice. You can talk to him yourself if you don't believe me," she said. "Hugh was drugged. I'd bet money that's how they pulled it off. His lab work was stolen so nobody'd see the test results."

"Maybe he was drunk," I suggested. "He might have pulled into the garage and fallen asleep."

She shook her head. "He didn't drink. He'd given that up."

"Did he have a problem with alcohol?"

"Once upon a time, he did," she said. "We *met* in a bar. Two in the afternoon, in the middle of the week. He wasn't even travelin'. He just liked to come watch the planes, he said. I should have suspected right then, but you know what it's like when you fall in love. You see what you want to see. It took me years to figure out how far gone he was. Finally I said I'd leave him if he didn't straighten up. He went into this program . . . not AA, but something similar. He got sobered up and that's how he stayed."

"Is there a chance he'd gone back to drinking? It wouldn't be unheard of."

"Not with him on Antabuse. He'da been sick as a pup."

"You're sure he took the stuff?"

"I gave it to him myself. It was like a little game we played. Every morning with his orange juice. He held his hand out and I gave him his pill and watched him swallow it right down. He wanted me to see he didn't cheat. He swore, the day he quit drinking, he'd never go back to it."

"How many people knew about the Antabuse?"

"I don't know. He never made a big deal of it. If people around him were drinking, he just said 'No thanks.' "

"Tell me what was happening the week he died."

"Nothing. It seemed like an ordinary week to me. He talked to Woody. Two days later, he was dead. After the funeral, I packed up, put everything in a U-Haul, and hit the road for home. This is where I've been ever since."

"And there was nothing among his things to suggest what was going on? No letter? A note?"

She shook her head. "I went through his desk the day he died, and I didn't see a thing."

12

The flight home was uneventful. I'd spent an hour and a half with Lyda, and the rest of the night in the airport terminal with its red carpeting, high glass ceiling, real trees, and an actual bird that flew back and forth, chirping incessantly. It was sort of like camping out, only I was sitting upright and I didn't have any wienies to roast. I made notes of my conversation with Lyda, which I'd transcribe for the files when I got home. I was inclined to believe Hugh Case had been murdered, though I had no idea how, why, or by whom. I also tended to think his death was related to current events at Wood/Warren, though I couldn't imagine what the connection might be. Lyda had promised to get in touch if she remembered anything of note. All in all, it was not an unproductive trip. It had generated more questions than it answered, but that was fine with me. As long as there are threads to unravel, I'm in business. The frustration starts when all the leads dry up and the roads turn out to be dead ends. With Hugh Case, I felt like I'd just found one of the corner pieces of a jigsaw puzzle. I had no idea what the final picture would look like, but at least I had a place to start.

I boarded the plane at 4:30 A.M. and arrived at LAX at 5:45. I had to wait for a 7:00 A.M. shuttle to Santa Teresa, and by the time I dragged my sorry ass home, I was dead on my feet. I let myself into the apartment an hour later, checked for messages (none), pulled my boots off, and curled up in the folds of my quilt, fully dressed.

At approximately 9:02, there was a knock at my door. I staggered up out of sleep and shuffled to the door, dragging my quilt behind me like a bridal train. My mouth tasted foul and my hair was standing straight up, as spiky as a punker's, only not as clean. I peered through the fish-eye, too clever to be caught unawares by an early-morning thug. Standing on my doorstep was my second ex-husband, Daniel Wade.

"Shit," I murmured. Briefly, I leaned my head against the door and then peeked again. All I could see in truncated form was his face in profile, blond hair curling around his head like an aura. Daniel Wade is quite possibly the most beautiful man I've ever seen—a bad sign. Beautiful men are usually either gay or impossibly narcissistic. (Sorry for the generalization, folks, but it's the truth.) I like a good face or an interesting face or a face with character, but not this sculpted perfection of his . . . the straight, well-proportioned nose, high cheekbones, strong jawline, sturdy chin. His hair was sun-bleached, his eyes a remarkable shade of blue, offset by dark lashes. His teeth were straight and very white, his smile slightly crooked. Get the picture, troops?

I opened the door. "Yes?"

"Hi."

"Hello." I gave him a rude stare, hoping he'd disappear. He's tall and slim and he can eat anything without gaining weight. He stood there in faded jeans and a dark-red sweatshirt with the sleeves pushed up. His skin had a golden sheen, tanned and windburned, so his cheeks glowed darkly. Just another boring California golden boy. The hair on his arms was bleached nearly white. His hands were tucked in his pockets, which was just as well. He's a jazz pianist with long, bony fingers. I fell in love with his hands first and then worked my way up.

"I've been in Florida." Good voice, too . . . just in case his

other virtues fail to excite. Reedy and low. He sings like an
angel, plays six instruments.

"What brought you back?"

"I don't know. Homesick, I guess. A friend of mine
was heading this way so I tagged a ride. Did I wake you
up?"

"No, I often walk around looking like this."

A slight smile here, perfectly timed. His manner seemed
hesitant, which was unusual for him. He was searching the
sight of me, looking (perhaps) for some evidence of the girl
I used to be.

"I like the haircut," he said.

"Gee, this is fun. I like yours, too."

"I guess I caught you at a bad time. I'm sorry about that."

"Uh, Daniel, could we skip to the punch line here? I'm
operating on an hour's sleep and I feel like shit."

It was clear he'd rehearsed this whole conversation, but in
his mind my response was tender instead of downright rude.
"I wanted you to know I'm clean," he said. "I have been for
a year. No drugs. No drinking. It hasn't been easy, but I really
have straightened up."

"Super. I'm thrilled. It's about bloody time."

"Could you knock off the sarcasm?"

"That's my natural way of speaking ever since you left. It's
real popular with men."

He rocked slightly on his heels, looking off across the yard.
"I guess people don't get a second chance with you."

I didn't bother to respond to that.

He tried a new tack. "Look. I have a therapist named Elise.
She was the one who suggested I clean up the unfinished
business in my life. She thought maybe you might benefit,
too."

"Oh, hey. That's swell. Give me her address and I'll write
her a bread-and-butter note."

"Can I come in?"

"Jesus Christ, Daniel, of course not! Don't you get it yet? I haven't seen you for eight years and it turns out that's not long enough."

"How can you be so hostile after all this time? I don't feel bad about you."

"Why would you feel bad? I didn't do anything to you!"

A look of injury crossed his face and his bewilderment seemed genuine. There's a certain class of people who will do you in and then remain completely mystified by the depth of your pain. He shifted his weight. This apparently wasn't going as he thought it would. He reached up to pick at a wood splinter in the door frame above my head. "I didn't think you'd be bitter. That's not like you, Kinsey. We had some good years."

"Year. Singular. Eleven months and six days, to be exact. You might move your hand before I slam the door on it."

He moved his hand.

I slammed the door and went back to bed.

After a few minutes, I heard the gate squeak.

I thrashed about for a while, but it was clear I wouldn't get back to sleep. I got up and brushed my teeth, showered, shampooed my hair, shaved my legs. I used to have fantasies about his showing up. I used to invent long monologues in which I poured out my sorrow and my rage. Now I was wishing he'd come back again so I could do a better job of it. Being rejected is burdensome that way. You're left with emotional baggage you unload on everyone else. It's not just the fact of betrayal, but the person you become . . . usually not very nice. Jonah had survived my tartness. He seemed to understand it had nothing to do with him. He was so blunt himself that a little rudeness didn't bother him. For my part, I really thought I'd made my peace with the past until I came face to face with it.

I called Olive Kohler and made an appointment to see her later in the day. Then I sat down at my desk and typed up my notes. At noon, I decided to get some errands done. Daniel was sitting in a car parked just behind mine. He was slouched down in the passenger seat, his booted feet propped up on the dashboard, a cowboy hat tilted over his face. The car was a ten-year-old Pinto, dark blue, dented, rusted, and stripped of its hubcaps. The sheepskin car-seat covers looked like badly matted dog. A decal on the bumper indicated that the car was from Rent-A-Ruin.

Daniel must have heard the gate squeak as I came out. He turned his head, pushing his hat back lazily. He sometimes affects that aw-shucks attitude. "Feeling better (Miss Kitty)?"

I unlocked my car and got in, started the engine and pulled away. I avoided the apartment for the rest of the day. I can't remember now half of what I did. Mostly I wasted time and resented the fact that I was not only out an office but banned from my own residence.

At 5:00, with the aid of a street map, I found the Kohlers' house on an obscure leafy lane in Montebello. The property was hidden by a ten-foot hedge, the driveway barred by an electronically controlled wrought-iron gate. I parked out on the street and let myself in through a wooden gate embedded in the shrubbery. The house was a two-story, English Tudor style, with a steeply pitched shingled roof, half-timbered gables, and a handsome pattern of vertical beams across the front. The lot was large, shaded with sycamores and eucalyptus trees as smooth and gray as bare concrete. Dark-green ivy seemed to grow everywhere. A gardener, a graduate of the Walt Disney school of landscape maintenance, was visible, trimming the shrubs into animal shapes.

The newspaper was resting on the doormat. I picked it up and then I rang the bell. I expected a maid, but Olive opened the door herself in a gray satin robe and low-heeled satin mules. I'd mostly seen those in Joan Crawford movies, and they looked like they'd be a trick to wear. I had brief visions of plopping around my apartment in backless bedroom slippers. Cigarette holder. Marcelled hair. I could have my eyebrows plucked back to ogee arches.

"Hello, Kinsey. Come in. Terry's on his way. I forgot we were due at a cocktail party at six." She stepped away from the door and I followed her in.

"We can do this another time if you like," I said. I handed her the paper.

"Thanks. No, no. This is fine. It's not for an hour anyway and the people don't live far. I've got to finish dressing, but we can talk in here." She glanced at the paper briefly and then tossed it on the hall table next to a pile of mail.

She clattered her way along the dark stone-tile hallway toward the master suite at the rear of the house. Olive was slim and blond, her shoulder-length hair blunt-cut and thick. I wondered sometimes if Ash was the only sister whose hair remained its natural shade. Olive's eyes were bright blue, her lashes black, her skin tone gold. She was thirty-three or so, not as brittle as Ebony, but with none of Ash's warmth. She was talking back over her shoulder to me.

"I haven't seen you for ten years. What have you been up to?"

"Setting up my own agency," I said.

"Married? Kids?"

"No, on both counts. You have kids?"

She laughed. "God forbid."

The bedroom we entered was spacious. Beamed ceiling, big stone fireplace, French doors opening onto a walled-in patio where a small deck had been added on. I could see a round, two-person hot tub, surrounded by ferns. A white Persian cat was curled up on a chaise, its face tucked into the circling plume of its tail.

The bedroom floor was polished teak with area rugs of a long white wool that probably came from yaks. The entire wall behind the bed was mirrored and I flashed on an image of Terry Kohler's sexual performances. What did Olive stare at, I wondered, while he watched himself? I glanced at the ceiling, checking to see if there was a cartoon tacked up there, like the one in my gynecologist's examining room: "Smile. It gives your face something to do!" This does not amuse.

I eased into an easy chair and watched while Olive moved into a walk-in closet the size of a two-car garage. Quickly she began to sort through a rack of evening clothes, rejecting sequined outfits, floor-length organza gowns, beaded jackets with long, matching skirts. I could see an assortment of shoes stacked in clear plastic boxes on the shelf overhead, and at one end of the rack, several fur coats of various lengths and types. She selected a knee-length cocktail dress with spaghetti straps and returned to the bedroom where she scrutinized her reflection. The dress was avocado green, infusing her skin with sallow undertones.

"What do you think?" she said, eyes still pinned to her own image in the glass.

"Makes you look green."

She stared at herself, squinting critically. "You're right. Here. You take this. I never liked it anyway." She tossed the dress on the bed.

"I don't wear clothes like that," I said uncomfortably.

"Take it. We'll have a New Year's Eve party and you can wear it then." She pulled out a black taffeta dress cut straight across the front. She stepped into it, then zipped it up the back in a motion that snapped everything into place. She was so slender I didn't see how the globelike breasts could possibly be hers. She looked like she'd had softballs surgically implanted on her chest. Hug a woman like that and she was bound to leave dents.

She sat down on the dressing-table bench and pulled on black panty hose, then slipped her feet into four-inch black spike heels. She looked gorgeous, all curves and flawless skin, the pale-blond hair brushing against her bare shoulders. She sorted through her jewelry box and selected clip-on diamond earrings shaped like delicate silver branches hung with sparkling fruit.

She returned to the closet and emerged in a soft white fur coat the same length as the dress. When she pulled the coat around her, she looked like a flasher decked out in white fox.

She half smiled when she caught my look. "I know what you're thinking, sweetie, but they were already dead when I got to the furrier's. Whether or not I bought the coat had no effect on their fates."

"If women didn't wear them, they wouldn't be killed in the first place," I said.

"Oh, bullshit. Don't kid yourself. In the wild, these animals get torn to shreds every day. Why not preserve the beauty, like a piece of art? The world's a vicious place. I don't pretend otherwise. And don't argue with me," she said firmly. She pointed a finger. "You came to talk, so talk." She slipped the coat off and tossed it on the bed, then sat down on the bench and crossed her legs. She eased off one high heel and let her shoe flap against the bottom of her foot.

I said, "How much do you know about the situation at Wood/Warren?"

She gestured impatiently. "Business is a bore. I use that section of the paper to line the cat box."

"You have no interest in the family split?"

"What split? You mean with Lance? I have nothing invested one way or the other. He and Ebony disagree. She wants me to vote with her. The way she explains it, it's to my advantage. Lance will have a fit, of course, but who gives a shit? He's had his chance."

"You're siding with her?"

"Who knows? Probably. She's smarter than he is and it's time for new blood. He's got his head in the toilet half the time."

"Meaning what?"

"Let me give you the lowdown on my brother, honey-bun. He's a salesman at heart. He can charm your socks off when it suits him. He's enthusiastic about anything that interests him, which isn't much. He has no head for figures. Absolutely none. He hates sitting in an office and he can't stand routine. He's good at generating business and lousy at follow-through. End transmission."

"You've seen this firsthand or is this Ebony's claim?"

"I hear about what happens at the plant every day. Terry's a workaholic and most of what he talks about is business."

"How do he and Lance get along?"

"They knock heads all the time. Terry's obsessive. It drives him crazy when people fuck up. Excuse the scientific term. Lance has poor judgment. Everyone knows that. Meet the woman he married if you have any doubts."

"What about the rest of the family? Can't they vote him out?"

"Nope. The rest of us combined only own forty-nine percent of the stock. Ebony wants to put the squeeze on him, but she can't actually force him out. She can bring him to heel, which I suspect is what she wants."

"I take it Bass isn't involved since he lives in New York."

"He shows up for board meetings occasionally. He enjoys playing mogul, but he's harmless enough. He and Lance are usually thick."

"Who will Ashley side with?"

"She could go either way. Obviously, Ebony's hoping she can persuade us all to mutiny."

"How does your mother feel? This couldn't sit well with her."

"She hates it. She wants Lance in charge. Not because he's good, but because it's less hassle."

"Do you think he's honest?"

"Lance? Are you kidding? No way."

"How do you and he get along?"

"I can't stand him. He's a very tense person and he's soooo paranoid. I hate to be around him. He gets on my nerves. He's my brother and I love him, don't get me wrong. I just don't like him much." She wrinkled her nose. "He always smells like garlic and sweat and that nasty Brut cologne. I don't know why men wear it. Such a turnoff."

"Have you heard any gossip about the warehouse blaze?"

"Just what Terry's told me. You know Lance borrowed money against the company two years ago and now he's losing his shirt. He'd love half a million bucks."

"Oh really. That's the first I heard of it."

She shrugged carelessly. "He went into the printing business, which is foolish in itself. I've heard printing and restaurants are the quickest way to go broke. He's lucky the warehouse burned down. Or is that the point?"

"Why don't you tell me?"

She rested her elbow on her knee and propped her chin up on her fist. "If you're looking for answers, I've just run out. I don't care about Lance. I don't care about Wood/Warren, to tell you the truth. Sometimes the politics amuse me in a soap-opera kind of way, like *Dynasty*, but it's still boring stuff."

"What *do* you care about?"

"Tennis. Travel. Clothes. Golf. What else is there?"

"Sounds like a fun life."

"Actually, it is. I entertain. I do charity work when I have the time. There are people who think I'm a spoiled, lazy bitch, but I have what I want. That's more than most can say. It's the have-nots who wreak havoc. I'm a real pussycat."

"You're fortunate."

"Like they say, there's no such thing as a free ride. I pay a price, believe me."

I could see what an exhausting proposition that must be.

We heard someone at the entrance, then footsteps along the hall. By the time Terry Kohler reached the bedroom door, he was already in the process of removing his coat and tie.

"Hello, Kinsey. Olive mentioned you'd be stopping by. Let me grab a quick shower and then we can talk." He looked at Olive. "Could you fetch us a drink?" he said, his tone peremptory.

She didn't exactly perk up and pant, but that's the impression she gave. Maybe her job was harder than I thought. I wouldn't do that for anyone.

13

I waited in the living room while Olive stepped into the kitchen. The place was handsome: beveled windowpanes, pecan paneling, a fieldstone fireplace, traditional furniture in damask and mahogany. Everything was rose and dusty pink. The room smelled faintly spicy, like carnations. I couldn't imagine the two of them sitting here doing anything. Aside from the conventional good taste, there was no indication that they listened to music or read books. No evidence of shared interests. There was a current copy of *Architectural Digest* on the coffee table, but it looked like a prop. I've never known rich people to read *Popular Mechanics*, *Family Circle*, or *Road & Track*. Come to think of it, I have no idea what they do at night.

Olive returned in ten minutes with a tray of hors d'oeuvres and a silver cooler with a wine bottle nestled in ice. Her entire manner had changed since Terry walked in the door. She still had an air of elegance, but her manner was tinged now with servitude. She fussed with small linen cocktail napkins, arranging them in a pattern near the serving plate she'd placed at one end of the coffee table. She'd prepared ripe figs stuffed with mascarpone cheese, triangles of phyllo, and chilled new potato halves topped with sour cream and caviar. If I called this my dinner, would all of my nutritional needs be met?

Olive crossed briskly to a sideboard and set out liquor bottles so we'd have a choice of drinks. The room was beginning to darken and she turned on two table lamps. The panels of her taffeta skirt made a silky scritching sound every time she moved. Her legs were well muscled and the spike heels threw her calves into high relief.

I glanced over to see Terry standing in the doorway, freshly showered and dressed, his gaze lingering on the picture she presented. He caught my eye, smiling with the barest suggestion of proprietorship. He didn't look like an easy man to please.

"Gorgeous house," I said.

Olive looked over with a rare smile. "Thanks," she said.

"Have a seat," he said.

"I don't want to hold you up."

Terry waved dismissively, as if the pending conversation took precedence. The gesture had the same ingratiating effect as someone who tells his secretary to hold all the calls. It's probably bullshit . . . maybe no one ever calls anyway . . . but it gives the visitor a feeling of importance.

"He'd never pass up a chance to talk business," Olive said. She handed him a martini and then glanced at me. "What would you like?"

"The white wine, if I may."

While I looked on, she opened the bottle, pouring a glass for me and then one for herself. She handed me mine and then eased out of her shoes and took a seat on the couch, tucking her feet up under her. She seemed softer, less egotistical. The role of helpmeet suited her, which surprised me, somehow. She was a woman who had no apparent purpose beyond indulging herself and pampering "her man." The notion seemed outdated in a world of career women and supermoms.

Terry perched on the arm of the couch, staring at me with guarded interest. He took charge of the conversation, a move he must have been accustomed to. His dark eyes gave his narrow face a brooding look, but his manner was pleasant.

He made only an occasional digital reference to the fact of his moustache. I've seen men who stroke their facial hair incessantly, as if it were the last remnant of a baby bunting, comforting and soft. "Lance says someone tried to frame you," he said. He ate a new-potato half and passed the plate to me.

"Looks that way," I said. I helped myself to a fig. Heaven on the tongue.

"What do you need from us?"

"For starters, I'm hoping you can fill me in on Ava Daugherty."

"Ava? Sure. What's she got to do with it?"

"She was there the day I did the fire-scene inspection. She also saw Heather give me the envelope full of inventory sheets, which have since disappeared."

His gaze shifted and I watched him compose his reply before he spoke. "As far as I know, Ava's straight as an arrow. Hardworking, honest, devoted to the company."

"What about Lance? How does she get along with him?"

"I've never heard them exchange a cross word. He's the one who hired her, as a matter of fact, when it was clear we needed an office manager."

"How long ago was that?"

"God, it must be two, three years now," he said. He looked down at Olive, sitting close by. "What's your impression? Am I reporting accurately?"

Olive shrugged. "Well, I wouldn't say she's crazy about him. She thinks he plays too much when he ought to be getting work done, but I don't think she'd devise any scheme to do him in." Olive passed the hors d'oeuvre tray to me. I thought it only gracious to sample something else, so I selected a potato half and popped it in my mouth.

"Who might?" I asked, licking sour cream from my thumb.

This shit was great. If they'd just leave the room for a minute, I'd have a go at the rest.

Both seemed to come up blank.

"Come on. He must have enemies. Somebody's gone to a lot of trouble over this," I said.

Terry said, "At the moment, I couldn't name one, but we can give it some thought. Maybe something will occur to us."

"What can you tell me about the Wood/Warren engineer who killed himself?"

"Hugh Case," Olive said.

Terry seemed surprised. "What brought that up? I just got a call from Lyda Case this afternoon."

"Really?" I said. "What did she have to say?"

"It wasn't what she said so much as her attitude. She was completely freaked out, screaming at the top of her lungs. Said his death was my fault."

Olive looked at him in disbelief. "Yours? What bullshit! Why would she say that?"

"I have no idea. She sounded drunk. Ranting and raving. Foulmouthed, shrill."

"That's curious," I said. "Is she here in town?"

Terry shook his head. "She didn't say. The call was long distance from the sound of it. Where's she live?"

"Dallas, I believe."

"I got the impression she intended to fly out. Do you want to talk to her if she shows up?"

"Yes, I'd like that," I said, careful to omit any reference to the fact that I'd met with her the night before. She hadn't seemed paranoid to me at all and she'd never mentioned Terry's name.

Olive stirred on the couch, shifting positions. "Just in time for New Year's. Everyone'll be here." She glanced at Terry. "Did I tell you Bass gets in tonight?"

A look of annoyance flashed across his face. "I thought he was broke. I hope you didn't pay his way."

"Me! Absolutely not. Ebony sends him money, but you wouldn't catch me doing it," she remarked. And then to me, "Bass and I had a falling-out at Thanksgiving and we haven't spoken since. He's got a big mouth in matters that are none of his business. I think he's loathsome, and he's just about that fond of me."

Terry glanced at his watch and I took that as my cue. "I should let you go if you've got a party," I said.

"I don't feel we've been any help," Olive said.

"Don't worry about it. I've got other sources. Just let me know if you come up with anything you think might pertain."

I left my card on the coffee table. Terry walked me to the door while Olive excused herself to fetch her coat. He watched her disappear into the bedroom. "I didn't want to mention this in front of her," he said, "but Lyda Case scared the hell out of me this afternoon."

"How so?"

"I don't want to make Olive nervous, but the woman threatened me. I don't think it has anything to do with Lance or I'd have said so up front. This is different. I don't know what it's about, but she really sounded cracked."

"What kind of threat?" I asked.

"Out of nowhere, she asked me how old I'd be on my next birthday. I didn't know what she was getting at, but when I told her I'd be forty-six, she said, 'Don't count on it.' And then she laughed like a fiend. Jesus, the sound made my blood run cold. I can't believe she was serious, but my God! What a thing to say."

"And you have no idea why she suddenly got in touch?"

"I haven't talked to her for years. Since Hugh died, I guess."

"I understand there's some question about the manner of his death."

"I've heard that too and I don't know what to think."

"How well did you know him?"

"I wouldn't say we were close, but I worked with him, oh, probably five years or so. He never struck me as the sort who'd commit suicide. Of course, you never know what someone under pressure will do."

"Pressure?"

"Lyda'd threatened to leave him. Hugh was a sweet guy, but he was terribly dependent on her and I think it just knocked the props out from under him."

"Why was she leaving? What was that about?"

"I wasn't privy to the details. Lance might know."

Olive reappeared, white fur coat across her shoulders, the green dress over her arm. Terry and I abandoned the topic of Lyda Case. He made no comment when she gave me the dress. Maybe Olive always gave away her clothes. The three of us left the house together, confining ourselves to small talk.

It was fully dark by then and the night was chilly. I turned on the heater in my car and drove to a pay phone in Montebello Village, putting a call in to Darcy at home. I wanted to stop off and see her before I went back to my place, but she told me Andy'd worked late, so she hadn't had a chance to search his office. She was going in early the next morning, and said she'd call if she came up with anything.

I hung up, realizing then how exhausted I felt. In addition to the jet lag, I was operating on a bad night's sleep, and the fragmentary nap I'd picked up this morning wasn't helping anything. I headed home. As I turned the corner onto my street, I spotted Daniel's rental car, still sitting at the curb in front of my apartment. I parked and got out. Even in the dark, I could see him slouched in the front seat, feet on the dash as they had been before. I was just opening the gate when he rolled down his window. "Can I talk to you?"

I felt something snappish rise up in me, but I forced it back down again. I don't like being bitchy, and I hated admitting to myself that he still had the power to distress. "All right," I said. I approached the car and halted about six feet away. "What is it?"

He unfolded himself and emerged from the car, leaning his elbows on the open car door. The pale glow from the street light gilded his cheekbones, touching off strands of silver in the cloud of blond hair.

"I'm in a bit of a bind," he said. His face was dappled with shadows that masked the remembered clear blue of his eyes. After eight years, it was amazingly painful just to be in his company.

I thought the safest course was to repeat information back to him without comment. "You're in a bind," I said. There was a brief silence wherein I assumed I was meant to quiz him on the nature of his problem. I clamped my teeth together, waiting.

He smiled ruefully. "Don't worry. I'm not going to ask you for money and I'm not trying to get in your pants."

"This comes as a big relief, Daniel. What *do* you want?" The bitchy tone was already back, but I swear I couldn't help myself. There's nothing more infuriating than a man who's manipulated your emotions once and now thinks he can do it again. I could still remember the charge that ran between us early in our relationship, sexual electricity infusing the very air we breathed. It had taken years for me to realize that I had generated most of it myself out of my own neediness. Maybe that's what was making me so churlish in retrospect. I was still chafing at myself for what a fool I'd been.

"I need a place to stash my gear," he said.

"What gear?"

He shrugged. "I got a two-thousand-dollar acoustic guitar I can't leave because the trunk lock is busted on the rental car I picked up. It'll get ripped off if it's in the back seat."

"You brought a guitar like that all the way from Florida?"

"I thought maybe I'd pick up a gig out here. I could use the bucks."

"What happened to your friend? I thought you got a ride with someone. Why not take it to his place? Or is it a woman? I guess I never asked you that."

"Well, no, it's a guy," he said. "The problem is, he doesn't actually live here in town. He was just passing through on his way to San Francisco and he won't be back till late on Sunday. That's why I had to rent a car of my own."

"Where are you staying? Don't you have a place?"

"I'm working on that. The town's booked solid because of the holidays. Meantime, I can't even pull into a gas station to take a leak without hauling everything in with me. It's just for a couple of days."

I stared at him. "You always do things like this, you know that? You're always in a bind, shifting your weight from foot to foot, hoping someone'll bail you out of the hole you're in. Try the Rescue Mission. Pick up a woman. That shouldn't be so tough. Or sell the damn thing. Why is it up to me?"

"It's not up to you," he said mildly. "It's a simple favor. What's the big deal?"

I ran out of steam. We'd had this same exchange a hundred times and he'd never heard me before. I might as well save my breath. I might as well give him what he wanted and get it over with. It was probably just an elaborate excuse to prolong our contact. "Never mind," I said. "No big deal. You can park the damn thing in a corner until Sunday and then I want it out of here."

"Sure. No problem. Thanks."

"I'm warning you, Daniel. If you've got a stash anywhere within six blocks of here, I'll call the cops."

"I'm clean. I told you that. You can look for yourself."

"Skip it," I said. I knew him well enough to know he wouldn't bluff on that, because he knew *me* well enough to know I'd have him thrown in the slammer if I caught him.

14

I took a couple of Tylenols and slept like a stone—deep, dreamless sleep that soothed my frazzled nerves and restored my good spirits. I was up at 6:00, ready to jog as usual. There was no sign of Daniel parked at my curb. I did a perfunctory stretch against the fence post and headed toward Cabana Boulevard.

The run felt great. The sky was a pearl gray streaked with pink. To my right, a dark-gray surf boomed against the hard-packed sand, leaving snowy froth in its wake. The wharf was mirrored in the glistening pools that remained when the waves receded. The sea seemed to shush the birds that shrieked overhead. This was the last day of the year and I ran with a sense of optimism the new year always brings. I'd find a way to sort it all out: Lance, Mac's suspicions about me, even Daniel's sudden appearance on my doorstep. I was alive and healthy, physically fit. Rosie's would open again on Monday. Henry would be home in another six days. I had the sassy green dress Olive had given me, and maybe a New Year's invitation if she came through as hoped. I did my three miles and slowed to a walk, cooling off as I headed home.

I showered and dressed in jeans as usual, savoring the morning at home. By then it was 7:00—too early for phone calls. I ate my cereal and read the *L.A. Times* over two cups of coffee. Daniel's guitar sat in the corner in mute testimony to his renewed presence in my life, but I ignored it for the most part.

Darcy called at 7:35 from California Fidelity. She'd done a thorough search. Andy's office was clean.

"Shit," I said. "What about a typewriter? I was hoping we could get a match on the phony fire-department report, but I didn't find one at his apartment."

"Maybe he keeps it in the trunk of his car."

"Oh, I like that. I'll see if I can find a way to check that out. In the meantime, keep an eye peeled. Maybe something will surface. Andy's gotta be tied into this business somehow. It would help a lot to know who he knows at Wood/Warren. Did you go through his Rolodex?"

"That won't help. He knows all those guys because that was his account. He's bound to have the number handy. I'll check it out, though. Maybe something else will come to light." She clicked off.

At 8:00, I put a call through to Lyda Case in Texas. Her roommate said she was out of town, maybe in California, but she wasn't sure. I left my number and asked her to have Lyda get in touch with me if she called home.

I called my pal at the credit bureau, but she was out until Monday. I had the feeling the rest of the day was going to come down about the same way. It was New Year's Eve day. As with Christmas Eve, businesses were closing early, people taking off at noon. Olive called me at 10:00 to say that she was indeed putting together an impromptu cocktail party. "It's mostly family and a few close friends. Half the people I called already had plans. Are you free? We'd love to have you, if you're not already tied up."

"Of course I'm not," I said. "I'd love to come." I hated to sound so eager, but in truth I was. I didn't want to spend this New Year's Eve alone. I was worried Daniel might start looking too good. "Can I bring anything?"

"Actually I could use some help," she said. "I gave the housekeeper the weekend off, so I'm throwing the whole thing together by myself. I can always use an extra set of hands."

"Well, I'm not a cook, but I can sure chop and stir. What time?"

"Four-thirty? I'll be back from the supermarket by then. Ash said she'd come about five to help, too. Everybody else will be coming about seven. We'll keep going till the food and alcohol give out."

"Great," I said. "And the green dress will be okay?"

"It better be. I'm giving this party so you can wear the damn thing."

I put a call through to Lance. I didn't like initiating the contact with him, but I had to hear his version of the situation with Hugh Case. As soon as he was on the line, I told him what I'd heard. The silence was weighty. "Lance?"

"I'm here," he said. He sighed heavily. "Jesus, I don't know how to deal with this. What the hell is going on? I heard rumors back then she thought I had something to do with his death. It's not true. It's completely untrue, but I don't have a way of proving it. Why would I do that? What could I possibly gain by killing him?"

"Wasn't he leaving the company?"

"Absolutely not. He talked about quitting. He said he wanted to start a company of his own. He even gave notice, but hell, Dad called him in and they had a long talk. Dad offered to make him a vice-president. Gave him a big raise and he was happy as a clam."

"When was this?"

"I don't know. A couple of days before he died."

"Didn't that strike you as peculiar?"

"Sure it did. She swore he didn't kill himself and I agreed. He wasn't the depressive type and he'd just made a hell of a deal for himself. Somehow she got it in her head that I killed the man. I wouldn't harm a soul. You gotta believe me. Somebody's working very hard to get me put away."

"Speaking of which, have you heard anything from California Fidelity?"

His tone changed. "Yeah, yesterday. They're turning everything over to the cops."

I could feel my stomach clench. "Really? Do they have enough to make a case?"

"I don't know. I hope not. Look, I need to talk to you privately and I can't do it here. It's important. Is there any way we can meet?"

I told him I'd be at Olive's later and we agreed to talk then. I wasn't anxious to be seen in his company, but he seemed insistent, and at that point, I didn't see how things could get worse. I wasn't guilty of conspiracy and I was tired of acting like I was. Worry was sitting in my chest like a weight, leaden and oppressive. I had to do something to get my mind off things.

I went out and bought a pair of high heels, anxiety translating into excitement as the day progressed. Being isolated that week had made me aware that I do have a few social impulses—buried deep, perhaps, under layers of caution, but part of me nevertheless. This was like dress-up time with the big kids, and I was looking forward to it. I'd begun to feel very charitable about Olive, whose life-style only yesterday had seemed superficial and self-indulgent. Who was I to judge? It was none of my business how she made her peace with the world. She'd fashioned a life out of tennis and shopping, but she managed to do occasional charity work, which was more than I could claim. She was right about one thing: the harm in the world is done by those who feel disenfranchised and abused. Contented people (as a rule) don't kite checks, rob banks, or kill their fellow citizens.

I thought about going to the gym, but decided to bag that idea. I hadn't done a workout since Tuesday, but I just didn't give a damn. I puttered and napped through the middle of the day.

At 3:00 I took a long bubble bath . . . well, I used dish-washing liquid, but it did foam right up. I washed my hair and combed it for a change. I did some stuff to my face that passed for makeup in my book, and then wiggled into underwear and panty hose. The dress was grand, and it fit like a charm, rustling the same way Olive's had the night before. I'd never had a role model for this female stuff. After my parents' death when I was five, I'd been raised by a maiden aunt, no expert herself at things feminine. I'd spent the days of my childhood with cap guns and books, learning self-sufficiency, which loomed large with her. By the time I reached junior high I was a complete misfit, and by high school I'd thrown in my lot with some bad-ass boys who cussed and smoked dope, two things I mastered at an early age. In spite of the fact that I'm a social oaf, my aunt instilled a solid set of values, which prevailed in the end. By the time I graduated, I'd straightened up my act and now I'm a model citizen, give or take a civil code or two. At heart, I've always been a prissy little moralist. Private investigation is just my way of acting out.

By 4:30, I was standing on the Kohlers' doorstep, listening to the door chime echo through the house. It didn't look as if anyone was there. There was mail jammed in the box, the newspaper and a brown paper-wrapped parcel on the mat. I peered into one of the long glass panels on either side of the front door. The foyer was dark and no lights were showing at the rear of the house. Olive probably wasn't home from the supermarket yet. The cat appeared from around the side of the house with her long white coat and flat face. Somehow she seemed like a girl to me, but what do I know? I said some cat-type things. She appeared unimpressed.

I heard a car horn toot. The electronic gate was rolled back

from the driveway and a white Mercedes 380 SL pulled in.
Olive waved and I moved toward the parking pad. She got
out of the car and walked around to the rear, looking very
classy in her white fur coat.

"Sorry I'm late. Have you been here long?"

"Five minutes."

She opened the trunk and picked up one grocery bag, then
struggled to lift a second.

"Here, let me help with that."

"Oh, thanks. Terry should be right behind me with the
liquor."

I took the bag, snagging up another one while I was at it.
There were two more in the trunk and another two bags visible
in the front seat. "God, how many people did you invite?"

"Just forty or so. It should be fun. Let's get these in and
we'll have Terry bring the rest. We've got a ton of work to
do."

She moved toward the front door while I brought up the
rear. There was a crunch of tires on gravel and Terry pulled
into the drive in a silver-gray Mercedes sedan. Must be nice,
I thought. The gate rolled shut. I waited while Olive emptied
the mailbox and shoved the stack of envelopes in the top of
her grocery bag. She picked up the newspaper and tucked
that in, too, then grabbed the parcel.

"You need help? I can take something else."

"I got it." She laid the parcel across the bag, securing it with
her chin while she fumbled for her house key.

The cat was sauntering toward the driveway, plumed tail
aloft. I heard the clink of liquor bottles as Terry set his bags
down on the concrete. He began to coil up a garden hose the
yardman had left on the walk.

"Break your neck on this thing," he said. Olive got the door
open and gave it a push. The telephone started to ring. I
glanced back as she tossed the parcel toward the hall table.

What happened next was too swift to absorb. There was a flash of light, a great burst that filled my visual field like a sun, followed by a huge cloud of white smoke. Shrapnel shot from a central point, spraying outward with a deadly velocity. A fireball seemed to curl across the threshold like a wall of water with a barrier removed, washing flames into the grass. Every blade of green in its path turned black. At the same time, I was lifted by a shattering low-frequency boom that hurtled me capriciously across the yard. I found myself sitting upright against a tree trunk like a rag doll, shoes gone, toes pointing straight up. I saw Olive fly past me as if she'd been yanked, tumbling in a high comic arc that carried her to the hedge and dropped her in a heap. My vision shimmered and cleared, a light show of the retina, accompanied by the breathless thumping of my heart. My brain, mute with wonder, failed to compute anything but the smell of black powder, pungent and harsh.

The explosion had deafened me, but I felt neither fear nor surprise. Emotions are dependent on comprehension, and while I registered the event, nothing made any sense. Had I died in that moment, I would not have felt the slightest shred of regret, and I understood how liberating sudden death must be. This was pure sensation with no judgment attached.

The front wall of the house was gone and a crater appeared where the hall table had been. The foyer was open to the air, surrounded by coronas of charred wood and plaster, burning merrily. Large flakes of pale blue and pale brown floated down like snow. Grocery items littered the entire yard, smelling of pickles, cocktail onions, and Scotch. I had taken in both sight and sound, but the apparatus of evaluation hadn't caught up with me yet. I had no idea what had happened. I couldn't remember what had transpired only moments before, or how this might relate to past events. Here we were in this new configuration, but how had it come to pass?

From the change in light, I guessed that my eyebrows and lashes must be gone and I was conscious of singed hair and flash burns. I put a hand up, amazed to find my limbs still functioning. I was bleeding from the nose, bleeding from both ears, where the pain was now excruciating. To my left, I could see Terry's mouth working, but no words were coming out. Something had struck him a glancing blow and blood poured down his face. He appeared to be in pain, but the movie was silent, sound reel flapping ineffectually. I turned to see where Olive was.

For one confused moment, I thought I saw a pile of torn foxes, their bloodied pelts confirming what she'd said the day before. It *is* true, I thought, these animals in the wild get ripped to shreds every day. The harsh splattering of red against the soft white fur seemed obscene and out of place. And then, of course, I understood what I was looking at. The blast had opened her body, exposing tangles of bloody flesh, yellow fat, and jagged bone along her backside. I closed my eyes. By then, the smell of black powder was overlaid with the scent of woodsmoke and cooked flesh. Carefully I pondered the current state of affairs.

Olive had to be dead, but Terry seemed okay, and I thought perhaps at some point he would come and help me up. No hurry, I thought. I'm comfy for now. The tree trunk provided back support, which helped, as I was tired. Idly, I wondered where my shoes had gone. I sensed movement, and when I opened my eyes again, confused faces were peering into mine. I couldn't think what to say. I'd already forgotten what was going on, except that I was cold.

Time must have passed. Men in yellow slickers pointed hoses at the house, swords of water cutting through the flames. Worried people crouched in front of me and worked their mouths some more. It was funny. They didn't seem to realize they weren't saying anything. So solemn, so animated, and so intent. Lips and teeth moving to such purpose with no visible effect. And then I was on my back, looking up into tree branches that wobbled through my visual field as I was borne away. I closed my eyes again, wishing that the reeling of the world would stop before I got sick. In spite of the fire, I was shivering.

15

Gradually my hearing returned, pale voices in the distance coming nearer until I understood that it was someone bending over me. Daniel, as radiant as an archangel, appeared above me. The sight of him was baffling, and I felt an incredible urge to put a hand to my forehead, like a movie heroine recovering from a swoon, murmuring, Where am I? I was probably dead. Surely, hell is having your former spouse that close again . . . flirting with a nurse. Ah, I thought, a clue. I was in a hospital bed. She was standing to his right, in polyester white, a vestal virgin with a bedpan, her gaze fixed on his perfect features in profile. I'd forgotten how cunning he was at that sort of thing. While he feigned grave concern for me, he was actually casting backward with his little sexual net, enveloping her in a fine web of pheromones. I moved my lips and he leaned closer. He said, "I think she's conscious."

"I'll get the doctor," the nurse said. She disappeared.

Daniel stroked my hair. "What is it, babe? Are you in pain?"

I licked my lips. "Asshole," I said, but it came out all garbled and I wasn't sure he got the drift. I vowed, in that moment, to get well enough to throw him out. I closed my eyes.

I remembered the flash, the deafening bang, Olive flying past me like a mannequin. She had looked unreal, arms crooked, legs askew, as lumpen as a sandbag flung through the air, landing with a sodden thump.

Olive must be dead. There wasn't any way to mend the parts of her turned inside out by the blast.

I remembered Terry with the blood gushing down his face. Was he dead, too? I looked at Daniel, wondering how bad it was.

Daniel sensed my question. "You're fine, Kin. Everything's okay. You're in the hospital and Terry's here, too," he said. And after a hesitation, "Olive didn't make it."

I closed my eyes again, hoping he'd go away.

I concentrated on my various body parts, hoping that all of them could be accounted for. Many treasured portions of my anatomy hurt. I thought at first I was in some sort of bed restraint, but it turned out to be an immobilizing combination of bruises, whiplash, IV fluids, painkillers, and pressure dressings on the areas where I had suffered burns. Given the fact that I'd been standing ten feet away from Olive, my injuries turned out to be miraculously insignificant—contusions and abrasions, mild concussion, superficial burns on my extremities. I'd been hospitalized primarily for shock.

I was still confused about what had happened, but it didn't take a 160 IQ to figure out that something had gone boom in a big way. A gas explosion. More likely a bomb. The sound and the impact were both characteristic of low explosives. I know now, because I looked it up, that low explosives have velocities of 3,300 feet per second, which is much faster than the average person tends to move. That short trip from Olive's front porch to the tree base was as close to free flight as I was ever going to get.

The doctor came in. She was a plain woman with a good face and sense enough to ask Daniel to leave the room while she examined me. I liked her because she didn't lapse into a slack-jawed stupor at the sight of him. I watched her, as trusting as a child while she checked my vital signs. She must have been in her late thirties, with haphazard hair, no makeup, gray eyes that poured out compassion and intelligence. She held my hand, lacing her cool fingers through mine. "How are you feeling?"

Tears welled up. I saw my mother's face superimposed on hers, and I was four again, throat raw from a tonsillectomy. I'd forgotten what it was like to experience the warmth radiated by those who tend the sick. I was saturated by a tenderness I hadn't felt since my mother died. I don't take well to helplessness. I've worked hard in my life to deny neediness, and there I was, unable to sustain any pretense of toughness or competence. In some ways it came as a great relief to lie there in a puddle and give myself up to her nurturing.

By the time she'd finished checking me, I was somewhat more alert, anxious to get my bearings. I quizzed her in a foggy way, trying to get a fix on my current state.

She told me I was in a private room at St. Terry's, having been admitted, through Emergency, the night before. I remembered, in fragments, some of it: the high keening of sirens as the ambulance swayed around corners, the harsh white light above me in the Emergency Room, the murmurs of the medical personnel assigned to evaluate my injuries. I remembered how soothing it was when I was finally tucked into bed: clean, patched up, pumped full of medications, and feeling no pain. It was now mid-morning of New Year's Day. I was still groggy, and I discovered belatedly that I was dropping off to sleep without even being aware of it.

The next time I woke, the IV had been removed and the doctor had been replaced by a nurse's aide who helped me onto the bedpan, cleaned me up again, changed my gown, and put fresh sheets on the bed, cranking me into a sitting position so I could see the world. It was nearly noon. I was famished by then and wolfed down a dish of cherry Jell-O the aide rustled up from somewhere. That held me until the meal carts arrived on the floor. Daniel had gone down to the hospital cafeteria for lunch, and by the time he got back, I'd requested a "No Visitors" sign hung on the door.

The restrictions must not have applied to Lieutenant Dolan, however, because the next thing I knew, he was sitting in the chair, leafing through a magazine. He's in his fifties, a big, shambling man, with scuffed shoes and a lightweight beige suit. He looked exhausted from the horizontal lines across his forehead to his sagging jawline, which was ill-shaved. His thinning hair was rumpled. He had bags under his eyes and his color was bad. I had to guess that he'd been out late the night before, maybe looking forward to a day of football games on TV instead of interviewing me.

He looked up from his magazine and saw that I was awake. I've known Dolan for maybe five years, and while we respect each other, we're never at ease. He's in charge of the homicide detail of the Santa Teresa Police Department, and we sometimes cross swords. He's not fond of private investigators and I'm not fond of having to defend my occupational status. If I could find a way to avoid homicide cases, believe me, I would.

"You awake?" he said.

"More or less."

He set the magazine aside and got up, shoving his hands in his coat pockets while he stood by my bed. All my usual sassiness had been, quite literally, blown away. Lieutenant Dolan didn't seem to know how to handle me in my subdued state. "You feel well enough to talk about last night?"

"I think so."

"You remember what happened?"

"Some. There was an explosion and Olive was killed."

Dolan's mouth pulled down. "Died instantly. Her husband survived, but he's blanking on things. Doctor says it'll come back to him in a day or two. You got off light for someone standing right in the path."

"Bomb?"

"Package bomb. Black powder, we think. I have the bomb techs on it now, cataloguing evidence. What about the parcel? You see anything?"

"There was a package on the doorstep when I got there."

"What time was that?"

"Four-thirty. Little bit before. The Kohlers were having a New Year's Eve party and she asked me to help." I filled him in briefly on the circumstances of the party. I could feel myself reviving, my thoughts gradually becoming more coherent.

"Tell me what you remember about the parcel."

"There isn't much. I only glanced at it once. Brown paper. No string. Block lettering, done with a Magic Marker from the look of it. I saw it upside down."

"The address facing the door," he said. He took out a little spiral-bound notebook and a pen.

"Right."

"Who's it sent to?"

"Terry, I think. Not 'Mr. and Mrs.' because the line of print wasn't that long. Even upside down, I'd have noticed the 'O' in Olive's name."

He was jotting notes. "Return address?"

"Uhn-un. I don't remember any postmark either. There might have been a UPS number, but I didn't see one."

"You're doing pretty good," he said. "The regular mailman says he only delivered hand mail yesterday, no packages at all. UPS had no record of a delivery to that address. They didn't even have a truck in the area. You didn't see anyone leave the premises?"

I tried to think back, but I was drawing a blank. "Can't help you there. I don't remember anyone on foot. A car might have passed, but I can't picture it."

I closed my eyes, visualizing the porch. There were salmon begonias in big tubs along the front. "Oh, yeah. The newspaper was on the doormat. I don't know how far up the walk the paperboy comes, but he might have seen the parcel when he was doing his route."

He made another note. "We'll try that. What about dimensions?"

I could feel myself shrug. "Size of a shirt box. Bigger than a book. Nine by twelve inches by three. Was there anything left of it?"

"More than you'd think. We believe there was gift wrap under the brown mailing paper. Blue."

"Oh sure," I said, startled. "I remember seeing flakes of brown and blue. I thought it was snow, but it must have been paper particles." I remembered what Terry had said to me. "Something else," I said. "Terry was threatened. He talked about it when I was there the night before. He had a phone call at the plant from a woman named Lyda Case. She asked him when his birthday was and when he told her, she said he shouldn't count on it."

I filled him in on the rest, unburdening the sequence of events from the first. For once, I loved offloading the information on him. This was big time . . . the heavy hitters . . . more than I could deal with by myself. When it came down to bombs, I was out of my league. Lieutenant Dolan was scratching notes at a quick clip, his expression that mask of studied neutrality all cops tend to wear—taking in everything, giving nothing back. He talked as if he was already on the witness stand. "So there's a chance she's in Santa Teresa. Is that what you're saying?"

"I don't know. He seemed to think she was coming out, but he was pretty vague on that point. He's here, too?" I asked.

"This floor. Other end of the hall."

"You care if I talk to him?"

"No, not a bit. Might help jog his memory."

After Lieutenant Dolan left, I eased into a sitting position on the edge of the bed, feet dangling over the side. My head was pounding at the sudden exertion. I sat and waited for the light show inside my head to fade. I studied as much of my body as I could see.

My legs looked frail under the lightweight cotton of the hospital gown, which tied at the back and let in lots of air. The pattern of bruises across my front looked like someone had taken a powder puff and dusted me with purple talc. My hands were bandaged and I could see an aura of angry red flesh along my inner arms where the burns tapered off. I held on to the handrail and slid off the bed, supporting myself on the bed table. My legs were trembling. I could almost bet they didn't want me getting up this way. I didn't think it was such a hot idea myself, the more I thought of it. Nausea and clamminess were chiming in with the pounding in my head and a fuzzy darkness was gathering along the periphery of my vision. I wasn't going to win an award for this so I sat back down.

There was a tap at the door and the nurse came in. "Your husband's out here. He says he has to leave and he'd like to see you before he goes."

"He's not my husband," I said automatically.

She put her hands in the pockets of her uniform—a tunic over white pants, no cap. I only knew she was a nurse because her plastic name tag had an R.N. after her name, which was Sharie Wright. I studied her covertly, knowing how much Daniel liked women with names like that. Debbie and Tammie and Cindie. Candie loomed large in there, too. I guess Kinsey qualified, now that I thought of it. Kinsie. Infidelity reduces and diminishes, leaving nothing where you once had a sense of self-worth.

"He's been worried sick," she said. "I know it's none of my business, but he was here all night. I thought you should be aware." She saw that I was struggling to get settled in the bed and she gave me a hand. I guessed that she was twenty-six. I was twenty-three when I married him, twenty-four when he left. No explanation, no discussion. The divorce was no-fault, served up in record time.

"Is there a way I can get a wheelchair? There's someone down the hall I'd like to see. The man who was admitted at the same time I was."

"Mr. Kohler. He's in three-oh-six at the end of the hall."

"How's he doing?"

"Fine. He's going home this afternoon."

"The policeman who was here a little while ago wants me to talk to him."

"What about your husband? He said it would only take two minutes."

"He's not my husband," I said, parrotlike, "but sure. Send him in. After he goes, could you find me a wheelchair? If I try to walk, I'll fall on my puss and have to sue this outfit."

She didn't think I was amusing and she didn't like the reference to lawsuits. She went out without a word. My husband, I thought. I should live so long.

16

He looked tired—an improvement, I thought. Daniel stood by my hospital bed, showing every minute of his forty-two years. "I know this won't sit well with you," he said, "but the doctor says she won't let you go home unless you have someone to look after you."

A feeling very like panic crept up in my chest. "I'll be fine in a day. I don't need anyone looking after me. I hate that idea."

"Well, I knew you would. I'm telling you what she said."

"She didn't mention it to me."

"She never had a chance. You were half zonked. She said she'd talk to you about it next time she made her rounds."

"They can't keep me here. That's disgusting. I'll go nuts."

"I already told her that. I just wanted you to know I'd be willing to help. I could get you signed out of here and settled at home. I wouldn't actually have to stay on the premises. That place of yours looks too small for more than one person anyway. But I could at least check on you twice a day, make sure you have everything you need."

"Let me think about it," I said grudgingly. But I could already see the bind I was in. With Henry gone, Rosie on vacation, and Jonah out of town, I'd be on my own. Truly, I wasn't feeling that good. I just couldn't make my body do what I wanted it to. The elderly, the feeble, and the infirm must experience the same exasperation and bewilderment. For once, my determination had nothing whatever to do with my proficiency. It was exhausting to sit up, and I knew perfectly well I couldn't manage much at home. Staying here was out of the question. Hospitals are dangerous. People make mistakes. Wrong blood, wrong medication, wrong surgeries, wrong tests. I was checking out of this place "toot sweet."

Daniel ran his hand across the top of my head. "Do what you want. I'll be back later."

He was gone again before I could protest.

I buzzed the nurses' station on the intercom.

A hollow voice came on. "Yes?"

"Can Mr. Kohler in three-oh-six have visitors?"

"As far as I know he can." The nurse sounded like she was talking into an old tin can, coughs and rustling in the background.

"Can I get a wheelchair? I'd like to go down and see him."

It was twenty minutes before anybody managed to find me one. In the meantime, I became aware that I was struggling with a depression generated by Olive's death. It wasn't as if we had had a relationship, but she'd been around on the borders of my life for years. I'd first seen her in high school when I met Ashley, but she'd left just before our junior year began. After that she was more rumor than fact . . . the sister who was always off somewhere else: boarding school, Switzerland, skiing in Utah with friends. I don't think we'd exchanged more than superficial chat until two days before, and then I'd found my opinion of her undergoing a shift. Now, death had smashed her like a bug, the blow as abrupt as a fly being swatted on a windowsill. The effect was jarring and the emotional impact hadn't worn off. I found myself turning images in my mind, trying to absorb the finality. I hadn't been consulted in the matter and I hadn't agreed. Death is insulting, and I resented its sudden appearance, like an unannounced visit from a boorish relative. I suspected the knot in my chest would be there for a long time; not grief per se, but a hard fist of regret.

I wheeled myself down the corridor to room 306. The door was closed and Bass was standing in the hall. He turned his head idly as I approached. Bass had the smooth good looks of someone in an eighteenth-century oil painting. His face was oval, boyish, his brow unlined, his eyes a barren brown. His mouth was sensual, his manner superior. Put him in a satin vest, a waistcoat, breeches, and leggings, and he might have been Blue Boy, grown slightly decadent. His hair was fine and dark, receding at the temples, worn slightly long and rather wispy where it gathered in a point on his forehead. He should have had an Afghan at his side, some creature with silky ears and a long, aristocratic snout.

"Hello, Bass. I'm Kinsey Millhone. Do you remember me?"

"Of course," he said. He bent down then and gave my cheek a social buss, more noise than contact. His expression was bleak. There was a dead time in the air, one of those uncomfortable stretched moments when you struggle to find something to say. His sister was dead. This was hardly the time for effusiveness, but I was puzzled by the awkwardness of our encounter.

"Where's Terry?"

Her glanced at the door. "He's having his dressing changed. They should be done shortly. He's going home as soon as the doctor signs the release. How are you? We heard you were down the hall."

"I'm all right. I'm sorry about Olive," I said, and I truly was.

"God, this is all so screwed up. I don't know what's going on."

"How's your mother doing? Is she holding up all right?"

"She'll be okay. She's a tough old bird. She's taking it pretty hard, but she's got a spine of steel. Ash is destroyed. She's been leveled. She and Olive were always just like this," he said, holding up crossed fingers. "What about you? You look like you took a beating."

"I'm all right. This is the first time I've been out of bed and I feel like shit."

"You're lucky to be alive, from what I hear."

"Lucky is right. I thought about picking the package up myself, but Olive's car pulled in and I went to help her with the groceries instead. Are you staying at your mother's?"

He nodded. "I got in Thursday night and then Olive called yesterday and said she was putting the party together. Seems like years ago. I was having a swim before I got dressed when Ebony showed up at the side of the pool. I couldn't figure out what was wrong with her. You know Eb. Always in control, never a hair out of place. Well, she looked like a wild woman. I pulled myself up on the side of the pool and she said a bomb had gone off at Olive's house and she was dead. I thought she was making the whole thing up. I laughed. It was so far-fetched, I couldn't help myself. She slapped the shit out of me and that's when I realized she was serious. What happened? Terry can't remember and the police won't tell us much."

I told him what I could, omitting the gruesome details of Olive's injuries. Even talking about it made me shake. I clamped my teeth shut, trying to relax. "Sorry," I said.

"It's my fault. I shouldn't have brought it up," he said. "I didn't mean to put you through it all over again."

I shook my head. "That's fine. I'm okay. Nobody's told me much either. Honestly, I think it helps. The blanks are frustrating." I was looking for a narrative thread to hang fragments on. I'd lost the night. Everything from 4:30 on had been deleted from my memory bank.

He hesitated for a moment and then filled me in on events

from his end. Ash had left. She was on her way to Olive's to help set up for the party. As soon as he heard about the explosion, he pulled some clothes on and he and Ebony jumped in the car. They arrived to find Terry being loaded into the ambulance. I was being bundled onto a stretcher, semiconscious. Olive was still lying near the shrubs, covered by a blanket.

Bass's recital of events was flat, like a news report. He was calm, his tone impersonal. He made no eye contact. I stared down the hall where a doctor with a somber expression was talking to an older couple sitting on a bench. The news must have been bad because the woman clutched and unclutched the purse in her lap.

I remembered then that I had seen Bass . . . one of the faces scrutinizing mine, bobbing above me like a balloon on a string. By then, shock had set in and I was shivering uncontrollably, in spite of the blankets they'd wrapped me in. I didn't remember Ebony. Maybe they had kept her out by the road, refusing to let her any closer to the carnage. The bomb had made tatters of Olive's flesh. Hunks of her body had been blown against the hedges, like clots of snow.

I put a hand against my face, feeling flushed with tears. Bass patted me awkwardly, murmuring nonsense, upset that he'd upset me, probably wondering how to get out of it. The emotion passed and I collected myself, taking a deep breath. "What about Terry's injuries?"

"Not bad. A cut on his forehead. Couple of cracked ribs where the blast knocked him into the garage. They wanted him in for observation, but he seems okay."

There was activity behind us and the door to Terry's room opened. A nurse came out bearing a stainless-steel bowl full of soiled bandages. She seemed enveloped in aromas of denatured alcohol, tincture of iodine, and the distinctive smell of adhesive tape.

"You can go in now. Doctor said he can leave any time. We'll get a wheelchair for him when he's ready to go down."

Bass went in first. I wheeled myself in behind. A nurse's aide was straightening the bed table where the nurse had been working. Terry was sitting on the edge of the bed, buttoning up his shirt. I caught sight of his taped ribs through the loose flaps of his shirt and I looked away. His torso was stark white and hairless, his chest narrow and without musculature. Illness and injury seem so personal. I didn't want to know the details of his frailty.

He looked battered, with a dark track sketched along his forehead where the stitches had been put in. One wrist was bandaged, from cuts perhaps, or burns. His face was pale, his moustache stark, his dark hair disheveled. He seemed shrunken, as if Olive's death had diminished him.

Ebony appeared in the doorway, taking in the scene with a cursory glance. She hesitated, waiting for the aide to finish. The room seemed unbearably crowded. I needed fresh air.

"I'll come back in a minute," I murmured. I wheeled myself out. Ebony followed me as far as the visitors' lounge, a small alcove with a green tweed couch, two matching chairs, an artificial palm and an ashtray. She took a seat, searching through her handbag for her cigarettes. She lit one, sucking in smoke as if it were oxygen. She looked totally composed, but it was clear that the hospital atmosphere unsettled her. She picked a piece of lint from the lap of her skirt.

"I don't understand any of this," she said harshly. "Who'd want to kill Olive? She never did anything."

"Olive wasn't the target. It was Terry. The package with the bomb in it was addressed to him."

Ebony's gaze shot up to mine and hung there. A pale wash of pink appeared in the dead white of her face. The hand with the cigarette gave a lurch, almost of its own accord, and cigarette ash tumbled into her lap. She rose abruptly, brushing at it.

"That's ridiculous," she snapped. "The police said there was nothing left of the package once the bomb went off." She stubbed the cigarette out.

"Well, there was," I said. "Besides which, I saw it. Terry's name was printed on the front, not hers."

"I don't believe it." A wisp of smoke drifted up from the crushed cigarette stub. She snatched it up again, working the live ember out with her fingertips. She was shredding the remains of the cigarette. The strands of raw tobacco seemed obscene.

"I'm just telling you what I saw. Olive could have been the target, but the package was addressed to him."

"Bullshit! That *bastard*! Don't tell me Olive died because she picked it up instead of him!" Her eyes suffused with tears and she struggled for control. She got up, pacing with agitation.

I turned the wheelchair slightly, tracking her course. "What bastard, Ebony? Who are you referring to?"

She sat down abruptly, pressing the butts of both palms against her eyes. "No one. I'm sorry. I had no idea. I thought someone meant to kill her, which was horrible enough. But to die by mistake. My God! At least she didn't suffer. They swear she died instantly." She sobbed once. She formed a tent of her hands, breathing hard into her palms.

"Do you know who killed her?"

"Of course not! Absolutely not! What kind of monster do you think I am? My own sister . . ." Her tone of outrage fell away and she wept earnestly. I wanted to believe her, but I couldn't be sure. I was tired, too close to events to sort out the false from the true. She lifted her face, which was washed with tears.

"Olive said she wasn't going to vote with you," I said, trying the possibility on her for size.

"You're such a bitch!" she shrieked at me. "How dare you! Get away from me!"

Bass appeared in the archway, his gaze turning to mine quizzically. I jammed backward on the push rim, pivoting in the wheelchair. I propelled myself down the corridor, passing a room where someone was calling for help in a low, hopeless tone. A clear plastic tube trailed from under the sheet to a gallon jug of urine under the bed. It looked like lemonade.

Olive usually brought the mail in. I'd seen her toss it on the hall table carelessly the day before. She might have been the intended victim even if the package *was* addressed to him. I really couldn't remember what she'd told me about who she was siding with in the power play between Ebony and Lance. Maybe he did it as a means of persuading the others to fall in line.

Darcy was waiting in my room when I got back. "Andy's gone," she said.

17

I eased myself back into bed while Darcy filled me in on the details. Andy had come whipping into the office at about 10:00 the day before. Mac had insisted on keeping office hours until 5:00, despite the fact that it was New Year's Eve day. Andy had a lunch meeting scheduled as well as a 2:00 appointment with one of the company vice-presidents. Darcy said Andy was in panic mode. She tried to give him his phone messages, but he cut her dead, hurried into his office, and began to load his personal items into his briefcase, along with his Rolodex. Next thing she knew, he was gone.

"It was too weird for words," she said. "He's never done anything like that before. And why the Rolodex? I'd already been through it and I didn't find a thing, but what made him think of that?"

"Maybe he's psychic."

"He'd have to be. Anyway, we didn't see him again for the rest of the day, so after work I hopped in my car and drove out to his place."

"You went all the way out to Elton?"

"Well, yeah. I just didn't like his attitude. He really had his undies in a bundle and I wanted to know what it was about. I didn't see his car parked anywhere near his apartment, so I went up and peeked in his front window. The place was a pigsty and all the furniture was gone. Maybe a card table in the living room, but that was it."

"That's all he's got," I said. "It looks like Janice took him for a bundle and she's clamoring for more."

"She can clamor all she wants, Kinsey, the man is gone. His next-door neighbor saw me peering in the window and he came out and asked me what I was up to. I told him the truth. I said I worked with Andy and we were worried because he left the office in a snit without telling us what to do about his appointments. This guy claims he saw Andy going down the steps yesterday morning with two big suitcases banging against his legs. This was maybe nine-thirty, something like that. He must have come straight to the office, packed up his stuff, and taken off. I called his place every couple of hours last night and again this morning. All I get is his machine."

I thought about it briefly. "Did the newspapers carry an account of Olive's death?"

"Not till this morning and he was gone by then."

I could feel a surge of energy, part restlessness, part dread. I pushed the covers back and swung my legs over the side of the bed. "I've gotta get out of here."

"Are you supposed to be up?"

"Sure. No problem. Check the closet and see if Daniel brought me any clothes." The green cocktail dress was gone, probably dissected by a pair of surgical scissors in the Emergency Room the night before, along with my tatty underwear.

"It's empty, except for this," she said. She held up my handbag.

"Great. We're in business. As long as I've got my keys, I can get some clothes when I get home. I assume you've got a car here."

"Can you leave without a doctor's permission?"

"I got it. She told Daniel I could go as long as he looked in on me, which he said he would."

Darcy studied me uncertainly, probably guessing what I said was part fib.

"God, don't worry about it, Darcy. It's not against the law to check out of a hospital. It's not a prison sentence. I'm a volunteer," I said.

"What about your bill?"

"Would you quit being such a stickler? My insurance pays for this so I don't owe them anything. They've got my address. They'll find me if they need to."

Darcy was clearly unconvinced, but she shrugged and helped me into the wheelchair, pushing me down the corridor toward the elevators. One of the nurse's aides stared at us as we went by, but I gave her a little wave and she apparently decided she didn't need to concern herself.

When we got downstairs, Darcy lent me her coat and left me in the glass foyer while she went to fetch the car. There I sat in my borrowed coat and little paper slippers, handbag in my lap. If my doctor walked by, I wasn't sure what I'd do. People passing through the foyer gave me cursory glances, but nobody said a word. Being sick is bullshit. I had work to do.

By 3:15 I was letting myself into my apartment, which already seemed to have the musty smell of neglect. I'd been gone one day, but it felt like weeks. Darcy came in behind me, her expression tinged with guilt when she saw that I was still shaky on my feet. I perched on the couch, momentarily clammy, and then set about getting dressed.

"What next?" she asked.

I was easing into my blue jeans. "Let's go into the office and see if Andy left anything behind," I said. I pulled on a sweatshirt and went into the bathroom, where I brushed my teeth. My reflection in the bathroom mirror showed a face marked by astonishment where my eyebrows used to be. My cheeks looked sunburned. I could see a few scrapes and bruises, but it was no big deal. I kind of liked having frizz across the front where my hair once was. I opened the medicine cabinet and took out my trusty nail scissors. I clipped the tape off my right arm and unwound the gauze, inspecting what was underneath. Looked okay to me. Burns do better in the open air, anyway. I took a painkiller just in case, and then waved dismissively at the sight of myself. I was fine.

I snagged the file folder I'd made after raiding Andy's trash. I put on some sweatsocks and tennis shoes, grabbing a jacket just before I locked up again. Santa Teresa usually gets chilly once the sun goes down and I wasn't sure how long I'd be gone.

Outside, it felt more like August than January. The sky was clear, the sun high overhead. There was no breeze at all, and the sidewalks were functioning like solar panels, absorbing the sunlight, throwing off heat. There was no sign of Daniel, for which I was grateful. He would no doubt have disapproved of my hospital defection. I spotted my little VW parked two doors down and I was glad somebody'd had the foresight to drive it back to my place. I wasn't up to driving yet, but it was nice to know the car was there.

Darcy drove us over to the office. There was scarcely any traffic. The whole downtown area seemed deserted, as if in the wake of nuclear attack. The parking lot was empty, except for a series of beer bottles clustered near the kiosk, the dregs of a New Year's Eve revelry.

We went up the back stairs. "You know what bothers me?" I asked Darcy as we climbed.

She unlocked the door to the building, glancing back at me. "What's that?"

"Well, suppose we assume Andy's guilty of conspiracy in this. It does look that way even though we don't have proof at this point, right?"

"I'd say so."

"I can't figure out why he agreed to it. We're talking major insurance fraud. He gets caught, it's his livelihood. So what's in it for him?"

"It has to be a payoff," Darcy said. "If Janice hosed him, he's probably desperate for cash."

"Maybe," I said. "It means somebody knew him well enough to think he'd tumble to a bribe. Andy's always been a jerk, but I never really thought of him as dishonest."

We'd reached the glass doors of California Fidelity. "What are you saying?" she asked as she unlocked the door and let us in. She flipped the overhead lights on and tossed her handbag on a chair.

"I don't really know. I'm wondering if something else was going on, I guess. He's in a perfect position to fiddle with the claim forms, but it's still a big risk. And why the panic? What went wrong?"

"He probably didn't count on Olive getting killed. That's gotta fit in somewhere," she said.

We went into Andy's office. Darcy watched with interest as I went through a systematic search. It looked like his business files were still intact, but all of his personal effects had been removed: the photograph of his kids that had sat on his desk, his leather-bound appointment calendar, address book, Rolodex, even the framed APSCRAP and MDRT awards he'd gotten some years before. He'd left a studio portrait of Janice, a five-by-seven color head shot, showing bouffant blond hair, a heart-shaped face, and a pointed chin. She did have a spiteful look about her, even grinning at the camera. Andy had blackened one front tooth and penned in some handsome hairs growing out of her nose. By widening her nostrils slightly, he'd created a piggy effect. The ever-mature Andy Motycka expressing his opinion of his ex-wife.

I sat in his swivel chair and surveyed the place, wondering how I was going to get a line on him. Where would he go and why take off like that? Had he made the bomb? Darcy was quiet, not wanting to interrupt my thought processes, such as they were.

"You have a number for Janice?" I asked.

"Yeah, at my desk. You want me to call and see if she knows where he is?"

"Let's do that. Make up an excuse if you can, and don't give anything away. If she doesn't know he's skipped out, let's don't tip it at this point."

"Right," Darcy said. She moved out to the reception area. I picked up the file I'd brought and pulled out all the papers. It was clear that Andy was in serious financial straits. Between Janice's harangue over the late support check, and the pink- and red-rimmed dunning notices, it was safe to assume that the pressure was on. I reread the various versions of his love letter to his inamorata. That must have been quite a Christmas Eve they'd had. Maybe he'd run away with her.

Andy's calendar pad still sat at the uppermost edge of his blotter, two date sheets side by side, connected by arched clips that allowed the pages to lie flat. He'd taken his leather month- by-month appointment book, but he'd left this behind. Ap- parently he made a habit of noting appointments on both places so his secretary could keep track of his whereabouts. I leafed back through the week, day by day. On Friday, De- cember 24, he'd circled 9:00 P.M. and penciled in the initial L. Was this his beloved? I worked my way back through the last six months. The initial cropped up at irregular intervals, with no pattern that I could discern.

I went out to the reception area, taking the calendar pad and the file folder with me.

Darcy was on the phone, in the midst of a chat with Janice, from what I gathered.

"Uh-hun. Well, I wouldn't know anything about that. I don't know him all that well. Uh-hun. What's your attorney telling you? I guess that's true, but I don't know what good it would do you. Look, I'm going to have to run, Janice. I've got somebody standing here waiting to use the phone. Uh-hun, I'd appreciate that and I'll let you know what we hear on this end. I'm sure he just went off for the weekend and forgot to mention it. Thanks much. You too. Bye-bye. Right."

Darcy replaced the receiver and let out a deep breath. "Good God, that woman can talk! It's lucky I called when I did because I got an earful. She's p.o.'d. He was supposed to come by last night and pick the kids up and he never showed. She was all set to go out and had to cancel her plans. No call, no apologies, nothing. She's convinced he's skipped town and she's all set to call the cops."

"Wouldn't do any good unless he's been missing seventy-two hours," I said. "He's probably shacked up somewhere with this bimbo he's so crazy about." I showed Darcy the letters I'd picked out of his trash.

It was wonderful watching her expression shift from amusement to distaste. "Oh God, would you let him suckle your hmphm-hmph?"

"Only if I doused it with arsenic first."

Darcy's brow wrinkled. "Her bazookas must be huge. He couldn't think what to compare 'em to."

I looked over her shoulder. "Well, 'footballs,' but he crossed that out. Probably didn't seem romantic."

Darcy shoved the papers back in the file. "That was titil-lating stuff. Oh, bad joke. Now what?"

"I don't know. He took his address book with him, but I do have this." I flipped through the calendar pad and showed her the penciled initials scattered through the months. I could see Darcy's mental wheels start to turn.

"Wonder if she ever called him here," she said. "She must have, don't you think?"

She opened her top right-hand desk drawer and took out the log for incoming telephone calls. It was a carbonless system with a permanent record in yellow overlaid by white perfo-rated originals. If a call came in for someone out of the office, she made a note of the date and time, the caller, and the return number, checking off one of the responses to the right, "Please call," "Will call back," or "Message." The top slip was then torn out and given to the relevant recipient. Darcy turned back to December 1.

It didn't take us long to find her. By comparing the log of Andy's calls with the calendar pad, we came up with one repeat caller who left a number, but no name, always a day or two prior to Andy's assignations . . . if indeed that's what they were.

"Do you keep crisscross around here?" I asked.

"I don't think so. We used to have one, but I haven't seen it for months."

"I've got last year's in my office. Let's see who's listed at this number. We better hope it's not a business."

I pulled my keys out of my handbag as Darcy followed me.

"You were supposed to turn those keys in," she said in mild reproof.

"Oh really? I didn't know that."

I unlocked my office door and moved to the file cabinet, pulling the crisscross from the bottom drawer. The number, at least the year before, belonged to last name Wilding, first name Lorraine.

"You think it's her?" Darcy asked.

"I know a good way to find out," I said. The address listed was only two blocks from my apartment, down near the beach.

"Are you sure you're okay? I don't think you should be running around like this."

"Don't sweat it. I'm fine," I said. The truth was, I wasn't feeling all that terrific, but I didn't want to lay my little head down until a few questions had been answered first. I was running on adrenaline—not a bad source of energy. When it ran out, of course, you were up shit creek, but for the time being it seemed better to be on the move.

18

I had Darcy drop me off. In an interview situation I prefer to work alone, especially when I'm not quite sure who I'm dealing with. People are easier to manage one on one; there's more room to ad-lib and more room to negotiate.

The apartment building was Spanish style, probably dating from the thirties. The red-tile roof had aged to the color of rust and the stucco had mellowed from stark white to cream. There were clumps of beaky-looking bird of paradise plants in front. A towering, sixty-foot pine tree enveloped the yard in shade. Bougainvillea was massed at the roofline, a tumble of magenta blossoms that spread out along the gutters and trailed like Spanish moss. Wood shutters, painted dark brown, flanked the windows. The loggia was chilly and smelled of damp earth.

I knocked at apartment D. There was no sign of Andy's car on the street, but there was still a possibility that he was here. I had no idea what I'd say if he appeared at the door. It was nearly 6:00 and I could smell someone's supper in the making, something with onions and celery and butter. The door opened and I felt a little lurch of surprise. Andy's ex-wife was staring out at me.

"Janice?" I said, with disbelief.

"I'm Lorraine," she said. "You must be looking for my sister."

Once she spoke, the resemblance began to fade. She had to be in her mid-forties, her good looks just beginning to dehydrate. She had Janice's blond hair and the same pointed chin, but her eyes were bigger and her mouth was more generous. So was her body. She was my height, probably ten pounds heavier, and I could see where she carried the excess. Her eyes were brown and she'd lined them with black, adding false lashes as dense as paintbrushes. She wore snug white twill shorts and a halter top. Her legs had been shapely once, but the muscles had taken on that stringy look that connotes no exercise. Her tan looked like the comprehensive sort you acquire at a tanning salon—the electric beach.

Andy must have been in heaven. I've known men who fall in love with the same type of woman over and over again, but the similarities are usually not so obvious. She looked hauntingly like Janice. The difference was that Lorraine was voluptuous where the former Mrs. Motycka tended toward the small, the dry, and the mean. Judging from Andy's letter, Lorraine was freer with her affections than Janice ever was. She did things to him that made his syntax turn to hiccups. I wondered if his affair with Lorraine came before or after his divorce. Either way, the liaison was dangerous. If Janice found out about it, she would extract a pretty price. It crossed my mind briefly that someone might have used this as leverage to secure his cooperation.

"I'm looking for Andy," I said.

"Who?"

"Andy Motycka, your brother-in-law. I'm from the insurance company where he works."

"Why look at me? He and Janice are divorced."

"He gave me this address in case I ever needed to get in touch."

"He did?"

"Why else would I be here?"

She looked at me with suspicion. "How well do you know Janice?"

I shrugged. "I don't really. I used to see her at company parties before they split. When you first opened the door, I thought it was her, you look so much alike."

She took that in and digested it. "What do you want Andy for?"

"He disappeared yesterday and no one seems to know where he went. Did he say anything to you?"

"Not really."

"Mind if I come in? Maybe we can figure what's happening."

"All right," she said reluctantly. "I suppose that's okay. He never told me he gave anyone this address."

She stepped back and I followed her into the apartment. A small tiled entry dropped down two steps into a large living room. The apartment looked as if it had been furnished from a rental company. Everything was new, handsome, and impersonal. A foot-high live spruce decked with candy canes sat on the glass-and-brass coffee table, but that was the only indication that Christmas had come and gone.

Lorraine flicked the television off and motioned me to a chair. The upholstery had the tough, rubbery feel of Scotchgarding. Neither tears, blood, nor spilled booze could penetrate such a finish. She sat down, giving the crotch of her shorts a pull so the inseam wouldn't bury itself in her private parts. "How'd you say you know Andy? Do you work for him?"

"Not really for him, but the same company. When did you see him last?"

"Three days ago. I talked to him on the phone Thursday night. He was taking his kids on New Year's Eve, so I wasn't going to see him till late tomorrow anyway, but he always calls, regardless of what's going on. When I didn't hear by this morning, I drove out to his place, but there's no sign of him. Why would you need him New Year's Day?"

I stuck as close to the truth as I could, filling her in on the fact that he'd departed Friday morning without giving any indication where he meant to go. "We need one of the files. Do you know anything about the claim he was working on? There was a fire out at Wood/Warren about a week ago and I think he was doing some of the paperwork."

There was a startled silence and the barriers shot up again. "Excuse me?"

"Did he mention that to you?"

"What'd you say your name was?"

"Darcy. I'm the receptionist. I think I've talked to you a couple of times on the phone."

Her manner became formal, circumspect. "I see. Well, Darcy, he doesn't talk to me about his work. I know he loves the company and he's fine at what he does."

"Oh, absolutely," said I. "And he's very well liked, which is why we were concerned when he went off without a word. We thought maybe some kind of family matter came up. He didn't say anything about going out of town for a few days?"

She shook her head.

Judging from her attitude, I was almost certain she knew about the scam. I was equally certain she'd never give a hint of confirmation.

She said, "I wish I could help you, but he never said a word to me. In fact, I'd appreciate a call myself when the man turns up. I don't like to have to sit here and fret."

"I don't blame you," I said. "You can reach me at this number if you need to, and I'll check back with you if I hear anything." I jotted down Darcy's name and my telephone number.

"I hope nothing's wrong." This seemed like the first sincere comment she'd made.

"I'm sure not," I said. Personally, I was betting something had scared the hell out of him and he'd taken off.

She'd had a few minutes now to focus on my browless,

burned face. "Uh, I hope this doesn't seem rude, but were you in some kind of accident?"

"A gas heater blew up in my face," I said. She made some sympathetic noises and I hoped the lie wouldn't come back to haunt me. "Well, I'm sorry I had to bother you on a holiday. I'll let you know if we hear from him." I got up and she rose as well, crossing with me to the front door.

I walked home through streets beginning to darken, though it was not quite 5:00. The winter sun had sunk and the air temperature was dropping with it. I was exhausted, secretly wishing I could check back into the hospital for the night. Something about the clean white sheets seemed inviting. I was hungry, too, and for once would have welcomed something more nutritious than peanut butter and crackers, which was what I was looking forward to.

Daniel's car was parked at the curb out in front of my apartment. I peered in, half expecting to find him asleep on the back seat. I went in through the gate and around the side of the building to Henry's backyard. Daniel was sitting on the cinder-block wall that separated Henry's lot from our neighbor's to the right. Daniel, his elbows on his knees, was blowing a low, mournful tune on an alto harmonica. With the cowboy boots, the jeans, and a blue-denim jacket, he might have been out on the range.

" 'Bout time you got home," he remarked. He tucked the harmonica in his pocket and got up.

"I had work to do."

"You're always working. You should take better care of yourself."

I unlocked my front door and went in, flipping on the light. I slung my handbag on a chair and sank down on the couch. Daniel moved into my kitchenette and opened the refrigerator.

"Don't you ever grocery-shop?"

"What for? I'm never home."

"Lord." He took out a stub of butter, some eggs, and a packet of cheese so old it looked like dark plastic around the edge. While I watched, he searched my kitchen cabinets, assembling miscellaneous foodstuffs. I slouched down on my spine, leaning my head against the back of the couch with my feet propped up on the ottoman. I was fresh out of snappy talk and I couldn't conjure up a shred of anger. This was a man I'd loved once, and though the feelings were gone, a certain familiarity remained.

"How come this place smells like feet?" he said idly. He was already chopping onions, his fingers nimble. He played piano the same way, with a careless expertise.

"It's my air fern. Somebody gave it to me as a pet."

He picked up the tag end of a pound of bacon, sniffing suspiciously at the contents. "Stiff as beef jerky."

"Lasts longer that way," I said.

He shrugged and extracted the three remaining pieces of bacon, which he dropped into the skillet with a clinking sound. "God, one thing about giving up dope, food never has tasted right," he said. "Smoke dope, you're always eating the best meal you ever had. Helps when you're broke or on the road."

"You really gave up the hard stuff?"

" 'Fraid so," he said. "Gave up cigarettes, gave up coffee. I do drink a beer now and then, though I notice you don't have any. I used to go to AA meetings five times a week, but that talk of a higher power got to me in the end. There isn't any power higher than heroin, you can take my word for it."

I could feel myself drifting off. He was humming to himself, a melody dimly remembered that blended with the scent of bacon and eggs. What could smell better than supper being cooked by someone else?

He shook me gently and I woke to find an omelet on a

warmed plate being placed in my lap. I roused myself, suddenly famished again.

Daniel sat cross-legged on the floor, forking up eggs while he talked. "Who lives in the house?"

"My landlord, Henry Pitts. He's off in Michigan."

"You got something goin' with him?"

I paused between bites. "The man is eighty-one."

"He have a piano?"

"Actually, I think he does. An upright, probably out of tune. His wife used to play."

"I'd like to try it, if there's a way to get in. You think he'd care?"

"Not at all. I've got a key. You mean tonight?"

"Tomorrow. I gotta be somewhere in a bit."

The way the light fell on his face, I could see the lines near his eyes. Daniel had lived hard and he wasn't aging well. He looked haggard, a gauntness beginning to emerge. "I can't believe you're a private detective," he said. "Seems weird to me."

"It's not that different from being a cop," I said. "I'm not part of the bureaucracy, that's all. Don't wear a uniform or punch a time clock. I get paid more, but not as regularly."

"A bit more dangerous, isn't it? I don't remember anyone ever tried to blow you up back then."

"Well, they sure tried everything else. Traffic detail, every time you pull someone over, you wonder if the car's stolen, if the driver's got a gun. Domestic violence is worse. People drinking, doing drugs. Half the time they'd just as soon waste you as one another. Knock on the door, you never know what you're dealing with."

"How'd you get involved in a homicide?"

"It didn't start out like that. You know the family, by the way," I said.

"I do?"

"The Woods. Remember Bass Wood?"

He hesitated. "Vaguely."

"His sister Olive is the one who died."

Daniel set his plate down. "The Kohler woman is *his* sister? I had no idea. What the hell is going on?"

I sketched it out for him, telling him what I knew. If I have a client, I won't talk about a case, but I couldn't see the harm here. Just me. It felt good, giving me a chance to theorize to some extent. Daniel was a good audience, asking just the right questions. It felt like old times, the good times, when we talked on for hours about whatever suited us.

Finally a silence fell. I was cold and feeling tense. I reached for the quilt and covered my feet. "Why'd you leave me, Daniel? I never have understood."

He kept his tone light. "It wasn't you, babe. It wasn't anything personal."

"Was there someone else?"

He shifted uneasily, tapping with the fork on the edge of his dinner plate. He set the utensil aside. He stretched his legs out in front of him and leaned back on his elbows. "I wish I knew what to tell you, Kinsey. It wasn't that I didn't want you. I wanted something else more, that's all."

"What?"

He scanned my face. "Anything. Everything. Whatever came down the pike."

"You don't have a conscience, do you?"

He broke off eye contact. "No. That's why we were such a mismatch. I don't have any conscience and you have too much."

"No, not so. If I had a conscience, I wouldn't tell so many lies."

"Ah, right. The lies. I remember. That was the one thing we had in common," he said. His gaze came up to mine. I was chilled by the look in his eyes, clear and empty. I could remember wanting him. I could remember looking at his face, wondering if there could ever be a man more beautiful. For some reason I never expect the people I know to have any talent or ability. I'd been introduced to Daniel and dismissed him until the moment I heard him play. Then I did a long double-take, astonished, and I was hooked. There just wasn't any place to go from there. Daniel was married to his music, to freedom, to drugs, and, briefly, to me. I was about that far down on the list.

I stirred restlessly. A palpable sexual vapor seemed to rise from his skin, drifting across to me like the scent of wood-smoke half a mile away. It's a strange phenomenon, but true, that in sleeping with men, none of the old rules apply to a man you've slept with before. Operant conditioning. The man had trained me well. Even after eight years, he could still do what he did best . . . seduce. I cleared my throat, struggling to break the spell. "What's the story on your therapist?"

"No story. She's a shrink. She thinks she can fix me."

"And this is part of it? Making peace with me?"

"We all have delusions. That's one of hers."

"Is she in love with you?"

"I doubt it."

"Must be early in the game," I said.

The dimple appeared and a smile flashed across his face, but it was mirthless, evasive, and I wondered if I hadn't touched on some pain of his. Now he was the restless one, glancing at his watch.

"I got to get," he said abruptly. He gathered both plates and the silverware, toting dishes to the kitchen. He'd cleaned up while he cooked, an old habit of his, so he didn't have much to do. By 7:00, he was gone. I heard the thunder and rattle of his car as he started it and pulled away.

The apartment seemed dark. Extraordinarily quiet.

I locked up. I took a bath, keeping the water away from my burns. I closed myself into the folds of my quilt and turned out the light. Being with him had brought back the pain in fossil form, evidence of ancient emotional life, embedded now in rock. I studied the sensations as I would some extinct sub-species, for the curiosity, if nothing more.

Being married to a doper is as close to loneliness as you can get. Add to that his chronic infidelity and you've got a lot of sleepless nights on your hands. There are certain men who rove, men who prowl the night, who simply don't show up for hours on end. Lying in bed, you tell yourself you're worried that he's wrecked the car again, that he's drunk or in jail. You tell yourself you're worried he's been rolled, mugged, or maimed, that he's overdosed. What really worries you is he might be with someone else. The hours creep by. From time to time, you hear a car approaching, but it's never his. By 4:00 A.M., it's a toss-up which is uppermost in your mind—wishing he would come home or wishing he were dead.

Daniel Wade was the one who taught me how to value solitude. What I endure now doesn't hold a candle to what I endured with him.

19

The memorial service for Olive was held at 2:00 P.M. on Sunday at the Unitarian Church, a spartan ceremony in a setting stripped of excess. Attendance was limited to family and a few close friends. There were lots of flowers, but no casket in evidence. The floors were red tile, glossy and cold. The pews were carved and polished wood, without cushions. The lofty ceiling of the church lent a sense of airiness, but the space was curiously devoid of ornamentation and there were no religious icons at all. Even the stained-glass windows were a plain cream with the barest suggestion of green vines curling around the edges. The Unitarians apparently don't hold with zealousness, piety, confession, penance, or atonement. Jesus and God were never mentioned, nor did the word "amen" cross anybody's lips. Instead of scriptures, there were readings from Bertrand Russell and Kahlil Gibran. A man with a flute played several mournful classical tunes and ended with a number that sounded suspiciously like "Send In the Clowns." There was no eulogy, but the minister chatted about Olive in the most conversational of tones, inviting those congregated to stand up and share recollections of her. No one had the nerve. I sat near the back in my all-purpose dress, not wanting to intrude. I noticed that several people nudged one another and turned to look at me, as if I'd achieved celebrity status by being blown up with her. Ebony, Lance, and Bass remained perfectly composed. Ash wept, as did her mother. Terry sat alone in the front row, leaning forward, head in his hands.

The whole group didn't occupy more than about the first five rows.

Afterward we assembled in the small garden courtyard outside, where we were served champagne and finger sandwiches. The occasion was polite and circumspect. The afternoon was hot. The sun was bright. The garden itself was gaudy with annuals, gold, orange, purple, and red marching along the white stucco wall that enclosed the churchyard. The stone-and-tile fountain plashed softly, a breeze occasionally blowing spray out onto the surrounding paving stones.

I moved among the mourners, saying little, picking up fragments of conversation. Some were discussing the stock market, some their recent travels, one the divorce of a mutual acquaintance who'd been married twenty-six years. Of those who thought to talk about Olive Wood Kohler, the themes seemed to be equally divided between conventional sentiment and cattiness.

". . . he'll never recover from the loss, you know. She was everything to him . . ."

". . . paid seven thousand dollars for that coat . . ."

". . . shocked . . . couldn't believe it when Ruth called me . . ."

". . . poor thing. He worshiped the ground she walked on, though I never could quite see it myself . . ."

". . . tragedy . . . so young . . ."

". . . well, I always wondered about that, as narrow as she was through the chest. Who did the work?"

I found Ash sitting on a poured-concrete bench near the chapel door. She looked drawn and pale, her pale-red hair glinting with strands of premature gray. The dress she wore was a dark wool, loosely cut, the short sleeves making her upper arms seem as shapeless as bread dough. In another few years she'd have that matronly look that women sometimes get, rushing into middle age just to get it over with. I sat down beside her. She held out her hand and we sat there together like grade-school kids on a field trip. "Line up in twos and no talking." Life itself is a peculiar outing. Sometimes I still feel like I need a note from my mother.

I scanned the crowd. "What happened to Ebony? I don't see her."

"She left just after the service. God, she's so cold. She sat there like a stone, never cried a tear."

"Bass says she was a mess when she first heard the news. Now she's got herself under control, which is probably much closer to the way she lives. Were she and Olive close?"

"I always thought so. Now I'm not so sure."

"Come on, Ashley. People deal with grief differently. You never really know what goes on," I said. "I went to a funeral once where a woman laughed so hard she wet her pants. Her only son had died in a car accident. Later, she was hospitalized for depression, but if you'd seen her then, you never would have guessed."

"I suppose." She let her gaze drift across the courtyard. "Terry got another phone call from that woman."

"Lyda Case?"

"I guess that's the one. Whoever threatened him."

"Did he call the police?"

"I doubt it. It came up a little while ago, before we left the house to come here. He probably hasn't had a chance."

I spotted Terry talking to the minister. As if on cue, he turned and looked at me. I touched Ash's arm. "I'll be right back," I said.

Terry murmured something and broke away, moving toward me. Looking at him was like looking in my mirror . . . the same bruises, same haunted look about the eyes. We were as bonded as lovers after the trauma we'd been through. No one could know what it was like in that moment when the bomb went off. "How are you?" he said, his voice low.

"Ash says Lyda Case called."

Terry took my arm and steered me toward the entrance to the social hall. "She's here in town. She wants to meet with me."

"Bullshit. No way," I whispered hoarsely.

Terry looked at me uneasily. "I know it sounds crazy, but she says she has some information that could be of help."

"I'm sure she does. It's probably in a box and goes boom when you pick it up."

"I asked her about that. She swears she didn't have anything to do with Olive's death."

"And you believed her?"

"I guess I did in a way."

"Hey, you were the one who told me about the threat. She scared the life out of you and here she is again. If you won't call Lieutenant Dolan, I will."

I thought he would argue, but he sighed once. "All right. I know it's the only thing that makes any sense. I've just been in such a fog."

"Where's she staying?"

"She didn't say. She wants to meet at the bird refuge at six. Would you be willing to come? She asked for you by name."

"Why me?"

"I don't know. She said you flew to Texas to talk to her. I can't believe you didn't mention that when the subject came up."

"Sorry. I guess I should have. That was early in the week. I was trying to get a line on Hugh Case, to see how his death fits in."

"And?"

"I'm not sure yet. I'd be very surprised if it didn't connect. I just can't figure out how."

Terry gave me a skeptical look. "It's never been proven he was murdered, has it?"

"Well, that's true," I said. "It just seems highly unlikely that the lab work would disappear unless somebody meant to conceal the evidence. Maybe it's the same person with a different motive this time."

"What makes you say that? Carbon-monoxide poisoning is about as far away from bombs as you can get. Wouldn't the guy use the same method if it worked so well the first time?"

I shrugged. "I don't know. If it were me, I'd do whatever was expedient. The point is, this is not something we should fool around with on our own."

I saw Terry's gaze focus on something behind me. I turned to see Bass. He looked old. Everybody had aged in the wake of Olive's death, but on Bass the lines of weariness were the least flattering—something puffy about the eyes, something pouty about the mouth. He had one of those boyish faces that doesn't lend itself to deep emotion. On him, sorrow looked like a form of petulance. "I'm taking Mother home," he said.

"I'll be right there," Terry said. Bass moved away and Terry turned back to me. "Do you want to call Lieutenant Dolan or should I?"

"I'll do it," I said. "If there's any problem, I'll let you know. Otherwise, I'll meet you down at the bird refuge at six."

I was home by 3:35, but it took me almost an hour to track down the lieutenant, who was certainly interested in having a chat with Lyda Case. He said he'd be there at 5:00 in an unmarked car, on the off-chance that she was feeling truly skittish about contact with the police. I changed into jeans and a sweatshirt and pulled on my tennis shoes. I was tired, and the residual pain from my injuries was like a slow leak from a tire, depleting. Over the course of the day, I could feel myself go flat. In some ways I shared Terry's sentiments. It was hard to believe Lyda was responsible for the package bomb, let alone her husband's death two years before. In spite of her accusations and the veiled threat to Terry, she didn't seem like the homicidal type, for whatever that's worth. I've been surprised by killers again and again, and I try not to generalize, but there it was. Maybe she was just what she claimed to be . . . someone with information that might be of help.

By the time I reached the meeting place, the sun was almost down. The bird refuge is a landscaped preserve near the beach, established to protect geese, swans, and other fowl. The forty-three-acre property abuts the zoo and consists of an irregular-shaped freshwater lagoon, surrounded by a wide lane of clipped grass through which a bike trail runs. There's a small parking lot at one end where parents bring little children with their plastic bags of old popcorn and stale bread. Male pigeons puff and posture in jerky pursuit of their inattentive female counterparts, who manage to strut along just one step away from conception.

I pulled into the lot and parked. I got out of my car. Sea gulls swirled and settled in an oddly choreographed dance of their own. Geese honked along the shore in search of crumbs while the ducks paddled through the still waters, sending out ripples around them. The sky was a deepening gray, the ruffled silver surface of the lagoon reflecting the rising wind.

I was glad when Lieutenant Dolan's car pulled in beside mine. We chatted idly until Terry appeared, and then the three of us waited. Lyda Case never showed. At 8:15, we finally gave it up. Terry took Dolan's number and said he'd be in touch if he heard from her. It was a bit of a letdown, as all three of us had hoped for a break in the case. Terry seemed grateful for the activity and I had to guess that it was going to be hard for him to spend his first night alone. He'd been in the hospital Friday night and with his mother-in-law on Saturday while the bomb squad finished their crime-scene investigation and a work crew came in to board up the front wall of the house.

My own sense of melancholy had returned in full force.

Funerals and the new year are a bad mix. The painkillers I'd been taking dulled my mental processes and left me feeling somewhat disconnected from reality. I needed companionship. I wanted lights and noise and a good dinner somewhere with a decent glass of wine and talk of anything except death. I fancied myself an independent soul, but I could see how easily my attachments could form.

I drove home hoping Daniel would appear again. With him, you never knew. The day he walked out of the marriage eight years before, he hadn't even left a note. He didn't like to deal with anger or recrimination. He said it bummed him out to be around people who were sad, depressed, or upset. His strategy was to let other people cope with unpleasantness. I'd seen him do it with his family, with old friends, with gigs that no longer interested him. One day he wasn't there, and you might not see him for two years. By then, you couldn't even remember why you'd been so pissed off.

Sometimes, as in my case, there'd be some residual rage, which Daniel usually found puzzling. Strong emotion is hard to sustain in the face of bafflement. You run out of things to say. Most of the time, in the old days, he was stoned anyway, so confronting him was about as productive as trying to discipline a cat for spraying on the drapes. He didn't "get it." Fury didn't make any sense to him. He couldn't see the connection between his behavior and the wrath that was generated as a consequence. What the man did really well was play. He was a free spirit, whimsical, inventive, tireless, sweet. Jazz piano, sex, travel, parties, he was wonderful at those . . . until he got bored, of course, or until reality surfaced, and then he was gone. I had never been taught how to play, so I learned a lot from him. I'm just not sure it was anything I really needed to know.

I found a parking spot six doors away. Daniel's car was parked in front of my place. He was leaning against the fender.

There was a paper bag with twine handles near his feet, a baguette of French bread sticking out of it like a baseball bat.

"I thought you might be gone by today," I said.

"I talked to my friend. It looks like I'll be here a couple days more."

"You find a place to stay?"

"I hope so. There's a little motel here in the neighborhood that will have a room free later. Some folks are checking out."

"That's nice. You can reclaim your stuff."

"I'll do that as soon as I know for sure."

"What's that?" I said, pointing at the baguette.

He looked down at the sack, his gaze following mine. "Picnic," he said. "I thought I'd play the piano some, too."

"How long have you been here?"

"Since six," he said. "You feel all right? You look beat."

"I am. Come on in. I hope you have wine. I could use some."

He pushed away from the car, toting the bag as he followed me through the gate. We ended up at Henry's, sitting on the floor in his living room. Daniel had bought twenty-five votive candles and he arranged those around the room until I felt like I was sitting in the middle of a birthday cake. We had wine, pâté, cheeses, French bread, cold salads, fresh raspberries, and sugar cookies the size of Frisbees. I stretched out afterward in a food-induced reverie while Daniel played the piano. Daniel didn't play music so much as he discovered it, calling up melodies, pursuing them across the keys, embroidering, embellishing. His background was in classical piano, so he warmed up with Chopin, Liszt, the intricacies of Bach, drifting over into improvisation without effort.

Daniel stopped abruptly.

I opened my eyes and looked at him.

His expression was pained. He touched at the keyboard

carelessly, a sour chord. "It's gone. I don't have it anymore. I gave up drugs and the music went with 'em."

I sat up. "What are you talking about?"

"Just what I said. It was the choice I had to make, but it's all bullshit. I can live without drugs, babe, but not without music. I'm not made that way."

"It sounded fine. It was beautiful."

"What do you know, Kinsey? You don't know anything. That was all technique. Mechanics. I got no soul. The only time music works is when I'm burning with smack, flying. This is nothing. Half-life. The other is better . . . when I'm on fire like that and give it all away. You can't hold back. It's all or nothin'."

I could feel my body grow still. "What are you saying?" Dumb question. I knew.

His eyes glowed and he pinched his thumb and index finger together near his lips, sucking in air. It was the gesture he always used when he was about to roll a joint. He looked down at the crook of his elbow and made a fist lovingly.

"Don't do that," I said.

"Why not?"

"It'll kill you."

He shrugged. "Why can't I live the way I want? I'm the devil. I'm bad. You should know that by now. There isn't anything I wouldn't do just for the hell of it . . . just to stay *awake*. Fuck. I'd like to fly again, you know? I'd like to feel good. I'll tell you something about being straight . . . it's a goddamn drag. I don't know how you put up with it. I don't know how you keep from hangin' yourself."

I crumpled up paper napkins and stuffed them in the sack, gathered paper plates, plastic ware, the empty wine bottle, cardboard containers. He sat on the piano bench, his hands held loosely in his lap. I doubted he'd live to see forty-three.

"Is that why you came back?" I asked. "To lay this on me? What do you want, permission? Approval?"

"Yeah, I'd like that."

I started blowing out candles, darkness gathering like smoke around the edges of the room. You can't argue with people who fall in love with death. "Get out of my life, Daniel. Would you just do that?"

20

I got up Monday morning at 6:00 and did a slow, agonizing five-mile jog. I was in bad shape and I had no business being out there at all, but I couldn't help myself. This had to be the worst Christmas I'd ever spent and the new year wasn't shaping up all that great as far as I could see. It was now January 3, and I wanted my life back the way it was. With luck, Rosie would reopen later in the day, and maybe Jonah would return from Idaho. Henry was flying home on Friday. I recited my blessings to myself as I ran, ignoring the fact that my body hurt, that I had no office at the moment, and a cloud of suspicion was still hanging over my head.

The sky was clear, a torpid breeze picking up. The day seemed unseasonably warm even at that hour, and I wondered if we were experiencing Santa Ana conditions, winds gusting in from the desert, hot drafts like the blast from an oven. It was the wrong time of year for it, but the air had that dry, dusty feel to it. The sweat on my face evaporated almost at once and my T-shirt was clinging to my back like a hot, soggy rag. By the time I got back to my neighborhood, I felt I'd blown some of the tension away. Kinsey Millhone, perpetual optimist. I jogged all the way to Henry's gate and took a few minutes walking back and forth, catching my breath, cooling down. Daniel's car was gone. In its place was a vehicle I hadn't seen before—a compact, judging from the shape, anonymous under a pale-blue cotton car cover. Off-street parking in the area is restricted and garages are rare. If I ever got a new car, I'd have to invest in a cover myself. I leaned against the fence, stretching my hamstrings dutifully before I went in to shower.

Lance Wood called me at 8:00. The background noise was that hollow combination of traffic and enclosure that suggests a phone booth.

"Where are you?" I asked, as soon as he'd identified himself.

"On a street corner in Colgate. I think my phone at work is tapped," he said.

"Have you had it checked?"

"Well, I'm not really sure how to go about it and I feel like a fool asking the phone company to come out."

"I'll bet," I said. "That's like asking the fox to secure the henhouse. What makes you think you've got a tap?"

"Odd stuff. I'll have a conversation and the next thing I know, something I've said is all over the place. I'm not talking about office gossip. It's something more insidious than that, like comments I've made to out-of-state customers that people here would have no way of knowing."

"Could it be a simple case of someone listening in? A lot of employees have access to the phones out there."

"Not my private line. It isn't like anything we do is top secret, but we all say things we'd rather not have spread around. Someone's making me look very bad. Is there some way you can check it out?"

"I can try," I said. "What about the phone itself? Have you tried unscrewing the mouthpiece?"

"Sure, but I don't know what the inside of a receiver's supposed to look like. I'm not picking up any odd noises or clicks, I will say that."

"You wouldn't if the tap is set up properly. It'd be virtually undetectable. Of course, it might not be that at all,"

I said. "Maybe the office itself is bugged."

"In which case, what? Is that something you can spot?"

"Sometimes, with luck. It's also possible to buy an electronic device that will scan for bugs. I'll see if I can locate one before I come out. Give me a couple of hours and I'll meet you at the plant. I've got some other things I probably ought to take care of first."

"Right. Thanks."

I took the next hour to type up my notes, clipping the newspaper article about the explosion to include with my files. I tried Lyda Case's telephone number in Texas on the off-chance that her roommate had heard from her. It would help if I knew how to find her here in Santa Teresa.

At 9:10, my phone rang. It was Darcy calling from California Fidelity and talking as if she had a hand cupped over the mouthpiece. "Big trouble," she said.

I could feel my heart sink. "Now what?"

"If I change the subject abruptly, you'll know Mac walked in," she murmured. "I overheard a conversation between him and Jewel. He says someone tipped the cops about the warehouse inventory. It looks like Lance Wood moved all the merchandise to another location before his warehouse burned down. The inventory he claimed reimbursement for was all worthless junk."

"That's bullshit," I said. "I saw some of it myself. I must have gone through five or six boxes when I inspected the place."

"Well, I guess he had a few real boxes seeded in among the fake. He's going to be charged, Kinsey. Arson and fraud, and you're being named as co-conspirator. Mac turned everything over to the D.A. this morning. I thought you'd like to know in case you need to talk to an attorney."

"What's the timetable? Do you know?"

"Mr. Motycka isn't in today, but I can leave a message on his desk," she said.

"Is that Mac?"

"He didn't say exactly, but we're expecting him some time today. Uh-hun. Yes, I'll do that. All right, thanks," she said and hung up.

I put a call through to Lonnie Kingman and alerted him. He said he'd check with the D.A.'s office and find out if a warrant was being issued. His advice was to surrender voluntarily, thus avoiding the ignominy and uncertainty of a public arrest.

"Jesus, I can't believe this is happening," I said.

"Well, it hasn't yet. Don't worry about it until I tell you to," he said.

I grabbed my handbag and car keys and headed out the door. I had disconnected my emotions again. There was no point in letting anxiety get in my way. I hopped in my car and drove over to an electrical-supply place on Granita. My knowledge of electronic surveillance was bound to be out-of-date, limited to information picked up in a crash course at the Police Academy nearly ten years before. The advances in miniaturization since then had probably revolutionized the field, but I suspected the basics were always going to be the same. Microphone, transmitter, recorder of some type, probably voice-activated these days. The planting can be done by a technician disguised as any commonly seen service person: telephone lineman, meter reader, cable-television installer. Electronic surveillance is expensive, illegal unless authorized by the court, and looks a lot easier on television than it is in real life. Bug detection is another matter altogether. It was always possible, of course, that Lance Wood was imagining the whole thing, but I doubted it.

The small all-band receiver I bought was about the size of

a portable radio. While not truly all-band, it was sufficient to cover most bugging frequencies—30–50 MHz and 88–108 MHz. If the bug in his office was wired, I was going to have to find the wire myself, but if the bug was wireless, the receiver would start emitting a high-pitched squeal when it was within range.

I drove out to Colgate with my windows rolled down, parched air whipping through the interior of the VW like a convection oven. The weather forecaster on the car radio seemed as baffled as I was. It felt like August, asphalt shimmering in the heat. January in Santa Teresa is usually our best month. Everything is green, flowers in full bloom, the temperatures in the low seventies, mild and pleasant. The time-and-temp sign on the bank building was showing 89 degrees and it wasn't yet noon.

I parked in front of Wood/Warren and went in. Lance came out of his office in a wilted shirt with the sleeves rolled up.

"Do we need to watch what we say once we go in there?" he asked, indicating the office door.

"I don't think so. Let's let 'em know we're hot on the trail. Maybe it'll shake 'em up."

Before we started work, I did a quick check of both interior and exterior office walls on the off-chance that someone had installed a spike mike, a small probe that can be inserted between the studs, or hidden in a hollow door, the door panel itself serving as a diaphragm to transmit sound. Lance's office was located in the right-front corner of the building. The construction on those two sides was block and fieldstone, which didn't lend itself to easy installation. Somebody would have had to drill through solid rock. Inside, one office wall was contiguous with the reception area, where the pickup unit would have been difficult to conceal. The fourth wall was clean.

Company employees watched the two of us incuriously as we moved through the preliminary phases of the search. If anyone was worried about surveillance equipment coming to light, there was no indication of it.

We went into the office. I examined the telephone first, taking the plate off the bottom, unscrewing the mouth and ear pieces. As far as I could tell, the instrument was clean.

"I take it it's not the phone," Lance said, watching me.

"Who knows? The bug might be downstream," I said. "I don't have any way to find out if somebody's tapped into the line at the pole. We'll have to operate on the premise that the bug's somewhere in the room. It's just a matter of coming up with it."

"What exactly are we looking for?" Lance asked.

I shrugged. "Microphone, transmitter. If you're being spied on by the FBI or the CIA, we probably won't find anything. I'm assuming those guys are good. On the other hand, if your eavesdropper's an amateur, the device might be fairly crude."

"What's that thing?"

"My handy little all-band receiver," I said. "This should pick up any sound being transmitted by the bug in a feedback loop that'll result in a high-pitched squeal. We'll try this first, and if nothing comes to light, we'll take the office apart item by item."

I flipped the receiver on and began to work my way through the popular bugging frequencies, moving around the office like someone dowsing for water. Nothing.

I tucked the debugger in the outside pocket of my handbag and started searching in earnest, working my way around the periphery of the room, then toward the center in an imaginary grid pattern that covered every square foot.

Nothing.

I stood for a moment, perplexed, my eye traveling along

the ceiling, down the walls, along the baseboard. Where was the sucker? I felt my attention tugged by the phone jack just to the right of the door. There was no telephone cord coming from it.

"What's that?"

"What? Oh. I had the jack moved when I changed the office around. The telephone used to be over there."

I got down on my hands and knees and inspected the jack. It looked okay. I took out my screwdriver and popped off the cover. A small section of the baseboard had been cut away. Tucked into the space was a microcassette recorder about the size of a deck of playing cards.

"Hello," I said. The tape gave a half-turn and stopped. I moved the microsensor button away from the voice-activated setting and placed the recorder on his desk. Lance sank heavily into his swivel chair. He and I exchanged a long look.

"Why?" he said, baffled.

"I don't know. You tell me."

He shook his head. "I can't even think where to start. I don't have enemies as far as I know."

"Apparently you do. And it isn't just you. Hugh Case is dead and Terry *would* have been if he'd picked up that package instead of Olive. What do the three of you have in common?"

"Nothing, I swear. We're all connected to Wood/Warren, but none of us even do the same kind of work. We make hydrogen furnaces. That's all we do. And Hugh died two years ago. Why then? If somebody wants control of the company, why kill off the key personnel?"

"Maybe that's not the motive. It could be something wholly unrelated to the work. Give it some thought. I'll talk to Terry and have him do the same. Maybe there's something you've overlooked."

"There must be," he said, his face florid with heat and

tension. He pushed at the tape recorder with one finger. "Thanks for this."

"Be careful. There could be another one. Maybe this one was planted someplace obvious to distract us from the other." I picked up my handbag and started toward the door, pausing at the threshold. "Get in touch if you think of anything. And if you hear from Lyda Case, let me know."

As I passed through the reception area, I did a detour to the right. This was the office where the engineers had their drafting tables. John Salkowitz glanced up at me from the rough diagram he was working on. "Can I help you?"

"Is Ava Daugherty here someplace?"

"She just left. She had some errands to run, but she should be right back."

I took out my business card and placed it on her desk. "Have her get in touch with me, if you would."

"Will do."

I was home again by 3:00, feeling hot and grimy from crawling the perimeter of Lance's office, peering under things. I let myself into my apartment and tossed my handbag on the couch. A piercing shriek started up and I jumped a foot, grabbing up my bag. I snatched the debugger out of the outside compartment and flipped the switch off. Jesus Christ, I'd scared myself to death! The silence was wonderful. I stood there, heart pounding, enjoying the air conditioning the sudden sweat had generated. I patted myself on the chest and blew out a big breath. I shook my head and moved into the kitchenette. I felt dry, longing for a beer. The apartment was as close and muggy as a sauna. I checked the refrigerator. I didn't even have a can of Diet Pepsi.

And then I paused, my head swiveling slowly toward the room behind me. I closed the refrigerator door and moved back to the couch. I picked up the debugger and flipped it on again, sweeping the room. The high-pitched squeal cut through the silence like a burglar alarm.

I crossed to the corner and stood there, looking down. I hunkered on my heels, running a hand carefully into the sound hole in Daniel's guitar. The tiny transmitter, no bigger than a matchbox, was affixed to the body of the instrument with tape. A chill started at the base of my spine and raced up my body. Daniel was somehow connected to the case.

21

It took me nearly two hours to find the voice-activated tape recorder, which turned out to be hidden on the sun porch that formerly connected my converted garage apartment to the main house. I wasn't sure how Daniel had gotten in. Perhaps he'd picked the lock, as I would have in his place. The tape was new, which meant he must have been there fairly recently, pulling out the old tape, inserting this one. I couldn't even remember what was going on when he had first appeared. It was appalling now to think of all the telephone conversations he must have picked up in the last few days. Even messages coming in on my answering machine would have been recorded and passed on, not to mention the lengthy discussion I'd had with him about the case itself. He'd been so interested, so astute in the questions he asked. I'd felt so gratified by his attention. Looking back, I could see that in his own way he'd tried to warn me. All that talk about what a liar he was. Had every word he said to me been false? I sat on my back step, turning the situation over in my mind. Who had put Daniel up to it? Lyda Case perhaps, or maybe Ebony. One or the other of them might have run into Daniel, the amoral, the promiscuous, bored and at loose ends, restless and sick of life. What difference would it make to him who he betrayed? He'd done me in before. One more time couldn't matter in the grand scheme of things. It was staggering to think of all the information that must have been passed down the line, just by listening in, just by assembling my end of telephone conversations. Maybe that's how Andy Motycka had figured out Darcy and I were onto him. *Something* had caused him to cut and run. Olive's death hadn't hit the papers until the day *after* he disappeared. Had he known what was going to happen? I had to find Daniel.

I gathered up his guitar, the transmitter, and the tape recorder, shoving everything in the back seat of the car, and then I started cruising the neighborhood, looking for his Rent-A-Ruin. I live one block from the beach in an area made up of motels and vintage California bungalows. I started at Cabana Boulevard and circled each block, checking the cars at every motel, scanning the restaurant parking lots along the beach. There was no sign of him. He'd probably lied about where he was staying, along with everything else.

At 5:00, I finally gave up and went home. As usual, I was forced to park several doors away. The intense heat of day was yielding to balminess and it felt like we were in for a warm night ahead. The sun had begun to drop and the combination of January twilight and the summery temperature was disconcerting and set my teeth on edge. I was turning in at my gate when I picked up the smell. Dead dog, I thought. Something fetid and rotten. I looked back at the street, thinking I'd spot some poor flattened creature on the pavement. Instead my attention was caught by the vehicle shrouded by the blue cotton car cover right out in front. I hesitated for a moment and then retraced my steps. The smell was stronger. Saliva began to collect involuntarily on the floor of my mouth. I swallowed, tears welling briefly, a fear reaction of mine. Gingerly, I lifted the car cover, pulling it up off the hood so that I could peer in through the windshield.

I jerked my hand away, making one of those sounds that have no translation in human speech.

Leaning against the window on the passenger side was the bloated face of Lyda Case, eyes bulging, tongue as fat and round and dark as a parakeet's, protruding slightly beyond puffy darkened lips. A scarf gaily printed with a surfing motif was nearly buried in the swollen flesh of her neck. I pulled the cover back over the windshield and went straight to my phone where I dialed 911 and reported the body. My voice sounded low and emotionless, but my hands were shaking badly. The sight of Lyda's face still danced in the air, a vision of death, wed to the smell of putrescence. The dispatcher assured me someone was on the way.

I went back out to the street. I sat on the curb to wait for the cops, guarding Lyda's body like some old loyal pooch. I don't think four minutes had passed before the black-and-white came barreling around the corner. I got up and moved to the street, holding an arm up like a crossing guard.

The two uniformed police who emerged were familiar, Pettigrew and Gutierrez, male and female. I knew they'd seen worse than Lyda Case . . . what beat cop hasn't? . . . but there was something repellent about the spectacle of this death. It looked like she'd been positioned so as to maximize the horror. The message was for me . . . mockery and macabre arrogance, an escalation of the terms between this killer and me. I hadn't taken Olive's death personally. I'd felt the loss, but I didn't believe I'd been targeted in any way. My presence there when the bomb went off was purely circumstantial. This was different. This was aimed at me. Someone knew where I lived. Someone had made very special arrangements to get her here.

The next two hours were filled with police routine, comforting procedures, as formalized as a dance. All of the responsibility belonged to someone else. Lieutenant Dolan appeared. I answered questions. The car turned out to be another rental, Hertz this time instead of Rent-A-Ruin. I'd first seen it this morning, as nearly as I could remember. No, I'd never seen it before. No, I hadn't seen any strangers in the area. Yes, I knew who she was, but she hadn't been in touch. No, I had no idea when or why she'd come to town except that she'd told Terry Kohler she had information for him. Dolan had waited with us at the bird refuge so he knew she hadn't showed up. She was probably already dead by then, her flesh beginning to bake in the toaster oven of the locked car.

Out of the corner of my eye, I watched the medical examiner do his preliminary examination of the body. The car doors were hanging open, the neighborhood perfumed by the stink of the corpse. By that time it was fully dark and neighbors were giving the crime scene a wide berth, watching from porches all up and down the street. Some were still in work clothes. Many held handkerchiefs to their faces, filtering the smell. The police personnel working directly with the body wore protective masks. Lights had been set up and the fingerprint technicians were going over every inch of the dark-blue car with white powder and brushes. Door handles, windows, dash, steering wheel, steering column, plastic seat covers. Since the rental car was probably cleaned up between uses, there was a good chance that any prints lifted would be significant. Easy to match, at any rate.

Pettigrew had gone into my apartment to contact the Hertz manager by phone.

Lyda was zipped into a body bag. The gases that had collected under her skin made her look like she'd suddenly gained fifty pounds, and for a moment, grotesquely, I worried she would burst. I got up abruptly and went inside. I poured myself a glass of wine and chugged it down like water. Officer Pettigrew finished his conversation and hung up the phone.

"I'm going in to take a shower if no one objects." I didn't wait for an answer. I grabbed a plastic garbage bag from the kitchen, closed myself into the bathroom and stripped, dropping every article of clothing, including my shoes, into the bag. I tied it shut and set it outside the bathroom door. I showered. I shampooed my hair. When I was done, I wrapped myself in a towel, searching my face in the mirror for reassurance. I couldn't shake the images. Lyda's features seemed to be superimposed on my own, the stench of her competing with the scent of shampoo and soap. Never had my own mortality seemed so immediate. My ego recoiled, incapable of contemplating its own surcease. There's nothing so astonishing or insulting to a soul as the suggestion that a day might come when it would not "be." Thus springs religion with comforts I couldn't accept.

By 9:00 the neighborhood had cleared again. Several prints, including a partial palm, had been lifted from the car, which had then been towed to the impound lot. The Hertz manager had appeared on the scene and the fingerprint technician had taken a set of his prints, as well as mine, for comparison. The crime-scene investigators would dust and vacuum the car like a crew of charwomen and then they'd begin the painstaking business of analyzing trace evidence.

In the meantime, I was too restless to stay at home. Any sense of refuge and safety I felt had been obliterated by the angle of Lyda's face, tilted so she seemed to be watching my gate. I hunched myself into a windbreaker and grabbed my handbag, depositing the sackful of fouled clothes in Henry's trash can on my way out. I cruised the neighborhood again, looking for Daniel's car, covering the same restaurant parking lots, the same motels. I still had his guitar in the back seat and I didn't think he'd skip out of town without retrieving it.

I hit pay dirt at the Beach View, which in fact only had a view of the backside of the adjacent motel. Daniel's ratty rented vehicle was parked in front of room 16, ground floor, rear. Parked beside it was a little red Alfa-Romeo convertible. Uneasily I turned to stare at it as I pulled in. I locked my car, pausing to check the glove compartment in the Alfa for the owner registration slip. Not surprisingly, the car belonged to Ashley Wood. My, my, my.

I knocked on Daniel's door. I could see that the lights were on, but there was a long wait. I was beginning to think they might have gone off somewhere on foot when the door opened and Daniel peered out. He was barefoot and shirtless, but he'd pulled on a pair of faded jeans. He looked slim-hipped and bronzed, his blond hair tousled as if he'd been asleep. His cheeks were flushed and the lines had been eased from around his eyes. He looked ten years younger, the haggard cast to his face magically erased. If he was surprised to see me, he gave no indication of it.

"Mind if I come in?" I asked.

He hesitated slightly and then stepped aside. I moved into the room, noting with grim amusement that the bathroom door was shut. The musky smell of sex still hung in the air like ozone after a rainstorm.

"I have your guitar in my car."

"You didn't have to do that. I told you I'd pick it up."

"It's no problem. I wanted to talk to you again, anyway." I strolled around the room, noting the roach clip, the darkened stub of a joint in the ashtray. "God, you got right to it, didn't you?" I remarked.

His gaze was watchful. He knew me well enough to realize I was in a mean mood. He said, "What's on your mind? I'm kind of tied up right now."

I smiled, wondering if he meant that literally. Bondage had never been part of his sexual repertoire, but who knew how Ash's tastes ran? "I found the transmitter. The tape recorder's in the car along with the guitar. I thought I might dump it all off the pier, but I'm too nice. I give you credit for balls, Daniel. It took a lot of fuckin' nerve to come waltzing back in my life and betray me again."

His expression altered, but at least he had the decency not to deny anything.

I moved to the bathroom door and opened it.

Bass was standing there. Something like pain shot through me, followed by the cessation of all feeling. Even rage was washed away in that moment of recognition. I thought about the last time I'd seen them together . . . Bass's twenty-first birthday party at the country club. Daniel's jazz combo had played for the occasion and I'd been invited, too, since I knew Ash. Two weeks later, Daniel was gone, without so much as a by-your-leave. I was looking at the reason. Who, I wondered, had seduced whom. Daniel was older than Bass by thirteen years, but that wasn't necessarily relevant. Not that it mattered anyway. Passion had ionized all the air in the room. I felt nearly giddy as I drank it in.

Bass had a towel wrapped around his waist. I found myself checking out the body Daniel found preferable to mine. Bass was pale, narrow through the chest, but he carried himself with perfect composure as he brushed by me.

"Hello, Kinsey." He paused at the ashtray and picked up the roach. He tilted his head, lighting it with a disposable Bic. He took a hit and held it out to Daniel, who declined with a slight shake of his head. The two men locked eyes, exchanging a look so filled with tenderness I had to drop my gaze.

Bass glanced over at me. "What brings you here?"

"Lyda Case is dead."

"Who?"

"Come on, Bass. Don't give me that shit. She was married to Hugh Case, who worked for Wood/Warren. Surely, you haven't forgotten him so soon."

Bass set the roach aside and moved to the bed. He stretched out, crossing his arms behind his head. The hair in his armpits was silky and black and I could see bite marks in the crook of his neck. When he spoke, his tone was mild and relaxed.

"No need to get ugly. I haven't been around for years. This has nothing to do with me," he said. "You're the one."

"*I* am? That's bullshit! I got backed into this business because of California Fidelity."

"So I heard. The D.A.'s office got in touch with Mother. You're being charged with insurance fraud."

"And you believe that," I said flatly.

"Hey, I can understand it. Lance got his tit in a wringer and needed some cash. Burning the warehouse was better than a bank loan. All he needed was a little help from you."

"Oh, really? You seem well informed for someone who's been gone. Who fills you in?"

"What's it to you?"

"You can't believe everything you hear, Bass. Sometimes you can't even believe your eyes. There's something going on here, and none of us has been smart enough to figure out what it is."

"I'm sure you'll come up with something. I understand you're very good at what you do."

I looked at Daniel. "How did you get sucked into this, or is that a bad choice of words?"

Daniel seemed uncertain how to reply so Bass answered for him. "We had to know what was going on. Obviously, you weren't going to tell us so we had to take steps." He paused to shrug. "We'll be turning the tapes over to the D.A., of course."

"Oh shit, yes. Of course. We who?"

"I'd rather not discuss that, in case you're inclined to retaliate," Bass said. "The point is, I knew Daniel and he knew you and it seemed like the logical way to gather information."

"And Andy Motycka? How does he fit in?"

"I don't know all the details on that. Why don't you tell me?"

"Well, I don't know the details either, Bass. My guess is that somebody pressured Andy into it. Maybe he got nervous when he found out that Darcy and I were onto him. Or maybe he got wind of Olive's death and felt like it was more than he had bargained for. Anyway, it looks like he's left town unless he's been murdered, too. Doesn't it bother you that Lyda Case died?"

"Why should it? I never knew the lady personally. Sure, I'm sorry she died, but I didn't have anything to do with it."

"How do you know you aren't next, Bass? Or maybe Daniel here? If you're not concerned about Olive, at least give some thought to your own vulnerability. You're dealing with someone who has less and less to lose."

"What makes you think he knows who it is?" Daniel said.

"What makes you think he doesn't?" I snapped.

22

When I got home, I turned on all of Henry's exterior lights, flooding his yard like a prison compound. I checked locks on all his doors and windows first and then secured my own. I cleaned and checked my little semiautomatic, loading eight cartridges into the magazine. It worried me that the sights were off. A gun is no protection if you can't control what it does. I stuck it in my handbag. I was going to have to leave it at a gun shop in the morning. Grimly I wondered if a gunsmith supplied loaners.

I brushed my teeth and washed my face, then surveyed my various burns, bruises, and minor cuts. I felt like shit, but I decided it was better to bypass the pain medication. I was afraid of sleeping deeply on the off-chance that someone might have a go at me. I was afraid, too, that Lyda Case might appear in my dreams unannounced.

I watched the digital clock flick its way through the night. Outside, the wind was hot and dry, teasing the palm fronds into rattling conspiracies. The air in my apartment seemed stifling, sounds muffled by the heat. Twice I got up and moved silently into the bathroom, where I stood in the shadows of the bathtub, peering out of the window. The tree branches bucked in the wind. Leaves scuttled along the street. Dust was funneled up out of nowhere into whirling spirals. Once a car passed slowly, its headlights fanning up against my ceiling. I pictured Daniel sheltered in the protective curve of Bass's body and I envied them their security. In the dead of night, personal safety seems more important than propriety.

I slept, finally, as the darkness was lifting to the soft gray of dawn. The wind had died and the ensuing silence was just as unsettling as the erratic creak of the live oak in my neighbor's yard. I woke at 8:15 with a start, disoriented by the sense of the day gone all wrong. I wanted to talk to Ava at Wood/ Warren as soon as the plant opened, which meant I'd have to skip my run. I was going to have to live with the brooding dread that was circulating through my bones. Exercise sweeps that away as nothing else can. Without the jog, I suspected the anxiety would accumulate. I dragged myself into the shower, then dressed and made a quick pot of coffee, double-strength, which I poured into a thermos and sipped as I drove the ten miles to Colgate.

Lance wasn't expected until after 10:00, and Terry was on a leave of absence, but Ava was at her desk, looking dark and sour. She'd had her cracked nail repaired and the color had shifted from harsh red to a mauve, with a chevron of dark maroon painted on each fingertip. Her outfit was purple jersey with a cross-chest bandolier of red, altogether dazzling, I thought.

"I left my business card yesterday. I was hoping you'd call," I said, taking a seat in the metal chair beside her desk.

"I'm sorry. We were swamped with work." She focused a look on me. All the flint was gone and worry had taken its place. The lady was in a mood to talk. She said, "I heard about Lyda Case on the radio this morning. I don't understand what's going on."

"Did you know Lyda?"

"Not really. I'd only talked to her a couple of times on the phone, but I was married to a man who killed himself. I know how devastating that can be."

"Especially when there was no way to have it verified," I

said. "You did know all his lab work disappeared within days."

"Well, I heard that, but I wasn't sure it was true. Suicide is sometimes hard to accept. People make things up without even meaning to. What happened to Lyda? The radio didn't say much except that her body'd been found. I can't tell you how shocked I was. It's horrible."

I told her the details, sparing little. Ordinarily I'd downplay the particulars, not wanting to pander to the public appetite for the gruesome specifics of violent death. With Ava, I felt the reality of the situation might loosen her tongue. She listened to me with distaste, her dark eyes filling with anxiety.

"Do you mind if I smoke?" she said.

"Not at all. Go ahead."

She opened the bottom drawer of her desk and pulled out her handbag. Her hands were trembling as she shook a Winston from the pack and lit it. "I've been trying to quit, but I just can't help myself. I stopped at the drugstore and picked up a pack on the way to work. I smoked two in the car." She took a deep drag. One of the engineers peered around from his drafting table as the smoke drifted toward him. She had her back turned so she missed the look of annoyance that crossed his face.

"Let's go back to Hugh's death," I said.

"I can't help you much with that. I'd only been with the company a few weeks before he died, so I hardly knew the man."

"Was there an office manager before you?"

Ava shook her head. "I was the first, which meant the office was a mess. Nobody did a thing. Filing alone was piled up to here. There was just one secretary. Heather was the receptionist, but all the day-to-day business was handled by Woody himself, or one of the engineers. It took me six months to get things squared away. Engineers may be obsessive, but not when it comes to paperwork." She took another drag, then tapped the small accumulation of ash from the end of her cigarette.

"What was the atmosphere like at the time? Was it tense? Was anybody caught up in an office dispute? A feud of any kind?"

"Not that I ever heard. Woody bid on a government contract and we were trying to get organized for that. . . ."

"Which entailed what?"

"Routine office procedure. Forms to be filled out, clearances, that kind of thing."

"What happened to the bid?"

"Nothing. The whole thing fell through. Woody had a heart attack, and after he died, Lance let the matter drop."

"What was it they were bidding on? I wonder if that ties in."

"I don't remember what it was. Hold on. I'll ask." Ava turned and scanned the room. John Salkowitz was passing through, blueprint in hand, apparently on his way to the rear of the plant. "John? Could I ask you about something over here?"

He detoured toward us, his expression clouding with concern when he caught sight of me. "What's the story on Lyda Case? My wife just called and said she heard about her on the news."

I gave him the shorthand version, putting it together with the question at hand. "I'm still trying to figure out how it ties into this business with Lance. There's gotta be a connection somewhere."

"He's not seriously being accused of insurance fraud, is he?"

"Looks that way. Along with me, I might add."

"Appalling," he said. "Well. I don't see how it could have any bearing on the contract we bid on, but I'll fill you in. We get a little trade paper called *Commerce Daily*, published by the government. It was Hugh's job to check it for any contract available for bid that might apply to us. He found one under heating equipment, requesting bids on a furnace for processing beryllium, which is used in the making of nuclear bombs and rocket fuel. It's hazardous work. We'd have had to build in a whole new venting system to accommodate CAL-OSHA, but if we got it, we'd have been in a position to bid on future contracts. Woody felt it was worth the expense of retooling. Not all of us agreed with him, but he was a shrewd man and you had to trust his instincts. Anyway, that's what we were going after."

"What would it have been worth to the company?"

"Quarter million bucks. Half a million maybe. More, of course, in the long run, if we bid on future work."

"What was the status of the bid when Hugh died?"

"I don't know. I guess we were gearing up. I know he'd gone down to the Federal Building in Los Angeles to pick up all the paperwork. Since it was the Department of Defense, we were going to need a company clearance, plus individual clearances. Hugh's death really didn't have much effect, but when Woody died on top of that, we lost heart."

"Could the company have handled the work with both men gone?"

"Probably, but of course Lance was just taking over, getting his feet wet. I guess we dropped the ball, but that's all it amounted to. We weren't out anything. We might not have been low bidder anyway, so it's all speculative."

"What about bids since?"

"That's an aspect of the business we haven't paid much attention to. We're on overload half the time as it is."

I looked at him, truly stumped. "And you don't think it's relevant?"

"If it is, I don't see how."

"Thanks for your time, at any rate. I may need to get back to you."

"Sure thing," he said.

Ava and I chatted a while longer, but the conversation seemed unproductive, except for one minor point. She mentioned, in passing, that Ebony had attended the memorial services for Hugh Case.

"I thought she was in Europe, married to some playboy named Julian."

"She was, but they came back to the States to visit every six months or so."

"How long had she been in town? Do you have any idea?"

Her look was blank. "Can't help you there. I was too new myself to sort out what was normal in that family."

"Maybe I can check it out," I said. "Thanks for your help."

Driving back into town, I was kicking myself. I'd falsely assumed that neither Ebony nor Bass could have been tied in to Hugh's death as both of them were out of the picture at the time—Ebony in Europe, Bass in New York. Now I wasn't sure. I stopped at a public phone booth and called the Woods' house. The maid answered. I was willing to talk to just about any member of the family, but that turned out to be problematic. Mrs. Wood was resting and had asked not to be disturbed. Ebony and Ashley had gone to the Santa Teresa Monument Company to look at memorial tablets for Miss Olive's gravesite. Bass was due back at any minute. Did I care to leave my name and number? I decided to hold off on that. I said I'd call again later and hung up without identifying myself. I hauled more change from my handbag and tried Darcy at the office. She had nothing new to report. I brought her up-to-date and we commiserated briefly on the blanks we were drawing. She said she'd leave word on my answering machine if anything developed. Fat chance, I thought.

I returned to my car and sat there at the curb. I poured the rest of the hot coffee into the thermos lid, sipping it with care. I was getting closer to the truth. I could feel it in my bones. I felt like I was circling, the orbits getting tighter as I approached the central point. Sometimes all it took was one tiny nudge and everything fell into place. But the balance was delicate, and if I pushed too hard, I might barge right past the obvious.

I didn't have that many trees to shake. I screwed the lid on the thermos and tossed it in the back seat. I started up the car and drove back into town again. Maybe Andy's mistress had heard from him. That might help. Fifteen minutes later, I was standing at her door, knocking politely. I wasn't sure if she worked or not. She was home, but when she opened the door, she didn't seem that thrilled to see me.

"Hi," said I. "I'm still looking for Andy and I wondered if you'd heard from him."

She shook her head. Some people think they can lie to me that way, without forming the actual falsehood with their lips. It's apparently part of an inner conviction that if they don't speak the lie aloud, they won't burn in hell.

"He never checked in to let you know he was okay?"

"I just said that, didn't I?"

"Seems odd to me," I remarked. "I half expected him to drop you a note, or make a quick phone call."

"Sorry," she said.

There was a tiny silence wherein she was hoping to close the door and be done with me.

"How'd he get that account anyway?" I asked.

"What account?"

"Wood/Warren. Did he know Lance pretty well or was it someone else in the family?"

"I have no idea. Anyway, he's the claims manager. I don't know that he sold the policy in the first place."

"Oh. Somehow I thought he did. I thought I saw that somewhere on one of the forms we processed. Maybe it was his account before he got promoted to claims manager."

"Are you through asking questions?" she said snappishly.

"Uh, well, actually I'm not. Did Andy know any of the Woods personally? I don't think you told me that."

"How do I know who he knew?"

"Just thought I'd take a flyer," I said. "It puzzles me that you're not worried about him. The man's been gone, what, four days? I'd be frantic."

"I guess that's the difference between us," she said.

"Maybe I'll check out at his place again. You never know. He might have stopped back at the apartment to pick up his clothes and his mail."

She just stared at me. There didn't seem a lot left to say.

"Well, off I go," I said cheerfully. "You've really been a peach."

Her goodbye was brief. Two words, one of which started with the letter "F." Her mama apparently hadn't taught her to be ladylike any more than mine had taught me. I decided to drive back out to Andy's place because, frankly, I couldn't think what else to do.

23

I headed out to the condominium complex where Andy lived, thrilled that I wasn't going to have to type up a report on the day's events. The truth was, I had no plan afoot, no strategy whatever for wrapping this business up. I didn't have a clue to what was going on. I was driving randomly from one side of the city to the other, hoping that I could shake something loose. I was also avoiding my apartment, picturing the gendarmes at my door with a warrant for my arrest. Andy represented one of the missing links. Someone had designed an elaborate scheme to discredit Lance and eliminate two key engineers at Wood/Warren. Andy had facilitated the frame-up, but once Olive was blown to kingdom come, he must have decided to blow town himself. If I could pinpoint the connection between Andy Motycka and the person who'd suckered him into it, then maybe I could figure out what the payoff was.

The electronic gates at The Copse stood open, and I passed through without attracting armed guards or vicious dogs. A tall, fair-haired woman in a jumpsuit was walking an apricot poodle, but she scarcely looked at me. I parked my car in the slot Andy had left in the wake of his departure. I trotted up to the second-floor landing and let myself in with the front-door key, which I knew from past experience he kept hidden on the cornice above the front door. I confess I sniffed the air apprehensively as I let myself in, mindful that Andy might have ended up in the same state as Lyda Case. The apartment smelled benign and the dust that had settled on the empty bookshelves attested to the fact that no one had been here for days.

I did a quick pass through the apartment to make sure it was unoccupied. I opened the rear sliding glass door, peered into each bedroom, then returned to the living room, where I drew the front drapes. I moved through the daylight gloom with curiosity. Andy lived on such spartan terms that his place had looked abandoned even when he was in residence. Now, however, the emptiness had the aura of a vacant lot, the wall-to-wall carpeting littered with paper scraps. In situations like this, I always long for the obvious—cryptic messages, motel receipts, annotated itineraries indicating where the missing might have gone. The various bits of paper on Andy's floor were none of the above and I was no wiser for having crawled around on my hands and knees reading them. The business of private investigation is fraught with indignities.

The medicine cabinet in his bathroom had been cleared out. Shampoo, deodorant, and shaving gear were gone. Wherever he was, he'd be clean-shaven and smell good. In his bedroom, all of the dirty clothes were gone and the blue plastic crates had been emptied of their contents. One tatty pair of boxer shorts remained, wild with fuchsia exclamation marks. I'm always amazed by men's underwear. Who could guess such things by looking at their sober three-piece suits? He'd left behind his bicycle, rowing machine, and the remaining moving cartons. There were still a few poorly folded sheets in the linen closet, one package of pizza rolls in the freezer. He'd taken the bottle of aquavit and the Milky Way bars, perhaps anticipating his life on the road as an endless round of sugar and alcohol abuse.

The card table was still in place, the answering machine on top, aluminum lawn chairs pulled up as if he'd had dinner guests for a banquet of Lean Cuisine. I sat down, propped my feet up on the adjacent chair, and surveyed Andy's make-shift office. There were still some pencils, a scratch pad, gummy white-out, unpaid bills. His answering machine turned out to be a duplicate of mine. I reached over and flipped open the side panel where the "oft-dialed" numbers were penned in. Of the sixteen spaces allotted, only six were filled. Andy was real imaginative. Fire, Police, California Fidelity, his ex-wife, a liquor store, and a pizza joint with free delivery.

I stared at the display on the answering machine, thinking about the features on this model. Carefully I pressed the asterisk button to the left of 0. On my machine, the * redials the last number called. With a flurry of notes up and down the scale, the machine redialed, the number displayed in green. It was vaguely familiar and I made a note of it. The line began to ring. Three times. Four.

Someone picked up. There was a whir and a pause as a machine on the far end of the line came to life.

"Hello. This is Olive Kohler at 555-3282. Sorry we're not here to take your call. I'm out at the supermarket at the moment, but I should be home at four-thirty or so. If you'll leave your number and a message, I'll get back to you as soon as I return. If you're calling with confirmations for the New Year's party, just leave your name and we'll see you this evening. 'Bye for now."

I could feel my heart thump. No one had changed the message since Olive's death, and there she was again, perpetually hung up in New Year's Eve day, leaving a verbal note before she went off to shop for the party that would never take place.

Perversely, I pressed the asterisk again. Four rings, and Olive answered, her voice sounding hollow but full of life. She was still going out to shop for the New Year's party, still requesting the caller's name, telephone number, and a message. " 'Bye for now," she said. I knew if I called a hundred

times, she'd still be saying " 'Bye for now" without ever knowing how final that farewell would be.

Andy's last phone call had been to her, but what did it
mean? A tiny jolt of memory shot through me. I saw Olive
unlock the front door, her arms loaded with groceries, the
package bomb, addressed to Terry, resting on top. As the
door swung open, the telephone had rung and that's why
she'd tossed the package in such haste. Maybe Andy knew the
package was waiting on the doorstep and had called to warn
them off.

I closed up Andy's apartment, got in my car, and headed
back to town, detouring en route to wolf down a fast-food
lunch. The Kohlers' house was the next logical stop, but as I
turned into the lane, I noticed a whisper of anxiety. I had
not, of course, been to the house since the bomb went off and
I was not eager to live through the trauma again. I parked
in front and gingerly stepped through the gap in the hedge
where the gate had been. Only the posts remained now, the
hardware twisted where the force of the bomb had wrenched
the heavy wooden gate from its hinges. In places the blast had
left the shrubbery completely bald.

I approached the house. Plywood sheets and two-by-fours
had been nailed across the yawning opening where the front
door had been. One of the columns supporting the porch
roof had been snapped in two and a clumsy six-by-six had
been rigged up in its place. The walkway was scorched, grass
sparse and blackened. Sawhorses and warning signs cautioned
folks to use the rear. I could still detect the faint briny smell
of the cocktail onions that had littered the yard like pearls.

I felt my gaze drawn irresistibly to the spot where Olive
had lain in a tumbled, bloody heap. I remembered then how
I'd offered to carry the package for her since her arms were
loaded with grocery bags. Her casual refusal had saved me.
Death sometimes passes us by that way, with a wink, a nod,

and an impish promise to return for us at another time. I
wondered if Terry felt the same guilt I did that she'd died in
our stead.

I was holding my breath, and I shook my arms out like a
runner in the middle of a race, moving then toward the rear
of the house. I knocked at the back door, cupping my hand
against the glass to see if Terry or the housekeeper was home.
There was no sign of anyone. I waited, then knocked again.
In the lower right-hand corner of the kitchen window there
was an alarm-company decal that said "Armed Response" across
the bottom. I stepped back so I could scan the area. There
was a red light showing on the alarm panel to the right, indicating that the system was armed. If the light was green,
any burglar would know it was safe to start work. I took a
business card from my handbag and sketched a quick note,
asking Terry to call me when he got home. I got in my car
again and drove to the Woods'. For all I knew, he was still
there.

Early-afternoon sunlight poured down on the house with
its dazzling white facade. The grass was newly cut, as short
and densely green as wool-pile carpeting. Beyond the bluffs,
the ocean was an intense navy blue, the surface feathered with
whitecaps that suggested a strong wind coming off the water.
The hot desert wind was blowing at my back, and the palms
tossed restlessly where the two met. Ash's little red sports car
was parked in the circular driveway, along with a BMW. There
was no sign of Terry's Mercedes. I walked around the house
to the long, low brick porch on the seaward side and rang the
bell.

The maid let me in and left me in the foyer while she went
to fetch Miss Ebony. I had asked for Ash, but I was willing
to take potluck. I wished fervently that I had a theory, but
this was still a fishing expedition. I couldn't be far from understanding the truth, but I had no clear concept what the

revelation might be. Under the circumstances, all I knew to do was persist, plowing through. Bass was the only member of the family I was hoping to avoid. Not that it made any difference at that point, but pride is pride. Who wants to make small talk with your ex-spouse's lover? I had to be careful that my sense of injury didn't get in the way of spotting his role in this.

"Hello, Kinsey."

Ebony was standing at the bottom of the stairs, her pale oval face as smooth as an egg, expressionless, composed. She was wearing a shirtwaist dress of black silk that emphasized her wide shoulders and slim hips, the long shapely legs. Her red spike heels must have added five inches to her height. Her hair was skinned back from the taut bones of her face. A swath of blusher on each cheek suggested high stress instead of the good health it was meant to convey. In the family mythology, she was the thrill-seeker, addicted to the sorts of treacherous hobbies that can spell early death: sky-diving, helicopter skiing, climbing the sheer faces of impossible cliffs. In the family dynamic, maybe she'd been designated to live recklessly, just as Bass lived with vanity, idleness, and self-indulgence.

I said, "I thought we should talk."

"About what?"

"Olive's death. Lyda Case is dead, too."

"Bass told me that."

My smile had a bitter feeling to it. "Ah. Bass. How did he get involved? Somehow I get the feeling you might have put a call through to him in New York."

"That's right."

"Dirty pool, Ebony."

She shrugged, undismayed. "It's your own damn fault."

"*My* fault?"

"I asked you what was going on and you wouldn't say. It's my family, Kinsey. I have a right to know."

"I see. And who thought about bringing Daniel into it?"

"I did, but Bass was the one who tracked him down. He and Daniel had an affair years ago, until Bass broke it off. There was unfinished business between them. Daniel was more than happy to accommodate him in the hope of rekindling the fires."

"Selling me out in the process," I said.

She smiled slightly, but her gaze was intent. "You didn't have to agree, you know. You must have had some unfinished business of your own or you wouldn't have been suckered in so easily."

"True," I said. "That was smart. God, he nicked right in there and gave you everything, didn't he?"

"Not quite."

"Oh? Something missing? Some little piece of the scheme incomplete?"

"We still don't know who killed Olive."

"Or Lyda Case," I said, "though the motive was probably not the same. I suspect she somehow figured out what was going on. Maybe she went back through Hugh's papers and came up with something significant."

"Like what?"

"Hey, if I knew that, I'd probably know who killed her, wouldn't I?"

Ebony stirred restlessly. "I have things to do. Why don't you tell me what you want."

"Well, let's see. Just in rambling around town, it occurred to me that it might help to find out who inherits Olive's stock."

"Stock?"

"Her ten voting shares. Surely, those wouldn't be left to someone outside the family. So who'd she leave 'em to?"

For the first time she was genuinely flustered and the color in her cheeks seemed real. "What difference does it make? The bomb was meant for Terry. Olive died by mistake, didn't she?"

"I don't know. Did she?" I snapped back. "Who stands to benefit? You? Lance?"

"Ash," came the voice. "Olive left all her stock to her sister Ashley." Mrs. Wood had appeared in the upstairs hall. I looked up to see her clinging to the rail, the walker close by, her whole body trembling with exertion.

"Mother, you don't have to concern yourself with this."

"I think I do. Come to my room, Kinsey." Mrs. Wood disappeared.

I glanced at Ebony and then pushed past her and went up the stairs.

24

We sat in her room near French doors that opened onto a balcony facing the sea. Sheer curtains were pulled across the doorway, billowing lazily in a wind that smelled of salt. The bedroom suite was dark and old, a clumsy assortment of pieces she and Woody must have salvaged from their early married years: a dresser with chipped veneer, matching misshapen lamps with dark-red silk shades. I was reminded of thrift-store windows filled with other people's junk. Nothing in the room would qualify as "collectible," much less antique.

She sat in a rocker upholstered in horsehair, frayed and shiny, picking at the fabric on the arms of the chair. She looked awful. The skin on her face had been blanched by Olive's death and her cheeks were mottled with liver spots and threaded with visible capillaries. She looked as though she'd lost weight in the last few days, the flesh hanging in pleats along her upper arms, her bones rising to the surface like a living lesson in anatomy. Even her gums had shrunk away from her teeth, the aging process suddenly as visible as in time-lapse photography. She seemed weighed down with some as yet unidentified emotion that left her eyes red-rimmed and lusterless. I didn't think she'd survive it, whatever it was.

She had clumped her way back to her room with the aid of her walker, which she kept close to her, holding on to it with one trembling hand.

I sat in a hard-backed chair near hers, my voice low. "You know what's going on, don't you?" I said.

"I think so. I should have spoken up sooner, but I so hoped my suspicions were groundless. I thought we'd buried the past. I thought we'd moved on, but we haven't. There's so much shame in the world as it is. Why add to it?" Her voice quavered and her lips trembled as she spoke. She paused, struggling with some inner admonition. "I promised Woody I wouldn't speak of it again."

"You have to, Helen. People are dying."

For a moment, her dark eyes sparked to life. "I know that," she snapped. The energy was short-lived, a match flaring out. "You do the best you can," she went on. "You try to do what's right. Things happen and you salvage what's left."

"Nobody's blaming you."

"I blame myself. It's my fault. I should have said something the minute things began to go wrong. I knew the connection, but I didn't want to believe it, fool that I am."

"Is this related to Woody?"

She shook her head.

"Who, then?"

"Lance," she whispered. "It started with him."

"Lance?" I said, disconcerted. It was the last name I expected to hear.

"You'd think the past could be diffused . . . that it wouldn't have the power to affect us so long after the fact."

"How far back does this go?"

"Seventeen years, almost to the day." She clamped her mouth shut, then shook her head again. "Lance was a hellion in his teens, rebellious and secretive. He and Woody clashed incessantly, but boys do that. Lance was at an age when *of course* he had to assert himself."

"Ash says he had a couple of scrapes with the law back then."

She stirred impatiently. "He was constantly in trouble. 'Acting out' they call it now, but I didn't think he was a bad boy.

I still don't. He had a troubled adolescence. . . ." She broke off, taking a deep breath. "I don't mean to belabor the point. What's done is done. Woody finally sent him off to military school, and after that he went into the army. We hardly saw him until he came home that Christmas on leave. He seemed fine by then. Grown up. Mature. Calm and pleasant and civil to us both. He became interested in the company. He talked about settling down and learning the business. Woody was thrilled." She fumbled in her pocket for a handkerchief, which she pressed to her lips, blotting the film of perspiration that had formed like dew.

So far she wasn't telling me a thing I didn't already know. "What happened?"

"That year . . . when Lance came home and things were going so well . . . that year . . . it was New Year's Day. I remember how happy I was things were off to such a good start. Then Bass came to us with the most preposterous tale. Somehow, in my heart, I suppose I've always blamed him. He spoiled everything. I've never really forgiven him, though it was hardly his fault. Bass was thirteen then. Sly. He knew about wickedness even at that age and he enjoyed it all so very much."

Still does, I thought. "What did he tell you?"

"He said he'd walked in on Lance. He came straight to us with that sneaky look in his eyes, pretending to be so upset when he knew exactly what he was about. At first, Woody didn't believe a word of it."

"He walked in on Lance doing what?"

There was a silence and then she pushed on, her voice dropping so low I was forced to lean closer. "With Olive," she whispered. "Lance and Olive. In her room on the bed. She was sixteen and so beautiful. I thought I'd die of the shame and embarrassment, the loathing at what was going on. Woody was crazed. He was in a towering rage. Lance swore it was innocent, that Bass misunderstood, but that was nonsense. Absurd to think we'd believe any such thing. Woody beat Lance to within an inch of his life. A fearful beating. I thought he'd kill him. Lance swore it only happened once. He swore he'd never lay another hand on her and he honored that. I know he did."

"That's when Olive was sent away to boarding school," I said.

Helen nodded.

"Who else knew about the incident?"

"No one. Just the five of us. Lance and Olive, Bass and Woody and me. Ebony was off in Europe. Ash knew something dreadful had happened, but she never knew what it was."

There was a silence. Helen smoothed the frayed fabric on the arm of the rocker where she'd picked strands loose. She glanced at me. Her expression seemed tinged with guilt, like an old dog that's piddled somewhere you haven't discovered yet. There was more, something she didn't want to own up to.

"What's the rest?" I asked. "What else?"

She shook her head, her cheeks turning pink in patches.

"Just tell me, Helen. It can't matter now."

"Yes, it does," she whispered. She'd begun to weep. I could see her clamp down, forcing her feelings back into the box she'd kept them in all these years.

I waited so long that I didn't think she meant to finish. Her hands began to shake in a separate dance of their own, a jitterbug of anxiety.

Finally she spoke. "Lance was lying about the two of them. It had gone on for years. Woody never knew, but I suspected as much."

"You suspected Lance was abusing her and you never interfered?"

"What could I say? I had no proof. I kept them away from each other whenever I could. He'd go off to summer camp. She'd stay with friends of ours in Maine. I never left them alone in the house. I hoped it was a phase, something that would disappear of its own accord. I thought if I called attention to it . . . I don't know what I thought. It was so unspeakable. A mother doesn't sit a boy down and discuss such things. I didn't want to pry, and Olive denied the slightest suggestion that anything was amiss. If she'd come to me, I'd have stepped in. Of course I would, but she never said a word. She might have been the one who initiated the contact for all I knew."

"How long did this go on?" I was having a hard time keeping the judgment out of my voice, afraid if she sensed the full range of my outrage, she'd clam up.

"Lance was obsessed with her almost from infancy. He was five when she was born and I was so relieved, you see, that he didn't resent her. It was just him and Ebony until Olive came along. He'd been the baby so I was delighted he seemed taken with her. It must have started as childish curiosity and advanced to something else. It did end once they were discovered. They could hardly tolerate each other's company these past few years, but by then the damage had been done. She had terrible problems."

"Sexual problems, I'd assume."

Helen nodded, cheeks coloring. "She also suffered deep depressions that would go on for months. All she did was run, run, run. Anything to escape the feelings. Play and spend. Spend and play. That's how she lived."

Rapidly I sorted through all the things I'd been told, processing the trivia I'd picked up in passing. "Olive said she and Bass had a falling-out when he was home for Thanksgiving. What was that about?"

"Something silly. I don't even remember now what the subject matter was. One of those ridiculous spats people get into when they've drunk too much. Bass was furious and wanted to get back at her, but it wasn't *about* anything. Petty temper, that's all."

I watched her carefully, making my mind a blank, trying to let the sense of this filter in. It had started with Lance, with Wood/Warren, talk of a takeover, evidence of insurance fraud. Someone had set Lance up and I'd been caught in the same trap. When Olive died, I'd assumed it was business-related, an accident. It was meant to look like that, but it wasn't. I felt the answer leap at me, so obvious once I knew what had gone on. "Oh shit," I said. "Bass told Terry, didn't he?"

"I think so," she said, almost inaudibly. "I don't think Terry's like the rest of us. He's not a well man. He doesn't seem right to me. Even when they met, he seemed 'off' somehow, but he was crazy about Olive. . . ."

" 'Obsessed' is the word I've heard applied," I broke in. "That he worshiped the ground she walked on."

"Oh, he adored her, there's no doubt of that. It was just what she needed and I thought it would all work out. She had such a low opinion of herself all her life. She couldn't seem to sustain a relationship until Terry came along. I thought she deserved a little happiness."

"You mean because she was 'damaged goods,' don't you? Tainted by what Lance had done."

"Well, she *was* tainted. Who knows what bestial appetites Lance had wakened in her?"

"That was hardly *her* fault."

"Of course not, but what nice boy was ever going to look at her if the truth came out? Terry seemed like a godsend."

"So the two of you decided not to say anything to him."

"We never spoke of it between us," she said tartly, "so we

could hardly speak of it to him. Why stir up trouble when everything was going so well?"

I got up abruptly and went to the phone, dialing Lieutenant Dolan's number at the Santa Teresa PD. The clerk said she'd put me through and I waited for Dolan's line to ring. Helen was right. What was done was done. There wasn't any point in blaming Bass. If anything, the blame lay with Helen and Woody. Olive died because Helen was too bloody polite to deal with the truth.

"Where's Terry now?" I said to Helen over my shoulder.

She was weeping openly. It seemed a little late for tears, but I didn't say so. "He was here a short while ago. He's on his way home."

When Dolan answered, I identified myself and laid it out for him, chapter and verse.

"I'll have him picked up for questioning," Dolan said. "We'll get a warrant so we can search the premises. He put that bomb together somewhere."

"He might have assembled it at work."

"We'll check that," he said. "Hang on." He put his hand across the mouth of the receiver and I could hear him issue an order to someone else in the room. He came back on the line. "Let me tell you what we have on this end. We got a match on the prints we lifted from the rental car Lyda Case was found in. They belong to a fellow named Chris Emms, who was charged with the murder of his foster mother twenty years ago. Blew her up with a package bomb he sent through the mail. The jury brought in a verdict of temporary insanity."

"Oh geez, I get it. No prison for him."

"Right. He was committed to the state hospital at Camarillo and escaped after eighteen months."

"And he was never picked up?"

"He's been free as a bird. I just talked to one of the staff docs and they're hunting up the old records to see what else they have on him."

"Was he really nuts or faking it?"

"Anybody who does what he did is nuts."

"Will you let the family know as soon as he's in custody?"

"Will do. I'll send somebody over in the meantime just in case he decides to come back."

"You better beef up security at Wood/Warren, too. He may make a try for Lance."

"Right," Dolan said. He broke off the connection.

I left Helen huddled in the rocker. I went downstairs, looking for Ebony, and told her what was going on. When I let myself out, she was on her way upstairs to see her mother. I couldn't imagine what they'd talk about. I had a flash of Olive sailing through the air, flying to oblivion. I just couldn't shake the image. I drove home feeling low, my perpetual state these days. I get tired of digging around in other people's dirty laundry. I'm sick of knowing more about them than I should. The past is never nice. The secrets never have to do with acts of benevolence or good deeds suddenly coming to light. Nothing's ever resolved with a handshake or a heart-to-heart talk. So often, humankind just seems tacky to me, and I don't know what the rest of us are supposed to do in response.

Under the bandages, my burns were chafed and fiery hot, throbbing dully. I glanced at myself in the rearview mirror. With my hair singed across the front and my eyebrows gone, I looked startled somehow, as if unprepared for the sudden conclusion to the case at this point. Quite true. I hadn't had time to process events. I thought about Daniel and Bass. Mentally I had to close the door on them, but it felt like unfinished business, and I didn't like that. I wanted closure, surcease. I wanted peace of mind again.

I pushed through the gate, pulling mail out of the box as I passed. I let myself into my place, and slung my handbag on the couch. I felt a desperate need to take a bath, symbolic as it was. It was only 4:00 in the afternoon, but I was going to scrub up and then go pound on Rosie's door. It was Tuesday and she was bound to be back in business by now. My neighborhood tavern usually opens at 5:00, but maybe I could sweet-talk her into letting me in early. I needed a heavy Hungarian dinner, a glass of white wine, and someone to fuss at me like a mother.

I paused at my desk and checked my answering machine. There were no messages. The mail was dull. Belatedly, I registered the fact that my bathroom door was closed. I hadn't left it that way. I never do. My apartment is small and the light from the bathroom window helps illuminate the place. I turned my head and I could feel the hair rise on the back of my neck. The knob rotated and the door swung open. That portion of the room was in shadow at that hour of day, but I could see him standing there. My spinal column turned to ice, the chill radiating outward to my limbs, which I couldn't will to move. Terry emerged from the bathroom and circled the couch. In his right hand he had a gun pointed right at my gut. I felt my hands rise automatically, palms up, the classic posture of submission guns seem to inspire.

Terry said, "Oops, you caught me. I expected to be gone by the time you got home."

"What are you doing here?"

"I brought you a present." He made a gesture toward the kitchenette.

Trancelike, I turned to see what he was pointing to. On the counter was a shoe box wrapped in Christmas paper, white HO HO HO's emblazoned on a dark-green background with a cartoon Santa swinging from each O. A preformed red satin bow was stuck to the lid. Surprise, surprise. Terry Kohler wanted me to have a box of death.

"Nice," I managed, though my mouth was dry.

"Aren't you going to open it?"

I shook my head. "I think I'll just leave it where it is. I'd hate to give it a bump."

"This one's on a timer."

I managed to loosen my jaw, but I couldn't form any words. Where had I put my gun? My mind was washed absolutely blank. I reached for the edge of my desk, supporting myself with my fingertips. Bombs are loud. The end is quick. I cleared my throat. "Sorry to interrupt you," I said. "Don't stick around on my account."

"I can stay for a minute. We could have a little chat."

"Why kill me?"

"It seemed like a good idea," he said mildly. "I thought you might like to go out with a bang, as opposed to a you-know-what."

"I'm surprised you didn't try for Lance."

"I have a package just like it in the car for him."

Probably in the bottom of my handbag, I thought. I'd meant to take it to the gun shop. Had I stuck it in the briefcase in the back seat of my car? If so, it was still out there and my ass was grass. "Do you mind if I sit?"

He did a quick survey of the area, making sure there weren't any rifles, bullwhips, or butcher knives within range. "Go ahead."

I moved to the couch and sank down without taking my eyes off him. He pulled my desk chair closer and sat down, crossing his legs. He was a nice-looking man, dark and lean, on the slight side. There was nothing in his manner to indicate how nuts he was. How nuts is he? I thought. How far gone? How amenable to reason? Would I trade my life for bizarre sexual favors if he asked? Oh sure, why not?

I was having trouble appraising the situation. I was home,

where I should have been safe. It wasn't even dark out. I really needed to pee, but it sounded like a ploy. And honest to God, I was embarrassed to make the request. It seemed advisable to try opening a dialogue, one of those conversations designed to ingratiate. "What's the timetable here?"

He glanced at his watch. "Ten minutes, more or less. The bomb should go off at four-thirty. I was worried you wouldn't get home in time," he said. "I can reset it, but I don't want to mess the wrapping paper up."

"I can understand that," I said. I checked the clock on my desk. 4:22. I could feel my adrenal gland squirt some juice into my veins. Terry didn't seem concerned. "You seem calm enough," I remarked.

He smiled. "I'm not going to be around when the damn thing goes off. They're dangerous."

"How can you keep me here? You'll have to shoot me first."

"I'll tie you up. I have some rope." I could see then that he had a coil of clothesline he'd tossed on the kitchen floor.

"You think of everything," I said. I wanted him to talk. I didn't want him to tie me up because then I'd be dead for sure. There wasn't going to be any way to hump and thump my way out. No broken glass by which I could saw through my ropes. No knives, no tricks, no miracles. "What if it goes off prematurely?"

"Too bad," he said with mockery, "but you know what Dylan Thomas said. 'After the first death, there is no other.'"

"How does Hugh Case fit in? Do you mind if I ask? I just want to know for the sake of it."

"I don't mind. We don't have anything else to talk about. Hugh was made the security officer after Woody bid on a government contract. We were all going to have to have clearances, but the guy went overboard. Forms, interviews, all these questions. He really took himself seriously. At first I thought it was all a game, but gradually I realized he was coming up with too many penetrating questions. He knew. Of course, he wanted my fingerprints. I stalled as long as possible, but I couldn't refuse. I had to kill him before he told Woody all the sordid details."

"About your mother."

"Foster mother," he corrected.

"Wouldn't somebody else have come up with the same information?"

"I'd figured a way around it, but I needed him out of the way for it to work."

"But you don't know that he was actually onto you."

"Oh, but I do and he was. I destroyed the file he kept at work, but he had a duplicate at home. Talk about a breach of security," he said. "That came to light just recently."

"Lyda found it."

"Now that was your fault. After you flew to Texas, she went through the papers she'd packed up and came across all the data on Chris Emms. She had no idea who he was, but she figured it was someone at the plant. She called me from Dallas and said she had some information Hugh had unearthed. I told her I'd be happy to take a look at it and help her figure out what to do with it. She made me promise not to mention it to Lance since she was so suspicious of him anyway."

"Nice," I said. "And the threat from her . . . you just made that up?"

"Yep."

"And the day we waited at the bird refuge, she was already dead out in front?"

"Righty-o," he said.

"How'd you kill Hugh?"

Terry shrugged indifferently. "Chloral hydrate. Then I strolled in and stole his blood and urine samples so it couldn't be traced."

"Takes nerve," I said.

"It had to be done and I knew I was right. I couldn't have him upsetting my life. What made me so mad afterwards, of course, is it was all for nothing. Olive had a past just as bad as mine. I didn't need to protect myself at all. I could have traded her, tit for tat, if she'd leveled with me."

"You must feel better now that she's gone. She's been paid in full, hasn't she?"

His face clouded. "I should have killed Lance and left her alive. I could have made her life miserable."

"I thought you'd already done that."

"Well, yes, but she didn't suffer nearly enough. And now she's off the hook."

"She did love you," I said.

"So what?"

"So nothing. I guess love doesn't count for much with you." I felt my eyes stray to the clock. 4:25.

"Not when it's based on lies and deceit," he said piously. "She should have told me the truth. She never shared the facts. She let me go right on believing our sex life was all my fault. She made me think I was inadequate when all the time it was her. Sometimes I think about him with his mouth all over her, feeding like a leech, sucking at her everywhere. Disgusting," he said.

"That was a long time ago."

"Not long enough."

"What about Andy Motycka? How'd you persuade him to help?"

"Money and threats. The carrot and the stick. Janice was hosing him for every cent he had. I paid him ten grand. Every time he got nervous, I reminded him that I'd be happy to tell Janice about Lorraine if he tried to back out."

"How'd you find out about her?"

"We've all known each other for years. The four of us went to UCST together before he and Janice got married. This was after I conjured up my new identity, of course. Once I settled on the frame-up, it didn't take much to figure out he was in the perfect position to assist me."

"Did you kill him too?"

"I wish I had. He ducked out on me, but I'll find a way to lure him back. He's not very smart."

Even with the tinnitus I suffer, I could have sworn I could hear the package bomb ticking merrily. I wet my lips. "Is there really a clock in there? Is that how it works?"

He glanced over at the kitchen counter. "It's not a complicated device. The one for Olive was more elaborate, but I had to make sure it would detonate on impact."

"It's amazing I wasn't killed then."

"Might have simplified things," he said.

I remembered then how he'd bent to recoil the hose lying on the walk. Any excuse to hang back out of range. I was beginning to feel strangely free. The time left was brief, but it was beginning to stretch and sag like a long strand of chewing gum. It seemed absurd to think I'd spend the last minutes of my life discussing trivial points with the man who was going to do me in. Oh hell, why not, you know? I flashed again to my brief flight off the front of Olive's porch while she soared beyond me like a bird. A death like that barely registers. What scared me was surviving, maimed and burned, living long enough to feel the loss of self. Time to make a move, I thought, regardless of the consequences. Once your life is threatened, what else do you have to lose?

I reached for my handbag. "I've got some tranqs in my bag. Do you mind?"

He seemed startled, waving his gun at me. "Leave it where it is."

"I'm a wreck, Terry. I really need a Valium. Then you can tie me up."

"No," he said peevishly. "Don't touch it. I mean it!"

"Come on. Indulge me. It's a small request."

I pulled the bag over and unzipped the top, rooting through the contents until I located the crosshatched ivory handle of my beloved .32 and eased the safety off. He couldn't believe I'd disobey him, but he couldn't seem to think what to do.

As he rose to his feet, I fired through the bottom of the handbag at a range of ten feet without any visible effect. He did jump as if I'd tossed hot gravy on his pants, but I didn't see blood and he didn't topple to the floor as I'd sincerely prayed he would. Instead, he roared to life, coming at me like a mad dog. I pulled the gun out of my purse to fire again, but he was on me, taking me with him to the floor. I saw his fist come at me, and I jerked to the right. The blow landed on my left ear, which rang with pain. I scrambled up, grabbing at the couch for support. I had no idea where my gun had gone, but he was aiming his at me. I snatched up my handbag and swung it. I caught him in the head. The momentum knocked him sideways.

He was blocking my passage to the front door, so I veered the other way and raced into the bathroom. I slammed the door after me, turned the lock, and hit the floor. He fired twice, bullets zinging through the door like bees. There was no way out. The bathroom window was right in the line of fire and I couldn't see anything to defend myself with. He started kicking at the door, savage blows that splintered the wood on impact. I saw his foot come through the panel and he kicked again. His hand shot through the hole and he fumbled for the lock. I jerked the lid off the toilet tank and cracked him a blow. I heard him yelp and he snatched his hand back through the hole. He fired again, screaming obscenities. Suddenly his face appeared in the gap, eyes roving wildly as he searched for my location. The nose of the gun peered at me. All I could think to do was to protect myself with the tank lid, holding it in front of me like a shield. The bullet slammed into it with a clang, the impact fierce enough to jolt the lid right out of my hands, breaking it in two. Terry started kicking at the door again, but the blows were losing force.

On the other side, I heard him fall heavily. I froze, astonished, gasping for breath. There wasn't time to wait to see if he was faking it. I flipped the lock, shoving at the door, which I couldn't budge. I dropped to my knees and peered at him through the panel. He was flat on his back, his shirt front drenched in red. Apparently I'd wounded him the first time I fired, but it had taken him this long to go down. Blood seeped from him like a slow leak from a worn tire. His chest was still heaving. Above his stertorous breathing I could hear the package ticking like a grandfather clock.

"Get out of the doorway! Terry, move!"

He was unresponsive. The clock on my desk said 4:29.

I shoved as hard as I could, but there was no budging him. I had to get out of there. Frantically I glanced around the room and then grabbed up one half of the broken toilet tank. I smashed at the window. Glass showered out into the front yard, leaving fangs of glass in the frame. I grabbed a towel and wedged it over the glass-ragged sill as I boosted myself up.

The boom from the explosion propelled me through the window like Superman in full flight. I landed on the grass with a whunk that knocked the wind right out of me. For a moment, I felt the panic of paralysis, wondering if I'd ever breathe again. Debris was raining down around me. I saw a hunk of the roof hover briefly above me, like a UFO. Then it began to tumble and bounce down through the intervening branches of a tree. A cloud of white smoke drifted into view and began to disperse. I angled my gaze up to the wall behind me, which seemed to be intact. My sofa bed was sitting in the driveway with the cushions askew. Perched on the arm was my perky green air fern looking like it had hopped up there by itself. I knew the whole front wall of my apartment would be gone, the interior a shambles, all my possessions destroyed. Lucky I don't have much in this world, I thought.

I was temporarily deaf again, but I was getting used to it. Eventually, with effort, I roused myself and went back inside to see if there was anything of Terry left.

Epilogue

Henry Pitts came home to find a crater where his rental unit had been. He was more distressed about my troubles in his absence than any damage to his property, which was covered by insurance. He has big plans now about building a new studio for me and he's already conferring with an architect. I managed to salvage a few articles of clothing, among them my all-purpose dress and my favorite vest. What could I complain about? As soon as I was on my feet again, I went back to work. Mac arranged for California Fidelity to refurbish my office as a way of making amends for my temporary suspension. Andy Motycka was fired and criminal charges were filed against him. The D.A.'s office probably whited my name out and typed his in its place. Within two days of the explosion, Daniel left with Bass. I can't say I felt much. After all I'd been through, his betrayal seemed beside the point.

In surveying the situation, I decided there was only one other matter that needed cleaning up. I conferred with Lieutenant Dolan in private about the five thousand dollars Terry'd deposited to my account. He advised me to keep my mouth shut, which I did.

Respectfully submitted,
Kinsey Millhone

"**F**" is for Fugitive

For Marian Wood
whose faith keeps me afloat

The author wishes to acknowledge the invaluable assistance of the following people: Steven Humphrey; Deputy District Attorney Robert P. Samoian, County of Los Angeles; Patricia Barnwell, M.D.; Alan S. Gewant, Pharm.D., and Barbara Long, La Cumbre Pharmacy; Jail Commander Pat Hedges, San Luis Obispo County Jail; Officer Eben Howard, Santa Barbara Police Department; John T. Castle, Castle Forensic Laboratories, Dallas, Texas; Vice President Peter Wisner and Financial Consultant Michael Karry, Merrill Lynch, Pierce, Fenner & Smith Inc.; Lieutenant and Mrs. Tony Baker, Santa Barbara County Sheriff's Department; Anne Reid; Florence Clark; Brent and Sue Anderson; Carter Blackmar; William Pasich and Barbara Knox; and Jerome T. Kay, M.D.

1

The Ocean Street Motel in Floral Beach, California, is located, oddly enough, on Ocean Street, a stone's throw from the sea wall that slants ten feet down toward the Pacific. The beach is a wide band of beige trampled with footprints that are smoothed away by the high tide every day. Public access is afforded by a set of concrete stairs with a metal rail. A wooden fishing pier, built out into the water, is anchored at the near end by the office of the Port Harbor Authority, which is painted a virulent blue.

Seventeen years ago, Jean Timberlake's body had been found at the foot of the sea wall, but the spot wasn't visible from where I stood. At the time, Bailey Fowler, an ex-boyfriend of hers, pleaded guilty to voluntary manslaughter. Now he'd changed his tune. Every violent death represents the climax of one story and an introduction to its sequel. My job was to figure out how to write the proper ending to the tale, not easy after so much time had elapsed.

Floral Beach has a population so modest the number isn't even posted on a sign anywhere. The town is six streets long and three streets deep, all bunched up against a steep hill largely covered with weeds. There may be as many as ten businesses along Ocean: three restaurants, a gift shop, a pool hall, a grocery store, a T-shirt shop that rents boogie boards, a Frostee-Freeze, and an art gallery. Around the corner on Palm, there's a pizza parlor and a Laundromat. Everything closes down after five o'clock except the restaurants. Most of the cottages are one-story board-and-batten, painted pale green or white, built in the thirties by the look of them. The lots are small and fenced, many with power boats moored in the side yards. Sometimes the boats are in better condition than the properties on which they sit. There are several boxy stucco apartment buildings with names like the Sea View, the Tides, and the Surf 'n' Sand. The whole town resembles the backside of some other town, but it has a vaguely familiar feel to it, like a shabby resort where you might have spent a summer as a kid.

The motel itself is three stories high, painted lime green, with a length of sidewalk in front that peters out into patchy grass. I'd been given a room on the second floor with a balcony that allowed me to look left as far as the oil refinery (surrounded by chain-link fence and posted with warning signs) and to my right as far as Port Harbor Road, a quarter of a mile away. A big resort hotel with a golf course is tucked up along the hill, but the kind of people who stay there would never come down here, despite the cheaper rates.

It was late afternoon and the February sun was setting so rapidly it appeared to be defying the laws of nature. The surf thundered dully, waves washing toward the sea wall like successive buckets of soapy water being sloshed up on the sand. The wind was picking up, but it made no sound, probably because Floral Beach has so few trees. The sea gulls had assembled for supper, settling on the curb to peck at foodstuffs spilling out of the trashcans. Since it was a Tuesday, there weren't many tourists, and the few hardy souls who had walked the beach earlier had fled when the temperature began to drop.

I left the sliding glass door ajar and went back to the table where I was typing up a preliminary report.

My name is Kinsey Millhone. I'm a private investigator, licensed by the state of California, operating ordinarily in the town of Santa Teresa, ninety-five miles north of Los Angeles. Floral Beach is another hour and a half farther up the coast. I'm thirty-two years old, twice married, no kids, currently unattached and likely to remain so given my disposition, which is cautious at best. At the moment, I didn't even have a legitimate address. I'd been living with my landlord, Henry Pitts, while my garage apartment was being rebuilt. My stay at the Ocean Street Motel was being underwritten by Bailey Fowler's father, who had hired me the day before.

I had just moved back into my office, newly refurbished by California Fidelity, the insurance company that accords me space in exchange for my services. The walls had been painted a fresh white. The carpeting was slate blue, a short-pile wool shag that cost twenty-five bucks a yard (exclusive of padding and installation, folks). I know this because I peeked at the invoice the day the carpet was laid. My file cabinet was in place, my desk arranged near the French doors as usual, a new Sparklett's water cooler plugged in and ready to provide both hot and cold trickling water, depending on which button I pushed. This was classy stuff and I was feeling pretty good, almost recovered from the injuries I'd sustained on the last case I worked. Since I'm self-employed, I pay my disability insurance before I even pay my rent.

My first impression of Royce Fowler was of a once-robust man whose aging processes had accelerated suddenly. I guessed him to be in his seventies, somewhat shrunken from an impressive six foot four. It was clear from the way his clothing hung that he'd recently dropped maybe thirty pounds. He looked like a farmer, a cowboy, or a roustabout, someone accustomed to grappling with the elements. His white hair was thinning, combed straight back, with ginger strands still visible along his ears. His eyes were ice blue, brows and lashes sparse, his pale skin mottled with broken capillaries. He used a cane, but the big hands he kept folded together on the crook of it were as steady as stone and speckled with liver spots. He'd been helped into the chair by a woman I thought might be a nurse or a paid companion. He didn't see well enough to drive himself around.

"I'm Royce Fowler," he said. His voice was gravelly and strong. "This is my daughter, Ann. My wife would have driven down with us, but she's a sick woman and I told her to stay at home. We live in Floral Beach."

I introduced myself and shook hands with them both. There was no family resemblance that I could see. His facial features were oversized—big nose, high cheekbones, strong chin—while hers were apologetic. She had dark hair and a slight overbite that should have been corrected when she was a kid.

The quick mental flash I had of Floral Beach was of summer cottages gone to seed and wide, empty streets lined with pickup trucks. "You drove down for the day?"

"I had an appointment at the clinic," he rumbled. "What I got, they can't treat, but they take my money anyway. I thought we should talk to you, as long as we're in town."

His daughter stirred, but said nothing. I pegged her at

forty-some and wondered if she still lived at home. So far, she'd avoided making eye contact with me.

I don't do well at small talk, so I shifted down a gear into business mode. "What can I do for you, Mr. Fowler?"

His smile was bitter. "I take it the name doesn't mean much to you."

"Rings a dim bell," I said. "Can you fill me in?"

"My son, Bailey, was arrested in Downey three weeks ago by mistake. They figured out pretty quick they had the wrong man, so they released him within a day. Then I guess they turned around and ran a check on him, and his prints came up a match. He was rearrested night before last."

I nearly said, "A match with what?" but then my memory gave a lurch. I'd seen an article in the local paper. "Ah, yes," I said. "He escaped from San Luis sixteen years ago, didn't he?"

"That's right. I never heard from him after the escape and finally decided he was dead. The boy nearly broke my heart and I guess he's not done yet."

The California Men's Colony near San Luis Obispo is a two-part institution; a minimum-security unit for old men, and a medium-security facility divided into four six-hundred-man sections. Bailey Fowler had apparently walked away from a work detail and hopped on the freight train that rumbled past the prison twice a day back then.

"How'd he get tripped up?"

"There was a warrant out on a fellow named Peter Lambert, the name he was using. He says he was booked, fingerprinted, and in the can before they realized they had the wrong man. As I understand it, some hot-shoe detective got a bug up his butt and ran Bailey's prints through some fancy-pants new computer system they got down there. That's how they picked up on the fugitive warrant. By a damn fluke."

"Bum deal for him," I said. "What's he going to do?"

"I hired him a lawyer. Now he's back, I want him cleared."

"You're appealing the conviction?"

Ann seemed on the verge of a response, but the old man plowed right over her.

"Bailey never went to trial. He made a deal. Pleaded guilty to voluntary manslaughter on the advice of this court-appointed PD, the worthless son of a bitch."

"Really," I said, wondering why Mr. Fowler hadn't hired a lawyer for him at the time. I also wondered what kind of evidence the prosecution had. Usually, the DA won't make a deal unless he knows his case is weak. "What's the new attorney telling you so far?"

"He won't commit himself until he sees the files, but I want to make sure he has all the help he can get. There's no such thing as a private detective up in Floral Beach, which is why we came to you. We need someone to go to work, dig in and see if there's anything left. Couple witnesses died and some have moved away. The whole thing's a damn mess and I want it straightened out."

"How soon would you need me?"

Royce shifted in his chair. "Let's talk money first."

"Fine with me," I said. I pulled out a standard contract and passed it across the desk to him. "Thirty dollars an hour, plus expenses. I'd want an advance."

"I bet you would," he said tartly, but the look in his eyes indicated no offense. "What do I get?"

"I don't know yet. I can't work miracles. I guess it

depends on how cooperative the county sheriff's department is."

"I wouldn't count on them. Sheriff's department doesn't
like Bailey. They never liked him much, and his escape
didn't warm any hearts. Made all those people look like
idiots."

"Where's he being held?"

"L.A. County Jail. He's being moved up to San Luis
tomorrow is what we heard."

"Have you talked to him?"

"Just briefly yesterday."

"Must have been a shock."

"I thought I was hearing things. Thought I'd had a
stroke."

Ann spoke up. "Bailey always told Pop he was innocent."

"Well, he is!" Royce snapped. "I said that from the first.
He never would have killed Jean under any circumstance."

"I'm not arguing, Pop. I'm just telling *her*."

Royce didn't bother to apologize, but his tone underwent
a change. "I don't have long," he went on. "I want this
squared away before I go. You find out who killed her and
I'll see there's a bonus."

"That's not necessary," I said. "You'll get a written report
once a week and we can talk as often as you like."

"All right, then. I own a motel up in Floral Beach. You
can stay free of charge for as long as you need. Take your
meals with us. Ann here cooks."

She flashed a look at him. "She might not want to take
her meals with us."

"Let her say so, if that's the case. Nobody's forcing her
to do anything."

She colored up at that but said nothing more.

Nice family, I thought. I couldn't wait to meet the rest. Ordinarily, I don't take on clients sight unseen, but I was intrigued by the situation and I needed the work, not for the money so much as my mental health. "What's the time-table here?"

"You can drive up tomorrow. The attorney's in San Luis. He'll tell you what he wants."

I filled out the contract and watched Royce Fowler sign. I added my signature, gave him one copy, and kept the other for my files. The check he took from his wallet was already made out to me in the amount of two grand. The man had confidence, I had to give him that. I glanced at the clock as the two of them left. The entire transaction hadn't taken more than twenty minutes.

I closed the office early and dropped my car off at the mechanic's for a tune-up. I drive a fifteen-year-old VW, one of those homely beige models with assorted dents. It rattles and it's rusty, but it's paid for, it runs fine, and it's cheap on gas. I walked home from the garage through a perfect February afternoon—sunny and clear, with the temperature hovering in the sixties. Winter storms had been blowing through at intervals since Christmas and the mountains were dark green, the fire danger laid to rest until summer rolled around again.

I live near the beach on a narrow side street that parallels Cabana Boulevard. My garage apartment, flattened by a bomb during the Christmas holidays, had now been re-framed, though Henry was being coy about the plans he'd drawn up. He and the contractor had had their heads bent together for weeks, but so far he'd declined to let me see the blueprints.

I don't spent a lot of time at home, so I didn't much

care what the place looked like. My real worry was that
Henry would make it too large or too opulent and I'd feel
obliged to pay him accordingly. My current rent is only
two hundred bucks a month, unheard-of these days. With
my car paid for and my office space underwritten by California Fidelity, I can live very well on a modest monthly
sum. I don't want an apartment too fancy for my pocket-
book. Still, the property is his and he can do with it as he
pleases. Altogether, I thought it best to mind my own business and let him do what suited him.

2

I let myself in through the gate and circled the new construction to Henry's patio in the rear. He was standing near the back fence, chatting with our next-door neighbor while he hosed down the flagstones. He didn't miss a beat, but his gaze flicked over to the sight of me, and a slight smile crossed his face. I never think of him as elderly, though he'd celebrated his eighty-second birthday on Valentine's Day, the week before. He's tall and lean, with a narrow face, and blue eyes the color of gas jets. He's got a shock of soft white hair that he wears brushed to one side, good teeth (all his), a year-round tan. His overriding intelligence is tempered with warmth, and his curiosity hasn't diminished a whit with age. Until his retirement, he worked as a commercial baker. He still can't resist making breads and sweet rolls, cookies and cakes, which he trades to merchants in the area for goods and services. His current passion is designing crossword puzzles for those little paperback publications you can pick up in a supermarket check-out line. He also clips coupons, priding himself on all the money he saves. At Thanksgiving, for instance, he managed to buy a twenty-three-pound turkey for only seven bucks. Then, of course, he had to invite fifteen people in to help him polish it off. If I had to find fault with him, I suppose I'd have to cite his gullibility, and a tendency to be passive when he ought to take a stand and fight. In some ways, I see myself as his protector, a notion that might amuse him, as he probably sees himself as mine.

I still wasn't used to living under the same roof with him. My stay was temporary, just until my apartment was finished, perhaps another month. Peripheral damage to his place had been speedily repaired, except for the sun porch, which was demolished along with the garage. I had my own key to the house and I came and went as I pleased, but there were times when the emotional claustrophobia got to me. I like Henry. A lot. There couldn't be anyone better-natured than he, but I've been on my own for eight years plus, and I'm not used to having anyone at such close range. It was making me edgy, as if he might have some expectation of me that I could never meet. Perversely, I found myself feeling guilty for my own uneasiness.

When I let myself in the back door, I could smell something cooking: onions, garlic, tomatoes, probably a chicken dish. A dome of freshly baked bread was resting on a metal rack. The kitchen table was set for two. Henry'd had a girlfriend briefly, who'd redecorated his kitchen. At the time, she'd been hoping to rearrange his life savings—twenty thousand in cash, which she thought might look better in her own bank account. She was thwarted, thanks to me, and all that remained of her, at this point, were the kitchen curtains, green print cotton tied back with green bows. Henry was currently using the color-coordinated table napkins for handkerchiefs. We never spoke of Lila, but I sometimes wondered if he didn't secretly resent my intrusion into his romance. Sometimes being fooled by love is worth the price. At least you know you're alive and capable of feeling, even if all you end up with is chest pain.

I moved through the hallway to the small back bedroom I was currently calling home. Just walking in the door had made me feel restless and I thought ahead to the trip to Floral Beach with relief. Outside, I heard the squawk of the faucet being turned off and I could picture Henry neatly recoiling the hose. The screen door banged, and in a moment I heard the creak of his rocker, the rustle of the newspaper as he folded it over to the sports section, which he always read first.

There was a small pile of clean clothes at the foot of the bed. I crossed to the chest of drawers and stared at myself in the mirror. I looked cranky, no doubt about it. My hair is dark and I cut it myself with a pair of nail scissors every six weeks. The effect is just about what you'd expect—ragged, inexpert. Recently, someone told me it looked like a dog's rear end. I ran my hands through my mop, but it didn't do much good. My brow was furrowed in a little knot of discontent, which I smoothed with one finger. Hazel eyes, dark lashes. My nose blows real good and it's remarkably straight, considering it's been broken twice. Like a chimp, I bared my teeth, satisfied to see them (more or less) lined up right. I don't wear makeup. I'd probably look better if I did something with my eyes—mascara, eyebrow pencil, eye shadow in two shades—but then I'd be forever fooling around with the stuff, which seems like a waste of time. I was raised, for the most part, by a maiden aunt whose notion of beauty care was an occasional swipe of cold cream underneath her eyes. I was never taught to be girlish, so here I am, at thirty-two, stuck with a face unadorned by cosmetic subterfuge. As it is, we could not call mine a beautiful puss, but it does the job well enough, distinguishing the front of my head from the back. Which was neither here nor there, as my appearance was not the source of my disquiet. So what was my problem?

I went back to the kitchen and paused in the doorway. Henry had poured himself a drink as he does every night; Black Jack on the rocks. He glanced at me idly and then did a proper double take, fixing me with a look. "What's wrong?"

"I got a job today up in Floral Beach. I'll probably be gone a week to ten days."

"Oh. Is that all? That's good. You need a change." He turned back to the paper, leafing through the section on local news.

I stood there and stared at the back of his head. A painting by Whistler came immediately to mind. In a flash, I understood what was going on. "Henry, are you mothering me?"

"What makes you say that?"

"Being here feels weird."

"In what way?"

"I don't know. Dinner on the table, stuff like that."

"I like to eat. Sometimes I eat two, three times a day," he said placidly. He found the crossword puzzle at the bottom of the funnies and reached for a ballpoint pen. He wasn't giving this nearly the attention it deserved.

"You swore you wouldn't fuss over me if I moved in."

"I don't fuss."

"You *do* fuss."

"You're the one fussing. I haven't said a word."

"What about the laundry? You've got clothes folded up at the foot of my bed."

"Throw 'em on the floor if you don't like 'em there."

"Come on, Henry. That's not the point. I said I'd do my own laundry and you agreed."

Henry shrugged. "Hey, so I'm a liar. What can I say?"

"Would you quit? I don't need a mother."

"You need a *keeper*. I've said so for months. You don't have a clue how to take care of yourself. You eat junk. Get beat up. Place gets blown to bits. I told you to get a dog, but you refuse. So now you got me, and if you ask me, it serves you right."

How irksome. I felt like one of those ducklings inexplicably bonded to a mother cat. My parents had been killed in a car wreck when I was five. In the absence of real family, I'd simply done without. Now, apparently, old dependencies had surfaced. I knew what *that* meant. This man was eighty-two. Who knew how long he'd live? Just about the time I let myself get attached to him, he'd drop dead. Ha, ha, the joke's on you, again.

"I don't want a parent. I want you as a friend."

"I am a friend."

"Well, then, cut the nonsense. It's making me nuts."

Henry's smile was benign as he checked his watch. "You've got time for a run before dinner if you quit mouthing off."

That stopped me. I'd really hoped to get a run in before dark. It was almost four-thirty, and a glance at the kitchen window showed I didn't have long. I abandoned my complaints and changed into jogging sweats.

The beach that day was odd. The passing stormclouds had stained the horizon a sepia shade. The mountains were a drab brown, the sky a poisonous-looking tincture of iodine. Maybe Los Angeles was burning to the ground, sending up this mirage of copper-colored smoke turning umber at the edge. I ran along the bike path that borders the sand.

The Santa Teresa coastline actually runs east and west. On a map, it looks like the ragged terrain takes a sudden left turn, heading briefly out to sea before the currents force it back. The islands were visible, hovering offshore, the channel dotted with oil rigs that sparkled with light. It's worrisome, but true, that the oil rigs have taken on an eerie beauty of their own, as natural to the eye now as orbiting satellites.

By the time I made the turnaround a mile and a half down the path, twilight had descended and the streetlights were ablaze. It was getting cold and the air smelled of salt, the surf battering the beach. There were boats anchored beyond the breakers, the poor man's yacht harbor. The traffic was a comfort, illuminating the grassy strip between the sidewalk and the bike path. I try to run every day, not from passion, but because it's saved my life more than once. In addition to the jogging, I usually lift weights three times a week, but I'd had to discontinue that temporarily, due to injuries.

By the time I got home, I was in a better mood. There's no way to sustain anxiety or depression when you're out of breath. Something in the sweat seems to bring cheer in its wake. We ate supper, chatting companionably, and then I went to my room and packed a bag for the trip. I hadn't begun to think about the situation up in Floral Beach, but I took a minute to open a file folder, which I labeled with Bailey Fowler's name. I sorted through the newspapers stacked up in the utility room, clipping the section that detailed his arrest.

According to the article, he'd been out on parole on an

armed-robbery conviction at the time his seventeen-year-old ex-sweetheart was found strangled to death. Residents of the resort town reported that Fowler, then twenty-three, had been involved in drugs off and on for years, and speculated that he'd killed the girl when he learned of her romantic entanglement with a friend of his. With the plea bargain, he'd been sentenced to six years in the state prison. He'd served less than a year at the Men's Colony at San Luis Obispo when he engineered his escape. He left California, assuming the alias of Peter Lambert. After a number of miscellaneous sales jobs, he'd gone to work for a clothing manufacturer with outlets in Arizona, Colorado, New Mexico, and California. In 1979, the company had promoted him to western division manager. He was transferred to Los Angeles, where he'd been residing ever since. The newspaper indicated that his colleagues were stunned to learn he'd ever been in trouble. They described him as hardworking, competent, outgoing, articulate, active in church and community affairs.

The black-and-white photograph of Bailey Fowler showed a man maybe forty years old, half-turned toward the camera, his face blank with disbelief. His features were strong, a refined version of his father's, with the same pugnacious jawline. An inset showed the police photograph taken of him seventeen years before, when he was booked for the murder of Jean Timberlake. Since then, his hairline had receded slightly and there was a suggestion that he may have darkened the color, but then again that might have been a function of age or the quality of the photograph. He'd been a handsome kid, and he wasn't bad looking now.

Curious, I thought, that a man can reinvent himself.

There was something enormously appealing in the idea of setting one persona aside and constructing a second to take its place. I wondered if serving out his sentence in prison would have had as laudatory an effect as being out in the world, getting on with his life. There was no mention of a family, so I had to guess he'd never married. Unless this new attorney of his was a legal wizard, he'd have to serve the remaining years of his original sentence, plus an additional sixteen months to two years on the felony escape charge. He could be forty-seven by the time he was released, years he probably wasn't interested in giving up without a fight.

The current paper had a follow-up article, which I also clipped. For the most part, it was a repetition of the first, except that a high school yearbook photo of the murdered girl was included along with his. She'd been a senior. Her dark hair was glossy and straight, cut to the shape of her face, parted in the middle and curving in softly at the nape of her neck. Her eyes were pale, lined with black, her mouth wide and sensual. There was the barest suggestion of a smile, and it gave her an air of knowing something the rest of us might not be aware of yet.

I slipped the clippings in the folder, which I tucked into the outside pocket of my canvas duffel. I'd stop by the office and pick up my portable typewriter en route.

At nine the next morning, I was on the road, heading up the pass that cuts through the San Rafael Mountains. As the two-lane highway crested, I glanced to my right, struck by the sweep of undulating hills that move northward, intersected by bare bluffs. The rugged terrain is tinted to a hazy blue-gray by the nature of the underlying rock. The land here has lifted, and now the ridges of shale and sandstone project in a visible spine called the Transverse Ranges. Geological experts have concluded that California, west of the San Andreas Fault, has moved north up the Pacific coast by about three hundred miles during the last thirty million years. The Pacific Plate is still grinding away at the continent, buckling the coastal regions in earthquake after earthquake. That we continue to go about our daily business without much thought for this process is either testimony to our fortitude or evidence of lunacy. Actually, the only quakes I've experienced have been minor temblors that rattle dishes on the shelf or set the coat hangers in the closet to tinkling merrily. The sensation is no more alarming than being shaken awake gently by someone too polite to call your name. People in San Francisco, Coalinga, and Los Angeles will have a different tale to tell, but in Santa Teresa (aside from the Big One in 1925) we've had mild, friendly earthquakes that do little more than slop some of the water out of our swimming pools.

The road eased down into the valley, intersecting Highway 101 some ten miles beyond. At 10:35, I took the Floral Beach exit, heading west toward the ocean through grassy, rolling hills dotted with oaks. I could smell the Pacific long before I laid eyes on it. Screeching sea gulls heralded its appearance, but I was still surprised by the breadth of that flat line of blue. I hung a left onto the main street of Floral Beach, the ocean on my right. The motel was visible three blocks away, the only three-story structure on Ocean Street. I pulled into a fifteen-minute parking space outside the registration office, grabbed my duffel, and went in.

3

The office was small, the registration desk blocking off
access to what I surmised were the Fowlers' personal quarters in the rear. My crossing the threshold had triggered
a soft bell.

"Be right out," someone called. It sounded like Ann.

I moved to the counter and peered to my right. Through
an open door, I caught a glimpse of a hospital bed. There
was the murmur of voices, but I couldn't see a soul. I heard
the muffled flushing of a toilet, pipes clanking noisily. The
air was soon scented with the artificial bouquet of room
spray, impossibly sweet. Nothing in nature has ever smelled
like that.

Several minutes passed. There was no seating available,
so I stood where I was, turning to survey the narrow room.
The carpeting was harvest gold, the walls paneled in knotty
pine. A painting of autumn birches with fiery orange and
yellow leaves hung above a maple coffee table on which a
rack of pamphlets promoted points of interest and local
businesses. I leafed through the display, picking up a brochure for the Eucalyptus Mineral Hot Springs, which I'd
passed on the road coming in. The advertisement was for
mud baths, hot tubs, and rooms at "reasonable" rates, whatever that meant.

"Jean Timberlake worked there in the afternoons after school," Ann said behind me. She was standing in the doorway, wearing navy slacks and a white silk shirt. She seemed more relaxed than she had in her father's company. She'd had her hair done and it fell in loose waves to her shoulders, steering the eye away from the slightly recessed chin.

I put the pamphlet back. "Doing what?" I asked.

"Maid service, part-time. She worked for us, too, a couple of days a week."

"Did you know her well?"

"Well enough," she said. "She and Bailey started dating when he was twenty. She was a freshman in high school." Ann's eyes were mild brown, her manner detached.

"A little young for him, wasn't she?"

Her smile was brief. "Fourteen." Any other comment was curtailed by a voice from the other room.

"Ann, is someone out there? You said you'd be right back. What's happening?"

"You'll want to meet Mother," Ann murmured in a way that generated doubts. She lifted a hinged section of the counter and I passed through.

"How's your father doing?"

"Not good. Yesterday was hard on him. He was up for a while this morning, but he's easily fatigued and I suggested he go back to bed."

"You've really got your hands full."

She flashed me a pained smile. "I've had to take a leave of absence."

"What sort of work?"

"I'm a guidance counselor at the high school. Who knows when I'll get back."

I let her lead the way into the living room, where Mrs.

Fowler was now propped up in the full-sized hospital bed. She was gray-haired and heavy, her dark eyes magnified by thick glasses in heavy plastic frames. She was wearing a white cotton hospital gown that tied down the back. The neck was plain, with SAN LUIS OBISPO COUNTY HOSPITAL inked in block letters along the rim. It struck me as curious that she'd affect such garb when she could have worn a bed jacket or a gown and robe of her own. Illness as theater, perhaps. Her legs lay on top of the bedclothes like haunches of meat not yet trimmed of fat. Her pudgy feet were bare, and her toes were mottled gray.

I crossed to the bed, holding my hand toward hers. "Hi, how are you? I'm Kinsey Millhone," I said. We shook hands, if that's what you'd call it. Her fingers were as cold and rubbery as cooked rigatoni. "Your husband mentioned you weren't feeling well," I went on.

She put her handkerchief to her mouth and promptly burst into tears. "Oh, Kenny, I'm sorry. I can't help myself. I'm just all turned around with Bailey showing up. We thought he was dead and here he comes again. I've been sick for years, but this has just made it worse."

"I can understand your distress. It's Kinsey," I said.

"It's what?"

"My first name is Kinsey, my mother's maiden name. I thought you said 'Kenny' and I wasn't sure you heard it right."

"Oh Lord. I'm so sorry. My hearing's nearly gone and I can't brag about my eyes. Ann, honey, fetch a chair. I can't think where your manners went." She reached for a Kleenex and honked into it.

"This is fine," I said. "I've just driven up from Santa Teresa, so it feels good to be on my feet."

"Kinsey's the investigator Pop hired yesterday."

"I know that," Mrs. Fowler said. She began to fuss with her cotton cover, plucking it this way and that, made restless by topics that didn't pertain to her. "I hoped to get myself all cleaned up, but Ann said she had errands. I hate to interfere with her any more than I have to, but there's just things I can't do with my arthritis so bad. Now, look at me. I'm a mess. I'm Ori, short for Oribelle. You must think I'm a sight."

"Not at all. You look fine." I tell lies all the time. One more couldn't hurt.

"I'm diabetic," she said, as though I'd asked. "Have been all my life, and what a toll it's took. I got tingling and numbness in my extremities, kidney problems, bad feet, and now I've developed arthritis on top of that." She held a hand out for my inspection. I expected knuckles as swollen as a prizefighter's, but they looked fine to me.

"I'm sorry to hear that. It must be rough."

"Well, I've made up my mind I will not complain," she said. "If it's anything I despise, it's people who can't accept their lot."

Ann said, "Mother, you mentioned tea a little while ago. How about you, Kinsey? Will you have a cup?"

"I'm all right for now. Thanks."

"None for me, hon," Ori said. "My taste for it passed, but you go ahead and fix some for yourself."

"I'll put the water on."

Ann excused herself and left the room. I stood there wishing I could do the same. What I could see of the apartment looked much like the office: gold high-low carpeting, Early American furniture, probably from Montgomery Ward. A painting of Jesus hung on the wall at the foot of the bed. He had his palms open, eyes lifted toward heaven—pained, no doubt, by Ori's home decorating taste. She caught my eye.

"Bailey gave me that pitcher. It's just the kind of boy he was."

"It's very nice," I replied, then quizzed her while I could. "How'd he get mixed up in a murder charge?"

"Well, it wasn't his fault. He fell in with bad company. He didn't do good in high school and after he got out, he couldn't find him a job. And then he ran into Tap Granger. I detested that no-account the minute I laid eyes on him, the two of 'em running around till all hours, getting into trouble. Royce was having fits."

"Bailey was dating Jean Timberlake by then?"

"I guess that's right," she said, apparently hazy on the details after so much time had passed. "She was a sweet girl, despite what everybody said about that mother of hers."

The telephone rang and she reached over to the bed table to pick it up. "Motel," she said. "Unh-hunh, that's right. This month or next? Just a minute, I'll check." She pulled the reservation book closer, removing a pencil from between the pages. I watched her flip forward into March, peering closely at the print. Her tone, as she conducted business, was completely matter-of-fact. Gone was the suggestion of infirmity that marked her ordinary speech. She licked the pencil point and made a note, discussing king-sized beds versus queen.

I took the opportunity to go in search of Ann. A doorway on the far wall led out into a hallway, with rooms opening off the central corridor in either direction. On the right, there was a staircase, leading to the floor above. I could hear water being run and then the faint tap of the teakettle on the burner in the kitchen to my left. It was hard to get a fix on the overall floor plan and I had to guess the apartment had been patched together from a number of motel rooms with the intervening walls punched out. The resulting town house was spacious, but jerry-built, with the traffic patterns of a maze. I peeked into the room across the hall. Dining room with a bath attached. There was access to the kitchen through what must have been an alcove for hanging clothes. I paused in the doorway. Ann was setting cups and saucers on an industrial-sized aluminum serving tray.

"Need any help?"

She shook her head. "Look around if you like. Daddy built the place himself when he and Mother first got married."

"Nice," I said.

"Well, it's not anymore, but it was perfect for them. Has she given you a key yet? You might want to take your bags up. I think she's putting you in room twenty-two upstairs. It's got an ocean view and a little kitchenette."

"Thanks. That's great. I'll take my bags up in a bit. I'm hoping to talk to the attorney this afternoon."

"I think Pop set up an appointment for you at one-forty-five. He'll probably want to tag along if he's feeling up to it. He tends to want to stage-manage. I hope that's all right."

"Actually, it's not. I'll want to go alone. Your parents seem defensive about Bailey, and I don't want to have to cope with that when I'm trying to get a rundown on the case."

"Yes. All right. I can see your point. I'll see if I can talk Pop out of it."

Water began to rumble in the bottom of the kettle. She took teabags from a red-and-white tin canister on the counter. The kitchen itself was old-fashioned. The linoleum was a pale gridwork of squares in beige and green, like an aerial view of hay and alfalfa fields. The gas stove was white with chrome trim, unused burners concealed by jointed panels that folded back. The sink was shallow, of white porcelain, supported by two stubby legs, the refrigerator small, round-shouldered, and yellowing with age, probably with a freezer compartment the size of a bread box.

The teakettle began to whistle. Ann turned the burner off and poured boiling water in a white teapot. "What do you take?"

"Plain is fine."

I followed her back into the living room, where Ori was struggling to get out of bed. She'd already swung her feet over the side, her gown hitching up to expose the crinkled white of her thighs.

"Mother, what are you doing?"

"I have to go sit on the pot again, and you were taking so long I didn't think I could wait."

"Why didn't you call? You know you're not supposed to get up without help. Honestly!" Ann set the tray down on a wooden serving cart and moved over to the bed to give her mother a hand. Ori descended ponderously, her wide knees trembling visibly as they took her weight. The two proceeded awkwardly into the other room.

"Why don't I go ahead and get my things out of the car?"

"Do that," she called. "We won't be long."

The breeze off the ocean was chilly, but the sun was out.

I shaded my eyes for a moment, peering at the town, where pedestrian traffic was picking up as the noon hour approached. Two young mothers crossed the street at a languid pace, pushing strollers, while a dog pranced along behind them with a Frisbee in his mouth. This was not the tourist season, and the beach was sparsely populated. Empty playground equipment was rooted in the sand. The only sounds were the constant shushing of the surf and the high, thin whine of a small plane overhead.

I retrieved my duffel and the typewriter, bumping my way back into the office. By the time I reached the living room, Ann was helping Ori into bed again. I paused, waiting for them to notice me.

"I need my lunch," Ori was saying querulously to Ann.

"Fine, Mother. Let's go ahead and do a test. We should have done it hours ago, anyway."

"I don't want to fool with it! I don't feel that good."

I could see Ann curbing her temper at the tone her mother used. She closed her eyes. "You're under a lot of stress," she said evenly. "Dr. Ortego wants you to be very careful till he sees you next."

"He didn't tell *me* that."

"That's because you didn't talk to him."

"Well, I don't like Mexicans."

"He's not Mexican. He's Spanish."

"I still can't understand a word he says. Why can't I have a real doctor who speaks English?"

"I'll be right with you, Kinsey," Ann murmured, catching sight of me. "Let me just get Mother settled first."

"I can take my bags up if you tell me where they go."

There was a brief territorial dispute as the two of them argued about which room to put me in. In the meantime,

Ann was taking out cotton balls, alcohol, and some sort of testing strip sealed in a paper packet. I looked on with discomfort, an unwilling witness as she swabbed her mother's fingertip and pierced it with a lancet. I could feel myself going nearly cross-eyed with distaste. I moved over to the bookcase, feigning interest in the titles on the shelves. Lots of inspirational reading and condensed versions of Leon Uris books. I pulled out a volume at random and leafed through, blocking out the scene behind me.

I waited a decent interval, tucked the book away, and then turned back casually. Ann had apparently read the test results from the digital display on a meter by the bed and was filling a syringe from a small vial of pale, milky liquid I presumed was insulin. I busied myself with a glass paperweight—a Nativity scene in a swirling cloud of snow. Baby Jesus was no bigger than a paper clip. God, I'm a sissy when it comes to shots.

From the rustling sounds behind me, I surmised they were done. Ann broke the needle off the disposable syringe and tossed it in the trash. She tidied up the bed table and then we moved out to the desk so she could give me my room key. Ori was already calling out a request.

4

By one-thirty, I had driven the twelve miles to San Luis Obispo and I was circling through the downtown area, trying to orient myself and get a feel for the place. The commercial buildings are two to four stories high and immaculately maintained. This is clearly a museum town, with Spanish and Victorian structures restored and adapted to current use. The storefronts are painted in handsome dark shades, many with awnings arching over the windows. The establishments seem to be divided just about equally between trendy clothing stores and trendy restaurants. Carrotwood trees border most avenues, with strings of tiny Italian lights woven into branches bursting with green. Any businesses not catering directly to the tourists seem geared to the tastes of the Cal Poly students in evidence everywhere.

Bailey Fowler's new attorney was a man named Jack Clemson, with an address on Mill, a block from the courthouse. I pulled into a parking space and locked my car. The office was located in a small, brown frame cottage with a pointed gable in the roof and a narrow wooden porch enclosed by trellises. A white picket fence surrounded the property, with a tangle of geraniums crowding in among the pales. Judging from the lettered sign affixed to the gate, Jack Clemson was the sole tenant.

I climbed the wooden porch steps and moved into the entrance hall now furnished as a reception area. A grandfather clock on the wall to my left gave the only sense of life, the brass pendulum snick-snacking back and forth mechanically. The former parlor on the right was lined with old-fashioned, glass-fronted oak bookcases. There was an oak desk with a typing ell, a swivel chair, a Xerox machine, but no secretary in sight. The screen on the computer monitor was blank, the surface of the desk neatly stacked with legal briefs and brown accordion files tied with string. Across the hall, the door to the matching parlor was shut. One of the buttons on the telephone was lighted and I could smell fresh cigarette smoke drifting out from somewhere in the back. Otherwise, the office seemed deserted.

I took a seat in an old church pew with a slot for hymnals underneath the bench. It was filled now with alumni journals from Columbia University Law School, which I leafed through idly. Presently, I heard footsteps and Clemson appeared.

"Miss Millhone? Jack Clemson. Nice to meet you. You'll have to pardon the reception. My secretary's out sick and the temp's still off at lunch. Come on back."

We shook hands and I followed him. He was maybe fifty-five and heavyset, one of those men who'd probably been considered portly since birth. He was short and squat, wide-shouldered and balding. His features were babified: sparse eyebrows and a soft, undefined nose with red dents along the bridge. A pair of tortoiseshell reading glasses were shoved up on his head, and strands of hair were standing straight up on end. His shirt collar was unbuttoned and his tie was loose. Apparently he hadn't had time to shave, and he scratched at his chin experimentally as if to gauge the morning's growth. His suit was tobacco brown, impeccably tailored, but wrinkled across the seat.

His office occupied the entire rear half of the building, and had French doors that opened out onto a sunny deck. Both of the dark green leather chairs intended for clients were piled high with legal briefs. Clemson scooped up an armload of books and files and set them on the floor, motioning for me to take a seat while he went around to the far side of the desk. He caught a glimpse of himself in the mirror hanging on the wall to his left, and his hand returned involuntarily to the stubble on his chin. He sat down and pulled a portable electric razor from his desk drawer. He flicked it on and began to slide it around his face with a practiced hand, mowing a clean path across his upper lip. The shaver buzzed like a distant airplane.

"I got a court date in thirty minutes. Sorry I can't spare you any more time this afternoon."

"That's all right," I said. "When does Bailey get in?"

"He's probably here by now. Deputy drove down this morning to bring him back. I made arrangements for you to see him at three-fifteen. It's not regular visiting hours, but Quintana said it's okay. It's his case. He was rookie of the year back then."

"What about the arraignment?"

"Eight-thirty tomorrow morning. If you're interested, you can come here first and walk over with me. That'll give us a chance to compare notes."

"I'd like that."

Clemson made a note on his desk calendar. "Will you be going back over to the Ocean Street this afternoon?"

"Sure."

He tucked the electric shaver away and closed the desk drawer. He reached for some papers, which he folded and slipped into an envelope, scrawling Royce's name across the front. "Tell Royce this is ready for his signature," he said.

I tucked the envelope in my handbag.

"How much of the background on this have you been told?"

"Not much."

He lit a cigarette, coughing into his fist. He shook his head, apparently annoyed by the state of his lungs. "I had a long talk this morning with Clifford Lehto, the PD who handled Fowler's case. He's retired now. Nice man. Bought a vineyard about sixty miles north of here. Says he's growing Chardonnay and Pinot Noir grapes. I wouldn't mind doing that myself one of these days. Anyway, he went through his old files for me and pulled the case notes."

"What's the story on that? Why'd the DA make a deal?"

Clemson gestured dismissively. "It was all circumstantial evidence. George De Witt was the district attorney. You ever run into him? Probably not. It would have been way before your time. He's a Superior Court judge now. I avoid him like the plague."

"I've heard of him. He's got political aspirations, doesn't he?"

"For all the good it's gonna do. He's into the sauce and it's the kiss of death. You never know which way he's gonna go on a case. He's not unfair, but he's inconsistent. Which is too bad. George was a hotdogger. Very flashy guy. He hated to bargain a high-publicity case, but he wasn't a fool. From what I hear, the Timberlake murder looked passable on the surface, but they were short of hard evidence. Fowler was known around town as a punk for years. His old man had thrown him out—"

"Wait a minute," I said. "Was this before he went to jail the first time or afterward? I thought he'd been convicted of armed robbery, but nobody's given me the story on that either."

"Shoot. All right, let me back up a bit. This was two, three years before. I got the dates here somewhere, but it matters not. The deal is, Fowler and a fellow named Tap Granger hooked up right around the time Fowler got out of high school. Bailey was a good-looking kid and he was smart enough, but he never got it together. You probably know the type. He was just one of those kids who seems destined to go sour. From what Lehto says, Bailey and Tap were doing a lot of drugs. They had to pay the local dope peddler, so they started bumping off gas stations. Nickel-and-dime jobs, and they're rank amateurs. Idiots. They're wearing panty hose on their heads, trying to act like big-time hoods. Of course, they got caught. Rupert Russell was the PD on that one and he did the best he could."

"Why not a private attorney? Was Bailey indigent?"

"In essence. He didn't have the dough himself and his old man refused to pop for any legal fees." Clemson took a drag of his cigarette.

"Had Bailey been in trouble as a juvenile?"

"Nope. His record was clean. He probably figured all he'd get was a slap on the wrist. This is armed robbery, you understand, but Tap carried the gun, so I guess Bailey thought somehow that let him off the hook. Unfortunately for him, the statute doesn't read that way. Anyway, when they offered him a deal, he turned 'em down cold, pleaded not guilty, and went to trial instead. Needless to say, the jury convicted and the judge got tough. Back then, robbery was one to ten in the state prison."

"That was still indeterminate sentencing?"

"Yeah, that's right. Back then, they had a Bureau of Prison Terms that would meet and set parole and actual date of release. We had a very liberal board of prison terms at that time. Hell, we had basically a much more liberal government in California. Those people who ran the board were appointed by the governor and Pat Brown Junior . . . well, skip that tale. Point is, these guys get one to ten, but they're out in two years. Everybody starts screaming and yelling because nobody was doing nine or ten years on a one-to-ten. Bailey only served eighteen months."

"Up here?"

"Nuh-unh. Down at Chino, the country club of prisons. He got out in August. Came back to Floral Beach and started looking for work without much luck. Pretty soon he was back doing drugs again, only it was cocaine this time, along with grass. Uppers, downers, you name it."

"Where was Jean all this time?"

"Central Coast High, senior year. I don't know if anybody filled you in on this girl."

"Not at all."

"She was illegitimate. Her mom's still around in Floral Beach. You might want to talk to her. She had a reputation as the town roundheel, the mother, this is. Jean was an only child. Cute kid, but I guess she had a lot of problems. As if the rest of us don't." He took another drag from his cigarette.

"She worked for Royce Fowler, didn't she?"

"Right. Bailey got out of prison and she took up with

him again. According to Lehto, Bailey claimed they were just good friends. The DA maintains they were lovers and Bailey killed her in a jealous rage when he found out she'd hooked up with Tap. Fowler says not so. It had nothing to do with Granger, even though Tap got out two months before he did."

"What about Granger? Is he still around?"

"Yeah, he operates the only gas station in Floral Beach. Owned by somebody else, but he's the manager, which is about all he can handle. He's not smart, but he seems steady enough. He was a wild one in his day, but he's mellowed out some."

I made a note about both Tap Granger and the Timberlake woman. "I didn't mean to interrupt. You were talking about Bailey's relationship with the girl after he got out of jail."

"Well, Bailey maintains the romance was over with. He and the girl hung out together and that was it. They were both outcasts anyway, Bailey because he'd been in prison, the Timberlake girl because her mother's such a slut. Besides which, the Timberlakes were poor. She was never going to amount to a hill of beans as long as she was stuck in Floral Beach. I don't know how much experience you've had with towns the size of Floral Beach. We're talking maybe eleven hundred people max, and most of 'em have been here since the year zip. Anyway, she and Bailey started running around together just like they did before. He says she was dallying with this other guy, involved in some affair that she was being real tight-lipped about. Claims she never would say who it was.

"The night she was killed, the two of 'em went out drinking. Hit about six bars in San Luis and two more in Pismo.

Around midnight, they came back and parked down at the beach. He says it was closer to ten, but a witness puts 'em there at midnight. Anyway, she was upset. They had a bottle and a couple of joints with 'em. They had a tiff and he says he left her there and stomped off. Next thing he knows, it's morning and he's in his room at the Ocean Street. These kids are swarming all over the beach down below, doing clean-up detail as part of some local church do-good project. He's sick as a dog . . . so hung over he was pukin' his guts out. She's still down on the beach, passed out over by the stairs . . . only when the clean-up crew gets close, they can see she's dead, strangled with a belt that turns out to be his."

"But anybody could have done it."

"Absolutely. Of course, Bailey was favored and they might have made it stick, but De Witt had had a string of wins and he didn't want to take a chance. Lehto saw an opportunity to bargain and since Bailey'd been burned once, he went along with the deal. On the armed robbery, he was guilty, went to trial, and got himself nailed. This time he claimed he was innocent, but he didn't like the odds so when they offered him a plea of manslaughter, he took it, just like that." Clemson snapped his fingers, the sound like the clean popping of a hollow stick.

"Could he have beaten the murder rap if he'd gone to trial?"

"Hey, who knows? Going to trial is a crapshoot. You put your money on the line every time. If you roll that seven or eleven, boy, you're feeling good. But if it comes out two, three, or twelve, you're the loser. The case generated a lot of publicity. Sentiment in town was running against him. Then you had Bailey's prior, no character witnesses to speak of. He was better off with the deal. Twenty years ago, he could've been given the death penalty, too, which is something you don't want to mess with if you can help it. Talk about rolling dice."

"I thought if you were charged with murder, they wouldn't reduce that."

"True, hypothetically, but that's not the way it works. It was just discretionary with the district attorney how he filed. What Lehto did was, he goes to De Witt and says, 'Look, George, I've got evidence my guy was under the influence at the time. Evidence from your own people.' He pulls out the police report. 'If you'll note in the record, when the officers arrested him, it states he appeared to be drowsy . . .' Blah, blah, blah. Clifford does this whole number and he can see George start to sweat. He's got his ego on the line and he doesn't want to go into court with a big hole in his case. As DA, you're expected to win ninety percent of the time, if not higher."

"So Bailey pleaded guilty to the manslaughter and the judge maxed him out," I said.

"Exactly. You got it, but we're only talkin' six years. Big deal. With time served and time off for good behavior, he might have been out in half that. The whole time, Fowler's thinking he got screwed, but he doesn't understand how lucky he was. Clifford Lehto did a hell of a job for him. I'd have done the same thing myself."

"What happens next?"

Clemson shrugged again, stubbing out his cigarette. "Depends on how Bailey wants to plead on the felony escape. What's he gonna say, 'No, I didn't escape'? Extenuating circumstances? He can always claim some prison goon was threatening his life, but that hardly explains where he's been all this time. The irony is, he should have hired some hotshot attorney the first couple rounds. At this point, it's not going to do him much good. I'll go to bat for him, but no judge in his right mind is going to set bail for some guy who's been on the lam sixteen years."

"What do you want from me in the meantime?"

Clemson got up and started pawing through the piles of paper on his desk. "I had my secretary pull all the clippings from the time of the murder. You might want to look at those. Lehto said he'd send down everything he's got. Police reports, list of witnesses. Talk to Bailey and see if he's got anything to add. You know the drill. Go back through the players and find me another suspect. Maybe we can develop evidence against somebody else and get Bailey off the hook. Otherwise, he's lookin' at a lot more years in the slammer unless I can persuade the judge no purpose would be served, which is what I'll try to do. He's been clean all this time, and personally, I can't see the point of puttin' him back in, but who knows? Here."

He unearthed an accordion file and handed it to me. I got to my feet and we shook hands again, chatting about other things as we left his office, walking toward the front. The office temp was sitting at her desk by then, trying to sustain an air of competence. She looked young and bewildered, out of her element in the world of habeas corpus, or corpuses of any kind.

"Oh yeah, one thing I almost forgot," Clemson said when we reached the porch. "What Jean was upset about that night? She was pregnant. Six weeks. Bailey swears it wasn't his."

5

I had about an hour to kill before I was due at the jail. I got out a city map and found the little dark square with a flag on it that marked the location of Central Coast High School. San Luis Obispo is not a large town, and the school was only six or eight blocks away. Lines painted on the main streets delineated a Path of History that I thought I might walk later in the week. I have an affection for early California history and I was curious to see the Mission and some of the old adobes as long as I was there.

When I reached the high school, I drove through the grounds, trying to imagine how it must have looked when Jean Timberlake was enrolled. Many of the buildings were clearly new: dark, smoke gray cinder block, trimmed in cream-colored concrete, with long, clean roof lines. The gymnasium and the cafeteria were of an earlier vintage, Spanish-style architecture done in darkening stucco with red tile roofs. On the upper level, where the road curved up and around to the right, there were modular units that had once served as classrooms and were now used for various businesses, Weight Watchers being one. The campus seemed more like a junior college than the high schools I'd seen. Rolling green hills formed a lush backdrop, giving the facility a feeling of serenity. The murder of a seventeen-

year-old girl must have been deeply distressing to kids accustomed to pastoral surroundings such as these.

From what I remember of high school, our behavior was
underscored by a hunger for sensation. Feelings were intense and events were played out in emotional extremes.
While the fantasy of death satisfied a craving for self-
drama, the reality was usually (fortunately) at some safe
remove. We were absurdly young and healthy, and though
we behaved recklessly, we never expected to suffer any
consequence. The notion of a real death, whether by accident or intent, would have pushed us into a state of perplexity. Love affairs provided all the theater we could
handle. Our sense of tragedy and our self-centeredness
were so exaggerated that we weren't prepared to cope with
any actual loss. Murder would have been beyond comprehension. Jean Timberlake's death probably still generated
discussion among the people she knew, giving rise to a
disquiet that marred the memories of youth. Bailey Fowler's sudden reappearance in the community was going to
stir it all up again: uneasiness, rage, the nearly incompre-
hensible feelings of waste and dismay.

On impulse, I parked the car and searched out the library, which turned out to be much like the one at Santa
Teresa High. The space was airy and open, the noise level
subdued. The vinyl floor tile was a mottled beige, polished
to a dull gleam. The air smelled like furniture polish, construction paper, and paste. I must have eaten six jars of
LePage's during my grade-school years. I had a friend who
ate pencil shavings. There's a name for that now, for kids
who eat inorganic oddities like gravel and clay. In my day,
it just seemed like a fun thing to do and no one ever gave
it a passing thought as far as I knew.

The library tables were sparsely occupied and the reference desk was being handled by a young girl with frizzy hair and a ruby drilled into the side of her nose. She had apparently been seized by a fit of self-puncturing because both ears had been pierced repeatedly from the lobe to the helix. In lieu of earrings, she was sporting the sort of items you'd find in my junk drawer at home: paper clips, screws, safety pins, shoelaces, wing nuts. She was perched on a stool with a copy of *Rolling Stone* open on her lap. Mick Jagger was on the cover, looking sixty if a day.

"Hi."

She looked at me blankly.

"I wonder if you can give me some help. I used to be a student here and I can't find my yearbook. Do you have any copies? I'd like to take a look."

"Under the window. First and second shelf."

I pulled the annuals from three separate years and took them to a table on the far side of a row of free-standing bookcases. A bell rang and the corridor began to fill with the rustling sound of students on the move. The slamming of locker doors was punctuated by the babble of voices, laughter bouncing off the walls with the harsh echo of a racquetball court. The ghostly scent of gym socks wafted in.

I traced Jean Timberlake's picture back, volume by volume, like the aging process in reverse. During her high school years, while the rest of California's youth were protesting the war, smoking dope, and heading for the Haight, the girls at Central Coast were teasing their hair into glossy towers, putting black lines around their eyes and white gloss on their lips. The junior girls wore white blouses and bouffant hair, which curved out in a heavily sprayed flip at the sides. The guys had damp-looking crewcuts and braces on their teeth. They couldn't have guessed how soon they'd be sporting sideburns, beards, bell-bottoms, and psychedelic shirts.

Jean never looked like she had anything in common with the rest. In the few group pictures where I spotted her, she never grinned and she had none of the bouncy-looking innocence of the Debbies and the Tammies. Jean's eyes were hooded, her gaze remote, and the faint smile that played on her mouth suggested a private amusement still evident after all these years. The blurb in the senior index listed no committees or clubs. She hadn't been burdened with scholastic honors or elective offices, and she hadn't bothered to participate in any extracurricular activities. I leafed through candid shots taken at various school functions, but I never did catch sight of her. If she went to football or basketball games, she must have hovered somewhere beyond the range of the school photographer. She wasn't in the senior play. All the prom pictures focused on the queen, Barbie Knox, and her entourage of beehived, white-lipped princesses. Jean Timberlake was dead by then. I jotted down the names of her more conspicuous classmates, all guys. I figured if the girls were still living in the area, they'd be listed in the phone book under married names, which I'd have to get somewhere else.

The principal at that time was a man named Dwight Shales, whose picture appeared in an oval on one of the early pages of the annual. The school superintendent and his two assistant superintendents were each pictured separately, seated at their desks, holding official-looking papers. Sometimes a member of the office staff, female, peered over some man's shoulder with interest, smiling perkily. The teachers had been photographed against a varied background of maps, industrial arts equipment, textbooks, and blackboards on which phrases had been writ large in chalk. I noted some of their names and specialties, thinking I might want to return at a later date to talk to one or two. A young Ann Fowler was one of four guidance counselors photographed on a separate page with a paragraph underneath. "These counselors gave extra time, thought, and encouragement to us as they helped us plan our program for the next year wisely or advised us when we had decisions to make regarding our future plans for jobs or college." I thought Ann looked prettier then, not as tired or as soured.

I tucked my notes away and returned the books to the shelves. I headed down the hallway, passing the nurse's office and the attendance office. The administrative offices were located near the main entrance. According to the name plate on the wall beside the door, Shales was still the school principal. I asked his secretary if I could see him, and after a brief wait, I was ushered into his office. I could see my business card sitting in the center of the blotter on his desk.

He was a man in his mid-fifties, medium height, trim, with a square face. The color of his hair had changed from blond to a premature white, and he'd grown it out from its original mid-sixties crewcut. His whole manner was authoritarian, his hazel eyes as watchful as a cop's. He had that same air of assessment, as if he were checking back through his mental files to come up with my rap sheet. I felt my cheeks warm, wondering if he could tell at a glance what a troublesome student I'd been in high school.

"Yes, ma'am," he said. "What can I do for you?"

"I've been hired by Royce Fowler in Floral Beach to look

into the death of a former student of yours named Jean Timberlake." I'd expected him to remember her without further prompting, but he continued to look at me with studied neutrality. Surely he couldn't know about the dope I'd smoked back then.

"You do remember her," I said.

"Of course. I was just trying to think if we'd held on to the records on her. I'm not sure where they'd be."

"I've just had a conversation with Bailey's attorney. If you need some kind of release . . ."

He gestured carelessly. "That's not necessary. I know Jack Clemson and I know the family. I'd have to clear it with the school superintendent, but I can't see that it'd be any problem . . . if we can locate 'em. It's the simple question of what we've got. You're talking more than fifteen years ago."

"Seventeen," I said. "Do you have any personal recollections of the girl?"

"Let me get clearance on the matter first and then I'll get back to you. You're local?"

"Well, I'm from Santa Teresa, but I'm staying at the Ocean Street in Floral Beach. I can give you the number . . ."

"I've got the number. I'll call you as soon as I know anything. Might be a couple of days, but we'll see what we can do. I can't make any guarantees."

"I understand that," I said.

"Good. We'll help you if we can." His handshake was brisk and firm.

At three-fifteen I headed north on Highway 1 to the San Luis Obispo County Sheriff's Department, part of a complex of buildings that includes the jail. The surround-

ing countryside is open, characterized by occasional towering outcroppings of rock. The hills look like soft humps
of foam rubber, upholstered in variegated green velvet.
Across the road from the Sheriff's Department is the California Men's Colony, where Bailey had been incarcerated
at the time of his escape. It amused me that in the pro-
motional literature extolling the virtues of life in San Luis
Obispo County, there's never any mention of the six thousand prisoners also in residence.

I parked in one of the visitors' slots in front of the jail.
The building looked new, similar in design and construction materials to the newer portions of the high school
where I'd just been. I went into the lobby, signs directing
me to the booking and inmate information section down
a short corridor to the right. I identified myself to the
uniformed deputy in the glass-enclosed office, where I
could see the dispatcher, the booking officer, and the computer terminals. To the left, I caught a glimpse of the
covered garage where prisoners could be brought in by
sheriffs' vehicles.

While arrangements were being made to bring Bailey
out, I was directed to one of the small, glass-enclosed booths
reserved for attorney-client conferences. A sign on the wall
spelled out the rules for visitors, admonishing us that there
could only be one registered visitor per inmate at any one
time. We were to keep control of children, and any rude
or boisterous conduct toward the staff was not going to be
tolerated. The restrictions suggested past scenes of chaos
and merriment I was already wishing I'd been privy to.

I could hear the muffled clanking of doors. Bailey Fowler appeared, his attention focused on the deputy who was
unlocking the booth where he would sit while we spoke.

We were separated by glass, and our conversation would be conducted by way of two telephone handsets, one on his side, one on mine. He glanced at me incuriously and then sat down. His demeanor was submissive and I found myself feeling embarrassed in his behalf. He wore a loosely structured orange cotton shirt over dark gray cotton pants. The newspaper photograph had shown him in a suit and tie. He seemed as bewildered by the clothing as he was by his sudden status as an inmate. He was remarkably good-looking: grave blue eyes, high cheekbones, full mouth, dark blond hair already in need of a cut. He was a tired forty, and I suspected circumstances had aged him overnight. He shifted in the straight-backed wooden chair, clasping his hands loosely between his knees, his expression empty of emotion.

I picked up the phone, waiting briefly while he picked up the receiver on his side. I said, "I'm Kinsey Millhone."

"Do I know you?"

Our voices sounded odd, both too tinny and too near.

"I'm the private investigator your father hired. I just spent some time with your attorney. Have you talked to him yet?"

"Couple of times on the phone. He's supposed to stop by this afternoon." His voice was as lifeless as his gaze.

"Is it all right if I call you Bailey?"

"Yeah, sure."

"Look, I know this whole thing's a bummer, but Clemson's good. He'll do everything possible to get you out of here."

Bailey's expression clouded over. "He better do something quick."

"You have family in L.A.? Wife and kids?"

"Why?"

"I thought there might be someone you wanted me to get in touch with."

"I don't have family. Just get me the hell out of here."

"Hey, come on. I know it's tough."

He looked up and off to one side, anger glinting in his eyes before the brief show of feeling subsided into bleakness again. "Sorry."

"Talk to me. We may not have long."

"About what?"

"Anything. When'd you get up here? How was the ride?"

"Fine."

"How's the town look? Has it changed much?"

"I can't make small talk. Don't ask me to do that."

"You can't shut down on me. We have too much work to do."

He was silent for a moment and I could see him struggle with the effort to be communicative. "For years, I wouldn't even drive through this part of the state for fear I'd get stopped." Transmission faltered and came to a halt. The look he gave me was haunted, as if he longed to speak, but had lost the capacity. It felt as if we were separated by more than a sheet of glass.

I said, "You're not dead, you know."

"Says you."

"You must have known it would happen one day."

He tilted his head, doing a neck roll to work the tension out. "They picked me up the first time, I thought it was all over. Just my luck there's a Peter Lambert out there wanted on a murder one. When they let me go, I thought maybe I had a chance."

"I'm surprised you didn't take off."

"I wish now I had, but I'd been free so long. I couldn't believe they'd get me. I couldn't believe anybody cared. Besides, I had a job and I couldn't just chuck it all and hit the road."

"You're some kind of clothing rep, aren't you? The L.A. papers mentioned that."

"I worked for Needham. One of their top salesmen last year, which is how I got promoted. Western regional manager. I guess I should have turned it down, but I worked hard and I got tired of saying no. It meant a move to Los Angeles, but I didn't see how I could get tripped up after all this time."

"How long have you been with the company?"

"Twelve years."

"What's their attitude? Can you count on them for any help?"

"They've been great. Real supportive. My boss said he'd come up here and testify . . . be a character witness and stuff like that, but what's the point? I feel like such a jerk. I've been straight all these years. Your proverbial model citizen. I never even got a parking ticket. Paid taxes, went to church."

"But that's good. That'll work in your favor. It's bound to make a difference."

"But it doesn't change the facts. You don't walk away from jail and get a slap on the wrist."

"Why don't you let Clemson worry about that?"

"I guess I'll have to," he said. "What are you supposed to do?"

"Find out who really killed her so we can get you off the hook."

"Fat chance."

"It's worth a shot. You got any ideas about who it might have been?"

"No."

"Tell me about Jean."

"She was a nice kid. Wild, but not bad. Mixed up."

"But pregnant."

"Yeah, well, the baby wasn't mine."

"You're sure of that." I framed it as a statement, but the question mark was there.

Bailey hung his head for a moment, color rising in his face. "I did a lot of booze back then. Drugs. My performance was off, especially after I got out of Chino. Not that it mattered. She was with some other guy by then."

"You were impotent?"

"Let's say, 'temporarily out of order.' "

"You do any drugs now?"

"No, and I haven't had a drink in fifteen years. Alcohol makes your tongue loose. I couldn't take the chance."

"Who was she involved with? Any indication at all?"

He shook his head again. "The guy was married."

"How do you know?"

"She told me that much."

"And you believed her?"

"I can't think why she would have lied. He was somebody respectable and she was underage."

"So this was somebody with a lot to lose if the truth came out."

"That'd be my guess. I mean, she sure didn't want to have to tell him she was knocked up. She was scared."

"She could have had an abortion."

"I guess . . . if it came to that. She only found out about the baby that day."

"Who was her doctor?"

"She didn't have one yet for that. Dr. Dunne was the family physician, but she had the pregnancy test at some clinic down in Lompoc so nobody'd know who she was."

"Seems pretty paranoid. Was she that well known?"

"She was in Floral Beach."

"What about Tap? Could the kid have been his?"

"Nope. She thought he was a jerk and he didn't like her much either. Besides, he wasn't married and it was nothing to him even if the kid had been his."

"What else? You must have given this a lot of thought."

"I don't know. She was illegitimate and she'd been trying to find out who her old man was. Her mom refused to tell her, but money came in the mail every month, so Jean figured he had to be around someplace."

"She saw the checks?"

"I don't think he paid by check, but she was getting a line on him somehow."

"Was she born in San Luis County?"

There was a jangle of keys and we both looked over to see the deputy at the door. "Time's up. Sorry to interrupt. You want more, Mr. Clemson has to make arrangements."

Bailey got up without argument, but I could see him zone out. Whatever energy our conversation had produced had already drained away. The numb look returned, giving him the air of someone not too bright.

"I'll see you after the arraignment," I said.

Bailey's parting look flickered with desperation.

After he left, I sat and jotted down some notes. I hoped he didn't have any suicidal tendencies.

6

Just to fill in another blank, I pulled into the gas station in Floral Beach and asked the attendant to top off my tank. While the kid was taking care of the windshield, I took my wallet and went into the office, where I studied the vending machine. Nothing but Cheetos for $1.25. Cheatos, I thought. There was no one at the desk, but I spotted someone working out in the service bay. I went to the door. The guy had a Ford Fiesta up on the lift, whipping lug nuts off the right rear wheel with an air-driven lug wrench.

"Can I get some change for the vending machine in here?"

"Sure thing."

The fellow set the wrench down and wiped his hands on a rag tucked into his belt. "Tap" was stitched in an embroidered script on the patch above his uniform pocket. I followed him back into the office. He moved in an aura of motor oil and tire smell, giving off that heady scent of sweat and gasoline fumes. He was wiry and small, with wide shoulders and a narrow butt, the type who might unveil a lavish tattoo when he took off his shirt. His dark hair was curly, combed into a crest on top, the sides swept into a ducktail in the back. He looked about forty, with a still-boyish face getting leathery around the eyes.

I handed him two dollars. "You know anything about VWs?"

He made eye contact for the first time. His were brown and didn't show much life. I suspected car woes were going to spark the only interest I'd be able to generate. He flicked a look out to the pumps, where the kid was just finishing up. "You got a problem?"

"Well, it may not be much. I keep hearing this high-pitched whine when I get up around sixty. Sounds kind of weird."

"You can hit sixty in a tin can like that?" he said.

A car joke. He grinned, punching open the register.

I smiled. "Well, yeah. Now and then."

"Try Gunter's in San Luis. He can fix you up." He dropped eight quarters into my palm.

"Thanks."

He moved back out to the service bay and I pocketed the change. At least I knew now who Tap Granger was. I paid for the gas and headed up two blocks to the motel.

As it turned out, I didn't talk to Royce at all that afternoon. He'd retired early, leaving word with Ann that he'd see me in the morning. I spoke briefly with her mother, filling her in on Bailey's current state, and then went on upstairs. I'd picked up a bottle of white wine on my way through San Luis and I stashed it in the small refrigerator in my room. I hadn't unpacked, and my duffel was tucked in the closet where I'd left it. I tend, on the road, to leave everything in a suitcase, digging out my toothbrush, shampoo, and clean clothing as the need arises. The room remains bare and unnaturally tidy, which appeals to a streak of monasticism in me. This room was spacious, the designated bedroom area separated from the living/dining/kitchenette by a partition. Factoring in the bathroom and a closet, it was bigger than my (former) apartment back home.

I rooted through the kitchen drawers until I came up with a corkscrew, and then I poured myself a glass of wine and took it out on the balcony. The water was turning a luminous blue as the light faded from the sky, and the dark lavender of the coastline was a vivid contrast. The sunset was a light show of deep pink and salmon shades, gradually sinking, as if by a dimmer switch, through magenta into indigo.

There was a tap at my door at six. I'd been typing for twenty minutes, though the information I'd collected, at this point, was scant. I screwed the lid on the white-out and went to the door.

Ann was standing in the corridor. "I wondered what time you wanted supper."

"Anytime's fine with me. When do you usually eat?"

"Actually, we can suit ourselves. I fed Mother early. Her meal schedule's pretty strict, and Pop won't eat until later, if he eats at all. I'm doing pan-fried sole for us, which is a last-minute thing. I hope you don't object to fish."

"Not at all. Sounds great. You want to join me in a glass of white wine first?"

She hesitated. "I'd like that," she said. "How's Bailey doing? Is he okay?"

"Well, he's not happy, but there's not much he can do. You haven't seen him yet?"

"I'll go tomorrow, if I can get in."

"Check with Clemson. He can probably set it up. It shouldn't be hard. Arraignment's at eight-thirty."

"I think I'll have to pass on that. Mother has a doctor's appointment at nine and I couldn't get back in time anyway.

Pop will want to go, if he's feeling okay. Could he go with you?"

"Sure. No problem."

I poured a glass for her and refilled my own. She settled on the couch, while I sat a few feet away at the tiny kitchen table where my typewriter was set up. She seemed ill at ease, sipping at her wine with an odd cast to her mouth, as if she'd been asked to down a glass of liniment.

"I take it you're not crazy about Chardonnay," I remarked.

She smiled apologetically. "I don't drink very often. Bailey's the only one who ever developed a taste for it."

I thought I'd have to pump her for background information, but she surprised me by volunteering a quick family time line. The Fowlers, she said, had never been enthusiastic about alcohol. She claimed this was a function of her mother's diabetes, but to me it seemed in perfect keeping with the dour fundamentalist mentality that pervaded the place.

According to Ann, Royce had been born and raised in Tennessee and the dark strains of his Scots heritage had rendered him joyless, taciturn, and wary of excess. He'd been nineteen at the height of the Depression, migrating west on a succession of boxcars. He'd heard there was work in the oilfields in California, where the rigs were springing up like a metallic forest just south of Los Angeles. He'd met Oribelle, en route, at a dime-a-dip dinner at a Baptist church in Fayetteville, Arkansas. She was eighteen, soured by disease, resigned to a life of scriptures and insulin dependency. She was working in her father's feed store, and the most she could look forward to was the annual trip to the mule market in Fort Smith.

Royce had appeared at the church that Wednesday night, having hopped off a freight in search of a hot meal. Ann said Ori still talked of her first sight of him, standing in the door, a broad-shouldered youth with hair the color of hemp. Oribelle introduced herself as he went through the supper line, piling his plate high with macaroni and cheese, which was her specialty. By the end of the evening, she'd heard his entire life story and she invited him home with her afterward. He slept in the barn, taking all his meals with the family. He remained a guest of the Baileys for two weeks, during which she was in such a fever pitch of hormones that she'd twice gone into ketoacidosis and had had to be briefly hospitalized. Her parents took this as evidence that Royce's influence was wicked. They talked to her long and hard about her giving him up, but nothing would dissuade her from the course she had set. She was determined to marry Royce. When her father opposed the courtship, she took all the money set aside for secretarial school and ran off with him. That was in 1932.

"It's odd for me to picture either one of them caught up in high passion," I said.

She smiled. "Me too. I should show you a photo. She was actually quite beautiful. Of course, I wasn't born until six years later—1938—and Bailey came along five years after me. Whatever heat they felt was burned out by then, but the bond is still strong. The irony is, we all thought she'd die long before him, and now it looks like he'll go first."

"What's actually wrong with him?"

"Pancreatic cancer. They're saying six months."

"Which he knows?"

"Oh yes. It's one of the reasons he's so thrilled about

Bailey's showing up. He talks about heartbreak but he doesn't mean a word of it."

"What about you? How do you feel?"

"Relieved, I guess. Even if he goes back to prison, I'll have someone to help me get through the next few months. The responsibility's been crushing ever since he disappeared."

"How's your mother handling this?"

"Badly. She's what they call a 'brittle' diabetic, which means she's always been in fragile health. Any kind of emotional upset is hard on her. Stress. I guess it gets to all of us one way or another, myself included. Ever since Pop was diagnosed as terminal, my life's been hell."

"You mentioned you were on a leave of absence from work."

"I had no choice. Someone has to be here twenty-four hours a day. We can't afford professional care, so I'm 'it.' "

"Rough."

"I shouldn't complain. I'm sure there are people out there who have it worse."

I shifted the subject. "You have any theories about who killed the Timberlake girl?"

Ann shook her head. "I wish I did. She was a student at the high school, as well as Bailey's girl."

"She spent a lot of time here?"

"A fair amount. Less while Bailey was off in jail."

"And you're convinced he had nothing to do with her death?"

"I don't know what to believe," she said flatly. "I don't want to think he did it. On the other hand, I've never liked the idea that the killer could still be around someplace."

"He won't like it either, now that Bailey's back in custody.

Somebody must have felt pretty smug all these years. Once the investigation's opened up, who knows where it'll go?"

"You're right. I wouldn't like to be in your shoes." She rubbed her arms as if she were cold and then laughed at herself uneasily. "Well. I better get back downstairs and see how Mother's doing. She was napping when I left, but she tends to sleep in short bursts. The minute her eyes open, she wants me Johnny-on-the-spot."

"Give me time to wash my face and I'll be right down." I walked her to the door. As I passed my handbag, I caught sight of the envelope Clemson had given me. "Oh. This is for your father. Jack Clemson asked me to drop it off." I plucked it out and handed it to her.

She glanced at it idly and then smiled at me. "Thanks for the drink. I hope I haven't bored you with the family history."

"Not at all," I said. "By the way, what's the story on Jean Timberlake's mother? Will she be hard to find?"

"Who, Shana? Try the pool hall. She's there most nights. Tap Granger, too."

After supper, I snagged a jacket from my room and headed down the back stairs.

The night was cold and the breeze coming off the Pacific was briny and damp. I shrugged into my jacket and walked the two blocks to Pearl's Pool Hall as if through broad daylight. Floral Beach, by night, is bathed in the flat orange glow of the sodium vapor lights that line Ocean Street. The moon wasn't up yet, and the ocean was as black as pitch. The surf tumbled onto the beach in an uneven fringe of gold, picking up illumination from the last reaches of the street lamps. A fog was rolling in and the air had the dense, tawny look of smog.

Closer to the pool hall, the quiet was broken by a raucous blast of country music. The door to Pearl's stood open and I could smell cigarette smoke from two doors away. I counted five Harley-Davidsons at the curb, all chrome and black leather seats, with convoluted tailpipes. The boys in my junior high school went through a siege of drawing machines like that: hot rods and racing cars, tanks, torture devices, guns, knives, and bloodlettings of all kinds. I should really check one day and find out how those guys turned out.

The pool hall itself was two pool tables long, with enough space between to allow folk to angle for a tricky shot. Both tables were occupied by bikers: heavyset men in their forties with Fu Manchu beards and long hair pulled back in ponytails. There were five of them, a family of road pirates on the move. The bar ran the entire length of wall to the left, the barstools filled with the bikers' girlfriends and assorted town folk. Walls and ceiling were covered with a collage of beer signs, tobacco ads, bumper stickers, cartoons, snapshots, and bar witticisms. One sign proclaimed Happy Hour from six to seven, but the hand-drawn clock under it had a 5 at every hour. A knee-slapper, that. Bowling trophies, beer mugs, and racks of potato chips lined the shelf behind the bar. There was also a display of Pearl's Pool Hall T-shirts on sale for $6.99. A leather biker's glove hung inexplicably from the ceiling, and a Miller Lite mirror on the wall was festooned with a pair of lady's underpants. The noise level was such that a hearing test might be in order later.

There was one empty stool at the bar, which I took. The

bartender was a woman in her mid-sixties, perhaps the very Pearl for whom the place was named. She was short, thick through the middle, with graying, permanent-curled hair chopped straight across the nape of her neck. She was wearing plaid polyester slacks and a sleeveless top, showing arms well muscled from hefting beer cases. Maybe, at intervals, she hefted some biker out the door by the seat of his pants.

I asked for a draft beer, which she pulled and served up in a Mason jar. Since the din made conversation impossible, I had plenty of time to survey the place in peace. I turned on the stool until my back was up against the bar, watching the pool players, casting an occasional eye at the patrons on either side of me. I wasn't really sure how I wanted to present myself. I thought for the time being I'd keep hush about my occupation and the reasons for my presence in Floral Beach. The local papers had carried front-page news about Bailey's arrest, and I thought I could probably conjure up talk on the subject without appearing too inquisitive.

Down to my left, near the jukebox, two women began to dance. The bikers' girlfriends made some rude observations, but no one seemed to pay much attention aside from that. Two stools over, a woman in her fifties looked on with a sloppy smile. I pegged her as Shana Timberlake, in part because no other woman in the bar looked old enough to have had a teenage daughter seventeen years before.

At ten, the bikers cleared out, motorcycles rocketing off down the street with diminishing thunder. The jukebox was between selections, and for a moment a miraculous silence fell across the bar. Someone said, "Whew, Lord!"

and everybody laughed. There were maybe ten of us left
in the place, and the tension level dropped to some more
familial feel. This was Tuesday night, the local hangout,
the equivalent of the basement recreation room at a church,
except that beer was served. There was no hard liquor in
evidence and my guess was that any wine on the premises
was going to come from a jug the size of an oil drum, with
about that much finesse.

The man on the stool next to mine on the right appeared
to be in his sixties. He was big, with a beer belly that pro-
truded like a twenty-five-pound bag of rice. His face was
broad, connected to his neck by a series of double chins.
There was even a roll of fat at the back of his neck where
graying hair curled over his shirt collar. I'd seen him flick a
curious look in my direction. The others in the bar seemed
known to one another, judging from the banter, which had
largely to do with local politics, old sporting grievances, and
how drunk someone named Ace had been the night before.
The sheepish Ace, tall, thin, jeans, denim jacket, and baseball cap, took a lot of ribbing about some behavior of his
with old Betty, whom he'd apparently taken home with
him. Ace seemed to revel in the accusations of misconduct,
and since Betty wasn't present to correct the impression,
everyone assumed that he'd gotten laid.

"Betty's his ex-wife," the man next to me said, in one of
those casual asides meant to include me in the merriment.
"She kicked him out four times, but she always takes him
back. Yo, Daisy. How about some peanuts down here?"

"I thought that was Pearl," I remarked, to keep the conversation alive.

"I'm Curtis Pearl," he said. "Pearl to my friends."

Daisy scooped what looked like a dog dish full of peanuts

from a garbage pail under the bar. The nuts were still in
the shell, and the litter on the floor suggested what we were
meant to do. Pearl surprised me by chomping down a peanut, shell and all. "We're talkin' fiber here," he said. "It's
good for you. I got a doctor believes in cellulose. Fills you
up, he says. Gets the old system powerin' through."

I shrugged and tried it myself. No doubt about it, the
shell had a lot of crunch and a sharp infusion of salt mingled nicely with the bland taste of the nut inside. Did this
count as grain, or was it the same as eating the panel from
a cardboard box?

The jukebox sparked to life again, this time a mellow
vocalist who sounded like a cross between Frank Sinatra
and Della Reese. The two women at the end of the bar
began to dance again. Both were dark-haired, both slim.
One taller. Pearl turned to look at them and then back at
me. "That bother you?"

"Why should I care?"

"Not what it looks like anyway," he said. "Tall one likes
to dance when she's feeling blue."

"What's she got to be unhappy about?"

"They just picked up the fellow killed her little girl a
few years back."

7

I watched her for a moment. At a distance of half the bar, she looked twenty-five. She had her eyes closed, head tilted to one side. Her face was heart-shaped, her hair caught up in a clip on top, the lower portion brushing across her shoulder in a rhythm with the ballad. The light from the jukebox touched her cheek with gold. The woman she was dancing with had her back to me, so I couldn't tell anything about her at all.

Pearl was sketching in the story for me with the practiced tone of frequent telling. No details I hadn't heard before, but I was thankful he'd introduced the subject without any further prompting on my part. He was just warming up, enjoying his role as tribal narrator. "You staying at the Ocean Street? I ask because this fella's dad owns that place."

"Really," I said.

"Yep. They found her down on the beach right in front," he said. Residents of Floral Beach had been telling this tale for years. Like a stand-up comedian, he had his timing down pat, knowing just when to pause, knowing just what response he'd get.

I had to watch what I said because I didn't want to imply I knew nothing of this. While I'm not averse to lying through my teeth, I never do it when I'm apt to be caught. People get crabby about that sort of thing. "Actually, I know Royce."

"Aw, then you know all about this."

"Well, some. You really think Bailey did it? Royce says no."

"Hard to say. Naturally, he'd deny anything of the sort. None of us want to believe our kids would kill someone."

"True enough."

"You have kids?"

"Unh-unh."

"My boy was the one who spotted the two of 'em pulling into the curb that night. They got out of the truck with a bottle and a blanket and went down the steps. Said Bailey looked drunk as a skunk to him and she wasn't much better off. Probably went down there to misbehave, if you get what I mean. Maybe she sprung it on him she was in a family way."

"Hey, there. How's that little Heinie car acting?"

I glanced back to see Tap behind me, a sly grin on his face.

Pearl didn't seem thrilled to see him, but he made polite noises with his mouth. "Say, Tap. What're you up to? I thought that old lady of yours didn't like you comin' in here."

"Aw, she don't care. Who's this we're talking to?"

"I'm Kinsey. How're you?"

Pearl raised an eyebrow. "You two know each other?"

"She had her bug in this afternoon and wanted me to take a look. Said it was kind of whiny up around sixty. Whiny Heinie," he said and got real tickled with himself. At close range, I could smell the pomade on his hair.

Pearl turned and stared at him. "You got something against the Germans?"

"Who, me?"

"My folks is German, so you better make it good."

"Naw, hell. I don't care. That Nazi business wasn't such a bad idea. Hey, Daisy. Gimme a beer. And hand me a bag of them barbecued potato chips. Big one. This gal looks like she could use a bite to eat. I'm Tap." He hiked himself up on the barstool to my left. He was the sort of man who saved his handshakes for meetings with other men. A woman, if known to him, might warrant a pat on the butt. As a stranger, I lucked out.

"What kind of name is Tap?" I asked.

Pearl cut in. "Short for tapioca. He's a real puddin' head."

Tap cut loose with a laugh again, but he didn't seem that amused. Daisy showed up with the beer and chips so I never did find out what Tap was short for.

"We're just talking about your old friend Bailey," Pearl said. "She's stayin' down at the Ocean Street and Royce is fillin' her head full of all kind of thing."

"Aw, that Bailey's something else," Tap said. "He's quick. He had a million schemes. Talk you into anything. We had us a good time, I can tell you that."

"I just bet you did," Pearl said. He was seated on my right, Tap on my left, the two of them conversing back and forth across me like a tennis match.

"Made more money than you ever seen," Tap said.

"Tap and him did a little business together in the old days," Pearl said to me, his tone confidential.

"Really. What kind of business?"

"Now come on, Pearl. She doesn't want to hear about that stuff."

"Eat a man's chips, you might want to know what kind of company you're in."

Tap was starting to squirm. "I straightened myself up now and that's a fact. I got me a good wife and kids and I keep my nose clean."

I leaned toward Pearl with mock concern. "What'd he do, Pearl? Am I safe with this man?"

Pearl loved it. He was looking for ways to prolong the aggravation. "I'd keep a hand on my wallet if I was you. Him and Bailey took to putting ladies' panties on their heads . . . stickin' up gas stations with their little toy guns."

"Pearl! Now, goddamn. You know that ain't true."

Tap apparently wasn't good at being teased about these things. His choice was to let the story stand, or make corrections that would perhaps have him looking even worse.

Pearl retracted his statement with all the contrition of a prosecuting attorney who knows the jury's already got the point. "Oh hell, I'm sorry. You're right, Tap. There was only the one gun," Pearl said. "Tap, here, carried it."

"Well, it wasn't my idea in the first place and the damn thing wasn't loaded."

"Bailey thought up the gun. It was Tap's idea about the ladies' underpants."

Tap made a stab at recovering. "This guy don't know ladies' pants from panty hose. That's his problem. We had stockings pulled over our faces."

"Kept gettin' runs in the hose," Pearl said, ad-libbing. "Spent all their profits at the five-and-dime buyin' more."

"Don't mind him. He's jealous is all. We got them panty hose off that wife of his. She put her legs up and they come right off." Tap snickered at himself. Pearl didn't seem to take offense.

I allowed myself to laugh, more from discomfort than amusement. It was odd being caught between these two male energies. It felt like the equivalent of two dogs barking at each other across the safety of a fence.

There was a commotion at the far end of the bar, and Pearl's attention strayed. Daisy, standing close to us, seemed to understand what it was about. "Jukebox is broke again. It's been eating quarters all day. Darryl claims he's down a dollar twenty-five."

"Give him back his money from the register and I'll take a look." Pearl eased off the stool and moved down to the jukebox. Shana Timberlake was still dancing, by herself this time, to music no one else could hear. There was a touch of exhibitionism in her grief, and a couple of guys playing pool were eyeing her with undisguised interest, calculating the odds of cashing in on her mood. I've known women like that, who use their troubles as a reason to get laid, as if sex were a balm with healing properties.

Once Pearl absented himself, the tension level in the air dropped by half and I could feel Tap relax. "Hey, Daze. Gimme another beer, here, babe. This is Crazy Daisy. She's worked for Pearl since before the rocks cooled."

Daisy glanced at me. "How about it? You ready for another one?"

Tap caught her eye. "Go ahead and make it two. On me."

I smiled briefly. "Thanks. That's nice."

"I didn't want you to think you were settin' here with a crook."

"He sure likes to hassle you, doesn't he?"

"Now that's the truth,". Tap said. He reared back and looked at me, surprised that anyone but he had picked up on it. "He don't mean any harm by it, but it gets on my nerves, I can tell you that. If this wasn't the only bar in town, I'd tell him to get . . . well, I'd tell him what he could do with it."

"Really. Anyone can make mistakes," I said. "I pulled all kinds of pranks when I was a kid. I'm just lucky I didn't get caught. Not that sticking up gas stations is a prank, of course."

"That ain't even the half of it. That's just what they nailed us for," he said. A slight note of bragging had crept into his tone. I'd heard it before, usually from men who longed for the remembered hype of past sports triumphs. I seldom thought of crime as a peak experience, but Tap might.

I said, "Listen, if we got nailed for everything we did, we'd all be in jail."

He laughed. "Hey, I like you. I like your attitude."

Daisy brought our beers and I watched while Tap pulled out a ten. "Run us a tab," he said to her.

She picked up the bill and moved back toward the register where I saw her make a note. Meanwhile, Tap studied me, trying to figure out where I was coming from. "I bet you never robbed nobody at gunpoint."

"No, but my old man did," I said easily. "Did time for it, too." Oh, I liked that. The lie rolled right off my tongue without a moment's thought.

"You're b.s.-in' me. Your old man did time? Don't give me that. Where?" The "where" came out sounding like "were."

"Lompoc," I said.

"That's federal," he said. "What'd he do, rob a bank?"

I pointed at him, aiming my finger like a gun.

"Goddamn," he said. "God*damn*." He was excited now,

as if he'd just found out my father was a former president. "How'd he get caught?"

I shrugged. "He'd been picked up before for passing bad checks, so they just matched the prints on the note he handed the teller. He never even had a chance to spend the money."

"And you never done any time yourself?"

"Not me. I'm a real law-and-order type."

"That's good. You keep that up. You're too nice to get mixed up with prison types. Women are the worst. Do all kind of things. I've heard tales that'd make your hair stand right up on end. And not the hair on your head neither."

"I'll bet," I said. I changed the subject, not wanting to lie any more than I had to. "How many kids you got?"

"Here, lemme show you," he said, reaching in his back pocket. He took out his wallet and flipped it open to a photo tucked in the window where his driver's license should have been. "That's Joleen."

The woman staring out of the picture looked young and somewhat amazed. Four little children surrounded her, scrubbed, grinning, and shiny-faced. The oldest was a boy, probably nine, snaggle-toothed, his hair still visibly damp where she'd combed it into a pompadour just like his dad's. Two girls came next, probably six and eight. A plump-armed baby boy was perched on his mother's lap. The picture had been shot in a studio, the five of them posed in the midst of a faux picnic scene complete with a red-and-white checked cloth and artificial tree branches over-head. The baby held a fake apple in one chubby fist like a ball.

"Well, they're cute," I said, hoping he didn't pick up on the note of astonishment.

"They're rascals," he said fondly. "This was last year. She's pregnant again. She's wishin' she didn't have to work, but we do pretty good."

"What's she do?"

"She's a nurse's aide up at Community Hospital on the orthopedic ward, night shift. She'll work eleven to seven. Then she gets home and I take off, drop the kids at school, and swing back around to the station. We got a babysitter for the little guy. I don't know quite what we'll do when the new one comes along."

"You'll figure something out," I said.

"I guess," he said. He flopped the wallet shut and tucked it back in his pocket.

I bought a round of beers and then he bought one. I felt guilty about getting the poor man sloshed, but I had another question or two for him and I wanted his inhibitions out of the way. Meanwhile, the population in the bar was thinning down from ten to maybe six. I noticed, with regret, that Shana Timberlake had left. The jukebox had been fixed and the volume of the music was just loud enough to guarantee privacy without being so obtrusive we'd be forced to shout. I was relaxed, but not as loose as I allowed Tap to think. I gave his arm a bump.

"Tell me something," I said soddenly. "I'm just curious."

"What's that?"

"How much money did you and this Bailey fellow net?"

"Net?"

"In round numbers. About how much you make? I'm just asking. You don't have to say."

"We paid restitution on two thousand some-odd dollar."

"Two thousand? Bulll. You made more than that," I said.

Tap flushed with pleasure. "You think so?"

"Even bumpin' off gas stations, you made more, I bet."

"That's all I ever saw," he said.

"That's all they caught you for," I said, correcting him.

"That's all I put in my pocket. And that's the honest truth."

"But how much else? How much altogether?"

Tap studied up on that one, extending his chin, pulling at his lip in a parody of deep thought. "In the neighborhood, I would say, of . . . would you believe, forty-two thousand six hunderd and six."

"Who got that? Bailey got that?"

"Oh, it's gone now. He never did see a dime of it neither, as far as I know."

"Where'd it come from?"

"Couple little jobs we pulled they never found out about."

I laughed with delight. "Well, you old devil, you," I said, and gave his arm another push. "Where'd it go?"

"Beats me."

I laughed again and he got tickled, too. Somehow, it seemed like the funniest thing either of us ever heard. After half a minute, the laughter trickled out and Tap shook his head.

"Whoo, that's good," he said. "I haven't laughed like that since I don't know when."

"You think Bailey killed that little girl?"

"Don't know," he said, "but I will tell you this. When we went off to jail? We give the money to Jean Timberlake to hold. He got out and next thing I know, she's dead and he says he don't know where the money's at. It was long gone."

"Why didn't you get it when the two of you got out?"

"Ah, no. Huh-unh. The cops prob'ly had their eye on us, waitin' to see if we'd make a move. Goddamn. Everybody figured he killed her for sure. Me, I don't know. Doesn't seem like him. Then again, she might of spent all the money and he choked her in a fit."

"Naw. I don't believe that. I thought Pearl said she was knocked up."

"Well, she was, but Bailey wouldn't kill her for that. What's the point? The money's all we cared about, and why in hell not? We done jail time. We paid. We get out and we're too smart to start throwin' cash around. We laid low. After she died, Bailey told me she was the only one knew for sure where it was and she never told. He didn't want to know in case he ever had to take a lie detector test. Gone for good by now. Or maybe it's still hid, only nobody knows where."

"Maybe he has it after all. Maybe that's what he's lived on the whole time he's been gone."

"I don't know. I doubt it, but I'd sure like to have me a little talk with him."

"What do you think, though? Honestly."

"The honest truth?" he said, fixing me with a look. He leaned closer, winking. "I think I gotta go see a man about a dog. Don't go 'way now." He eased off the stool. He turned and pointed a finger at me solemnly like a gun. I fired a digit right back at him. He proceeded to the john, walking with the exaggerated nonchalance of a man who's drunk.

I waited fifteen minutes, nursing my beer, with an occasional glance at the door to the unisex facility. The woman who'd been dancing with Shana Timberlake was now playing pool with a kid who looked eighteen. It was nearly midnight by then, and Daisy started cleaning off the bar with a rag.

"Where'd Tap go?" I said when she had worked her way down within range of me.

"He got a phone call and took off."

"Just now?"

"Few minutes ago. He still owes a couple bucks on that tab."

"I'll take care of it," I said. I laid a five on the bar and waved away any change.

She was looking at me. "You know Tap's the biggest bullshitter ever lived."

"I gathered as much."

Her gaze was dark. "He might have been in trouble some years ago, but these days he's a decent family man. Nice wife and kids."

"Why tell me? I'm not hustling his buns."

"Why all the questions about the Fowler boy? You been pumping him all night."

"I talked to Royce. I'm curious about this business with his son, that's all."

"What's it to you?"

"It's just something to jaw about. There's nothing else going on."

She seemed to soften, apparently satisfied at the benevolence of my intent. "You here on vacation?"

"Business," I replied. I thought she'd pursue it, but she let the subject drop.

"We close about this time weeknights," she said. "You're welcome to stay while I lock up in back, but Pearl doesn't like anyone around when I close out the register."

I realized then that I was the last person in the place. "I

guess I better let you get on with it, then. I've had enough anyway."

The fog had curled right up to the road, obscuring the beach in a bunting of yellow mist. In the distance, a foghorn repeated its warning note. There were no cars passing and no sign of anyone on foot. Behind me, Daisy flipped the dead bolt and turned off the exterior lights, leaving me on my own. I walked briskly back to my motel room, wondering why Tap hadn't said good-bye.

8

Bailey's arraignment was scheduled for room B of the Municipal Court, on the lower level of the San Luis Obispo County Courthouse on Monterey Street. Royce rode with me. He didn't really seem well enough for the trip into town, but he was determined to have his way. Since Ann was taking her mother to the doctor that morning and couldn't accompany us, we tried to minimize the exertions he'd be subjected to. I dropped him out in front, watching as he made his way painfully up the wide concrete steps. We had arranged for him to wait for me in the airy lobby coffee shop with its skylights and potted ficus plants. I had already briefed him in the car coming over and he'd seemed satisfied with the state of my inquiries to that point. Now I wanted the opportunity to bring Jack Clemson up to speed.

I left my car parked in a small private lot behind the attorney's office, a block away. Clemson and I walked over to the courthouse together, using the time to talk about Bailey's frame of mind, which he found worrisome. With me, Bailey had seemed to alternate between numbness and despair. By the time he and Clemson chatted later in the day, his mood had darkened considerably. He was convinced he was never going to beat the escape charge. He was certain he'd end up at the Men's Colony again and equally certain he'd never survive incarceration.

"The guy's a basket case," Jack said. "I can't seem to talk any sense into him."

"But what are his chances, realistically?"

"Hey, I'm doing what I can. Bail's been set at half a million bucks, which is ridiculous. We're not talkin' Jack the Ripper here. I'll enter a motion to reduce. And maybe I can talk the prosecuting attorney into letting him plead to escape for the minimum. The time'll be added on, of course, but there's no way around that."

"And if I come up with some convincing evidence that someone else killed Jean Timberlake?"

"Then I'd move to set aside the original plea, or maybe file a coram nobis. Either way, we'd be set."

"Don't count on it, but I'll do what I can."

He flashed a smile at me, holding up crossed fingers.

When we got to the courthouse, he left me in the lobby while he went down to meet with the prosecuting attorney and the judge in chambers. The coffee shop was really no more than a wide expanse of central lobby, jammed with people now, the press in evidence. Royce was seated at a small table near the stairs, his hands folded across the top of his cane. He seemed tired. His hair had that matted, slightly sweaty cast of someone in ill health. He had ordered coffee, but it sat in the cup looking cold and untouched. I took a seat. The waitress swung by with a fresh pot of coffee, but I shook my head. Royce's anxiety enveloped the table like a sour, hopeless scent. He was clearly a proud man, accustomed to bending the world to his will. Bailey's arraignment already bore all the trappings of a public spectacle. The local paper had been running the story of his capture on the front page for days, and the local radio stations made mention of it at the top of each hour and again in the quick news summaries on the half hour.

A crew with a minicam passed just to the right of us, heading down the stairs without realizing Bailey Fowler's father was sitting within camera range. He turned a baleful eye on them and the ensuing smile was bitter and brief.

"Maybe we better go on down," I said.

We descended the stairs, walking slowly. I controlled an urge to give him physical support, sensing that he might take offense. His stoicism had a hint of self-mockery to it. He was grimly amused to have prevailed thus far, forcing his body to do his bidding regardless of the cost.

The corridor below was lined on one side with big plate-glass windows, with two exits into a sunken courtyard. Both the interior passageway and the exterior stairways were filling with spectators, some of whom seemed to recognize Royce as we passed. There was a silent parting in the crowd; gazes averted as we made our way into the courtroom. In the third row, people squeezed together to make room for us. There was the same hushed murmuring as in a church before services start. Most had dressed in their Sunday best, and the air seemed to stir with conflicting perfumes. No one spoke to Royce, but I could sense the rustling and nudging going on all around us. If he was humbled by the reaction, he gave no sign. He had been a respected member of the community, but Bailey's notoriety had tainted him. To have a son accused of murder is the same as being accused of a crime oneself—parental failure of the direst sort. Unfair though it may be, there is always that unspoken question: What did these people do to turn this once-in-

nocent child into a cold-blooded killer of another human
being?

I had checked the docket posted in the upstairs corridor.
There were ten other arraignments scheduled that morning in addition to Bailey's. The door to the judge's chambers was closed. The court clerk, a slim, handsome woman
in a navy blue suit, was seated at a table below and to the
right of the judge's bench. The court reporter, also female,
sat at a matching table to the left. There were a dozen
attorneys present, most in dark, conservatively cut suits, all
with white shirts, muted ties, black shoes. Only one was
female.

While we waited for the proceedings to begin, I scanned
the crowd. Shana Timberlake was seated across the aisle
from us, one row back. Under the flat fluorescent lights,
the illusion of youth vanished and I could see the dark
streaks at the corners of her eyes, suggesting age, weariness, too many nights in bad company. She was wide-shouldered, heavy-breasted, slender through the waist and hips,
wearing jeans and a flannel shirt. As mother of the victim,
she was free to dress any way she liked. Her hair was nearly
black, with a few strands of silver here and there, combed
straight back from her face and held with a clip on top.
She turned her hot, dark eyes on me and I looked away.
She knew I was with Royce. When I glanced back, I could
see her gaze lingering on him with a blunt appraisal of his
physical condition.

One other woman caught my attention as she came down
the aisle. She was in her early thirties, sallow, thin, wearing
an apricot knit dress with a big stain across the hem. She
had on a white sweater and white heels with short white
cotton socks. Her hair was a dishwater blond, held back

with a wide, tatty-looking headband. She was accompanied by a man I assumed was her husband. He appeared to be in his mid-thirties, with curly blond hair and the sort of pouty good looks I've never liked. Pearl was with them, and I wondered if this was the son he'd referred to who had seen Bailey with Jean Timberlake the night she was killed.

There was a faint escalation of murmurs at the rear of the courtroom and I turned my head. The crowd's attention focused in the way it does at a wedding when the bride appears, ready to begin her walk down the aisle. The prisoners were being brought in and the sight was oddly disturbing: nine men, handcuffed, shackled together, shuffling forward with their leg chains. They wore jail garb: unconstructed cotton shirts in orange, light gray, or charcoal, and gray or pale blue cotton pants with JAIL stenciled across the butt, white cotton socks, the type of plastic sandals known as "jellies." Most of them were young: five Latinos and three black guys. Bailey was the only white. He seemed acutely self-conscious, high color in his cheeks, his eyes downcast, the modest star of this chorus line of thugs. His fellow prisoners seemed to take the proceedings for granted, nodding to the scattering of friends and relatives. Most of the spectators had come to see Bailey Fowler, but nobody seemed to begrudge him his status. A uniformed deputy escorted the men into the jury box up front, where their leg chains were removed in case one of them had to approach the bench. The prisoners settled in, like the rest of us, to enjoy the show.

The bailiff went through his "all rise" recital, and we dutifully rose as the judge appeared and took his seat. Judge McMahon was in his forties and bristled with efficiency. Trim and fair-haired, he looked like the kind of man who played handball and squash, and risked dropping dead of a heart attack despite his prior history of perfect health. Bailey's case was being called next to last, so we were treated to a number of minor procedural dramas. A translator had to be summoned from somewhere in the building to aid in the arraignments of two of the accused who spoke no English. Papers had been misfiled. Two cases were kicked over to another date. Another set of papers had been sent but never received, and the judge was irked about that because the attorney had no proof of service and the other side wasn't ready. Two additional defendants, out on OR, were seated in the audience and each stepped forward in turn as his case was called.

At one point, one of the deputies pulled out a set of keys and unlocked an accused's handcuffs so that he could talk to his attorney at the back of the room. While that conference was going on, another prisoner engaged the judge in a lengthy discussion, insistent on representing himself. Judge McMahon was very opposed to the idea and spent ten minutes warning and admonishing, advising and scolding. The defendant refused to budge. The judge was finally forced to concede to the fellow's wishes since it was his right, but he was clearly cross about the matter. Through all of this, an undercurrent of restlessness was agitating the spectators into side-conversations and titters of laughter. They were primed for the lead act, and here they were, having to suffer through this second-rate series of burglaries and sexual assault cases. I half expected them to start clapping in unison, like a movie audience when the film is delayed.

Jack Clemson had been leaning against the wall in murmured conversation with the attorney next to him. As the time approached for Bailey's case to be called, he broke away and crossed the room. He spoke to the deputy and she unlocked Bailey's handcuffs. The two of them had just stepped to one side when there was a shout from the back. The judge's head snapped up and everybody turned simultaneously. A man in a red ski mask stood in the doorway, brandishing a sawed-off shotgun. The effect was electric, a ripple running through the room.

"FREEZE!" he yelled. "Everybody just hold it right there."

He fired once, apparently to make his point. The boom from the gun was deafening and the blast took one of the overhead lights right off its chain and sent it crashing to the floor. Shattered glass rained down like a cloudburst, and people screamed and scrambled for cover. A baby started shrieking. Everybody hit the floor, including me. Bailey's father was still sitting upright, immobilized by surprise. I reached up and grabbed him by the shirt front. I pulled him down to the floor with me, sheltering him with my body weight. He struggled, trying to get up, but in his condition it didn't take much to subdue him. I glanced over in time to see one of the deputies belly-crawl up the aisle to my right, shielded from the gunman's view by the wooden benches.

I'd caught a glimpse of the gunman and I could have sworn it was Tap, his hands shaking badly. He seemed too small to be a threat, his entire body tensed by fear. The true menace was the shotgun, with its broad, lethal spray, the indiscriminate destruction if his finger slipped. Any unexpected movement might startle him into firing. Two women on the other side of Royce were burbling hysterically, clinging to one another like lovers.

"BAILEY, COME ON! GET THE FUCK OUTTA

HERE!!" the gunman screamed. His voice broke from fright and I felt a chill as I peered over the seat. It had to be Tap.

Bailey was transfixed. He stared in disbelief and then he was in motion. He leaped the wooden railing and ran, pounding down the aisle toward the rear door while Tap blasted again. A large framed photograph of the governor jumped off the wall, disintegrating as the pellets ripped through glass, wood frame, and matting in a spray of white. A second round of wails and screams erupted from the crowd. Bailey had disappeared by then. Tap cracked the shotgun and jammed in two more shells as he backed out of the courtroom. I heard running. An outside door slammed and then there were shouts and the sound of shots.

In the courtroom, there was chaos. The clerk and the court reporter were nowhere to be seen and I could only guess that the judge had made his way out of the room at floor level, crawling on his hands and knees. Once the immediate threat was gone, people surged forward in a panic, shoving toward the bench, pushing through to the safety of the judge's chambers beyond. Pearl was hustling his son and daughter-in-law out the fire exit, setting off an alarm bell that clanged at a piercing pitch.

More screams sounded from the corridor, where some-one was shouting incomprehensibly. I headed in that di-rection, bent double until I could get a sense of what was happening. If more gunfire broke out, I didn't want to get caught by flying bullets. I passed a woman bleeding badly from the glass shards that had cut into her face. Someone was already applying pressure to the worst of her wounds, while beside her, two little children huddled together and wept. I reached the rear door and pushed out. Shana Timberlake was leaning against the wall to my left, her face blanched, the shadows under her eyes as emphatic as stage makeup.

Outside, police sirens were already spiraling against the morning air.

Through the big plate-glass walls that formed one side of the corridor, I could see uniformed police officers spilling down the steps into the courtyard outside. Several women screamed in continuous shrill tones, as if the shooting had unleashed years of suppressed anguish. The jam of hysterical people in the hallway surged forward and then parted abruptly.

Tap Granger lay on his back, his arms flung out like he was taking a sunbath. The red ski mask had been pulled back off his face and it rested on the back of his head, as flabby as a rooster's crest. He wore a short-sleeved shirt and I could see where his wife had ironed the creases in. His arms looked skinny. His whole body looked dead. Bailey was nowhere in sight.

I went back into the courtroom, aware for the first time that I was crunching my way through broken glass and grit. Royce Fowler was on his feet, swaying uncertainly among the rows of empty benches. His mouth trembled.

"Tell me you had nothing to do with this," I said to him.

"Where's Bailey? Where's my boy? They'll shoot him down like a dog."

"No, they won't. He's unarmed. They'll find him. I take it you didn't know this was going to happen."

"Who was that in the mask?"

"Tap Granger. He's dead."

Royce sank onto the bench and lowered his head into

his hands. The debris underfoot made a crackling sound. Looking down, I realized the floor was littered with white specks.

I stared in confusion, then bent down and picked up a handful. "What is this?" I said. Comprehension came in the same moment, but it still made no sense. Tap's shotgun shells had been loaded with rock salt.

9

By the time we got back to the motel, Royce was close to collapse and I had to help him into bed. Ann and Ori had heard the news in the doctor's office and they came straight home, pulling in soon after I did. Bailey Fowler was being billed as "a killer on the loose, believed armed and dangerous." The streets of Floral Beach already looked deserted, as if in the wake of some natural disaster. I could practically hear the doors slamming all up and down the block, little children jerked to safety, old ladies peering out from behind their curtains. Why anyone thought Bailey would be foolish enough to come back to his parents' house, I don't know. The sheriff's department must have considered it a good possibility because a deputy, in a tan uniform, stopped by the motel and had a long, officious chat with Ann, one hand on his gun butt, his gaze shifting from point to point, searching (I assumed) for some indication that the escapee was being harbored on the premises.

As soon as the patrol car pulled away, friends began to arrive with solemn expressions, dropping off casseroles. Some of these people I'd seen at the courthouse and I couldn't tell if their appearance was motivated by sympathy or a craven desire to be part of the continuing drama. Two neighbor ladies came, introduced to me as Mrs. Emma and Mrs. Maude, aging sisters who'd known Bailey since he was a boy. Robert Haws, the minister from the Baptist church, appeared along with his wife, June, and yet another woman who introduced herself as Mrs. Burke, the owner of the Laundromat two blocks away. She just popped over for a minute, she said, to see if there was anything she could do. I was hoping she'd offer cut rates on the Fluff 'n' Fold, but apparently this didn't occur to her. Judging from Mrs. Maude's expression, she disapproved of the store-bought frozen cheesecake the Laundromat lady handed over so blithely. Mrs. Maude and Mrs. Emma exchanged a look that suggested this was not the first time Mrs. Burke had flaunted her lack of culinary zealousness. The phone rang incessantly. Mrs. Emma appointed herself the telephone receptionist, fielding calls, keeping a log of names and return numbers in case Ori felt up to it later.

Royce refused to see anyone, but Ori entertained from her bed, repeating endlessly the circumstances under which she'd heard the news, what she'd first thought, when the facts had finally penetrated, and how she'd commenced to howl with misery until the doctor sedated her. Whatever Tap Granger's fate or her son's fugitive status, she experienced events as peripheral to "The Ori Fowler Show," in which she starred. Before I had a chance to slip out of the room, the minister asked us to join him in a word of prayer. I have to confess, I've never been taught proper prayer etiquette. As far as I can tell, it consists of folded hands, solemnly bowed heads, and no peeking at the other supplicants. I don't object to religious practices, per se. I'm just not crazy about having someone else inflict their beliefs on me. Whenever Jehovah's Witnesses appear at my door, I always ask for their addresses first thing, assuring them that I'll be around later in the week to plague them with my views.

While the minister interceded with the Lord in Bailey Fowler's behalf, I absented myself mentally, using the time to study his wife. June Haws was in her fifties, no more than five feet tall and, like many women in her weight class, destined for a sedentary life. Naked, she was probably dead white and dimpled with fat. She wore white cotton gloves with some sort of amber-staining ointment visible at the wrist. With her face blocked out, hers were the kind of limbs one might see in a medical journal, illustrative of particularly scabrous outbreaks of impetigo and eczema.

When Reverend Haws's interminable prayer had come to a close, Ann excused herself and went into the kitchen. It was clear that the appearance of servitude on her part was actually a means of escaping whenever she could. I followed her and, in the guise of being helpful, began to set out cups and saucers, arranging Pepperidge Farm cookies on plates lined with paper doilies while she hauled out the big stainless-steel coffee urn that usually sat in the office. On the kitchen counter, I could see a tuna casserole with crushed potato chips on top, a ground beef and noodle bake, and two Jell-O molds (one cherry with fruit cocktail, one lime with grated carrots), which Ann asked me to refrigerate. It had only been an hour and a half since Bailey fled the courthouse in a blaze of gunfire. I didn't think gelatin set up that fast, but these Christian ladies probably knew tricks with ice cubes that would render salads and desserts in record time for just such occasions. I pictured a section in the ladies' auxiliary church cookbook for Sudden Death Quick Snacks . . . using ingredients one could keep on the pantry shelf in the event of tragedy.

"What can I do to help?" June Haws asked from the

kitchen door. With her cotton gloves, she looked like a pallbearer, possibly for someone who had died recently from the same skin disease. I moved a plate of cookies just out of range and pulled a chair out so she could have a seat.

"Oh, not for me, hon," she said. "I never sit. Why don't you let me take over, Ann, and you can get off your feet."

"We're doing fine," Ann said. "If you can keep Mother's mind off Bailey, that's all the help we need."

"Haws is reading Scriptures with her even as we speak. I can't believe what that woman's been through. It's enough to break your heart. How's your daddy doing? Is he all right?"

"Well, it's been a shock, of course."

"Of course it has. That poor man." She looked over at me. "I'm June Haws. I don't believe we've been introduced."

Ann broke in. "I'm sorry, June. This is Kinsey Millhone. She's a private detective Pop hired to help us out."

"Private *detective*?" she said, with disbelief. "I didn't think there was such a thing, except on television shows."

"Nice to meet you," I said. "I'm afraid the work we do isn't quite that thrilling."

"Well, I hope not. All those gun battles and car chases? It's enough to make my blood run cold! It doesn't seem like a fit occupation for a nice girl like you."

"I'm not that nice," I said modestly.

She laughed, mistaking this for a joke. I avoided any further interaction by picking up a cookie plate. "Let me just take these on in," I murmured, moving toward the other room.

Once in the hallway, I slowed my pace, caught between

Bible readings in the one room and relentless platitudes in the other. I hesitated in the doorway. The high school principal, Dwight Shales, had appeared while I was gone, but he was deep in conversation with Mrs. Emma and didn't seem to notice me. I eased into the living room where I handed the cookie plate to Mrs. Maude, then excused myself again and headed toward the office. Reverend Haws was intoning an alarming passage from the Old Testament full of besiegedness, pestilence, consuming locusts, and distress. Ori's lot must have seemed pretty tame by comparison, which was probably the point.

I went up to my room. It was almost noon and my guess was the assembled would hang around for a hot lunch. With luck, I could slip down the outside stairs and reach my car before anybody realized I was gone. I washed my face and ran a comb through my hair. I had my jacket over my arms and a hand on the doorknob when somebody knocked. For a moment I flashed on the image of Dwight Shales. Maybe he'd gotten the okay to talk to me. I opened the door.

Reverend Haws was standing in the corridor. "I hope you don't mind," he said. "Ann thought you'd probably come up here to your room. I didn't have an opportunity to introduce myself. I'm Robert Haws of the Floral Beach Baptist Church."

"Hi, how are you?"

"I'm just fine. My wife, June, was telling me what a nice chat she had with you a short while ago. She suggested you might like to join us for Bible study over at the church tonight."

"How nice," I said. "Actually, I'm not sure where I'll be tonight, but I appreciate the invitation." I'm embarrassed to admit it, but I was mimicking the warm, folksy tone they all used with one another.

Like his wife, Reverend Haws appeared to be in his fifties, but aging better than she was, I thought. He was round-faced, handsome in a Goody-Two-Shoes sort of way: bifocals with wire frames, sandy hair streaked with gray, cut full (with just the faintest suggestion of styling mousse). He was wearing a business suit in a muted glen plaid and a black shirt with a clerical collar that seemed an affectation for a Protestant. I didn't think Baptists wore things like that. He had all the easy charm of someone who spent his entire adult life on the receiving end of pious compliments.

We shook hands. He held on to mine and gave it a pat, making lots of Christian eye contact. "I understand you're from Santa Teresa. I wonder if you know Millard Alston from the Baptist church there in Colgate. He and I were seminarians together. I hate to tell you how long ago that's been."

I extracted my hand from his moist grip, smiling pleasantly. "The name doesn't sound familiar. Of course, I don't have much occasion to be out in that direction."

"What's your congregation? I hope you're not going to tell me you're an ornery Methodist." He said this with a laugh, just to show what a wacky sense of humor he had.

"Not at all," I said.

He peered toward the room behind me. "Your husband traveling with you?"

"Uh, no. Actually he's not." I glanced at my watch. "Oh golly. I'm late." The "golly" rather stuck in my throat, but it didn't seem to bother him.

He put his hands in his pants pockets, subtly adjusting

himself. "I hate to see you run off so soon. If you're in Floral Beach come Sunday, maybe you can make it to the eleven-o'clock service and then join us for lunch. June doesn't cook anymore because of her condition, but we'd enjoy having you as our guest at the Apple Farm Restaurant."

"Oh gee. I wish I could, but I'm not sure I'll be here for the weekend. Maybe another time."

"Well, you're a tough little gal to pin down," he said. His manner was a trifle irritated and I had to guess he was unaccustomed to having his unctuous overtures rebuffed.

"I sure am," I said. I put on my jacket as I moved out into the corridor. Reverend Haws stepped aside, but he was still standing closer to me than I would have liked. I pulled the door shut behind me, making sure it was locked. I walked toward the stairs and he followed me.

"Sorry to be in such a rush, but I have an appointment." I'd cut the warm, folksy tone to a minimum.

"I'll let you get on your way, then."

The last I saw of him, he was standing at the head of the exterior stairs, looking down at me with a chilly gaze that contradicted his surface benevolence. I started my car and then waited in the parking slot until I'd seen him walk by, returning to the Fowlers. I didn't like the idea of his being anywhere near my room if I was off the premises.

I drove half a mile along the two-lane access road that connected Floral Beach to the highway, another mile due north. I reached the entrance to the Eucalyptus Mineral Hot Springs and turned into the parking lot. The brochure in the motel office indicated that the sulfur-based springs had been discovered in the late 1800s by two men drilling for oil. Instead of the intended rigs, a spa was built, serving as a therapeutic center for ailing Californians who arrived by train, alighting at the tiny station just across the road. A staff of doctors and nurses attended the afflicted, offering cures that included mud baths, nostrums, herbal treatments, and hydroelectric therapy. The facility flourished briefly and then fell into disuse until the 1930s, when the present hotel was constructed on the site. A second incarnation occurred in the early seventies when spas became fashionable again. Now, in addition to the fifty or so hot tubs that dotted the hillside under the oak and eucalyptus trees, there were tennis courts, a heated pool, and aerobics classes available, along with a full program of facials, massage, yoga instruction, and nutritional counseling.

The hotel itself was a two-story affair, a curious testament to thirties architecture, art deco Spanish, complete with turrets, sensuously rounded corners, and walls of block glass. I approached the office by way of a covered walk, the air chilled by deep shade unrelieved by sunlight. At close range, the building's stucco exterior showed bulging cracks that snaked up from the foundations to the terracotta roof tiles that had aged to the color of cinnamon. The sulfurous aroma of the mineral springs blended dankly with the smell of wet leaves. There was the suggestion of subtle leakages, something permeating the soil, and I wondered if, later, drums of poisonous wastes would be excavated from the spot.

I took a quick detour, climbing a set of steep wooden stairs that cut up along the hill behind the hotel. There were gazebos at intervals, each sheltering a hot tub sunk into a wooden platform. Weathered wooden fences were strategically placed to shield the bathers from public view. Each alcove had a name, perhaps to facilitate some scheduling procedure in the office down below. I passed "Serenity," "Meditation," "Sunset," and "Peace," uncomfortably aware of how similar the names were to the "sleep rooms" in certain funeral homes of my acquaintance. Two of the tubs were empty, littered with fallen leaves. One had an opaque plastic cover lying on the surface of the water like a skin. I picked my way down the steps again, thankful that I wasn't in the market for a hot soak.

At the main building, I pushed through glass doors into the reception area. The lobby seemed more inviting, but it still had the feel of a YWCA in need of funds. The floors were a mosaic of black and white tiles, the smell of Pine-Sol suggesting a recent swabbing with a wet mop. From the far reaches of the interior, I could hear the hollow echoes of an indoor pool where a woman with a German accent called out authoritatively, "Kick! Resist! Kick! Resist!" Her commands were punctuated by a torpid splashing that called to mind the clumsy mating of water buffalo.

"May I help you?"

The receptionist had emerged from a small office behind me. She was tall, big-boned, one of those women who probably shopped in the "full figured" department of women's clothing stores. She must have been in her late forties, with white-blond hair, white lashes, and pale, unblemished skin. Her hands and feet were large, and the shoes she wore were the prison-matron-lace-up sort.

I handed her my business card, introducing myself. "I'm looking for someone who might remember Jean Timberlake."

She kept her eyes pinned on my face, her expression blank. "You'll want to talk to my husband, Dr. Dunne. Unfortunately, he's away."

"Can you tell me when he's expected back?"

"I'm not certain. If you leave a number, I can have him call when he returns."

We locked eyes. Hers were the stony gray of winter skies before snow. "What about you?" I said. "Did you know the girl yourself?"

There was a pause. Then, carefully, "I knew who she was."

"I understand she was working here at the time of her death."

"I don't think this is something we should discuss"—she glanced down at the card—"Miss Millhone."

"Is there some problem?"

"If you'll tell me how to reach you, I'll have my husband get in touch."

"Room twenty-two at the Ocean Street Motel in—"

"I know where it is. I'm sure he'll call if he has time."

"Wonderful. That way we won't have to bother about subpoenas." I was bluffing, of course, and she might have guessed as much, but I did enjoy the pale wash of color that suffused her cheeks. "I'll check back if I don't hear from him," I said.

It wasn't until I reached the car again that I remembered the owners mentioned in the brochure I'd seen. Dr. and Mrs. Joseph Dunne had bought the hotel the same year Jean Timberlake died.

10

It was 12:35 when I swung back around to the main street of Floral Beach and parked my car out in front of Pearl's Pool Hall. Weekday business hours were listed as 11:00 A.M. to 2:00 A.M. The door stood open. Last night's air tumbled out in a sluggish breeze that smelled of beer spills and cigarettes. The interior was stuffy, slightly warmer than the ocean-chilled temperature outside. I caught sight of Daisy at the back door, hauling out a massive plastic sack of trash. She gave me a noncommittal look, but I sensed that her mood was dark. I took a seat at the bar. I was the only customer at that hour. Empty, the place seemed even more drab than it had the night before. The floors had been swept and I could see peanut shells and cigarette butts in a heap near the broom, waiting to be nudged into the dustpan propped nearby. The back door banged shut and Daisy reappeared, wiping her hands on the toweling she'd tucked in her belt. She approached warily, her gaze not quite meeting mine. "How's the detective work?"

"I'm sorry I didn't identify myself last night."

"What's it to me? I don't give a damn who you are."

"Maybe not, but I wasn't quite straight with Tap and I feel bad about that."

"You look real tore up."

I shrugged. "I know it sounds lame, but it's the truth. You thought I was hustling him, and in a way, I was."

She said nothing. She stood and stared at me. After a while she said, "You want a Co'-Cola? I'm having one."

I nodded, watching as she picked up a couple of Mason jars and filled them from the hose dispenser under the bar She set mine in front of me.

"Thanks."

"I hear by the grapevine Royce hired you," she said. "What'd he do that for?"

"He's hoping to have Bailey cleared of the murder charge."

"He'll have a hell of a time after what happened this morning. If Bailey's innocent like he claims, why take off?"

"People get impulsive under pressure. When I talked to him at the jail, he seemed pretty desperate. Maybe when Tap showed up, he saw a way out."

Daisy's tone was contemptuous. "Kid never did have a lick of sense."

"So it would seem."

"What about Royce? How's he doing?"

"Not that well. He went right to bed. A lot of people are over there with Ori."

"I don't have much use for her," Daisy said. "Anybody heard from Bailey?"

"Not as far as I know."

She busied herself behind the bar, running a sink full of hot soapy water and a second sink full of rinse water. She began to wash Mason jars left over from the night before, her motions automatic as she ran through the sequence, setting clean jars to drain on a towel to the right. "What'd you want with Tap?"

"I was curious what he had to say about Jean Timber-lake."

"I heard you askin' him about the stickups them two pulled."

"I was interested in whether his version would match Bailey's."

"Did it?"

"More or less," I said. I studied her as she worked, wondering why she was suddenly so interested. I wasn't about to mention the $42,000 Tap claimed had disappeared. "Who called him here last night? Did you recognize the voice?"

"Some man. Not anyone I knew right off. Might have been someone I'd talked to before, but I couldn't say for sure. There was something queer about the whole conversation," she remarked. "You think it was related to the shooting?"

"It almost had to be."

"That's what I think, too, the way he tore out of here. I'd be willing to swear it wasn't Bailey, though."

"Probably not," I said. "He wouldn't have been permitted to use the jail phone at that hour and he couldn't have met with Tap in any event. What made the call seem so queer?"

"Odd voice. Deep. And the speech was kind of drug out, like someone who'd had a stroke."

"Like a speech impediment?"

"Maybe. I'd have to think about that some. I can't quite put my finger on it." She was silent for a moment and then shook her head, shifting the subject. "Tap's wife, Joleen, is who I feel sorry for. Have you talked to her?"

"Not yet. I guess I will at some point."

"Four little kids. Another due any day."

"Nasty business. I wish he'd used his head. There's no way he could have pulled it off. The deputies are always armed. He never had a chance," I said.

"Maybe that's the way they wanted it."

"Who?"

"Whoever put him up to it. I knew Tap since he was ten years old. Believe me, he wasn't smart enough to come up with a scheme like that on his own."

I looked at her with interest. "Good point," I said. Maybe Bailey was meant to get whacked at the same time, thus eliminating both of them. I reached into my jeans pocket and pulled out the list of Jean Timberlake's classmates. "Any of these guys still around?"

She took the list, pausing while she removed a pair of bifocals from her shirt pocket. She hooked the stems across her ears. She held the paper at arm's length and peered at the names, tilting her head back. "This one's dead. Ran his car off the road about ten years back. This fella moved up to Santa Cruz, last I heard. The rest are either here in Floral Beach or San Luis. You going to talk to every one of 'em?"

"If I have to."

"David Poletti's a dentist with an office on Marsh. You might want to start with him. Nice man. I've known his mother for years."

"Was he a friend of Jean's?"

"I doubt it, but he'd probably know who was."

As it turned out, David Poletti was a children's dentist who spent Wednesday afternoons in the office, catching up on his paperwork. I waited briefly in a pastel-painted reception suite with scaled-down furniture and tattered issues of *Highlights for Children* stacked on low tables, along

with *Jack and Jill* and *Young Miss*. Of special interest to me
in the last was a column called "Was My Face Red!" in
which young girls gushingly related embarrassing moments—most of which were things I'd done not that long
ago. Knocking a full cup of Coke off a balcony railing was
one. The people down below really yell, don't they?

Dr. Poletti's office staff was composed of three women
in their twenties, Alice-in-Wonderland types with big eyes,
sweet smiles, long straight hair, and nothing threatening
about them. Soothing music oozed out of the walls like
whiffs of nitrous oxide. By the time I was ushered into his
inner office, I would almost have been willing to sit in a
tot-sized dental chaise and have my gums probed with one
of those tiny stainless-steel pruning hooks.

When I shook hands with Dr. Poletti, he was still wearing
a white jacket with an alarming bloodstain on the front.
He caught sight of it about the same time I did, and peeled
his jacket off, tossing it across a chair with a soft, apologetic
smile. Under the jacket he was wearing a dress shirt and
a sweater vest. He indicated that I should take a seat while
he shrugged into a brown tweed sport coat and adjusted
his cuffs. He was maybe thirty-five, tall, with a narrow face.
His hair frizzed in tight curls already turning gray along
the sides. I knew, from his yearbook pictures, that he'd
played high school basketball and I imagined sophomore
girls gushing over him in the cafeteria. He wasn't technically handsome, but he had a certain appeal, a gentleness
in his demeanor that must have been reassuring to women
and little kids. His eyes were small and drooped slightly at
the corners, the color a mild brown behind lightweight
metallic frames.

He sat down at his desk. A color studio portrait of his

wife and two young boys was prominently displayed, probably to dispel any fantasies his staff might entertain about
his availability. "Tawna says you have some questions about
an old high school classmate. Given recent events, I'm assuming it's Jean Timberlake."

"How well did you know her?"

"Not very well. I knew who she was, but I don't think I
ever had a class with her." He reached for a set of plaster-
of-Paris impressions that sat on his desk, upper plate positioned above the lower in a jutting overbite. He cleared
his throat. "What sort of information are you looking for?"

"Whatever you can tell me. Bailey Fowler's father hired
me to see if I could come up with some new evidence. I
thought I'd start with Jean and work forward from there."

"Why come to me?"

I told him about my conversation with Daisy and her
suggestion that he might be of help. His manner seemed
to shift, becoming less suspicious, though a certain wariness
remained. Idly he lifted the mold's upper plate and stuck
his finger in, feeling the crowded lower incisors. If I had
banged a fist down on the mold, I could have bitten his
finger off. The thought made it hard to concentrate on
what he was saying. "I've been thinking a lot about the
murder since Bailey Fowler's arrest. Terrible thing. Just
terrible."

"Were you in that group of kids who found her, by any
chance?"

"No, no. I'm a Catholic. That was the youth group from
the Baptist church."

"The one in Floral Beach?"

He nodded and I made a mental note, thinking of Reverend Haws. "I've heard she was a bit free with her favors,"
I said.

"That's the reputation she had. Some of my patients are young girls her age. Fourteen, fifteen. They just seem so immature. I can't imagine them sexually active and yet I'm sure some of them are."

"I've seen pictures of Jean. She was a beautiful girl."

"Not in any way that served her. She wasn't like the rest of us. Too old in some ways, innocent in others. I guess she thought she'd be popular if she put out, so that's what she did. A lot of guys took advantage." He paused to clear his throat. "Excuse me," he said. He poured himself half a tumbler of water from the thermos sitting on his desk. "You want some water?"

I shook my head. "Anybody in particular?"

"What?"

"I'm wondering if she was involved with anyone you knew."

He gave me a bland look. "Not that I recall."

I could feel the arrow on my bullshit meter swing up into the red. "What about you?"

A baffled laugh. "Me?"

"Yeah, I was wondering if you got involved with her." I could see the color come and go in his face, so I ad-libbed a line. "Actually, someone told me you dated her. I can't remember now who mentioned it, but someone who knew you both."

He shrugged. "I might have. Just briefly. I never dated her steadily or anything like that."

"But you were intimate."

"With Jean?"

"Dr. Poletti, spare me the wordplay and tell me about your relationship. We're talking about things that happened seventeen years ago."

He was silent for a moment, toying with the plaster jaw,

which seemed to have something on it he had to pick off. "I wouldn't want this to go any further, whatever we discuss."

"Strictly confidential."

He shifted in his chair. "I guess I've always regretted my association with her. Such as it was. I'm ashamed of it now because I knew better. I'm not sure she did."

"We all do things we regret," I said. "It's part of growing up. What difference does it make after all this time?"

"I know. You're right. I don't know why it's so hard to talk about."

"Take your time."

"I did date her. For a month. Less than that. I can't say my intentions were honorable. I was seventeen. You know how guys are at that age. Once word got out that Jeannie was an easy lay, we became obsessed. She did things we'd never even heard about. We were lined up like a pack of dogs, trying to get at her. It was all anybody ever talked about, how to get in her pants, how to get her in ours. I guess I was no better than the other guys." He shot me an embarrassed smile.

"Go on."

"Some of 'em didn't even bother going through the motions. Just picked her up and took her out to the beach. They didn't even take her out on a date."

"But you did."

He lowered his gaze. "I took her out a few times. I felt guilty even doing that. She was kind of pathetic . . . and scary at the same time. She was bright enough, but she wanted desperately to believe someone cared. It made you feel sheepish, so you'd get together with the guys afterward and bad-mouth her."

"For what you'd done," I supplied.

"Right. I still can't think about her without feeling kind of sick. What's strange is I can still remember things she did." He paused for a moment, eyebrows going up. He shook his head once, blowing out a puff of air. "She was really outrageous . . . insatiable's the word . . . but what drove her wasn't sex. It was . . . I don't know, self-loathing or a need to dominate. We were at her mercy because we wanted her so much. I guess our revenge was never really giving her what she wanted, which was old-fashioned respect."

"And what was hers?"

"Revenge? I don't know. Creating that heat. Reminding us that she was the only source, that we could never have enough of her or anything even halfway like her for life. She needed approval, some guy to be nice. All we ever did was snicker about her behind her back, which she must have known."

"Did she get hung up on you?"

"I suppose. Not for long, I don't think."

"It would help if you could tell me who else might have been involved with her."

He shook his head. "I can't. You're not going to get me to blow the whistle on anybody else. I still hang out with some of those guys."

"How about if I read you some names off a list?"

"I can't do that. Honestly. I don't mind owning up to my own part in it, but I can't implicate anybody else. It's an odd bond and something we don't talk about, but I'll tell you this—her name gets mentioned, we don't say a word, but we're all thinking the same damn thing."

"What about guys who weren't friends of yours?"

"Meaning what?"

"At the time of the murder, she was apparently having an affair and got herself knocked up."

"Don't know."

"Make a guess. There must have been rumors."

"Not that I heard."

"Can you ask around? Somebody must know."

"Hey, I'd like to help, but I've probably already said more than I should."

"What about some of the girls in your class? Someone must have been clued in back then."

He cleared his throat again. "Well. Barb might know. I could ask her, I guess."

"Barbara who?"

"My wife. We were in the same class."

I glanced at the photograph on his desk, recognizing her belatedly. "The prom queen?"

"How'd you know about that?"

"I saw some pictures of her in the yearbook. Would you ask her if she could help?"

"I doubt if she knows anything, but I could mention it."

"That'd be great. Have her give me a call. If she doesn't know anything about it, she might suggest someone who would."

"I wouldn't want anything said about . . ."

"I understand," I said.

I gave him my card with a little note on the back, with my telephone number at the Ocean Street. I left his office feeling faintly optimistic and more than a little disturbed. There was something about the idea of grown men haunted by the sexuality of a seventeen-year-old girl that seemed riveting—both pitiable and perverse. Somehow the glimpse he'd given me of the past made me feel like a voyeur.

11

At two o'clock I slipped up the outside stairs at the motel
and changed into my running clothes. I hadn't had lunch,
but I was feeling supercharged, too wired to eat. After the
hysteria at the courthouse, I'd spent hours in close contact
with other human beings and my energy level had risen
to an agitated state. I pulled on my sweats and my running
shoes and headed out again, room key tied to my laces.
The afternoon was slightly chilly, with a haze in the air.
The sea blended into the sky at the horizon with no line
of demarcation visible between. Southern California sea-
sons are sometimes too subtle to discern, which I'm told is
disconcerting to people who've grown up in the Midwest
and the East. What's true, though, is that every day is a
season in itself. The sea is changeable. The air is trans-
formed. The landscape registers delicate alterations in
color so that gradually the saturated green of winter
bleaches out to the straw shades of summer grass, so quick
to burn. Trees explode with color, fiery reds and flaming
golds that could rival autumn anywhere, and the charred
branches that remain afterward are as bare and black as
winter trees in the East, slow to recover, slow to bud
again.

I jogged along the walkway that bordered the beach. There was a sprinkling of tourists. Two kids about eight were dodging the waves, their shrieks as raucous as the birds that wheeled overhead. The tide was almost out and a wide, glistening band divided the bubbling surf from the dry sand. A twelve-year-old boy with a boogie board slid expertly along the water's edge. Ahead, I could see the zigzagging coastline, banded with asphalt where the road followed the contours of the shore. At the road's end was the Port San Luis Harbor District, a fuel facility and launching area that serviced the local boats.

I reached the frontage road and angled left, jogging along the causeway that spanned the slough. Up on the hill to my right was the big hotel with its neatly trimmed shrubs and manicured lawns. A wide channel of seawater angled back along the fairways of the hotel's golf course. The distance was deceptive and it took me thirty minutes to reach the cul-de-sac at the end of the road where the boats were launched. I slowed to a walk, catching my breath. My shirt was damp and I could feel sweat trickling down the sides of my face. I've been in better shape in my life and I didn't relish the misery of regaining the ground I'd lost. I did the turnaround, watching with interest as three men lowered a pleasure craft into the water from a crane. There was a fishing trawler in drydock, its exposed hull tapering to a rudder as narrow as the blade of an ice skate. I found a spigot near a corrugated metal shed and doused my head, drinking deeply before I headed back, my leg muscles protesting as I increased my pace. By the time I reached the main street of Floral Beach again, it was nearly four and the February sun was casting deep shadows along the side of the hill.

I showered and dressed, pulling on jeans, tennis shoes, and a clean turtleneck, ready to face the world.

The Floral Beach telephone directory was about the size of a comic book, big print, skimpy on the Yellow Pages, light on advertising space. There was nothing to do in Floral Beach and what there was, everybody knew about. I looked up Shana Timberlake and made a note of her address on Kelley, which, by my calculation, was right around the corner. On my way out, I peered into the motel office, but everything was still.

I left my car in the slot and walked the two blocks. Jean's mother lived in what looked like a converted 1950s motor court, an inverted U of narrow frame cottages with a parking space in front of each. Next door, the Floral Beach Fire Department was housed in a four-car garage painted pale blue with dark blue trim. By the time I got back to Santa Teresa, it would seem like New York City compared with this.

There was a battered green Plymouth parked beside unit number one. I peered in the window on the driver's side. The keys had been left in the ignition, a big metal initial T dangling from the key ring—for Timberlake, I assumed. Trusting, these folk. Auto theft must not be the crime of choice in Floral Beach. Shana Timberlake's tiny front porch was crowded with coffee cans planted with herbs, each neatly marked with a Popsicle stick labeled with black ink: thyme, marjoram, oregano, dill, and a two-gallon tomato sauce can filled with parsley. The windows flanking the front door were opened a crack, but the curtains were drawn. I knocked.

Presently, I heard her on the other side. "Yes?"

I talked through the door to her, addressing my remarks

to one of the hinges. "Mrs. Timberlake? My name is Kinsey Millhone. I'm a private detective from Santa Teresa. I wonder if I might talk to you."

Silence. Then, "You the one Royce hired to get Bailey off?" She didn't sound happy about the idea.

"I guess that's one interpretation," I said. "Actually, I'm in town to look into the murder. Bailey says now he's innocent."

Silence.

I tried again. "You know, there never was much of an investigation once he pled guilty."

"So what?"

"Suppose he's telling the truth? Suppose whoever killed her is still running around town, thumbing his nose at the rest of us?"

There was a long pause and then she opened the door.

Her hair was disheveled, eyes puffy, mascara smeared, nose running. She smelled like bourbon. She tightened the sash on her flowered cotton kimono and stared at me blearily. "You were in court."

"Yes."

She swayed slightly, working to focus. "You believe in justice? You b'lieve justice is done?"

"On occasion."

"Yeah, well, I don't. So what's there to talk about? Tap's been shot down. Jean's choked to death. You think any of this is going to bring my daughter back?"

I said nothing, but I kept my gaze on her, waiting for her to wind down.

Her expression darkened with contempt. "You prob'ly don't even have kids. I bet you never even had a dog. You look like somebody breezing through life without a care in this world. Stand there talking about 'innocence.' What do you know about innocence?"

I kept my temper intact, but my tone was mild. "Let's put it this way, Mrs. Timberlake. If I had a kid and somebody'd killed her, I wouldn't be drunk in the middle of the day. I'd be out pulling this town apart until I found out who did it. And then I'd manufacture some justice of my own if that's what it took."

"Well, I can't help you."

"You don't know that. You don't even know what I want."

"Why don't you tell me?"

"Why don't you invite me in and we'll talk."

She glanced back over her shoulder. "Place looks like shit."

"Who cares?"

She focused on me again. She could barely stand up. "How many kids you got?"

"None."

"That's how many I got," she said. She pushed the screen door open and I stepped in.

The place was essentially one long room with a stove, sink, and refrigerator lined up at the far end. Every available surface was stacked with dirty dishes. A small wooden table with two chairs divided the kitchen from the living room, one corner of which was taken up by a brass bed with the sheets half pulled off. The mattress sagged in the middle and it looked as if it would erupt in a symphony of springs if you sat on it. I caught a glimpse of bathroom through a curtained doorway to the right. On the other side of the bathroom, there was a closet, and beyond that was the back door.

I followed her to the kitchen table. She sank into one of the chairs and then got up again, frowning, and moved with great care to the bathroom where she threw up at length. I hate listening to people throw up. (This is big news, I'll bet.) I moved over to the sink and cleared the dirty dishes out, running hot water to mask the sounds coming from the bathroom. I squirted dish-washing liquid into the tumbling water and watched with satisfaction as a cloud of bubbles began to form. I slid plates into the depths, tucking silverware around the edges.

While the dishes soaked, I emptied the garbage, which consisted almost exclusively of empty whiskey bottles and beer cans. I peered into the refrigerator. The light was out and the interior smelled like mold, the metal racks crusted with what looked like dog doo. I closed the door again, worried I was going to have to take a turn in the bathroom with her.

I tuned an ear to Shana again. I heard the toilet ga-lumphing and, after that, the reassuring white noise of a shower being run. Being an incurable snoop at heart, I turned my attention idly to the mail stacked up on the kitchen table. Since I was being mother's little helper, I felt almost entitled to nose around in her business. I walked my fingers through some unopened bills and junk mail. Nothing of interest on the face of it. There was only one piece of personal mail, a big square envelope postmarked Los Angeles. A greeting card? Curses. The envelope was sealed so tight I couldn't even pick the flap loose. Nothing visible when I held it to the light. No scent. Shana's name and address were handwritten in ink, a genderless script that told me nothing about the person who'd penned it. Reluctantly I tucked it back and returned to the sink.

By the time I had the dishes clean and piled in a perilous mound in the rack, Shana was emerging from the bathroom, her head wrapped in one towel and her body in another. Without any modesty at all, she dried herself off and got dressed. Her body was much older than her face. She sat down at the kitchen table in jeans and a T-shirt, barefoot. She looked exhausted, but her skin was scrubbed and her eyes had cleared to some extent. She lit an unfiltered Camel. This lady took smoking seriously. I didn't think unfiltered cigarettes were available these days.

I sat down across from her. "When did you last eat?"

"I forget. I started drinking this morning when I got back. Poor Tap. I was standing right there." She paused and her eyes filled with tears again, her nose turning pink with emotion. "I couldn't believe what was happening. I just lost it. Couldn't cope. I wasn't crazy about him, but he was an okay guy. Kind of dumb. A goofball who made awful jokes. I can't believe this is starting all over. What was he thinking about? He must have been nuts. Bailey comes back to town and look what happens. Somebody else dead. This time it's his best friend."

"Daisy figures somebody put Tap up to it."

"Bailey did," she snapped.

"Just wait," I said. "He got a telephone call last night at Pearl's. He talked briefly and then took off."

She blew her nose. "Must have been after I left," she said, unconvinced. "You want some coffee? It's instant."

"Sure, I'll have some."

She left her cigarette on the lip of the ashtray and got up. She filled a saucepan with water and stuck it on the back burner, turning on the gas. She extracted two coffee mugs from the dish rack. "Thanks for cleaning up. You didn't have to do that."

"Idle hands . . ." I said, not mentioning that I'd also managed a little of the devil's work.

She unearthed a jar of instant coffee and a couple of spoons, which she set on the table while we waited for the water to boil. She took another drag from her cigarette and blew the smoke toward the ceiling. I could feel it settle around me like a fine veil. I was going to have to shampoo my hair again and change my clothes.

She said, "I still say Bailey killed her."

"Why would he do that?"

"Why would anybody else?"

"Well, I don't know, but from what I've heard, he was the only real friend she had."

She shook her head. Her hair was still wet, separated into long strands that dampened the shoulders of her T-shirt. "God, I hate this. Sometimes I wonder how she would have ended up. I've thought about that a lot. I never was much of a mom in terms of the ordinary stuff, but that kid and I were close. More like sisters."

"I saw some pictures of her in the yearbook. She was beautiful."

"For all the good it did. Sometimes I think her looks were what caused all her problems."

"Do you know who she was involved with?"

She shook her head. "I didn't know she was pregnant until I heard about the coroner's report. I knew she was sneakin' out at night, but I have no idea where she went. And what was I supposed to do, nail the door shut? You can't control a kid that age. I guess maybe I should correct myself. We'd always *been* close. I thought we still were. If she was in trouble, she could have come to me. I'd have done anything for her."

"I heard she'd been trying to find out about her father."

Shana shot me a startled look, then covered her surprise with business. She stubbed out her cigarette and moved over to the stove, where she picked up a pot holder and shifted the saucepan unnecessarily. "Where'd you hear that?"

"Bailey. I talked to him at the jail yesterday. You never told her who her father was?"

"No."

"Why not?"

"I made a deal with him years ago and I kept my part. I might have broken down and told her, but I couldn't see what purpose it'd serve."

"Did she ask?"

"She might have mentioned it, but she didn't seem all that intent on the answer and I didn't think much of it."

"Bailey thought she was getting a line on the guy. Was there a way she could have tracked him down?"

"Why would she do that when she had me?"

"Maybe she wanted acknowledgment, or maybe she needed help."

"Because she was pregnant?"

"It's possible," I said. "As I understand it, she'd just had it confirmed, but she must have suspected if her period was late. Why else go all the way to Lompoc for a test?"

"I have no idea."

"What if she'd found him? What would his reaction have been?"

"She didn't find him," she said flatly. "He'd have told me."

"Unless he didn't want you to know."

"What are you getting at?"

"*Somebody* killed her."

"Well, it wasn't him." Her voice had risen and I could see the heat in her face.

"It could have been an accident. He might have been upset or incensed."

"She's his daughter, for God's sake! A seventeen-year-old girl? He'd never do such a thing. He's a nice man. A prince."

"Why not take responsibility if he was so nice?"

"Because he couldn't. It wasn't possible. Anyway, he did. He sent money. Still does. That's all I ever asked."

"Shana, I need to know who he is."

"It's none of your business. It's nobody's business except his and mine."

"Why all the secrecy? What's the big deal? So he's married. So what?"

"I didn't say he was married. You said that. I don't want to discuss it. He's got nothing to do with this, so just drop it. Ask me any more about him and I'll throw your ass out the door."

"What about Bailey's money? Did she ever mention that?"

"What money?"

I watched her carefully. "Tap told me the two of them had a stash nobody knew about. They asked her to hold it till they got out of jail. That's the last anybody heard of it."

"I don't know about any money."

"What about Jean? Did she seem to spend more than she might have made at work?"

"Not that I ever saw. If she'd had some, you wouldn't have caught her livin' like this."

"You were living here at the time of her death?"

"We had an apartment a couple blocks over, but it wasn't much better."

We talked on for a bit, but I couldn't elicit any more information. I got back to my room at six o'clock, not much smarter than I was when I'd started out. I typed up a report, fudging the language to disguise the fact that I hadn't gotten much.

12

I ate an early dinner with the Fowlers that night. Ori's meals had to come at fixed intervals to keep her blood sugar on track. Ann had made a beef stew, with salad and French bread, all of it yummy, I thought. Royce had problems with the meal. His illness had sapped his appetite along with his strength, and some deep-seated impatience made it hard for him to tolerate social occasions in any event. I couldn't imagine how it must have been to grow up with a man like him. He was gruff to the point of churlishness except when Bailey's name was mentioned, and then he shifted into a sentimentality he made no attempt to disguise. Ann didn't show much reaction to the fact that Bailey was the preferred child, but then she'd had a lifetime to get used to it. Ori, wanting to be certain Royce's illness didn't outshine her own, picked at her food, not complaining about it, but sighing audibly. It was obvious she was feeling "poorly," and Royce's refusal to inquire about her health only caused her to double her efforts. I made myself inconspicuous, tuning out the content of their conversation so I could concentrate on the interplay between them. As a child, I didn't experience much in the way of family and I usually find myself somewhat taken aback to see one at close range. "The Donna Reed Show" this was not. People talk about "dysfunctional" families; I've never seen any other kind. I turned up my interior volume control.

Ori put her fork down and pushed her plate back. "I best get things picked up. Maxine's coming by in the morning."

Ann took note of how much Ori'd eaten, and I could see her debating whether to speak up or not. "Did she switch days again? I thought she came on Mondays."

"I asked her to come special. Time to spring-clean."

"You don't have to do that, Mother. Nobody does any spring cleaning out here."

"Well, I know I don't *have* to. What's that got to do with it? Place is a mess. Dirt everywhere. It gets on my nerves. I may be an invalid, but I'm not infirm."

"Nobody said you were."

Ori plowed right on. "I still have some use, even if it's not appreciated."

"Of course you're appreciated," Ann murmured dutifully. "What time's she coming?"

"About nine, she said. We'll have to tear this whole place apart."

"I'll take care of my room," Ann said. "Last time she was in there, I swear she went through everything I owned."

"Well, I'm sure Maxine wouldn't do that. Besides, I already told her to do the floors in there and take down the drapes. I can't turn around and tell her the opposite."

"Don't worry about it. I'll tell her myself."

"Don't you hurt her feelings," Ori warned.

"All I'm going to do is tell her I'll clean my own room."

"What do you have against the woman? She's always liked you."

Royce stirred irritably. "Goddamn it, Ori. There's such

a thing as privacy. If she doesn't want Maxine in her room, then so be it. Keep her out of my room, too, while you're at it. I feel the same way Ann does."

"Well, pardon me, I'm sure!" Ori snorted.

Ann seemed surprised by Royce's support, but she didn't dare comment. I'd seen his loyalties alter inexplicably, but there didn't seem to be any pattern to the shift. As a result, she was often caught up short or in some way made to look foolish.

Ori was now annoyed and her face was set with stubbornness. She lapsed into silence. Ann studied her dinner plate. I was casting about desperately for a reason to excuse myself.

Royce focused on me. "Who'd you talk to today?"

I hate being quizzed at the table. It's one of the reasons I choose to eat alone. I mentioned my conversation with Daisy and the brief interview with the dentist. I was detailing some of the background information I'd picked up on Jean when he cut me off.

"Waste of time," he said.

I paused, losing my train of thought. "That isn't clear."

"I'm not paying you to talk to that pansy of a dentist."

"Then I'll do it on my own time," I said.

"Man's an idiot. Never had a thing to do with Jean. Wouldn't give her the time of day. Thought he was too good. She told me that herself." Royce coughed into his fist.

"He did date her briefly."

Ann's face lifted. "David Poletti did?"

"Do what I say and leave him out of this."

"Pop, if Kinsey thinks he might provide useful information, why not let her pursue it?"

"Who's paying the woman, you or me?"

Ann retreated into silence. Ori gestured with impatience and struggled to her feet. "You have ruint this meal," she snapped at him. "Just go on to bed if you can't be civil to our company. Lord a day, Royce, I can't stand no more of your crankiness."

Now the pouting crossed the table from Ori to Royce. Ann got up and moved to the kitchen counter, probably driven by the same tension that was making my stomach hurt. My orphanhood was becoming more appealing by the minute.

Ori snatched her cane and began to hobble toward the living room.

"Sorry for the interruption. Her temper's kind of short," he said to me.

"Is not," she fired back over her shoulder.

Royce ignored her so he could concentrate on me. "That's all you talked to? Daisy and that . . . tooth fairy?"

"I spoke to Shana Timberlake."

"What for?"

Ori paused at the door, not wanting to miss a trick. "Maxine says she's took up with Dwight Shales. Can you believe that?"

"Oh, Mother. Don't be ridiculous. Dwight wouldn't have anything to do with her."

"It's the truth. Maxine saw her getting out of his car over by the Shop 'n' Go last Saturday."

"So what?"

"At six A.M.?" Ori said.

"Maxine doesn't know what she's talking about."

"She most certainly does. She was right about Sarah Brunswick and her yardman, wasn't she?"

Royce turned around and stared at her pointedly. "Do you *mind*?" Ann's face was beginning to flush darkly as the conflict between the two sparked to life again. He turned back to me. "What's Shana Timberlake got to do with my son?"

"I'm trying to find out who fathered Jean's baby. I gather he was married."

"She mention any names?" Royce asked. Ann had returned with a fresh basket of bread, which she passed to him. He took a piece and passed the basket on to me. I placed it on the table, unwilling to be distracted by ritual gestures.

"She says Jean didn't tell her, but she must suspect someone. I'll let a little time pass and try her again. Bailey indicated Jean was trying to find out who her own father was, and that might open up some possibilities."

Royce pinched his nose, sniffing, and then he waved the idea away. "Probably some trucker she took up with. Woman never was particular. Long as a fella had money in his pocket, she'd do anything he asked." A second mild bout of coughing shook him and I had to wait till it had passed before I responded.

"If it was a trucker, why conceal his identity? It almost has to be somebody in the community, and probably somebody respectable."

"Hogwash. Nobody respectable would be caught dead with that whore. . . ."

"Somebody who didn't want it known, then," I said.

"Bullshit! I don't believe a word of it—"

I cut him off in a flash. "Royce, I know what I'm doing. Would you just back off and let me get on with it?"

He stared at me dangerously, his face growing dark. "What?"

"You hired me to do a job and I'm doing it. I don't want to have to justify and defend every move."

Royce's temper flared like lighter fluid squirted on a fire. His hand shot out and he pointed a shaking finger in my face. "I'm not taking any sass from you, sis!"

"Great. And I won't take any sass from you. Either I do this my way or you can find somebody else."

Royce came halfway out of his chair, leaning on the table. "How dare you talk to me that way!" His face was flaming and his arms trembled where they bore his weight.

I sat where I was, watching him remotely through a haze of anger. I was on the verge of a comment so rude that I hesitated to voice it, when Royce started to cough. There was a pause while he tried to suppress it. He sucked in a breath. The coughing doubled. He pulled out a handkerchief and clamped it across his mouth. Ann and I both gave him our undivided attention, alerted by the fact that he couldn't seem to get his breath. His chest heaved in a wrenching spasm that gathered momentum, flinging him about.

"Pop, are you all right?"

He shook his head, unable to speak, his tongue protruding as the coughing shook him from head to toe. He wheezed, clutching at his shirt front as if for support. Instinctively, I reached for him as he staggered backward into his chair, struggling for air. It was suffocating to watch. The coughing tore at him, bringing up blood and phlegm. Sweat broke out on his face.

Ann said, "My God." She rose to her feet, hands cupped across her mouth. Ori was transfixed in the doorway, horrified by what was happening. Royce's whole body was wracked. I banged on his back, grabbing one arm, which I held aloft to give his lungs room to inflate.

"Get an ambulance!" I yelled.

Ann turned a blank look on me and then mobilized herself sufficiently to reach for the phone, punching 911. She kept her eyes pinned on her father's face while I loosened his collar and fumbled with his belt. Through a rush of adrenaline, I heard her describe the situation to the dispatcher on the other end, reciting the address and directions.

By the time she put the phone down, Royce was gaining control, but he was soaked in perspiration, his breathing labored. Finally the coughing subsided altogether, leaving him pale and clammy-looking, his eyes sunken with exhaustion, hair plastered to his scalp. I wrung a towel out in cold water and wiped his face. He started to tremble. I murmured nonsense syllables, patting at his hands. There was no way Ann and I could lift him, but we managed to lower him to the floor, thinking somehow to make him more comfortable. Ann covered him with a blanket and tucked a pillow under his head. Ori stood there in tears, mewing helplessly. She seemed to grasp the severity of his illness for the first time and she cried like a three-year-old, giving herself up to grief. He would go first. She seemed to understand that now.

In the distance we heard the sirens from the emergency vehicle. The paramedics arrived, taking in the situation with a practiced eye, their demeanor so studiously neutral that the crisis was reduced to a series of minor problems to be solved. Vital signs. Oxygen administered and an IV started. Royce was hefted with effort onto a portable gurney, which was angled out of the room to the vehicle at the curb. Ann went with him in the ambulance. The next thing I knew, I was alone with Ori. I sat down abruptly. The room looked as if it had been ransacked.

I heard a tentative voice from the office. "Hello? Ori?"

"That's Bert," Ori murmured. "He's the night manager."

Bert peered into the living room. He was maybe sixty-five, slight, no more than five feet tall, dressed in a suit he must have bought in the boy's wear department. "I saw the ambulance pull away. Is everything all right?"

Ori told him what had happened, the narrative apparently restoring some of the balance in her universe. Bert was properly sympathetic, and the two swapped a few long-winded tales about similar emergencies. The phone started to ring and he was forced to return to the front desk.

I got Ori into bed. I was worried about her insulin, but she wouldn't discuss it so I had to drop the subject. The episode with Royce had thrown her into a state of clinging dependency. She wanted physical contact, incessant reassurances. I made her some herb tea. I dimmed the lights. I stood by the bed while she clutched my hand. She talked on about Royce and the children at length while I supplied questions to keep the conversation afloat. Anything to get her mind off Royce's collapse.

She finally drifted off to sleep, but it was midnight before Ann got back. Royce had been admitted and she'd stayed until he was settled. A number of tests had been scheduled for first thing in the morning. The doctor was guessing that the cancer had invaded his lungs. Until the chest Xrays came back, he couldn't be sure, but things weren't looking good.

Ori stirred. We'd been speaking in whispers, but it was clear we were disturbing her. We moved out through the kitchen and sat together on the back steps. It was dark out there, the building shielding us from the smudged yellow of the streetlights. Ann pulled her knees up and rested her head wearily on her arms. "God. How am I going to get through the next few months?"

"It'll help if we can get Bailey cleared."

"Bailey," she said. "That's all I hear about." She smiled bitterly. "So what else is new?"

"You were what, five when he was born?"

She nodded. "Mom and Pop were so thrilled. I'd been sickly as an infant. Apparently, I didn't sleep more than thirty minutes at a stretch."

"Colic?"

"That's what they thought. Later, it turned out to be some kind of allergy to wheat. I was sick as a dog . . . diarrhea, ferocious stomach aches. I was thin as a stick. It seemed to straighten out for a while. Then Bailey came along and it started all over again. I was in kintergarden by then and the teacher decided I was just acting up because of him."

"Were you jealous?" I asked.

"Absolutely. I was horribly jealous. I couldn't help myself. They doted on him. He was everything. And of course he was good . . . slept like an angel, blah, blah, blah. Meanwhile, I was half-dead. Some doctor caught on. I don't even know now who it was, but he insisted on a bowel biopsy and that's when they diagnosed the celiac disease. Once they took me off wheat, I was fine, though I think Pop was always half-convinced I'd done it out of spite. Ha. The story of my life." She glanced at her watch. "Oh hell, it's almost one. I better let you go."

We said our good-nights and then I went upstairs. It wasn't until I was ready for bed that I realized someone had been in my room.

13

What I spotted was the partial crescent of a heel print on the carpet just inside the sliding door. I don't even know now what made me glance down. I had gone into the kitchen to pour myself a glass of wine. I popped the cork back in the bottle and tucked it in the refrigerator door. I crossed to the sliding glass door and opened the drapes, then flipped the lock and slid the door open about a foot, letting in a dense shaft of ocean breeze. I stood for a moment, just breathing it all in. I loved the smell. I loved the sound the ocean made and the line of frothy silver curling up onto the sand whenever a wave broke. The fog was in and I could hear the plaintive moo of the foghorn against the chill night air.

My attention strayed to a small kink in the hem of the drape. There was a trace of wet sand adjacent to the metal track in which the door rode. I peered at it, uncomprehending. I set my wineglass aside and went down on my hands and knees to inspect the spot. The minute I saw what it was, I got up and backed away from the door, whipping my head around so I could scan the room. There was no place anyone could hide. The closet consisted of an alcove without a door. The bed was bolted to the wall and quite low, framed in at the bottom with wood strips mounted flush with the carpeting. I'd just come out of the bathroom, but I checked it again, moving automatically. The frosted-glass shower door was open, the stall empty. I knew I was alone, but the sense of that other presence was so vivid that it made my hair stand on my arms. I was seized by an involuntary tremor of fear so acute that it generated a low sound in my throat, like a growl reflex.

I surveyed my personal belongings. My duffel seemed untouched, though it was perfectly possible that someone had eased a sly hand among the contents. I went back to the kitchen table and checked my papers. My portable Smith-Corona was sitting open as it had been, my notes in a folder to the left. Nothing was missing as far as I could tell. I couldn't tell if the papers had been disturbed because I hadn't paid any particular attention to them when I tucked them away. That had been before supper, six hours ago.

I checked the lock on the sliding glass door. Now that I knew what I was looking for, the tool marks were unmistakable and I could see where the aluminum frame had been forced out around the bolt. The lock was a simple device in any event, and hardly designed to withstand brute force. The thumb bolt still turned, but the mechanism had been damaged. Now the latch lever didn't fully meet the strike plate, so that any locking capacity was strictly illusory. The intruder must have left the bolt in its locked position and used the corridor door for egress. I got the penlight out of my handbag and checked the balcony with care. There were additional traces of sand near the railing. I peered the one floor down, trying to figure out how someone could have gotten up here—possibly through one of the rooms on the same floor, climbing from balcony to balcony. The motel driveway ran right under my room and led to covered parking along the perimeter of the court-yard formed by the four sides of the building. Someone could have parked in the driveway, then climbed up on the car roof, and from there swung up onto the balcony. It wouldn't have taken long. The driveway might have been blocked temporarily, but at this hour there was little or no traffic. The town was shut down and the tenants of the motel were probably in for the night.

I called down to the desk, told Bert what had happened, and asked him to move me to another room. I could hear him scratch his chin. His voice, when it came, was papery and frail.

"Gee, Miss Millhone. I don't know what to tell you this time of night. I could move you first thing tomorrow morning."

"Bert," I said, "someone broke into my room! There's no way I'm going to stay here."

"Well. Even so. I'm not sure what we can do at this hour."

"Don't tell me you don't have another room somewhere. I can see the 'vacancy' sign from here."

There was a pause. "I suppose we *could* move you," he said skeptically. "It's awful late, but I'm not saying we can't. When do you think it might have happened, this break-in you're referring to?"

"What difference does it make? The lock on the sliding glass door's been jimmied. I can't even get it to shut prop-erly, let alone lock."

"Oh. Well, even so. Things can fool you sometimes. You know some of those fittings have warped over the years. Doors down here, some of them at any rate, you have to—"

"Could you connect me with Ann Fowler, please?"

"I believe she's asleep. I'd be happy to come up myself and take a look. I don't believe you're in danger. I can understand your concern, but you're up on the second floor there and I don't see how anyone could get up on that balcony."

"Probably the same way they got up here in the first place," I said snappishly.

"Unh-hunh. Well, why don't I come up there and take a look? I guess I can leave the desk for a minute. Maybe we can figure something out."

"Bert. Goddamn it, I want another room!"

"Well, I can see your point. But now there's the question of liability, too, you know. I don't know if you've considered it in that light. Truth is, we've never had any kind of break-in all the years I've been here, which is, oh . . . nearly eighteen years now. Over at the Tides, it's different of course . . ."

"I . . . want . . . another . . . room," I said, giving full measure to each syllable.

"Oh. Well." A pause here. "Let me check and see what I can do. Hang on and I'll pull the registration."

He put me on hold, giving me a restful few minutes in which to get my temper under control. In some ways it felt better to be irritated than unnerved.

He cut back into the line. I could hear him flipping through registration cards in the background, probably licking his thumb for traction. He cleared his throat. "You can try the room next door," he said. "That's number twenty-four. I can bring you up a key. Connecting door might be open if you want to give it a try. Unless, of course, you got some notion that's been tampered with, too. . . ."

I hung up on him, which seemed preferable to going mad.

I hadn't paid much attention to the fact that my room connected to the one next door to it. Access to room 24 was actually effected through two doors with a kind of air space between. I unlocked the door on my side. The second door was ajar, the room in shadow. I flashed my penlight around. The room was empty, orderly, with the slightly musty smell of carpeting that's been dampened too often by the trampling of summer feet. I found the switch and turned the light on, then checked the sliding door that opened out onto the balcony adjacent to mine.

Once I determined the room could be secured, I tossed my few loose personal items into my duffel and moved it next door. I gathered up my typewriter, papers, wine bottle. Within minutes, I was settled. I pulled some clothes on, took my keys and went down to the car. My gun was still locked in my briefcase in the backseat. I stopped in at the office and picked up the new room key, curtly refusing to engage with Bert in any more of his rambling dialogues. He didn't seem to mind. His manner was tolerant. Some women just seem to worry more than others, he remarked.

I took the briefcase up to my room, where I locked the door and chained it. Then I sat at the kitchen table, loaded seven cartridges in the clip, and smacked it home. This was my new handgun. A Davis .32, chrome and walnut, with a five-and-a-quarter-inch barrel. My old gun had gotten blown to kingdom come when the bomb went off in my apartment. This one weighed a tidy twenty-two ounces and already felt like an old friend, with the added virtue that the sights were accurate. It was 1:00 A.M. I was feeling a deadly rage by then and I didn't really expect to sleep. I turned the light out and pulled the fishnet drapes across the glass doors, which I felt compelled to keep locked. I peered out at the empty street. The surf was pounding monotonously, the sound reduced to a mild rumble through the glass. The muffled foghorn intoned its hollow warning to any boats at sea. The sky was dense with clouds, moon and stars blanked out. Without fresh air coming in, the room felt like a prison cell, stuffy and dank. I left my clothes on and got in bed, sitting bolt upright, my gaze pinned on the sliding glass doors, half expecting to see a shadowy figure slip over the railing from below. The sodium-vapor streetlights washed the balcony with a tawny glow. The incoming light was filtered by the curtains. The neon "vacancy" sign had begun to sputter off and on, causing the room to pulsate with red. Someone knew where I was. I'd told a lot of people I was staying at the Ocean Street, but not which room. I got up again and padded over to the table, where I picked up my file notes and tucked them in my briefcase. From now on, I'd take them with me. From now on, I'd tote the gun with me, too. I got back in bed.

At 2:47 A.M. the phone rang and I jumped a foot, unaware that I'd been asleep. The jolt of adrenaline made my heart clatter in my chest like a slug of white-hot metal on a stone floor. Fear and the shrilling of the phone became one sensation. I snatched up the receiver. "Yes?"

His tone was low. "It's me."

Even in the dark, I squinted. "Bailey?"

"You alone?"

"Of course. Where *are* you?"

"Don't worry about that. I don't have much time. Bert knows it's me, and I don't want to take a chance on his calling the cops."

"Forget it. They can't get a trace on a call that fast," I said. "Are you all right?"

"I'm fine. How are things there, pretty bad?"

I gave him a brief rundown on what was happening. I didn't dwell on Royce's collapse because I didn't want to worry him, but I did mention that someone had broken in. "Was it you, by any chance?"

"Me? No way. This is the first time I've been out," he said. "I heard about Tap. God, poor bastard."

"I know," I said. "What a chump he was. It looks like he didn't even have a real load in the gun. He was firing rock salt."

"Salt?"

"You got it. I checked the residue at the scene. I don't know if he realized what it was or not."

"Jesus," Bailey breathed. "He never had a chance."

"Why did you take off? That was the worst move you could possibly have made. They probably have every cop in the state out. Were you the one who set it up?"

"Of course not! I didn't even know who it was at first, and then all I could think to do was get the hell out of there."

"Who could have put him up to it?"

"I have no idea, but somebody did."

"Joleen might know. I'll try to see her tomorrow. In the meantime, you can't stay on the loose. They've got you listed as armed and dangerous."

"I figured as much, but what am I supposed to do? The minute I show up, they're going to blow me off the face of the earth, same as Tap."

"Call Jack Clemson. Turn yourself in to him."

"How do we know it wasn't him set me up?"

"Your own attorney?"

"Hey, if I die, it's over. Everybody's off the hook. Anyway, I gotta get myself out of here before—" I heard an intake of breath. "Hang on." There was a silence. His end of the conversation had reverberated with the hollow echo of a phone booth. Now I heard the metal bi-fold door squeak. "All right, I'm back. I thought there was somebody out there, but it doesn't look like it."

"Listen, Bailey. I'm doing what I can, but I could use some help."

"Like what?"

"Like what happened to the money from the bank job you did?"

A pause. "Who told you about that?"

"Tap, last night at the pool hall. He says you left it with Jean, but then the last he heard, the whole forty-two thousand had disappeared. Could she have taken it herself?"

"Not Jean. She wouldn't have done that to us."

"What was the story she told you? She must have said something."

"All I know is she went to lay hands on it and the whole stash was gone."

"Or so she said," I put in.

I could hear him shrug. "Even if she did take it, what was I going to do, turn her in to the cops?"

"Did she tell you where she'd hidden it?"

"No, but I got the impression it was somewhere up there at the hot springs where she worked."

"Oh, great. Place is huge. Who else knew about the money?"

"That's all as far as I know." He hissed into the phone. I could feel my heart do a flip-flop. "What's wrong?"

Silence.

"Bailey?"

He severed the connection.

Almost immediately, the phone rang again. A sheriff's deputy advised me to remain where I was until a car could pick me up. Good old Bert. I spent the rest of the night at the county sheriff's department, being variously questioned, accused, abused, and threatened—quite politely, of course—by a homicide detective named Sal Quintana, who wasn't in a much better mood than I was at that point. A second detective stood against the wall, using a broken wooden match to clean the plaque off his teeth. I was certain his dental hygienist would applaud his efforts when he saw her next.

Quintana was in his mid-forties, with closely cropped black hair, big, dark eyes, and a face remarkable for its impassivity. Dwight Shales's face had the same deadpan look: obdurate, unresponsive, aggressively blank. This man was probably twenty pounds overweight, with a shirt size that hadn't quite conceded the point. The extra weight across his back had pulled his sleeves up an inch, and where his wrist extended, there were already a few gray hairs mingled with the black. He had good teeth, and my assessment of his looks might have been upgraded if he'd smiled. No such luck. He seemed to be operating on the theory that Bailey Fowler and I were in cahoots.

"You're crazy," I said. "I only saw the man once."

"When was that?"

"You know when. Yesterday. I signed in at the desk. You've got it right there in front of you."

His gaze flicked down to the papers on the table. "You want to tell us what you talked about?"

"He was depressed. I tried to cheer him up."

"You fond of Mr. Fowler?"

"That's none of your business. I'm not under arrest and I'm not charged with anything, right?"

"That's right," he said patiently. "We're just trying to understand the situation here. I'm sure you can appreciate that, given the circumstances." He paused while the second detective leaned down and murmured something indistinct. Quintana looked back at me. "I believe you were present in the courtroom when Mr. Fowler escaped. You have any contact with him at the time?"

"None. Zippity-doo-dah."

He didn't react at all to my flippancy. "When you spoke with Mr. Fowler on the telephone, did he give you any indication where he was calling from?"

"No."

"Was it your impression he was still in the area?"

"I don't know. I guess so. He could have called from anyplace."

"What'd he tell you about the escape?"

"Nothing. We didn't talk about that."

"You have any idea who picked him up?"

"I don't even know which direction he went. I was still in the courtroom when the shots were fired."

"What about Tap Granger?"

"I don't know anything about Tap."

"You spent enough time with him the night before," he remarked.

"Yeah, well, he wasn't that informative."

"You know who might have paid him off?"

"Somebody paid Tap off?" I said.

Quintana was unresponsive, simply waiting me out.

"He didn't even mention the arraignment. I was astonished when I turned around and realized it was him."

"Let's get back to Bailey's phone call," Quintana said.

"I've covered most of it."

"What else was said?"

"I told him to get in touch with Jack Clemson and turn himself in."

"He say he'd do that?"

"Uh, no. He didn't seem real thrilled at that, but maybe he'll have a change of heart."

"We're having a hard time believing he could disappear without a trace. He almost had to have assistance."

"Well, he didn't get it from me."

"You think somebody's hiding him?"

"How do I know?"

"Why'd he get in touch?"

"I have no idea. The call was interrupted before he got to that."

We continued in this monotonous, circular fashion till I thought I'd drop. Quintana was unfailingly civil, unsmiling, persistent—nay, relentless—and finally agreed to let me go back to the motel only after he'd milked me of all conceivable information. "Miss Millhone, let me make one thing crystal clear," he said, shifting in his seat. "This is a police matter. We want Bailey Fowler back in custody. I better not find out you're helping him in any way. Do you understand that?"

"Absolutely," I said.

He gave me a look that said he doubted my sincerity.

I staggered back to bed at 6:22 A.M. and slept until nine, which was when Ann tapped on my door and got me up.

14

Ann was on her way to the hospital to see her father. The house cleaner, Maxine, had been delayed, but swore she'd be there by ten. In the meantime, Ann felt Ori was too anxious to be left alone. "I've called Mrs. Maude. She and Mrs. Emma agreed to sit with Mother, but neither one can make it till this afternoon. I feel like a dog asking you to fill in . . ."

"Don't worry about it. I'll be right down."

"Thanks."

I still had my clothes on, so I didn't have to waste any time getting dressed. I brushed my teeth and threw some water on my face, ignoring the dark smudges around my eyes. There was a time in my youth when staying up all night had felt adventuresome. Dawn then was exhilarating and there didn't seem to be any end to the physical resources at my command. Now the lack of sleep was creating an odd high that foreshadowed a stomach-churning descent. I was still on the upswing, gathering momentum as I dragged my body out. Coffee might help, but it would only postpone the inevitable crash. I was going to pay for this.

Ori was sitting up in bed, fussing with the ties on her

gown. Paraphernalia on the night table and the faint scent
of alcohol indicated that Ann had done Ori's glucose test
and had already administered her morning dose of insulin.
The trace of blood streaked on the reagent strip had dried
to a rusty brown. Old adhesive tape was knotted up on the
bed tray like a wad of chewing gum. Stuck to it was a cotton
ball with a linty-looking dot of red. This before breakfast.
Mentally, I could feel my eyes cross, but I bustled about
in my best imitation of a visiting nurse. I was accustomed,
from long experience, to steeling myself to the sight of
violent death, but this residue of diabetic odds and ends
nearly made my stomach heave. Resolutely, I swept it all
into a plastic wastebasket and tucked it out of sight, tidying
pill bottles, water glass, carafe, and Ace bandages. Usually,
Ori had her legs bound in heavy pink stretch wraps, but
she was apparently airing them today. I avoided the sight
of her mottled calves, the ice-cold feet in which so little
circulation pumped, the blue-gray toes, dry and cracked.
She had an ulcerated area about the size of a nickel on the
inside aspect of her right ankle.

"I think I'll sit down a minute," I murmured.

"Well, honey. You're pale as a ghost. Go out to the
kitchen and get a glass of juice."

The orange juice helped and I ate a piece of toast, cleaning up the kitchen afterward as a way of avoiding the
woman in the other room. Three thousand hours of investigative training hadn't quite prepared me for a sideline
as a drudge. I felt like I'd spent half my time on this case
washing dirty dishes. How come Magnum, P.I., never had
to do stuff like this?

At twenty minutes after ten, Maxine appeared, cleaning
supplies in a plastic bucket on her arm. She was one of

those women with an extra hundred pounds wobbling around her body like a barrel made of flesh. She had one eyetooth the size and color of a rusty nail. Without any pause, she took out a dustrag and began to work her way around the room. "Sorry I'm late, but I couldn't get that old car to start to save my neck. I finally called and asked John Robert to come over with a set of jumper cables, but it took him a good half hour just to get there. I heard about Royce. God love his heart."

"I'm going to have Ann take me over there this evening," Ori said. "Provided I feel well enough."

Maxine just clucked and shook her head. "I tell you," she said. "And I bet you haven't heard a word from Bailey. No telling where he's at."

"Aw, and I'm worried sick. I never even laid eyes on him after all this time. And here he's took off again."

Maxine made a face that conveyed sympathy and regret, then flapped her dustrag to indicate a shift in tone. "Mary Burney's making a perfect fool of herself. Windows boarded up, big lock on the gate, convinced he'll go over there and carry her off."

"Well, whatever for?" Ori asked, completely mystified.

"I never said she had brains, but then half the people I talked to are loading their guns. Radio says he 'may be seeking refuge among former acquaintances.' Just like that. 'May be seeking refuge.' Now, if that's not the silliest thing I ever heard. I told John Robert, 'Bailey's got more sense than that,' I said. 'For one thing, he doesn't know Mary Burney from a hole in the ground and besides which, he wouldn't go anywhere near that place of hers because it backs right up to the National Guard Armory. Chain-link fence and all what kind of thing. Floodlights? Lord God,'

I said. 'Bailey may be a criminal, but he's not a *re*tard.' "

As soon as I could decently insert myself into the conversation, I told Ori I'd be taking off. Maxine got conspicuously quiet, hoping no doubt to pick up some information she could pass along to John Robert and Mary Burney next chance she had. I avoided giving any indication where I meant to go. The last glimpse I had of them, Maxine was handing Ori a fistful of junk mail to sort through while she applied Lemon Pledge to the top of the bookshelf where the mail had been stacked.

Tap Granger's widow lived on Kaye Street in a one-story frame house with a screened-in porch. The exterior was painted an ancient turquoise trimmed in buttercup, the porch steps eaten through by something that left ominous holes in the wood. She came to the door looking pale and thin, except for the belly that jutted out in front of her like a globe. Her nose was a dull pink from tears, her eyes swollen, with all the makeup cried off. Her hair had the tortured appearance of a recent home permanent. She wore faded jeans that hung on her narrow behind, a sleeveless T-shirt that left her bare arms bony-looking and puckered from the chilly morning air. She had a plump baby affixed to one hip, his massive thighs gripping her bulk like a horseman preparing to post. The pacifier in his mouth looked like some kind of plug you might pull if you wanted to let all the air out. Solemn eyes, runny nose.

"I'm sorry to bother you, Mrs. Granger. My name's Kinsey Millhone. I'm a private investigator. Could I talk to you?"

"I guess," she said. She couldn't have been much more than twenty-six, with the lackluster air of a woman drained of youth. Where was she going to find someone who'd take on another man's five kids?

The house was small and rustic, the construction crude, but the furnishings looked new. All Sears Revolving Charge Account items, still under warranty. The couch and two matching Barcaloungers were green Naugahyde, the coffee table and the two end tables flanking the couch were blond wood laminate, still unscarred by little children's shoes. The squat table lamps had pleated shades still wrapped in clear cellophane. She'd be paying it all off till the kids were in high school. She sat down on one couch cushion, which buckled up slightly and let out a sigh as the air was forced out. I perched on the edge of one lounge chair, uneasy about the half-eaten Fluffer-nutter sandwich that kept me company on the seat.

"Linnetta, quit doin' that!" she sang out suddenly, though there didn't seem to be anyone else in the room. I realized belatedly that the twanging sound of a kid jumping up and down on a bed had just ceased. She shifted the baby, setting him on his feet. He swayed, clutching at her jeans, the pacifier wriggling around in his mouth as he started working it with a little humming sound.

"What'd you want?" she said. "The police have been here twice and I already told 'em everything I know."

"I'll try to be brief. It must be hard on you."

"Doesn't matter," she shrugged. The stress of Tap's death had made her face break out, her chin splotched and fiery pink.

"Did you know what Tap was getting involved in yesterday?"

"I knew he had some money, but he said he won a bet with this guy who finally paid up."

"A bet?"

"Might not have been true," she said, somewhat defensively, "but God knows we needed it and I wasn't about to ask after it too close."

"Did you see him leave the house?"

"Not really. I'd come in from work and I went straight to bed as soon as him and the kids left. I guess he dropped Ronnie and the girls off and then took Mac to the sitters. He must have drove into San Luis Obispo after that. I mean, he had to, since that's where he ended up."

"But he never said anything about the breakout or who put him up to it?"

"I wouldn't have stood for it if I'd known."

"Do you know how much he was paid?"

Her eyes became wary in the blank of her face. She began to pick idly at her chin. "Nuh-unh."

"No one's going to take it back. I just wondered how much it was."

"Two thousand," she murmured. God, a woman with no guile, married to a man with no sense. Two thousand dollars to risk his life?

"Are you aware that the shotgun shells were loaded with rock salt?"

Again, she gave me that cagy look. "Tap said that way nobody'd get hurt."

"Except him."

Light dawned in that faraway world of the 98 IQ. "Oh."

"Was the shotgun his?"

"Nuh-unh. Tap never had a gun. I wouldn't have one in the house with these kids," she said.

"Do you have any idea at all who he was dealing with?"

"Some woman, I heard."

That got my attention. "Really."

Back went the hand to her chin. Pick, pick. "Somebody saw 'em together at the pool hall night before he died."

It took a split second. "Shit, that was *me*. I was trying to get a lead on this Bailey Fowler business and I knew they'd been friends."

"Oh. I thought maybe him and some woman . . ."

"Absolutely not," I said. "In fact, he spent half the time showing me pictures of you and the kids."

She colored faintly, tears welling. "That's sweet. I wish I could help. You seem awful nice."

I took out my card and jotted down the number of the motel on the back. "Here's where I'll be for the next couple of days. If you think of anything, get in touch."

"Are you coming to the funeral? It's tomorrow afternoon at the Baptist church. It should be a good turnout because everybody liked Tap."

I had my doubts about that, but it was clearly something she needed to believe. "We'll see. I may be tied up, but I'll be there if I can." My recollection of Reverend Haws made attendance unlikely, but I couldn't rule it out. I'd been present at a number of funerals over the last several months, and I didn't think I could endure another. Organized religion was ruined for me when I was five years old, subjected to a Sunday-school teacher with hairs sticking out of her nose and bad breath. Trust me to point that out. The Presbyterians had suggested the Vacation Bible School at the Congregational Church down the road. Since I'd already been expelled by the Methodists, my aunt was losing heart. Personally, I was looking forward to another flannel board. You could make Baby Jesus with some fuzzies on his back and stick him right up in the sky like a bird, then make him dive-bomb the manger.

Joleen left the baby sidestepping his way down the length
of the couch while she walked me to the door. The bell
rang almost simultaneously with her opening it. Dwight
Shales stood on the doorstep, looking as surprised as we
were. His glance shifted from her face to mine and then
back again. He nodded at Joleen. "Thought I'd stop by
and see how you were."

"Thanks, Mr. Shales. That's real nice of you. This is,
unh . . ."

I held my hand out. "Kinsey Millhone. We've met." We
shook hands.

"I remember," he said. "I just stopped by the motel, as
a matter of fact. If you can hold on a minute, we can have
a chat."

"Sure," I said. I stood there while he and Joleen talked
briefly. From their conversation, I gathered that she'd been
at the high school not that many years before.

"I just lost my wife, and I know how it feels," he was
saying. The authoritarian air I remembered was gone. His
pain seemed so close to the surface, it made tears well up
in Joleen's eyes again.

"I appreciate that, Mr. Shales. I do. Mrs. Shales was a
nice woman and I know she suffered something fierce. You
want to come in? I can fix you some tea."

He glanced at his watch. "I can't right this minute. I'm
late as it is, but I'll stop by again. I wanted you to know
we're all thinking of you over at the high school. Can I
help you with anything? You have enough money?"

Joleen seemed completely overwhelmed, nose turning
rosy, her voice cracking when she spoke. "I'm all right.
Mom and Daddy are coming up from Los Angeles tonight.
I'll be fine as soon as they get here."

"Well, you let us know if there's anything we can do. I

can have one of the senior girls look after the kids tomorrow afternoon. Bob Haws said the services are scheduled for two."

"I'd appreciate the help. I hadn't even thought about who'd be keeping the kids. Will you be at the funeral? Tap'd be awful glad."

"Of course, I'll be there. He was a fine man and we were all proud of him."

I followed him out to the street, where his car was parked. "I pulled school records on Jean Timberlake," he said. "If you want to stop by the office, you can see what we've got. You have a car? I can give you a lift."

"I better take mine. It's back at the motel."

"Hop in. I'll drop you off."

"Are you sure? I don't want to hold you up."

"Won't take a minute. I'm headed back in that direction anyway."

He held the door for me and I got in, the two of us chatting inconsequentially during the brief ride back to the Ocean Street. I could have walked, but I has trying to ingratiate myself with the man in the hope that he might have personal recollections of his own to add to whatever data I found in Jean's file.

Ann had returned from the hospital and I saw her peer out of the office window as we pulled up. She and Shales exchanged a smile and a wave and she disappeared.

I stepped out of the car, leaning back toward the open window. "I have another errand to run and then I'll pop by."

"Good. Meanwhile, I'll check and see if any of the staff have information to contribute."

"Thanks," I said.

As he took off, I turned to find Ann right behind me. She seemed surprised to see him pull away. "He's not coming in?"

"I think he had to get back to the school. I just ran into him over at Joleen Granger's. How's your father?"

Reluctantly, Ann's gaze flicked back to my face. "About what you'd expect. Cancer's spread to his lungs, liver, and spleen. They're saying now he probably has less than a month."

"How's he taking it?"

"Poorly. I thought he'd made his peace, but he seemed real upset. He wants to talk to you."

My heart sank. It was the last thing I needed, a conversation with the doomed. "I'll try to get up there sometime this afternoon."

15

I sat in the vestibule outside Dwight Shales's office, variously picking my way through the papers in Jean Timberlake's school file and eavesdropping on an outraged senior girl who'd been caught in the restroom shampooing her hair. Apparently the drill in disciplinary matters was for the culprit to use the pay phone in the school office to notify the appropriate parent about the nature of the offense.

". . . Well, guy, Mom. How was I to know? I mean, big fuckin' deal," she said. ". . . Because I didn't have time! Guuuyyy . . . Well, nobody ever told me . . . It's a fuckin' free country. All I did was wash my hair! . . . I did noooot . . . I'm not smarting off! Yeah, well, you have a big mouth, too." Her tone shifted here from exasperation to extreme martyrdom, voice sliding up and down the scale. "Okaaay! I said, okay. Oh, right, Mom. God . . . Why'n't you ground me for life. Right. Oh, rilly, I'm sure. Fuck you, okay? You are such an asshole! I just hate you!!" She slammed the phone down resoundingly and burst noisily into tears.

I suppressed a temptation to peer around the corner at her. I could hear the low murmur of a fellow conspirator.

"God, Jennifer, that is just *so* unfair," the second girl said.

Jennifer was sobbing inconsolably. "She is such a bitch. I hate her fuckin' guts. . . ."

I tried to picture myself at her age, talking to my aunt like that. I'd have had to take out a loan for the ensuing dental work.

I leafed through Jean's Scholastic Aptitude Test scores, attendance records, the written comments her teachers had added from time to time. With the weeping in the background, it was almost like having Jean Timberlake's ghost looking on. She certainly seemed to have had her share of grief in high school. Tardiness, demerits, detention, parent-teacher conferences scheduled and then canceled when Mrs. Timberlake failed to show. There were repeated notes from sessions with first one and then another of the four school counselors, Ann Fowler being one. Jean had spent a large part of her junior year consigned to Mr. Shales's office, sitting on the bench, perhaps sullenly, perhaps with the total self-possession she seemed to display in the few yearbook photographs I'd seen. Maybe she'd sat there and recollected, in tranquillity, the lewd sexual experiments she'd conducted with the boys in the privacy of parked cars. Or maybe she'd flirted with one of the senior honors students manning the main desk. From the moment she reached puberty, her grade point average had slid steadily downward despite the contradictory evidence of her IQ and past grades. I could practically feel the heat of noxious hormones seeping through the pages, the drama, confusion, finally the secrecy. Her confidences in the school nurse ceased abruptly. Where Mrs. Berringer had jotted down folksy notes about cramps and heavy periods, advising a consultation with the family physician, there was suddenly concern about the girl's mounting absenteeism. Jean's problems didn't go unnoticed or unremarked. To the credit of the faculty, a general alarm seemed to sound. From the paper trail left behind, it looked as if every effort had been made to bring her back from the brink. Then, on November 5, someone had noted in dark blue angular ink that the girl was deceased. The word was underlined once, and after that, the page was blank.

"Is that going to help?"

I jumped. Dwight Shales had emerged from his inner office and he stood now in the door. The weeping girl was gone, and I could hear the tramp of footsteps as the students passed between classes. "You scared me," I said, patting myself on the chest.

"Sorry. Come into the office. I've got a conference scheduled at two, but we can talk till then. Bring the file."

I gathered up Jean's records and followed him in.

"Have a seat," he said.

His manner had changed. The easygoing man I'd seen earlier had disappeared. Now he seemed guarded, careful of his words, all business—slightly curt, as if twenty years of dealing with unruly teenagers had soured him on everyone. I suspected his manner tended toward the autocratic anyway, his tone edged with combativeness. He was used to being in charge. On the surface, he was attractive, but his good looks were posted with warning signs. His body was trim. He had the build and carriage of a former military type, accustomed to operating under fire. If he was a sportsman, I'd peg him as an expert in trap and skeet shooting. His games would be handball, poker, and chess. If he ran, he'd feel compelled to lower his finish by a few seconds each time out. Maybe once he'd been open, vulnerable or soft, but he was shut down now, and the only evidence I'd seen of any warmth at all was in his dealings with Joleen. Apparently his wife's death had ruptured the bounds of his self-control. In matters of mourning, he could still reach out.

I took a seat, placing the fat, dog-eared manila folder on the desk in front of me. I hadn't found anything startling, but I'd made a few notes. Her former address. Birth date, social security number, the bare bones of data made meaningless by her death. "What did you think of her?" I asked him.

"She was a tough little nut. I'll tell you that."

"So I gathered. It looks like she spent half her time in detention."

"At least that. What made it frustrating—for me, at any rate, and you're welcome to talk to some of the other teachers about this—is that she was a very appealing kid. Smart, soft-spoken, friendly—with adults, at any rate. I can't say she was well liked among her classmates, but she was pleasant to the staff. You'd sit her down to have a chat and you'd think you were getting through. She'd nod and agree with you, make all the proper noises, and then she'd turn around and do exactly what she'd been reprimanded for in the first place."

"Can you give me an example?"

"Anything you name. She'd ditch school, show up late, fail to turn in assignments, refuse to take tests. She smoked on campus, which was strictly against the rules back then, kept booze in her locker. Drove everybody up the wall. It's not like what she did was worse than anybody else. She simply had no conscience about it and no intention what-

ever of cleaning up her act. How do you deal with someone
like that? She'd say anything that got her off the hook. This
girl was convincing. She could make you believe anything
she said, but then it would evaporate the minute she left
the room."

"Did she have any girlfriends?"

"Not that I ever saw."

"Did she have a rapport with any teacher in particular?"

"I doubt it. You can ask some of the faculty if you like."

"What about the promiscuity?"

He shifted uncomfortably. "I heard rumors about that,
but I never had any concrete information. Wouldn't surprise me. She had some problems with self-esteem."

"I talked with a classmate who implied that it was pretty
steamy stuff."

Shales wagged his head reluctantly. "There wasn't much
we could do. We referred her two or three times for professional counseling, but of course she never went."

"I take it the school counselors didn't make much progress."

"I'm afraid not. I don't think you could fault us for the
sincerity of our concern, but we couldn't force her to do
anything. And her mother didn't help. I wish I had a nickel
for every note we sent home. The truth is, we liked Jean
and thought she had a chance. At a certain point, Mrs.
Timberlake seemed to throw up her hands. Maybe we did,
too. I don't know. Looking back on the situation, I don't
feel good, but I don't know how we could have done it any
differently. She's just one of those kids who fell between
the cracks. It's a pity, but there it is."

"How well do you know Mrs. Timberlake at this point?"

"What makes you ask?"

"I'm being paid to ask."

"She's a friend," he said, after the barest hesitancy.

I waited, but he didn't amplify. "What about the guy Jean was allegedly involved with?"

"You've got me on that. A lot of stories started circulating right after she died, but I never heard a name attached."

"Can you think of anything else that might help? Someone she might have taken into her confidence?"

"Not that I recall." A look crossed his face. "Well, actually, there was one thing that always struck me as odd. A couple times that fall, I saw her at church, which seemed out of character."

"Church?"

"Bob Haws's congregation. I forget who told me, but the word was she had the hots for the kid who headed up the youth group over there. Now what the hell was his name? Hang on." He got up and went to the door to the main office. "Kathy, what was the name of the boy who was treasurer of the senior class the year Jean Timberlake was killed? You remember him?"

There was a pause and a murmured response that I couldn't quite hear.

"Yeah, he's the one. Thanks." Dwight Shales turned back to me. "John Clemson. His dad's the attorney representing Fowler, isn't he?"

I parked in the little lot behind Jack Clemson's office, taking the flagstone path around the cottage to the front. The sun was out, but the breeze was cool and the pittosporum shading the side yard were being hedged up by a man in a landscape company uniform. The Little Wonder electric trimmer in his hands made a chirping sound as he passed it across the face of the shrub, which was raining down leaves.

I went up on the porch, pausing for a moment before I let myself in. All the way over, I'd been rehearsing what I'd say, feeling not a little annoyed that he'd withheld information. Maybe it would turn out to be insignificant, but that was mine to decide. The door was ajar and I stepped into the foyer. The woman who glanced up must have been his regular secretary. She was in her forties, petite—nay, toy-sized—hair hennaed to an auburn shade, with piercing gray eyes and a silver bracelet, in a snake shape, coiled around her wrist.

"Is Mr. Clemson in?"

"Is he expecting you?"

"I stopped by to bring him up to date on a case," I said. "The name is Kinsey Millhone."

She took in my outfit, gaze traveling from turtleneck to jeans to boots with an almost imperceptible flicker of distaste. I probably looked like someone he might represent on a charge of welfare fraud. "Just a moment, I'll check." Her look said, *Not bloody likely*.

Instead of buzzing through, she got up from her desk and tippy-tapped her way down the hall to his office, flared skirt twitching on her little hips as she walked. She had the body of a ten-year-old. Idly, I surveyed her desk while she was gone, scanning the document that she was working from. Reading upside down is only one of several obscure talents I've developed working as a private eye. ". . . . And he is enjoined and restrained from annoying, molesting, threatening, or harming petitioner . . ." Given the average marriage these days, this sounded like pre-nups.

"Kinsey? Hey, nice to see you! Come on back."

Clemson was standing in the door to his office. He had his suit jacket off, shirt collar unbuttoned, sleeves rolled up, and tie askew. The gabardine pants looked like the same ones he'd had on two days ago, bunched up in the seat, pleated with wrinkles across the lap. I followed him into his office in the wake of cigarette smoke. His secretary tippy-tapped back to her desk out front, radiating disapproval.

Both chairs were crowded with law books, tongues of scrap paper hanging out where he'd marked passages. I stood while he cleared a space for me to sit down. He moved around to his side of the desk, breathing audibly. He stubbed out his cigarette with a shake of his head.

"Out of shape," he remarked. He sat down, tipping back in his swivel chair. "What are we going to do with that Bailey, huh? Guy's a fuckin' lunatic, taking off like that."

I filled him in on Bailey's late-night call, repeating his version of the escape while Jack Clemson pinched the bridge of his nose and shook his head in despair. "What a jerk. No accounting for the way these guys see things."

He reached for a letter and gave it a contemptuous toss. "Look at this. Know what that is? Hate mail. Some guy got put away twenty-two years ago when I was a PD. He writes me every year from jail like it's something I did to him. Jesus. When I was in the AG's office, the AG did a survey of prisoners as to who they blamed for their conviction— you know, 'why are you in prison and whose fault is it?' Nobody ever says, 'It's my fault . . . for being a jerk.' The number-one guy who gets blamed is their own lawyer. 'If I'da had a real lawyer instead of a PD, I'da got off.' That's the number-one guy, okay? His own lawyer. The number-two guy that was blamed was the witness who testified against him. Number three—are you ready?—is the judge who sentenced him. 'If I'da had a fair judge, this woulda never happened.' Number four was the police who investigated the case, the investigating officer, whoever caught 'im. And way down there at the bottom was the prosecuting attorney. Less than ten percent of the people they surveyed could even remember the prosecutor's name. I'm in the wrong end of the business." He snorted and leaned forward on his elbows, shoving files around on his desk. "Anyway, skip that. How's it going from your end? You comin' up with anything?"

"I don't know yet," I said carefully. "I just talked to the principal at Central Coast High. He tells me he saw Jean at the Baptist church a couple of times in the months before she was killed. Word was she was infatuated with your son."

Dead silence. "Mine?" he said.

I shrugged noncommittally. "Kid named John Clemson. I assume he's your son. Was he the student leader of the church youth group?"

"Well, yeah, John did that, but it's news to me about her."

"He never said anything to you?"

"No, but I'll ask."

"Why don't I?"

A pause. Jack Clemson was too much the professional to object. "Sure, why not?" He jotted an address and a telephone number on a scratch pad. "This is his business."

He tore the leaf off and passed it across the desk to me, locking eyes with me. "He's not involved in her death."

I stood up. "Let's hope not."

16

The business address I'd been given turned out to be a seven-hundred-square-foot pharmacy at one end of a medical facility half a block off Higuera. The complex itself bore an eerie resemblance to the padres' quarters of half the California missions I'd seen: thick adobe walls, complete with decorator cracks, a long colonnade of twenty-one arches, with a red tile roof, and what looked like an aqueduct tucked into the landscaping. Pigeons were misbehaving up among the eaves, managing to copulate on a perilously tiny ledge.

The pharmacy, amazingly, did not sell beach balls, lawn furniture, children's clothing, or motor oil. To the left of the entrance were tidy displays of dental wares, feminine hygiene products, hot water bottles and heating pads, corn remedies, body braces of divers kinds, and colostomy supplies. I browsed among the over-the-counter medications while the pharmacist's assistant chatted with a customer about the efficacy of vitamin E for hot flashes. The place had a faintly chemical scent, reminiscent of the sticky coating on fresh Polaroid prints. The man I took to be John Clemson was standing behind a shoulder-high partition in a white coat, his head bent to his work. He didn't look at me, but once the customer left, he murmured something to his assistant, who leaned forward.

"Miss Millhone?" she said. She wore pants and a yellow polyester smock with patch pockets, one of those uniforms that would serve equally for a waitress, an au pair, or an LVN.

"Yes."

"You want to step back here, please? We're swamped this morning, but John says he'll talk to you while he works, if that's all right."

"That's fine. Thanks."

She lifted a hinged portion of the counter, holding it for me while I ducked underneath and came up in a narrow alleyway. The counter on this side was lined with machinery: two computer monitors, a typewriter, a label maker, a printer, and a microfiche reader. Storage bins below the counter were filled with empty translucent plastic pill vials. Ancillary labels on paper rolls were hung in a row, stickers cautioning the recipient: SHAKE WELL; THIS RX CANNOT BE REFILLED; WILL CAUSE DISCOLORATION OF URINE OR FECES; EXTERNAL USE ONLY; and DO NOT FREEZE. On the right were the drug bays, floor-to-ceiling shelves stocked with antibiotics, liquids, topical ointments and oral medications, arranged alphabetically. I had, within easy reach, the cure for most of life's ills: depression, pain, tenderness, apathy, insomnia, heartburn, fever, infection, obsession, and dizziness, excitability, seizures, histrionics, remorse. Given my poor night's sleep, what I needed were uppers, but it seemed unprofessional to whine and beg.

I'd expected John Clemson to look like his father, but he couldn't have been more different. He was tall and lean, with a thatch of dark hair. His face, in profile, was thin

and lined, his cheeks sunken, cheekbones prominent. He
had to be my age, but he had a worn air about him, an
aura of weariness, ill health, or despair. He made no eye
contact, his attention fixed on the task in front of him.
Using a spatula, he was sliding pills, by fives, across the
surface of a counting tray. With a rattle, he tumbled pills
into a groove on the side, funneling them into an empty
plastic vial, which he sealed with a child-proof cap. He
affixed a label, set the vial aside, and started again, working
with the same automatic grace as a dealer in Vegas. Thin
wrists, long, slender fingers. I wondered if his hands would
smell of PhisoDerm.

"Sorry I can't interrupt what I'm doing," he said mildly.
"What can I help you with?" His tone had a light mocking
quality, as if something amused him that he might or might
not reveal.

"I take it your father called. How much did he tell
you?"

"That you're investigating the murder of Jean Timberlake at his request. I know, of course, that he was hired to
represent Bailey Fowler. I don't know what you want with
me."

"You remember Jean?"

"Yes."

I had hoped for something a little more informative, but
I was willing to press. "Can you tell me about your relationship with her?"

His mouth curved up slightly. "My relationship?"

"Somebody told me she used to hang out at the Baptist
church. As I understand it, you were a classmate of hers
and headed up the youth group back then. I thought
maybe the two of you developed a friendship."

"Jean didn't have friends. She had conquests."

"Were you one?"

A bemused smile. "No."

What was the damn joke here? "Do you remember her coming to church?"

"Oh yes, but it wasn't me she was interested in. I wish I could say it was. She was very particular, our Miss Timberlake."

"Meaning what?"

"Meaning she'd never have tumbled for the likes of me."

"Oh, really? Why is that?"

He turned his face. The whole right side was disfigured, right eye missing, the lid welded shut by shiny pink and silver scar tissue that extended from his scalp to his jaw. His good eye was large and dark, filled with self-awareness. The missing eye created the illusion of a constant wink. I could see now that his right arm was also badly scarred.

"What was it?"

"Automobile accident when I was ten. The gas tank blew up. My mother died and I was left looking like this. It's better now. I've had surgery twice. Back then, the church was my salvation, literally. I was baptized when I was twelve, dedicating my life to Jesus. Who else would have me? Certainly not Jean Timberlake."

"Were you interested in her?"

"Sure, I was. I was seventeen years old and doomed to be a virgin for life. My bad luck. Good looks ranked high with her because she was so beautiful herself. After that came money, power . . . sex, of course. I thought about her incessantly. She was so completely venal."

"But not with you?"

He went back to his work, sliding pills into the trough. "Unfortunately not."

"Who, then?"

The lips curved up again in that nearly beatific smile. "Well, let's see now. How much trouble should I make?"

I shrugged, watching him carefully. "Just tell me the truth. What else can you do?"

"I could keep my mouth shut, which is what I've done to date."

"Maybe it's time to speak up," I said.

He was quiet for a moment.

"Who was she involved with?"

His smile finally disappeared. "The Right Reverend Haws. What a pal he turned out to be. He knew I lusted after her, so he counseled me in matters of purity and self-control. He never mentioned what he did with her himself."

I stared at him. "Are you sure of that?"

"She worked at the church, cleaning Sunday-school rooms. Wednesdays at four o'clock before choir practice started, he would pull his pants down around his knees and lie back across his desk while she worked on him. I used to watch from the vestry . . . Mrs. Haws, our dear June, suffers from a peculiar stigmata that originated just about that time. Resistant to treatment. I know because I fill the prescriptions, one right after the other. Amusing, don't you think?"

A chill rippled down my back. The image was vivid, his tone matter-of-fact. "Who else is aware of this?"

"No one, as far as I know."

"You never mentioned it to anybody at the time?"

"Nobody asked, and I've since left the church. It turned out not to be the kind of comfort I was hoping for."

.   .   .

The San Luis county clerk's office is located in the annex, right next door to the County Courthouse on Monterey. It was hard to believe that only yesterday we were all convening for Bailey's arraignment. I found a parking place across the street, inserted coins in the meter, then headed past the big redwood and into the annex entrance. The corridor was lined with marble, a cold gray with darker streaks. The county clerk's office was on the first floor, through double doors. I set to work. Using Jean Timberlake's full name and the date of birth I'd pulled from her school records, I found the volume and page number listing her birth certificate. The records clerk looked up the original certificate and, for eleven dollars, made me a certified copy. I didn't much care if it was certified or not. What interested me was the information it contained. Etta Jean Timberlake was born at 2:26 A.M. on June 3, 1949, 6 lbs., 8 oz., 19 inches long. Her mother was listed as gravida 1, para 1, fifteen years old and unemployed. Her father was "unknown." The attending physician was Joseph Dunne.

I found a public phone and looked up his office. The number rang four times and then his answering service picked up. He was out on Thursdays, not due in again till Monday morning at ten. "Do you know how I can reach him?"

"Dr. Corsell's on call. If you'll leave your name and number, we can have him get in touch."

"What about the Hot Springs? Could Dr. Dunne be up there?"

"Are you a patient of his?"

I set the receiver back in the cradle and let myself out of the booth. Since I was already downtown, I debated briefly about stopping by the hospital to see Royce. Ann had said he was asking for me, but I didn't want to talk to him just yet. I drove back toward Floral Beach, taking one of the back roads, an undulating band of asphalt that wound past ranches, walled tract "estates," and new housing developments.

There were very few cars in the spa's parking lot. The hotel couldn't be doing enough business to sustain the good doctor and his wife. I angled my VW in close to the main building, noting as I had before the dense chill in the air. The sulfur smell of spoiled eggs conjured up images of some befouled nest.

This time I bypassed the spa entrance and went around to the front, up wide concrete stairs to the wraparound porch. A row of chaise longues lent the veranda the look of a ship's deck. Under a canopy of oaks, the ground sloped down gradually, leveling out then for a hundred yards until it met the road. On my left, in an area cleared of trees, I caught a glimpse of the deserted swimming pool in a flat oblong of sunlight. Two tennis courts occupied the only other portion of the property graced with sun. The surrounding fence was screened by shrubs, but the hollow *pok . . . pok* suggested that at least one court was in use.

I pushed through a double-wide door of carved mahogany, the upper half inset with glass. The lobby was built on a grand scale, rimmed with wooden balustrades, flooded with light from two translucent glass skylights. The main salon was currently undergoing renovation. The carpeting was obscured by yards of gray canvas dropcloth, speckled with old paint. Scaffolding erected along two walls suggested that the wood paneling was in the process of being sanded and refinished. Here, at least, the harsh smell of varnish overrode the pungent aroma of the mineral springs that burbled under the property like a cauldron.

The registration desk ran the width of the lobby, but there was no one in evidence. No reception clerk, no bellman, no painters at work. The silence had a quality about it that caused me to glance back over my shoulder, scanning the second-floor gallery. There was no one visible. Shadows hung among the eaves like spiderwebs. Wide, carpeted hallways extended on either side of the desk back into the gloomy depths of the hotel. I waited a decent interval in the silence. No one appeared. I pivoted, doing a one-eighty turn while I surveyed the place. Time to nose around, I thought.

Casually, I ambled down the corridor on the right, my passage making no sound on the densely carpeted floors. Halfway down the hall, glass-paned doors opened into a vast semicircular dining room with a wooden floor, furnished with countless round oak dining tables and matching ladder-backed chairs. I crossed to the bay windows on the far side of the room. Through the watery ripples of old glass, I saw the tennis players leave the courts, heading my way.

There were two sets of wooden swinging doors down to my left. I tiptoed the length of the room and peered into the hotel kitchen. A dull illumination from the kitchen windows cast a gray light against the expanses of stainless-steel counter. Stainless-steel fixtures, chrome, old linoleum. Heavy white crockery was stacked on open shelves. The room might have been a museum exhibit—the "moderne" style revisited, the kitchen of the future, circa 1966. I moved back toward the corridor. The murmur of voices.

I slipped into the triangle formed by the dining room

door and the wall, pressing myself flat. Through the hinged
crack, I saw Mrs. Dunne pass in a tennis outfit, racket under
one arm. She had legs about as shapely as a pair of Doric
columns, capped by the rims of her underpants, which
extended unbecomingly from the flounce of short skirt. A
varicose vein wound along one calf like a vine. Not one
strand of her white-blond hair was out of place. I assumed
her companion was her husband, Dr. Dunne. They were
gone in a flash, voices receding. The only impression I had
of him was of curly white hair, pink skin, and portliness.

As soon as they'd disappeared from sight, I slipped out
of my hiding place and returned to the lobby. A woman
in a burnt orange hotel blazer was now standing at the
registration desk. Her gaze flicked toward the corridor
when she saw me emerge, but she was apparently too
schooled in proper desk-clerk behavior to quiz me about
where I'd been.

"I was just having a look around," I said. "I may want
to book a room."

"The hotel's closed for three months for renovation.
We'll be open again April first."

"Do you have a brochure?"

"Certainly." She reached under the counter, automatically producing one. She was in her thirties, probably with
a degree in hotel management, no doubt wondering if she
was wasting her professional training in a place that smelled
like a faulty garbage disposal. I glanced at the pamphlet
she'd handed me, a match for the one I'd seen at the motel.

"Is this Dr. Dunne around? I'd like to talk to him."

"He just came in from the tennis courts. You must have
passed him in the hall."

I shook my head, baffled. "I didn't see anyone."

"Just a moment. I'll ring."

She picked up an in-house telephone, turning away from me so I couldn't read her lips while she murmured to someone on the other end. She replaced the receiver. "Mrs. Dunne will be right out."

"Great. Uh, do you have a rest room close by?"

She pointed toward the corridor to the left of the desk. "Second door down."

"I'll be right back."

I was telling a little fib. The minute I was out of sight I race-walked down the corridor to the far end where it met a transverse corridor with administrative offices on either side. All of them were empty except for one. A nice brass plaque identified it as Dr. Dunne's. I went in. He didn't seem to be there, but the chair was piled with sweaty tennis togs, and I could hear the patter of a shower being run behind a door marked Private. I took the liberty of a stroll around his desk while I waited for him. I let my fingers tippy-toe among his papers, but there was nothing of interest. A detail man had been there and had left some samples of a new anticholinergic, with accompanying literature. The glossy color enlargement showed a duodenal ulcer as large as the planet Jupiter. Oh, barf. Picture that sucker sitting in your gut.

The file cabinets were locked. I had hoped to explore his desk drawers, but I didn't want to push my luck. Some people get cranky when you snoop around like that. I cupped one hand to my ear. Shower off. Ah, that was good. The doctor and I were going to have a little chat.

17

Dr. Dunne emerged from the bathroom fully dressed, wearing kelly green slacks with a white belt, a pink and green plaid sports shirt, white loafers, pink socks. All he needed was a white sportcoat to constitute what's known as a "full Cleveland," very popular among middle-aged bon vivants in the Midwest. He had a full head of white hair, still damp, combed straight back. Tendrils were already curling up around his ears. His face was full, his complexion hot pink, eyes very blue under unruly white brows. He was probably six foot two, toting an extra fifty pounds' worth of rich food and drink, which he carried in the front like six months' worth of pregnancy. How come all the men in this town were out of shape?

He stopped in his tracks when he caught sight of me. "Yes, ma'am," he said, in response to some question I hadn't asked him yet.

I infused my tone with warmth, feigning graciousness. "Hi, Dr. Dunne. I'm Kinsey Millhone," I said, extending my hand. He responded with a minimal squeeze, three fingers pressing mine.

"Personnel's down the hall, but we're not hiring presently. The hotel won't open for business until April first."

"I'm not looking for work. I need some information about a former patient of yours."

His eyes took on that doctor-privilege look. "And who would that be?"

"Jean Timberlake."

His body language switched over to a code I couldn't read. "Are you with the police?"

I shook my head. "I'm a private detective, hired by—"

"I can't help you, then."

"Mind if I sit?"

He stared at me blankly, accustomed to his pronouncements being taken as law. He probably never had to deal with pushy people like me. He was protected from the public by his receptionist, his lab tech, his nurse, his billing clerk, his answering service, his office manager, his wife— an army of women keeping Doctor safe and untouched. "I must not have made myself clear, Miss Millhone. We have nothing to discuss."

"Sorry to hear that," I said equably. "I'm trying to find out who her father was."

"Who let you in here?"

"The desk clerk just talked to your wife," I said, which was true but not relevant.

"Young lady, I'm going to have to ask you to leave. There's no way in the world I'd give you information about the Timberlakes. I've been the personal physician to that family for years."

"I understand that," I said. "I'm not asking you to breach confidentiality—"

"You most certainly are!"

"Dr. Dunne, I'm trying to get a line on a murder suspect. I know Jean was illegitimate. I've got a copy of the birth certificate, listing her father as unknown. I don't see any reason to protect the man if you know who he was. If you don't, just say so and save us both some time."

"This is a damn outrage, barging in on me like this! You have no right to pry into that poor girl's past. Excuse me," he said darkly, crossing to the door. "Elva!" he yelled. "El!!"

I could hear someone thumping purposefully down the corridor. I put a business card on the edge of his desk. "I'm at the Ocean Street Motel if you decide to help."

I was halfway out the door when Mrs. Dunne appeared. She was still in tennis clothes, her pale cheeks flushed. I could see that she recognized me from my first visit to the place. My return wasn't greeted with the delight I had hoped for. She was holding her racket like a hatchet, the wooden rim edgewise. I eased away, keeping an eye on her. I don't usually feel that threatened by horsey women with big legs, but she had already stepped across the line into my psychological space. She moved forward a step, standing so close now I could smell her breath, no big treat.

"I was hoping to get some help on a case, but I guess I was wrong."

"Call the police," she said flatly to him.

Without any warning, she lifted the racket like a samurai sword.

I skipped back as the racket swopped down at me. "Whoa, lady! You better watch that," I said.

She struck out at me again, missing.

I had dodged in reflex. "Hey! Knock it off!"

She whacked at me again, fanning the air within an inch of my face. I jerked back. This was ludicrous. I wanted to laugh, but the racket had hissed with a savagery that made my stomach lurch. I danced backward as she advanced.

She swatted again with the Wilson and missed. Her face had taken on an expression of avid concentration, eyes glittering, lips parted slightly. Behind her, I was dimly aware that Dr. Dunne's attitude had shifted from wariness to concern.

"Elva, that's enough," he said.

I didn't think she'd heard him, or if she had, she didn't care. The racket whacked at me sideways, wielded this time like a broadax. She shifted her weight, her grip two-handed as she sliced diagonally, and sliced again.

Whack, whack!

Missing me by a hair's breadth and only because I was quick. She was totally focused and I was afraid if I turned to run, she'd catch me in the back of the head. Take a crack like that and you're talkin' blood, folks. Not a fatal impact, but one you'd prefer to skip.

Up came the racket again. The wood rim descended like a blade, too swift this time to evade. I took the brunt of it on my left forearm, raised instinctively to shield my face. The racket connected with a cracking sound. The blow was like a white flash of heat up my arm. I can't say I felt pain. It was more like a jolt to my psyche, unleashing aggression.

I caught her in the mouth with the heel of my hand, knocking her back into him. The two of them went down with a mingled yelp of surprise. The air around me felt white and empty and clean. I grabbed her shirt with an unholy strength, hauling her to her feet. Without any thought at all, I punched her once, registering an instant later the smacking sound as my fist connected with her face.

Somebody snagged my arm from behind. The desk clerk was hanging on to me, screaming incoherently. My left hand was still knotted in Elva's shirt. She tried to backstroke out of range, arms flailing as she yodeled with fear, eyes wide.

My self-control reasserted itself and I lowered my fist. She fairly crowed with relief, staring at me with astonishment. I don't know what she'd seen in my face, but I knew what I'd seen in hers. I felt giddy with power, happiness surging through me like pure oxygen. There's something about physical battle that energizes and liberates, infusing the body with an ancient chemistry—a cheap high with a sometimes deadly effect. A blow to the face is as insulting as you can get, and there's no predicting what you'll garner in return. I've seen petty barroom disputes end in death over a slap on the cheek.

Her mouth was already puffy, her teeth washed with blood. Exhilaration peaked and drained at the sight. Now I could feel pain throb in my arm and I bent with the pulse of it, panting hard. The bruise was a sharp blue vertical line, red welt spreading its blood cloud under the skin. I would swear I could see a raised line where the gut had been strung along the edge of the racket. Set upon by an evil-tempered tennis buff. It was all so damn dumb. Lucky I hadn't interrupted her at a round of golf. She'd have pounded me to a pulp with her pitching wedge. My knuckles were stinging where the skin had ripped. I hoped her rabies vaccinations were up to date.

Elva began to cry piteously, adopting the victim stance when it was she who had tried to savage me! I felt something stir and I yearned to go after her again, but the truth was I hurt, and the need to tend to myself took precedence. Dr. Dunne shepherded his wife into his office. The desk clerk in the orange blazer scurried after them while I leaned against the wall, trying to catch my breath. He might have been calling the sheriff's department, but I didn't much care.

In a moment the doctor returned, full of soothing apologies and solicitous advice. All I wanted was to get the hell out of there, but he insisted on examining my arm, assuring me it wasn't broken. God, did the man think I was an idiot? Of course it wasn't broken. He steered me into the hotel infirmary where he cleaned my battered hand. He was clearly worried, and that interested me more than anything that had transpired so far.

"I'm sorry you and Elva had a falling-out." He dabbed a stinging disinfectant on my hand, his gaze flicking quickly to my face to see if I'd react.

I said, "You know women. We get into these little tiffs." The irony was apparently lost on him.

"She's protective. I'm sure she didn't mean to offend. She was so upset, I had to give her a sedative."

"I hope you've got all your hand tools locked up. I'd hate to see the lady with a crescent wrench."

He began to put his first-aid supplies away. "I think we should try to forget the incident."

"Easy for you to say," I said. I was flexing my right hand, admiring the way the butterfly Band-Aid closed the cleft in my knuckle formed by Elva's front teeth. "I take it you still won't give me information on Jean Timberlake."

He had crossed the room to the sink, where he was washing his hands, his back turned. "I saw her that day," he said tonelessly. "I explained as much to the police at the time."

"The day she was killed?"

"That's right. She came to my office when she got the results of her pregnancy test."

"Why not have you run the test to begin with?"

"I couldn't tell you that. Perhaps she was embarrassed about the predicament she was in. She said she'd pleaded with the Lompoc doctor to abort her. He'd turned her down and I was next on her list."

He dried his hands thoroughly and hung the towel on the rack.

"And you refused?

"Of course."

"Why 'of course'?"

"Aside from the fact that back then abortion was illegal, it's something I would never do. Her mother survived an illegitimate pregnancy. No reason this girl couldn't have done the same. The world doesn't end, though she didn't seem to see it that way. She said it would ruin her life, but that simply wasn't true."

While he talked, he unlocked a cabinet and took out a big jar of pills. He shook five into a small white envelope, which he handed to me.

"What are these?"

"Tylenol with codeine."

I couldn't believe I'd need painkillers, but I tucked the envelope in my handbag. In my line of work, I get bashed around a lot. "Did you tell Jean's mother what was going on?"

"Unfortunately, no. Jean was a minor and I should have informed her mother, but I agreed to keep the matter confidential. I wish now I'd spoken up. Maybe things would have turned out differently."

"And you have no idea who Jean's father was?"

"I'd try ice on that arm," he said. "If the swelling persists, come back and see me. At the office, if you don't mind. There'll be no charge."

"Did she give you *any* indication who she was involved with?"

Dr. Dunne left the room without another word.

I scrounged a long-sleeved shirt out of the backseat of my car and pulled it on over my T-shirt so the rainbow of bruises on my arm wouldn't show. I sat there for a moment, leaning my head back against the seat, trying to marshal my forces for whatever was coming next. I was done in. It was only four o'clock and I felt as if the day had gone on forever. So many things bothered me. Tap with his shotgun shells loaded with rock salt. The $42,000 unaccounted for. Someone was maneuvering, slipping in and out like a dim figure in the fog. I had caught glimpses, but there was no way to identify the face. I pulled myself upright and started the car, heading into town again so I could talk to Royce.

I found the hospital on Johnson, just a few blocks from the high school, the architecture chunky and nondescript. No design awards for this one.

Royce was on the medical-surgical floor. The soles of my boots squeaked faintly against the highly polished vinyl tiles. I passed the nurses' station, following the room numbers. Nobody paid any attention to me as I made my way down the hall, averting my eyes when I passed an open door. The sick, the injured, and the dying have very little privacy as it is. Out of the corner of my eye, I could see that most of them lay abed in a cluster of flower arrangements, get-well cards propped open, their television sets on. I could smell green beans. Hospitals always smell like canned vegetables to me.

I came to Royce's room. I paused just outside the door

and disconnected my feelings. I went in. Royce was asleep. He looked like a captive, sides pulled up around his bed, an IV like a tether connecting him to a pole. A clear blue plastic oxygen cone covered his nose. The only sound was the breath whiffling through his lips in an intermittent snore. His teeth had been taken away from him, lest he bite himself to death. I stood by the bed and watched him.

He'd been sweating and his white hair was lank, plastered in long strands across his forehead. His hands lay palms-up on the covers, large and raw, fingers twitching now and then. Was he dreaming, like a dog, of his hunting days? In a month he'd be gone, this ornery mass of protoplasm driven by countless irritations, by dreams, by desires unfulfilled. I wondered if he'd live long enough to have what he wanted most—his son, Bailey, whose fate he'd entrusted to my care.

18

At five-thirty I was knocking on Shana Timberlake's door, already convinced there was no one home. Her battered green Plymouth was no longer in the drive. The cottage windows were dark and the drawn front curtains had that blank look of no occupancy. I tried the knob without luck, always interested in the notion of an unsupervised inspection of the premises, a specialty of mine. I did a quick detour around to the back, checking the rear door. She'd put a second bag of trash out, but I could see through the kitchen window that the dirty dishes were piling up again and the bed was unmade. The place looked like a flophouse.

I went back to the motel. What I wanted most in the world was to lay my little head down and go to sleep, but I couldn't see a way to pull that off. I had too much work to do, too many troubling questions yet to ask. I stepped into the office. As usual, the desk was unmanned, but I could hear Ori on the telephone in the family living room. I slipped under the counter and knocked politely on the door frame. She glanced up, catching sight of me, and motioned me in.

She was taking reservations for a family of five, negotiating a sofa bed, a crib, and a cot with variations in the room rate. Maxine, the cleaning lady, had come and gone with very little evidence of her effectiveness. All she'd done, as far as I could see, was to clear off a few surfaces, leaving a residue of furniture oil in which dust was settling. The counterpane on Ori's hospital bed was now littered with junk mail, news clippings, and old magazines, along with that mysterious collection of coupons and fliers that seems to accumulate on end tables everywhere. The wastebasket beside the bed was already spilling over. Ori was idly sorting and discarding as she talked. She concluded her business and set the telephone aside, fanning herself with a windowed envelope.

"Aw, Kinsey. What a day it's been. I think I'm comin' down with something. Lord only knows what. Everybody I talk to has the twenty-four-hour flu. I feel so achy all over and my head's about to bust."

"I'm sorry to hear that," I said. "Is Ann around?"

"She's inspecting some rooms. Every time we get a new maid we have to check and double-check, makin' sure the job's done right. Of course, the minute one's trained, off she goes again and you have to start from scratch. Well, look at you. What'd you do to your hand there, poke it through a winda screen?"

I glanced at my knuckles, trying to think of a convincing fib. I didn't think I'd been hired to punch out the local doctor's wife. Bad form, and I was embarrassed now that I'd lost control of myself. Fortunately, my ills were of only passing interest, and before I could answer, she was back to her own.

She scratched at her arm. "I got this rash," she said, mystified. "Can you see them little bumps? Itch? It's like to drove me insane. I never heard of any kind of flu like that, but I don't know what else it could be, do you?"

She held her arm up. I peered dutifully, but all I could see were the marks she'd made while clawing at herself. She was the kind of woman who would launch, any minute, into a long monologue about her bowels, thinking perhaps that her flatulence had some power to fascinate. How Ann Fowler survived in this atmosphere of medical narcissism was beyond me.

I glanced at my watch. "Oh gee, I better get upstairs."

"Well, I'm not gonna let you do that. You sit right down here and visit," Ori said. "With Royce gone, and my arthritis acting up, I don't know where my manners have went. We never had a chance to get to know one another." She patted the side of the bed as if I might be a lucky pup, allowed at last on the furniture.

"I wish I could, Ori, but you know I have to—"

"Oh no, you don't. It's after five o'clock and not even supper time yet. Why would you have to run off at this hour?"

My mind went blank. I stared at her mutely, unable to think of any plausible excuse. I have a friend named Leo who became phobic about old ladies after one wrapped a turd in waxed paper and put it in his trick-or-treat bag. He was twelve at the time and said that aside from spoiling Halloween for him, it ruined all his candy corn. He never could trust old folks after that. I'd always been fond of the elderly, but now I was developing much the same distaste.

Ann appeared in the doorway, a clipboard in hand. She shot me a distracted look. "Oh, hello, Kinsey. How are you?"

Ori launched right in, not wanting to let anybody else establish a conversational beachhead. She held her arm out again. "Ann, honey, look at this here. Kinsey says she's never seen anything like this in her life."

Ann gave her mother a look. "Could you just wait a minute, please."

Ori didn't seem to pick up on the prickliness. "You're going to have to go to the bank first thing in the morning. I paid Maxine out of petty cash and there's hardly anything left."

"What happened to the fifty I gave you yesterday?"

"I just told you. I paid Maxine with that."

"You paid her fifty dollars? How long was she here?"

"Well, you needn't take that tone. She come at ten and didn't leave till four and she never set down once except to eat her lunch."

"I bet she ate everything in sight."

Ori seemed offended. "I hope you don't begrudge the poor woman a little bite of lunch."

"Mother, she worked six hours. What are you paying her?"

Ori, uneasy on this point, began to pluck at the covers. "You know her son has been sick, and she says she doesn't see how she can keep cleaning for six dollars an hour. I told her we could go to seven."

"You gave her a raise?"

"Well, I couldn't very well tell her no."

"Why not? That's ridiculous. She's slow as molasses and she does shitty work."

"Well, pardon *me*, I'm sure. What's wrong with you?"

"Nothing's wrong! I've got problems enough. The rooms upstairs were a mess, and I had to do two of them again—"

Ori cut in. "That's no reason to snap at me. I told you not to hire the girl. She looked like some kind of foreigner with that black hair braided down the back."

"Why do you do this? The minute I walk in the door,

you're all over me. I've asked you and asked you to give
me time to catch my breath! But oh no . . . whatever you
want is the most important thing in the world."

Ori shot me a look. This was the kind of treatment a
sick old woman was subjected to. "I was just trying to help,"
she said, her voice quavering.

"Oh stop that!" Ann said. She left the room in exasperation. A moment later, we could hear her in the kitchen
banging drawers and cabinet doors. Ori wiped at her eyes,
making certain I noticed how upset she was.

"I have to make a phone call," I murmured and eased
out of the room before she could enlist my support.

I went upstairs, feeling out of sorts. I had never worked
for such unpleasant people in my life. I locked myself in
my room and lay down on the bed, too exhausted to move
and too unsettled to sleep. The tensions of the day were
piling up, and I could feel my head begin to pound from
the lack of sleep. Belatedly, I realized I'd never eaten lunch.
I was starving.

"God," I said aloud.

I got out of bed, stripped, and headed for the shower.
Fifteen minutes later, I was dressed in fresh clothes and
on my way out. Maybe a decent dinner would help get me
back on track. It was absurdly early, but I never eat at a
fashionable hour anyway, and in this town the concept
would be wasted.

Floral Beach has a choice of restaurants. There's the
pizza parlor on Palm Street, and on Ocean, there's the
Breakwater, the Galleon, and the Ocean Street Café, which
is open for breakfast only. A line was already forming
outside the Galleon. I gathered the Early Bird Special
drew crowds from as far away as two blocks. The sign in-

dicated "Family-Style Dining," which means no booze is served and there are shrieking kids on booster seats banging spoons.

I pushed into the Breakwater, heartened by the notion of a full bar. The interior was a mix of nautical and Early American: maple captain's chairs, blue-and-white-checked cloths on the tables, candles in fat red jars encased in the kind of plastic webbing it's fun to fiddle with while you talk. Above the bar, fishing nets were draped across the wooden spokes of a ship's wheel. The hostess was dressed in a mock pilgrim's costume, which consisted of a long skirt and a tight bodice with a low-cut neckline. She had apparently donned an Early American push-up bra because her perky little breasts were forced together like two patty-pan squash. If she leaned over too far, one was going to pop right out. A couple of guys at the bar kept an eye on her, hoping against hope.

Aside from those two, the place was nearly deserted and she seemed relieved to have some business. She seated me in the no-smoking section, which is to say between the kitchen and the pay phone. The menu she handed me was oversized, bound with a tasseled cord, and featured steak and beef. Everything else was deep-fried. I was wrestling with the choice of 'plump shrimp, litely battered & served with our chef's own secret sause,' or 'tender sea scallops, batter-coated, litely sauteed and served with a zesty sweet 'n' sour dip,' when Dwight Shales materialized at my table. He looked as if he'd showered and changed clothes, too, in preparation for a big, hot night on the town.

"I thought that was you," he said. "Mind if I sit down?"

"Be my guest," I said, indicating the empty seat. "What's the story here? Should I have eaten at the Galleon?"

He pulled out a chair and sat down. "The same people own both."

"Well, then, how come the line's so long over there, and this place is empty?"

"Because it's Thursday and the Galleon offers free barbecued ribs as an appetizer. The service is always lousy, so you're not missing anything."

I surveyed the menu again. "What's good here?"

"Not much. All the seafood is frozen and the chowder comes out of cans. The steak is passable. I order the same thing every time I come. Filet mignon, medium rare, with a baked potato, tossed salad with bleu cheese, and apple pie for dessert. If you have two martinis up front, you'll think it's the fourth best meal you ever ate. Up from that is any quarter pounder with cheese."

I smiled. He was flirting, a hitherto unsuspected aspect of his personality. "You're joining me, I hope."

"Thanks. I'd like that. I hate to eat alone."

"Me, too."

The waitress appeared and we ordered drinks. I confess I was curing my fatigue with a martini on the rocks, but it was quick and efficient and I enjoyed every minute of it. While we talked, I did a covert assessment of him. It interests me how people's looks change as you get to know them. The first flash is probably the most accurate, but there are occasions when a face undergoes a transformation that seems almost magical. With Dwight Shales, there seemed to be a more youthful persona submerged in a fifty-five-year-old shell. His hidden self was becoming more visible to me as he talked.

I listened with both eyes and one ear, trying to discern what was really going on. Ostensibly, we were discussing how we spent our leisure time. He gravitated toward backpacking, while I tended to amuse myself with the abridged California Penal Code and textbooks on auto theft. While his mouth made noises about an assault of ticks on a recent day hike, his eyes said something else. I disconnected my brain and fine-tuned my receiver, picking up his code. This man was emotionally available. That was the subliminal message.

A chunk of lettuce dropped off my fork and my mouth closed on the bare tines. Ever the sophisticate. I tried to act as though I preferred to eat my salad that way.

Midway through the meal, I changed the tenor of the conversation, curious what would happen if we talked about something personal. "What happened to your wife? I take it she died."

"Multiple sclerosis. She went into remission numerous times, but it always caught up with her. Twenty years of that shit. Toward the end, she couldn't do anything for herself. She was luckier than most, if you want to look at it that way. Some patients are rapidly incapacitated, but Karen wasn't in a wheelchair until the last sixteen months or so."

"I'm sorry. It sounds grim."

He shrugged. "It was. Sometimes it looked like she had it licked. Long periods symptom-free. The hell of it was she was misdiagnosed early on. She'd been plagued by minor health problems, so she started seeing a local chiropractor for what she thought was gout. Of course, once he got hold of her, he mapped out a whole bullshit program that only postponed her getting real help. Class three subluxation. That's what he said it was. I should have sued his ass off, but what's the point?"

"She wasn't a patient of Dr. Dunne's, by any chance?"

He shook his head. "I finally forced her to see an internist in town and he referred her to UCLA for a workup. I guess it didn't matter in the final analysis. Things probably would have come out the same, either way. She handled it much better than I did, that's for sure."

I couldn't think of a thing to say to him. He talked about her for a while and then went on to something else.

"May I ask you about your relationship with Shana Timberlake?"

He seemed to debate briefly. "Sure, why not? She's become a good friend. Since my wife died, I've spent a lot of time with her. I'm not having an affair with the woman, but I do enjoy her company. I know tongues in town are wagging, but to hell with it. I'm too old to worry about that sort of thing anymore."

"Have you seen her today? I've been trying to track her down."

"No, I don't think so."

I looked over to see Ann Fowler coming in the door. "Oh, there's Ann," I said.

Dwight turned and caught her eye, motioning to her with pleasure. As she approached, he got up and borrowed a chair from a nearby table and moved it over to ours. The dark mood was still with her. She radiated tension, her mouth looking pinched. If Dwight was aware of it, he gave no sign.

He held her chair. "Would you like a drink?"

"Yes, sherry." She signaled for the waitress before he had a chance. He sat down again. I noticed she was avoiding eye contact with me. And drinking? That seemed odd.

"Have you eaten?" I asked.

"You could have told me you wouldn't be with us for dinner tonight."

I felt my cheeks heat at her tone. "I'm sorry. It didn't even occur to me. I was going to take a nap when it dawned on me I hadn't eaten all day. I took a quick shower and came straight over here. I hope I didn't put you out."

She didn't bother to reply to that. I could see that unconsciously she'd adopted her mother's strategy, hanging on to her martyrdom and milking it. I'm not crazy about this as a mode of interaction.

The waitress arrived and asked Ann what she wanted. Before she disappeared, Dwight snagged the woman's attention. "Hi, Dorothy. Has Shana Timberlake been in today?"

"Nope. Not that I've seen. She's usually here for lunch, but she may have gone in to San Luis. Thursday's her day to shop."

"Well, if you see her, tell her to give me a buzz if you would."

"Will do." Dorothy moved away from the table, and he turned back to us.

"How are you, Dwight?" Ann said, with forced pleasantness. It was clear she was cutting me right out of the loop.

I was too tired to play games. I finished my coffee, tossed a twenty on the table, and excused myself.

"You're leaving us?" Dwight said, with a quick look at his watch. "It's not even nine-thirty."

"It's been a long day and I'm beat."

We went through our good-night maneuvers, Ann being only minimally more polite than she had been. Her sherry arrived as I left the table and headed for the door. I thought Dwight seemed slightly disappointed at my departure, but I might have been kidding myself. Martinis bring out the latent romantic in me. Also headaches, if anybody's interested.

19

The night was clear. The moon was a pale gold, with gray patches forming patterns across the face of it like bruises on a peach. The door to Pearl's Pool Hall was standing open as I passed, but there were no pool players in evidence and just a handful of people at the bar. The jukebox was playing a country-western tune of some haunting melodic sort. There was one couple on the dance floor, the woman stony-faced as she looked over the man's shoulder. He was doing a hip-swaying two-step, moving her in a circle while she pivoted in place. I slowed, recognizing them from the arraignment. Pearl's son and daughter-in-law. On an impulse, I went in.

I perched on a barstool and turned so I could watch them. He seemed self-absorbed. She was bored. They reminded me of one of those middle-aged couples I see in restaurants whose interest in one another has long ago expired. He was wearing a tight, white T-shirt that bowed slightly at the waist where his love handles bulged out. His jeans were low-slung, too short for the heel on his cowboy boots. His hair was a curly blond, damp from all the styling mousse, which I had to guess was going to smell as pungent as buffalo musk. His face was smooth and full, with a pug nose, a sulky mouth, and an expression that suggested he was very smitten with himself. This guy spent a lot of time in front of bathroom mirrors, combing his hair while he decided which side of his mouth to hang his cigarette from. Daisy approached, her gaze following mine.

"That's Pearl's son and daughter-in-law?"

"Yep. Rick and Cherie."

"Happy-looking pair. What's he do?"

"A welder at a company makes storage tanks. He's an old friend of Tap's. She works for the telephone company, or at least she did. She quit a couple weeks back and they been squabbling ever since. Want a beer?"

"Sure, why not?"

Pearl was on the far end of the room in a conversation with a couple of guys in bowling shirts. He nodded when he saw me, and I gave him a wave. Daisy brought my beer in a frosty Mason jar.

The dance number ended. Cherie left the dance floor, with Rick close behind. I put a couple of bucks on the bar and crossed to their table just as they sat down. Close up, her features were delicate, her blue eyes set off by dark lashes and brows. She might have been pretty if she'd had the resources. As it was, she was thin in a way that spoke of poor nutrition: bony shoulders, bad coloring, lifeless hair pulled back with a couple of plastic barrettes. Her fingernails were bitten right down to the quick. The wrinkles in her sweater suggested that she'd snatched it, in passing, from a pile on the bedroom floor. Both Rick and Cherie smoked.

I introduced myself. "I'd like to talk to you, if you don't mind."

Rick lounged in his seat, hooking his arm over the back

of his chair while he checked me out. His legs were now extended insolently into my path. The pose was probably meant to look macho, but I suspected his waistband had jammed his stomach right up against his spleen and he was affording himself some relief. "I heard about you. You're that private detective old man Fowler hired." His tone was knowing. Nobody was going to put one over on him.

"Could I sit down?"

Rick motioned me to a chair, which he kicked out with his foot—his notion of etiquette. I sat down. Cherie didn't seem thrilled with my company, but at least it saved her being alone with him. "So what's the deal?" he said.

"The deal?"

"Yeah. What do you want with me?"

"Information about the murder. I understand you saw Bailey and Jean together the night she was killed."

"What of it?"

"Can you tell me what happened? I'm trying to get a feel for what was going on."

From the far side of the room, I saw Pearl's attention focus on our table. He extracted himself from his conversation and ambled over. He was a big man, so that even the exertion of crossing the room left him breathing heavily. "I see you've met my boy and his wife."

I rose halfway from my seat and shook his hand. "How are you, Pearl? Are you joining us?"

"Could." He pulled out a chair and took a seat, signaling to Daisy to bring him a beer. "You fellas want anything?"

Cherie shook her head. Rick ordered another beer.

"How about you?" Pearl said to me.

"I'm fine."

He held up two fingers and Daisy began to fill a jar from

the dispenser hose at the bar. Pearl turned back to me. "They catch Bailey yet?"

"Not as far as I know."

"Heard Royce had him a heart attack."

"An attack of some kind. I'm not sure what it was. He's in the hospital now, but I haven't really talked to him."

"Fella's not long for this world."

"Which is why I hope to wrap this thing up," I said. "I was just asking Rick about the night he saw Jean Timberlake."

"Sorry to interrupt. You go right ahead."

"Not much to tell," Rick said uncomfortably. "I drove by and spotted the two of 'em getting out of Bailey's truck. They looked drunk to me."

"They were staggering?"

"Well, not that, but hanging on to each other."

"And that was midnight?"

Rick made a visual reference to his father, who had turned at Daisy's approach. "Could have been a little after that, but right around there." Daisy put the two beers on the table and went back to the bar.

"You see any cars passing? Anybody else on the street?"

"Nuh-unh."

"Bailey says it was ten o'clock. I'm puzzled by the discrepancy."

Pearl intervened. "Coroner put the time of death close to midnight. Naturally, Bailey'd like everybody to believe he was home in bed by then."

I glanced at Rick. He should have been home in bed himself. "You were how old, seventeen at the time?"

"Who, me? I'se a junior in high school."

"You'd been out on a date?"

"I'd been at my grammaw's and I was on my way home. She'd had a stroke and Dad wanted me to stay with her till the visiting nurse got there." Rick lit another cigarette.

Cherie's face was expressionless, except for an occasional flicker of the mouth—meaning what? She checked her nails and decided to give herself a manicure with her teeth.

"Which was when?"

"Ten after twelve. Something like that."

Pearl spoke up again. "Nurse on the early shift called in sick so I had Rick sit in till the other one got there."

"I take it your grandmother lived in the neighborhood."

"Why all the questions?" Rick asked.

"Because you're the only witness who can actually put him at the scene."

"Of course he was there. He admits that himself. I saw the two of 'em get out of his truck."

"It couldn't have been somebody else?"

"I know Bailey. I've known him all my life. He wasn't any farther away than here to there. The two of 'em drove down to the beach and he parked and they got out and went down the steps." Rick's eyes strayed back to his father's face. He was lying through his teeth.

"Excuse me," Cherie said. "Does anybody mind if I bug out? I got a headache."

"You go on home, baby," Pearl said. "We'll be there in a bit."

"Nice meeting you," she said to me briefly, as she got up. She didn't bother to say anything to Rick. Pearl watched her departure, clearly fond of her.

I caught Rick's eye again. "Did you see anybody coming in or out of the motel?" I knew I was being persistent, but I figured this might be the only chance I'd get to question him. His father's presence probably didn't help, but what was I going to do?

"No."

"Nothing out of the ordinary?"

"I already told you that. It was just regular. Normal."

Pearl spoke up. "You've about exhausted the subject, haven't you?"

"Looks like it," I said. "I keep hoping I'll pick up a lead."

"It'd be nothin' more than damn luck after all this time."

"Sometimes I can make luck," I said.

Pearl leaned forward, thrusting his double chins at me. "I'll tell you something. You're never going to get anywhere with this. It's no point. Bailey's confessed and, by God, it's gonna stick. Royce don't want to believe he's guilty and I can understand that. He's near dead and he doesn't want to go to his grave with a cloud hanging over him. I feel sorry for the old fool, but that doesn't change the facts."

"How do we even know what the facts are at this point?" I said. "She died seventeen years ago. Bailey disappeared the year after that."

"My point exactly," Pearl said. "This is old news. A dead horse. Bailey admitted he was guilty. He could've been out by now instead of starting all over. Look at him. He's taken off again. Who knows where, doing who knows what. We might any of us be in danger. We don't know what's going through his head."

"Pearl, I don't want to argue with you, but I won't give up."

"Then you're a bigger fool than he is."

I'd just about had my fill of argumentative old men. Who asked him? "I appreciate your assessment. I'll keep that in mind." I glanced at my watch. "I better get back."

Neither Rick nor Pearl seemed sorry to see me go. I could feel their eyes on me as I left the place, giving me the kind of look that makes you want to step up your pace a bit.

I walked the two blocks to the motel. It was just after ten, and two black-and-whites were parked side by side across the street. Two young cops were leaning on the fenders, coffee cups in hand while their radio kept up a running account of what was going on in town. I kept thinking about Rick. I knew he was lying, but I had no idea why. Unless he killed her himself. Maybe he'd made sexual advances and she'd laughed him off. Or maybe he'd just been trying to look important at the time, the last man who'd seen Jean Timberlake alive. It was bound to lend him status in a community the size of Floral Beach.

I took my keys out as I went up the outside stairs. It was dark on the second-floor landing, but I caught a whisper of cigarette smoke. I stopped.

There was someone standing in the shadow of the vending machine across from my room. I reached for the penlight in my handbag and flicked it on.

Cherie.

"What are you doing here?"

She stepped out of the dark, the dim glow of the flashlight washing her face with white. "I'm sick of Rick's b.s."

I moved to my door and unlocked it, glancing back at her. "You want to come in and talk?"

"I better not. If he gets home and I'm out, he'll want to know where I've been."

"He's been lying, hasn't he?"

"It wasn't midnight when he saw them. It was closer to ten. He was on his way to see me. He knew if his Daddy found out he'd left his granny by herself, he'd get the crap beat outta him."

"So what happened then, he left and went back?"

"Right. He got back by the time the visiting nurse showed up for her shift. Later, when it turned out Jean Timberlake had been murdered, he said he saw her and Bailey. He just blurted it out before he realized how much trouble he'd be in. So then he had to make the time different so he wouldn't get his ass whipped."

"And Pearl still doesn't know?"

"I'm not sure about that. He's real protective of Rick, so maybe he suspects. It didn't seem like it mattered, once Bailey pleaded guilty. He said he killed her, so nobody really cared what time it was."

"Did Rick tell you what really happened?"

"Well, he did see 'em get out of the truck and go down to the beach. He told me that at the time, but Bailey really could have gone back to his room and passed out like he claimed."

"Why are you telling me?"

"It's no skin off my butt. I'm leaving him anyway, first chance I get."

"You never told anyone else?"

"With Bailey gone all those years, who was I going to tell? Rick made me swear I'd keep my mouth shut and I've done it, but I can't stand listening to any more bull. I want my conscience clear and then I'm heading out."

"Where will you go if you leave Floral Beach?"

She shrugged. "Los Angeles. San Francisco. I got a hundred bucks for the bus and I'll just see how far it goes."

"Is there any chance Rick could have been involved with her?"

"I don't think he killed her, if that's what you mean. I wouldn't stick with him if I thought he did that. Anyway, the cops know he lied about the time and they never cared."

"The cops knew?"

"Sure, I'd assume so. They probably saw her themselves. Ten o'clock, they're always down at the beach. That's where they have their coffee break."

"Jesus, people in this town have sure been content to make Bailey the scapegoat."

Cherie stirred restlessly. "I have to get home."

"If you think of anything else, will you let me know?"

"If I'm still around, I will, but don't count on it."

"I appreciate that. Take care."

But she was gone.

20

It was eleven o'clock when I finally eased into bed. Exhaustion was making my whole body ache. I lay there, acutely aware of my heartbeat as it pulsed in my throbbing forearm. This would never do. I hauled myself into the bathroom and washed down some Tylenol with codeine. I didn't even want to think about the day's events. I didn't care what had happened seventeen years ago or what would happen seventeen years hence. I wanted healing sleep in excessive doses, and I finally gave myself up to a formless oblivion, undisturbed by dreams.

It was 2:00 A.M. when the ringing telephone woke me from the dead. I picked up the receiver automatically and laid it on my ear. I said, "What."

The voice was labored and slow, low-pitched, gravelly, and mechanically slurred. "You bitch, I'm going to tear you apart. I'm going to make you wish you'd never come to Floral Beach. . . ."

I slammed the phone down and snatched my hand back before the guy got out another word. I sat straight up, heart thudding. I'd been sleeping so soundly that I didn't know where I was or what was going on. I searched the shadows, disoriented, tuning in belatedly to the sound of

the ocean thundering not fifty yards away, discerning in
the tawny reflection of the streetlights that I was in a motel
room. Ah yes, Floral Beach. Already, I was wishing I'd
never come. I pushed the covers back and padded, in my
underpants and tank top, across the room, peering out
through the sheers.

The moon was down, the night black, surf tumbling its
pewter beads along the sand. The street below was deserted. A comforting oblong of yellow light to my left suggested that someone else was awake—reading, perhaps, or
watching late-night TV. As I watched, the light was flicked
off, leaving the balcony dark.

The phone shrilled again, causing me to jump. I crossed
to the bed table and lifted the receiver cautiously, placing
it against my ear. Again, I heard the muffled, dragging
speech. It had to be the same voice Daisy had heard at
Pearl's when someone called to ask for Tap. I pressed a
hand to my free ear, trying to pick up any background
sounds from the caller's end of the line. The threat was
standard fare, real ho-hum stuff. I kept my mouth shut
and let the voice ramble on. What kind of person made
crank calls like this? The real hostility lay in the disruption
of sleep, a diabolical form of harassment.

The repeat call was a tactical error. The first time, I'd
been too groggy to make the sense of it, but I was wide
awake now. I squinted in the dark, blanking out the message so I could concentrate on the mode. Lots of white
noise. I heard a click, but the line was still alive. I said,
"Listen, asshole. I know what you're up to. I'll figure out
who you are and it won't take me long, so enjoy." The
phone went dead. I left mine off the hook.

I kept the lights off while I pulled my clothes on in haste

and gave my teeth a quick brushing. I knew the trick. In my handbag I carry a little voice-activated tape recorder with a variable speed. If you record at 2.4 centimeters per second and play back at 1.2, you can produce the same effect: that sullen, distorted, growling tone that seems to come from a talking gorilla with a speech impediment. There was no way to guess, of course, how the voice would sound if it were played back at the proper speed. It could be male or female, young or old, but it almost had to be a voice I would recognize. Else, why the disguise?

I unlocked my briefcase and took out my little .32, loving the smooth, cold weight of it against my palm. I'd only fired the Davis at the practice range, but I could hit damn near anything. I tucked my room key in my jeans pocket and eased the door open a crack. The corridor was dark, but it had an empty feel to it. I didn't really believe anyone would be there. People who intend to kill you don't usually give fair warning first. Murderers are notoriously poor sports, refusing to play by the rules that govern the rest of us. These were scare tactics, meant to generate paranoia. I didn't take the death-and-dismemberment talk very seriously. Where could you rent a chain saw at this time of night? I pulled the door shut behind me and slipped down the stairs.

The light was on in the office, but the door leading into the Fowlers' living quarters was closed. Bert was asleep. He sat behind the counter in a wooden chair, his head angled to one side. The snores flapping through his lips sounded like a whoopee cushion, flat and wet. His suitcoat was neatly arranged on a wire hanger on the wall. He'd pulled on a cardigan, with cuffs of paper toweling secured by rubber bands to protect his sleeves. From what, I wasn't sure. He didn't seem to have any work to do aside from manning the desk for late-night arrivals.

"Bert," I said. No response. "Bert?"

He roused himself, giving his face a dry scrub with one hand. He looked at me blearily and then blinked himself awake.

"I take it the calls I just got didn't come through the switchboard," I said. I watched while the electrical circuits in his brain reconnected.

"Excuse me?"

"I just received two calls. I need to know where they came from."

"Switchboard's closed," he said. "We don't put calls through after ten o'clock." His voice was hoarse from sleep and he had to cough to clear his throat.

"News to me," I said. "Bailey called me the other night at two A.M. How'd he manage that?"

"I connected him. He insisted on that or I wouldn't have done. I hope you understand about my contacting the sheriff. He's a fugitive from—"

"I know what he is, Bert. Could we talk about the calls that just came in?"

"Can't help you there. I don't know anything about that."

"Could someone ring my room without coming through the switchboard?"

He scratched at his chin. "Isn't any way I know of. You can phone out, but you can't phone in. Ask me, the whole business is a pain in the neck. Over at the Tides, they don't even have phones in the rooms. System costs more than it's worth anyhow. We had this one installed a few years back, and then half the time it's down. What's the point?"

"Can I see the board?"

"You're welcome to take a look, but I can tell you right

now no calls came through. I been on duty since nine o'clock and there hasn't been a one. I've been doing accounts payable. Phone hasn't made a peep."

I could see a pile of envelopes tucked in the box for outgoing mail. I ducked under the counter. The telephone console was on one end, eighteen inches wide, with a numbered button for every room. The only light showing was my room, 24, because I'd left my phone off the hook. "You can tell when a phone's in use by the light?"

"By the light," he said, "that's correct."

"What about room-to-room? Couldn't a motel guest bypass the switchboard and dial direct?"

"Only if they knew your room number."

I thought back to all the times I'd given out my business card in the last couple of days, the telephone number at the Ocean Street neatly jotted on the back—my room number too, in some cases . . . but which? "If a phone's in use, you can't tell from the light whether a call is to the outside, room-to-room, or off the hook, right?"

"That's right. I could flip that switch and listen in, but of course that'd be against the rules."

I studied the console. "How many rooms are occupied?"

"I'm not at liberty to say."

"What, we have national security at stake here?"

He stared at me for a moment and then indicated with a put-upon air that I could check the registration cards in the upright file. While I flipped through, he hovered, wanting to be certain I didn't pocket anything. Fifteen rooms out of forty were occupied, but the names meant nothing. I don't know what I'd expected.

"I hope you're not fixing to change rooms again," he said. "We'd have to charge extra."

"Oh, really. Why is that?"

"Motel policy," he said, giving his pants a hitch.

Why was I egging him on? He looked as if he was about to launch into a discourse on management strategies over at the Tides. I said good night and went back upstairs.

There was no possibility of sleep. The phone began to make plaintive little sounds as though it were sick, so I replaced the receiver and disconnected the instrument at the jack. I left my clothes on as I had the night before, pulling the spread over me for warmth. I lay awake, staring at the ceiling while I listened to muffled noises through the wall: a cough, a toilet flushing. The pipes clanked and groaned like a clan of ghosts. Gradually, sunlight replaced the streetlights and I became aware that I was drifting in and out of consciousness. At seven I gave it up, dragged myself into the shower, and used up my allotment of hot water.

I tried the Ocean Street Café for breakfast, downing cups of black coffee with the local paper propped up in front of me so I could eavesdrop on the regulars. Faces were beginning to look familiar. The woman who ran the Laundromat was sitting at the counter, next to Ace, who was getting ragged again about his ex-wife, Betty, seated on his other side. There were two other men I recognized from Pearl's.

I was in a booth near the front, facing the plate-glass windows, with a view of the beach. Joggers were trotting along the wet-packed sand. I was too tired to do a run myself, though it might have perked me up. Behind me, the customers were chatting together as they probably had every day for years.

"Where you think he's at?"

"Lord only knows. I hope he's left the state. He's dangerous."

"They better catch him quick is all I can say. I'll shoot his ass if I see him anywheres around here."

"I bet he's got you peekin' under your bed at night."

"I peek every night. 'At's the only thrill I get. I keep hopin' to find somebody peekin' back at me." The laughter was shrill, underscored with anxiety.

"I'll come over there and help you out."

"Big help you'd be."

"I would. I got me a pistol," Ace said.

" 'At's not what Betty says."

"Yeah, he's loaded half the time, but that don't mean his pistol works."

"Bailey Fowler shows his face, you'll see different," Ace said.

"Not if I get him first," one of the other men said.

The front page of the local newspaper was a rehash of the case to date, but the tone of the coverage was picking up heat. Photographs of Bailey. Photographs of Jean. An old news photo of the crime scene, townspeople standing in the background. The faces in the crowd were blurred and indistinct, seventeen years younger than they looked today. Jean's body, barely visible, was covered with a blanket. Trampled sand. Concrete steps going up on the right. There was a quote from Quintana, who sounded pompous even then. Probably bucking for sheriff since he joined the department. He seemed like the type.

I wolfed down my breakfast and went back to the motel.

As I went up the outside stairs, I saw one of the maids knocking on the door of room 20. Her cart was parked nearby, loaded with fresh linens, vacuum cleaner mounted on the back.

"Maid service," she called. No answer.

She was short, heavyset, a gold-capped tooth showing

when she smiled. Her passkey didn't turn in the lock so she moved on to the room I'd been in before Bert had so graciously consented to the change. I let myself into room 24 and closed the door.

My bed was a tumble of covers that beckoned invitingly. I was buzzing from coffee, but under the silver shimmer of caffeine my body was leaden from weariness. The maid knocked at my door. I abandoned all hope of sleep and let her in. She moved into the bathroom, a plastic bucket in hand, filled with rags and supplies. Nothing feels so useless as hanging around while someone else cleans. I went down to the office.

Ori was behind the counter, clinging shakily to her walker while she sorted through the bills Bert had left in the box for outgoing mail. She was wearing a cotton duster over her hospital gown.

Ann called from the other room. "Mother! Where are you? God . . ."

"I'm right here!"

Ann appeared in the doorway. "What are you doing? I told you I want to do your blood test before I go up to see Pop." She caught sight of me and smiled, her dark mood gone. "Good morning."

"Good morning, Ann."

Ori was leaning heavily on Ann's supporting arm as she began to shuffle into the living room.

"You need some help?" I asked.

"Would you please?"

I slipped under the counter, supporting Ori on the other side. Ann moved the walker out of her mother's path and together we walked her back to the bed.

"Do you have to go to the bathroom while you're up?"

"I guess I best," she said.

We did a slow walk to the bathroom. Ann got her settled on the commode and then stepped into the hall, closing the door.

I glanced at Ann. "Could I ask you a couple of questions about Jean while I've got you here?"

"All right," she said.

"I took a look at her school records yesterday and I noticed that you were one of the counselors who worked with her. Can you tell me what those sessions were about?"

"Her attendance, primarily. The four of us did academic counseling—college prep requirements, dropping or adding classes. If a kid didn't get along with a teacher or wasn't performing up to snuff, we'd step in and test sometimes, or settle disputes, but that was the extent of it. Jean was obviously in trouble scholastically and we talked about the fact that it was probably connected to her home life, but I don't think any of us actually felt qualified to play shrink. We might have recommended she see a psychologist, but I know I didn't try to function with her in that capacity."

"What about her relationship to the family? She hung out here quite a bit, didn't she?"

"Well, yes. During the time she and Bailey dated."

"I get the impression both your parents were fond of her."

"Absolutely. Which only made it awkward when I tried to approach her professionally at school. In some ways, the ties were too close to permit any objectivity."

"Did she ever confide in you as a friend?"

Ann frowned. "I didn't encourage it. Sometimes she complained about Bailey—if the two of them weren't getting along—but after all, he was my brother. I was hardly going to jump in and take her side. I don't know. Maybe I should have made more of an effort with her. I've often asked myself that."

"What about other faculty or staff? Anybody else she might have confided in?"

She shook her head. "Not that I ever knew."

We heard the toilet flush. Ann stepped back into the bathroom while I waited in the hall. When Ori emerged, we maneuvered her back into the living room.

She shrugged off her duster and then we struggled to get her into bed. She must have weighed two hundred eighty pounds, all ropey fat, her skin paper white. She smelled fusty and I had to make a conscious effort not to register my distaste.

Ann began to assemble alcohol, cotton wipe, and lancet. If I had to watch this procedure again, I'd pass out.

"Mind if I use the phone?"

Ori spoke up. "I need to keep this line free for business."

"Try the one in the kitchen," Ann said. "Dial nine first."

I left the room.

21

From the kitchen, I tried Shana Timberlake's number, but got no answer. Maybe I'd stop by her place again in a bit. I intended to press her for information when I caught up with her. She held a big piece of the puzzle, and I couldn't let her off the hook. The telephone book was on the kitchen counter. I looked up Dr. Dunne's office number and tried that next. A nursey-sounding woman picked up on the other end. "Family practice," she said.

"Oh, hi. Is Dr. Dunne in the office yet?" I'd been told he was out until Monday. My business was with her.

"No, I'm sorry. This is Doctor's day at the clinic in Los Angeles. Can I be of help?"

"I hope so," I said. "I was a patient of his some years ago and I need records of the illness I was seeing him for. Can you tell me how I'd go about getting those?"

Ann came into the kitchen and moved to the refrigerator, where she removed the glass vial of insulin and stood rolling it in her palms to warm it.

"When would this have been?"

"Uhm, oh gee, 1966 actually."

"I'm sorry, but we don't keep records that far back. We consider a file inactive if you haven't seen Doctor in five years. After seven years, records are destroyed."

Ann left the room. I'd miss the injection altogether if I strung this out long enough.

"And that's true even if a patient is deceased?" I asked.

"Deceased? I thought it was your medical records we were talking about," she said. "Could I have your name please?"

I hung up. So much for Jean Timberlake's old medical chart. Frustrating. I hate dead ends. I returned to the living room.

I hadn't stalled long enough.

Ann was peering at the syringe, holding it needle up, while she tapped to make sure there were no bubbles in the pale, milky insulin. I eased toward the door, trying to be casual about it. She looked up as I passed. "I forgot to ask, did you see Pop yesterday?"

"I stopped by late afternoon, but he was asleep. Did he ask for me again?" I tried to look every place, but at her.

"They called this morning," she said irritably. "He's raising all kinds of hell. Knowing him, he wants out." She swiped alcohol on the bald flesh on her mother's thigh.

I fumbled in my handbag for a Kleenex as she plunged the needle home. Ori visibly jumped. My hands were clammy and my head was already feeling light.

"He's probably making everybody's life miserable." She was blabbing on, but the sound was beginning to fade. Out of the corner of my eye, I saw her break the needle off the disposable syringe, dropping it in the wastebasket. She began to clean up cotton wads, the paper from the lancet. I sat down on the couch.

She paused, a look of concern crossing her face. "Are you all right?"

"I'm fine. I just feel like sitting down," I murmured. I'm

sure death creeps up on you just this way, but what was I going to say? I'm a bad-ass private eye who swoons in the same room with a needle? I smiled at her pleasantly to show I was okay. Darkness was crowding my peripheral vision.

She went on about her business, heading toward the kitchen to return the insulin. The minute she left the room, I hung my head down between my knees. They say it's impossible to faint while you're doing this, but I've managed it more than once. I glanced at Ori, apologetically. She was moving her legs restlessly, unwilling, as usual, to concede that anybody might feel worse than she did. I was trying not to hyperventilate. The creeping darkness receded. I sat up and fanned myself as if this was just something I did every day.

"I don't feel good," she said. She scratched at her arm, her manner agitated. What a pair we made. Apparently her mythical rash was acting up again and I was going to have to make a medical evaluation. I sent her a wan smile, which I could feel turning to perplexity. She was wheezing now, a little mewing sound coming from her throat as she clawed at her arm. She looked at me with alarm through thick glasses that magnified the fear in her eyes.

"Oh Lord," she rasped. "It couldn't . . ." Her face was ashen, swelling visibly, hot pink welts forming on her neck.

"What is it, Ori? Can I get you anything?"

Her distress was accelerating so quickly I couldn't take it in. I crossed to the bed and then yelled toward the kitchen. "Ann, could you come in here? Something's wrong."

"Be right there," she called. I could tell from her tone I hadn't conveyed any sense of urgency.

"Ann! For God's sake, get in here!"

Suddenly I knew where I'd seen this before. When I was eight and went to Donnie Dixon's birthday party next door. He was stung by a yellow jacket and was dead before his mother reached the backyard.

Ori's hands went to her throat, her eyes rolling wildly, sweat popping out. It was clear she wasn't getting air. I tried to help, but there was nothing I could do. She grabbed for me like a drowning woman, clutching my arm with such force that I thought she'd tear off a hunk of flesh.

"Now what?" Ann said.

She appeared in the doorway, wearing an expression that was a mix of indulgence and irritation at her mother's latest bid for attention. She paused, blinking as she tried to assimilate the sight before her. "What in the world? Mother, what's wrong? Oh my God!"

I don't think more than two minutes had passed since the attack began. Ori was convulsing, and I could see a flood of urine spread along the bedding under her. The sounds she made were none that I had ever heard from a human being.

Ann's panic was a singing note that rose from low in her throat. She snatched up the phone, fumbling in her haste. By the time she had dialed 911, Ori's body was bucking as if someone were administering electric shock treatments.

It was clear the 911 dispatcher had picked up the call. I could hear a tiny female voice buzz across the room like a fly. Ann tried to respond, but the words turned into a scream as she caught sight of her mother's face. I was frantically trying CPR techniques, but I knew there wasn't any point.

Ori was still, her eyes wide and blank. She was already beyond medical help. I looked at the clock automatically

for time of death. It was 9:06. I took the phone out of
Ann's hand and asked for the police.

About 20 percent of all people die under circumstances
that would warrant an official inquiry into the cause of
death. The burden of determining cause and manner of
death usually falls to the first police officer to appear on
the scene. In this case, Quintana must have been alerted
to the call because within thirty minutes the Fowlers' living
quarters had been taken over by sheriff's department personnel: Detective Quintana and his partner, whose name
I still didn't know, the coroner, a photographer, two evidence techs, a fingerprint tech, three deputies securing the
area, and an ambulance crew waiting patiently until the
body could be removed. Any matter related to Bailey Fowler was going to be subject to official scrutiny.

Ann and I had been separated shortly after the first
county sheriff's car arrived. Clearly, no one wanted us to
confer. They were taking no chances. For all they knew,
we'd just conspired in the murder of Ori Fowler. Of course,
if we'd been brash enough to kill her, you'd think we'd also
have been smart enough to get our stories straight before
we called the cops. Maybe it was only a question of making
sure we didn't contaminate each other's account of events.

Ann, wan and shaken, sat in the dining room. She had
wept briefly and without conviction while the coroner went
through the motions of listening for Ori's heart. Now she
was subdued, answering in low tones as Quintana questioned her. She seemed numbed by circumstance. I'd seen
the reaction countless times when death is too sudden to
be convincing to those most affected by it. Later, when the
finality of the event sinks in, grief breaks through in a noisy
torrent of rage and tears.

Quintana flicked a look in my direction as I passed the door. I was on my way to the kitchen, escorted by a female deputy whose law-enforcement paraphernalia must have added ten inches to her waist measurement; heavy belt, portable two-way radio, nightstick, handcuffs, keys, flashlight, ammunition, gun and holster. I was reminded uncomfortably of my own days in uniform. It's hard to feel feminine in a pair of pants that make you look like a camel from the rear.

I took a seat at the kitchen table. I kept my face neutral, trying to act as if I wasn't sucking in every detail of the crime scene activity. I was frankly relieved to be out of sight of Ori, who was beached in death like an old sea lion washed up on the sand. She couldn't even be cold yet, but her skin was already suffused with the bleached, mottled look of decay. In the absence of life, the body seems to deteriorate before your very eyes. An illusion, of course—perhaps the same optical trickery that makes the dead appear to breathe.

Ann must have told them about injecting the insulin, because an evidence technician came into the kitchen within minutes and removed the vial of insulin, which he bagged and labeled. Unless the local labs were a lot more sophisticated than usual in a town this size, the insulin, plus all the samples of Ori's blood, urine, gastric content, bile, and viscera would probably be shipped off to the state crime lab in Sacramento for analysis. Cause of death was almost certainly anaphylactic shock. The question was, what had triggered it? Surely not the insulin after all these years—unless somebody'd tampered with the vial, a not unreasonable guess. Death might have been accidental, but I doubted it.

I looked over to the back door, where the thumb latch

on the lock had been turned to the open position. From what I'd seen, the motel office was seldom secured. Windows were left open, doors unlocked. When I thought back to all the people who'd been trooping through the place, it seemed clear that anybody could have sauntered over to the refrigerator for a peek. Ori's diabetes was common knowledge, and her insulin dependency was the perfect means of delivering a fatal dose of who-knew-what. Ann's administering the injection would only add guilt to her grief, a cruel postscript. I was curious as to what Detective Quintana was going to make of it.

As if on cue, he ambled into the kitchen and took a seat at the table across from me. I wasn't looking forward to a chat with him. Like many cops, he took up more than his share of psychological space. Being with him was like being in a crowded elevator, stuck between floors. Not an experience you seek out.

"Let's hear how you tell it," he said.

To give him credit, he seemed more compassionate than he had before, perhaps in deference to Ann. I launched into my account with all the candor I could muster. I had nothing to hide, and there wasn't any point in playing games with the man. I started with the telephone harassment in the dead of night and proceeded to the moment when I'd taken the receiver from Ann and asked for the police. He took careful notes, printing rapidly in a style that mimicked an italic typeface. By the time he finished quizzing me, I found myself trusting his thoroughness and his attention to detail. He flipped his notebook closed and tucked it in his coat pocket.

"I'm going to need a list of the people who've been in and out of here the last couple of days. I'd appreciate your help with that. Also, Miss Fowler says the family doctor isn't in the office on Fridays. So, you might keep an eye on her. She looks like she's one step away from collapse. Frankly, you don't look all that hot yourself," he said.

"Nothing that a month of sleep won't cure."

"Give me a call if anything comes up."

He gave instructions to the deputy in charge. By the time he left, much of the dusting, bagging, tagging, and picture-taking was finished and the CSI team was packing up. I found Ann still seated at the dining room table. Her gaze traveled to my face when I entered the room, but she registered no response.

"Are you all right?" I asked.

No reply.

I sat down next to her. I would have taken her hand, but she didn't seem like the type you could touch without asking permission first. "I know Quintana must have asked you this, but did your mother have allergies?"

"Penicillin," she said dully. "I remember she had a very bad reaction to penicillin once."

"What other medications was she taking?"

Ann shook her head. "Just what's on the bed table, and her insulin, of course. I don't understand what happened."

"Who knew about the allergy?"

Ann started to speak and then shook her head.

"Did Bailey know?"

"He would never do such a thing. He couldn't have . . ."

"Who else?"

"Pop. The doctor . . ."

"Dunne?"

"Yes. She was in his office when she had the first bad reaction."

"What about John Clemson? Is his the pharmacy she uses?"

She nodded.

"People from the church?"

"I suppose. She didn't make a secret of it, and you know her. Always talking about her illnesses . . ." She blinked and I saw her face suffuse with pink. Her mouth tightened, turning downward as the tears welled in her eyes.

"I'm going to call someone to come sit with you. I've got things to do. You have a preference? Mrs. Emma? Mrs. Maude?"

She curled in on herself and laid her cheek against the tabletop as if she might go to sleep. Instead she wept, tears splashing onto the polished wood surface like hot wax. "Oh God, Kinsey. I did it. I can't believe it. I actually stood there and injected the stuff. How am I going to live with that?"

I didn't know what to say to her.

I went back into the living room, avoiding the sight of the bed, which was empty now, linens stripped off and carted away with the rest of the physical evidence. Who knew what they might find in the bedding? An asp, a poisonous spider, a suicide note shoved down among the dirty sheets.

I called Mrs. Maude and told her what had happened. After we went through the obligatory expressions of shock and dismay, she said she'd be right over. She'd probably make a few quick telephone calls first, rounding up the usual members of the Family Crisis Squad. I could practically hear them crushing up potato chips for the onslaught of tuna casseroles.

As soon as she'd arrived and taken over responsibility for the office, I went upstairs to my room, locked the door, and sat down on the bed. Ori's death was confusing. I couldn't figure out what it meant or how it could possibly fit in. Fatigue was pressing down on me like an anvil, nearly crushing me with its weight. I knew I couldn't afford to go to sleep, but I wasn't sure how much longer I could go on.

The phone shrilled beside me. I hoped to God it wasn't going to be another threat. "Hello?"

"Kinsey, it's me. What the hell is going on?"

"Bailey, where are you?"

"Tell me what happened to my mother."

I told him what I knew, which didn't sound like much. He was silent for so long I thought he'd hung up. "Are you there?"

"Yes, I'm here."

"I'm sorry. Really. You never even got to see her."

"Yeah."

"Bailey, do me a favor. You have to turn yourself in."

"I'm not going to do that till I know what's going on."

"Listen to me—"

"Forget it!"

"Goddamn it, just hear me out. Then you can do anything you want. As long as you're on the street, you're going to take the blame for whatever happens. Can't you see that? Tap gets blown to hell and you take off like a shot. Next thing you know, your mother's dead, too."

"You know I didn't do it."

"Then turn yourself in. If you're in custody, at least you can't be blamed if something else goes wrong."

Silence. Finally he said, "Maybe. I don't know. I don't like this shit."

"I don't either. I hate it. Look, just do this. Call Clemson and see what he has to say."

"I know what he'll say."

"Then take his advice and do the smart thing for once!" I banged the phone down.

22

I had to get some air. I locked the door behind me and left the motel. I crossed the street and sat down on the sea wall, staring down at the stretch of beach where Jean Timberlake had died. Behind me, Floral Beach was laid out in miniature, six streets long, three streets wide. It bothered me somehow that the town was so small. It had all happened right here in the space of these eighteen blocks. The very sidewalks, the buildings, the local businesses—it all must have been much the same back then. The townspeople were no different. Some had moved away, a few had died. In the time I'd been here, I'd probably talked to the killer myself at least once. It was an affront somehow. I turned and looked back at the section of town that I could see. I wondered if someone in one of the little pastel cottages across the street had seen anything that night. How desperate could I get? I was actually contemplating a door-to-door canvass of the citizens of Floral Beach. But I had to do something. I glanced at my watch. It was after one o'clock. Tap Granger's funeral service was scheduled for two. He'd have a good turnout. The locals had talked of little else since he was gunned down. Who was going to miss this climactic event?

I crossed back to the motel, where I picked up my car and drove a block and a half to Shana Timberlake's. She'd been out when I'd called this morning, but she'd have to be home now and dressing for Tap's funeral if she intended to go. I pulled in across the street. The little wood-frame cottages in her courtyard had all the charm of army barracks. Still no Plymouth in the driveway. Her front curtains were still as they had been before. Two days' worth of newspapers were now piled near the porch. I knocked at her door, and when I got no response, I slyly tried the knob. Still locked.

An old woman stood on the porchlet of the cottage next door. She watched me with the baggy eyes of a beagle hound.

"Do you know where Shana went?"

"What?"

"Is Shana here?"

She gestured impatiently, turned away, and banged back into her place. I couldn't tell if she was mad because she couldn't hear me or because she didn't give a damn what Shana did. I shrugged and left the front porch, walking between the two cottages to the rear.

Everything looked the same, except that some animal—a dog, or maybe a raccoon—had tipped over her garbage cans and spread her trash around. Very classy stuff. I climbed the porch steps and peered in the kitchen window as I had before. It seemed clear that Shana hadn't been home for days. I tried the back door, wondering if there was any reason to break in. I couldn't think of one. It is, after all, against the law, and I don't like to do it unless I can anticipate some benefit.

As I went down the steps, I noticed a square white envelope among the papers littering the yard. The same one I'd been sniffing at the other day when I talked to her? I picked it up. Empty. Shoot. Gingerly, I began to sort through the garbage. And there it was. The card was a reproduction of a still life, an oil painting of opulent roses in a vase. There was no printed message, but inside, somebody had penned "Sanctuary. 2:00. Wed." Whom could she have met with? Bob Haws? June? I tucked the card in my handbag and drove over to the church.

The Floral Beach Baptist Church (Floral Beach's only church, if you want to get technical) was located at the corner of Kaye and Palm streets—a modest-sized white frame structure with various outbuildings attached. A concrete porch ran the width of the main building, with white columns supporting the composition roof. One thing about the Baptists, they're not going to waste the congregation's money on some worthless architect. I'd seen this particular church design several times before, and I pictured ecclesiastical blueprints making the rounds for the price of the postage. A florist's truck was parked out on the street, probably delivering arrangements for the funeral.

The double doors were standing open and I went inside. There were several paint-by-the-numbers-style stained-glass windows, depicting Jesus in an ankle-length nightgown that would get him stoned to death in this town. The apostles had arranged themselves at his feet, looking up at him like curly haired women with simpering expressions. Did guys really shave back then? As a child, I never could get anybody to answer questions like that.

The interior walls were white, the floor covered in beige linoleum tile. The pews were decorated with black satin bows. Tap Granger's coffin had been placed down near the front. I could tell Joleen had been talked into paying more than she could afford, but that's a tough pitch to resist when you're in the throes of grief. The cheapest coffin in the showroom is inevitably a peculiar shade of mauve and looks as if it's been sprayed with the same stuff they use on acoustic ceilings to cut the sound.

A woman in a white smock was placing a heart-shaped wreath on a stand. The wide lavender ribbon had "Resting In The Arms Of Jesus" written on it in a lavish gold script. I could see June Haws in the choir loft, rocking back and forth as she played the pipe organ with much working of the feet. She was playing a hymn that sounded like a tender moment in a vintage daytime soap, singing to herself in a voice with more tweeter than woofer. The bandages on her hands made her look like something newly risen from the dead. She stopped playing as I approached, and turned to look at me.

"Sorry to interrupt," I said.

She put her hands in her lap. "That's all right," she said. There was something placid about her, despite the fact that the tincture of iodine was working its way up her arms. Was it spreading, this plague, this poison ivy of the soul?

"I didn't know you doubled as the organist."

"Ordinarily, I don't, but Mrs. Emma's sitting with Ann. Haws went over to the hospital to counsel Royce. I guess the doctors told him about Oribelle. Poor soul. A reaction to her medication, was it? That's what we were told."

"Looks that way. They'll have to wait for the lab reports to be sure."

"God love her heart," she murmured, picking at the gauze wound around her right arm. She'd taken her gloves off so she could play. Her fingers were visible, sturdy and plain, the nails blunt-cut.

I took the card out of my bag. "Did you talk to Shana Timberlake here a couple of days ago?"

Her eyes flicked to the card and she shook her head.

"Could your husband have met with her?"

"You'll have to ask him about that."

"We haven't had a chance to talk about Jean Timberlake," I remarked.

"She was a very misguided girl. Pretty little thing, but I don't believe she was saved."

"Probably not," I said. "Did you know her well?"

She shook her head. Some sort of misery had clouded her eyes and I waited to see if she would speak of it. Apparently not.

"She was a member of the youth group here, wasn't she?"

Silence.

"Mrs. Haws?"

"Well, Miss Millhone. You're a mite early for the service, and I'm afraid you're not dressed properly for church," Bob Haws said from behind me.

I turned. He was in the process of shrugging himself into a black robe. He wasn't looking at his wife, but she seemed to shrink away from him. His face was bland, his eyes cold. I had a vivid flash of him stretched out across his desktop, Jean performing her volunteer work.

"I guess I'll have to miss the funeral," I said. "How's Royce?"

"As well as can be expected. Would you like to step into the office? I'm sure I can help you with any information you might be pressing Mrs. Haws for."

Why not? I thought. This man gave me the creeps, but we were in a church in broad daylight with other people nearby. I followed him to his office. He closed the door. Reverend Haws's ordinarily benevolent expression had already been replaced by something less compassionate. He stayed on his feet, moving around to the far side of his desk.

I surveyed the place, taking my time about it. The walls were pine-paneled, the drapes a dusty-looking green. There was a dark green plastic couch, the big oak desk, a swivel chair, bookcases, various framed degrees, certificates, and biblical-looking parchments on the walls.

"Royce asked me to deliver a message. He's been trying to get in touch. He won't be needing your services. If you'll give me an itemized statement, I'll see that you're paid for the time you've put in."

"Thanks, but I think I'll wait and hear it from him."

"He's a sick man. Distraught. As his pastor, I'm authorized to dismiss you on the spot."

"Royce and I have a signed contract. You want to take a peek?"

"I dislike sarcasm and I resent your attitude."

"I'm skeptical by nature. Sorry if that offends."

"Why don't you state your case and leave the premises."

"I don't have a 'case' to state at this point. I thought maybe your wife might be of help."

"She has nothing to do with this. Any help you get will have to come from me."

"Fair enough," I said. "You want to tell me about your meeting with Shana Timberlake?"

"Sorry. I never met with Mrs. Timberlake."

"What do you think this means, then?" I said. I held the card up, making sure the penned message was visible.

"I assure you I have no idea." He busied himself, needlessly straightening some papers on his desk. "Will there be anything else?"

"I did hear a rumor about you and Jean Timberlake. Maybe we should discuss that as long as I'm here."

"Any rumor you may have heard would be difficult to substantiate after all this time, don't you think?"

"I like difficulty. It's what makes my job fun. Don't you want to know what the rumor is?"

"I have no interest whatever."

"Ah well," I said. "Perhaps another time. Most people are curious when gossip like this circulates. I'm glad to hear it doesn't trouble you."

"I don't take gossip seriously. I'm surprised you do." He gave me a chilly smile, adjusting his shirt cuffs under the wide sleeves of the robe. "Now, I think you've taken up enough of my time. I have a funeral to conduct and I'd like to have time alone to pray."

I moved to the door and opened it, turning casually. "There was a witness, of course."

"A witness?"

"You know, somebody who sees somebody else do something naughty."

"I'm afraid I don't follow. A witness to what?"

I fanned the air with a loose fist, using a hand gesture he seemed to grasp right away.

His smile was losing wattage as I closed the door behind me.

Outside, the air seemed mercifully warm. I got in my car and sat for a few minutes. I leafed through my notes, looking for unturned stones. I don't even know what I was hoping to find. I reviewed the information I'd jotted down when I went through Jean Timberlake's school records. She'd lived on Palm then, just around the corner from where I sat. I craned around in the seat, wondering if it was worth it to go have a look. Oh hell, why not? In lieu of hard facts, I might as well hope for a psychic flash.

I started the VW and headed for the old Timberlake address. It was only one block down, so I could have left the car where it was, but I thought I'd better free up a parking space for the hearse. The building was on the left, two stories of shabby, pale green stucco jammed up against a steep embankment.

As I approached, I realized there was nothing much to see. The building was abandoned, the windows boarded up. On the left, a wooden staircase angled up to the second floor, where a balcony circled the perimeter. I climbed the stairs. The Timberlakes had lived in number 6, in the shadow of the hill. The whole place looked dreary. The front door of their apartment had a perfect round hole where the knob should have been. I pushed the door open. The veneer had been splintered, leaving stalagmites of lighter wood showing along the bottom edge.

The windows here were still intact, but so grimy that they might as well have been boarded up. The incoming light was filtered by dust. Soot had settled on the linoleum floors. The kitchen counters were warped, the cabinet doors hanging by their hinges. Mouse pellets suggested recent occupancy. There was only one bedroom. The back door opened off this bedroom onto the rear of the building, where the balcony connected to a clumsy stairway anchored to the side of the hill. I looked up. The sheer sides of the dirt embankment were eroded. Dense vines spilled over the lip of the hill maybe thirty feet above. Up there, at the top, I caught a glimpse of a private residence that boasted a spectacular view of the town, with the ocean stretching off to the left and a gentle hill on the right.

I returned to the apartment, trying to roll back the years in my mind. Once this place had been furnished, not grandly perhaps, but with an eye to modest comfort. From gouges in the floor, I could guess where the couch had been. I suspected they'd used the dining ell as a sleeping alcove, and I wondered which of them had slept there. Shana had mentioned Jean's sneaking out at night.

I passed through the bedroom to the back door and studied the rear stairs, letting my eye follow the line of ascent. She might have used these, climbing up to the street above, where her various boyfriends could have picked her up and dropped her off again. I tested the crude wooden handrail, which was flimsily constructed and loose after years of disuse. The risers were unnaturally steep and it made climbing hazardous. Many of the balusters were gone.

I trudged upward, huffing and puffing my way to the top. A chain-link fence ran along the crest of the embankment. There was no gate now, but there might have been at one time. Carefully I turned my head, looking back over the neighborhood from above the rooftops. The view was heady—treetops at my feet, the town spread out below—creating a mild vertigo. A parked car was about the size of a bar of soap.

I studied the house in front of me, a two-story frame-and-glass structure with a weathered exterior. The yard was immaculate and beautifully landscaped, complete with a swimming pool, decking, a hot tub, a Brown-Jordan glass-topped table and chairs. Situated anyplace else in town, the property would have required shielding shrubs for privacy. Up here, the owners could enjoy an unobstructed 180-degree view.

I struck off to the right, clinging to the fence as I made my way along the narrow path that skirted the property. When I reached the lot line on the right, I followed the fence, which defined the vacant lot next door. The street beyond was the last stretch of a cul-de-sac, with only one other house in sight. As far as I'd seen, this was Floral Beach's only classy neighborhood.

I approached the house from the front and rang the bell. I turned and stared out at the street. Up here on the hill, the sun beat down unmercifully on the chaparral. There were very few trees and there was very little to cut the wind. The ocean was visible perhaps a quarter of a mile away. I wondered if the fog stretched this far; could be desolate in its way. I rang the bell again, but there was apparently no one home. Now what?

The word "Sanctuary" was nagging at me. I'd assumed it meant the church, but there was another possibility. The hot tubs up at the mineral springs all had names like that. Maybe it was time for another visit with the Dunnes.

23

The parking lot at the mineral springs was empty except for two service trucks, one from a pool company and the other a high-sided pickup with gardening tools visible in the bed. I could hear the whine of a wood chipper somewhere on the property, and I assumed brush was being cleared. I approached the spa from the rear, as I had on my first visit to the place.

The reception area was quiet and there was no one at the desk. Maybe everyone was off at Tap's funeral. I checked the bulletin board. The schedule of classes showed nothing for Friday afternoons. I was not above nosing around on my own as long as I was there, but I had an uneasy feeling I might run into Elva Dunne.

I poked my head out into the corridor, hoping to spot a stairway that would lead to the hotel lobby above. There didn't seem to be anyone around at all. Well, gee whiz, folks, what was I supposed to do? Casually, I eased behind the desk. Taped to the counter on the right was a plot map of all the hot tubs on the hill. Curling lines represented the winding paths between the spas. A band across the top of the map was marked as a fire lane. I let my fingers do the walking, past "Peace," "Serenity," "Tranquillity," and

"Composure." A real snore, this place. "Sanctuary" was a little two-person tub located way up on the far corner of the hill. According to the schedule lying open on the desk, no one was booked into "Sanctuary" on Wednesday afternoon, or on any day after that. I flipped back a week. Nothing. My guess was that Shana's rendezvous was 2:00 A.M. instead of P.M. and probably not officially listed anyplace. I did a quick search of the drawers, which yielded nothing of significance. A cardboard box on the counter, labeled "Lost & Found," contained a silver bracelet, a plastic hairbrush, a set of car keys, and a fountain pen. I checked the pigeonholes to the left and then felt myself do a double take. The car keys in the lost-and-found box had a big metal T attached to the key ring. Shana's.

I heard footsteps in the corridor. I did a quick tippy-toe out from behind the desk. I grabbed the door open and turned, timing my entrance so it looked like I was just arriving as Elva and Joe Dunne walked into the reception area. Elva's face went blank when she caught sight of me. I pulled the card out of my handbag. Dr. Dunne seemed to know what it was right away. He patted her arm and murmured something, probably letting her know he'd take care of any dealings either of them might have to have with me. She continued on into the little side office. Dr. Dunne took me by the elbow and steered me out the door. I hadn't really wanted to go in that direction.

"This is not a good idea," he was murmuring in my left ear. He still held my arm, trotting me toward the parking lot.

"I thought this was your day at the clinic down in Los Angeles."

"I had to do a great deal of talking to persuade Mrs.

Dunne not to file assault charges against you," he said, apropos of nothing. Or was it meant to be a threat?

"Let her go for it," I said. "Make sure she does it before my knuckle heals. And while we're at it, let's have the cops take a look at this." I pulled my sleeve up far enough for him to see the pattern of bruises left by Madame's tennis serve. I jerked my arm out of his grasp and held the card up. "Want to talk about this?"

"What is it?"

"Oh, come on. It's the card you sent Shana Timberlake."

He shook his head. "I never saw that in my life."

"Excuse my language, Doctor, but that's a fuckin' fib. You wrote her last week when you were down in L.A. You must have heard about Bailey's arrest and thought the two of you better have a chat. What's the deal? Can't you just pick the phone up and call your lady love?"

"Please lower your voice."

When we reached the parking lot, he glanced back at the building. I followed his gaze, catching sight of his wife peering at us through the office window. She realized we'd spotted her, and withdrew. Dr. Dunne opened my car door on the driver's side as though to usher me in. His manner was uneasy and his eyes kept shifting to the building behind us. I pictured Mrs. Dunne belly-crawling through the bushes with a knife between her teeth.

"My wife is a paranoid schizophrenic. She's violent."

"I'll say! So what?"

"She handles all the books. If she found I'd put a call through to Shana, she'd . . . well, I don't know what she'd do."

"I'll bet I could guess. Maybe she was jealous of Jean and wrapped a belt around her neck."

His ruddy complexion glowed pinker from within, as if
a bulb had gone on behind his face. Perspiration was collecting in the crevices in his neck. "She would never do
such a thing," he said. He took a handkerchief from his
hip pocket and mopped at his forehead.

"What *would* she do?"

"This has nothing to do with her."

"What's the story, then? Where's Shana?"

"She was supposed to meet me here Wednesday night.
I was late getting up there. She never showed, or she might
have left early. I haven't spoken to her, so I don't know
where she was."

"You'd meet her here on the *premises*?" My voice fairly
squeaked with incredulity.

"Elva takes a sleeping pill every night. She never wakes."

"As far as you know," I said tartly. "I take it your affair
is ongoing?"

I saw him hesitate. "It's not an affair in that sense of the
word. We haven't been sexual with one another for years.
Shana's a dear woman. I enjoy her company. I'm entitled
to friendship."

"Oh, right. I conduct all my friendships in the dead of
night."

"Please. I'm begging you. Get in your car and go. Elva
will want to know every word we said."

"Tell her we were talking about Ori Fowler's death."

He stared at me. "Ori's dead?"

"Oh yeah. This morning she got what was probably a
penicillin shot. She went to heaven right after that."

For a moment he didn't say a word. The look on his face
was more convincing than denial. "What was the circumstance?"

I did a quick verbal sketch of the morning's events. "Does Elva have access to penicillin?"

He turned abruptly and started walking toward the building.

I wasn't going to let him off the hook that easily. "You were Jean Timberlake's father, weren't you?"

"It's over. She's dead. You'll never prove it anyway, so what difference does it make?"

"My question exactly. Did she know who you were when she asked for the abortion?"

He shook his head, walking on.

I scooted after him. "You didn't tell her the truth? You didn't even offer to help?"

"I don't want to discuss it," he said, biting off the words.

"But you do know who she was involved with, I bet."

"Why ruin a promising career?" he said.

"Some guy's career meant more than her *life?*"

He reached the door to the reception area and went in. I debated going in, but I couldn't see any purpose in pursuing the point. I needed corroboration first. I reversed myself, heading for my car. I glanced back over my shoulder. Mrs. Dunne was standing at the window again, her expression inscrutable. I wasn't sure if my voice had carried that far or not, and I didn't care. Let them sort it out. I wasn't worried about him. He knew how to look out for himself. It was Shana I was worried about. If she hadn't showed up at all Wednesday night, then where had her car keys come from? And if she'd arrived for their meeting as planned, then where the hell had she gone?

I drove back to the motel. Bert was handling the desk. Mrs. Emma and Mrs. Maude had taken charge of the Fowlers' living room. They stood side by side, plump women in their seventies, one in purple jersey, the other in mauve. Ann was resting, they said. They'd taken the liberty of having Ori's bed moved into Royce's room. The living room had been restored to some former arrangement of furniture and geegaws. It seemed enormous somehow after the overbearing presence of the hospital bed with its cranks and side rails. The bed table was gone. The tray of medications had been removed by the police. Nothing could have eradicated Ori more effectively.

Maxine had arrived, and she seemed faintly mystified to be there with no responsibility to clean. "I'll make some tea," she murmured the minute I arrived.

We were all using our library voices. I found myself mimicking that tone they all used—saccharine, solicitous, patently maternal. Actually, I was discovering that it was useful for situations like this. Mrs. Maude was all set to bring me a little lunch, but I demurred.

"I have something to take care of. I may be gone for a while."

"Well now, that's just fine," Mrs. Emma said, patting my hand. "We'll take care of everything here, so don't you worry about that. And if you want a bite to eat later, we can fix you a tray."

"Thanks." We all exchanged sorrowful smiles of a long-suffering sort. Theirs were more sincere than mine, but I must say Ori's death had generated a nagging sensation down in my gut. Why had she been murdered? What could she possibly have known? On the face of it, I couldn't see how her death bore any relation to Jean Timberlake's.

Bert appeared in the doorway and gave me a look. "Call for you," he said. "It's that lawyer fella."

"Clemson? Great. I'll take it in the kitchen. Can I pick it up in there?"

"Suit yourself," he said.

I moved into the kitchen and picked up the phone. "Hi, it's me," I said. "Hang on." I paused decently and then said, "Thanks, Bert. I've got it." There was a little click. "Go ahead."

"What was that about?" Clemson asked.

"It's not worth going into. How are things with you?"

"Interesting development. I just got a call from June Haws at the church. You never heard this from me, but apparently she's been hiding Bailey all along."

"He's with her?"

"That's the problem. He was. The sheriff's department is starting a house-to-house search. I guess a deputy came to her door and next thing she knew, Bailey'd bolted. She doesn't know where he's gone. Have you heard from him?"

"Not a word."

"Well, stick around. If he gets in touch, you gotta talk him into turning himself in. With word out on his mom's death, the town's going nuts. I'm worried about his safety."

"Me too, but what am I supposed to do?"

"Just stay by the phone. This is critical."

"Jack, I can't. Shana Timberlake's missing. I saw her car keys at the hot springs and I'm going up after dark to take a look."

"Screw Shana. This is more important."

"Then why don't you come over here yourself? If Bailey calls, you can talk to him."

"Bailey doesn't trust me!"

"Why is that, Jack?"

"Damned if I know. If he heard me on the phone, he'd be gone again in a flash, convinced the line was tapped. June says aside from her, you're the only one he trusts."

"Look, this may not take me long. I'll be back as soon

as possible and touch base with you then. If I hear from Bailey, I'll talk him in. I swear."

"He *has* to surrender."

"Jack, I know that!" I felt a flash of irritation as I hung up the phone. Why was the guy suddenly on my case? I knew the kind of jeopardy Bailey Fowler was in.

I turned to leave the kitchen. Bert was standing in the hall. He moved into the kitchen as if he'd been in motion all along. "Miss Ann wants some water," he mumbled.

Bullshit, I thought. You little snoop.

I went upstairs to my room and changed into my jogging shoes. I tucked my penlight, my picks, and my room key in my jeans pocket. I wasn't sure I'd need the picks, but I thought I should be prepared. I debated about my little .32. When I bought the Davis, I got myself a custom-fitted Alessi shoulder rig, adjusted so that the holster and weapon would lie snugly against my left side, just under the breast. I yanked my shirt off and strapped the rig into place. I pulled a black turtleneck over it and studied the effect in the bathroom mirror. It would do.

I tried Shana's first, just to be sure she hadn't come back in the meantime. Still no one home and no sign she'd been there. I took one of the side streets that arched up over the hill, intersecting Floral Beach Road on the far side of town. The funeral cortege for Tap Granger had probably taken this same route and I was anxious to be off the road before they returned. I did a slow trot north, toward 101. The two-lane road smelled of eucalyptus, hot sun, and sage. A pale brown grasshopper kept pace with me for a bit, darting from one weed top to the next. On my right was a narrow, rocky ditch, a low wire fence, and then the grassy hillside, strewn with boulders. Live oaks provided an occasional patch of shade. The stillness was broken only by the shrill peeping of the birds.

I heard a vehicle approaching from around a bend up ahead. A Ford pickup barreled into view, slowing when the driver caught sight of me. It was Pearl, with his son, Rick, beside him in the passenger seat. I slowed to a walk and then halted for him. The old man's big, beefy arm hung out the open window. He was wearing a short-sleeved blue dress shirt and a tie that he'd pulled loose so he could unbutton his collar.

"Hello, Pearl. How are you?" I said, giving Rick a nod.

"You missed the funeral," Pearl said.

"I didn't know Tap that well and I felt like the service should be reserved for his friends. You're just coming back?"

"Everybody else is still at the grave site, I guess. Me and Rick ducked out early so's we can open the pool hall for the wake. Joleen says it's what he'd want. What are you up to? Out for some exercise?"

"That's right," I said. I had to leap right over the image of the wake itself—french fries and a pony keg. I mean, was that class or what? Rick murmured something to his father.

"Oh yeah. Rick wants to know if you've seen Cherie."

"Cherie? I don't think so." I figured she was on a bus to Los Angeles, but I didn't say that.

"She was supposed to go with us, but she went off to the store and hadn't come back by the time we left. You see her, tell her we're at the pool hall." He checked the rearview mirror. "I better get out of the way here before somebody plows into me. Why don't you stop by for a beer when you get done with your jog?"

"I'll do that. Thanks."

Pearl pulled away and I began to trot. As soon as the truck was out of sight, I crossed the ditch and hopped over the wire fence. I climbed straight up, heading for the cover of the trees. In two more minutes I had reached the crest and was peering down the slope toward the mineral springs hotel, half obscured in the eucalyptus grove.

The tennis courts were empty. From where I crouched, I couldn't see the swimming pool, but I was very much aware of the work crew: three men and a wood chipper just off to my right. I found a natural hideaway in the shadow of some rocks and settled in to wait. In the absence of people, reading matter, and ringing telephones, exhaustion crept over me and I sank into sleep.

The sun began to drop in the sky about four. It was technically winter, which, in California, means the perfect days are cut from fourteen hours to ten. In past years, February usually brought the rains, but that was changing of late. The hillside was quiet now, the work crew apparently gone. I scrambled out of my hiding place, reassured myself of some privacy, and peed in some bushes, taking care not to wet my good jogging shoes. My only objection to being female is that I can't pee standing up.

I took up a position where I could watch the hotel. An unmarked police car pulled into the parking lot at one point: Quintana and his partner on the move again. Or maybe Elva had filed a complaint. That'd be rich. Fifteen minutes later, they came out again and took off. As darkness gathered in the trees, a few lights came on. Finally, at seven, I began to traverse the hill, heading for the fire lane that cut across the top of the property. From there I could angle down to the hotel from the rear. I used my penlight sparingly, picking my way with care through heavy brush, twigs snapping underfoot. I was hoping the work crew had cleared a nice path for me, but they'd apparently been laboring farther down on the hill.

I stumbled onto the fire lane, a packed dirt road just wide enough to admit one vehicle. I moved to the left, trying to calculate where the hotel was in relation to me. The whole backside of the building was apparently dark, and it was tricky to calculate my exact location. I risked the penlight. The shallow beam picked up an object looming in my path. I stopped dead. Ahead of me, nearly obscured by overhanging branches, was Shana's battered Plymouth.

24

I circled the car, which looked vaguely sinister on the path, like the hulking carcass of some inexplicable beast. All four tires were flat. Someone hadn't wanted Shana to go anywhere. I would almost have been willing to bet she was dead, that she'd arrived for her rendezvous with Dunne and had somehow never left. I lifted my head. The woods were chilly, smelling of leaf mold, damp mosses, and sulfur. The dark was intense, the night sounds eradicated, as if my very presence were a warning to the cicadas and tree frogs whose songs had been stilled. I didn't want to find her. I didn't want to look. Every bone in me was aching with the certainty that her body was here somewhere.

I could feel my stomach churn as I flashed the narrow beam from the penlight across the front seat of Shana's car. Nothing. I checked the backseat. Empty. I stared at the trunk lid. I didn't think my lock picks would work, so if the trunk was locked, I was going to have to go down to the office, break in, lift Shana's car keys from the lost-and-found box, and come back. I pressed the catch and the trunk swung open. Empty. I let out the breath I'd been holding unconsciously. I left the lid up, not wanting to risk the noise I'd make slamming it shut. "Sanctuary" had to be somewhere close.

I tried to picture the plot map for the spas in this area. I flashed the penlight across the close-growing shrubs, looking for a path. Foliage that appeared to be a vivid green by day now had the matte, washed-out look of construction paper. A set of packed dirt steps, shored up by railroad ties, descended through a gap in the bushes.

I went down. A rustic wood arrow indicated that "Aerie" was just off to my left. I passed "Haven" and "Tip Top." "Sanctuary" was the fourth hot tub from the summit. I remembered then that it was located at the end of a long, twisted path, with two smaller paths branching off it. The leaves underfoot were soggy and made scarcely any sound, but I noticed I was leaving marshy prints in my wake. When I reached "Sanctuary," I played the penlight across the ground. There were three cigarette butts trampled among the leaves. I hunkered down, bending close. Camel unfiltered. Shana's brand.

The silence was undercut by the intermittent high whining of a siren out on the highway. An erratic breeze, as moist as the inside of an ice chest, rattled among the tree branches. With the strong odor from the mineral springs in the air, it was difficult to discern any other scent. I've been known to find bodies with my nose, but not in this case.

The spa had a bi-fold insulated cover pulled over it with a plastic handhold along the rim. I hesitated for a moment and then lifted it. A dense sulfurous cloud wafted into my face. The water in the redwood tub was pitch black, as still as glass. Mist hovered on the surface. I could feel my mouth purse. I wasn't going to put my hand in there, folks. I wasn't going to plunge my arm in up to the elbow, feeling around to determine if Shana's body was submerged in the depths. I experienced a nearly physical sensation of undulating hair, soft and feathery, at my fingertips. At the back of my mind, it did occur to me that if Shana'd been killed and then dumped in here, she'd be floating by now, buoyed by accumulating gases . . . sort of like a pool toy. I could feel my eyes cross. Sometimes I sicken myself with my own thoughts.

At knee height, there was a wooden door that apparently opened onto the heater and pump works tucked away out of sight. I pulled the door open. The body had been jammed in feet first. She unfolded from the waist, her bloody head coming to rest against my foot, sightless eyes staring up at me. A sound came up in my throat like bile.

"Don't move!"

I jumped, whipping around, a hand against my lurching heart.

Elva Dunne was standing there, flashlight in her left hand.

"Jesus, Elva. You scared the shit out of me," I snapped.

She glanced briefly at Shana, not nearly as startled by the sight as I had been. Belatedly, I noticed that she had a little .22 semiautomatic pointed at my gut. Gun buffs are dismissive of a .22, apparently convinced that a weapon doesn't count unless it's capable of blowing a fist-sized hole through a board. Unfortunately, Elva hadn't heard about this and she looked as if she was ready to drill me a second belly button right above the first. Let a little .22 slug rip around in your gut and see how good you feel. It'll bounce off bone like a tiny bumper car, tearing up every organ in its path.

"I got a phone call from some guy who said Bailey Fowler was up here," she said. "Just stay where you are and don't move or I'll shoot."

I raised my hands like they do in the movies, thinking to reassure her. "Hey, no Bailey. It's just me and I'm cool," I said. I gestured at Shana's body. "I hope you don't think I did that."

"Bullshit. Of course you did. Why else would you be here?"

I could hear the siren now in its winding approach on the road down below. Somebody must have called the cops as well. Mention Bailey's name and you got service real quick. "Look, put the gun down. Honest to God, I saw Shana's keys in the lost-and-found box this afternoon. I figured she must have been here at some point, so I thought I'd check it out."

"Where's the weapon? What'd you do, hit her with a baseball bat?"

"Elva, she's been dead for days. She was probably killed Wednesday night. If I'd just done it, the blood would be bright red and, uh, you know . . . spurting." I hate it when people can't comprehend the elementary stuff.

Elva's gaze jumped around and she shifted nervously. Dr. Dunne had said she was a paranoid schizophrenic, but what does that mean? I thought all those people were tripping out on Thorazine these days, as placid as rocks. This woman was big, one of those ham-shouldered Nordic types. I already knew she was as weird as they come. If she'd whacked at me with a Wilson, what was she going to do with a gun in her hand? Two deputies, with flashlights, were zigzagging up the path from below. Things were not looking good.

I let my eyes drift toward her pants, and lifted my eyebrows a bit. "Oh wow. I wouldn't worry about it, but there's a spider the size of a meatball crawling down your leg."

She had to look. How could she not?

I kicked upward, my running shoe lifting the gun right out of her hand. I saw the .22 do a high, tumbling somersault and disappear into the dark. I rammed into her, knocking her ass-over-teakettle right after it. She yelped as she tumbled backward, crashing down the hill.

The first of the deputies had apparently reached the midpoint of the hill. I shoved my penlight in my pocket and ran like hell. I wasn't sure where I was going, but I hoped to get there quick. I angled up through the trees, headed for the fire lane, figuring I could run for a while unimpeded. Shana's Plymouth was blocking the overgrown lane, so even if they managed to get a sheriff's car up here, they'd have trouble getting through. I was making too much noise to hear if anyone was behind me, but it seemed smarter to assume the cops were close on my heels. I quickened my pace, sailing over the trunk of a tree in my path.

The fire lane began to climb steeply, dead-ending in a gate with a wire fence that stretched away on either side. I took a flying leap, put a hand on the gatepost and arched my back, catching my foot as I tried to clear the top. I smacked down with an "Oof!" rolled, and got up again, suppressing a moan. The fall had rammed the Davis right into my ribs. Much pain.

I plugged on, heading upward. The hill leveled out in a rugged pasture dotted with scrub oak and manzanita. The moon wasn't full, but there was enough of it to illuminate the choppy field through which I ran. I must have been a quarter of a mile from the road, in an area inaccessible to vehicles. I was desperately in need of rest. I looked over my shoulder. There was no sign of pursuit. I slowed to a jog and searched out a depression in the grass.

I sank down, winded, blotting my sweaty brow on the sleeve of my turtleneck. Some winged creature swooped down close to me and then cruised away, temporarily mistaking me for something edible. I hate nature. I really do. Nature is composed entirely of sticks, dirt, fall-down places, biting and stinging things, and savageries too numerous to list. And I'm not the only one who feels this way. Man has been building cities since the year oughty-ought, just to get away from this stuff. Now we're on our way to the moon and other barren spots where nothing grows and you can pick up a rock without having something jump out at you. The quicker we get there, the better, as far as I'm concerned.

Time to move. I staggered to my feet again and began to trot, wishing I had a plan. I couldn't go back to the motel—the sheriff's department was going to be there in ten minutes flat—but without my car keys and some bucks, what was I going to do? It occurred to me I might have been better off hanging out with Elva until the deputies arrived, taking my chances with the law. Now *I* was a fugitive, and I didn't like it much.

A flash of Shana's face popped into my head. She'd been bludgeoned to death, from the look of her, shoved into the narrow space under the hot tub until someone could dispose of her—if that was the intent. Maybe that's what Elva had trudged up there in the dark to do. I couldn't decide if I should believe her claim about the phone call. Had *she* killed Shana Timberlake? Killed her daughter seventeen years before that? Why the lag time? And why Ori Fowler? Given Elva as the killer, I couldn't come up with a scenario in which Ori's death made any sense. Could the phone call have been meant to trap me up there? As far as I knew, the only two people who were aware of where I'd be were Jack Clemson and Bert.

I halted again. The ground was beginning to slant downward, and I found myself squinting through the dark at a sharp drop-off. Below, a gray ribbon of road curled along the base of the hill. I had no idea where it led, but if the cops were smart, they'd be calling for backup cars, which might be cruising by any minute, hoping to cut me off. I scrambled down the rocky incline as fast as I could, half-humping, half-sliding on my backside, preceded by a tiny landslide of loose stones and dirt. I could hear approaching sirens as I skidded the last few feet. I was panting from exhaustion, but I didn't dare stop. I hightailed it across the road, reaching the far side just as the first black-and-white rounded the bend maybe six hundred yards away.

I plunged into the brush, hugging the ground as I bellycrawled my way through the weeds. Once I was safely in the cover of the trees, I paused to reorient myself, rolling over on my back. Against the encroaching fog bank I could see the reflection of the vapor lights that lined Ocean Street. Floral Beach wasn't far. Unfortunately, what lay between me and the town was the posted property belonging to the oil refinery. I studied the eight-foot chain-link fence. Strands of barbed wire were strung along the top. No crossing that. Big oil storage tanks loomed up on the far side, painted in pastel shades, like a series of cakes.

I was still close enough to the road that I could hear the squawking of the sheriff's cars in position along the berm. Lights raked the hillside. I hoped the suckers hadn't brought dogs. That was all I'd need. I crawled to the base of the fence, clinging to it doggedly as I pushed on. In the dark, it served not only as a guide, but as a needed support.

More warning signs. This was a hard hat area . . . and me with no hard hat. I was winded and sweating, my hands torn, nose beginning to run. The smell of the ocean was getting stronger and I took comfort from that.

Abruptly, the fence took a hard cut left. What opened up in front of me was a dirt path strewn with trash, a lovers' lane perhaps. I didn't dare use my penlight. I was still in the hills above Floral Beach, but I was getting closer to the town. In less than a quarter of a mile, I found myself at the tag end of the lane that spilled into a cul-de-sac. Oh glory, now I knew where I was. This was the bluff above Jean Timberlake's old apartment building. Once I reached the wooden stairway, I could climb down to the rear door of her place and hide. To my right, I spotted the glass-and-frame house where I'd knocked earlier. Lights were on inside.

I skirted the house, groping my way along the property line, marked by waist-high shrubs. As I passed the kitchen window, I caught sight of the occupant looking straight out at me. I dropped, realizing belatedly that the guy must be standing at the kitchen sink. The window would be throwing his own reflection back at him, effectively blocking out the sight of me, I hoped. Cautiously I rose and peered closer. Dwight Shales.

I blinked, debating with myself. Could I trust him? Was I safer up here with him or hiding in the abandoned building below? Oh hell, this was no time to be shy. I needed help.

I doubled back to the front porch and rang the bell. I kept an eye on the street, worried a patrol car would cruise into sight. At some point they were going to realize I'd slipped through the net. Given the impenetrability of the oil company property, this was probably the logical place to end up. The porch light came on. The front door opened. I turned to look at him. "Kinsey, my God. What happened to you?"

"Hello, Dwight. Can I come in?"

He held the door open, stepping back. "Are you in some kind of trouble?"

"That would cover it," I said. My explanation was worthy of a box top, twenty-five words or less, tendered while I followed him through the foyer—all raw woods and modern art. We went down a step into the living room, which was dead ahead: two stories of glass looking out toward the view. The roof of Jean's apartment building wasn't visible, but I could see the lights of Floral Beach stretching almost as far as the big hotel on the hillside half a mile away.

"Let me get you a drink," he said.

"Thanks. Do you mind if I clean up?"

He nodded to his left. "Straight down the hall."

I found the bathroom and ran some water, scrubbing my hands and face. I blotted my face dry, staring at myself in the bathroom mirror. I had a big scratch on my cheek. My hair was matted with dirt. I found a comb in his medicine cabinet and ran it through my mop. I peed, brushed myself off, washed my hands and face again, and returned to the living room where Dwight handed me some brandy in a softball-sized snifter.

I took it neat and he poured me a second.

"Thanks," I said. I could feel the liquor defining my insides as it eased through. I had to breathe with my mouth open for a bit. "Whew! Great."

"Sit down. You look beat."

"I am," I said. I glanced anxiously toward the front door. "Are we visible from the street?"

The narrow panels on either side of the front door were frosted glass. It was the exposed living room that bothered me. I felt as if I were on stage. He crossed the room and closed the drapes. The room was suddenly much cozier and I relaxed a bit.

He sat down in the chair across from me. "Tell me again."

I went back through the story, filling in the details. "I probably should have just waited for the cops."

"You want to go ahead and call them and turn yourself in? The phone's right there."

"Not yet," I said. "That's what I kept telling Bailey, but now I know how he felt. They'd just keep me up all night, hounding me with questions I don't have the answers for."

"What are you going to do?"

"Don't know. Get my head together and see if I can figure this out. You know, I was up here earlier and knocked on the door, but you weren't home. I wanted to ask if anybody up here ever saw Jean using the stairs."

"The stairs?"

"Up from the Timberlakes' apartment. It was right down there." I found myself pointing to the floor to indicate the base of the bluff.

"Oh, that's right. I'd forgotten about that. Talk about small towns. I guess none of us are that far from anybody else."

"That's for sure," I said. At the back of my mind, uneasiness was beginning to stir. Something about his response wasn't quite ringing true. Maybe it was his manner, which was suddenly too studiously casual to be believable. Pretending to be "normal" is a lot harder than you'd think. Did it mean anything, his having lived this close? "You forgot Jean Timberlake lived thirty feet away?"

"No big deal," he said. "I think they only lived there a few months before she died." He set his brandy snifter on the coffee table. "You hungry? I'd be happy to fix you something to eat."

I shook my head, easing him back toward the subject that interested me. "I realized this afternoon that the back door of the Timberlake apartment opened right onto the stairs. I figure she could easily have used the road up here as a rendezvous point for the guys she screwed around with. You never saw her up here?"

He considered the possibility, searching his memory. "No, I don't believe so. Is it that important?"

"Well, it could be. If somebody saw Jean, they might have also seen the guy she was having the affair with."

"Come to think of it, I did see cars up here at night on occasion. I guess it never occurred to me it might be somebody waiting to pick her up."

I love bad liars. They work so hard at it and the effort is so transparent. I happen to lie well myself, but only after years of practice. Even then, I can't pull it off every time. This guy didn't even come close. I sat and looked at him, giving him time to reconsider his position.

He frowned with concern. "By the way, what's the story on Ann's mother? Mrs. Emma called about an hour ago and told me Bailey switched the medication. I couldn't believe it . . ."

"Excuse me, could we get back to Jean Timberlake first?"

"Oh, sorry. I thought we were done, and I've been awfully worried about Ann. It's unbelievable what she's been through. Anyway, go ahead."

"Were you fucking Jean Timberlake yourself?"

The word was just right, crude and to the point. He let out a little laugh of disbelief, like he must not have heard me right. "What?"

"Come on. 'Fess up. Just tell me the truth. I'd really like to know."

He laughed again, shaking his head as though to clear it. "My God, Kinsey. I'm a high school principal."

"I know what you are, Dwight. I'm asking you what you did."

He stared at me, apparently annoyed that I'd persist. "This is ridiculous. The girl was seventeen."

I said nothing. I returned a look of such skepticism that his smile began to fade. He got up and poured himself another drink. He held the brandy bottle toward me, mutely asking me if I wanted more. I shook my head.

He sat down again. "I think we should move on to something more productive. I'm willing to help, but I'm not going to play any games with you." He was all business now. The meeting was called to order and we were going to get serious. No more silly bullshit. "I'd have to be crazy to get involved with a student," he went on. "Jesus. What an idea." He rolled his shoulders. I could hear the joint pop. I knew he wanted to convince me, but the words carried no conviction.

I dropped my gaze to the tabletop, pushing my empty snifter an inch. "We're all capable of astonishing ourselves when it comes to sex."

He was silent.

I focused on him intently.

He recrossed his legs. Now it was him, not looking at me.

"Dwight?"

He said, "I thought I was in love with her."

Careful, I thought. Take care. The moment is fragile and his trust is tenuous. "It must have been a tough time. Karen was diagnosed with MS right about then, wasn't she?"

He set the glass down again and his gaze met mine. "You have a good memory."

I kept silent.

He finally took up the narrative thread. "She was actually in the process of being evaluated, but I think we knew. It's staggering how something like that affects you. She was bitter at first. Withdrawn. In the end, she was better about it than I was. God, I couldn't believe it was happening, and then I turned around and Jean was there. Young, lusty, outrageous."

He was quiet for a moment.

I said nothing, letting him tell it his way. He didn't need any prompting from me. This was a story he knew by heart.

"I didn't think Karen would survive anyway because the first round was acute. She seemed to go downhill overnight. Hell, I didn't think she'd live till spring. In a situation like that, your mind leaps ahead. You get into survival mode. I remember thinking, 'Hey, I can make it. The marriage isn't that great, anyway.' I was only what, thirty-nine? Forty? I had a lot of years ahead of me. I figured I'd marry again. Why not? We weren't perfect, the two of us. I'm not sure we were even very well suited to each other. The MS changed all that. When she died, I was more in love with her than I'd ever been."

"And Jean?"

"Ah, but Jean. Early on"—he paused to shake his head—"I was crazy. I must have been. If that relationship had ever become public knowledge . . . well, it would have ruined my life. Karen's, too . . . what was left of it."

"Was the baby yours?"

"I don't know. Probably. I wish I could say no, but what could I do? I only found out about it after Jean died. I can't imagine what the consequences would have been . . . you know . . . if the pregnancy had come to light."

"Yeah, unlawful sexual intercourse being what it is."

"Oh God, don't say that. Even now the phrase is enough to make me sick."

"You kill her?"

"No. I swear. I was capable of a lot of craziness back then, but not that."

I watched him, sensing that he was telling the truth. This wasn't a killer I was listening to. He might have been desperate or despairing. He might have realized after the fact how perilous his situation was, but I didn't hear the kind of rationalization killers get into. "Who else knew about the pregnancy?"

"I don't know. What difference would it make?"

"I'm not sure. You can't really be certain the baby was yours. Maybe there was somebody else."

"Bailey knew about it."

"Aside from him. Couldn't someone else have heard?"

"Well, sure, but so what? I know she showed up at the school very upset and went straight to the counselor's office."

"I thought the guidance counselors only handled academic matters—college prep requirements and stuff like that."

"There were exceptions. Sometimes we had to screen personal problems and refer kids out for professional counseling."

"What would have been done then, if Jean had asked for help?"

"We'd have done what we could. San Luis has social agencies set up for things like that."

"Jean never talked to you herself?"

He shook his head. "I wish she had. Maybe I could have done something for her, I don't know. She had her crazy side. We're not talking about a girl who'd agree to an abortion. She never would have given that baby up and she wouldn't have kept quiet. She'd have insisted on marriage, regardless of the price. I have to tell you—I know it sounds horrible, but I have to say this—I was relieved when she died. Enormously. When I understood the risk I'd taken . . . when I saw what I had at stake. It was a gift. I cleaned up my act right then. I never screwed around on Karen again."

"I believe you," I said. But what was bothering me? I could feel an idea churning, but I couldn't quite sense what it was.

Dwight was going on. "It was a bit of a rude awakening when I heard the stories going around after she'd been killed. I was naïve enough to think we had something special between us, but that turned out not to be the case."

I kept picking at it like a bone. "So if she didn't turn to you for help, she could have turned to somebody else."

"Well, yes, but she didn't have much time for that, as I understand. She had the test done in Lompoc and got the results that afternoon. By midnight she was dead."

"How long does it take to make a phone call?" I said. "She had hours. She could have called half the guys in Floral Beach and some in San Luis, too. Suppose it was someone else? Suppose you were just a cover for another relationship? There must have been other guys with just as much to lose."

"I'm sure it's possible," he said, but he sounded dubious.

The phone rang, a harsh sound in the stillness of the big house. Dwight leaned back, reaching over to pick up the receiver from the end table by the couch. "Hello? Oh, hi."

His face had brightened with recognition and I saw his eyes stray to my face as the person on the other end of the line went on. He was making "unh-hunh" noises while someone rattled on. "No, no, no. Don't worry. Hang on. She's right here." He held the phone out and I took it. "It's Ann," he said.

"Hi, Ann. What's happening?"

Her voice was cold and she was clearly upset. "Well. At long last. Where the hell have *you* been? I've been looking for you for hours."

I found myself squinting at the phone, trying to determine the reason for the tone she had taken. What was wrong with her? "Is there a deputy with you?" I asked.

"I think we could say that."

"You want to wait and call me back when he goes?"

"No, I don't, dear. Here's what I want. I want you to get your ass down here right away! Daddy checked himself out of the hospital and he's been bugging me ever since. WHERE HAVE YOU BEEN?" she shrieked. "Do you have any idea . . . do you have any IDEA what's been going on? DO YOU? Goddamn it! . . ."

I held the phone away from my ear. She was really building up a head of steam here. "Ann, stop that. Calm down. It's too complicated to go into right now."

"Don't give me that. Don't you dare ever, ever give me that."

"Don't give you what? What are you so upset about?"

"You know perfectly well," she snapped. "What are you doing over there? You listen to me, Kinsey. And you listen good . . ."

I started to interrupt, but she'd just put a palm across the mouthpiece, talking to someone in the background. The deputy? Oh hell, was she telling him where I was?

I replaced the receiver in the cradle.

Dwight was looking at me with perplexity. "You okay? What was that about?"

"I have to go to San Luis Obispo," I said carefully. It was a lie, of course, but it was the first thing that occurred to me. Ann had told them where I was. Within minutes this whole cul-de-sac would be blocked off, the neighborhood swarming with deputies. I had to get out of there, and I didn't think it was wise to let him know where I was headed.

"San Luis?" he said. "What for?"

I moved toward the front door. "Don't worry about it. I'll be back in a bit."

"Don't you need a car?"

"I'll get one."

I closed the door behind me, leaped off the porch, and ran.

25

The Ocean Street Motel was only four blocks away. It wasn't going to take the cops long. I kept to the pavement until I caught the sound of a vehicle accelerating up the hill. I took a dive into the bushes as a black-and-white sped into view, heading straight for Dwight's place. Lights flashing, no siren. A second black-and-white gunned up the hill after the first. Hotdoggers. The deputy in the second car was probably twenty-two. Big career ahead of him, careening through Floral Beach legally. He must have been having the time of his life.

The solution to so many problems seems obvious once you know where to look. My conversation with Dwight had generated a shift in my mind-set and the questions that had troubled me before now seemed to have answers that made perfect sense. Some of them, at any rate. I needed confirmation, but at least now I had a working premise. Jean Timberlake had been murdered to protect Dwight Shales. Ori Fowler had died because she was meant to die . . . to get her out of the way. And Shana? I thought I understood why she had died, too. Bailey was supposed to take the rap for all of it, and he'd fallen for it like a chump. If he'd had sense enough not to run—if he'd just stayed put—he couldn't have been blamed for everything that'd happened since.

I approached the motel from the rear, through a vacant lot filled with weeds and broken glass. Many of the motel windows were ablaze with lights. I could imagine all the uproar caused by the presence of sheriffs' cars. I suspected there was still a deputy posted somewhere close, probably just outside my room. I reached the Fowlers' back door. The kitchen light was on, and I could see the shadow of someone moving around in the back part of the apartment. A little black-and-white television now sat on the counter, a taped newscast flickering across the empty room. Quintana was making mouth noises on the courthouse steps. Must have been this afternoon. A picture of Bailey Fowler followed. He was being led, in handcuffs, to a waiting vehicle. On came the announcer, turning to the weather map. I tried the kitchen door. Locked. I didn't want to stand out there trying to pick the lock.

I circled the building, hugging the outside wall, checking darkened windows for one left ajar. What I found instead was a side door that was located just across from the stairway inside the back hall. The knob turned in my hand and I pushed the door open cautiously. I peered in. Royce, in a ratty bathrobe, was shuffling down the hall toward me, slump-shouldered, eyes on his slippers. I could hear the hum of his weeping, broken by intermittent sighs. He was walking his grief like a baby, back and forth. He reached the door to his room and turned, shuffling back toward the kitchen. Now and then he murmured Ori's name, voice breaking off. Lucky is the spouse who dies first, who never has to know what survivors endure. Royce must have signed himself out of the hospital after Reverend Haws paid his call. Ori's death had pushed him past struggling. What did he care if he sped death along?

The lights from the living room gave the uncomfortable sense of other people very near. I could hear two women in the dining room, talking in low tones. Was Mrs. Emma still with Ann? Royce was reaching the kitchen, where I knew he'd turn again, coming back.

I closed the door behind me, crossed to the stairs, and took them two at a time, moving silently. I should have put two and two together when I saw that the maid's master key wouldn't open room 20. That room had probably been sealed off, part of the Fowlers' apartment upstairs.

The second floor was dark, except for a window on the landing through which a soft yellow light now spilled. I was disoriented. Somehow this didn't look the way I'd expected it to. There was a short corridor to my left, ending in a door. I crossed to it, stopped, and listened carefully. Silence. I tried the knob and pushed the door open a crack. Cold air wafted in. I was facing the exterior corridor that ran right by my room. I could see the vending machine and the outside stairs. To my immediate left was room 20, next to that room 22, where I'd spent my first night. There was no sign of a deputy on duty. Did I dare simply mosey down, use my key, and go in? What if the deputy was waiting inside?

I reached around and tried the knob from the outside. Ah, locked. Once I went out this door, I couldn't get back in unless I jammed it open. I stayed where I was, easing the door shut. The door to my left was unlocked. I slipped inside, taking out my penlight. Like the rest of the Fowlers' living quarters, this had once been a regular motel room, converted now to office space.

Sliding glass doors along the front opened onto a second-floor balcony overlooking Ocean Street. The drapes were open and I could make out a desk, a swivel chair, bookcases, a reading lamp. I swept the room with the narrow beam of the penlight, getting my bearings. The book titles were half fiction, half college textbooks in psychology. Ann's.

On the desk was a photo of Ori in her youth. She really had been beautiful, with large luminous eyes. I searched the desk drawers. Nothing of interest. Checked the closet alcove, which was filled with summer clothing. The bathroom held nothing. The door that connected this room to room 20 was locked. Locked doors are always more interesting than the other kind. This time I got out my set of key picks and set to work. In TV shows, people pick locks with remarkable ease. Not so in real life, where you have to have the patience of a saint. I was working in the dark, clamping the penlight in my mouth like a cigar while I used the rocker pick in my left hand and the wire in my right. Sometimes I do this efficiently, but that's usually when the light is good. This time it took forever, and I was sweating from the tension when the lock finally gave.

Room 20 was a duplicate of the one I'd occupied. This was Ann's bedroom, the one Maxine was not to clean. I could see why. On the closet floor, dead ahead, was a Ponsness-Warren shot shell reloader with a built-in wad guide, an adjustable crimp die, and two powder reservoirs filled with rock salt. I crossed to the closet and hunkered down, inspecting the device, which looks like a cross between a bird feeder and a cappuccino machine, and is designed to pack a shell with anything you like. A blast of rock salt, at close range, usually ends up buried under your skin where it stings like a son of a bitch, but doesn't do much else. Tap had found out just how ineffectual salt can be in staving off the sheriff's deputies.

I had really hit the jackpot. On the floor beside the reloader was a microcassette recorder with a tape in it. I pressed the rewind button and then pressed play, listening to a familiar voice slowed down to a series of quite nasty gravel-throated threats. I rewound, switched the tape speed, and tried it again. The voice was clearly Ann's, spelling out her intentions with an ax and a chain saw. The whole thing sounded stupid, but she must have had a ball. "I am going to get you. . . ." We used to do shit like this as kids. "I am going to cut your head off. . . ." I smiled grimly, remembering the night those calls had come through. I'd taken comfort from the fact that someone two doors away was wide awake like me. The square of light had looked so cozy at that hour. All the time she'd been in here, dialing room-to-room, part of her campaign of psychological abuse. At this point I couldn't even remember when I'd had an uninterrupted night's sleep. I was being carried on adrenaline and nerve, the momentum of events sweeping me willy-nilly down the path. The night my room was broken into, all she'd had to do was use her passkey and jimmy up the sliding glass door afterward so it would look like the point of entry. I got to my feet and checked the shelf above. In a shoebox, I found a windowed envelope addressed to "Erica Dahl" containing quarterly dividends and year-end tax summaries for IBM stock. There must have been more than a hundred such envelopes neatly packed into the box, along with a social security card, driver's license, and passport—with Ann Fowler's photograph affixed. The statements from Merrill Lynch showed a $42,000 investment in shares of IBM back in 1967. With stock splits in the intervening years, the shares had more than doubled in value. I noticed that "Erica" had dutifully paid taxes on the interest that accrued from year to year. Ann Fowler was too shrewd to get tripped up by the IRS.

I flashed the penlight through her living room and kitchenette, doing a one-eighty turn. When the narrow beam crossed the bedstead, I caught an oval of white and flashed the light back over it again. Ann was propped up in bed watching me. Her face was dead pale, her eyes enormous, so filled with lunacy and hate that my skin crawled. I felt as if I'd been pierced with an icy arrow, the chill spreading from the core of my body to my fingertips. In her lap she held a double-barreled shotgun, which she raised and pointed right at my chest. Probably not rock salt. I didn't think the spider story was going to work with her.

"Finding everything you need?" she asked.

I raised my hands just to show I knew how to behave. "Hey, you're pretty good. You almost got away with it."

Her smile was thin. "Now that you're 'wanted,' I can do it, don't you think?" she said conversationally. "All I have to do is pull the trigger and claim trespass."

"And then what?"

"You tell me."

I hadn't quite worked the whole story out, but I knew enough to make a flying guess. Why you have chats with killers in circumstances like these is because you hope against hope you can (1) talk them out of it, (2) stall until help arrives, or (3) enjoy a few more moments of this precious commodity we call life, which consists (in large part) of breathing in and out. Hard to do with your lungs blown out your back.

"Well," said I, hoping to make a short story long, "I

figure once your daddy dies and you unload this place, you'll take the proceeds, add them to the profits from the forty-two thou you stole, and sail off into the sunset. Possibly with Dwight Shales, or so you hope."

"And why not?"

"Why not, indeed? Sounds like a great plan. Does he know about it yet?"

"He will," she said.

"What makes you think he'll agree?"

"Why wouldn't he? He's free now. And I will be, too, as soon as Pop dies."

"And you think that constitutes a relationship?" I said, astonished.

"What do *you* know about relationships?"

"Hey, I've been married twice. That's more than you can say."

"You're divorced. You don't know dick."

I had to shrug at that.

"I bet Jean was sorry she confided in you."

"Very. At the end, she put up quite a fight."

"But you won."

"I had to. I couldn't have her ruining Dwight's life."

"Assuming it was his," I said.

"The babe? Of course it was."

"Oh great. No problem, then. You're completely justified," I said. "Does he know how much you've done for him?"

"That's our little secret. Yours and mine."

"How did you know where Shana would be Wednesday night?"

"Simple. I followed her."

"But why kill the woman?"

"Same reason I'm going to kill you. For screwing Dwight."

"She was going up there to meet Joe Dunne," I said. "Neither one of us screwed Dwight."

"Bullshit!"

"It's not bullshit. He's a nice enough guy, but he's not my type. He told me himself he and Shana were just friends. It was strictly platonic. They hadn't even screwed *once!*"

"You liar. You think I don't know what's been going on? You sashay into town and start coming on to him, riding around in his car, having cozy dinners . . ."

"Ann, we were talking. That's all it was."

"Nobody's going to get in my way, Kinsey. Not after all I've been through. I've worked too hard and waited too long. I've sacrificed my entire adult life, and you're not going to spoil things now that I'm almost free."

"Well, listen, Ann . . . if I may say so, you're as crazy as a bug. No offense, but you are looney-tunes, completely cuckoo-nuts." I was just making mouth noises while I thought about my gun. My little Davis was still in the holster tucked up against my left breast. What I wanted to do was take it out and plug her right between the eyes—or someplace fatal. But here's the way I figured it. By the time I reached up under my turtleneck, snatched the gun out, pointed it, and fired, that shotgun of hers would have taken off my face. And how was I going to get the gun, feign a heart attack? I didn't think she'd fall for it. My eyes had adjusted to the dark, and since I could see her perfectly, I had to guess she could see me just as well.

"Mind if I turn off the penlight? I hate to use up the batteries," I said. The beam was pointed at the ceiling, and my arms were getting tired. Probably hers, too. A shotgun like that weighs a good seven pounds—not easy to hold steady, even if you're used to lifting weights.

"Just stay where you are and don't move."

"Wow, that's just what Elva said."

Ann reached over and turned on the bedside lamp. She looked worse in the light. She had a mean face, I could see that now. The slightly receding chin made her look like a rat. The shotgun was a twelve-gauge, over-and-under, and she seemed to know which end did the hurt.

Dimly, I became aware of a shuffling sound in the hall. Royce. When had he come upstairs? "Ann? Aw, Annie, I found some pictures of your mother I thought you'd like. Can I come in?"

I saw her eyes flick toward the door. "I'll be down in a minute, Pop. We can look at them then."

Too late. He had pushed the door open, peering in. He had a photograph album in his arms, and his face held such innocence. His eyes seemed very blue. His lashes were sparse, still wet from his tears, his nose red. Gone was the gruffness, the arrogance, the dominance. His illness had made him frail, and Ori's death had knocked him to his knees, but here he came again, an old man full of hope. "Mrs. Maude and Mrs. Emma are looking for you to say good night."

"I'm busy right now. Will you take care of it?"

He caught sight of me. He must have wondered what I was doing with my hands in the air. His attention strayed to the shotgun Ann held at shoulder height. I thought he was going to turn and shuffle out again. He hesitated, uncertain what to do next.

I said, "Hello, Royce. Guess who killed Jean Timberlake?"

He glanced at me and then looked away. "Well." His gaze

slid over to Ann as if she might deny the accusation. She got up from the bed and reached behind him for the door.

"Go on downstairs, Pop. I have something to do and then I'll be down."

He seemed confused. "You're not going to hurt her."

"No, of course not," she said.

"She's going to shoot my ass!" I said.

His gaze strayed back to hers, looking for reassurance.

"What do you think she's doing with that shotgun? She's going to kill me dead and then claim trespass. She told me so."

"Pop, I caught her going through my closet. The cops are after her. She's in cahoots with Bailey, trying to help him get away."

"Oh, don't be a silly. Why would I do that?"

"Bailey?" Royce said. It was the first time tonight I'd seen comprehension in his eyes.

"Royce, I've got proof he's innocent. Ann's the one who killed Jean—"

"You *liar!*" Ann cut in. "The two of you are trying to take Pop for everything he's worth."

God, I couldn't believe this. Ann and I were squabbling like little kids, each of us trying to persuade Royce to be on our side. "Did too." "Did not." "Did too."

Royce put a trembling finger to his lips. "If she's got proof, maybe we should hear what it is," he said, talking almost to himself. "Don't you think so, Annie? If she can prove Bailey's innocent?"

I could see the rage begin to stir at the mention of his name. I was worried she would shoot and argue with her daddy afterward. The same thought apparently occurred to him. He reached for the shotgun. "Put it down, baby."

Abruptly, she backed away. "DON'T TOUCH ME!"

I could feel my heart start to thud, afraid he'd yield. Instead, he seemed to focus, gathering his strength.

"What are you doing, Ann? You can't do that."

"Go on. Get out of here."

"I want to hear what Kinsey has to say."

"Just do what I tell you and get the hell out!"

He clamped a hand on the barrel. "Give me that before you hurt someone."

"No!" Ann snatched it out of his reach.

Royce lunged, grabbing it. The two of them struggled for possession of the shotgun. I was immobilized, my attention fixed on the big black 8 of the two barrels that pointed first at me, then the floor, ceiling, weaving through the air. Royce should have been the stronger, but illness had sapped him and Ann's rage gave her the edge. Royce jerked the gun by the stock.

Fire spurted from the barrel, and the blast filled the room with powder smell. The shotgun thumped to the floor as Ann screamed.

She was looking down in disbelief. Most of her right foot had been blown away. All that was left was a torn stump of raw meat. I could feel heat rip through me as though the sensation were mine. I turned away, repelled.

The pain must have been excruciating, blood pumping out. What color she had left drained from her face. She sank to the floor, speechless, her body rocking as she clutched herself. Her cries dropped to a low, relentless pitch.

Royce backed away from her, his voice feeble with regret. "I'm sorry. I didn't mean to do that. I tried to help."

I could hear people pounding up the stairs: Bert, Mrs.

Maude, a young deputy I'd never seen. Another kid. Wait until he got a load of this.

"Get an ambulance!" I yelled. I was pulling a pillowcase off the bed, wadding it against her mangled foot, trying to stanch the blood spewing everywhere. The deputy fumbled with his walkie-talkie while Mrs. Maude babbled, wringing her hands. Mrs. Emma had pushed into the room behind her, and she began to shriek when she saw what was going on. Maxine and Bert were both white-faced, holding on to each other. Belatedly, the deputy herded all of them into the corridor and closed the door again. Even through the wall I could hear Mrs. Emma's shrill cries.

Ann was lying on her back by then, one arm flung across her face. Royce clung to her right hand, rocking back and forth. She was weeping like a five-year-old. "You were never there for me . . . you were never there. . . ."

I thought about my papa. I was five when he left me . . . five when he went away. An image came to me, a memory repressed for years. In the car, just after the wreck, when I was trapped in the backseat, wedged in tight, with the sound of my mother's weeping going on and on and on, I had reached around the edge of the front seat, where I found my father's hand, unresisting, passive, and soft. I tucked my fingers around his, not understanding he was dead, simply thinking everything would be all right as long as I had him. When had it dawned on me that he was gone for good? When had it dawned on Ann that Royce was never going to come through? And what of Jean Timberlake? None of us had survived the wounds our fathers inflicted all those years ago. Did he love us? How would we ever know? He was gone and he'd never again be what he was to us in all his haunting perfection. If love is what injures us, how can we heal?

Epilogue

The case against Bailey Fowler has been dismissed. He turned himself in when he heard news of Ann's arrest. She was charged with two counts of first-degree murder in the deaths of Ori Fowler and Shana Timberlake. The DA's office may never be able to assemble sufficient evidence to prosecute her for the death of Jean Timberlake.

Two weeks have passed. I'm now back in my office in Santa Teresa, where I've itemized expenses. With the hours I put in, my mileage, and meals, I'm billing Royce Fowler for $1,832 against the two grand he advanced. We chatted about it by phone and he's told me to keep the change. He's still hanging on to life with all the stubbornness he can muster and at least Bailey will be with him during his last weeks.

I find that I'm looking at Henry Pitts differently these days. He may be the closest thing to a father I'll ever have. Instead of viewing him with suspicion, I think I'll enjoy him for the time we have left, whatever that may be. He's only eighty-two, and God knows, my life is more hazardous than his.

Respectfully submitted,
Kinsey Millhone